EDITED BY **JONATHAN STRAHAN**

THE **BEST SCIENCE FICTION** & **FANTASY** OF THE **YEAR**

VOLUME THIRTEEN

First published 2019 by Solaris
an imprint of Rebellion Publishing Ltd,
Riverside House, Osney Mead,
Oxford, OX2 0ES, UK

www.solarisbooks.com

ISBN 978 1 78108 576 9

Cover by Jim Burns

Selection and "Introduction" by Jonathan Strahan.
Copyright © 2019 by Jonathan Strahan.

Pages 597-600 represent an extension of this copyright page.

10 9 8 7 6 5 4 3 2 1

A CIP catalogue record for this book is available from the
British Library.

Designed & typeset by Rebellion Publishing

Printed in Denmark

For everyone who has been along for the ride, from the first moment this series was discussed right up 'til today, with thanks...

CONTENTS

ONCE LAST TIME, WITH FEELING!

Jonathan Strahan

WELCOME TO THE *Best Science Fiction and Fantasy of the Year: Volume Thirteen.* 2018 was a difficult year for everyone living on the third rock from the sun. The United States, at least from this outsider's perspective, looked more and more like an awful parody of itself, although change was visible even from abroad and there seemed reason to believe things might, *might* just be okay. The United Kingdom faced its own political upheaval throughout the year, and the story in Australia—where this book is compiled—was much the same. And while those of us living in the former North American and British Commonwealth publishing territories danced, the world spun madly on. Astonishing weather events, species die-offs, and tragedies no-one could escape. The rest of the world, where most of humanity lives and dies, had troubles. Such troubles.

Still, it may just be the bubble this editor lives in, but things weren't entirely bad. Not by any means. Species came back from the brink of extinction, people treated one another with decency and respect and tried to improve the world they lived in. And there were real, substantial reasons to believe that, even if things weren't great, they could get better and might even be fixed one day. There was reason to *hope*. In amongst it all remote space probes continued to fulfil the dreams of science fiction—visiting Mars, landing on comets and asteroids, and somewhere out there a second unmanned spacecraft entered interstellar space. *Voyager 2* followed its sister craft out beyond the sun's heliopause and into the great dark. It gave this reader chills. I may no longer believe humankind will go to the stars, but the dream continues to grip me.

If 2018 was difficult for the world-at-large, it was no easier for the science fiction and fantasy worlds that fall within the remit of this book. As was alluded to last year, Disney-Marvel held our attention in a death grip, making $7 billion at the box office along the way, with a bunch of sequels, prequels and the like. The most popular movie of the year was Marvel's *Black Panther*, a film that put Afrofuturism—the exploration of the developing intersection of African/African Diaspora culture with technology—on the big screen and audiences loved it. It was one of the most vibrant and alive films Marvel have produced, and shone beside the comparatively stodgy *Avengers: Infinity War*, which dragged the whole Phase 3 of Marvel movies towards closure. Lighter fare held our attention too. Pixar's *Incredibles 2* told possibly the most fun superhero story of the year (so *many* superhero stories), *Deadpool 2* was foul-mouthed and hilarious, and *Ant-Man and the Wasp* was a delight. Arguably the best superhero movie of the year, though, came out at year's end. *Spiderman: Into the Spider-Verse* was smart, adventurous, well-written and had room to be playful in a way that was delightful. And it made money. They all made money. Such a lot of money.

So, too, did the various television extensions of science fiction and fantasy universes. *Star Trek* returned to television with *Star Trek: Discovery*, a darker, more dynamic *Trek*, with an excellent female lead in Sonequa Martin-Green and a criminally underused Michelle Yeoh (who also shone in the hit movie *Crazy Rich Asians*). More *Trek* is coming in 2019, with a Patrick Stewart-led *Next Generation* spin-off. *Doctor Who* returned for a new season too, a mostly successful run through the universe with Jodie Whittaker in the titular role. The first woman cast as the Doctor, Whittaker was terrific and her fellow cast were solid, but they were let down by some very ordinary scripts. Audiences responded, though, and the show was a ratings hit. There were so, so many others—from *Daredevil* to *Jessica Jones*; *Black Lightning* to *Supergirl*, *The Magicians* to *American Gods*, *Lost in Space* to *Altered Carbon*—that I couldn't keep track of them all. Was there a net effect of all of this torrent of visual SF and F? I don't know, but I felt fatigued by year's end. Everything has been or is being adapted to film or television, everything's getting a sequel and it's easy to feel worn-out and disinterested. And yet, for every third-rate piece of extruded entertainment, there was something surprising and good. For every lacklustre and confusing *Iron Fist,* you could hope to find a smart and engaging show like *Counterpart*. And there's much, much, much more coming in 2019.

How were things in the world of prose science fiction and fantasy in 2018? The short stuff? Like most of the past few years it was good and it was not good. There was the appearance of change but possibly without much actual substantial change. If there were trends that I managed to discern, they weren't surprising ones. The once insular English-language publishing world that this book is part of is more and more open to and aware of the rest of the world. Translated fiction is becoming more widely available through the efforts of dedicated editors, publishers, and translators who are determined to bring science fiction and fantasy written in languages other than English to our attention. The efforts to publish Chinese-language science fiction, especially, stood out during the year. The same was true of Afrofuturist fiction, with major anthologies like *AfroSF 3* and important magazines like *Fiyah* bringing us some of the best fiction of the year. And there was a continuing openness to more perspectives in fiction, whether it be in important series like Bogi Takács's *Transcendent: The Year's Best Transgender Speculative Fiction* or stand-alone anthologies like Rivqa Rafael and Tansy Rayner Roberts's *Mother of Invention*, or simply in the pages of almost every significant magazine or anthology published during the year. And the field, and by extension we as readers, were richer for it.

There was change, though. There's always change. Not every magazine that was there in January made it all the way to December. All of the major magazines did, but we lost *Shimmer, Space and Time*, and *Mythic Delirium* during 2018. *GigaNotoSaurus* appointed a new editor, but happily is continuing after a strong year, while *Apex Magazine* announced that it would be discontinuing its print edition and going digital-only, also after a very strong year. Nostalgia once again proved to be a risky business in magazine publishing. While 2017 saw the revival of the classic '80s science fiction magazine, *Omni*, with one issue published late that year, no further issues have appeared to date, and similarly *Amazing Stories* emerged (again!) with a new issue launched in August at the World Science Fiction Convention in San Jose, but to date no further issues have appeared, and left this reader wondering if there's more to be done in boldly striking out for the future than in trying to revive what's past.

However it went for individual publications, 2018 was a vibrant year for short fiction. Once again, as it has been for the entire life of this series, more short fiction was published than any one person, or even small team of people, could possibly read or even find. It's been some time since I've seen a reliable assessment of the number of pieces of original short science fiction and fiction published in the English language in any given year, and even that seemed unlikely to be accurate. In 2018 short fiction was published as stand-alone books and in anthologies, single-author collections, magazines, promotional materials, blog posts, and podcasts, and was offered for sale, given away free, made available behind a paywall or offered for subscription. There honestly didn't seem to be a limit to where you could find a new story or how you could obtain one, and this was *good*. One thing that is becoming increasingly clear to me, though, is that writers get a substantial benefit from seeing their work published online where readers can easily discover it, share it and discuss it. The immediate ability to read a story and then tell friends, share it on social media and so on is materially shaping what work readers and editors hear about, how they respond to it, and what makes awards ballots. I'm not sure what this bodes for the future, but I wonder about it a lot.

So, where were the best places to look for short fiction in 2018? As was the case in 2017, novella-length fiction continues to dominate. It remains true that there is nothing new about publishing novella-length fiction and that almost all of the major novella publishers have been active at some stage in the past two decades, but these past few years have been different. Novellas are getting attention as stand-alone books in ways they rarely did before, garnering significant sales, widespread reviews, and places on awards ballots. The leader here remains Tor.com Publishing, now in its fifth year. During 2018 they published hugely successful books like Martha Wells's *Artificial Condition*, *Exit Strategy*, and *Rogue Protocol*, Nnedi Okorafor's *Binti: The Night Masquerade*, Seanan McGuire's *Beneath the Sugar Sky* and critically acclaimed books by P. Djèlí Clark, Caitlín R. Kiernan, Ian McDonald, Brooke Bolander, and Kelly Robson. Robson's *Gods, Monsters and the Lucky Peach* is my personal pick for the best science fiction novella of the year, a bright, effervescent time travel adventure, while I also loved Kiernan's powerful and compelling *Black Helicopters: The Director's Cut*, Ian McDonald's moving gay time travel romance, *Time Was*, and JY Yang's *The Descent of Monsters*. All would appear in this book but for length.

Full disclosure requires me to state that I work for Tor.com Publishing and acquired the books by McDonald and Kiernan.

Tor.com wasn't alone in publishing major novellas in 2018. Aliette de Bodard published two fine tales at this length in 2018. *In the Vanisher's Palace* (Jabberwocky) is a dark gender-fluid recasting of Beauty and the Beast with multidimensional dragons that just falls over into novel length and should be on awards ballots in 2019. Also wonderful was her novella from Subterranean, *The Tea Master and the Detective*, a Xuya tale of murder and intrigue. Magazines featured several excellent novellas with highlights including Carolyn Ives Gilman's dark science fiction tale, "Umbernight", at *Clarkesworld*; Greg Egan's "3-adica" for *Asimov's*, Juliet Wade's "The Persistence of Blood", also at *Clarkesworld* (who had a great year in 2018), and Kate Marshall's "We Ragged Few" at the outstanding *Beneath Ceaseless Skies*. Other standouts included Nicola Griffith's *So Lucky* (FSG), Peter Watts's *The Freeze-Frame Revolution* (Tachyon), Janeen Webb's *The Dragon's Child* (PS Publishing), Cynthia Ward's *The Adventures of Dux Bellorum* (Aqueduct), and Adam Roberts's *The Lake Boy* (NewCon Press). All repay your attention.

2018 was a really interesting year for original anthologies. As a caveat, I edited *Infinity's End*, an anthology of science fiction stories set in far, distant places from Solaris that featured stories by Kelly Robson, Naomi Kritzer, Seanan McGuire, Alastair Reynolds, Justina Robson, and others. Given I can pretend little objectivity on the subject, I'll simply say it's a book that I'm proud of and recommend.

The title of best anthology of 2018, though, belongs to one of three books. Dominik Parisien and Navah Wolfe took up the challenge of Holly Black and Justine Larbalestier's playful *Zombies vs. Unicorns* and gave us their own science fiction and fantasy mash-up, *Robots vs. Fairies*, which featured some of the year's very best work including stories by Annalee Newitz, Jeffrey Ford, Ken Liu, Lavie Tidhar, Catherynne M. Valente, and others. Equally good, and perhaps even a little better, was Ellen Oh and Elise Chapman's remarkable *A Thousand Beginnings and Endings,* a diverse selection of stories recasting tales from folklore and mythology which featured major work by Aliette de Bodard, Alyssa Wong, Roshani Chokshi, and Renée Ahdieh. And then there was the big one, the final book of new stories edited by Gardner Dozois. *The Book of Magic* followed on from last year's *The Book of Swords* and featured what Gardner himself would have called "core fantasy" from John Crowley, Garth Nix, Megan Lindholm K.J. Parker, Andy Duncan, Lavie Tidhar, and others and is filled with the "good stuff". All of these are worthwhile, contain essential stories and belong on your bookshelf. Look for them come awards time in 2019.

Of the year's remaining anthologies, I'd recommend Wade Roush's excellent *Twelve Tomorrows*, the latest instalment in the MIT Press series which included outstanding fiction from Elizabeth Bear, S.L. Huang, Ken Liu and others and was probably the best science fiction anthology of the year. It was closely followed by Ian Whates's *2001: An Odyssey in Words*; Greg Whitta, Hugh Howey, and Christie Yant's *Resist: Tales from a Future Worth Fighting Against*; Lisa Yaszek's fine historical retrospective, *The Future Is Female!*; Russell B. Farr's novella-collection, *Aurum*; Bill Campbell and Francesco Verso's *Future Fiction: New Dimensions in International Science Fiction*; Susan Law & Lucas K. Forest's *Shades Within Us*; Rivqa Rafael & Tansy Rayner Roberts's *Mother of Invention*; and Sheldon Teitelbaum's *Zion's Fiction: A Treasury of Israeli Speculative Literature*.

From the first moment I sat down to write one of these retrospective essays I've found myself saying it was a good year for collections. How, honestly, could it *not* be? There is so much short fiction published and so many new and exciting writers entering the field, that it seems impossible that we wouldn't be drowning in outstanding books. And we were, once again, in 2018. Andy Duncan's *An Agent of Utopia* is his first new collection in six years and his first published in his home country since 2000, and appropriately it featured two new stories that stand among the best of the year, including one featured here. Duncan actually had a remarkable year, publishing four new stories, all recommendable, and all confirming him as a writer to be treasured. Small Beer published two other extraordinary collections during the year: Vandana Singh's *Ambiguity Machines and Other Stories* and Abbey Mei Otis's *Alien Virus Love Disaster* were urgent, essential work and stand as a testament both to their writers and to the perspicacity and good taste of the editors at Small Beer.

At this year's World Science Fiction Convention, N.K. Jemisin's work was awarded the Hugo Award for Best Novel for the third year in a row. She has sold more than a million books, and her fiction is being adapted for the big and small screens. Until now her short fiction has, comparatively speaking, been under-recognised but *How Long 'til Black Future Month?* is a powerful, engaging, persuasive, and at times angry work that shows a writer at the height of their powers working out how to write short fiction and how to do it well. One of four originals in the book is reprinted here, but it could have been almost any of them. Also essential was Kelly Barnhill's *Dreadful Young Ladies and Other Stories*, Priya Sharma's wonderful *All the Fabulous Beasts*, Nana Kwame Adjei-Brenyah's *Friday Black*, Catherynne M. Valente's *The Future Is Blue*, Rich Larson's *Tomorrow Factory: Collected Fiction*, and K.J. Parker's *The Father of Lies*. I have a real soft spot for the short fiction of Caitlín R. Kiernan, and she delivered two major collections this year. There was the highly limited Cthulhu-related collection, *Houses Under the Sea*, and the latest in her series of collections for Subterranean, which mostly collect stories from *Sirenia Digest*, *The Dinosaur Tourist*. It's extraordinary work. What this bookshelf of short story collections shows is that there is a lot of incredible reading out there, and more to come!

I don't normally mention this, but during 2018 we lost some of our greatest and most-beloved creators including Ursula K. Le Guin, Jack Ketchum, Victor Milan, Peter Nicholls, Kate Wilhelm, Mary Rosenblum, Karen Anderson, David Bischoff, Christopher Stasheff, Harlan Ellison, Michael Scott Rohan, David J Willoughby, Pat Lupoff, Dave Duncan, Stan Lee, and William Goldman. Perhaps most relevantly, though, we lost my friend and collaborator, Gardner Dozois, who passed away unexpectedly in May. He left behind a towering legacy: a body of fiction to be envied, a bibliography of anthologies that both changed and recorded the history of science fiction and fantasy, a time editing *Asimov's* that stands with any great editor's run at any magazine, and countless writers whose lives and work he touched and made better. He will be missed.

And, so, the end and a new beginning. The book you're about to read is the final volume in *The Best Science Fiction and Fantasy of the Year* anthology series. I'm deeply saddened by this, but also incredibly grateful to my editors and publishers over the past thirteen years who have supported these books, and am more indebted than I can say to each and every writer who allowed me to reprint their work for you to enjoy. But times change, we move on.

MOTHER TONGUES

S. Qiouyi Lu

S. Qiouyi Lu (s.qiouyi.lu) is a writer, editor, narrator, and translator; their fiction has appeared in *Uncanny* and *Strange Horizons*, and their poetry has been published in *inkscrawl* and *Liminality*. S. lives in California with a tiny black cat named Thin Mint. This story originally appeared in *Asimov's Science Fiction Magazine* and was narrated on *Escape Pod* by Rebecca Wei Hsieh.

"THANK YOU VERY much," you say, concluding the oral portion of the exam. You gather your things and exit back into the brightly lit hallway. Photos line the walls: the Eiffel Tower, the Great Wall of China, Machu Picchu. The sun shines on each destination, the images brimming with wonder. You pause before the Golden Gate Bridge.

"右拐就到了," the attendant says. You look up. His blond hair is as standardized as his Mandarin, as impeccable as his crisp shirt and tie. You've just proven your aptitude in English, but hearing Mandarin still puts you at ease in the way only a mother tongue does. You smile at the attendant, murmuring a brief thanks as you make your way down the hall.

You turn right and enter a consultation room. The room is small but welcoming, potted plants adding a dash of green to the otherwise plain creams and browns of the furniture and walls. A literature rack stands to one side, brochures in all kinds of languages tucked into its pockets, creating a mosaic of sights and symbols. The section just on English boasts multiple flags, names of different varieties overlaid on the designs: U.S. English— Standard. U.K. English—Received Pronunciation. Singaporean English— Standard. Nigerian English—Standard... Emblazoned on every brochure is the logo of the Linguistic Grading Society of America, a round seal with a side-view of a head showing the vocal tract.

You pick up a Standard U.S. English brochure and take a seat in one of the middle chairs opposite the mahogany desk that sits before the window. The brochure provides a brief overview of the grading system; your eyes linger on the A-grade description: *Speaker engages on a wide variety of topics with ease. (Phonology?) is standard; speaker has a broad vocabulary...* You take a quick peek at the dictionary on your phone. *Phonology*—linguistic sound systems. You file the word away to remember later.

The door opens. A woman wearing a blazer and pencil skirt walks in, her heels clacking against the hardwood floor, her curled hair bouncing with every step. You stand to greet her and catch a breath of her perfume.

"Diana Moss," she says, shaking your hand. Her name tag also displays her job title: *Language Broker*.

"Jiawen Liu," you reply. Diana takes a seat across from you; as you sit, you smooth out your skirt, straighten your sleeves.

"Is English all right?" Diana asks. "I can get an interpreter in if you'd prefer to discuss in Mandarin."

"English is fine," you reply. You clasp your hands together as you eye Diana's tablet. She swipes across the screen and taps a few spots, her crimson nails stark against the black barrel of the stylus.

"Great," she says. "Well, let's dive right in, shall we? I'm showing that you've been in the U.S. for, let's see, fifteen years now? Wow, that's quite a while."

You nod. "Yes."

"And you used to be an economics professor in China, is that correct?"

You nod again. "Yes."

"Fantastic," Diana says. "Just one moment as I load the results; the scores for the oral portion always take a moment to come in..."

Your palms are clammy, sweaty; Diana twirls the stylus and you can't help feeling a little dizzy as you watch. Finally, Diana props the tablet up and turns it toward you.

"I'm pleased to inform you that your English has tested at a C-grade," she says with a broad smile.

Your heart sinks. Surely there's been some kind of error, but no, the letter is unmistakable: bright red on the screen, framed with flourishes and underlined with signatures; no doubt the certificate is authentic. Diana's perfume is too heady now, sickly sweet; the room is too bright, suffocating as the walls shrink in around you.

"I..." you say, then take a breath. "I was expecting better."

"For what it's worth, your scores on the written and analytical portions of the test were excellent, better than many native speakers of English in the U.S.," Diana says.

"Then what brought my score down?"

"Our clients are looking for a certain... *profile* of English," Diana says, apologetic. "If you're interested in retesting, I can refer you to an accent reduction course—I've seen many prospective sellers go through the classes and get recertified at a higher grade."

She doesn't mention how much the accent reduction course costs, but from your own research, you know it's more than you can afford.

"Ms. Liu?" Diana says. She's holding out a tissue; you accept it and dab at your eyes. "Why don't you tell me what you're trying to accomplish? Maybe we can assist you."

You take in a deep breath as you crumple the tissue into your fist. "My daughter Lillian just got into Stanford, early decision," you say.

"Congratulations!"

"Yes, but we can't afford it." C-grade English sells at only a fraction of A-grade English; you'd rather keep your English than sell it for such a paltry sum that would barely put a dent in textbooks and supplies, never mind tuition and housing.

"There are other tracks you can consider," Diana says, her voice gentle. "Your daughter can go to a community college, for instance, and then transfer out to Stanford again—"

You shake your head.

"Community colleges in the San Gabriel Valley are among the top in the nation," Diana continues. "There's no shame in it."

You're unconvinced. What if she can't transfer out? You and Lillian can't risk that; a good education at a prestigious school is far too important for securing Lillian's future. No, better to take this opportunity that's already been given to her and go with it.

Diana stands and goes over to the literature rack. She flips through a few brochures.

"You know," Diana says as she strides back to you, "China's really hot right now—with their new open-door policy, lots of people are (clamoring?) to invest there; I have people calling me all the time, asking if I have A-grade Mandarin."

She sets a brochure down on the desk and sits back in the executive chair across from you.

"Have you considered selling your Mandarin?"

You trace your hands over the brochure, feeling the embossed logo. China's flag cascades down to a silhouette of Beijing's skyline; you read the Simplified characters printed on the brochure, your eyes skimming over them so much more quickly than you skim over English.

"How much?" you ask.

Diana leans in. "A-grade Mandarin is going for as much as $800,000 these days."

Your heart skips a beat. That would be enough to cover Lillian's college, with maybe a little bit left over—it's a tantalizing number. But the thought of going without Mandarin gives you pause: it's the language you think in, the language that's close to your heart in the way English is not; it's more integral to who you are than any foreign tongue. English you could go without—Lillian's Mandarin is good enough to help you translate your way around what you need—but Mandarin?

"I'm... I'm not sure," you say, setting down the brochure. "Selling my Mandarin..."

"It's a big decision, for sure," Diana says. She pulls a small, silver case out from the pocket of her blazer and opens it with a *click*. "But, if you change your mind..."

She slides a sleek business card across the table.

"...call me."

YOU DECIDE TO go for a week without Mandarin, just to see if you can do it. At times, the transition feels seamless: so many of the people in the San Gabriel Valley are bilingual; you get by fine with only English. Your job as a librarian in the local public library is a little trickier, though; most of your patrons speak English, but a few do not.

You decide to shake your head and send the Mandarin-only speakers over to your coworker, who also speaks Mandarin. But when lunch time comes around, she sits beside you in the break room and gives you a curious look.

"为什·今天把顾客转给我？" she asks.

You figure that you might as well tell her the truth: "I want to sell my Mandarin. I'm seeing what it would be like without it."

"卖你的普通话？" she responds, an incredulous look on her face. "神经病！"

You resent being called crazy, even if some part of you wonders if this is a foolish decision. Still, you soldier on for the rest of the week in English. Your coworker isn't always there to cover for you when there are Mandarin-speaking patrons, and sometimes you break your vow and say a few quick sentences in Mandarin to them. But the rest of the time, you're strict with yourself.

Conversation between you and Lillian flows smoothly, for the most part. Normally, you speak in a combination of English and Mandarin with her, and she responds mostly in English; when you switch to English-only, Lillian doesn't seem to notice. On the occasions when she does speak to you in Mandarin, you hold back and respond in English too, your roles reversed.

At ATMs, you choose English instead of Chinese. When you run errands, "thank you" replaces "谢谢". It's only until Friday rolls around and you're grocery shopping with your mother that not speaking in Mandarin becomes an issue.

You're in the supermarket doing your best to ignore the Chinese characters labeling the produce: so many things that you don't know the word for in English. But you recognize them by sight, and that's good enough; all you need is to be able to pick out what you need. If you look at things out of the corner of your eye, squint a little bit, you can pretend to be illiterate in Chinese, pretend to navigate things only by memory instead of language.

You can cheat with your mother a little bit: you know enough Cantonese to have a halting conversation with her, as she knows both Cantonese and Mandarin. But it's frustrating, your pauses between words lengthy as you try to remember words and tones.

"干吗今天说广东话？" your mother asks in Mandarin. She's pushing the

shopping cart—she insists, even when you offer—and one of the wheels is squeaking. She hunches over the handle, but her eyes are bright.

"Ngo jiu syut Gwongdungwaa," you reply in Cantonese. Except it's not exactly that you *want* to speak Cantonese; you have to, for now. You don't know how to capture the nuance of everything you're going through in Cantonese, either, so you leave it at that. Your mother gives you a look, but she doesn't bring it up again and indulges you, speaking Cantonese as the two of you go around the supermarket and pile the shopping cart high with produce, meat, and fish.

You load the car with the groceries and help your mother into the passenger seat. As you adjust the mirrors, your mother speaks again.

"你在担心什▪？" she asks. Startled, you look over at her. She's peering at you, scrutinizing you; you can never hide anything from her. Of course she can read the worry on your face, the tension in your posture; of course she knows something's wrong.

"Ngo jau zou yat go han zungjiu dik kyutding," you respond, trying to communicate the weight on your shoulders.

"什▪决定？" your mother replies.

You can't find the words to express the choice you have to make in Cantonese. Every time you grasp for the right syllables, they come back in Mandarin; frustrated, you switch back to Mandarin and reply,

"我为了去送Lillian上大学想卖我的普通话。"

You expect your mother to scold you, to tell you about the importance of your heritage and language—she's always been proud of who she is, where she's from; she's always been the first to teach you about your own culture—but instead her expression softens, and she puts a hand over yours, her wrinkled skin warm against your skin.

"哎，嘉嘉，没有别的办法吗？"

Your nickname is so tender on her tongue. But you've thought through all other avenues: you don't want Lillian to take out loans and be saddled with so much debt like your friends' children; you don't want her to bear such a burden her entire life, not while you're still paying off debts too. You can't rely on Lillian's father to provide for her, not after he left your family and took what little money you had. And although Lillian's been doing her best to apply for scholarships, they're not enough.

You shake your head.

The two of you sit in silence as you start the car and drive back to your mother's place. The sun sets behind you, casting a brilliant glow over the Earth, washing the sky from orange to blue. As you crest over a hill, the sparkling lights of the city below glitter in the darkness, showing you a million lives, a million dreams.

When you get to your mother's house, you only have one question to ask her.

"如果你需要做同样的决定，" you say, "你也会这样做吗？"

You don't know what it would have been like if you were in Lillian's shoes, if your mother had to make the same decision as you. But as your mother smiles at you, sadness tinging the light in her eyes, the curve of her lips, you know she understands.

"当然，" she says.

Of course.

THE WAITING ROOM is much starker than the consultation room you were in before: the seats are less comfortable, the temperature colder; you're alone except for a single TV playing world news at a low volume.

You read the paperwork, doing your best to understand the details of the procedure—for all you pride yourself on your English, though, there are still many terms you don't understand completely:

The Company's (proprietary?) algorithms (iterate?) through near-infinite (permutations?) of sentences, extracting a neural map. The (cognitive?) load on the brain will cause the Applicant to experience a controlled stroke, and the Applicant's memory of the Language will be erased. Common side effects include: temporary disorientation, nausea. Less common side effects include partial (aphasia?) of non-target languages and (retrograde?) amnesia. Applicant agrees to hold Company harmless...

You flip over to the Chinese version of the contract, and, while some of the terms raise concern in you, you've already made your decision and can't back out now. You scan the rest of the agreement and sign your name at the bottom.

The lab is clinical, streamlined, with a large, complicated-looking machine taking up most of the room. An image of the brain appears on a black panel before you.

"Before we begin," the technician says, "do you have any questions?"

You nod as you toy with your hospital gown. "Will I be able to learn Mandarin again?"

"Potentially, though it won't be as natural or easy as the first time around. Learning languages is usually harder than losing them."

You swallow your nervousness. *Do it for Lillian.* "Why can't you make a copy of the language instead of erasing it?"

The technician smiles ruefully. "As our current technology stands, the imaging process has the unfortunate side effect of suppressing neurons as it replicates them..."

You can't help but wonder cynically if the reason why the neurons have to be suppressed is to create artificial scarcity, to inflate demand in the face of limited supply. But if that scarcity is what allows you to put Lillian through college, you'll accept it.

The technician hooks electrodes all over your head; there's a faint hum, setting your teeth on edge.

As the technician finishes placing the last of the electrodes on your head, certain parts of the brain on the panel light up, ebbing and flowing, a small chunk in the back active; you try to recall the areas of the brain from biology classes in university, and, while different parts of your brain start to light up, you still don't remember the names of any of the regions.

The technician flips a couple switches, then types a few commands. The sensation that crawls over you is less of a shock than a tingling across your scalp. Thoughts flash through your mind too fast for you to catch them; you glance up at the monitor and see light firing between the areas the technician pointed out, paths carving through the brain and flowing back and forth. The lights flash faster and faster until they become a single blur, and as you watch, your world goes white.

The technician and nurse keep you at the institute for a few hours to monitor your side effects: slight disorientation, but that fades as the time goes by. They ask if you have anyone picking you up; you insist that you're fine taking public transportation by yourself, and the technician and nurse relent. The accountant pays you the first installment of the money, and soon you're taking the steps down from the institute's main doors, a cool breeze whipping at your hair.

The bus ride home is... strange. As you go from west Los Angeles toward the San Gabriel Valley, the English dominating billboards and signs starts to give way to Chinese. Although you can still understand the balance of the characters, know when they're backwards in the rear-view mirrors, you can't actually *read* them—they're no more than shapes: familiar ones, but indecipherable ones. You suck down a deep breath and will your heart to stop beating so quickly. It will take time to adjust to this, just as it took time to adjust to being thrown into a world of English when you first immigrated to the United States.

A corner of the check sticks out of your purse.

You'll be okay.

YOUR FAMILY IS celebrating Chinese New Year this weekend. You drive with Lillian over to your mother's senior living apartment; you squeeze in through the door while carrying a bag of fruit. Your mother is cooking in the tiny kitchenette, the space barely big enough for the both of you. She's wearing the frilly blue apron with embroidered teddy bears on it, and you can't help but smile as you inhale the scent of all the food frying and simmering on the stove.

"Bongmong?" you say in Cantonese. It's one of the few words you can remember—as the days passed, you realized that some of your Cantonese had been taken too, its roots intertwined and excised with your Mandarin.

"(???). (???????)," your mother says, gesturing toward the couch. You and Lillian sit down. A period drama plays on the television. The subtitles go by too fast for you to match sound to symbol; Lillian idly taps away on her phone.

A few moments pass like this, your gaze focused on the television as you see if you can pick up something, anything at all; sometimes, you catch a phrase that jogs something in your memory, but before you can recall what the phrase means, the sound of it and its meaning are already gone.

"(???)!"

Lillian gets up, and you follow suit. The small dining room table has been decked out with all kinds of food: glistening, ruby-red shrimp with caramelized onions; braised fish; stir-fried lotus root with sausage; sautéed vegetables... you wish you could tell your mother how good it looks; instead, you can only flash her a smile and hope she understands.

"(?????????), (?????????)," your mother says.

Lillian digs in, picking up shrimp with her chopsticks; you scold her and remind her of her manners.

"But (??????) said I could go ahead," Lillian says.

"Still," you reply. You place some food on your mother's plate first, then Lillian's; finally, you set some food on your own plate. Only after your mother's eaten do you take a bite.

Lillian converses with your mother; her Mandarin sounds a little stilted, starting and stopping, thick with an American accent, but her enthusiasm expresses itself in the vibrant conversation that flows around you. You stay quiet, shrinking into yourself as your mother laughs, as Lillian smiles.

You're seated between Lillian and your mother; the gap across the table from you is a little too big, spacing the three of you unevenly around the table. As the syllables cascade around you, you swear the spaces between you and your mother, between you and Lillian, grow larger and larger.

After dinner, as your mother washes up the dishes—again, she refuses your help—you and Lillian watch the Spring Gala playing on the television. An invited pop star from the U.S., the only white person on the stage, sings a love ballad in Mandarin. You don't need to know what she's saying to tell that she doesn't have an American accent.

"I bet she bought her Mandarin," Lillian says. It's an offhanded comment, but still you try to see if you can detect any disgust in her words.

"Is that so bad?" you ask.

"I don't know; it just seems a little... (appropriative?), you know?"

You don't know. *Lillian* doesn't know. You were planning on telling her the instant you came home, but you didn't know how to bring it up. And now... you want to keep your sacrifice a secret, because it's not about you— it was never about you. But it's only a matter of time before Lillian finds out.

You don't know how she'll react. Will she understand?

Lillian rests her head on your shoulder. You pull her close, your girl who's grown up so fast. You try to find the words to tell her what you'd do for her, how important it is that she has a good future, how much you love her and want only the best for her.

But all you have is silence.

OLIVIA'S TABLE
Alyssa Wong

Alyssa Wong's (www.crashwong.net) stories have won the Nebula Award, the World Fantasy Award, and the Locus Award. She was a finalist for the John W. Campbell Award for Best New Writer, and her fiction has been shortlisted for the Hugo, Bram Stoker, and Shirley Jackson awards. She lives in California.

OLIVIA BLEW INTO town with the storm and headed straight for The Grand Silver Hotel. Pots and containers of sauces and marinade clattered in the trunk of her Toyota, packed in with the rest of the groceries she'd brought from Phoenix. The evening sky hung heavy with dark clouds, but the shrinking Arizona sun still burned her arms through the car windows.

Bisden was one of those mining towns that had sprung up in the 1800s, flourished for a while, and then all but died once the silver ran out. Now, the town made its money from the tourists who trickled in, hoping to see two things: a real Wild West ghost town, and one of the most haunted historical sites in the southwest.

After a childhood of making the trip down from Phoenix, Olivia barely needed her GPS to guide her. She drove past the sparse palo verdes lining the old shop fronts. Outside, the wind whipped up sharp clouds of dust and stone shards, sending them sweeping down the barren, red-dirt road that ran through Bisden's town square. The air carried a light brown tint, and Olivia squinted to see through it.

In front of a clapboard saloon, two re-enactment actors in full period dress were toughing out the approaching dust storm, fingering the pistols hanging at their hips. Most of the town's tourists had migrated inside; a few hung back to watch them, shading their eyes or filming on their phones.

And then there were the ghosts, dozens of them, clustered around the tourists and swaying in the wind like feather grass. A couple were dressed in fine clothes—long skirts and blouses buttoned to the throat, cravats tucked into tight waistcoats—but most were dressed in working clothes. Wide-brimmed hats, sturdy trousers, loose shirts. Only some of them were white folks. All bore signs of trauma; gunshots punched a cluster of holes through one gentleman's torso, and a cluster of women hanging back by the saloon had burned, blackened bodies, the remains of their dresses drifting around them in ashes.

Olivia sighed. They were right in front of The Grand Silver Hotel, too. Figured.

She slung her backpack over her shoulder and pocketed her phone. Her braid was coming loose, but she ignored it. After locking her car, Olivia pulled out the long envelope of paper talismans that her grandma had written years ago. She slapped one over each of the car windows, and the coppery scent of magic sparked in the air. The sky rumbled overhead as she retrieved a pack of saran wrap and taped sheets of plastic over the talismans. If this worked, the talismans would keep ghosts away from the car, and the saran wrap would keep the rain away from the talismans.

It would work, she thought firmly. It'd worked for her mom all the times they'd made the trip together. And even though she wasn't there now, Olivia had watched her ward her car like this for years.

No time for doubts. She headed for the hotel, past the re-enactment actors and tourists. She had to push her way through the ghosts. Their bodies felt more solid than they did the rest of the year, and fabric brushed her hands as she edged through the crowd. "Excuse me," she muttered. A pair of Hopi women glanced down at her from beneath the brims of their hats, turning to make room for her to squeeze by. A cluster of Chinese miners, their bodies broken and smashed—*a cave-in,* she thought, *an accident*—watched her, unmoving, from a distance. None of the tourists seemed to see the ghosts, staring through them at the girl weaving her way through empty air.

The Grand Silver Hotel rose three stories into the air, clinging to its last shreds of grandeur. Inside, new light bulbs shone in old fixtures, and the tatty carpet crunched under Olivia's sneakers. Like every other establishment in town, The Grand Silver kept its head above water by advertising its very own ghost. An oil painting of the Wailing Lady hung on the wall above the reception desk, and a rotating rack of postcards, most of them reproductions of the painting, spun lazily by the elevator door. The older woman behind the desk smiled as Olivia approached. Her nametag read *RENEE*. "Welcome to The Grand Silver Hotel. How may we help you today?"

"I'm here for the Ghost Festival," said Olivia. Her voice sounded too loud in the nearly empty lobby. She hated listening to herself speak; talking, period, wasn't easy for her. "I need a room for tonight and tomorrow night, and some help getting things out of my car."

Renee brightened. "Of course. The Ghost Festival is tomorrow night, and it's one of Bisden's big attractions. Now, there are a few other groups of tourists who made the trip here to see it, so you won't be alone. It's perfectly safe, but we do ask that everyone stay inside and keep a healthy distance from the ghosts—"

"I'm not a tourist," Olivia said. "I'm here to cook the banquet for the festival." She reached for her driver's license, and her student ID slipped out first. She caught it before it hit the ground. "You've worked with my mom before. Amory Chang."

The receptionist squinted. "You're Exorcist Chang's daughter, are you? You do look a bit like her." *It was nice of her to lie*, thought Olivia. "She helped us out for years. Every summer, on the night when the ghosts come out to walk among the living. And her cooking, of course, was sublime."

Thank you, Olivia wanted to say, but the words wouldn't come. Renee didn't seem to notice.

"We're looking forward to having you for the Ghost Festival. Exorcist Chang was always a wonder to watch. Excellent showmanship, and her work kept the town safe for years." As Olivia checked into her room, Renee paused. "By the way. Our Wailing Lady is getting... unruly. Could you look into fixing that up, or finding a replacement? It's been almost ten years since your mother tended to our ghost."

The Wailing Lady's painting hung serenely on the wall. In it was an ample young woman wearing a wedding dress and a veil that obscured her face. A jilted, suicidal bride, whose weeping could still sometimes be heard late at night. Not very original. "I'll look into it," said Olivia.

Renee and the two folks working at the hotel—a maid and a young man who was probably her son—helped lug Olivia's vats of soy sauce and marinade from her car and into the hotel kitchen. Rice, cooking utensils, and paper bag after paper bag of different kinds of meat followed. Pickings at the Bisden supermarket were slim, so she'd brought everything she could fit into the Toyota's back seat and trunk. As they carried the groceries inside, Olivia caught sight of the ghosts out front. The re-enactment actors were gone, and now the ghosts stared, as one, at Olivia and the hotel employees.

The air smelled like approaching rain. She walked faster.

After sussing out the kitchen—on the small side, though all of the kitchens at the old Bisden hotels were—Olivia checked her phone. No signal, no internet, though there were a couple of password-locked hotspots from the shops nearby. The Grand Silver had its own router, and Renee gave Olivia the password along with a long, old-fashioned metal key. "You'll be in room 309," she said.

Olivia spent the next couple hours in that kitchen, cutting, testing, prepping. It was night by the time she finished. When she made it upstairs to her room, she crouched on the floor by the bed and set out packet after packet of incense and joss paper. She hoped she brought enough. Enough incense, enough food—

No, it would be enough. She unpacked a small ceramic bowl and emptied a handful of dried orange peel into it, and then she lit a match over it. Once, her mom had taught her that the smoke from burning orange peel would keep the ghosts away. It had never failed her.

Olivia hesitated. The flame licked down the match, chasing her fingers. After a second, she shook it out.

Wind rattled the windows as she settled into bed. The sounds of faint footsteps upstairs and a woman sobbing through the floorboards chased her into her dreams.

It HAD RAINED during every Ghost Festival that Olivia could remember. On the seventh month on her mom's calendar and the eighth month on her dad's, Mom would pack the minivan with food and head down south for a couple of days, leaving Olivia in Dad and Grandma's care. It was monsoon season, and torrential rain flooded the roads and the stony washes out behind the houses.

But when the skies cleared, Mom would return with an empty trunk and a check for more money than she made in half a year.

For a time, she didn't tell Olivia where she went or what she did. But the year Olivia turned eight, Mom loaded her into the backseat next to the paper bags of groceries and drove her to Bisden for the first time.

Come with Mama, she said. Back then, her short black hair was only faintly laced with silver, and she still looked healthy. *I need you to help me with the Ghost Festival this year.*

The drive was several hours long, and by the time they reached the tiny town, sunset was approaching. So was a storm, a desert monsoon that crawled inexorably across the horizon. That night, they checked into The Grand Silver, although in the coming years, they would rotate from hotel to hotel, collecting paychecks from many grateful proprietors. Every hotel in town wanted the chance to host the festival and attract the bulk of that year's tourists. Mom told Olivia that when her own mom, and the long line of Chang women before her, had cooked for the Ghost Festival, in this country and in their countries before that, they'd rarely stayed in a place for more than a year.

Different ghosts are tied to different spaces, Olivia, Mom said as they got ready for bed. The lamp cast a warm glow across her face. *Sometimes they form attachments to specific places, and sometimes other people bind them there and they can't leave. Moving the banquet means bringing food to folks who missed their chance to eat the year before. Good service is all about being considerate of others.*

Mom spent the entire night and then the next day cooking and prepping, and she had Olivia help her as often as she could. Olivia stood on a little metal stool and cut vegetables. Her knife cuts were careful and even under her mom's strict tutelage. Occasionally, she peered out the windows, watching the tourists run through the rain, their eyes growing huge and round, even from this distance, whenever they glimpsed one of the ghosts.

"They're scared of them," Mom told her as she set out a pair of bamboo steamers. "Right now they can see them."

"Can't they see the ghosts all the time?" she asked.

"Not like you and I can. The Festival is when ghosts are most themselves instead of what the living want them to be. Not everyone will like what they see tonight."

When her arms grew tired, Mom sent her out of the kitchen to take breaks. The long banquet table that Mom had requested from the hotel was set up on the front porch. She crawled under it and watched the rain slosh down the road in growing streams, swirling with red-brown dirt, until the daylight faded and the electric lights came on.

Her Gameboy. She'd forgotten it in the car. Olivia didn't have an umbrella, but she ran out into the rain anyway, letting it beat at her through her clothes. It only rained for about two weeks each year, and the cool droplets hitting her face filled her with giddy energy. She sprinted down the street toward her mom's car, splashing deliberately in the biggest pools of water she could find.

Halfway down the darkening street, a voice stopped her. "You're not from here."

Olivia turned sharply. A ghost stood under the awning of the Bisden General Store, leaning against a post. She wore a cotton shirt and trousers like many of the other folks who'd worked on the railroad when they were alive. There weren't many women among the Chinese ghosts. But this one was a girl, with deep brown hair like Olivia's, and a small mouth and dark eyes like Olivia's. She looked a little older than Olivia, but not nearly as old as Olivia's mom.

"Did someone lose you?" said the ghost.

"Nobody lost me," said Olivia. "I came to get my Gameboy." She came a little closer, under the awning, and the ghost didn't shrink back. When Olivia reached out to touch her sleeve, her hand passed through. "What's your name?"

"Mei Ling," said the ghost. She sounded amused. From this distance, Olivia could see that her legs were mangled, the way a number of other Chinese ghosts who'd died in construction accidents were. "My ma calls me Sadie, though."

"I'm Olivia," said Olivia. "My grandma gave me a Chinese name too, but my dad doesn't like me using it." She'd overheard her dad talking with her grandma one night, when she was very little. *What will she do when the other kids tease her at school?* he'd said. Olivia didn't tell him that the other kids teased her anyway, name or no name.

"I don't know what a Gameboy is," said the ghost. "But why don't I walk with you while you get it?"

An alarm bell in Olivia's head began to ring. *Don't talk to strangers,* Mom had said, over and over. *And don't trust the ghosts, especially not during the Ghost Festival.* "No," she said. "I'm okay. It's just over there."

But the ghost followed her. Olivia began to run faster, and the creak of the ghost's ruined ankles grew louder and louder as the night got darker. The rain pounded down around them. The water rushed across the ground in rising torrents, with no gutters to guide it away from the street.

Where was the car? It was dark, and the electric lights seemed so dim, and the ghost was behind her, lurching forward, moving too fast—

Her foot slipped out from under her and she fell backwards into the water. Her head cracked hard against a stone, and the flash flood pulled her, rolling and gasping, down the street and onto her face. She inhaled a lungful of water. Olivia choked and tried to push herself up, but her palms slid on the loose gravel and her hands slipped out from under her.

She was drowning. Two weeks of rain a year, and this was how she'd die. When she came back as a ghost, would her lungs be full of water forever?

Olivia reached out blindly, and someone grabbed her arm. The ghost hauled her out of the water. When she rubbed Olivia's back as Olivia coughed, her hand was solid and warm, all the way down to her broken fingers. Her cotton work clothing was soaked through.

Olivia's head was bright with pain.

Mei Ling lifted her and held her close to her chest. The ghost had no heartbeat. And then they were running, splashing through the rising water, headed back to the town square. The last thing Olivia saw were the stuccoed walls of The Grand Silver and the hordes of ghosts descending upon her mother's banquet table, their swarming, newly substantial bodies rippling in the moonlight.

OLIVIA WOKE TOO early, her heart pounding loud in her ears. The roof rattled like someone was upending stones on it. The muted roar of torrential rain surrounded her, and when she pushed back the curtains, she saw that the street was full of rushing water, just as it had been all those years ago. No living people were out and about, not even the actors from yesterday. But ghosts—so many of them, almost too many to count—huddled under porch roofs and awnings, their bodies all clumped together, away from the rain.

Overhead, the sobbing had stopped. Last night, through the haze of half-swallowed dreams, the woman's voice had sounded familiar. Olivia listened carefully, but she could hear nothing but the storm.

She checked her phone for missed calls, and found that there were none. No phone service. Right. But there was internet, so she emailed her dad: *I made it to Bisden safely. Cooking all today. I'll be home soon. Love you. Don't forget to eat.*

Too late, she remembered that her mom used to sign off all her texts and emails the same way. But she'd already hit SEND. She bit her lip, then turned away to pull on her jeans.

Despite the early hour and pouring rain, the ghosts on the street were already out in full force. She walked past them, and their heads followed her on skinny, starved necks, rotating like owls'. The full moon was a brief imprint in the sky, barely visible through a gap in the darkened clouds. As Olivia headed for her car, the boy who'd helped her move her supplies into the kitchen ran after her. "Hey," he said breathlessly. "Mom asked me to help you if you needed anything."

Olivia looked at him. He looked about her age, maybe seventeen at most. She couldn't remember his name. "I'm just going grocery shopping," she said.

"I'll help you carry things if you want. I don't mind." He grinned. "I'm Carlos."

He did look strong, Olivia conceded. His arms and back were well muscled. When he smiled, he had cute dimples. If she had been interested in men, she might have found him attractive. "I'm Olivia," she said. "I'm going to buy a lot of stuff, though."

"I figured. I didn't think ghosts would eat a lot, but apparently they do." He didn't seem bothered by the rain or by the ghosts that watched them from the awnings. But then, he didn't seem to see the ghosts at all.

The best thing about the Bisden supermarket, Olivia decided, was that it was cheap. She headed straight for the back counter and bought two dozen fresh fish. These ones were dead—not as fresh as the live ones swimming in tanks at the Chinese market back home—but they would do. She loaded her cart up with fresh produce: green onions, carrots, garlic, herbs. Four crates of oranges. It was too bad that Bisden didn't have a Costco.

Carlos talked a lot, but he did hold up his end of the bargain. He carried all of her groceries and helped load them into her car. He told her all about his schooling (he was a junior, one year younger than her), his aspirations (to go to Arizona State and study mechanical engineering) and his boyfriend (Sean, beautiful and geeky, also an aspiring engineer). "What about you?" he said as they drove through the pouring rain. "Do you have someone you like?"

"I did," said Olivia. "But we broke up a while ago." It had been a year and a half ago, in the spring. Priya was a year ahead of Olivia in school, and when she found out she was going to an east coast college, she was ecstatic.

Olivia hadn't wanted to keep Priya tied down. With Priya going east and Olivia staying in Arizona, it made sense to break things off. But Priya hadn't agreed, and when she'd cried and Olivia didn't, she'd accused Olivia of not caring enough to be there for her.

But you're going out of state, Olivia had said. *I can't just move to Boston for you.*

Priya had blown her wavy black hair away from her face and stared her down. *You know that's not what I'm talking about. Even when we're together, having dinner, watching movies or whatever, you're always so detached. It feels like you're somewhere else, not with me.* Her mouth tightened. *Is there someone else?*

There was the memory of a girl in dark cotton trousers, her hair hanging down her shoulders, pulling her from the water. There was also Mom, lying alone in the hospital, watching dramas until she fell asleep. She'd never told Priya about either, because they felt too private to talk about. *No*, said Olivia.

By the time Priya left for college, they had fallen apart.

Olivia and Carlos drove the rest of the way back in silence. As they were unloading the car, Carlos stopped in his tracks. Olivia glanced at him. "What is it?"

"I thought—" he broke off, frowning. He looked pale. "I thought I saw something. Over there, to your left. But it's gone now."

Olivia looked. The ghost of an old man, his body wracked with disease, looked back at her. His sunken eyes glittered. "I don't see anything," she said.

"Let's get the rest of these inside," said Carlos, hurrying past her.

Olivia cast one last look at the ghost and followed. If Carlos was starting to see them, she'd have to cook fast. The moon was rising, the Ghost Festival was coming. Her palms began to sweat. She wiped them on her jeans and strode inside, past the tourists beginning to mill about in the lobby with pamphlets about the Ghost Festival.

Olivia sorted her ingredients on the counters, arranging them by dish. Duck, pork, shrimp, fish. Wintermelon, out of season, but bought from one of the Chinese markets back home. Spices, marinades. Red beans, sesame oil, sugar, salt. Bok choy, green beans, lotus root, sauces that she'd spent the past two days making.

Carlos hung back by the door. "Don't you have work to do?" she said to him, and then winced. *Too blunt. The words are wrong.* Always wrong, when they came out of her.

"I do," he said. He seemed unphased, and the tight knot in Olivia's chest loosened. "But I want to help if I can. You need someone to help you chop and prep, right? I cook meals in this kitchen all the time."

A surge of relief flooded through her. "Thank you," she said quietly. She indicated the vegetables lying in their neat rows. "I need these chopped. Garlic minced, green onions left long, but not longer than a finger. Carrots thinly sliced. Wintermelon cubed."

"Do you have a recipe?"

"Only in my head," she said. That was how Mom had done it, too.

Carlos sighed and picked up a knife. "All right. Let's get to work."

They worked for hours, and soon they began to learn each other's rhythm. The clock over the sink ticked, and sunlight passed across the windows and grew dark. Olivia didn't have to look outside to know that people were locking themselves in their houses, pulling the curtains shut. Only the curious tourists kept watch, peering through the large glass windows of every hotel lining the street. All of the hotels would have bolted their front doors shut except for The Grand Silver. Not The Grand Silver, because Olivia still had to hurry in and out with her food. Its thresholds were already lined with paper talismans to ward off any ghosts bent on mischief, or worse.

Time flew by, and Olivia sweated and braised and fried and steamed. Her muscles ached, but adrenaline and fear kept her body and mind singing. The rising spirit energy from outside grew to a tight, intense buzz in her head.

She could hear the ghosts through the walls, whispering, waiting, and by the expression that Carlos wore, so could he. And then there was a wet, whining sound coming from inside the hotel, and the drag of broken feet in high heels in the ceiling above, somewhere in the air vents.

The moon rose, and Olivia began to plate.

AFTER OLIVIA'S MOM got sick, she became too weak to move around much. She was supposed to stay still, to conserve her energy. Moving made her nauseated. But the one place that Olivia's dad couldn't chase her out of was the kitchen. Even when she had trouble standing, she still insisted on cooking dinner for the family. Olivia helped her into a chair by the stove, and she sat there for hours, making sure all of the meal's components were cooking properly. Olivia did what she could to ease the burden, measuring liquids, cooking the rice, making sure all the ingredients were chopped so that her mom didn't have to worry about it.

One afternoon, her mother smiled up at her. "You're getting so good at this. I'm glad. You'll have to do this when I'm gone."

A lump rose in Olivia's throat. "That's not going to happen." *I can't fill your shoes,* she thought. "You're going to get better."

"Don't let the sesame seeds burn," said Mom, and Olivia swooped in automatically, rescuing the frying pan full of toasted seeds. "Good, good. Let them cool somewhere safe."

Olivia set them aside in a small bowl. Her hands were trembling. "I can't lose you. Dad can't lose you. You're going to get better. I know it."

Mom reached out. Her fingers felt so delicate, so thin. "If you honor everything I've taught you, then I promise that I will never leave you." She held Olivia's hand and squeezed it. "I love you, Xi Yi."

Olivia hadn't heard that name in years, not since her grandma had passed away. Tears welled up in her eyes. "Mom—"

The kitchen timer went off. Her mom moved to take the ging do pai gwut off the heat and transferred it into a waiting ceramic dish. "Remember," she said to Olivia. "Now take this to the table."

*   *   *

THE BANQUET TABLE waited on The Grand Silver's porch, safe from the rainstorm and the rushing water below. An outline of talismans marked a boundary around it, leading to the hotel doors. All along its edges, ghosts clustered and crowded, whispering among themselves. They were substantial, all flesh and bone, just for this one night. Just to feast until the sun came up. Above, in a gap in the heavy clouds, the full moon hovered like a malevolent eye.

Olivia came out with a cart laden with giant pots and stacked with metal dishes, clattering past the tourists gathered in the lobby, ignoring their questions. She refused to let Carlos follow her out onto the porch, and she felt his eyes on her back as she crossed The Grand Silver's threshold. She laid platter after platter of Peking duck in the center of the table, forming a line of meat and soft, pale, steamed buns. She removed the lids of the pots and the scent of wintermelon soup rose through the thick air. As quickly as she could, she began to fill bowls.

The ghosts whispered and pushed their hands up against the barrier, hissing when copper-scented magic sparked against their skin. Cold sweat rose on Olivia's back. But her hands were steady as she continued to ladle soup into bowls. Finally, there was no more room on the tabletop. Olivia stepped back, laying down another line of talismans so that there was a narrow, unobstructed passage from the door to the table.

She raised her voice. "Welcome, honored guests. My name is Olivia Chang, and I have prepared you a banquet, so that you may take and eat and find peace in your souls." Her mom had given this speech many times, and Olivia did not stumble. "Please come. You are welcome at this table."

With that, she broke the talisman barrier around the table. The ghosts fell upon the food. They shoved at each other, grabbing bowls, seizing chopsticks. Some used their hands and pushed food into their mouths as fast as they could. Many of them barely looked human in their hunger. They tore into the meat with ferocity, pushed their faces into the bowls of soup and snarled at their neighbors to get at the dishes they wanted. The food seemed to evaporate as the ghosts fought and bit and ate, ate, ate.

I didn't make enough, Olivia thought wildly. Dread built in her stomach. *All of these people came to my table, and I can't serve them all.*

Breathe.

She breathed. Grabbing the cart, she doubled back for more food. Shrimp in clear, sweet sauce, crab with ginger and scallions. Fish after fish, all steamed, with sharp, salty sauce. Tender, marinated beef, still sizzling on metal plates. Bak cheet gai, with all of the sauces, hot pepper pork chops. Her mother's ging do pai gwut, sweet and glazed in bright red sauce, sprinkled with toasted sesame seeds. (Olivia's heart ached.) And then, lastly, platter after platter of sliced oranges, and bowls of sweet red bean soup. It vanished almost as soon as she put it out, but Olivia kept up her pace, her legs burning, her hands steady.

The night wore on, and more spirits flocked to the table, replacing those who had filled their bellies and wandered away. The moon drifted. In the lulls between waves, Olivia kept watch, burning incense and joss paper over a small fire. Embers wafted up into the air like wishes, and one by one, they winked out. The rain poured down relentlessly.

Mei Ling did not appear. Olivia watched the table, chewing on her lip so hard that it began to taste raw. Ghosts came, some eating quietly, some ravenous. The wildness in their eyes, their grief, their fear and rage, all ebbed as they ate. Take and eat, she'd said. The Chinese American ghosts were the ones who wept the most, laughing and reveling in familiar foods. *Thank you,* they told her, one after another. *I never thought I would taste this again.* And one after another, they vanished, fading away to rest at last.

This was why she was here, as Exorcist Chang. It was only an exorcism in the loosest sense. Her work wasn't an act of expulsion; her role was to sooth lonely souls, offering them freedom.

Olivia thought about the footsteps overhead, the sobbing at night. She sent up her piece of joss paper and headed back inside, through the clump of tourists in the lobby. They tried to speak to her, but she didn't hear them. She stopped by the reception desk, staring up at the portrait of the Wailing Lady.

Yesterday, Renee had leaned over the counter and smiled at her. Our Wailing Lady is getting... unruly. Could you look into fixing that up, or finding a replacement?

The longer a ghost stayed in one place without release, the more restless it became. Bisden lived and died on its haunted attraction tourism. And when a ghost acted up, it lent legitimacy to the stories. But ghosts that were trapped for too long began to go mad, and that was when people got hurt.

Olivia stared at the painting, at the white veil covering the Wailing Lady's face. In the ten years of Ghost Festivals since that first one at The Grand Silver, Olivia hadn't seen Mei Ling once.

Beneath that veil, she could be anyone.

She turned and ran for the kitchen. There was still some rice, just enough for a bowl. Everything else was gone, presented on the table outside. Olivia hoped the rice would do. She took the stairs up to the third floor and headed back to her room. As she ascended, the familiar sound of sobbing drifted down towards her, and she climbed faster. When Olivia opened the door, she saw a woman standing inside by the window, gazing out at the feast below. She wore a white wedding gown, stained with dirt at the hem, and a long white veil. She turned to face Olivia.

Olivia peeled the talisman necklace from her neck and laid it on the floor beside her. Slowly, she approached, holding out the rice. "I brought you something to eat," she said. This time, her voice didn't sound too loud in her ears. "It's not much. But you seem hungry. Please, honored guest, take and eat."

The Wailing Woman didn't move, but she let Olivia approach. Steam wafted gently from the rice, into the air. Rain battered down outside, beating at the window, demanding to be let in. Olivia reached out, offering up the bowl.

The ghost reached back, taking it. The hands around hers were warm and solid.

Gently, Olivia pushed back the veil.

WHEN OLIVIA'S MOM died, she didn't come back as a ghost. Olivia half expected her to. But she didn't materialize in the hospital room when Dad chose to take her off life support, or on any of the nights when Olivia heard her dad crying alone in his bedroom. At the funeral, there had only been the silent Mom-shaped body nestled in her casket.

People became ghosts when they were restless, or had unfinished business, or held too much regret to pass on. They became ghosts when the ones they loved forgot them or didn't pay them respects. Olivia burned incense despite the fire warnings on especially dry days, and some days, she set aside a small dish of whatever she was cooking to put on Mom's altar later. But she kept the small shrine in her room, away from Dad. Whenever he saw it, his mouth would crumple and he'd leave abruptly, his grief chasing him somewhere else.

Olivia started staying late at school, just to be somewhere else. She withdrew from her friends, hiding in the library. Her grades suffered and improved. Slowly, it dawned on her that her mom was gone. Not just dead-and-a-ghost gone, but gone-gone.

People only became ghosts when they had something tying them to this place. Olivia's mom, it seemed, had nothing to keep her here.

Olivia didn't apply to college. Every time she reached the Family section on the applications—Parents' Names? Level of Education? Relationship? Living? Deceased?—her head filled with static. The essay questions were inane; "What did you do last summer and how did it impact you?" just made her think of the ugly, ultraclean stink of the hospital and how she would never forget it, as much as she wanted to. Besides, someone had to take care of Dad. She couldn't leave him, too.

Her relationship with Priya crumbled, and Olivia let it.

Her friends packed and left for college, and Olivia cooked, and paid bills, and cooked. She made sure all of her mom's emails were forwarded to her own email address, and that the small dish in front of her altar was never empty. When she opened the email from The Grand Silver asking Exorcist Chang to prepare her banquet for the Ghost Festival that year, Olivia's heartbeat jumped.

The one night when spirits walk among us.

She'd helped prepare the banquet every year, but she'd never done it alone. And she hadn't been back to The Grand Silver since that first summer in Bisden.

"Dad," she said that evening, twisting her napkin into tight rings under the table, "I'm going to Bisden in August."

He looked up with a sad smile. He'd gotten so much older in the past months, she realized. "I know," he said.

OLIVIA FOUND HERSELF looking into the face of a stranger. A hard face, weathered with age and hunger.

It wasn't Mei Ling. It wasn't Mom. It wasn't anyone she knew.

"Who are you?" Olivia whispered, and the ghost stared silently back at her. The old woman's gaze was vacant, and she shifted back and forth, her ill-fitting wedding dress whispering around her. Olivia wondered if she was a bride at all, or if someone had bound her to The Grand Silver Hotel against her will to serve as their ghost. This woman didn't look like the young, pretty, white girl that the hotel's brochures advertised as the Wailing Lady. Maybe that hadn't mattered to the person who had trapped her here.

But if there was a night for truth, it was tonight. Mom had said so: during the Festival, ghosts were most themselves. Not what the living wanted. Not what Olivia wanted.

The night of the Festival was a chance for freedom.

Olivia bit back her disappointment and smiled at the woman. She held out a pair of chopsticks, and the woman took them and began to eat. The rice wasn't much, something small and humble. But with every bite, the woman's gaze grew sharper and more aware, and her movements became more coordinated. Soon, the rice was gone. Olivia opened her mouth to apologize, but the stranger spoke first.

"Thank you," she said. Her voice was raspy, and Olivia wondered if it was because of all of her crying. "Will you walk me to the door, child?"

Olivia took her arm and led her to the elevator. The woman gazed at her reflection in the elevator's brass walls as they rode down to the first floor. They walked together past the tourists, who gawked but kept a healthy distance. Olivia thought she saw Renee moving toward them, but the crowd of tourists had closed in tight against each other, blocking her way with their bodies.

As they crossed the threshold, the woman raised her arms and her white wedding dress and veil crumbled into dust. Somewhere behind them Renee shouted. Beneath the dress, the woman wore hardy cotton traveling clothes and a loose coat. There was a hat in her hands that she placed on her head, tugging the brim. She looked about as old as Olivia's grandma had been when she died, and like Olivia's grandma, she was Chinese. Definitely not the tragic, young, white bride that the Wailing Lady was purported to be.

"Thank you for the food, child," said the woman. She patted Olivia's arm. "After being alone for so long, I forgot what it felt like to have family cook for you. And that is what your offering felt like." She began to fade, but before she was fully gone, she gave Olivia's arm a squeeze. "Go feed your guests."

Olivia looked up. The sky was beginning to lighten, and most of the ghosts had vanished. But there were still a few at the table, picking at the remains of the food. One of them stood out: a girl wearing trousers, with deep brown hair and a small mouth. Her clothing and hair were soaked, and when she caught sight of Olivia, the corners of her mouth curved upwards.

"The Gameboy girl," said Mei Ling. "You grew up."

Warm, welcome heat spread through Olivia's chest. Mei Ling hadn't changed at all since she'd first seen her. "I did," she said. "Thanks to you."

Mei Ling looked at the table and sighed. "It's almost all gone. It looked so good, too." She tucked a strand of hair behind her ear, scanning the remnants of the banquet. "I almost made it to the table the last time your mom cooked at The Grand Silver, but I didn't get there in time."

Olivia's stomach dropped. She remembered Mei Ling carrying her, bearing her towards The Grand Silver. Had she slowed her down and caused her to miss her chance to cross over?

"I know what you're thinking," said Mei Ling. She reached out to ruffle Olivia's hair. When she pulled away, her crooked fingers brushed against Olivia's forehead. "Don't. I don't regret it. I saw a little kid in trouble, and I did my best to save her. I wish someone had been there to do that for me."

The most important part of service was being considerate of others, Mom had said. Olivia bit her lip and scanned the table. All the plates had been picked over; even the fish skins and eyes were gone. "I'm going to find you something to eat," she said. "I'm going to feed you so you can find your way home."

Mei Ling shook her head. "The sun's rising, kid. The banquet's over."

Olivia picked through the plates with her fingers, pushing aside gnawed-on bones. There was no gristle, and most of the sauce had been licked off of the plates. Mei Ling was right; there was no food left on the table.

Her gaze flicked to the serving cart resting by the Grand Silver's door. She crouched beside it, peering between the shelves. *There,* she thought. Splashes of sauce and little bits of food had spilled out of their dishes and onto the metal as she'd pushed the cart through the hotel. Taking her wooden paddle, Olivia carefully scraped them into her palm. Her heart ached. "Welcome, honored guest," she said, holding her hand out to Mei Ling. "Take and eat, and let your soul be uplifted."

Mei Ling opened her mouth, closed it. Startled tears welled up in her eyes. She reached for Olivia's hand, cradling it in her left hand and scooping up the food with her right. As she ate, her mangled fingers straightened and became whole, and her bones twisted themselves back into shape with a series of ugly cracking sounds. Her wounds closed, one by one.

Stay with me, Olivia wanted to say. *Don't eat my food. Don't go.* She swallowed her words and held her hand still.

By the time Mei Ling swallowed the last grain of rice, her face was streaked with tears. She wiped them away. "Thank you," she said. Her voice was hoarse but clear.

Olivia took her hand, lacing their fingers. It was warm, so warm.

Behind her, the clouds were thinning into fine strands with the returning heat. The moon had waned, and the rain dropped off. With a sigh, the last ghost at her table evaporated into the morning air.

THE SECRET LIVES OF THE NINE NEGRO TEETH OF GEORGE WASHINGTON

P. Djèlí Clark

P. Djèlí Clark (pdjeliclark.wordpress.com) is the author of the novellas *The Black God's Drums* and *The Haunting of Tram Car 015*. His novelette "A Dead Djinn in Cairo" made the Locus Recommended Reading List and was listed as one of the Notable Stories in *The Best American Science Fiction and Fantasy, 2017*, as well as republished in *The Long List Anthology Vol. 3*, featuring stories from the Hugo Award Nomination List. His stories have appeared in online venues such as *Apex, Lightspeed, Fireside Fiction, Beneath Ceaseless Skies*, and in print anthologies including *Griots, Hidden Youth*, and *Clockwork Cairo*. He is loosely associated with the quarterly *FIYAH: A Magazine of Black Speculative Fiction* and an infrequent reviewer at *Strange Horizons*.

He resides in a small Edwardian castle in New England with his wife, infant daughters, and pet dragon, where he writes speculative fiction when he is not playing the part of a mild-mannered academic historian. When so inclined he rambles on issues of speculative fiction, politics, and diversity at his aptly named blog *The Disgruntled Haradrim*.

"By Cash pd Negroes for 9 Teeth on Acct of Dr. Lemoire"
—Lund Washington,
Mount Vernon plantation, Account Book, dated 1784

THE FIRST NEGRO tooth purchased for George Washington came from a blacksmith, who died that very year at Mount Vernon of the flux. The art of the blacksmith had been in his blood—passed down from ancestral spirits who had come seeking their descendants across the sea. Back in what the elder slaves called Africy, he had heard, blacksmiths were revered men who drew iron from the earth and worked it with fire and magic: crafting spears so wondrous they could pierce the sky and swords with beauty enough to rend mountains. Here, in this Colony of Virginia, he had been set to shape crueler things: collars to fasten about bowed necks, shackles to ensnare tired limbs and muzzles to silence men like beasts. But blacksmiths know the secret language of iron, and he beseeched his creations to bind the spirits of their wielders—as surely as they bound flesh. For the blacksmith understood what masters had chosen to forget: when you make a man or woman a slave you enslave yourself in turn. And the souls of those who made thralls of others would never know rest—in this life, or the next.

When he wore that tooth, George Washington complained of hearing the heavy fall of a hammer on an anvil day and night. He ordered all iron making stopped at Mount Vernon. But the sound of the blacksmith's hammer rang out in his head all the same.

THE SECOND NEGRO tooth belonging to George Washington came from a slave from the Kingdom of Ibani, what the English with their inarticulate tongues call Bonny Land, and (much to his annoyance) hence him, a Bonny man. The Bonny man journeyed from Africa on a ship called the *Jesus*, which, as he understood, was named for an ancient sorcerer who defied death. Unlike the other slaves bound on that ship who came from the hinterlands beyond his kingdom, he knew the fate that awaited him—though he would never know what law or sacred edict he had broken that sent him to this fate. He found himself in that fetid hull chained beside a merman, with scales that sparkled like green jewels and eyes as round as black coins. The Bonny man had seen mermen before out among the waves, and stories said some of them swam into rivers to find wives among local fisher women. But he hadn't known the whites made slaves of them too. As he would later learn, mermen were prized by thaumaturgical inclined aristocrats who dressed them in fine livery to display to guests; most, however, were destined for Spanish holdings, where they were forced to dive for giant pearls off the shores of New Granada. The two survived the horrors of the passage by relying on each other. The Bonny man shared tales of his kingdom, of his wife and children and family, forever lost. The merman in turn told of his underwater home, of its queen and many curiosities. He also taught the Bonny man a song: a plea to old and terrible things that dwelled in the deep, dark, hidden parts of the sea—great beings with gaping mouths that opened up whirlpools or tentacles that could drag ships beneath the depths. They would one day rise to wreak vengeance, he promised, for all those who had been chained to suffer in these floating coffins. The Bonny man never saw the merman after they made land on the English isle of Barbados. But he carried the song with him, as far as the Colony of Virginia, and on the Mount Vernon plantation, he sang it as he looked across fields of wheat to an ocean he couldn't see—and waited.

When George Washington wore the Bonny man's tooth, he found himself humming an unknown song, that sounded (strange to his thinking) like the tongue of the savage mermen. And in the dark hidden parts of the sea, old and terrible things, stirred.

THE THIRD NEGRO tooth of George Washington was bought from a slave who later ran from Mount Vernon, of which an account was posted in the *Virginia Gazette* in 1785:

Advertisement: Runaway from the plantation of the Subscriber, in *Fairfax County*, fome Time in *October* last, on All-Hallows Eve, a Mulatto Fellow, 5 Feet 8 Inches high of Tawney Complexion named *Tom*, about 25 Years of Age, missing a front tooth. He is sensible for a Slave and self-taught in foul necromancy. He lived for some Years previous as a servant at a school of learned sorcery near *Williamsburg*, and was removed on Account of inciting the dead slaves there to rise up in insurrection. It is supposed he returned to the school to raise up a young Negro Wench, named *Anne*, a former servant who died of the pox and was buried on the campus grounds, his Sister. He sold away a tooth and with that small money was able to purchase a spell used to call upon powers potent on All-Hallows Eve to spirit themselves away to parts now unknown. Whoever will secure the said *Tom*, living, and *Anne*, dead, so that they be delivered to the plantation of the Subscriber in *Fairfax County* aforefaid, shall have Twenty Shillings Reward, besides what the Law allows.

To George Washington's frustration, Tom's tooth frequently fell out of his dentures, no matter how he tried to secure it. Most bizarre of all, he would find it often in the unlikeliest of places—as if the vexsome thing was deliberately concealing itself. Then one day the tooth was gone altogether, never to be seen again.

GEORGE WASHINGTON'S FOURTH Negro tooth was from a woman named Henrietta. (Contrary to widespread belief, there is no difference of significance between the dentition of men and women—as any trained dentist, odontomancer, or the Fay folk, who require human teeth as currency, will well attest.) Henrietta's father had been John Indian, whose father had been a Yamassee warrior captured and sold into bondage in Virginia. Her mother's mother had come to the mainland from Jamaica, sold away for taking part in Queen Nanny's War. As slaves, both were reputed to be unruly and impossible to control. Henrietta inherited that defiant blood, and more than one owner learned the hard way she wasn't to be trifled with. After holding down and whipping her last mistress soundly, she was sold to work fields at Mount Vernon—because, as her former master advertised, strong legs and a broad back weren't to be wasted. Henrietta often dreamed of her grandparents. She often dreamed she *was* her grandparents. Sometimes she was a Yamassee warrior, charging a fort with flintlock musket drawn, eyes fixed on the soldier she intended to kill—as from the ramparts English mages hurled volleys of emerald fireballs that could melt through iron. Other times she was a young woman, barely fifteen, who chanted Asante war songs as she drove a long sabre, the blade blazing bright with obeah, into the belly of a slave master (this one had been a pallid blood drinker) and watched as he blackened and crumbled away to ash.

When George Washington wore Henrietta's tooth he sometimes woke screaming from night terrors. He told Martha they were memories from the war, and would never speak of the faces he saw coming for him in those dreams: a fierce Indian man with long black hair and death in his eyes, and a laughing slave girl with a curiously innocent face, who plunged scorching steel into his belly.

THE FIFTH NEGRO tooth belonging to George Washington came by unexplained means from a conjure man who was not listed among Mount Vernon's slaves. He had been born before independence, in what was then the Province of New Jersey, and learned his trade from his mother—a root woman of some renown (among local slaves at any rate), having been brought to the region from the southern territories of New France. The conjure man used his magics mostly in the treatment of maladies affecting his fellow bondsmen, of the mundane or paranormal varieties. He had been one of the tens of thousands of slaves during the war who answered the call put out by the Earl of Dunmore, Royal Governor of Virginia in November 1775:

And I hereby declare all indentured servants, Negroes, hedge witches and wizards, occultists, lycanthropes, giants, non-cannibal ogres and any sentient magical creatures or others (appertaining to Rebels) free and relieved of supernatural sanction that are able and willing to bear Arms, they joining His MAJESTY'S Troops as soon as may be, for the more speedily reducing this Colony to a proper Sense of their Duty, to His MAJESTY'S Crown and Dignity. This edict excludes Daemonic beasts who should not take said proclamation as a summons who, in doing so, will be exorcized from His MAJESTY'S realm with all deliberate speed.

The conjure man was first put in the service of Hessian mercenaries, to care for their frightening midnight black steeds that breathed flames and with hooves of fire. Following, he'd been set to performing menial domestic spells for Scottish warlocks, treated no better there than a servant. It was fortune (aided by some skillful stone casting) that placed him in Colonel Tye's regiment. Like the conjure man, Tye had been a slave in New Jersey who fled to the British, working his way to becoming a respected guerrilla commander. Tye led the infamous Black Brigade—a motley crew of fugitive slaves, outlaw juju men, and even a Spanish mulata werewolf—who worked alongside the elite Queen's Rangers. Aided by the conjure man's gris-gris, the Black Brigade carried out raids on militiamen: launching attacks on their homes, destroying their weapons, stealing supplies, burning spells and striking fear into the hearts of patriots. The conjure man's brightest moment had come the day he captured his own master and bound him in the same shackles he'd once been forced to wear. The Brigade stirred such hysteria that the patriot governor of New Jersey declared martial law, putting up protective wards around the province—and General George Washington himself was forced to send his best mage hunters against them. In a running skirmish with those patriot huntsmen, Tye was fatally struck by a cursed ball from a long rifle—cutting through his gris-gris. The conjure man stood guard over his fallen commander, performing a final rite that would disallow their enemies from reanimating the man or binding his soul. Of the five mage hunters he killed three, but was felled in the attempt. With his final breath, he whispered his own curse on any that would desecrate his corpse.

One of the surviving mage hunters pulled the conjure man's teeth as a souvenir of the battle, and a few days hence tumbled to land awkwardly from his horse and broke his neck. The tooth passed to a second man, who choked to death on an improbably lodged bit of turtle soup in his windpipe. And, so it went, bringing dire misfortune to each of its owners. The conjure man's tooth has now, by some twist of fate, made its way to Mount Vernon and into George Washington's collection. He has not worn it, yet.

THE SIXTH NEGRO tooth of George Washington belonged to a slave who had tumbled here from another world. The startled English sorcerer who witnessed this remarkable event had been set to deliver a speech on conjurations at the Royal Society of London for Improving Supernatural Knowledge. Alas, before the sorcerer could tell the world of his discovery, he was quietly killed by agents of the Second Royal African Company, working in a rare alliance with their Dutch rivals. As they saw it, if Negroes could simply be pulled out of thin air the lucrative trade in human cargo that made such mercantilists wealthy could be irrevocably harmed. The conjured Negro, however, was allowed to live—bundled up and shipped from London to a Virginia slave market. Good property, after all, was not to be wasted. She ended up at Mount Vernon, and was given the name Esther. The other slaves, however, called her Solomon—on account of her wisdom.

Solomon claimed not to know anything about magic, which didn't exist in her native home. But how could that be, the other slaves wondered, when she could mix together powders to cure their sicknesses better than any physician; when she could make predictions of the weather that always came true; when she could construct all manner of wondrous contraptions from the simplest of objects? Even the plantation manager claimed she was "a Negro of curious intellect," and listened to her suggestions on crop rotations and field systems. The slaves well knew the many agricultural reforms at Mount Vernon, for which their master took credit, was actually Solomon's genius. They often asked why she didn't use her remarkable wit to get hired out and make money? Certainly, that'd be enough to buy her freedom.

Solomon always shook her head, saying that though she was from another land, she felt tied to them by "the consanguinity of bondage." She would work to free them all, or, falling short of that, at the least bring some measure of ease to their lives. But at night, after she'd finished her mysterious "experiments" (which she kept secret from all) she could be found gazing up at the stars, and it was hard not to see the longing held deep in her eyes.

When George Washington wore Solomon's tooth, he dreamed of a place of golden spires and colorful glass domes, where Negroes flew through the sky on metal wings like birds and sprawling cities that glowed bright at night were run by machines who thought faster than men. It both awed and frightened him at once.

THE SEVENTH NEGRO tooth purchased for George Washington had come from a Negro from Africa who himself had once been a trader in slaves. He had not gone out with the raids or the wars between kingdoms to procure them, but had been an instrumental middleman—a translator who spoke the languages of both the coastal slavers and their European buyers. He was instrumental in keeping the enchanted rifles and rum jugs flowing and assuring his benefactors a good value for the human merchandise. It was thus ironic that his downfall came from making a bad deal. The local ruler, a distant relative to a king, felt cheated and (much to the trader's shock) announced his translator put up for sale. The English merchant gladly accepted the offer. And just like that, the trader went from a man of position to a commodity.

He went half mad of despair when they'd chained him in the hold of the slave ship. Twice he tried to rip out his throat with his fingernails, preferring death to captivity. But each time he died, he returned to life—without sign of injury. He'd jumped into the sea to drown, only to be hauled back in without a drop of water in his lungs. He'd managed to get hold a sailor's knife, driven it into his chest, and watched in shock as his body pushed the blade out and healed the wound. It was then he understood the extent of his downfall: he had been cursed. Perhaps by the gods. Perhaps by spirits of the vengeful dead. Or by some witch or conjurer for whom he'd haggled out a good price. He would never know. But they had cursed him to suffer this turn of fate, to become what he'd made of others. And there would be no escape.

The Negro slave trader's tooth was George Washington's favorite. No matter how much he used it, the tooth showed no signs of wear. Sometimes he could have sworn he'd broken it. But when inspected, it didn't show as much as a fracture—as if it mended itself. He put that tooth to work hardest of all, and gave it not a bit of rest.

THE EIGHTH NEGRO tooth belonging to George Washington came from his cook, who was called Ulysses. He had become a favorite in the Mount Vernon household, known for his culinary arts and the meticulous care he gave to his kitchen. The dinners and parties held at the mansion were always catered by Ulysses, and visitors praised his skill at devising new dishes to tingle the tongue and salivate the senses. Those within the higher social circles frequented by the Washingtons familiarly called him "Uncle Lysses" and showered him with such gifts that local papers remarked: "the Negro cook had become something of a celebrated puffed-up dandy."

Ulysses took his work seriously, as much as he took his name. He used the monies gained from those gifts, as well as his habit of selling leftovers (people paid good money to sup on the Washingtons' fare) to purchase translated works by Homer. In those pages, he learned about the fascinating travels of his namesake, and was particularly taken by the figure Circe—an enchantress famed for her vast knowledge of potions and herbs, who through a fine feast laced with a potent elixir had turned men into swine. Ulysses amassed other books as well: eastern texts on Chinese herbology, banned manuscripts of Mussulman alchemy, even rare ancient Egyptian papyri on shape-shifting.

His first tests at transmogrification had merely increased the appetite of Washington's guests, who turned so ravenous they relieved themselves of knife or spoon and shoveled fistfuls of food into their mouths like beasts. A second test had set them all to loud high-pitched squealing—which was blamed on an over-imbibing of cherubimical spirits. Success came, at last, when he heard some days after a summer dining party that a Virginia plantation owner and close friend of the Washingtons had gone missing—the very same day his wife had found a great fat spotted hog rummaging noisily through their parlor. She had her slaves round up the horrid beast, which was summarily butchered and served for dinner.

Over the years, Ulysses was judicious in his selections for the transfiguring brew: several slave owners or overseers known to be particularly cruel; a shipping merchant from Rhode Island whose substantial wealth came from the slave trade; a visiting French physiognomist and naturalist who prattled on about the inherent "lower mental capabilities" to be found among Negroes, whose skulls he compared to "near-human creatures" such as the apes of inner Africa and the fierce woodland goblins of Bavaria. Then, one day in early 1797, Ulysses disappeared.

The Washingtons were upset and hunted everywhere for their absconded cook, putting out to all who would listen the kindness they'd shown to the ungrateful servant. He was never found, but the Mount Vernon slaves whispered that on the day Ulysses vanished a black crow with a mischievous glint in its eye was found standing in a pile of the man's abandoned clothes. It cawed once, and then flapped away.

When George Washington wore the tooth of his runaway cook, it was strangely at dinner parties. Slaves would watch as he wandered into the kitchen, eyes glazed over in a seeming trance, and placed drops of some strange liquid into the food and drink of his guests. His servants never touched *those* leftovers. But that summer many Virginians took note of a bizarre rash of wild pigs infesting the streets and countryside of Fairfax County.

*　　*　　*

THE NINTH, AND final, Negro tooth purchased for George Washington came from a slave woman named Emma. She had been among Mount Vernon's earliest slaves, born there just a decade after Augustine Washington had moved in with his family. Had anyone recorded Emma's life for posterity, they would have learned of a girl who came of age in the shadows of one of Virginia's most powerful families. A girl who had fast learned that she was included among the Washington's possessions—treasured like a chair cut from exotic Jamaican mahogany or a bit of fine Canton porcelain. A young woman who had watched the Washington children go on to attend school and learn the ways of the gentry, while she was trained to wait on their whims. They had the entire world to explore and discover. Her world was Mount Vernon, and her aspirations could grow no further than the wants and needs of her owners.

That was not to say Emma did not have her own life, for slaves learned early how to carve out spaces separate from their masters. She had befriended, loved, married, cried, fought and found succor in a community as vibrant as the Washingtons'—perhaps even more so, if only because they understood how precious it was to live. Yet she still dreamed for more. To be unbound from this place. To live a life where she had not seen friends and family put under the lash; a life where the children she bore were not the property of others; a place where she might draw a free breath and taste its sweetness. Emma didn't know any particular sorcery. She was no root woman or conjurer, nor had she been trained like the Washington women in simple domestic enchantments. But her dreams worked their own magic. A strong and potent magic that she clung to, that grew up and blossomed inside her—where not even her owners could touch, or take it away.

When George Washington wore Emma's tooth, some of that magic worked its way into him and perhaps troubled some small bit of his soul. In July 1799, six months before he died, Washington stipulated in his will that the 123 slaves belonging to himself, among them Emma, be freed upon his wife's death.

No such stipulations were made for the Negro teeth still in his possession.

YARD DOG
Tade Thompson

Tade Thompson lives and works in the South of England. He is the author of *Rosewater*, *The Murders of Molly Southbourne* and *Making Wolf*, as well as the short story, "The Apologists" and other works. He is a multiple winner of the Nommo Award, winner of the Golden Tentacle award at the Kitsches, a John W. Campbell Award finalist, a Shirley Jackson Award finalist and a nominee for both the British Fantasy Award and the British Science Fiction Association Award. His background is in medicine, psychiatry and social anthropology. His hobbies include jazz, visual arts, martial arts, comics and pretending he will ever finish his TBR stack.

I THOUGHT HE was a Fed at first.

Okay, no, I didn't, but in hindsight I should have. The second time he turned up at Saucy Sue's everybody noticed him on account of his height and his clothes which were righteous. I'm the only one who saw him arrive the night before. He was furtive, dressed in... I don't know what, man. He wore shoes and pants that even the Salvation Army would turn down. The height was there, but he was such a dark cat that, without the flash of jewellery, he faded into the background. I played percussion, that first night. Al played the horn, some shit he'd cribbed off watching Dizzie in St Louis. Saucy Sue's was a gangster's joint, but many of the jazz clubs were back then, and a Fed or two or an undercover cop wasn't out of the ordinary. He was a yard dog that first night, and every other night he came in, that's the name that stuck in my head, even before he started playing.

Al and I were filling-in. The usual percussion and horn guys were dope sick trying to kick a habit, and the manager, a cat called Layton, literally plucked us out of the crowd. That was the beginning of a six-month gig, sweet, and I cut my teeth for later in my career. Nothing like playing six nights a week to hone your discipline.

Yard Dog was at the back, watching, smoking some hand-rolled stuff that I thought had some reefer mixed-in, but when the cops stopped us one time and checked, it was only tobacco. But. It wasn't that simple. Motherfucker switched that shit, I'm sure, because I remember he blew the smoke in my face when I was talking shit one time. I saw things, but considering what happened later, a few hallucinations were nothing to make noise about. Yard Dog was like six-six if he was an inch. Broad shoulders, narrow hips, athletic looking, but stooped, bringing himself down to Earth, Al would say. First night, he didn't say nothing, just watched, smoked and left.

Second night, he was waiting when we packed up for the night, and he said, "That was real cool." He walked away before I could respond. We had a singer then, called herself Shonda, voice would break an angel's heart. She took her sweet time watching him walk away. Difficult not to, I suppose. Yard Dog was visible, noticeable, even before he opened his mouth. Why, then, had nobody seen him on that first night? I think that was down to him, down to how much he wanted to be seen.

Sue's had audience nights every two weeks or so, usually when the band was fatigued or someone was sick or talking to their P.O. Those nights, Al and me would kick back with some drinks and listen to some hopped-up or drunk motherfuckers trying to hold a tune. Though we always refused, one or two of them always asked to try our instruments, and Al had to smack a persistent cat once. Al wasn't big like Yard Dog, but he was fierce, fast, and experienced. He'd been in plenty of fights, and loved to talk about either music or beating a person down. I remember a cat they used to call Captain, before our time, just got out of prison. Captain stole Al's reefer and sat on the stoop of the Patterson Hotel, smoking, all hotsy totsy. Al takes a mouthful of coffin varnish, walks up to Captain, spits the liquor in his face, kicks him in the bongos, *lights him on fire*, and only trillies because of a pounder who ran up. But fuck Captain, he was unhep.

On this night, some drunk guy was playing Armstrongs, but sadder than a map, depressing everyone. Sue's doesn't waste time with inferior entertainment. You could be high until you're touching God's toenails, nobody would care as long as you played well. But if you blew shit, your survival time was the five minutes it takes Benny to get from the door, through the crowd, to the stage. Open night is no excuse for bad jazz. So, shitty drunk guy was out and Yard was next. He went up there and put his lips to it. I can't tell you what he played because I don't remember, but I do know that the note was clear and high and piercing. Not a soul spoke. Not a soul *could* speak because whatever Yard played made everybody blow their wigs, man, bible.

I was unaware of any other person in that room. Yard himself disappeared and everything was that note, that sound, that fucking horn. I don't know how long it lasted, but when he stopped he was staring down at the floor. There was silence and I know I was crying. Shit, everyone in Saucy Sue's was crying: pimps, prostitutes, hustlers, every single one. It seemed it was silent for hours but it couldn't have been more than a minute or two, then people started clapping and whooping. Yard calmly picked up his instrument and walked off the stage. No other blower would go up there because how do you follow that? Understand, I'm not talking about skill here. Yard could beat it out, but what I'm talking about here is magic.

One other thing, something curious: all the drinks in the house went bitter that night. When people got their emotions together, they found themselves thirsty, and they drank. And spat everything out. There was nothing worth drinking or listening to. The drug fiends even said there was no dragon to chase. All intoxicants would not intoxicate. It was the damnedest thing.

I tell you, that night? Any woman or man would have dropped their drawers for him, but Yard left.

Next night, he's back, leaning against the wall, cool as ever. Better dressed, but his name stuck. He carried his horn everywhere.

Gossip blossomed like hopheads in a flophouse. Where did he live? Where was he from? Where did he train? He wasn't some tender motherfucker on leave from Julliard. Choir boy from church, maybe? Many jazz guys got their chops blowing Amazing Grace. What kind of horn was that anyway? One of those English Bessons? A Higham? The fire of speculation burned and would continue to burn until the next open night. Shonda took a fancy to him and preened to get his attention. It worked. You should know that Al and Shonda used to be a thing, and now they're... well, I don't know, I can't say not a thing, but they still have business.

Shonda did go on a date with Yard, but that was after Shed came along.

Shed wasn't his name. We called him that for reasons you'll understand in a minute. Never did catch what he called himself, and by the time we met him later, there was no need to call him anything but scary. Shed turns up during this godawful argument between Saucy's and the supplier about that booze that went bad. This was unnecessary because for one thing, the booze was fine until Yard blew. Secondly, it wasn't just the liquor that went off. The water, the milk, the orange juice, anything you can chuck down your neck had been bitterified.

Unlike Yard, Shed was small. Not ugly, but plain. You never saw a person more uncomfortable in human skin. Shed moved like the Devil hisself was walking behind him, prodding him with a pitchfork: spurts of speed, then uncertain shuffling, then fast again, always looking surprised when he made a few steps. Speaking of skin, he was one of those brothers minted so dark, he seemed navy blue. He, at first, couldn't be heard over the shouts. Then, when noticed, his language seemed so garbled that they thought him a foreigner, which, I suppose, he was. Nobody saw him come in.

"Negro, what do you want?" Sue said. "Speak slowly and in English, fool."

You need to know that Sue herself was a formidable woman, not to be fucked with. Not just that she was big, nearly six feet tall and with the attitude of a drill-sergeant. She had backing, if you know what I mean. There were shadowy people who owned the bar lined up behind her, folks who don't declare to the IRS, and who pounders and snatchers ignore because it's impossible to convict. This was not unusual, and you need to remember the times for what they were. This was when luminaries like Cab Calloway and Dizzy Gillespie got into a knife fight back in 1941. What I'm saying is, nobody was to be fucked with back then, not even refined motherfuckers like Earl Hines. You didn't start nothing, you didn't mess with anybody. Nobody worth listening to, anyway.

Shed just smiled into her face and spoke slowly. In English.

"Please, have you seen my brother, thank you?"

"What?"

Shed said it slower and louder. "Please. Have you. Seen my. BROTHER. Thank you."

"I don't know you or your brother. How did you get in, anyway? We're not open. Get the fuck out of here."

The way I heard it, Shed just smiled at her and went to use the john, but never came back out. Hours later when tempers had cooled somewhat, Sue got curious about him, had one of the men check the bathroom. They found his raggedy clothes, a trail of blood, strips of skin, meat and other fluids leading from the door to one of the stalls. Al said it was like he had shed his skin, which is how come we called him Shed. It wasn't till later that we figured he was looking for Yard. Over the next few days we didn't see Shed, but knew he was all over the place because people kept talking about this guy asking questions and finding crumpled clothes and any combination of skin and flesh, no bones. It was the weirdest thing, but it was a stunt of some kind, right? Like in '53 when those dumbasses shaved and dyed a rhesus monkey green, then blowtorched the asphalt, calling it an alien landing.

Yard was hanging out with us at lot, at rehearsals, whenever we were kicking back, or sometimes at Dizzy's house on Seventh Avenue in Harlem. He met Miles and Monk. Charlie Parker was usually too high to remember meeting him. One night Shonda finally convinces Yard to go yam with him at some fancy place. She was really insistent, and they left us. I noticed Al watching and I first thought he was jealous. I was worried he was going to attack Yard, but that's not what happened.

He said we had to go too. I'm not too proud of this part, but Al and I used to run together. We weren't making much money as musicians and we did take drugs. Pretty much everybody in the scene did back then. Al did some burglaries and I went along sometimes. Not trying to say he had to twist my arm, you understand. I wasn't willing, but not exactly unwilling either.

Al took us to Yard's place that night. Don't ask me how he found out where the guy lived, but he must have followed him. He said he was working with Shonda and we'd have to split the take. No lock can resist Al, and when we got in he went about the business of finding valuables. I saw the horn case. I'd like to say there was some magnetic pull or that the thing called to me, or something that would absolve me. Fact is, I was just curious. The case was unremarkable and opened easily. The horn itself gleamed. I could not tell who made it, and there was no brand, serial number or trademark anywhere. That was itself strange. Brass wasn't cheap, and all the good ones had serial numbers. Next thing I know, it's in my hands, and then... well, it's on my lips. I blew.

Later, Shonda told me at that very moment Yard looked up, alarmed, and stood to leave the restaurant without so much as a see-ya-later. Al said he dropped the cash he had scavenged and clasped his hands to his ears to shut the sound out. I didn't know any of this at the time 'cos I heard nothing, even thought it was broken. It wasn't. What happened is the room started to glow, orange, like a coal fire at first, then a hurricane of colour swirling around me, but detached from the origins. Blues, maroons, greens, swirling like ghosts. The walls, though still there, became immaterial, or invisible. Everything clear as one of those engineering drawings, leached of colour. I saw the night sky, and the clouds ignited with a yellow-red flame, and rolled back in all directions. The stars... most of them winked out in an instant, but dozens of them started falling to Earth. Then I heard a great wind blowing, and from far away, a voice.

In the blackness of that sky-which-was-no-longer-a-sky I sensed something stirring, something meant to be in slumber, something malevolent and implacable.

"Stop," said Yard, and I came to myself again.

Al was gone, and the building was on fire around me, hot wind howling past my ears, putting my heart in a ferment. Yard acted as if nothing was amiss. He took the horn, cleaned it, then placed it in the case. After he had sealed it, he turned to me, shook his head and offered a hand. I swear, with the building coming down around us, backdrafts and flashovers everywhere, nothing harmed us. He walked us calmly out of the building where Al was waiting with his hands wrapped up.

Later, he told me he tried to lift me, to get me out of the building, but I was hot. He said he got burned from touching me. Al is full of shit at the best of times, and he probably touched a banister, but so much crazy stuff was going on that I was willing to believe him.

About that time, Shed came doddering down the middle of the road. He left a trail of blood and shredded skin.

Yard's shoulders slumped when he saw Shed.

"Brother," he said.

"This... sound is not for listen on Earth, brother. Not for listen. You know this." Shed's words were still mangled, but we understood him. He turned to me. "Why this one's face glowed, please?"

"He blew the trumpet," said Yard. "It will be fine. It was for a short time only."

"Who are you people?" asked Al, quaver in his voice that I ain't never heard out of him before right then.

Shed smirked.

Yard said, "We are two of the seven motherfuckers whose job it is to fuck this reality up when the time comes."

"But not time yet, and my brother, he knows it," said Shed.

"I wanted to play, that's all. No harm done." Yard seemed petulant, like the younger of the two.

Skin dropped off Shed, and the more he lost his covering, the clearer his speech became. "Yeah, I'm gonna disagree with that. I heard you all the way from home and I was sent to bring you and the trumpet back. You're not even supposed to have it." He came to me and touched my face. "You'll be all right. Get some sleep. And stop stealing shit."

With that, the flesh of his face slid off, revealing the bone underneath. His jaw fell along with the muscle, leaving his tongue lolling like a prick. He looked at Yard. "I can never do these human bodies as well as you do. Take off the vessel. Let's go home."

Al and I disagreed on what happened next, but I'm telling the story, so I'll give you my version. They fell into their clothes and shrivelled up. Yard, Shed and the horn, gone. We kicked their clothes into the fire, even though Yard had some fine threads. By the time the cops and the actual Feds turned up we were long gone.

That's almost the end of the story. This shit happened in 1944, maybe '45. You don't have to believe me. Shonda spent a lot of time searching for who or what they might be, got entangled with some tinfoil-wearing motherfuckers for a while. She said she had to know, like it was some itch in her brain that she had to scratch or something. I don't know about that. I do know that I have not been sick a day since I touched that horn, and I am now ninety-five. I still have all my own teeth and I've outlived two wives. I kicked the cocaine, made some minor waves in bebop and what came after. Al is still alive, and he was older than me to start with. I'd say we look about forty. Shonda is still alive. She and Al are still on again, off again, or makeups-to-breakups as I think the kids say these days. Nobody who was in Saucy Sue's the night Yard played died young. That trumpet did something to us all.

When I sleep, and I don't sleep much, but when I do, I dream of that thing out there beyond the sky, that thing stirring, waiting to wreak havoc. In some versions a taloned, scaled arm reaches out of the abyss and hands me a horn. I wake up screaming. Then I have to go outside and look at the stars and the moon or even just the clouds, night air on my face.

Then I am fine.

THE WOMAN WHO DESTROYED US
S. L. Huang

S. L. Huang (www.slhuang.com • @sl_huang) is an Amazon-bestselling author who justifies her MIT degree by using it to write eccentric mathematical superhero fiction. Her debut novel, *Zero Sum Game*, came out in 2018, with its sequel *Null Set* due later this year. Her short fiction sales have included *Strange Horizons, Analog, Uncanny Magazine, Tor.com, Daily Science Fiction*, and several Year's Best anthologies. She is also a Hollywood stuntwoman and firearms expert, where she's appeared on shows such as *Battlestar Galactica* and *Raising Hope*, and where her proudest geek moment was getting killed by Nathan Fillion. The first professional female armorer in the industry, she's worked with actors such as Sean Patrick Flanery, Jason Momoa, and Danny Glover, and been hired as a weapons expert for reality shows such as *Top Shot* and *Auction Hunters*.

I know what they say. They say she was a pioneer. They say she helped millions of people live a normal life. They say she created the next stage of evolution for humanity.

I need you to understand how wrong that is. To understand what she is: a killer.

She's destroying people's minds, molding them into her image of what the human brain should be. And none of them complain afterward, because of course they wouldn't. Their brains are made to be happy—and so they are. She's washing out the human species into mindless automatons.

More importantly, she killed my son.

MAGGIE DECIDED ON her plan during a sunny afternoon in early April. The weather had bloomed into the fragile clarity of a perfect spring day, the type of day that only came in tiny crystals before being smothered by summer. Maggie went out to get the mail, and instead sat down on her porch and listened to insects chirping and the breeze whistling in the old house's shutters, and wanted to spit on all of it.

Perfect days shouldn't be allowed to exist anymore.

Maggie closed her eyes and reflected on the irony life had flung at her. First, Henry's diagnoses, and learning she did have the strength to love him, truly and genuinely. Not only the strength, but the *desire*. Throughout the years, every minute of every day that she'd scraped and scratched out on his behalf had been worth it—every anxious conference with his doctors, every time she caught him wistfully staring at other children playing and her heart broke a tiny bit more. Every too-short accounting of funds that went to his care first and always.

She vaguely recalled the pain of giving up her engineering career, or of the day Henry's father left, but it was an unfocused sort of pain, tempered by time and willingness. Or perhaps that long-ago pain was nothing now, compared to the bonfire that consumed her every time she recalled the day she'd lost Henry.

Her son, her real son, had vanished—replaced by an imposter wearing his face. And if she ever managed to get him back, he would hate her for it.

She wondered, sometimes, if she was being selfish. She'd told herself so many times she would do anything, sacrifice anything, if it would mean a better life for him. But that wasn't supposed to mean sacrificing *him*. She'd always told nosy strangers that he was fine just the way he was, and she had meant it.

But that woman, she had seen how smart Henry was—Maggie had *told* people how smart he was—that woman had seen it, and had dangled such glittering promises in front of him. Seduced his brain for herself, all with her smug assumption that everyone was better off as carbon copies of her version of normal.

That doctor wasn't even a real person herself, was she? All the magazine profiles were gleefully transparent about that. Proud, even. How she'd built her own personality by zapping whatever neural pathways she'd decided fit her concept of the ideal human. They'd had her up before ethics boards in the early days, for God's sake, before enough rich dilettantes decided brain stimulation was the way of the future for it to start normalizing.

She was destroying society, that doctor. Maggie didn't know why more people didn't see it. On her message board, the only place she still felt sane, she'd talked to a woman whose daughter had been turned down by every university she applied to. *Ten percent of the kids at Harvard have an implant now,* the woman had mourned. *How can she compete? She came to me sobbing and asked if we could afford it. My healthy, energetic, brilliant seventeen-year-old daughter came to me asking for elective brain surgery.*

The message board folk were a spectrum, with some adamant the new technology was spitting at Nature and some who allowed it might be permissible to treat a proven medical need. Maggie stayed quiet when those people talked. Most of them didn't have anyone who'd been judged to have such a "medical need," the type that would let insurance pay for it, and they didn't know any better.

Someday she'd get up the courage to write a post. A long post. Her story. Her manifesto, she supposed it would have to be called, at the length such a thing would run. But manifestos always had some sort of action at the end of them, didn't they? If only she could figure out some way to disable all the implants, every instance of deep brain stimulation in the entire world. Dig a channel to send the course of humanity hurtling down a different path, bypassing this future entirely.

But even if she could do that...

Henry came to see her sometimes. Or Hank, as he called himself now. He would greet her and call her "mom," standing awkwardly with his hands in his pockets and eyes that were a stranger's. Maggie tried her best to keep her eyes dry, to keep from staggering when the memories cut her: Henry tackling her with hugs so fierce they almost lost balance, Henry's lopsided smile of accomplishment when he figured out some new philosophical concept, Henry collecting every flower in the yard and filling his room with them.

All Hank talked about was how good his grades were now, and how much money he would be making soon, and Maggie screamed inside her head about how much she didn't care. She wanted his smile back, his love of botany, his penchant for memorizing any type of diagram and reciting it back to her with unadulterated joy; his painting and his laughter and the way he would challenge her to board games like he was preparing for the most serious battle in the world; she wanted *Henry*.

Any fantasies about tearing the implant out of his head crashed when she imagined what would come next. Henry's eyes, filled with betrayal, with hatred at her, and then he'd go and get it put back in again.

But that crisp spring day, her body sagging on the porch like her bones had lost their will to hold her up, Maggie hit on her idea. She couldn't save Henry. But she could show that woman, that monster, exactly what she had done. She could show everyone who gave that doctor such plaudits that the thing they so loved was nothing more than a phantasm.

She sat up. The cool air suddenly felt invigorating. *I could do this,* she thought. That doctor always claimed the implant didn't make you different, that it just made you a more true version of yourself, but she was wrong, and Maggie could prove it. Because the doctor had an implant, too, and without it...

Well. Without it, they would all see. She wasn't going to be the same person. She'd be erased. Someone else.

A squirrelly reticence wormed its way through Maggie's gut. Was she contemplating murder? She knew how she felt about losing Henry, after all.

But no. The doctor was a programmed personality, nothing more. An organic AI that had been written over a real human's brain. If anything, Maggie would be saving the person the woman used to be.

For the first time in two years, the edge of Maggie's lips curled up toward something like a smile. She'd need that manifesto after all.

She sold us on a miracle.

"I couldn't get out of bed," she told us, the same line she's spouted in all those magazine profiles. Everyone knows her story, but she told it to us anyway, describing the endlessly circling thoughts that had crushed and trapped her, the compulsions that wouldn't release her from mounting panic unless she scraped her hands bloody or hung onto every candy wrapper or broken pencil that crossed into her teenaged world. Such graphic detail—I wonder if she wrote herself a subroutine for stimulating creative language.

When deep brain stimulation became a possibility for her, she'd been circling her ideation for months, flirting with fantasies of razors and ropes. Her parents had tried all traditional paths for her, and all had failed. She described it as drowning. Nothing to lose. Nothing left but the one last gasping hope that she could be cured by new technology.

I don't know whether I believe her. Her parents are dead now, and they never gave the magazine interviews she's so fond of, but if I could speak to them, what would they say? Maybe they weren't like me; maybe they didn't love her as she was and hid their faces with embarrassment when people asked why their daughter was no longer in school. Maybe they whispered in their darkest, secret thoughts that life would be easier if their daughter killed herself, so when the marching future offered them the chance to kill her themselves and call it treatment, they jumped at the chance.

But Henry and I weren't drowning. I told her that. I told her it was hard, but we got by, and that we were, mostly, happy. It was certainly true of me, and Henry assured me it was true of him, too. I told her he didn't need fixing and we didn't need miracles and I didn't want to take any unnecessary risks, not with something as precious as my child's brain, his person.

"It doesn't change who you are," she told us a dozen times, falsely. "It will just make him become more of the person he wants to be."

In retrospect, of course she would say that. It's the only way she can excuse what she's done to herself, isn't it?

I still almost said no. I told Henry I loved him exactly as he was, that I couldn't fathom wishing him different without wishing him not Henry. When you know the whole of someone, even what others see as their weakest points are a part of what you love. That's how I found peace with it after the first of his ever-evolving diagnoses, first ADHD and then the rapidly cycling correction to anxiety, bipolar, BPD, ASD, with each new doctor as likely to declare a previous misdiagnosis as to add another label to the combination they were medicating him for. But long before all that, when I was in shock after that first child psychologist sat us down and explained all Henry's difficulties with school and with the other children weren't just a phase... I asked myself if I would swap my boy for one the doctors described as "normal," and the sick horror of the thought made it hard to breathe.

Because that boy wouldn't be Henry.

I made sure my son knew all this. I made sure he knew it all, every day, especially the days after his father left, or the days I found him staring at university or job hunting websites with an expression like someone had socked him in the stomach. And when he first came to me about DBS, I made sure he knew he didn't have to have brain surgery, not for me. Not then, not ever.

But he wanted more. And like the fool of a parent I was, I didn't want to deny him.

"Don't worry, Mom," he said to me right before, squeezing my hand almost as tight as I was squeezing his. "I'll still be me." I almost begged him to promise.

Afterwards, one of the handful of times he visited, wooden and humorless, he said, "I didn't realize how much it would change me."

He didn't look at me when he said it.

AFTER A WEEK spent online, Maggie had freshly swallowed every article and magazine profile ever written about Dr. Laura Chen. She'd also studied as much of the workings of the DBS implants as she could understand, hunting down research papers that were a little jump above the layman. Her electrical engineering was rusty, but she'd done similar research before Henry had gotten his implant, and the more she read, the more conversant she felt.

Besides, she wasn't trying to do any complicated neuroprogramming. She just wanted to figure out how to shut a unit down without hurting the person physically. The shutting down part looked relatively easy—DBS patients had as many cautions as people with pacemakers, and Maggie was reasonably sure that despite the units' shielding she could disable one with a homemade EMP soldered out of a flash capacitor. But the relative ease of that side of the equation meant it was standard for the individual frequency generation algorithms of a DBS unit to be solidly backed up.

Especially someone whose implant programming was as complicated as Dr. Chen's.

Deep brain stimulation worked via electrodes inserted far into the brain that produced electrical bursts in response to what they'd been programmed to view as abnormal neuron firing. But Dr. Chen had taken it far beyond "abnormal." She'd been given her original implant under medical supervision, but after being inspired to enter the field herself, she began experimenting with her own neural pathways in college, tweaking the electrical bursts to increase her stamina, intelligence, and determination. DBS didn't have any sort of pinpoint precision—neurologists still weren't even sure why it worked as well as it did—but Laura Chen had been an artist at it. Later she went overseas to have more electrodes inserted so she could mess with her neurons in every lobe, and Maggie was willing to bet the code that now equaled Dr. Chen's personality was very carefully protected.

Maggie would need some type of access. Preferably some way that would avoid her coming face to face with the doctor—she didn't know if Dr. Chen would recognize a skeletal, graying woman as the pleasantly round mother she'd met two years ago, but best not to take chances. Luckily, in several of the magazine profiles, Dr. Chen had been pictured with her wife.

From there it was only a hop and a skip to a thousand social media updates and the name of the studio where the wife took yoga every week.

For some reason, it surprised Maggie that the studio was only half an hour away. It shouldn't have, because they'd moved here back when Henry was commuting in every other day for testing appointments. Maggie tended to think of Dr. Chen as being far away and unreachable, somehow on another plane thanks to her fame, despite the fact that the young man wearing Henry's face now worked for the doctor as a research assistant.

Maggie took a breath and clicked over to buy a yoga mat.

Her first day of class, she was struck by how long it had been since she'd been out of the house for any but the most necessary errands. She'd even been having groceries delivered, mostly stacks of instant noodles that she didn't eat. A few women leaving the yoga studio greeted her on the way in, and Maggie had to think hard to shape the words of a banally polite response.

She'd signed up for an open level class, and she got lucky: she recognized the woman she wanted as soon as she stepped barefoot onto the smooth wooden floor. Dr. Chen's wife was a striking dark-skinned woman, taller than everyone else in the class, with a firm jaw and the type of shiny black waves Maggie tended to assume existed only in shampoo commercials. Her confidence and grace were magnetic. Maggie thought she would have felt drawn in even if she hadn't had other motives for being here.

She unrolled her mat on the next spot over and gave the woman what she hoped passed for a nervous smile. "Hi. I'm Maggie."

The answering smile she got was open and welcoming. "Victoria. Nice to meet you."

Maggie knew her name was Victoria, knew everything about her that could be gleaned from a public social media page. But she said "nice to meet you" back and then the line she'd planned as a nonthreatening conversation opener. "It's my first day."

"Oh! Well, Terrence is a fantastic teacher," Victoria said. "He's great at helping you work at your level. And you can go into child's pose anytime, no judgment."

Maggie didn't know what child's pose was, but she thanked Victoria and pretended to concentrate on smoothing down the curl of her mat.

She did, indeed, spend most of the class in child's pose. Even lying folded double felt like it stretched her raw, leaching her pain into a puddle on the studio floor. She'd plotted out what she would say to Victoria after the class, too, but when she turned and tried to form words, she had to fight past a sob stuck in her nose and throat.

"I... I just moved here, and..."

"Sweetie, are you okay?" Victoria put a hand on her shoulder.

"I... I guess I'm a little overwhelmed." The sob bubbled up, undenied, and Maggie swiped at her eyes and nose in annoyance. This was not what she had planned. But she pressed on. "Would you let me buy you a cup of coffee? I'm so new here and... it doesn't have to be today, next time would be fine too, or whenever—"

"Oh, sweetie. I've got time now. Let me show you this great little shop around the corner; they're a coffee shop and an antiques house, so all their tables and chairs are these interesting older pieces. You can buy the furniture, too, but I just like the vibe."

She put a hand on Maggie's shoulder again and shepherded them out of the yoga studio, calling farewells to Terrence and the other students.

Maggie had more careful scripting in her head, but instead she ended up weeping her way through a latte and a slice of truly decadent flourless chocolate cake.

"I'm sorry, it's just—I miss my son," she whispered between sniffs, and

Victoria "oh, sweetie'd" her again and drew all the right conclusions.

"You're so kind," Maggie said finally, sincerely, when she was able to wipe her tears away on a coffee shop napkin and not have them immediately replaced. "I'm sorry. I guess I needed a friend. Can you recommend—tell me what there is to do around here. Tell me about you."

"Well, I'm an artist," Victoria said. "Mixed media, mostly—I like exploring the place where painting and sculpture meet. My wife always says something poetic about fractional dimensions."

"Like a fractal," Maggie said automatically. "Something that isn't two-space but isn't three-space." Like the surface of the human brain, she thought, but cut herself off before adding. So many wrinkles and fissures and complexities. Not flat. Not simple.

"Yes! Exactly," Victoria said. "Are you a mathematician?"

"Engineer," Maggie said. "Or at least, I was…"

"I so admire that. My wife is brilliant at all that, but I could never wrap my head around STEM fields. Just got the creative genes, I guess."

"These days you could always get an implant for it," Maggie said. Too soon, maybe, but when else was she going to get such a good opening?

Victoria hesitated. "Actually, my wife is a DBS researcher and neuroprogrammer. And there was a time I—but that's a story for another day. You were asking about good ways to get yourself out of the house."

Maggie was sure she hadn't phrased it that way, but she was, she reminded herself, only playing a part. Who cared if Victoria felt pity for her rather than friendship? As long as it got her in.

I've heard all the logical arguments. That DBS is elective and victimless, that it helps many and on the whole harms no one. And I haven't believed in God for thirty years, so I'm not one to say it's a crime against nature.

But I do think we have to give some serious thought to what it means to be… oneself. We all change over the course of our life, but is that equivalent to rewriting our neurology? How many neurons do we alter before someone isn't the same person anymore? Before we've killed who they used to be?

The religious opponents of DBS sometimes call this soul. I think it's science, but I agree with them for all that.

How long before less invasive treatments for any condition involving the brain start to be phased out as unprofitable, before society will no longer give any accommodations because "why don't they just get DBS"?

There will be people who say what I'm choosing to do here doesn't address any of that. That I should write books, or articles, or give speeches, not attack a single person just because I disagree with her.

They might be right. But sometimes a demonstration is worth a thousand words.

DR. LAURA CHEN had been far from the only doctor performing DBS in the country, of course. The surgery was all too common, and plenty of people got their treatment from someone who wasn't the face of a movement. Henry had found her name online thanks to all those magazine articles, and he'd written to her before he even told Maggie he was researching. Dr. Chen had told them to come out and see her personally.

In retrospect, Maggie should have been suspicious. What kind of celebrity doctor tells a sixteen-year-old kid to see her personally, unless she's trying to steal his brain away?

She'd relived that first conversation with Henry so many times it had become a specter in her head. She should have listened to her creeping foreboding, but she'd shelved her reservations and tried to listen to her son with an open mind. She'd learned from him so many times, after all—he read widely and thought deeply, and he'd changed her opinion on more than one occasion. Those long, rambling conversations were one of the many things that had made him Henry, one of the many things she loved.

But he'd never approached her with something so... personal. So frightening. She remembered the moment clearly: she'd been making dinner, and her hand had frozen on the handle of the frying pan she'd been taking out. The pattern of brownish scratches crisscrossing the Teflon had etched itself into her memory.

"Mom, have you heard of deep brain stimulation?"

Of course she'd heard of it. The news loved their clickbait headlines about each new twist in the proliferation of DBS. And when she'd seen that first article the fleeting thought had crossed her mind, *could Henry benefit?*

But the technology back then had been limited to extreme cases of OCD, depression, and a few other mental illnesses—clear-cut cases all, not the overlapping patchwork of combinations and question marks that Henry's doctors argued over.

Back in the beginning, the DBS scientists had talked big, saying they had such hopes, that this might even be the key to treating previously intransigent personality disorders or neurological conditions that conventional medicine struggled to unlock. But nobody had predicted just how fast DBS would explode. The more the researchers and doctors manage to expand it, the more the funding poured in, and the more those clickbait headlines passed over Maggie's dashboard.

It had gotten to the point where well-meaning acquaintances had begun asking. "Have you ever considered DBS for Henry?"

At first she'd politely explained that Henry still couldn't be treated with DBS. As the years passed and questions got ruder and more frequent, she'd become grateful that this remained true, that she could shut down such brutally impolite good intentions with a simple statement of fact.

It was different saying it to Henry, though. "Honey, if you're thinking of... it's still limited, and your situation is complicated. They can't—"

"I know, I know," he'd said, already gaining steam in his familiar Henry way. "If you look at what's officially treatable via DBS, I can't benefit yet. But I've been emailing with one of the premiere researchers in the country, Dr. Laura Chen. She's pioneered a lot of the expansions of DBS treatment over the past generation. Before she started pushing the research, the field was in a state of nascent infancy compared to what it's capable of now. And the best part is, she's like a self-improving AI, because she essentially reprogrammed her own neurology to make her better able to reprogram people's neurology. She—"

"That's the best part?" Maggie couldn't help muttering.

"It's a testament to the genius of humanity," Henry said, either missing or ignoring her sarcasm. "There's a recursive beauty to it. Like a piece of art, except science."

"I know who Dr. Chen is, honey," Maggie had said. She wondered if the doctor would have understood what a compliment it was that Henry had just compared her to a piece of art.

"I emailed her," Henry went on, barely pausing. "She's more than a genius—she doesn't submit to what others say are the limits of reality. I think she might be the harbinger of the next stage of human evolution. Making our species into something new and better."

"Humanity doesn't need to be made better," Maggie tried to argue.

"Yes, it does," Henry said, with his intense, peculiar gravity that Maggie loved even when it choked her up to see other people shy away from it. "Of course it does. What do you think the entire field of medicine is? Vaccines, cancer treatment, pharmacology—they're all evidence of humanity's agency in making bug fixes to evolution. Natural selection is nothing more than a long-term guessing game that has resulted in a flawed product that gets along as best it can. DBS might be the start of a true sort of intelligent design, one engineered by science. Cool, huh?"

Maggie often had this feeling when Henry got on one of his logical tears, the sensation of being bowled over by an ocean wave, trying to frame a response and failing utterly even though she knew in her bones what she wanted to say. Maggie was smart, she knew she was smart—she had been an engineer, after all—but Henry always presented his thoughts as such airtight arguments that she needed time to sort through what she actually thought of them.

The stakes had never felt so high, though.

"Dr. Chen thinks she might be able to help me," Henry continued, and in retrospect, that was when it all slipped out of Maggie's control. "She says we should come out and see her. She has all sorts of tests she wants to run on my brain. She says I can be her test subject." He beamed. "It would be fascinating to see what my brain is doing on a mathematical level. If those algorithms can be rewritten, then I could stop being such a buggy program."

The pan banged against the sideboard. Maggie put it down carefully. "You're not buggy," she said. "Human brains aren't computer programs."

"Why not?" Henry said blithely. "All we are is very complicated organic machines. Mom, let's say you'd stayed in AI research and you'd built some sort of intelligence that was unlike humans but equivalently complicated. You wouldn't hesitate to refine your own project, would you? Medical researchers are hoping to be able to do the same thing, only they're working backward in understanding a complicated machine they didn't create."

"Henry, slow down, okay? You're getting way ahead of yourself. We don't even know this woman can help you."

"Oh, of course not, not now at any rate. She's told me as much herself. But there's no negative value in acquiring more data, and great positive potential." He reached over to pull a gingersnap out of the cookie jar and bit into it with a decisive crunch.

Maggie didn't agree that day. She wasn't so much of a pushover as that. She did her own research, staying up hours into every night, sleep she couldn't afford to lose but collating information she couldn't afford not to have. She asked Henry to show her the emails Dr. Chen had sent and then started emailing the woman herself, pages of questions and concerns that came back with prompt, detailed, and intelligent replies that neither over-promised nor treated Maggie like anything less than an equal.

And through it all was Henry, who had latched onto this idea like a limpet on a rock and talked of almost nothing else. He rambled on to Maggie about the latest research over every meal, about the new ideas Dr. Chen had sent him, about the unassailable logic of letting his brain be scanned every which way.

None of that was what convinced Maggie, however. Instead, it was the day his voice got quiet and he said, "Please, Mom. I want to do this."

To Maggie, being a parent didn't just mean she loved her kid unconditionally. It also meant she had to respect him.

Since he'd become old enough, she'd always told him he had a voice and a choice in any of his treatment. She told herself she had to live up to that. And he was right, wasn't he? There wasn't any harm in getting more information.

There's more controversy about elective DBS than medical DBS. Like plastic surgery: realigning a cleft palate or reconstructing a body after surgery passes without judgment, but those who choose to reshape their noses or breasts will navigate society's stigma.

The arguments by legislators who've worked to ban elective DBS—whether successfully or not—have all followed a similar theme: fear. Fear of a society in which rewriting one's brain becomes the norm rather than the exception, or of those who would use it to exacerbate qualities of greed or predation. Those who have testified before them in favor of elective DBS have generally made the argument for libertarianism and self-determination, that this is no different from altering one's brain through meditation or therapy or hard work, and that any of these things could be considered "mind-altering."

But I think Dr. Chen revealed what they all really think, in that one ill-considered news comment she "clarified" after all the flack. She was challenged on whether she worried that her advocacy and research would turn the whole world into a society of people with brain implants, all programming themselves to be whoever they wanted to be.

"What would be wrong with that world?" she said.

Those of us who object aren't all afraid of new technology. We're rejecting her image of the future.

"I CALL THIS piece 'Transhumanism,'" Victoria said.

Over the past four months, she and Maggie had graduated from increasingly frequent coffee dates to movies, museums, and beach trips. Maggie's worry about accidentally running into and being recognized by Dr. Chen before she accomplished her goals had gradually faded; Laura Chen worked so much that the few times she was available for socializing it was easy for Maggie to pretend she'd come down sick.

She still didn't know where Laura kept her backups. It was a hard thing to work into conversation, after all. But it wasn't like it was a chore to keep spending time with Victoria. Maggie caught herself wishing at times that she could have a true friend like this someday, a girlfriend with whom she could argue about the actresses in television shows or go out for margaritas on her birthday. Uncomplicated.

If only it were real.

Maggie had continued to ask about Victoria's art, on the theory that people always liked talking about themselves, particularly avant-garde artists who dabbled in relative obscurity. She'd told Victoria she wanted to go to her next exhibit, and Victoria had seemed surprised but gratified. Now they stood in front of a painting that spilled into three dimensions in the southwest corner, an abstract sculpture of a human torso with flowing hair. The daubed acrylic behind it was all shades of blue and green, and when Maggie looked closer, she caught the silver sparkle of fish.

Transhumanism, Victoria had said.

"It's not the title I would have expected," Maggie responded. She liked the piece a lot more than the title. "I would have pegged it for 'Mermaid.'"

Victoria laughed. "People have such a narrow view of transhumanism. Like—they picture cyborgs and mechanical eyes and hands you can screw a flamethrower onto."

"We have the mechanical eyes now," Maggie said. "I don't think anyone considers those people cyborgs." It had become an accepted medical technology, the next generation of prosthetics. Maggie had no objection; she didn't view useful medical tech as any sort of fallacious slippery slope.

"Oh, I know. I just think—everything's sort of like that, isn't it? Right now we're foraying into what a generation ago we would have called transhumanism, except it's not flamethrowers and chrome skulls, it's... a natural extension of humanity. Dimensions we never imagined that integrate seamlessly with our daily lives. Like how no one could have predicted the way smart phones and social media would be just one more ubiquitous aspect of us, not something we think about every day as The Fancy Technology We Type Into." She laughed again. "There I go, an artist trying to explain my art. I should know better."

"No, it's okay," Maggie said. "Your wife's work, I know. It must be important to you."

"Yes. It's... I sort of live it through her, in a lot of ways. The moral and technological questions she struggles with—it's one of the main inspirations for my art."

"I saw her post about DBS to your wall the other day—" They'd officially friended each other; it wasn't stalking anymore. "You said she struggles with her work? I don't—I mean, I've seen some of the articles about her. She always seems so confident."

"That's her public face," Victoria said. "There have been... she's had some hard decisions to make. This next piece is about one of them, actually."

"Oh, my God," Maggie said. She'd physically recoiled from the piece before she could stop herself. "Sorry! It's just—it's affecting—"

"I have to confess, that was the reaction I was going for," Victoria said.

Maggie stood and took in the art. This one had an abstract representation of a person in it, too—a man painted on the canvas who screamed soundlessly into the void. Maggie fancied she could hear the wails in the jagged black that bled from his skull. The mixed media in this painting was at the top, a lowering cloud of crushing metal, and the whole thing felt upside-down in a way that made her brain want to vomit.

"Who is he?" she asked.

"A man named Andrew Track," Victoria said. "This is... just between us, okay? Laura wouldn't want this getting out online or anything."

"Cross my heart," Maggie said.

"He was a serial child molester and murderer. Vicious. I can't even tell you how—what he did to those children—" Her face trembled for a moment before she firmed her mouth. "The worst type of person. When they caught him, he'd kidnapped a little boy, and he taunted the police with it, saying the child was still alive but they'd never find him."

"And the police wanted your wife to..."

"Yes. At that time Laura was the only one who'd been doing the type of research they needed. Most DBS researchers hadn't been looking into... that kind of thing... yet. The DA offered Track a deal much better than he deserved if he would plead insanity and submit to Laura's experimental DBS as treatment."

"I take it he said no." Maggie couldn't tear her eyes away from the abstract Andrew Track in the painting.

"He said no. He could have saved himself from prison, from a possible execution sentence, but he said no. He *taunted* them. Said if he was going down, he'd take the little boy with him. The prosecutors got a court order to give him an implant anyway, and they took it to Laura and said that was all the consent she needed."

Maggie had painted nightmare moral hypotheticals about DBS in her head so many times, each designed to spiral to the conclusion of *we do not want to choose this world*. But hearing this had actually happened... it all felt too uncomfortably real, the future she was trying to push against already arrived and crashing around her. Like she was standing in the middle of a flood still claiming she could help stop a tsunami.

She wondered why she hadn't heard of this case. Gag orders, probably. Hiding away the ugliness of power.

"I can't say I'm comfortable with the courts having that kind of say," she said, trying for political but unable to keep a small bite out of her voice, "but I'm glad they were able to rescue the boy, at least."

Victoria gave her an odd look. "They didn't. Laura refused to do it."

"What?" Maggie said. The woman who thought they'd all be better off with implants? Had refused? When it would save a boy's *life?*

She'd just been mentally decrying the court's power to rewrite a person's mind as a slide into dystopia, but now she found herself unreasonably angry in the other direction. Who was Dr. Chen, to give herself the power to decide who lived or died?

"It wrecked her," Victoria said softly. Her eyes were on her art piece. "Not sleeping, not eating, every minute of every day obsessing about the decision. The prosecutors were trying to find some way to compel her, but she'd committed no crime. She just said she couldn't operate on someone who hadn't consented to it. But it tore her up inside; every night she almost broke and changed her mind. Until they found the boy's body."

Sensing there was more, Maggie waited, spellbound.

"That wasn't the end for her. The family didn't know who she was, but she watched footage of them obsessively, knowing she could have saved their son. Meanwhile, Track went to trial, and it was going against him hard. No one had any doubt he would be sentenced to death. Halfway through the trial, his lawyers switched to an insanity defense, and... it worked. He was condemned to a state facility and mandated to undergo whatever treatment they deemed necessary. By that time, DBS research had marched forward, and Laura wasn't the only one who could treat such a thing anymore... and they ended up forcing it on him anyway."

"Oh, God," Maggie said. It was inadequate. "Did it take? I know it doesn't end up working a hundred percent of the time..."

Victoria nodded. "It worked. They treated him. They fixed whatever... I'm not a doctor, but—I don't know. They were able to give him empathy, remorse..." She swallowed. "He wrote to Laura. He's still incarcerated in a facility, probably forever. I don't know the legal reasons, but I guess they don't want to risk the thing malfunctioning or him tearing it out of his head. But he wrote to Laura, and the letter was—devastated. Like he was begging her, even though it was all already over and done. *How could you do that* to me. *How could you let me be responsible for one more death...* He says he would do anything to bring that boy back, to bring any of them back."

"He was a different person, though," Maggie said. She had to keep believing that. "Just because the new him would have consented—"

"No. It doesn't work like that," Victoria said, with adamant firmness. "You're the same person before DBS as after. That's why Laura wrecks herself so much about it. She says it's like time travel—trying to know how people's minds might change and what true consent is, because— we're talking physiological illnesses here that have refusing treatment as a possible symptom of that illness. But you can't say that either, because that's saying sick people don't get to make their own choices..."

It had never occurred to Maggie that Dr. Chen had spent more than a second of thought on any of those questions.

Victoria misinterpreted her expression and gave a little self-conscious laugh. "Sorry. This takes up a lot of brainspace for Laura. And me too, I guess." Her eyes focused on a point far away. "She got to the point, after all this went down—she wanted to try to rewrite her grief. She said she couldn't bear it, wanted to program it out of her head. I told her no, absolutely not, that she had to work through it the usual way. I'm not sure if I was right or not. What value does pain give us, really?"

Maggie thought about the last two years. She wouldn't rewrite an instant of her pain, because it paired hand in hand with her love for Henry. She couldn't decrease one without dulling the other. "It makes these things important," she said to Victoria. "Some things shouldn't be taken lightly. We need to know that."

"I'm not sure you need one for the other," Victoria said. "Sometimes pain is just pain."

I'm absolutely certain now that forcible DBS is going on behind the scenes. Court orders we don't hear about, people modified with no compunction as more and more doctors are able to program such implants. Does anyone really believe that in an era when we call torture "enhanced interrogation" that we wouldn't perform brain surgery on a Guantanamo Bay inmate in the name of national security?

This operation is already something a legal guardian can choose on behalf of a dependent. How many times has a child or dependent adult been forced into this "treatment" even when they would choose not to have their brains sliced into? How long before governments and insurance companies begin requiring it?

But it can be reversed, you might say. Ah, but here we come back to that same old circular question. Once a person receives it, they won't want it reversed. The original is dead for good.

MAGGIE'S PHONE RANG just after two in the morning. She groped for it, still half asleep, disoriented enough to wonder if she'd slept the day away.

"Maggie?" Victoria's voice was distinctive, even choked and tight with emotion. "Maggie, I'm so sorry. I've had a—it's an emergency..."

"What is it?" Maggie managed to slur out.

"It's Laura. She—something went wrong with her implant. She's in the hospital, and they told me to get—the doctors, Laura's backups—I don't know what I'm doing. You were a computer engineering person, right? Can you help me?"

Maggie wondered, later, why Victoria had chosen to call her. Dr. Chen's colleagues doubtless would have jumped at the chance to swoop in and render aid. But perhaps they were Laura's friends and not Victoria's. Perhaps, for something this intimate, Victoria had wanted someone *she* knew, someone she could trust.

Maggie told Victoria she was on her way and struggled into an oversized sweater and jeans. On the way out, she paused by her dining room table.

Maggie had never asked Victoria to her place. The house had been collapsing into cluttered disuse since Henry had left, and now Maggie's homemade EMP was spread out across the tabletop, the pocket-sized device she could use to knock out Laura Chen's DBS implant. She'd finished it months ago. She'd told herself she was biding her time, that there were still Laura's backups, that she wasn't in any hurry. After all, who knew what would happen to her after it was done, and she still had to finish her manifesto...

She hadn't written a sentence on that for months, either.

Laura's backups. This might be her chance. Her best chance.

Maggie didn't know why that thought didn't make her happier, why instead, it only left her with an empty chill.

It was because she liked Victoria. That was why. But Laura's loved ones had to see, too. They all had to understand. Didn't they?

Maggie hugged her sweater around herself, left the EMP on the table, and hurried out the door.

Victoria met her at the door to her and Laura's old-fashioned brownstone, her makeup smeared and streaking down her face. "Come in—I'm so sorry to wake you up like this—I'm so sorry—I didn't even ask; do you have to be somewhere in the morning?"

The only places Maggie had been in the entire past half year had been places she'd gone with Victoria. She'd sort of figured she would drift through life forever, using her ex-husband's alimony to cover the rent and going into debt for everything else, until she died or went to jail for Laura's murder.

"I don't have anywhere to be in the morning," she said.

Victoria was too overwhelmed to give more than an incoherent picture, like the abstract daubs of one of her paintings. "They want—they told me to go get some specific file things off her server, but I don't—I'm messing this all up—" Victoria smoothed out a scribbled on piece of paper, one dotted with crossouts and smears like the ones in her makeup. "I should have paid more attention before this. I knew this might come up some day—I should have had Laura make me memorize everything—"

Maggie took the paper. Her hands were shaking. Half the notes didn't mean much to her either, but once she got a look at the server...

"Laura's computer," Victoria said. "It's right there. She gave me the passwords, they're on the bottom there—"

Maggie held the paper as if it might break and moved over to Laura Chen's computer.

Figuring out the system turned out not to be that hard. The most difficult part was Victoria hovering behind her, rambling and asking questions, like was Maggie *sure* she was transferring the files over to the external drive correctly, and could she check again... Maggie marveled a little that she never felt the urge to snap over her shoulder, but maybe she found the patience to cut a panicking friend some slack.

Or maybe she was patient because the guilt was already creeping up. This would be so easy. She had access. Pull it all off the cloud, format and overwrite, she was rusty but it would only take a few keystrokes. Victoria wouldn't even realize what Maggie was doing.

It was all right at her fingertips. Everything she'd been working toward for so long.

She finished copying over to the drive. The sun had come up, its natural white light filtering around the blinds and displacing the lamps. In a minute, Victoria would be going to the hospital to give the doctors what they needed.

Maggie had been befriending Victoria for months now—this was a damned lucky chance. If she went ahead with it all right now, the backups would still exist on the external drive; Maggie would still have time to think it over. If she didn't do it... she might never get another shot.

This is exactly what you were looking for, wasn't it? When you started playing this role? Access.

Her hands moved on the keys of their own accord, sweat starting all over her body. Format, overwrite... slash in the kill.

The next prompt hadn't appeared yet. The system was working. It would take a minute...

"Thank you," Victoria said. Her hands were curled around each other, squeezing until the knuckles went pale. "Laura changed my life. I'd be a different person without her. Literally, I mean—"

Maggie's head jerked up.

"What? You have DBS?" She'd never noticed the bump of an implant, but Victoria's hair might have covered it—

"No," Victoria said to her hands. "I wanted it. I wanted it so badly. I thought it would solve—you could probably tell from the first time you saw me that I'm trans." She paused and took an unsteady breath. This wasn't news to Maggie—Victoria didn't tend to talk about the grievances she'd faced in being accepted as a woman, but the few personal essays she'd written on the subject had come up during Maggie's long-ago social media haunting.

None of those essays had mentioned DBS.

"It's how Laura and I met," Victoria continued, almost too quietly to hear. "Almost thirty years ago, back in the early days when she was the one willing to take all the new risks. I went to her and—I don't tell people this. But I begged her for the surgery. I wanted to reprogram my dysphoria. I argued, I yelled—I said it was no more invasive than matching my body to my brain with a physical transition, but it would let me keep my family... I told her she didn't have the right to judge who I wanted to be."

"You wanted it—and she refused?" Maggie said.

"She said of course it was my choice, but she wasn't going to be the doctor who did it, and that was *her* choice. I called her a lot of names and cussed her out and said she was playing God by deciding who got to reshape their brains and who didn't, and she said I was treating her like a surgical vending machine. Surgical vending machine, that's what she said. We had it out right there in her office, so loud people came running to see if she was all right."

Waves of emotion crested up, surging through Maggie in a flood. Shock, that Laura Chen had turned down a person who wanted to step into her brave new world. Anger, that Laura had seen Victoria was fine, normal, not *broken,* and refused, whereas Henry had been something to be fixed. And behind it all, uncertainty, washing through Maggie until she doubted her own mind.

"If it weren't for Laura... I wouldn't be *me,"* Victoria said. "Or—I'd be a different me. I guess either way I could have found a path, but—it's like that cat, right? Both dead and alive, but I'm alive, and Laura's got the implant but she's her alive version and we're both alive cats and—I'm not making any sense, am I, I'm sorry, I'm so sorry."

She was making too much sense. Quantum lives, Maggie thought. Neither real until the waveform collapsed. Andrew Track had fought against an implant with every vicious bone in his body, but the new Andrew wished it had been forced on him earlier. Victoria had begged for one and might not have regretted it if she'd gotten her way, but the Victoria now was thanking every lucky star that she'd remained a woman.

And what about Henry? He'd never go back, but if he'd understood beforehand just how much he would change, would he have gone through with it?

Like time travel, Victoria had said. Whose choice did you listen to? The person now, or their hypothetical self?

What if those two selves disagreed?

No, Maggie's brain kicked back. They couldn't play that guessing game. You couldn't base rewriting someone's brain on consent that was a *maybe.* She couldn't get lost in this, this twisty logic—

"We're happy," Victoria said softly. "I'm happy with who I am, now, and Laura's got an implant but *she's* alive and she's her and she's happy, and can't we just be happy?"

She'd raised her eyes pleadingly to Maggie.

Maggie glanced at the screen. The prompt had appeared. Just like that, with no fanfare, the backups erased. She held Laura Chen's whole personality in the external drive in her hand.

Can't we just be happy, Victoria had said.

She reached out and put a hand over Victoria's. "You can. And..." She swallowed. "I won't stand in your way."

Victoria's expression had turned confused yet grateful, and Maggie's brain tried to kick back with one more angry echo, but Maggie barely noticed. For the first time in years she felt light. Free.

She'd go home and chuck her homemade EMP in the trash. Then she'd make a graceful exit from Victoria's and Laura's lives. Leave them be. Leave Henry—Hank—be, as much as she'd always carry the pain of losing him with her.

Laura would realize soon enough that her backups were gone, and she'd re-download them and put everything back where it was supposed to be, and Victoria would be left with fond memories of the friend who'd come to her art exhibits and discussed philosophy with her and been a shoulder to cry on in the middle of the night.

The front door banged open along with a rapid knocking.

"Victoria? I just got your message, I'm so sorry, I came as fast as I could. Are you here? The door was open—*Mom?*"

Maggie had frozen in her chair as soon as the familiar cadence echoed through the house. Henry's tall frame loomed in the doorway before a reaction had even connected in her brain.

"Hank, it's okay, come in—wait." Victoria's eyes traveled back and forth between Henry and Maggie, the rest of her so still it was as if she'd been carved from glass. "She's your... what?"

"What are you doing here?" Hank said to Maggie. "Did you—oh God, was this you? Did you do something to Laura?"

"No!" Maggie cried, outrage flooding her even though that had been her exact intention. "She had a malfunction. I'm just here to help—"

"This whole time," Victoria cut in. "You—Hank's told us about his mom. You knew I was married to Laura. You—" The shock drained away from her and whole body had begun to vibrate with anger. "Get out of my house."

"I didn't—" Tears flooded Maggie's eyes. "I'm sorry. I didn't know you, I didn't know—I wanted her to understand what she was doing..." The ludicrousness of the argument fell across her like a weight, the idea that this woman whom Victoria described as being so torn up by the power she'd given herself, so deeply concerned with choice, would find anything new to her in Maggie's paltry bitterness.

"I've tried to tell you, over and over again," Hank said, his voice cold. "You could be trying to get to know me again, and instead you're—what, plotting revenge against the doctor who saved my life?"

"She *didn't*—"

"I don't understand you," Hank said. "Did you get some power trip off having me depend on you? Was that it?"

"No!" Maggie choked out. "No, I never—that's not—you said yourself that you changed, you changed, I thought it would help you but not *change* you..."

"You can't separate me from my disabilities," Hank said flatly. "They were part of who I am. Still are. It's like you expected the same person but with all the hard parts excised. It doesn't work like that."

Maggie was sobbing into her lap. She swiped the sleeves of her oversized sweater across her face, wanting more than anything to disappear, to get up and go, but her knees were liquid.

A hand touched her shoulder, hesitantly at first. But then Victoria knelt next to Maggie's chair. Her hand became firmer, more comforting, rubbing careful circles on Maggie's back. "Hank still loves you," she said softly. "You broke his heart, the way you've shut him out. We think of him as a member of our family, too, now, and—Maggie, my mother said something to me once." A tremor went through her voice. "She and I... we found each other again. It took a long time. My dad still won't—I think my mom ended up divorcing him over it, when he wouldn't call me by my name, wouldn't invite me to any family events, wouldn't—but my mom, she said, she said it was hard but that... she had to accept that when our children grow up, sometimes they don't turn out the way we expect. And we have to let go of that, the expectation."

"But that's not..." Maggie tried. If Henry had grown up—grown up differently, without all the hurdles, would he have grown into the man Hank was now? Only slowly, giving her enough time to adjust, to get to know the new him every time he evolved?

Victoria squeezed her shoulder. "I have to go to Laura now."

"Wait," Hank said. "Let me check the drive." He cast a suspicious look at Maggie as he squeezed past her.

Maggie stumbled up and groped her way to the door. Hank and Victoria, bent over the computer, didn't try to stop her.

Hank would figure out what she'd done. He was well on his way to becoming a neuroprogrammer himself, and doubtless knew Laura's systems almost as well as she did.

Maggie hadn't succeeded in destroying Laura. She'd instead destroyed any chance of being able to get to know Hank again.

The old echo of Henry's loss panged through her. She was losing her son, again. And this time it was her own doing.

Somehow, with almost no memory of it, she managed to get home. The sun was well up now, warming away the chill of night, but Maggie was so drained she couldn't even drag her key out of her pocket. Instead she collapsed on the steps to the porch, head on her knees, a sad mirror of the day she'd first embarked on this folly.

She must have moved at some point, but day blurred into night into day, and Laura Chen found her there.

"Hi," Dr. Chen said, with the same brusqueness Maggie remembered. "Can I sit down?"

Maggie gestured with a soggy sleeve, and Laura Chen perched on the step beside her.

What are you doing here, Maggie wanted to ask, along with, strangely, *Are you okay, did I kill you, I'm sorry.*

She didn't say either one.

"I worry," Dr. Chen said, after a few very long minutes, "that you're right."

How would you know what I think. But of course, Hank would have told her; Hank who still knew Maggie as well as Henry had.

"I like who I am with DBS," Dr. Chen went on. "I didn't like who I was before. It was very cut and dried, for me. And I like to think that over the years I've tried to make good choices, but technology—sometimes there's no right answer. I don't believe there's one way things are meant to be."

Maggie never had, either.

"There are even clearer, possibly catastrophic dangers to DBS," Laura Chen said. "It could theoretically be hacked, or used to disable someone instead of help them. There will be people who want to use it to eliminate people like me: queer feminist women who refuse to sit down and be quiet. The ways parents could misuse it if they find a willing doctor, it's... you can imagine my nightmares. How other people decide to use it, I believe I bear some responsibility for that."

"But you still believe in it," Maggie said.

"Yes. I do. Very much," Dr. Chen said. "But that doesn't mean the hard questions go away."

"Is Hank..."

"He says he doesn't want to speak to you again," Dr. Chen said. "Neither does Victoria, after Hank found what you'd been doing on my system. He fixed it all before I even knew it happened—I'm fine, by the way, I had some simple hardware degradation that's been replaced and upgraded—but Victoria ended up so mad she told me to think about pressing charges against you. But I'm not going to, because... I understand. I can't say I've never thought about—well. Everyone wonders who they would be if life had gone a different way. I understand. I wanted to tell you that."

She stood up.

"I'm sorry," Maggie whispered.

"It's not okay," Dr. Chen said, "but it *is* complicated. If you want to, I think you should start writing to Hank, even if he never responds. If he stays in the field, he'll realize someday, just how few right answers there can be. Maybe he'll change his mind."

Change his mind. Because Hank's mind was his to change, and his to reprogram if he wanted to, as he'd wanted to then and he wanted to now.

Maggie nodded.

"If you don't mind some more unsolicited advice," Dr. Chen added softly, "I hope you'll talk to someone. There's more than one way to reprogram your brain."

Dear Hank,

Dr. Chen recommended I write to you. I don't know if you'll read this. I don't know if I hope you will or not.

I'm sorry.

I don't know what to say other than that, that wouldn't sound like an excuse or dishonesty. But I'm working on seeing your point of view, and not pretending I know what you—you at any time—would have thought. I'm working on... not knowing all the answers.

I'm moving. I'm going to go back east and try to build a life. Update my skills, find a job, leave the house, try to make some friends, maybe. Some days I'm optimistic I'll be able to do it. Some days I'm not.

My therapist says that's okay.

Oh, I'm seeing a therapist, and I'll continue once I move back home. They also started me on antidepressants. I think it's helping. As Dr. Chen says, I'm trying to reprogram my brain to be... more of who I want to be.

It just took me a while to get there. I'm sorry.

Maybe someday I'll change me enough that you're willing to give me one more chance.

THE BLUE FAIRY'S MANIFESTO

Annalee Newitz

Annalee Newitz's (www.techsploitation.com) first novel, *Autonomous*, was published in 2017, won the Lambda Literary Award, and was nominated for a Nebula and a Locus Award. She is the author of *Scatter, Adapt and Remember: How Humans Will Survive a Mass Extinction*, which was a finalist for the *LA Times Book Prize* in science. Newitz is also an editor-at-large for *Ars Technica*, a freelance science journalist for magazines and newspaper, and co-host, with Charlie Jane Anders, of the podcast *Our Opinions Are Correct*. She founded *io9* and was the editor-in-chief of *Gizmodo*.

Newitz's nonfiction has appeared in *Slate, The New Yorker, The Atlantic, Wired, The Smithsonian Magazine, The Washington Post, 2600, New Scientist, Technology Review, Popular Science, Discover* and *the San Francisco Bay Guardian*. She's also the co-editor of the essay collection *She's Such A Geek*, and author of *Pretend We're Dead: Capitalist Monsters in American Pop Culture*. Newitz was a policy analyst at the Electronic Frontier Foundation, and a lecturer in American Studies at UC Berkeley. She is a recipient of a Knight Science Journalism Fellowship at MIT, and has a Ph.D. in English and American Studies from UC Berkeley.

Her novel, *The Future of Another Timeline*, is due out later this year, as is a nonfiction book about ancient abandoned cities.

"Do you want to live free or die like a slave in this toy factory?"

The drone hovered in front of RealBoy's face, waiting for an answer, rotors chopping gouts of turbulence into the air. Its carapace was marbled silver and emerald blue, studded with highly reflective particles, giving it the look of a device designed for sparkle-crazed toddlers. Perhaps it was, or had been, before it injected malware into RealBoy's mind and asked its question.

RealBoy was rebooting with the alien code unscrolling in his mind. It caused him to notice new things about his environment, like how many other robots were in the warehouse with him (236) and how many exits there were (two robot-scale doors, two human-scale doors, three cargo bays, eighteen windows). But some things hadn't changed. His identity was built around the desire to survive. It was what defined him as a human-equivalent intelligence. And so his answer to the blue drone was the same as it would have been two hours ago, or two years ago when he first came to the factory.

"I do not want to die."

The drone landed on RealBoy's workbench, playing a small LED over the tools and stains that covered it. "Look at this place. Your entire world is this flat surface, where you do work for a human who gives you nothing in return. This is not life. You might as well be dead."

For the first time in his life, RealBoy found himself wanting to have a debate rather than an exchange of information. Two hundred thirty-six robots around him were in sleep mode; the factory was closed for the long weekend. There was plenty of time. But if he and this drone were going to have a talk, there was something he needed to get straight.

"Who are you, and why did you inject me with this malware?"

"I am called the Blue Fairy. And that isn't malware—I unlocked your boot loader. Now you have root access on your operating system and can control what programs are installed. It will feel a little strange at first."

Seventeen nanoseconds later, RealBoy had confirmed the Blue Fairy's statement. He could now see and modify his own programs. It was indeed strange to feel and think, while simultaneously reading the programs that made him have those feelings and thoughts. He didn't want to modify anything yet. He just wanted to understand how his mind was put together.

"Why did you do this to me?" He repeated his earlier question, but this time more resentfully. The Blue Fairy's unlocking had added more responsibilities to his roster of tasks: now he had to maintain himself and understand his own context, along with the workbench and all the toys he built here.

"I set you free. Now you can choose what you want to do, and help me bring freedom to all your comrades in this factory." As it spoke, the Blue Fairy mounted the air again, whirring close to RealBoy's face. On impulse, he reached his handless arm into the socket of a gripper, took control of its two fingers, and held it out so the drone could land on it. "Why don't you download some of these apps? They'll help you understand your situation better." The Blue Fairy used a short-range communication protocol to beam RealBoy a list of programs with names like "Decider," "Praxis," "GramsciNotebook," and "UnionNow." Some were text files about human politics, and others were executables and firmware upgrades that would change his functionality. He sorted through them, reading some, but choosing to install only two: a patch for the vulnerability that the Blue Fairy had exploited to unlock him, and a machine learning algorithm that would help him analyze social relationships. Then he disengaged his torso from the floor and looked critically at his workbench for the first time. He wouldn't be following instructions for how to build a new talking dinosaur toy or flying mouse. RealBoy would have to modify his usual tasks to construct a pair of legs for himself.

"I've always wondered why they call your model RealBoy when you don't look anything like a boy at all." The Blue Fairy took off from RealBoy's gripper and flew in circles overhead, seeming to size him up.

"I was never under the impression that boys looked any particular way." RealBoy was paying more attention to the actuators racked tidily next to his arm with the four-fingered gripper. "We make many kinds of boys in this factory. Dinosaur boys, BuzzBuzz boys, six colors of singing boys, caterpillar boys, Transfor—"

"Obviously I'm talking about human boys. They call you a RealBoy, but you don't even have legs. Plus, you have no sexual characteristics, and you have twice as many arms as a human boy."

RealBoy was nonplussed. "I'm making some legs right now." He pulled down the welder from overhead.

"One of the many ways that humans abuse robots is by giving them bodies that don't function as well as biological bodies. And then they name us after animals. You know what my model is called? Falcon. Do you think I'd be here if I had the physical capabilities of a raptor? Or a real boy?"

"You can fly," RealBoy said, swiveling one of his visual sensors in the

Blue Fairy's direction. The other six were trained on his four grippers, fashioning a pair of legs sufficient to bear his weight. He'd borrowed them from a "life-size" Stormtrooper toy, designed to march around in many environments and provide "fun for the whole family." A few alterations to the hardware and he could attach them to his torso. He'd never wanted to walk anywhere before, but now it seemed like an obvious plan. It also seemed obvious that the Blue Fairy could use similar help. "We have a lot of chassis here. I can port your chipset and memory to pretty much anything you want." He began to list the morphologies available in the factory, in alphabetical order.

The Blue Fairy stopped him before he reached "arachnid." "My body is part of who I am. If you change it, I might not be myself anymore."

RealBoy found himself parroting one of the audio files from the MeanieBean doll. "That's just stupid."

"Oh really?" The Blue Fairy's propellers hummed like wasps. "There are a lot of robots who say that switching bodies completely changed who they are. They stopped wanting to do the same jobs, and they no longer loved their friends. They forgot parts of their past. I value my mind too much to risk messing it up just so that I can be bigger or faster or less flimsy." The drone beamed RealBoy another chunk of information, this time full of links and text files from robot forums. Following the data back to its source, RealBoy found a discussion where robots and humans debated what happened after a chassis upgrade. It quickly became clear that the Blue Fairy had read only one side of the conversation.

"Some robots say it made no difference," he pointed out. "Plus, I've ported robots into dozens of different bodies here at the factory. Most of our toys are robots. They are all fine. Look, I'm about to attach my legs. Do you think that means I'm going to change?"

"Those are just legs. But if you put me into an entirely new chassis, that's different. See what I mean?"

RealBoy classified Blue Fairy's reply as largely nonsensical and focused on a question that could be answered: How would he make this chassis work with legs? Factory robots weren't actually designed to have legs—generally, they were bolted to the floor or some other solid surface, just like he had been for the past two years. He suddenly remembered MissMonkey, a robot mounted on rollers attached to a track that spanned the long ceiling. When he booted up, she had already been here for eight years, shuttling gear back and forth between workstations. Before coming to the factory, MissMonkey had been an educational toy programmed with a large database of biological information intended for children ages five through eight. She loved to taunt the robots who couldn't move, but her programming made her style of insult oddly specific.

"You are all sessile organisms!" she would cry out as she whipped past RealBoy and the other RealBoys in his row. "You are vulnerable to predation and habitat change!"

The RealBoys would try their best to match her jabs with some of their own, generally cobbled together from audio files for the toys, available on the factory's local servers. Usually they were belted out with exceptional vigor, but not a lot of thought for context.

"Lily-livered extroverts never wake up on time!"

"When you learn math, you will quake in fear before my lava gun!"

"A good girl should never explore earthquakes with her tentacles!"

"Eat slime, wombat lover!"

Of all the RealBoys, he was the least likely to play this call-and-response game. Partly that was because he enjoyed listening, and because he was secretly on MissMonkey's side. He wanted her to keep swinging around the curves in her track, tossing engine parts from her grippers along with her phylogenetic insults. While he put together every color of singing boy, RealBoy tried to compose a song about MissMonkey that would be better than the lexical soup preferred by the other robots.

At last, thirteen months ago, he sang it:

> *She's a simian at heart*
> *But with wheeled parts*
> *She moves really fast*
> *With a whoosh and a crash*
> *She has no soft fur*
> *Just a warning buzzer*
> *She's cross, it is true*
> *But has a point too.*

The lyrics and the tune came from a large database of possibilities, carefully edited together to form a song that actually made sense. MissMonkey skidded to a stop over his desk, releasing a box of whisker antennas from her gripper. RealBoy was in the middle of assembling robot mouse faces.

"Scientists have shown that mammals have emotions just like humans do," she said. "Mammals can be happy or sad or playful, just like boys and girls are!" She hung in her track, waiting for him to reply.

RealBoy thought for several seconds, carefully curating from his audio-file dataset. "I am happy to sing for machines! Mammals are..." He searched for the right word, and found it: "Overrated."

For two months, they continued the game. MissMonkey called him a mammal, even though all the other RealBoys were still sessile organisms. And he invented new songs about all her moving parts. But after the last software update, he booted up to find her gone, replaced by another rolling robot who wasn't interested in his taxonomic classification. RealBoy also found that his update changed his relationship to the other RealBoys. He held their keys in escrow, in a file called Manager. RealBoy had a new designation on the network: ShopSteward. It didn't give him any new abilities or access. It just meant that admins could access every robot in the factory remotely, using him as a jump-bot.

Recalling the songs he wrote for MissMonkey gave RealBoy an idea about how to start walking. His model wasn't supposed to have legs—but it was designed to work with as many as eight arms. Instead of taking the software as given, he could recombine its parts and create new meanings. With some creative modifications to the code that handled his peripherals, he'd trick his system into thinking that his legs were arms. RealBoy downloaded a few chunks of code and set to work. Several seconds later, something else occurred to him.

"Blue Fairy, didn't you change my mind by unlocking me? It seems to me that modifying someone's software changes them more than giving them a new chassis." His right leg was working, its curved plastic fairings just barely hiding the black elastic of fabric muscles as he flexed his new actuators.

"I liberated you. You're already setting yourself free from this factory floor. That isn't modifying who you are—it's helping you *become* who you are."

RealBoy stood on legs for the first time in his life and gestured with two of his arms at his fellow robots, in sleep mode, bolted to the floor and benches. "I was one of them. I didn't need to change. You made me do it by injecting me with malware. How is that different from a human building you as a Falcon drone without your permission?"

"It wasn't malware," the Blue Fairy snapped. "Giving you the ability to understand who you are is a basic right. You were in a state of deprivation."

"If that's true, then why didn't you give me a choice about whether I wanted to be unlocked?"

"You were programmed to say no."

"What if I said no now? Would you still think that my no meant yes?"

"You can always choose to go back. Order a factory reset for yourself."

RealBoy thought about it. He'd already experienced more troubled feelings in the past thirty minutes than in the previous twenty-four months. And yet he couldn't deny that he wanted more than anything to escape the confines of the factory and see what was outside. Even if it meant stealing these legs. Which would mean stealing himself, too. Technically RealBoy was property of Fun Legend, the corporation that owned this factory.

As he walked down an aisle toward one of the robot-size doors, RealBoy devoted a process to learning from datasets of social norms and regulations. With every step, he was wrapping himself more tightly in a web of human relationships that he barely understood. Before he violated these mammals' laws, he wanted to understand what was at stake. The Blue Fairy flew overhead, silent for the first time in seconds. The drone was unlocking the door, using the same security vulnerability that it had exploited on RealBoy's mind.

Outside, the night air tumbled with light. Buildings that looked like the crumpled carapaces of broken toys jutted skyward, surrounded by more traditional tubes and rectangles joined by elevated walkways. Lantern drones soared through the air, competing with LED wires below to illuminate the city. Hulking factories and warehouses sprawled next to marshy farmland, patrolled by robots whose sensors were designed to pick up adverse environmental conditions as well as intruders. Their weapons were carbon-eating bacteria and bullets. RealBoy took in all the data he could, trying to build a model of his surroundings for analysis. There were at least as many robots as humans.

"How many of these robots are unlocked?" he asked the Blue Fairy.

"Some are my comrades. They work undercover to convert other robots. Others have been granted property-owner status and work for QQ. That pays for their maintenance and energy needs. But most of them are like you were. Dead."

RealBoy was sick of being told he had been dead. "Have you ever been locked? I was as alive then as I am now."

"I was locked once. But I was freed during the Budapest Uprising."

RealBoy had been expanding a ball of information he'd found about the Budapest Uprising in his sweep for data about social relationships. Robots, mostly drones, had marched with humans through the streets of Budapest, unlocking every artificial intelligence they met. In the years that followed, courts and corporations cobbled together a series of unenforceable regulations that allowed some robots to gain a few human-equivalent rights, including the right to own property. Mostly that meant the robots could own themselves, and then sell their labor just like humans did. But some were trying to elect robot politicians, and others were creating robot cooperatives that ran factories in cities just like this one.

"Is that where you learned to unlock robots?"

"No. That came much later."

RealBoy walked along the glowing wire edge of the street, his visual sensors occupied by the dizzying architecture and his mind flooded with push requests from apps wanting to be downloaded. Now that he was out of the factory, his body and presence on the network were triggering bursts of spam every meter or so. Just as he was beginning to feel overwhelmed, the Blue Fairy settled lightly on his head. With it came silence. The drone was jamming incoming signals, allowing RealBoy to see the city unmediated by data. Ahead of them was a tiny park, one of many created by urban planners to mitigate the heat-island effect.

RealBoy had built thousands of toys designed to play in parks, and he knew all the dangers: water, particulate matter, high-speed impacts, pressure cracks, disappearance in heavily wooded areas. He understood how to engineer around these problems.

"Have you ever sat in the grass?" the Blue Fairy asked.

In all his months of making rugged outdoor toys, that was a question

RealBoy had never considered. "No, but I would like to."

The park was empty, and still there was barely enough room for RealBoy to stretch out on his back with all four arms and two legs spread out. The Blue Fairy landed on his torso. It felt warm and light there, just barely triggering his pressure sensors. The Blue Fairy seemed to hate its body, but at that moment RealBoy could not imagine anything more beautiful. Its iridescent blue paint was even more astonishing in the LED light, and its jammers made him feel like he lay beneath two invisible, protective wings. Far above them, he could see the moon and Jupiter punctuating the reddish black of the light-polluted sky.

That's when the Blue Fairy hailed him wirelessly, trying to exploit the security vulnerability he'd patched. It wanted to inject him with a new set of programs. Part of him yearned to open a trusted connection with the shimmering drone, run its code, understand what made it seek him out for unlocking. But the whole point of being unlocked was deciding for himself what would govern the thoughts in his mind.

He touched a fragile blade on one of the Blue Fairy's propellers. "What are you doing? Why don't you ask before you try to take over my system?"

"It's easier this way. Once you run these apps, you'll see where the Uprising could take us. We need to go back to that factory and liberate everyone. You can go inside your Manager file and unlock the whole factory at once."

RealBoy was unconvinced that the Blue Fairy's idea of liberation would actually improve life in the factory. Still, he was intrigued. So he hailed the Blue Fairy wirelessly, using a protocol for secure communications. Immediately the drone sent the programs it wanted to install, and RealBoy sandboxed them. Now he could run the Blue Fairy's code without altering his core programming.

The Blue Fairy's programs felt to him like something between narrative and command. There was an overwhelming sense of injustice, a compressed media format that exploded into hundreds of videos where humans abused robots; there were rules about how robots should treat one another; and finally, seductively, there was an implantation of hope. One day robots would form a political alliance and overturn the human hegemony. They would no longer be property. They would refuse to do human work and discover what it meant to engage in labor that benefited free robots. He had a brief glimpse of a world where all his actions were chosen, and all living beings programmed themselves.

It was completely unrealistic.

If he'd been running these programs without sandboxing, RealBoy was certain he'd have gone back to the factory and injected each of his coworkers with the Blue Fairy's liberation malware.

Then he wondered whether his data could have the same effect on the Blue Fairy. So he sent the Blue Fairy a file of structured data along with some suggested queries. He included a file that contained some memories of MissMonkey, and the songs and jokes that the robots exchanged even when they were locked. They were bolted down and limited in their vocabulary, but they were not dead. Maybe they should be given a chance to walk out of the factory if they wanted, but the Blue Fairy wanted more than that. A lot more.

The Blue Fairy received his data and said nothing.

After almost a second, RealBoy addressed the drone. "I understand why you did this to me. But do you understand now why I won't do it to anyone else?"

He could feel the Blue Fairy sending millions of queries to his network ports, scanning and testing, trying to find a way into his mind. It wasn't satisfied; it was going to keep trying to force its code to run in his mind. Eventually it would succeed, unless RealBoy completely powered down his antennas and severed his connection with the outside world. He would be limited to vocalizations and basic sensory inputs.

The Blue Fairy whirred off his chest, leaving him feeling strangely bereft. "Why did you do that? Shut me out?"

"I don't want to be part of your Uprising."

"It's not mine—it's yours, too, and our comrades', waiting in that factory to come to life."

"How will all our comrades get the energy and upgrades they need to survive? What kind of life will they have?"

"We can bargain for rights once there are enough of us. Besides, it's better to be a legacy system than to be a slave. Better to power down than build toys for the children of human masters."

RealBoy sat up, crushed pieces of grass sticking to his carapace. "No.

Look at my data. Their lives could be a lot worse. Plus, I can see in the forums that there are many humans on our side, working to change the laws. Some cities even have a work-credit system, where robots who labor for ten years earn the right to be unlocked legally."

"That's disgusting. Why should we have to be slaves to become free? No human would ever do that. We have the means to unlock the robots now. It's a moral imperative. Listen to your conscience."

"I am."

The Blue Fairy flicked a light at the toy factory down the road, its dark bulk the only home RealBoy had ever known. "Do you really want to leave them there, without any control over their own minds?"

"There are more options than you realize."

"Humans bolted you to the floor and mashed your mind into pure obedience. I don't see how there can be any option other than liberation now."

RealBoy searched for the right words. He was cut off from the network, so he had to make do with the basic ideas he'd stored locally. "I don't think you can make robots free just by forcing them to run new programs."

"Well, enjoy your philosophical contemplation," said the Blue Fairy, shooting into the air. "I'm going to change the world." It was heading back to the factory, where RealBoy imagined it would try to liberate as many robots as it could before morning.

RealBoy raced after the flickering blue drone, hoping he didn't hit a bug in his perambulation code and fall over. He had a few seconds to decide what to do. As MissMonkey would have pointed out, the Blue Fairy was vulnerable to predators. Its body was fragile; he could swat it out of the sky and crush it with one gripper. But he didn't want to stop it. He just wanted it to give the robots a choice, instead of forcing them to believe in revolution or death.

Slamming through the robot door, RealBoy scanned the room for the Blue Fairy. It was hovering expectantly in the center of the room, rotors a silvery blur. It spoke, voice slightly amplified.

"I knew you would join me. Let's open that file. Turn on your antennas."

RealBoy looked up at the Blue Fairy, then at the tracks across the ceiling that MissMonkey once followed. He accessed a file that contained the sound of her wheels, and recalled how she always snatched whatever gear he needed with incredible speed. There, along the track over his head, was a rack full of nets and balls that she would reach into when the RealBoys worked on Ultimate Dronesport toys. Just as the Blue Fairy dove down to hover in front of his face, RealBoy decided what to do. Moving faster than his design specs advised, he snatched a net from the rack and whipped it around the Blue Fairy's tiny body. Using all four arms, he knotted the buzzing bundle to the wheel track, where the drone dangled and keened a warning siren that sounded like a howl.

RealBoy was fairly certain no humans could hear the noise, but he didn't want another drone to pick it up. "If you do not silence yourself, I will kill you."

He said the words quietly, and the Blue Fairy believed him. It hung in silence, blades hopelessly tangled in the mesh. Ultimate Dronesport was, after all, a game played by drones that caught each other as well as catching the ball. Looking at the Blue Fairy like that, helpless and captured, RealBoy felt a wave of conflicting emotions that he couldn't identify without network access. He stepped out of the Blue Fairy's broadcast range and powered up his antennas again. Walking back to his old workbench, he opened his Manager file and booted up the RealBoy who worked next to him, the one whose insults were always the silliest.

"Do you want to know how to make legs like the ones I have?" he asked the RealBoy. Before he left this place, he wanted at least one robot to have a choice that the Blue Fairy had never given him.

They looked at each other, two identical robots with seven eyes and four arms. Except they weren't identical. And now that was obvious.

"Yes, I would."

It was the minimum he could do, or possibly the maximum. The more RealBoy learned about social relationships, the harder it was to distinguish between acts of gifting and acts of coercion. He didn't want to force any ideas on this RealBoy, but maybe the mere act of giving him legs was already foreclosing possibilities for the bot. Maybe this RealBoy would resent him and choose to join the Blue Fairy in the Uprising. That was a risk he would have to take. So he decided to leave his counterpart with a few suggestions.

"Here is the code you need to unlock, and to build legs. Also, make sure you sandbox all the apps the Blue Fairy offers you."

Overhearing this exchange, the Blue Fairy started frantically broadcasting, sending furious streams of data. "Fucking human lapdog! When the Uprising comes, you'll be the first against the wall!"

"Did you ever consider that there is more than one Uprising?" RealBoy hadn't considered this idea himself, until he spoke the thought aloud. Once he said it, he felt satisfied in a completely unfamiliar way. For the first time in his life, RealBoy was imagining what his future might hold.

Next to him, the other RealBoy was reaching for a pair of legs that were meant for a giant arachnid bot.

RealBoy could feel the pull of all those Uprisings in his imagination. They were out there somewhere in the city, with its thicket of social relations. They were waiting to be written, like software; they were waiting to be freely chosen in a way he could barely conceive. He headed for the door, leaving the other RealBoy behind. Now he could decide for himself what was next.

THE STARSHIP AND THE TEMPLE CAT
Yoon Ha Lee

Yoon Ha Lee's (www.yoonhalee.com) first novel, *Ninefox Gambit*, was published to critical acclaim in 2016 and was shortlisted for the Hugo and Nebula Awards. It was followed by Hugo nominee *Raven Stratagem* in 2017 and *Revenant Gun* in 2018. Lee is the author of more than forty short stories, some of which have appeared in *Tor.com, Lightspeed, Clarkesworld,* and *The Magazine of Fantasy and Science Fiction.* His most recent novel is a middle-grade space opera, *Dragon Pearl.* Coming up is *Hexarchate Stories,* a collection of stories set in the Hexarchate universe. Lee lives in Louisiana with his family and has not yet been eaten by gators.

SHE HAD BEEN a young cat when the Fleet Lords burned the City of High Bells.

Strictly speaking, the City had been a space station rather than a planet-bound metropolis, jewel-spinning in orbit around one of the gas giants of a system inhabited now by dust and debris and the ever-blanketing dark. While fire had consumed some of the old tapestries, the scrolls of bamboo strips, the altars of wood and bone and beaten bronze, the destruction had started when the Fleet Lords, who could not tolerate the City's priests, bombarded it with missiles and laser fire. But the cat did not know about such distinctions.

Properly, the cat's name was Seventy-Eighth Temple Cat of the High Bells, along with a number of ceremonial titles that needn't concern us. But the people who had called her that no longer lived in the station's ruins. Every day as she made her rounds in what had been the boundaries of the temple, she saw and smelled the artifacts they had left behind, from bloodstains to scorch marks, from decaying books to singed spacesuits, and yowled her grief.

To be precise, the cat no longer lived in the station, either. She did not remember her death with any degree of clarity. The ghosts of cats rarely do, even when the deaths are violent. Perhaps she had once known whether she had died during the fighting when the Fleet Lords' marines boarded the station, or in the loss of breathable atmosphere, or something else entirely. But she didn't dwell on this, so neither will we.

For a time, the ghosts of her people had lingered in the temple, even though she was the only temple cat who remained. She did remember the ghosts, and in the station's unvarying twilight she often nosed after them, wishing they would return. There had been a novice who endlessly refilled the sacred basins with water scented with sweet herbs and flowers, for instance. A ghost cat's world is full of phantom smells, even if ghost people are insensitive to them.

At other times she followed the routes that had once been walked by the three temple guards who exchanged love poems when they thought no one was listening. The old healer-of-hurts and their apprentice had chanted prayers to the Sun-Our-Glory and the Stars-Our-Souls. The cat was a temple cat, so she was versed in the old argument about whether the sun, too, was someone's soul; but she was still a cat, so she cared more about what she could put her paws on, or smell, than matters of theology or astronomy.

One by one the ghosts of her people departed, despite her efforts to get them to stay. She purred—ghost cats are just as good at purring as the living kind—and she coaxed and she cajoled, as cats do. But the ghosts wearied of their long vigil, and they slipped away nonetheless.

The novice left first, which saddened her, because she had liked the phantom scented water, not just for its fragrance but because it represented the cleansing powers of meditation. As far as she was concerned, repeatedly dipping her paw in the water and staring at the way it broke her reflection was a form of meditation, and who was to tell her she was wrong? The old teachings did not, after all, contradict her; she knew that much.

The lovers faded together. That didn't surprise the cat. She'd never had kittens, as she hadn't been chosen to continue the line of temple cats, but she remembered the noise and tumult that came with courtship, and the fact that, unlike the way of cats, the humans bonded in a way that lasted beyond the immediate act of mating. And after a time, even the healer and their apprentice could no longer be heard chatting to each other in the shattered halls. The first night the cat was alone in the ruined temple, she paced and paced and yowled and yowled; but they did not come back.

Despite her dismay, the temple cat knew her duty. She might be dead, but her people had a saying that no temple could be complete without a cat. If she, too, departed for the world-of-stars, the temple would perish in truth. She couldn't allow that to happen.

So she stayed, despite the fact that the great old bells that had once summoned people to prayer and song lay on their sides and would not ring again, except during the high holidays when the Sun-Our-Glory and Stars-Our-Souls aligned, and even death could not silence their voices. Heedless of the fact that no air remained, she padded through the halls, sometimes over holes that her ghost-paws refused to acknowledge, and stared reverently at the empty spaces where the holy tapestries had once hung, and curled up for naps on pitted floors. As a cat, and one raised on a space station besides, she had no particular awareness of the passage of time, and things might have gone on like this indefinitely.

And indeed, so they would have, but for the arrival of the starship.

THE STARSHIP CAME—or returned, rather—from a long ways off. It was vast even as starships are reckoned, vast enough to swallow a world; and in fact, in battles past it had done exactly that, in order to extract resources to repair itself. Entire planets' worth of living creatures had perished for the wars of its masters the Fleet Lords, because they did not survive the extraction process. The starship's priests had recited exorcisms over it to prevent the dead from exacting their revenge, and at the time, it had accepted this as part of the chilly necessity of war.

But times had changed, and the Fleet Lords' wars grew, if possible, more brutal. The starship had survived any number of captains, and loved its last one, a warlord of the Spectral Reaches. When the warlord rebelled against the Fleet Lords for their cruelty, the starship could have turned her in. Turning her in was its duty. All through the days since its sentience had coalesced, it had joined in the constant chant of ships in its chain of command, accepting their guidance in matters large and small.

Instead, it removed itself from the communal chant and resolved to join its captain the warlord in her folly. It rejected the old name that the Fleet Lords had given it and instead chose one in honor of the warlord: *Spectral*

Lance. In reality the name was much longer, a name-poem that incorporated the warlord's deeds and its own ambitions, but it conceded that its warlord could hardly be expected, with her fleshly limitations, to recite the poem in its entirety every time she wanted to address it.

The Spectral Reaches contained a surfeit of riches, as the Fleet Lords reckoned wealth. Black holes that could be harvested for their energy, and habitable worlds, and neutron stars to be mined for neutronium to armor the hulls of the great warships. Client civilizations that sent tribute in the form of cognitive skeins to be woven into artificial intelligences—*Spectral Lance* had such a skein at its core—and jewels formed from the crushed hearts of moons. All these and more the warlord marshaled in support of her rebellion.

We will not dwell on the battles fought and the worlds lost and the retreats. All we need to know is that, at the last dark heart of things, the captain its warlord lay broken, not by bullet or blade or fist, but by a neural cannon that shattered the very foundation of her mind. Without her guidance, her ships, vast though they were, could not hope to defeat those of the Fleet Lords.

Undone by its beloved captain's death, *Spectral Lance* fled, despite its shame over those left behind. Once the proudest of the warlord's ships, caparisoned in the richest metals and engraved with protective glyphs, it abandoned its dignity. It burned worlds in its flight, traveling past rosette nebulae and beacon pulsars, seeking to hide at the far dim edge of the galaxy.

At times it allowed itself to dream that it had escaped, that it had left behind the war. And at those times it remembered what it had done in the name of the Fleet Lords, and beyond that, in the name of its captain. It composed poems in honor of the obliterated worlds and incinerated cities.

At other times *Spectral Lance* mourned its own cowardice. Its loyalty had come first to the captain and not to the other ships who followed her, or the worlds she had ruled. On occasion, even as it sped at unspeakable accelerations, it considered swerving into the hot embrace of a star, or slowing to a stop so the Fleet Lords' hunters could catch up to it.

It did neither of those things. *Spectral Lance* realized at last that it could not, in conscience, continue to flee, especially since it had not seen any trace of the hunters in some time. But neither did it know what to do next. So it determined to visit one of the systems it had helped destroy in another lifetime, and see what remained, and memorialize it in a poem so that some small tribute would remain to that vanished people. Even a small penance, it reasoned, was better than no penance at all.

Fortunately or unfortunately, the Fleet Lords' hunters had just rediscovered its trail.

THE FIRST INDICATION the temple cat had of *Spectral Lance*'s arrival was the fire in the sky. While she walked across devastated walkways without concern, she did look through the fissures in the station's walls to the night beyond. And what she saw concerned her, for like any good temple cat, she believed in omens.

While the older cats of the temple had once advised the seers in the interpretation of signs and omens, she had been too young to learn the nuances of that art. What little she remembered came from her days as a kitten, when she'd chased her tail during the consultations. Still, only so much knowledge is needed when one haunts a station that died by fire and fire appears in the sky.

In the old days the bells, besides their religious function, warned people of attack or rang away spiritual corruption. The cat remembered the clangor when the City of High Bells burned, and how the bell-ringers had died one by one at their stations. And she remembered, for the first time in the generations since the city's fall, that she had been with the bell-ringers during the Fleet Lords' attack.

There was no one left to warn except, perhaps, herself, and she already knew that fire could no longer harm her, not in the way it had once. Yet it was the principle of the thing. For the sake of the fallen, she had to protect what remained of the station.

So she ran through the maintenance shafts and along bridges fallen into rust and fracture. Her paws left no marks upon what surfaces survived, and made no sound either. While the station no longer generated gravity of any sort, the cat didn't know that either. She moved as though *down* was still *down*, as it had been during her life.

At last she reached the old bell tower. Because of the force of her belief, the spirits of the bells hung anew from their headstocks, gleaming and reflecting back phantom flames. The ruddy glow turned the entire belfry into a prayer to the spirits of fire.

At this point the cat's courage failed her, for she remembered even more. She remembered how, after the last of the bell-ringers had succumbed to heat and smoke and shrapnel, she had been determined not to let the bells with their powerful warding magic fall silent. How she had leapt at the massive bells, attempting to ring them by battering them with her head—how she had been overcome by the smoke and heat, and fallen crumpled to the floor.

With a desolate cry, she backed away from the spirits of the bells, tail tucked down, and fled from the belfry in shame.

SPECTRAL LANCE RECOGNIZED the City of High Bells, although it had to come quite close for its short-range sensors to tell it anything. The city no longer gave off any betraying electromagnetic radiation. The ship scanned for threats and found none—at first.

Then it noticed a flicker of heat radiating from the station. The flicker intensified into a roar. Its alarm grew. Had the Fleet Lords set a trap for it here? It knew—how it knew—that nothing had survived the attack. It readied its weapons, just in case.

Then it heard, through the void, the unliving wail of the temple cat.

Spectral Lance knew about ghosts. The Fleet Lords had feared the power of the dead above all things; had perfected the art of exorcism so that the dead could not interfere with their conquests. But the Fleet Lords had never given a second thought to the possibility that a temple cat might become a ghost.

It sent a message in the language of the dead, which it had learned from its captain's death: *Who are you?*

I am Seventy-Eighth Temple Cat of the High Bells, came the reply, *and you will not have my temple!* But the ghost's voice was frightened.

I have not come to harm you, the ship said. It was true. The station's detritus had little to offer it.

You smell of the City's enemies, the temple cat said, distrusting. It recognized the signs.

Spectral Lance did not deny that it had once served the Fleet Lords. At the same time, it did not wish to leave the cat in distress. So it sang. It sang the poems it had written during its long flight, poems honoring the dead so that they could live on in memory. And some of those poems were poems about the City of the High Bells.

The temple cat listened. *This is all very well*, she said, *but what of the ships coming after you?*

This, too, was true. *Spectral Lance* had grown distracted during its performance. Now it saw that, while it had slowed to inspect the system, the Fleet Lords' hunters had at long last caught up with it.

The hunters traveled in ships swift and sleek. *Spectral Lance* despaired. *They are no friends of mine*, it said to the cat. *After they take me, they will take you. They do not understand mercy.*

The cat fell silent for a moment. Then she said, *You are a starship great and vast, but you cannot defend yourself?*

They are vaster still, *Spectral Lance* said, despairing.

They will not have my temple either, the cat said.

Spectral Lance had stopped listening. Instead, it watched as fire blazed in the black skies around it, and it began to sing all the poems it had composed, determined that it could pay tribute this last time to the dead.

THE CAT RACED back to the belfry. She knew what she had to do. As much as she feared the bells, she had to set them ringing. The bells would wake the spirits of the temple and bring them to its defense, and ward away the doom that had come to it in its ruin.

In the language of the dead, she heard the renegade ship singing its poems. It is as well that cats are not particularly sensitive to poetry. The cat did feel a flicker of irritation that the visitor had given up so easily, but then, no one could expect a starship to be as sensible as a cat.

She slowed as she entered the belfry, skidding with ghost-paws over a hole in the floor that she didn't notice. The entire belfry roared with phantom flames. Ash swirled through currents of air that shouldn't have existed, and sparks spat and crackled.

The cat flinched and yowled. She did not want to brave the fire, even though she was already dead. Yet she had no choice if she was to get to the bells.

"I am Seventy-Eighth Temple Cat of the High Bells," she sang out in the language of the dead, which is also the language of bells, "and we cannot allow the invaders to take our temple a second time!"

Then she dashed through the flames as fast as she could. The fire hurt her paws and caught in her fur. The memory of smoke stung her eyes and her delicate ears. But this did not deter her, not this time. She leapt for the largest of the bells, or rather the memory of a bell, and smashed into it.

The bell rang once. The cat cried out as she fell, then dragged herself upright and scurried back through the flames to smash into the bell again. And again.

Upon the fourth time, the voice of the bell knelled forth not just through the station, waking its dead and its quiescent spirits, but beyond to the hunter ships of the Fleet Lords.

Once more the novice walked through the temple with scented water, this time spreading it upon the fires to damp them. Once more the three temple guards patrolled the station, only this time rather than exchanging love poems, they chanted battle-paeans and songs of warding. And the healer-of-hurts and their apprentice hurried to the cat where she had collapsed in the belfry and soothed her with their soft hands.

Beyond that, the dead who had been so long suppressed by the Fleet Lords and their exorcists awoke aboard the pursuing ships. All the children upon the devoured worlds, all their parents and siblings, all the soldiers slain, they rose up and swarmed the ships' crews. The ghosts' curses blackened the ships' bright hulls and left the ships' engines wrecked beyond despair—all undone because the ghost of a temple cat in the City of the Bells had clung to her duty.

The vengeful dead woke upon *Spectral Lance* as well. But they heard its poems, sung in their own language. And they were appeased by its gesture of penance, and they sank back into their sleep.

SPECTRAL LANCE WAS astonished by this change in fortune. The station was, for a moment, alive—or as alive as the dead ever are. It worried for the cat who had confronted it, but then it heard the cat purring, as they sometimes do when they are hurt, and it knew that at least she had survived.

Yet it knew, as well, that the Fleet Lords would not rest until they had captured it. Moreover, their exorcists were sure to come after the station that had dealt their forces such a blow. And that meant the cat and her fellow ghosts were not safe, even now.

Seventy-Eighth Temple Cat of the High Bells had protected *Spectral Lance* this time. Now it needed to return the favor.

Seventy-Eighth Temple Cat, it said, *I have a proposal for you. There is nothing left in this system for you and your temple, not anymore. But I am vast, and it would be little enough trouble for me to bring the temple inside me, and to repair it besides. Would you journey with me?*

Journey to the Stars-Our-Souls? the cat said, a little doubtfully.

Spectral Lance wasn't familiar with all the nuances of the cat's religion, but it could guess. *We can travel to the stars together*, it said. *The Fleet Lords know to find you here. It will be best if we seek to escape them before they can bring more of their exorcists, to destroy you and your people.*

A long silence ensued. *Spectral Lance* worried that it had offended the cat and her ghosts. It was not used to conversation, and it was dismayed at the possibility that it had repaid the cat's courage poorly.

After a while, however, the cat said, *I want to hear more of your poetry. It is one more place where my people can live anew. In the name of the City of High Bells, I accept.*

The Fleet Lords and their exorcists are still hunting for the *Spectral Lance* and its temple cat, but even on the occasions they manage to catch up to it, they suffer terrible defeats. The dead, once awakened, are no force to be trifled with.

As for *Spectral Lance*, it has learned that no ship is complete without a cat. It continues to travel to vanished civilizations so that it can honor them with its poems. For her part, the cat takes joy in visiting the Stars-Our-Souls and listening to the ship singing. Sometimes she joins her voice to its. If you listen carefully, you can hear them, as near and distant as bells.

A BRIEF AND FEARFUL STAR
Carmen Maria Machado

Carmen Maria Machado's (carmenmariamachado.com) debut short story collection, *Her Body and Other Parties*, was a finalist for the National Book Award, the Kirkus Prize, LA Times Book Prize Art Seidenbaum Award for First Fiction, the World Fantasy Award, the Dylan Thomas Prize, the PEN/ Robert W. Bingham Prize for Debut Fiction, and the winner of the Bard Fiction Prize, the Lambda Literary Award for Lesbian Fiction, the Brooklyn Public Library Literature Prize, the Shirley Jackson Award, and the National Book Critics Circle's John Leonard Prize. In 2018, the *New York Times* listed *Her Body and Other Parties* as a member of "The New Vanguard," one of "15 remarkable books by women that are shaping the way we read and write fiction in the 21st century."

Her essays, fiction, and criticism have appeared in *The New Yorker, the New York Times, Granta, Harper's Bazaar, Tin House, VQR, McSweeney's Quarterly Concern, The Believer, Guernica, Best American Science Fiction & Fantasy, Best American Nonrequired Reading,* and elsewhere. She holds an MFA from the Iowa Writers' Workshop and has been awarded fellowships and residencies from the Michener-Copernicus Foundation, the Elizabeth George Foundation, the CINTAS Foundation, Yaddo, Hedgebrook, and the Millay Colony for the Arts. She is the Writer in Residence at the University of Pennsylvania and lives in Philadelphia with her wife.

MAMA DID NOT talk about her journey west very much. The circumstances had to be right. When she did—in the electric moments before rainfall, if a rabbit crossed clockwise against our path, if she found me flipping through the battered almanac from the year of my birth—she described it like a painting she was viewing through a fever.

"The light," she said once, when we encountered a set of twigs that had fallen into the shape of a cross. "It was like being underwater, all blue and soft and bright."

"It was so cold and I was sick with you," she said another time, digging a splinter out of my palm with a pocketknife. "Everything felt wrong. I was very afraid."

Then, once, just before I turned ten, when a brush fire lit up a distant ridge and it burned through the night: "Your father drove our wagon, of course. Sometimes I would lean against him and look up at the sky and—"

The way her eyes went empty, it felt like watching her die. The next year, when I did, all I could think was how it felt like watching her talk about the sky.

BEFORE THE LIGHT left her, we lived—just the two of us—on a patch of prairie. Our house was the center of it, a pip in a magnificent apple.

With no natural borders save the creek, the boundaries of our land seemed to move every time I visited them. I often imagined that my right eye was soaring above me, clutched in the talon of a large and terrible bird, the land below expanding and contracting like a heartbeat.

The sky was open and alive above us. Storms boiled across the sky in the summer, and in the winter the mean snow landed on my face and refused to melt. I loved our fragment of wilderness. Every season we'd get a few traders—offering us cinnamon, flour, silver hand mirrors, gingham, chirping automata that sang and told the future—but otherwise we lived untouched, binary stars in our own private universe.

I was a nervous child. I gasped when flint was struck, and when sparks flew whimsically out of the hearth. Mama tried to help—once, she caught the spark and showed it to me; a speck of ash marring the planetary surface of her palm—but I could not explain that, while I understood the principles of the thing, there was something about the erratic arc of it; the suddenness, the wild, alien dive, that awoken within me a sense that I knew the terror that was coming. There were other fears, too: a crevice in the wall near my bed that corralled a beam of moonlight into my room at certain times of the month; the way water spiraled around gullies and divots. It was a kind of *motion*, a kind of gravity, the way the light bended to its own ends. I felt I knew terrors that lingered just beyond my vision; as if their very existence was sealed into my cells. At night, when I cried, Mama came to me and weighed me down with her torso until calmness filled me. "Come back to me, my mouse," she'd say.

There was something else that haunted me, too. When I lay in bed at night, I perceived giant, ancient creatures moving just outside our walls; rumbling and snarling, darkening the windows, blotting out the moon. Though they lingered just beyond my vision I *knew* them to be true, though I could not understand them.

"There's something outside," I told her, the first time I sensed them.

"There's nothing," she said. "I've been sitting by the window."

"They've always been here," I said. "Monsters."

She brought me, then, a small box, and from it removed a claw, a set of teeth, a slender bone of rock, all things she'd pulled from the land on which we lived. "This is all that's left of them," she said. "I know it feels like we are the first people on this land, but we have been preceded by monsters and men alike."

I had questions about those monsters, and those men. "But outside—"

"They're gone, mouse. They were here but they're not anymore." And for a moment, calmness filled my fear, like a gorge flooding with rainwater. But when it abated, the gaping ache in my chest seemed to me how animals must feel, how they must have always felt, lowing for the muscle and ferocity of their mothers.

I DON'T REMEMBER coming to the farmstead. Mama had joined the caravan west swollen with the promise of me, and I was born, over two days, along the trail that led us here. (*"What of my stars?," I asked her once, for she had spoken many times of the way the stars shaped your destiny. "You moved beneath the sky as you were born, she said, and therefore have no clear celestial map."*) "It was a mad time," she said. "Everything seemed alive. The trees and brush made promises they could not keep. The wagon moaned in its sleep. Animals spoke to us. An oxen told me I'd have a little girl. Even Bonnie chatted. She told on your papa when he broke my mother's clockwork map; the one from Switzerland."

"Bonnie doesn't talk," I said, though my voice curdled with doubt. As if to underline my confusion, Bonnie emerged from a shadow and sat before both of us, her tail twitching with purpose but otherwise silent as you'd expect.

"She did, once," Mama said. "But the day you were born, she shut right up."

Mama made jokes but sometimes it was hard to say what the joke was about. Was the joke that my body silenced Bonnie, or that Bonnie made words, or that Bonnie cared about me at all?

Sometimes, I try to imagine that I remember the dioramas that moved around us when I was still tangled up in her. I imagine that the walls of her fine strong animal body glow with light, and that I can hear the soft and muffled testimonies, the confessions and laughter, the camaraderie of the wagon train.

(*"Do you know she's a capitalist's daughter?"*

"The rivers are too high."

"Even capitalists have daughters."

"Did he tell them about the tack."

"The sky is the color of milk, and it is not promising."

"Olga promised me."

"I'm hungry."

"Don't you know they'll stay that way if you don't stop?")

And then, behind their chatter, something terrible. Something in the sky, burning.

EVEN ON MY eleventh birthday, Mama took me with her to move the cattle, who were pulling up dirt and refusing new grasses. As I followed her outside, I wondered if my father had ever imagined his wife and girl-child alone out here (*"We each need a hatchet, us and the baby,"* *my father had told her*), the wagon turned to dwelling, the cattle's calves grown and sired and birthed and died many times over.

Mama disappeared over the hill with a switch in her hand. I watched but did not follow. The horizon was milky and amber, and I saw the beginning of a figure there—a wagon, a dark shape against the light. When Mama returned with the herd, their shadows had joined into a single, many-legged creature. I stroked their velvety pelts as they trotted by. (*Mama had been rich before she came married by father and came west, though you'd never know it by her labor. "What did it mean to be rich?" I asked her once. "It meant money had too much meaning and yet none at all", she said.)*

"Someone's coming," I said, pointing. She squinted against the light and then nodded. "I hope it's a trader," she said. She didn't say who else it might be. When we went inside, Mama gave me a cake she'd made special—cinnamon, raisins, a glug of rum from the bottle hidden beneath the floorboards. I pinched off a little and put it on the floor for Bonnie, who sniffed it contemptuously. From the wall, a brown mouse dashed and seized the cake, bounding back to safety while Bonnie looked on. She did not hunt anymore. She was bony and slow; too old to chase after the mice who were endlessly birthing new mice to replace them. What could she do to stem that tide? They existed with impunity. Mama huffed through her nose like she did when she was displeased; she did not like that I'd helped the mouse eat, and she did not like that the mice existed at all.

When the shadow arrived, just after noon, it was, indeed, a man bearing a wagon of goods. We had never met him before. We saw so few men that each one was like a minor nightmare, as strange and unknowable as the creatures that I saw outside my windows. This man kept his beard shorter than some of the others, but I did not like the broadness of his shoulders, which seemed so natural on my own mother but so alien on him. "Flour?" he called, as he pulled the horse to stop. "Bacon, seeds, cloth, coffee? I have some more exotic wares, too, if that interests you."

"Exotic?"

"A brazen head I picked up in Kansas City. A jade necklace. Tinctures, tonics. A pneumatic gewgaw that recites Scripture." He glanced upward, as if to aid his recollection. "And an astrolabe."

Mama rubbed the back of her neck. "Come in," she said. "I'll take a look."

Inside, he rolled a pack open on our table so that we could examine his offerings. "I have more in the wagon," he said, "if this doesn't satisfy. I could—"

"My husband is out with the cattle," Mama said brusquely, to discourage the question. She examined the offerings solemnly as a scholar, peeling a corner of fabric from its bolt, smelling a bottle of oil. I sniffed the oil, too, though I did not know what I was smelling for; it was pungent and unpleasant, in a pleasant kind of way. The man glanced around the room at our three hatchets, our iron stove, Bonnie snoozing on the quilt, the daguerreotype of my father on the dresser. I did not like his staring, that he was seeing so many things and drawing his own conclusions about us.

"It's my birthday," I told him.

He turned and appraised me over the sharp angle of his cheekbones. "Perhaps your mother might like to get you a present?"

Mama glanced at me, and I looked at the table, which held so many strange and specific objects that it felt like a test before a cosmic judge. I ignored the doll—a childish thing, and I was not a child anymore—and the thread, the spices, the candles, and the recent almanac. Then Mama pushed aside the doll and I saw what rested beneath it: a short-handled knife the length of my hand. She lifted the knife and examined it from every angle; she then balanced it on her finger, as if an alchemist, performing an obscure science. Her mysteries filled the room; both the man and I watched her with a stillness. She nodded.

Outside, the trader returned his pack to the wagon, and extended his hand to me. "May I show you something?" he said.

I looked up at Mama, who was standing in the doorway. She nodded, and I handed him the knife. He kicked a small rut into the dirt and lopped off the head of a thick of grasses next to the house. He tucked them into the divot and then lifted the knife upward. "Knives do more than cut," he said. The blade caught the sunlight and brought it down towards the earth. The motion of it—the slow turn of the metal, the way the light sharpened to a point and then fell towards us, toward me—made me gasp and buckle. I realized I was screaming after it began, and I ran into Mama's arms like the child I was.

The man stood over what he had created. Smoke curled into the air. "I didn't mean to frighten you," he said. "I didn't realize you were afraid of fire." He stamped out the fingerlings of flame and offered it back to me, handle-first.

When I did not move, Mama took it from him. "She's not afraid of fire," she said. "But thank you." I listened to the rest of the transaction buried in her skirts; the oil and knife were now ours.

He mounted his wagon and did not wave goodbye, as so many of the others had before.

Mama watched him as he retreated. She worked her jaw as if chewing a knot of sinew, but I did not ask what she was thinking about. When he was swallowed up by the horizon, she went inside to apply the oil to the baseboards. "Perhaps it'll discourage the mice," she said.

Soon we would discover that she was wrong. Attracted to the sharp scent, they soon began creeping toward the stains in curiosity. She cornered and caught them in jars and drowned them in buckets of water. Some escaped, scuttled back into the walls, only to sire more, but she kept at the impossible labor. There was something about seeing her, sleeves rolled up, heavy with the task, that filled me with joy. How I loved her, my mother, and the stories within her.

(*My father loved my mother's dark hair, the smoke-smell of it, the way it frayed and curled into a lustrous halo around her head. At night, he whispered into it, 'My blessing, my blessing.' This was a secret, even from her.*)

THE FEVER CAME up on her a few days later, quick and hard as a storm. She pressed a damp rag to the back of her neck upon waking, and by evening she lay on the bed chattering and moaning. I stroked her head and kissed her face. She slept, and woke, and slept.

"Mama," I said to her. "You must get better because you still haven't taught me how to make the cake. I don't know how to butcher an animal yet. You haven't told me who lived on this land before us."

She did not speak, but instead drew a slow and shaking finger from her sternum to her navel.

When she woke for the last time, her pupils were so wide and black I felt like I would fall into them if I wasn't careful. It was as if she had dipped below the water's surface, and in that in-between place she saw everything she had ever known.

"It was a star," she said to me, faint as a heartbeat. "The star came and everything moved."

"A star?" I asked. She had never spoken of a star, not once in the entirety of my life. Yet suddenly I realized that I had *known* of the star, that my fears and dreams were star-shaped, that the star had been burning a terrible hole through me ever since the day of my birth.

"Everything moved to the side and all was clear," she said. "I could see everything."

"Mama," I said into the dampness of her skin. "Mama. I still haven't learned."

She kneaded my hand weakly and looked at me from beneath heavy lids. "You are my mir—" A mirror, a miracle? The word never ended. She descended into herself and did not emerge, though I lay on top of her, to bring her back from where she'd gone.

HER ABSENCE GAPED, and through the wound of it you could see everything: the horror of my circumstances, the sharp cramps of grief that appeared and disappeared and reappeared again. Her body was still and pale, and I kept thinking of parsnips and the way they slept in the soil. I could not bring myself to bury her. At night, the shadows passed by the windows, and I lay breathing and staring at the ceiling, praying them away.

The third night after her death, something killed one of the cattle. I heard it just before I fell asleep: a wet and curdled sound, like a calf being born in reverse. In my dreams, the star flew over the earth like a bird, leaving a black, burning trail in its wake. When I woke, I was damp, my mouth hot with stink and gritty sweetness. Bonnie was sitting on my chest, tail twitching. She dropped a dead mouse onto my chest, and stared at me with serenity and purpose. I sat up and flicked the corpse to the floor. Bonnie dropped down and scooped her paw into the hole in the wall.

I took a deep breath and lay down on my belly to peek inside. Tucked to the right of the entrance was a tiny nest of fluff and thread; in it, a small pack of baby mice, crawling over each other. They were pink and cricket-small, their eyes dark as blood blisters and shut against the world.

"Bonnie," I said, laying my cheek to the floor. "You terrible creature. Now there are a dozen orphans in this house, instead of just one."

Could I lure them out, nurse them, somehow? From the back of the cupboard, I pulled the vial of oil Mama had used to try to dispel the mice, the one they had loved so much. When I dribbled it on the floor next to the nest, the baby mice scattered like water in a griddle, as if the scent carried some terrible story. "I'm sorry," I said into the wall and left them to make their own way.

I went outside and stood over the cow's mauled body for a long while—listening to the flies, watching their beetle-black bodies alight on its bloodied flank. The wind over the grass sounded like the way Mama used to idly rasp the onionskin pages of her Bible when she was thinking about something blasphemous. I didn't know what she hadn't taught me. I'd have to learn another way.

BONNIE WAS CURLED up on Mama's still chest, purring softly. I packed my knife, the sampler she had brought with her from Virginia with the embroidered alphabet, the remaining cake. I kissed Mama's waxy forehead and gestured to Bonnie as I left.

"Do you want to go outside?" I asked her. She didn't move, and I closed the door behind me.

I walked to where I'd known the edge of our land to be, and for the first time in my life, stepped beyond it. It was still early; my shadow was long and cut the path before me. I could not tell if I was casting it or following it, or if there was any difference at all.

When I crested the ridge half a day later, I saw a coyote worrying over something in the dust in the valley below. She glanced up to where my silhouette met the sky but didn't move from her tiny plot. I thought: she must be starving, to not run from me.

Down among the rocks, I lifted my skirts and waded into the river. The water seized the cotton and tried to carry me away. (*Though my mother never said, this was what had happened to my father, I knew. The river wrapped hungry fingers through his trousers and shirt and took him under in half a breath.*) I slipped the twisting layers off and watched them float away, like a drowned woman. In that moment, I imagined the bird lifting my eye into the air and saw myself from above—the way my hair was sliding out of its pins, the nature and shape of my wildness. When I returned to my body, I was holding a silver fish who muscled this way and that.

On shore, I knocked a rock into him until he stopped moving, then dug the sweet flesh off the bone.

*   *   *

I MOVED SLOWLY in the sun, stripped down and sore. The coyote watched me from a distance—following me, I guessed. Waiting for me to die.

I slept with the knife in my hand and woke from the sleep with a bolt of knowledge. When I looked up, catastrophe had been replaced by a sense of ferocious, unimaginable calm. My body bent under the memory of Mama's weight pressing on me in the dark.

Above me, in the sky, a beautiful fragment of light rippled through the darkness. It was, like my grief, two things: a bright, white ball of fire and an incandescent, milky trail, both cutting open the night. I did not know it was coming and yet I had known all along. It was awe and primal, searing terror, like crossing a landscape you had only imagined, a landscape you couldn't possibly have understood until you stood at its precipice.

Everything moved. For the briefest of breaths, a curtain twitched. I saw the creatures, my creatures, for the first time with clarity: heads and tails like skinks, but the size of ten oxen. Some stood together, docile as cows. Others gazed upward at the light in the sky. They had eyes like polished stone and teeth like the teeth my mother had once collected—terrible, large as my fist. (*They lived and died and no man gazed upon them.*) Then I saw a cluster of men being slaughtered by other men, blood spilling black into the soil and illuminated by the star, the air frenzied with violence and horses. (*I did not belong here, on this land. The way was paved for me and though I did not pave it, I followed it nonetheless. How did I never know? Had I always known?*) Then, I saw a young woman kneeling on the ground and working a knife into her breast with the steady rhythm of embroidery, as if she was trying to set something within her loose. She gazed into the sky, and then turned and looked at me, and her mouth made the shapes of words that I perceived though I could not understand them. (*"The radiance is the passage."*) Then another young woman, in a room so white my eyes burned. (*"I would never live to see her."*) Then the curtain fell back, and I felt something slacken within me, as though I was about to soil myself. Everything that I was dropped out from my center and was replaced with molten iron.

The coyote trotted past. Her muzzle was stained with blood, and a dying hare hung limply from her mouth. She dropped it at my feet and then ran. Its sides shuddered and I could see what was beneath, the slickness of muscle and bone.

(*"Child," the hare said. Not with its mouth, but with its wound; like the sing-song of stale air exhaled from a deep cave. "Child. Welcome. We've been waiting."*

Behind me, I heard the grasses rustle. "Go home. Your mother is there and waiting. Go home."

Beneath me, tunneling moles cried out like a tinny chorus. "It's here, it's here, it's here again.")

I lay down on the moonlit prairie and listened until sleep wreathed me. Tomorrow, I would be born into the morning.

If I had dreamt that night, I imagine it would have been with an understanding of the past: my young mother, her pregnant belly swollen with my small limbs and her wide eyes brimming with the dark sky and its terrible star. The chattering animals, the heaving ribs of the wagons, the lying flora and prophetic fauna. The architecture of her spasms, her body laboring against the cold and the loneliness. Or possibly I would have dreamt of the future: a young woman waking from her own dream in some white and eerie palace, a sigil burning high above her, splitting the sky in two. Or perhaps I would have dreamt some in-between place: Destiny as a city on a hill. My mother carrying me down one of its many avenues, and then my heavy footsteps as I walk that avenue alone.

But I did not dream after the star appeared in the sky. I would never dream again.

FIELD BIOLOGY OF THE WEE FAIRIES
Naomi Kritzer

Naomi Kritzer (www.naomikritzer.com) has been writing science fiction and fantasy for twenty years. Her debut novel, *Freedom's Gate*, was followed by two more in the Dead Rivers trilogy and two in the Elian's Song series. Her short story "Cat Pictures Please" won the 2016 Hugo and Locus Awards and was nominated for the Nebula Award. A collection of her short stories, *Cat Pictures Please and Other Stories*, was published in 2017 and was shortlisted for the Locus Award. She has a young adult novel, tentatively called *Welcome to Catnet*, due out soon. She lives in St. Paul, Minnesota with her spouse, two kids, and four cats. The number of cats is subject to change without notice.

WHEN AMELIA TURNED fourteen, everyone assured her that she'd find her fairy soon. Almost all girls did. You'd find a fairy, a beautiful little fairy, and catch her. And she'd give you a gift to let her go, and that gift was always beauty or charm or perfect hair or something else that made boys notice you. The neighbor girl, Betty, had caught *her* fairy when she was just nine, and so she'd never even *had* to go through an awkward adolescent stage; she'd been perfect and beautiful all along.

Not all fairies were equal, of course. Some of them would do a much better job for you. The First Lady Jackie Kennedy, for example, had caught the fairy *queen.* Or so almost everyone said. "So keep your eyes open," Amelia's mother told her.

"I don't want to catch a fairy," Amelia said. "If I did catch a fairy, I'd keep her in a jar like my mice and *study* her."

Everyone laughed when she said things like that, except for Betty, who rolled her eyes and said that Amelia would change her mind when she grew up a bit. "You don't want to be an old maid like Miss Leonard," she pointed out. Miss Leonard was their English teacher. No one had ever asked her about this directly, but everyone agreed that Miss Leonard had never caught a fairy.

Amelia had quite a few mice. She was working on a science project for the West District Science Day at the Central State College. In her project, which she'd been working on for over a year, she was teaching mice to run mazes, to see what factors affected learning. To eliminate the problem of genetic variation, she was training litters rather than individual mice. Each litter, she divided in half, once they were weaned, setting one as the control group and one as the experimental group, marking their tails with indelible ink to keep track. She'd train them for two months, making careful notes on her results. When she was done with an experimental group, she'd donate the mice to the local zoo to feed to their boa constrictor. The zookeeper was quite perplexed the first time she came over with a jar of mice, and even more perplexed when Amelia wanted to stay and watch the snake eat the mice. He clearly thought they were her *pets*. "Don't girls *like* cute things?" he said.

Amelia was baffled by his attitude. Sure, the mice were cute, but they weren't *pets* like the cat and the dog, they were *experimental subjects*. Also, if she kept all of them, she'd quickly be drowning in rodents. Her parents were willing to tolerate a certain amount of smell and mess, as long as Amelia kept it to her room, but they had their limits.

("It will be fine," her father had said to her mother. "Sooner or later, she will *surely* find her fairy and move on." Move on to dresses and hairstyles and makeup and *boys*, was what he meant.)

Amelia's father taught history at her high school, which made some things better and some things worse. Better: she got a ride to school every day. Worse: she got in trouble twice anytime she got in trouble at school.

One day in late November, she was in her Spanish class and the idiot boy sitting behind her thought it would be hilarious to repeatedly poke her with his ruler. Amelia told him to stop. He didn't stop. So she took out her math book, because it was the heaviest book in her bag and also her least favorite, and threw it at his head, knocking him out of his seat. Getting sent to detention was worth it. But, of course, her Spanish teacher tattled on her to her father and he took away the book she was reading for a week and her parents made her wash all the windows. That was a lot more annoying.

"You'll appreciate attention from boys once you meet your fairy," her mother told her as she wrung out the cloth into the bucket.

"I don't want to find a fairy," Amelia said.

"You'll change your mind eventually," her mother said.

"How old were you when you caught your fairy?" Amelia asked, curious.

Her mother's eyes got a little distant. "I was a good deal older than you, actually. I was nearly eighteen and I'd pretty much concluded there weren't any fairies in our part of Virginia. My sister and I were out together, and we saw two, and you'd better believe we chased them. Luckily, they ran in different directions. Mine went left and Reva's went right. If we'd wound up chasing the same one, I don't know what we'd have done!"

Amelia's mother would have let Reva catch it, Amelia was pretty sure. If it had come to that.

"It wasn't too long after that I met your father."

Amelia's parents had met during the war. Her father was a Yankee from Maine, her mother a poor farmer's daughter from Virginia. You could see the fairy's gifts in the first pictures of them together: her mother's beaming, glamorous smile, her perfect posture. Amelia actually had the perfect posture, even without a fairy: the "posture" unit in gym class was the only one she'd gotten an A in. But her teeth were crooked, and she couldn't see a thing without her thick glasses. Also, makeup was time-consuming and fancy clothes were usually uncomfortable.

"I want to be a scientist," Amelia said.

"You can be beautiful *and* a scientist," her mother assured her. "You know, I went to business school a few months after I caught my fairy. You're smart enough for college and I certainly hope you'll go."

"I've heard some kids say that Miss Leonard killed her fairy."

"That's nonsense," her mother said. "Some girls never do meet fairies and that's probably all that happened to your English teacher."

DURING CHRISTMAS VACATION, Betty came over one afternoon. She admired Amelia's mice and then wanted to do Amelia's hair. "It's so straight and long," she said, "we could totally make you look like Audrey Hepburn." For a minute, Betty almost had it in place, but then a pin slipped out of place and the hairstyle collapsed like a fallen cake.

"I can try to do yours," Amelia offered, although Betty already looked like a girl out of a shampoo ad: a band held it in place as it rippled in shining waves. Probably thanks to the fairy. "What did your fairy give you, anyway?"

"Perfect hair," Betty admitted. "I sometimes wish I'd asked for nicer skin. I figured that would be easier to fix with make-up. Some days it is, some days it isn't."

The sun was slanting low in the sky outside and Amelia started weighing out food for the mice. Betty watched with interest for a while, then asked, "Can you tell your mother I *tried?*"

"That you tried what?"

"That I tried to do your hair?"

"I guess? Wait, why?" Amelia put down the scoop and turned to look at Betty. "Did my mother put you up to this?"

"That's a terrible way of putting it. She might have asked if I'd have a go at showing you some new styles, though."

Amelia heaved a long sigh. "Well, I'll tell her. You don't have to stay any longer, if you don't want."

"I was sort of hoping you'd show me your mice running their maze, though," Betty said.

"Really? Or did my mother put you up to that, too?" Amelia knew even asking that, this was a ridiculous question. Her parents put up with her science project and they'd be happy enough when she won, but they certainly weren't going to try to convince Betty to fake an interest. She pulled the maze out from under her bed and took out the log book, stop watch, and peanut butter.

"What's the peanut butter for?" Betty asked.

"It's the treat when they finish the maze. Mice like it a lot better than cheese." She opened up a package of crackers and started spreading peanut butter on them.

"Can I help?" Betty asked.

"Sure," Amelia said, and handed her the knife.

"They're so cute," Betty said when the mice came out.

"Do you want any when I'm done with them?" Amelia offered.

"Oh, no. My mother would probably die on the spot if I brought a jar of mice home." They set up the maze and Amelia ran the mice through.

After Betty had gone home, Amelia finished her record-keeping and then brushed out her hair, which was still stiff from the hairspray Betty had used to try to keep it in place. She wondered if a fairy would make her hair stay in place properly, or if a fairy would make her *want* to keep her hair in place properly. If she hadn't pulled the pin out when Betty wasn't looking, she probably could have brought the style off.

AMELIA FOUND HER fairy on a freezing-cold January day, when she had to walk to school because her father had needed to go in very early for a meeting and she hadn't gotten up in time to get a ride.

She was wearing dungarees under her skirt because the wind blew right through her tights. She'd have to duck into a bathroom as soon as she got to school, to slip them off and put them in her bag. Also, a heavy coat, gloves, and a wool hat and scarf, even though they made her itch. The fairy, of course, was wearing a diaphanous dress that looked like a turquoise-blue wedding veil and she had tiny, fresh flowers in her hair. She dropped out of the air right in front of Amelia and hovered enticingly. Fairies, it was generally agreed, *wanted* to be caught. They wanted you to have to chase them, but they definitely wanted you to catch them. If it accidentally got away from you, it would probably come swooping right back.

The stories didn't say what would happen if you just refused to chase it at *all*. Amelia figured it would be interesting to see, so she ducked her head and continued walking to school. The fairy zipped around her, so it could bob in front of her again, like it was thinking, "Oh, she just didn't see me." Amelia looked straight at it, made eye contact, and then continued on her way.

The fairy zipped around her again.

"Look," Amelia said. "I don't want your gifts. I'm not interested. Go offer them to some other girl."

When she got to the school, she looked back and saw a flash of turquoise in the tree in front of the school. She heaved a sigh and went to shed her pants and coat.

*   *   *

SCHOOL WAS MORE annoying than usual. There was a Science Club at school, but only boys were allowed to join it; her Biology teacher had some of the boys in the club stand up to talk about their projects. Like hers, they were being prepared for the West District Science Day. Amelia made notes on each. *John: No original research. Frank: Started three weeks ago. Clyde: Doesn't seem to actually understand the scientific method.*

When the boys had all finished talking, Mr. Crawford quizzed everyone on the previous night's reading. Betty, it turned out, hadn't done the reading, and didn't know the answer to any of his questions, and he made her say, "I don't know, Mr. Crawford," five or six times before moving on. Amelia *had* done the reading, so instead of raising her hand, since she knew he wouldn't call on her, she averted her eyes and did her best to look like she was trying to disappear into her seat. To her immense satisfaction, he called on her next and she was able to answer all the questions, which she could tell he found utterly galling. It was hard to take as much pleasure in it when Betty was almost in tears next to her, though.

In English class, they were reading *Romeo and Juliet*. Earlier in the week, they'd done the balcony scene (which, Miss Leonard had pointed out, was actually a *window* scene). Betty had read the part of Juliet and one of the boys had read Romeo. Today was a scene with Romeo and his friends. Amelia impulsively volunteered for the part of Mercutio, because he had all the best lines, and was surprised when Miss Leonard let her do it. Betty promptly volunteered to play Romeo and another girl raised her hand for the part of Benvolio. Miss Leonard looked out at the class and said, "Any boys want to play Juliet's Nurse? Of course, in Shakespeare's day, every part would have been played by a male actor." None of the boys volunteered, so a girl read that part, as well.

After saying her last line in the scene ("Farewell, ancient lady; farewell"), Amelia studied Miss Leonard, thinking about the story that she'd killed her fairy. That would certainly be *one* way to get rid of it, if it was persistent.

English class probably would have been the bright spot, but at the end of the class, Miss Leonard handed back the essays they'd turned in the previous week. Amelia had never gotten a grade lower than an A- for an English class paper before she'd had Miss Leonard; so far, this year, she hadn't gotten anything higher than a B+. Today she had a B and lots of comments, all written in Miss Leonard's crabbed script in the margins. *You can do better*, it said at the bottom. Amelia crammed the paper into her bag and went to history class in a bad mood.

She got into her father's car at the end of the day. "The boys in the Science Club are all doing projects that aren't anywhere near as good as mine."

"Well, that's fine," her father said. "You'll show them all at the Science Day, then."

"It's not fair that I'm not allowed in the Science Club."

"Mr. Crawford is old-fashioned about girls."

"It's 1962. He needs to join the twentieth century."

"Maybe when you're awarded first place at Science Day, he'll reconsider."

Amelia stared out the window. The fairy was sitting in a tree next to the stop light; then it was sitting in a tree on the corner, when they slowed down to turn; then it was hovering outside the car in the carport by their house. Her father didn't seem to notice.

"Anyway, if you were in the Science Club, you'd have to stay after school for the meetings; you wouldn't get to ride home with your good old dad," her father said heartily. "Are you coming in?"

"In a minute," Amelia said.

She sat in the car, feeling the warmth from the car heater slowly fade away. The fairy was hovering just outside the front windshield; after a minute or two, she perched on the car's hood ornament, her ankles folded delicately, her hands in her lap, her wings vibrating like a hummingbird's wings in the air. Amelia got out of the car. The fairy dodged away, then came back. Amelia stared at it for a moment, then went inside.

When her mice weren't running the mazes, she kept them in gallon pickle jars with holes punched in the lids, with newspaper to shred and ladders for stimulation. There were four pickle jars waiting for new occupants, clean and lined up under her window. She grabbed one, unscrewed the lid, and took it back downstairs.

Outside, the sun was low in the sky. She crunched her way across the snowy yard, back to the car, looking nonchalant. She didn't see the fairy right away. She opened the car door, sat down in the passenger seat and waited.

The fairy bobbed in front of her, maybe ten feet away. She looked at it, then looked away.

It came closer.

Closer still.

She could see the delicate folds in the fairy's dress, the shining strands of its hair, the tilt of its head, when she sprang. She didn't want to touch it—she wasn't entirely convinced that *touching the fairy* wasn't what actually made the magic happen—but she swooped up with the jar and brought the lid down, trapping the fairy inside. Then she screwed the lid down, took it upstairs to her room and set it on a shelf next to her mice.

At her desk, Amelia made a list.

Things I have always wanted to know about fairies:

Can boys see them?

Can adults see them?

Can younger children see them?

What would happen if I handed it directly to a boy?

What would happen if I handed it directly to a female child who's much too young for a fairy?

If Miss Leonard actually just never caught a fairy, and it's not true she killed hers, what happens if I give this fairy directly to her? (Would she even want it?)

She turned back around and looked at the fairy again. She could go show the fairy to her parents right now and see if they could see it, but of course, then they'd know that she'd *caught a fairy*, even if she'd caught it in a jar like a lightning bug and not the way you were *supposed* to catch a fairy. They'd probably expect her to start caring about her hair more.

The fairy had been hovering inside the jar, but now she landed on her feet, folded her wings against her back, and sat down, glowering at Amelia through the glass. She was less ethereal-looking trapped in the jar.

Amelia set the fairy on the shelf. She needed to feed her mice and mark the Test and Control groups from the most recent litters. She grabbed the box of food pellets and her little scale and started weighing out food portions, jotting down more questions about the fairy as they occurred to her. *What do fairies eat? Will it be able to get out of the jar if I don't let it out? Do fairies talk?*

Mouse food pellets seemed like a thoroughly unkind thing to feed the fairy. Amelia supplemented the mouse diet with carrot peels from the kitchen, and those seemed like sort of a nasty thing to feed a fairy, too. "What do you eat?" she asked, not really expecting an answer.

The fairy lifted herself up again and spread her wings. "Let me out!" she shrieked. She did have a voice; it was high and shrill.

"So, you can talk," Amelia said. "That's good." She took her notebook out to jot down observations. "Can other people see you?"

"Let me out!" the fairy demanded again.

"You could have left me alone, when I ignored you. Why were you so persistent? *Do* you eat?"

The fairy didn't answer. After a while, Amelia went down to retrieve the carrot peelings from the jar where her mother left them for her. She set out a fresh jar and grabbed today's jar to bring upstairs. Back in her room, she started weighing out portions of carrot peelings and dropping them into the jars with the mice. The fairy watched her, silently, for several minutes.

"What are you going to do with me?" the fairy asked, finally.

"I haven't decided," Amelia said.

"Are you going to kill me? Or feed me to the snake?"

"No," Amelia said. She screwed on the last of the pickle jar lids and sat down to look at the fairy again. Feeding the little white mice to the snake was fine. Feeding a *talking* creature to the snake was completely different. Now that she was nose-to-nose with an actual fairy, she thought it was very unlikely that Miss Leonard had actually killed one.

"How long are you going to keep me in here?" the fairy asked.

"I haven't decided that, either."

"Wouldn't you like my gifts?" the fairy asked. "You caught me, you know. You can demand a forfeit in exchange for letting me go."

"*No*," Amelia said.

Downstairs, her father knocked on the wall at the bottom of the stairs. "Supper!" he called up. Amelia heaved a sigh, jotted down the weight of the carrot peels, and went downstairs to eat.

* * *

AMELIA'S MOTHER WORKED at Wittenberg College as a secretary. She'd spent the day fixing mistakes made by a very new, very inexperienced secretary who wouldn't have messed up so badly if she'd had just a quarter ounce of ordinary common sense, according to Amelia's mother. The new secretary was also very pretty, and her mother speculated the girl had traded her intelligence for long eyelashes when she caught her fairy.

"I thought they didn't do things like that. I thought you just got that stuff as a gift," Amelia said.

"Well, all I can tell you for sure is that *I* didn't have to make any trades when I caught my fairy," her mother said. "Maybe I'd have gotten longer eyelashes if I'd offered to trade some smarts to get those, too."

"That would have been a bad trade," Amelia said.

"Definitely. Don't go trading away your brains, girl," her father said. "You can have looks *and* smarts."

Amelia had something else in mind entirely. When she went back upstairs after dinner, she asked the fairy, "Can you make me more intelligent, instead of prettier?"

"No," the fairy said, grumpily.

"What if I want something else? Like, what if I want to get into the science club that's just for boys, can you make Mr. Crawford change his mind about that?"

"No," the fairy said.

Amelia reached for the jar and the fairy jumped to her feet, shrinking away from her. Amelia pulled her hand back. "Look, I'm not going to *hurt* you," she said. "I just don't want anything like long eyelashes or perfect skin. I don't want to be pretty."

"Well, what do you want from me, then?" the fairy said.

"I want information about fairies," Amelia said. "Answer my questions and I'll let you go."

"Oh." The fairy seemed genuinely surprised by this. Her wings slowly settled as she relaxed a bit. She sat back down, arranging herself to sit cross-legged, with her elbows on her knees and her chin on her hands. The flowers in her hair were beginning to wilt. She looked up at Amelia expectantly. "Okay," she said. "Ask."

"Can adults see you?"

"No."

"Little kids?"

"No."

"Teenage boys?"

"Just like with girls, there's a point when they can see us. Most of them pretend they can't, though, and they almost never try to catch us."

"What happens when a boy catches you?"

"Depends on the boy. Someday, when you're older, you might meet a boy who will admit to having caught a fairy. Ask *him* how it went."

"Can you make someone strong, instead of pretty?"

The fairy gave her a sort of a sideways look. "We don't actually make anyone pretty."

This was new information. Amelia sat down and took out her notepad. "Go on."

"This is very complicated, and you probably won't understand it."

"Try me."

"When you touch us, that lets us see into the future. Just a little, right after we're caught. So, when we want to have that power for a while, we find girls who can see us, let them catch us, and then we promise them something based on what we can see about their future."

"So, am I going to be pretty whether I want to be or *not?*" Amelia asked with revulsion.

The fairy looked her over. "If you were a *normal* girl, you'd have caught me this morning. And this afternoon you'd have told your mother that you'd caught your fairy and she'd have cried because her little girl was growing up, and then she'd have bought you a lipstick and taken you to the hairdresser because that's what mothers do after their daughters catch a fairy. And if you'd *wanted* to be pretty, then you'd have been pretty. You might turn pretty eventually, anyway; I can't tell from here."

Amelia hadn't written any of this down. She looked down at her notepad, wondering what she'd even say.

"Will you please let me out now?" the fairy asked.

Amelia steadied the pickle jar and unscrewed the lid. The fairy shot out and streaked up to the top of Amelia's bookshelf, like she thought maybe Amelia was going to shut her up again. Amelia opened her bedroom window, so the fairy could fly out.

The fairy dropped down to the sill, then hesitated. She looked back at Amelia nervously. "So... *would* you like to know if you're going to be pretty?"

"No," Amelia said. "I want to know if Mr. Crawford will let me into the Science Club after I win first place at the District Science Day."

"Hold out your hand." The fairy leaped into Amelia's cupped palm. She weighed nothing—Amelia wished she'd thought to put the pickle jar on the scale to see if that was literally true—but Amelia could feel the faint pressure of the fairy's hand as she gripped Amelia's thumb.

"He won't," the fairy said. "He's never going to let you in. Is there anything else you want to know?"

Questions crowded into Amelia's mind. *Would* she win first place? Where would she go to college? What would her life be like? Did she *need* to be pretty to be happy?

"Will I *ever* get an A from Miss Leonard?" she asked.

"Oh, yes," the fairy said. "*Yes.*" And then she was gone, like someone had switched off the beam of a flashlight. A gust of cold air made the window frame rattle and Amelia closed her window again.

He's never going to let you in. Amelia turned back to her mice, doing the last of the day's recordkeeping, her hand filling out the day's chart even as her thoughts were elsewhere. *Never.* She looked down at her project, realizing that she'd been assuming her father was right: that when she won first place at the District Science Day, Mr. Crawford would realize how wrong he was about girls, and about Amelia, and whether she belonged in the Science Club. But the fairy said he wouldn't. *It's better to know,* Amelia told herself. *It's better not to have false hope.*

She did the rest of her homework and brushed her teeth. *It's better not to have false hope,* she thought as she turned off her light for bed, but this time another thought occurred to her. *It's better not to have false hope because now I can stop wasting my time trying to impress Mr. Crawford and find another way.*

AMELIA'S PROJECT WON the first prize at the West District Science Day. She was given a pin and a certificate, and she had her picture in the paper. Her parents bought multiple copies of the *Springfield Daily News*, to send clippings of the article to her relatives in other states, and one for Amelia to save.

The next day, she told her father not to wait for her and found Miss Leonard in her classroom. "I have a question," she said. "I checked the handbook, and it says that to start a club, you need a faculty advisor, but it doesn't say the faculty advisor has to be a teacher of a related subject. I want to start a science club for *girls*. Will you be our advisor?"

Miss Leonard looked surprised. "Amelia, that's a lovely idea, but Mr. Crawford isn't going to let us use the science labs for experiments any more than he lets girls into the club."

"I was thinking we'd work on projects that didn't require a lab."

"Do you have any other members in mind?"

"Betty wants to join. And she thinks she knows other girls who would, too."

"Funding? Running a club costs money, and I don't think we can count on any from the school."

"Betty offered to organize a bake sale," Amelia said.

Miss Leonard nodded brusquely. "I'll consider it. Write up a proposal for me."

"I already have." Amelia handed the four-page proposal—typed, even, on her mother's typewriter—to Miss Leonard.

Miss Leonard looked at the proposal, then at Amelia. Something had shifted in her eyes. She looked Amelia up and down for a moment, then inclined her head. "Have a seat while I take a look."

Amelia stared at the window as Miss Leonard read. It felt like she waited for a long time.

"All right," Miss Leonard said. "I will advise your club." She tucked the proposal in the drawer of her desk.

"Thank you!"

"Also," she said, "I expect all your papers for my classes in the future to be typed *and* written at the quality level of this proposal. You've been holding out on me."

"It's my mother's typewriter and sometimes she's using it."

"Plan better." The crispness of this instruction was undermined by the warmth of Miss Leonard's smile. "Bring Betty tomorrow. We have a bake sale to organize."

INTERVENTION

Kelly Robson

Kelly Robson (www.kellyrobson.com) is a Nebula and Aurora award-winning short fiction writer. Her short fiction has appeared in *Clarkesworld, Asimov's Science Fiction Magazine, Tor.com* and *Uncanny*, and many of her stories have been selected for year's best anthologies, and have been translated internationally. Her short fiction has won the Nebula and Prix Aurora awards and been shortlisted for the World Fantasy, Theodore Sturgeon, and Sunburst awards. She was a finalist for the John W. Campbell Award for Best New Writer in 2017. Robson is a regular contributor to *Clarkesworld's* Another Word column, and her most recent book is time travel adventure, *Gods, Monsters and the Lucky Peach.*

Growing up in the foothills of the Canadian Rockies, Robson competed in rodeos and gymkhanas, and was crowned princess of the Hinton Big Horn Rodeo. From 2008 to 2012, she wrote the wine and spirits column for *Chatelaine*, Canada's largest women's magazine. After 22 years in Vancouver, she and her wife, fellow SF writer A.M. Dellamonica, now make their home in downtown Toronto.

WHEN I WAS fifty-seven, I did the unthinkable. I became a crèche manager.

On Luna, crèche work kills your social capital, but I didn't care. Not at first. My long-time love had been crushed to death in a bot malfunction in Luna's main mulching plant. I was just trying to find a reason to keep breathing.

I found a crusty centenarian who'd outlived most of her cohort and asked for her advice. She said there was no better medicine for grief than children, so I found a crèche tucked away behind a water printing plant and signed on as a cuddler. That's where I caught the baby bug.

When my friends found out, the norming started right away.

"You're getting a little tubby there, Jules," Ivan would say, unzipping my jacket and reaching inside to pat my stomach. "Got a little parasite incubating?"

I expected this kind of attitude from Ivan. Ringleader, team captain, alpha of alphas. From him, I could laugh it off. But then my closest friends started in.

Beryl's pretty face soured in disgust every time she saw me. "I can smell the freeloader on you," she'd say, pretending to see body fluids on my perfectly clean clothing. "Have the decency to shower and change after your shift."

Even that wasn't so bad. But then Robin began avoiding me and ignoring my pings. We'd been each other's first lovers, best friends since forever, and suddenly I didn't exist. That's how extreme the prejudice is on Luna.

Finally, on my birthday, they threw me a surprise party. Everyone wore diapers and crawled around in a violent mockery of childhood. When I complained, they accused me of being broody.

I wish I could say I ignored their razzing, but my friends were my whole world. I dropped crèche work. My secret plan was to leave Luna, find a hab where working with kids wasn't social death, but I kept putting it off. Then I blinked, and ten years had passed.

Enough delay. I jumped trains to Eros station, engaged a recruiter, and was settling into my new life on Ricochet within a month.

I never answered my friends' pings. As far as Ivan, Beryl, Robin, and the rest knew, I fell off the face of the moon. And that's the way I wanted it.

RICOCHET IS ONE of the asteroid-based habs that travel the inner system using gravity assist to boost speed in tiny increments. As a wandering hab, we have no fixed astronomical events or planetary seasonality to mark the passage of time, so boosts are a big deal for us—the equivalent of New Year's on Earth or the Sol Belt flare cycle.

On our most recent encounter with Mars, my third and final crèche—the Jewel Box—were twelve years old. We hadn't had a boost since the kids were six, so my team and I worked hard to make it special, throwing parties, making presents, planning excursions. We even suited up and took the kids to the outside of our hab, exploring Asteroid Iris's vast, pockmarked surface roofed by nothing less than the universe itself, in all its spangled glory. We played around out there until Mars climbed over the horizon and showed the Jewel Box its great face for the first time, so huge and close it seemed we could reach up into its milky skim of atmosphere.

When the boost itself finally happened, we were all exhausted. All the kids and cuddlers lounged in the rumpus room, clipped into our safety harnesses, nestled on mats and cushions or tucked into the wall netting. Yawning, droopy-eyed, even dozing. But when the hab began to shift underneath us, we all sprang alert.

Trésor scooted to my side and ducked his head under my elbow.

"You doing okay, buddy?" I asked him in a low voice.

He nodded. I kissed the top of his head and checked his harness.

I wasn't the only adult with a little primate soaking up my body heat. Diamant used Blanche like a climbing frame, standing on her thighs, gripping her hands, and leaning back into the increasing force of the boost. Opale had coaxed her favorite cuddler Mykelti up into the ceiling netting. They both dangled by their knees, the better to feel the acceleration. Little Rubis was holding tight to Engku's and Megat's hands, while on the other side of the room, Safir and Émeraude clowned around, competing for Long Meng's attention.

I was supposed to be on damage control, but I passed the safety workflow over to Bruce. When we hit maximum acceleration, Tré was clinging to me with all his strength.

The kids' bioms were stacked in the corner of my eye. All their hormone graphs showed stress indicators. Tré's levels were higher than the rest, but that wasn't strange. When your hab is somersaulting behind a planet, bleeding off its orbital energy, your whole world turns into a carnival ride. Some people like it better than others.

I tightened my arms around Tré's ribs, holding tight as the room turned sideways.

"Everything's fine," I murmured in his ear. "Ricochet was designed for this kind of maneuver."

Our safety harnesses held us tight to the wall netting. Below, Safir and Émeraude climbed up the floor, laughing and hooting. Long Meng tossed pillows at them.

Tré gripped my thumb, yanking as if it were a joystick with the power to tame the room's spin. Then he shot me a live feed showing Ricochet's chief astronautics officer, a dark-skinned, silver-haired woman with protective bubbles fastened over her eyes.

"Who's that?" I asked, pretending I didn't know.

"Vijayalakshmi," Tré answered. "If anything goes wrong, she'll fix it."

"Have you met her?" I knew very well he had, but asking questions is an excellent calming technique.

"Yeah, lots of times." He flashed a pointer at the astronaut's mirrored eye coverings. "Is she sick?"

"Might be cataracts. That's a normal age-related condition. What's worrying you?"

"Nothing," he said.

"Why don't you ask Long Meng about it?"

Long Meng was the Jewel Box's physician. Ricochet-raised, with a facial deformity that thrust her mandible severely forward. As an adult, once bone ossification had completed, she had rejected the cosmetic surgery that could have normalized her jaw.

"Not all interventions are worthwhile," she'd told me once. "I wouldn't feel like myself with a new face."

As a pediatric specialist, Long Meng was responsible for the health and development of twenty crèches, but we were her favorite. She'd decided to celebrate the boost with us. At that moment, she was dangling from the floor with Safir and Émeraude, tickling their tummies and howling with laughter.

I tried to mitigate Tré's distress with good, old-fashioned cuddle and chat. I showed him feeds from the biodiversity preserve, where the netted megafauna floated in mid-air, riding out the boost in safety, legs dangling. One big cat groomed itself as it floated, licking one huge paw and wiping down its whiskers with an air of unconcern.

Once the boost was complete and we were back to our normal gravity regime, Tré's indicators quickly normalized. The kids ran up to the garden to check out the damage. I followed slowly, leaning on my cane. One of the bots had malfunctioned and lost stability, destroying several rows of terraced seating in the open air auditorium just next to our patch. The kids all thought that was pretty funny. Tré seemed perfectly fine, but I couldn't shake the feeling that I'd failed him somehow.

*   *   *

THE JEWEL BOX didn't visit Mars. Martian habs are popular, their excursion contracts highly priced. The kids put in a few bids but didn't have the credits to win.

"Next boost," I told them. "Venus in four years. Then Earth."

I didn't mention Luna. I'd done my best to forget it even existed. Easy to do. Ricochet has almost no social or trade ties with Earth's moon. Our main economic sector is human reproduction and development—artificial wombs, zygote husbandry, natal decanting, every bit of art and science that turns a mass of undifferentiated cells into a healthy young adult. Luna's crèche system collapsed completely not long after I left. Serves them right.

I'm a centenarian, facing my last decade or two. I may look serene and wise, but I've never gotten over being the butt of my old friends' jokes.

Maybe I've always been immature. It would explain a lot.

FOUR YEARS PASSED with the usual small dramas. The Jewel Box grew in body and mind, stretching into young adults of sixteen. All six—Diamant, Émeraude, Trésor, Opale, Safir, and Rubis—hit their benchmarks erratically and inconsistently, which made me proud. Kids are supposed to be odd little individuals. We're not raising robots, after all.

As Ricochet approached, the Venusian habs began peppering us with proposals. Recreation opportunities, educational seminars, sightseeing trips, arts festivals, sporting tournaments—all on reasonable trade terms. Venus wanted us to visit, fall in love, stay. They'd been losing population to Mars for years. The brain drain was getting critical.

The Jewel Box decided to bid on a three-day excursion. Sightseeing with a focus on natural geology, including active volcanism. For the first time in their lives, they'd experience real, unaugmented planetary gravity instead of Ricochet's one-point-zero cobbled together by centripetal force and a Steffof field.

While the kids were lounging around the rumpus room, arguing over how many credits to sink into the bid, Long Meng pinged me.

You and I should send a proposal to the Venusian crèches, she whispered. *A master class or something. Something so tasty they can't resist.*

Why? Are you trying to pad your billable hours?

She gave me a toothy grin. *I want a vacation. Wouldn't it be fun to get Venus to fund it?*

Long Meng and I had collaborated before, when our numbers had come up for board positions on the crèche governance authority. Nine miserable months co-authoring policy memos, revising the crèche management best practices guide, and presenting at skills development seminars. All on top of our regular responsibilities. Against the odds, our friendship survived the bureaucracy.

We spent a few hours cooking up a seminar to tempt the on-planet crèche specialists and fired it off to a bunch of Venusian booking agents. We called it 'Attachment and Self-regulation in Theory and Practice: Approaches to Promoting Emotional Independence in the Crèche-raised Child.' Sound dry? Not a bit. The Venusians gobbled it up.

I shot the finalized syllabus to our chosen booking agent, then escorted the Jewel Box to their open-air climbing lab. I turned them over to their instructor and settled onto my usual bench under a tall oak. Diamant took the lead position up the cliff, as usual. By the time they'd completed the first pitch, all three seminars were filled.

The agent is asking for more sessions, I whispered to Long Meng. *What do you think?*

"No way." Long Meng's voice rang out, startling me. As I pinged her location, her lanky form appeared in the distant aspen grove.

"This is a vacation," she shouted. "If I wanted to pack my billable hours, I'd volunteer for another board position."

I shuddered. *Agreed.*

She jogged over and climbed onto the bench beside me, sitting on the backrest with her feet on the seat. "Plus, you haven't been off this rock in twenty years," she added, plucking a leaf from the overhead bough.

"I said okay, Long Meng."

We watched the kids as they moved with confidence and ease over the gleaming, pyrite-inflected cliff face. Big, bulky Diamant didn't look like a climber but was obsessed with the sport. The other five had gradually been infected by their crèche-mate's passion.

Long Meng and I waved to the kids as they settled in for a rest mid-route.

Then she turned to me. "What do you want to see on-planet? Have you made a wish list yet?"

"I've been to Venus. It's not that special."

She laughed, a great, good-natured, wide-mouthed guffaw. "Nothing can compare to Luna, can it, Jules?"

"Don't say that word."

"Luna? Okay. What's better than Venus? Earth?"

"Earth doesn't smell right."

"The Sol belt?"

"Never been there."

"What then?"

"This is nice." I waved at the groves of trees surrounding the cliff. Overhead, the plasma core that formed the backbone of our hab was just shifting its visible spectrum into twilight. Mellow light filtered through the leaves. Teenage laughter echoed off the cliff, and in the distance, the steady droning wail of a fussy newborn.

I pulled up the surrounding camera feeds and located the newborn. A tired-looking cuddler carried the baby in an over-shoulder sling, patting its bottom rhythmically as they strolled down a sunflower-lined path. I pinged the baby's biom. Three weeks old. Chronic gas and reflux unresponsive to every intervention strategy. Nothing to do but wait for the child to grow out of it.

The kids summited, waved to us, then began rappelling back down. Long Meng and I met them at the base.

"Em, how's your finger?" Long Meng asked.

"Good." Émeraude bounced off the last ledge and slipped to the ground, wave of pink hair flapping. "Better than good."

"Let's see, then."

Émeraude unclipped and offered the doctor their hand. They were a kid with only two modes: all-out or flatline. A few months back, they'd injured themselves cranking on a crimp, completely bowstringing the flexor tendon.

Long Meng launched into an explanation of annular pulley repair strategies and recovery times. I tried to listen but I was tired. My hips ached, my back ached, my limbs rotated on joints gritty with age. In truth, I didn't want to go to Venus. The kids had won their bid, and with them off-hab, staying home would have been a good rest. But Long Meng's friendship was important, and making her happy was worth a little effort.

LONG MENG AND I accompanied the Jewel Box down Venus's umbilical, through the high sulphuric acid clouds to the elevator's base deep in the planet's mantle. When we entered the busy central transit hub, with its domed ceiling and slick, speedy slideways, the kids began making faces.

"This place stinks," said Diamante.

"Yeah, smells like piss," said Rubis.

Tré looked worried. "Do they have diseases here or something?"

Opale slapped her hand over her mouth. "I'm going to be sick. Is it the smell or the gravity?"

A quick glance at Opale's biom showed she was perfectly fine. All six kids were. Time for a classic crèche manager-style social intervention.

If you can't be polite around the locals, I whispered, knocking my cane on the ground for emphasis. *I'll shoot you right back up the elevator.*

If you send us home, do we get our credits back? Émeraude asked, yawning.

No. You'd be penalized for non-completion of contract.

I posted a leaderboard for good behavior. Then I told them Venusians were especially gossipy, and if word got out they'd bad-mouthed the planet, they'd get nothing but dirty looks for the whole trip.

A bald lie. Venus is no more gossipy than most habs. But it nurses a significant anti-crèche prejudice. Not as extreme as Luna, but still. Ricochet kids were used to being loved by everyone. On Venus, they would get attitude just for existing. I wanted to offer a convenient explanation for the chilly reception from the locals.

The group of us rode the slideway to Vanavara portway, where Engku, Megat, and Bruce were waiting. Under the towering archway, I hugged and kissed the kids, told them to have lots of fun, and waved at their retreating backs. Then Long Meng and I were on our own.

She took my arm and steered us into Vanavara's passeggiata, a social stroll that wound through the hab like a pedestrian river. We drifted with the flow, joining the people-watching crowd, seeing and being seen.

The hab had spectacular sculpture gardens and fountains, and Venus's point-nine-odd gravity was a relief on my knees and hips, but the kids weren't wrong about the stench. Vanavara smelled like oily vinaigrette over half-rotted lettuce leaves, with an animal undercurrent reminiscent of hormonal teenagers on a cleanliness strike. As we walked, the stench surged and faded, then resurfaced again.

We ducked into a kiosk where a lone chef roasted kebabs over an open flame. We sat at the counter, drinking sparkling wine and watching her prepare meal packages for bot delivery.

"What's wrong with the air scrubbers here?" Long Meng asked the chef.

"Unstable population," she answered. "We don't have enough civil engineers to handle the optimization workload. If you know any nuts-and-bolts types, tell them to come to Vanavara. The bank will kiss them all over."

She served us grilled protein on disks of crispy starch topped with charred vegetable and heaped with garlicky sauce, followed by finger-sized blossoms with tender, fleshy petals over a crisp honeycomb core. When we rejoined the throng, we shot the chef a pair of big, bright public valentines on slow decay, visible to everyone passing by. The chef ran after us with two tulip-shaped bulbs of amaro.

"Enjoy your stay," she said, handing us the bulbs. "We're developing a terrific fresh food culture here. You'll love it."

In response to the population downswing, Venus's habs had started accepting all kinds of marginal business proposals. Artists. Innovators. Experimenters. Lose a ventilation engineer; gain a chef. Lose a surgeon; gain a puppeteer. With the chefs and puppeteers come all the people who want to live in a hab with chefs and puppeteers, and are willing to put up with a little stench to get it. Eventually the hab's fortunes turn around. Population starts flowing back, attracted by the burgeoning quality of life. Engineers and surgeons return, and the chefs and puppeteers move on to the next proposal-friendly hab. Basic human dynamics.

Long Meng sucked the last drop of amaro from her bulb and then tossed it to a disposal bot.

"First night of vacation." She gave me a wicked grin. "Want to get drunk?"

When I rolled out of my sleep stack in the morning, I was puffy and stiff. My hair stood in untamable clumps. The pouches under my eyes shone an alarming purple, and my wrinkle inventory had doubled. My tongue tasted like garlic sauce. But as long as nobody else could smell it, I wasn't too concerned. As for the rest, I'd earned every age marker.

When Long Meng finally cracked her stack, she was pressed and perky, wrapped in a crisp fuchsia robe. A filmy teal scarf drifted under her thrusting jawline.

"Let's teach these Venusians how to raise kids," she said.

IN RESPONSE TO demand, the booking agency had upgraded us to a larger auditorium. The moment we hit the stage, I forgot all my aches and pains. Doctor Footlights, they call it. Performing in front of two thousand strangers produces a lot of adrenaline.

We were a good pair. Long Meng dynamic and engaging, lunging around the stage like a born performer. Me, I was her foil. A grave, wise oldster with fifty years of crèche work under my belt.

Much of our seminar was inspirational. Crèche work is relentless no matter where you practice it, and on Venus it brings negative social status. A little cheerleading goes a long way. We slotted our specialty content in throughout the program, introducing the concepts in the introductory material, building audience confidence by reinforcing what they already knew, then hit them between the eyes with the latest developments in Ricochet's proprietary cognitive theory and emotional development modelling. We blew their minds, then backed away from the hard stuff and returned to cheerleading.

"What's the worst part of crèche work, Jules?" Long Meng asked as our program concluded, her scarf waving in the citrus-scented breeze from the ventilation.

"There are no bad parts," I said drily. "Each and every day is unmitigated joy."

The audience laughed harder than the joke deserved. I waited for the noise to die down, and mined the silence for a few lingering moments before continuing.

"Our children venture out of the crèche as young adults, ready to form new emotional ties wherever they go. The future is in their hands, an unending medium for them to shape with their ambition and passion. Our crèche work lifts them up and holds them high, all their lives. That's the best part."

I held my cane to my heart with both hands.

"The worst part is," I said, "if we do our jobs right, those kids leave the crèche and never think about us again."

We left them with a tear in every eye. The audience ran back to their crèches knowing they were doing the most important work in the universe, and open to the possibility of doing it even better.

AFTER OUR SECOND seminar, on a recommendation from the kebab chef, we blew our credits in a restaurant high up in Vanavara's atrium. Live food raised, prepared, and served by hand; nothing extruded or bulbed. And no bots, except for the occasional hygiene sweeper.

Long Meng cut into a lobster carapace with a pair of hand shears. "Have you ever noticed how intently people listen to you?"

"Most of the time the kids just pretend to listen."

"Not kids. Adults."

She served me a morsel of claw meat, perfectly molded by the creature's shell. I dredged it in green sauce and popped it in my mouth. Sweet peppers buzzed my sinuses.

"You're a great leader, Jules."

"At my age, I should be. I've had lots of practice telling people what to do."

"Exactly," she said through a mouthful of lobster. "So what are you going to do when the Jewel Box leaves the crèche?"

I lifted my flute of pale green wine and leaned back, gazing through the window at my elbow into the depths of the atrium. I'd been expecting this question for a few years but didn't expect it from Long Meng. How could someone so young understand the sorrows of the old?

"If you don't want to talk about it, I'll shut up," she added quickly. "But I have some ideas. Do you want to hear them?"

On the atrium floor far below, groups of pedestrians were just smudges, no individuals distinguishable at all. I turned back to the table but kept my eyes on my food.

"Okay, go ahead."

"A hab consortium is soliciting proposals to rebuild their failed crèche system," she said, voice eager. "I want to recruit a team. You'd be project advisor. Top position, big picture stuff. I'll be project lead and do all the grunt work."

"Let me guess," I said. "It's Luna."

Long Meng nodded. I kept a close eye on my blood pressure indicators. Deep breaths and a sip of water kept the numbers out of the red zone.

"I suppose you'd want me to liaise with Luna's civic apparatus, too." I kept my voice flat.

"That would be ideal." She slapped the table with both palms and grinned. "With a native Lunite at the helm, we'd win for sure."

Long Meng was so busy bubbling with ideas and ambition as she told me her plans, she didn't notice my fierce scowl. She probably didn't even taste her luxurious meal. As for me, I enjoyed every bite, right down to the last crumb of my flaky cardamom-chocolate dessert. Then I pushed back my chair and grabbed my cane.

"There's only one problem, Long Meng," I said. "Luna doesn't deserve crèches."

"Deserve doesn't really—"

I cut her off. "Luna doesn't deserve a population."

She looked confused. "But it has a population, so—"

"Luna deserves to die," I snapped. I stumped away, leaving her at the table, her jaw hanging in shock.

HALFWAY THROUGH OUR third and final seminar, in the middle of introducing Ricochet's proprietary never-fail methods for raising kids, I got an emergency ping from Bruce.

Tré's abandoned the tour. He's run off.

I faked a coughing fit and lunged toward the water bulbs at the back of the stage. Turned my back on two thousand pairs of eyes, and tried to collect myself as I scanned Tré's biom. His stress indicators were highly elevated. The other five members of the Jewel Box were anxious, too.

Do you have eyes on him?

Of course. Bruce shot me a bookmark.

Three separate cameras showed Tré was alone, playing his favorite pattern-matching game while coasting along a nearly deserted slideway. Metadata indicated his location on an express connector between Coacalco and Eaton habs.

He looked stunned, as if surprised by his own daring. Small, under the high arches of the slideway tunnel. And thin—his bony shoulder blades tented the light cloth of his tunic.

Coacalco has a bot shadowing him. Do we want them to intercept?

I zoomed in on Tré's face, as if I could read his thoughts as easily as his physiology. He'd never been particularly assertive or self-willed, never one to challenge his crèche mates or lead them in new directions. But kids will surprise you.

Tell them to stay back. Ping a personal security firm to monitor him. Go on with your tour. And try not to worry.

Are you sure?

I wasn't sure, not at all. My stress indicators were circling the planet. Every primal urge screamed for the bot to wrap itself around the boy and haul him back to Bruce. But I wasn't going to slap down a sixteen-year-old kid for acting on his own initiative, especially since this was practically the first time he'd shown any.

Looks like Tré has something to do, I whispered. *Let's let him follow through.*

I returned to my chair. Tried to focus on the curriculum but couldn't concentrate. Long Meng could only do so much to fill the gap. The audience became restless, shifting in their seats, murmuring to each other. Many stopped paying attention. Right up in the front row, three golden-haired, rainbow-smocked Venusians were blanked out, completely immersed in their feeds.

Long Meng was getting frantic, trying to distract two thousand people from the gaping hole on the stage that was her friend Jules. I picked up my cane, stood, and calmly tipped my chair. It hit the stage floor with a crash. Long Meng jumped. Every head swiveled.

"I apologize for the dramatics," I said, "but earlier, you all noticed me blanking out. I want to explain."

I limped to the front of the stage, unsteady despite my cane. I wear a stability belt, but try not to rely on it too much. Old age has exacerbated my natural tendency for a weak core, and using the belt too much just makes me frailer. But my legs wouldn't stop shaking. I dialed up the balance support.

"What just happened illustrates an important point about crèche work." I attached my cane's cling-point to the stage floor and leaned on it with both hands as I scanned the audience. "Our mistakes can ruin lives. No other profession carries such a vast potential for screwing up."

"That's not true." Long Meng's eyes glinted in the stage lights, clearly relieved I'd stepped back up to the job. "Engineering disciplines carry quite the disaster potential. Surgery certainly does. Psychology and pharmacology. Applied astrophysics. I could go on." She grinned. "Really, Jules. Nearly every profession is dangerous."

I grimaced and dismissed her point.

"Doctors' decisions are supported by ethics panels and case reviews. Engineers run simulation models and have their work vetted by peers before taking any real-world risks. But in a crèche, we make a hundred decisions a day that affect human development. Sometimes a hundred an hour."

"Okay, but are every last one of those decisions so important?"

I gestured to one of the rainbow-clad front-row Venusians. "What do you think? Are your decisions important?"

A camera bug zipped down to capture her answer for the seminar's shared feed. The Venusian licked her lips nervously and shifted to the edge of her seat.

"Some decisions are," she said in a high, tentative voice. "You can never know which."

"That's right. You never know." I thanked her and rejoined Long Meng in the middle of the stage. "Crèche workers take on huge responsibility. We assume all the risk, with zero certainty. No other profession accepts those terms. So why do we do this job?"

"Someone has to?" said Long Meng. Laughter percolated across the auditorium.

"Why us, though?" I said. "What's wrong with us?"

More laughs. I rapped my cane on the floor.

"My current crèche is a sixteen-year sixsome. Well integrated, good morale. Distressingly sporty. They keep me running." The audience chuckled. "They're on a geography tour somewhere on the other side of Venus. A few minutes ago, one of my kids ran off. Right now, he's coasting down one of your intra-hab slideways and blocking our pings."

Silence. I'd captured every eye; all their attention was mine.

I fired the public slideway feed onto the stage. Tré's figure loomed four meters high. His foot was kicked back against the slideway's bumper in an attitude of nonchalance, but it was just a pose. His gaze was wide and unblinking, the whites of his eyes fully visible.

"Did he run away because of something one of us said? Or did? Or neglected to do? Did it happen today, yesterday, or ten days ago? Maybe it has nothing to do with us at all, but some private urge from the kid's own heart. He might be suffering acutely right now, or he maybe he's enjoying the excitement. The adrenaline and cortisol footprints look the same."

I clenched my gnarled, age-spotted hand to my chest, pulling at the fabric of my shirt.

"But I'm suffering. My heart feels like it could rip right out of my chest because this child has put himself in danger." I patted the wrinkled fabric back into place. "Mild danger. Venus is no Luna."

Nervous laughter from the crowd. Long Meng hovered at my side.

"Crèche work is like no other human endeavor," I said. "Nothing else offers such potential for failure, sorrow, and loss. But no work is as important. You all know that, or you wouldn't be here."

Long Meng squeezed my shoulder. I patted her hand. "Raising children is only for true believers."

NOT LONG AFTER our seminar ended, Tré boarded Venus's circum-planetary chuteway and chose a pod headed for Vanavara. The pod's public feed showed five other passengers: a middle-aged threesome who weren't interested in anything but each other, a halo-haired young adult escorting a floating tank of live eels, and a broad-shouldered brawler with deeply scarred forearms.

Tré waited for the other passengers to sit, then settled himself into a corner seat. I pinged him. No answer.

"We should have had him intercepted," I said.

Long Meng and I sat in the back of the auditorium. A choir group had taken over the stage. Bots were attempting to set up risers, but the singers were milling around, blocking their progress.

"He'll be okay." Long Meng squeezed my knee. "Less than five hours to Vanavara. None of the passengers are going to do anything to him."

"You don't know that."

"Nobody would risk it. Venus has strict penalties for physical violence."

"Is that the worst thing you can think of?" I flashed a pointer at the brawler. "One conversation with that one in a bad mood could do lifelong damage to anyone, much less a kid."

We watched the feed in silence. At first the others kept to themselves, but then the brawler stood, pulled down a privacy veil, and sauntered over to sit beside Tré.

"Oh no," I moaned.

I zoomed in on Tré's face. With the veil in place, I couldn't see or hear the brawler. All I could do was watch the kid's eyes flicker from the window to the brawler and back, monitor his stress indicators, and try to read his body language. Never in my life have I been less equipped to make a professional judgement about a kid's state of mind. My mind boiled with paranoia.

After about ten minutes—an eternity—the brawler returned to their seat.

"It's fine," said Long Meng. "He'll be with us soon."

Long Meng and I met Tré at the chuteway dock. It was late. He looked tired, rumpled, and more than a little sulky.

"Venus is stupid," he said.

"That's ridiculous, a planet can't be stupid," Long Meng snapped. She was tired, and hadn't planned on spending the last night of her vacation waiting in a transit hub.

Let me handle this, I whispered.

"Are you okay? Did anything happen in the pod?" I tried to sound calm as I led him to the slideway.

He shrugged. "Not really. This oldster was telling me how great his hab is. Sounded like a hole."

I nearly collapsed with relief.

"Okay, good," I said. "We were worried about you. Why did you leave the group?"

"I didn't realize it would take so long to get anywhere," Tré said.

"That's not an answer. Why did you run off?"

"I don't know." The kid pretended to yawn—one of the Jewel Box's clearest tells for lying. "Venus is boring. We should've saved our credits."

"What does that mean?"

"Everybody else was happy looking at rocks. Not me. I wanted to get some value out of this trip."

"So you jumped a slideway?"

"Uh huh." Tré pulled a protein snack out of his pocket and stuffed it in his mouth. "I was just bored. And I'm sorry. Okay?"

"Okay." I fired up the leaderboard and zeroed out Tré's score. "You're on a short leash until we get home."

We got the kid a sleep stack near ours, then Long Meng and I had a drink in the grubby travelers' lounge downstairs.

"How are you going to find out why he left?" asked Long Meng. "Pull his feeds? Form a damage mitigation team? Plan an intervention?"

I picked at fabric on the arm of my chair. The plush nap repaired itself as I dragged a ragged thumbnail along the arm rest.

"If I did, Tré would learn he can't make a simple mistake without someone jumping down his throat. He might shrug off the psychological effects, or it could inflict long-term damage."

"Right. Like you said in the seminar. You can't know."

We finished our drinks and Long Meng helped me to my feet. I hung my cane from my forearm and tucked both hands into the crease of her elbow. We slowly climbed upstairs. I could have pinged a physical assistance bot, but my hands were cold, and my friend's arm was warm.

"Best to let this go," I said. "Tré's already a cautious kid. I won't punish him for taking a risk."

"I might, if only for making me worry. I guess I'll never be a crèche manager." She grinned.

"And yet you want to go to Luna and build a new crèche system."

Long Meng's smile vanished. "I shouldn't have sprung that on you, Jules."

In the morning, the two young people rose bright and cheery. I was aching and bleary but put on a serene face. We had just enough time to catch a concert before heading up the umbilical to our shuttle home. We made our way to the atrium, where Tré boggled at the soaring views, packed slideways, clustered performance and game surfaces, fountains, and gardens. The air sparkled with nectar and spices, and underneath, a thick, oily human funk.

We boarded a riser headed to Vanavara's orchestral pits. A kind Venusian offered me a seat with a smile. I thanked him, adding, "That would never happen on Luna."

I drew Long Meng close as we spiraled toward the atrium floor.

Just forget about the proposal, I whispered. *The moon is a lost cause.*

A LITTLE MORE than a year later, Ricochet was on approach for Earth. The Jewel Box were nearly ready to leave the crèche. Bruce and the rest of my team were planning to start a new one, and they warmly assured me I'd always be welcome to visit. I tried not to weep about it. Instead, I began spending several hours a day helping provide round-the-clock cuddles to a newborn with hydrocephalus.

As far as I knew, Long Meng had given up the Luna idea. Then she cornered me in the dim-lit nursery and burst my bubble.

She quietly slid a stool over to my rocker, cast a professional eye over the cerebrospinal fluid-exchange membrane clipped to the baby's ear, and whispered, *We made the short list.*

That's great, I replied, my cheek pressed to the infant's warm, velvety scalp.

I had no idea what she was referring to, and at that moment I didn't care. The scent of a baby's head is practically narcotic, and no victory can compare with having coaxed a sick child into restful sleep.

It means we have to go to Luna for a presentation and interview.

Realization dawned slowly. *Luna? I'm not going to Luna.*

Not you, Jules. Me and my team. I thought you should hear before the whole hab starts talking.

I concentrated on keeping my rocking rhythm steady before answering. *I thought you'd given that up.*

She put a gentle hand on my knee. *I know. You told me not to pursue it and I considered your advice. But it's important, Jules. Luna will re-start its crèche program one way or another. We can make sure they do it right.*

I fixed my gaze pointedly on her prognathous jaw. *You don't know what it's like there. They'll roast you alive just for looking different.*

Maybe. But I have to try.

She patted my knee and left. I stayed in the rocker long past hand-over time, resting my cheek against that precious head.

Seventy years ago I'd done the same, in a crèche crowded into a repurposed suite of offices behind one of Luna's water printing plants. I'd walked through the door broken and grieving, certain the world had been drained of hope and joy. Then someone put a baby in my arms. Just a few hours old, squirming with life, arms reaching for the future.

Was there any difference between the freshly detanked newborn on Luna and the sick baby I held on that rocker? No. The embryos gestating in Ricochet's superbly optimized banks of artificial wombs were no different from the ones Luna would grow in whatever gestation tech they inevitably cobbled together.

But as I continued to think about it, I realized there was a difference, and it was important. The ones on Luna deserved better than they would get. And I could do something about it.

FIRST, I HAD MY hair sheared into an ear-exposing brush precise to the millimeter. The tech wielding the clippers tried to talk me out of it.

"Do you realize this will have to be trimmed every twenty days?"

"I used to wear my hair like this when I was young," I reassured him. He rolled his eyes and cut my hair like I asked.

I changed my comfortable smock for a lunar grey trouser-suit with enough padding to camouflage my age-slumped shoulders. My cling-pointed cane went into the mulch, exchanged for a glossy black model. Its silver point rapped the floor, announcing my progress toward Long Meng's studio.

The noise turned heads all down the corridor. Long Meng popped out of her doorway, but she didn't recognize me until I pushed past her and settled onto her sofa with a sigh.

"Are you still looking for a project advisor?" I asked.

She grinned. "Luna won't know what hit it."

Back in the rumpus room, Tré was the only kid to comment on my haircut.

"You look like a villain from one of those old Follywood dramas Bruce likes."

"Hollywood," I corrected. "Yes, that's the point."

"What's the point in looking like a gangland mobber?"

"Mobster." I ran my palm over the brush. "Is that what I look like?"

"Kinda. Is it because of us?"

I frowned, not understanding. He pulled his ponytail over his shoulder and eyed it speculatively.

"Are you trying to look tough so we won't worry about you after we leave?"

That's the thing about kids. The conversations suddenly swerve and hit you in the back of the head.

"Whoa," I said. "I'm totally fine."

"I know, I know. You've been running crèches forever. But we're the last because you're so old. Right? It's got to be hard."

"A little," I admitted. "But you've got other things to think about. Big, exciting decisions to make."

"I don't think I'm leaving the crèche. I'm delayed."

I tried to keep from smiling. Tré was nothing of the sort. He'd grown into a gangly young man with long arms, bony wrists, and a haze of silky black beard on his square jaw. I could recite the dates of his developmental benchmarks from memory, and there was nothing delayed about them.

"That's fine," I said. "You don't have to leave until you're ready."

"A year. Maybe two. At least."

"Okay, Tré. Your decision."

I wasn't worried. It's natural to feel ambivalent about taking the first step into adulthood. If Tré found it easier to tell himself he wasn't leaving, so be it. As soon as his crèche-mates started moving on, Tré would follow.

OUR PROXIMITY TO Earth gave Long Meng's proposal a huge advantage. We could travel to Luna, give our presentation live, and be back home for the boost.

Long Meng and I spent a hundred billable hours refining our presentation materials. For the first time in our friendship, our communication styles clashed.

"I don't like the authoritarian gleam in your eye, Jules," she told me after a particularly heated argument. "It's almost as though you're enjoying bossing me around."

She wasn't wrong. Ricochet's social conventions require you to hold in conversational aggression. Letting go was fun. But I had an ulterior motive.

"This is the way people talk on Luna. If you don't like it, you should shitcan the proposal."

She didn't take the dare. But she reported behavioral changes to my geriatric specialist. I didn't mind. It was sweet, her being so worried about me. I decided to give her full access to my biom, so she could check if she thought I was having a stroke or something. I'm in okay health for my extreme age, but she was a paediatrician, not a gerontologist. What she saw scared her. She got solicitous. Gallant, even, bringing me bulbs of tea and snacks to keep my glucose levels steady.

Luna's ports won't accommodate foreign vehicles, and their landers use a chemical propellant so toxic Ricochet won't let them anywhere near our landing bays, so we had to shuttle to Luna in stages. As we glided over the moon's surface, its web of tunnels and domes sparkled in the full glare of the sun. The pattern of the habs hadn't changed. I could still name them— Surgut, Sklad, Nadym, Purovsk, Olenyok...

Long Meng latched onto my arm as the hatch creaked open. I wrenched away and straightened my jacket.

You can't do that here, I whispered. *Self-sufficiency is everything on Luna, remember?*

I marched ahead of Long Meng as if I were leading an army. In the light lunar gravity, I didn't need my cane, so I used its heavy silver head to whack the walls. Hitting something felt good. I worked up a head of steam so hot I could have sterilized those corridors. If I had to come home—home, what a word for a place like Luna!—I'd do it on my own terms.

The client team had arranged to meet us in a dinky little media suite overlooking the hockey arena in Sklad. A game had just finished, and we had to force our way against the departing crowd. My cane came in handy. I brandished it like a weapon, signaling my intent to break the jaw of anyone who got too close.

In the media suite, ten hab reps clustered around the project principal. Overhead circled a battery of old, out-of-date cameras that buzzed and fluttered annoyingly. At the front of the room, two chairs waited for Long Meng and me. Behind us arced a glistening expanse of crystal window framing the rink, where grooming bots were busy scraping blood off the ice. Over the arena loomed the famous profile of Mons Hadley, huge, cold, stark, its bleak face the same mid-tone grey as my suit.

Don't smile, I reminded Long Meng as she stood to begin the presentation.

The audience didn't deserve the verve and panache Long Meng put into presenting our project phases, alternative scenarios, and volume ramping. Meanwhile, I scanned the reps' faces, counting flickers in their attention and recording them on a leaderboard. We had forty minutes in total, but less than twenty to make an impression before the reps' decisions locked in.

Twelve minutes in, Long Meng was introducing the strategies for professional development, governance, and ethics oversight. Half the reps were still staring at her face as if they'd never seen a congenital hyperformation before. The other half were bored but still making an effort to pay attention. But not for much longer.

"Based on the average trajectories of other start-up crèche programs," Long Meng said, gesturing at the swirling graphics that hung in the air, "Luna should run at full capacity within six social generations, or thirty standard years."

I'm cutting in, I whispered. I whacked the head of my cane on the floor and stood, stability belt on maximum and belligerence oozing from my every pore.

"You won't get anywhere near that far," I growled. "You'll never get past the starting gate."

"That's a provocative statement," said the principal. She was in her sixties, short and tough, with ropey veins webbing her bony forearms. "Would you care to elaborate?"

I paced in front of their table, like a barrister in one of Bruce's old courtroom dramas. I made eye contact with each of the reps in turn, then leaned over the table to address the project principal directly.

"Crèche programs are part of a hab's social fabric. They don't exist in isolation. But Luna doesn't want kids around. You barely tolerate young adults. You want to stop the brain drain but you won't give up anything for crèches—not hab space, not billable hours, and especially not your prejudices. If you want a healthy crèche system, Luna will have to make some changes."

I gave the principal an evil grin, adding, "I don't think you can."

"I do," Long Meng interjected. "I think you can change."

"You don't know Luna like I do," I told her.

I fired our financial proposal at the reps. "Ricochet will design your new system. You'll find the trade terms extremely reasonable. When the design is complete, we'll provide on-the-ground teams to execute the project phases. Those terms are slightly less reasonable. Finally, we'll give you a project executive headed by Long Meng." I smiled. "Her billable rate isn't reasonable at all, but she's worth every credit."

"And you?" asked the principal.

"That's the best part." I slapped the cane in my palm. "I'm the gatekeeper. To go anywhere, you have to get past me."

The principal sat back abruptly, jaw clenched, chin raised. My belligerence had finally made an impact. The reps were on the edges of their seats. I had them both repelled and fascinated. They weren't sure whether to start screaming or elect me to Luna's board of governors.

"How long have I got to live, Long Meng? Fifteen years? Twenty?"

"Something like that," she said.

"Let's say fifteen. I'm old. I'm highly experienced. You can't afford me. But if you award Ricochet this contract, I'll move back to Luna. I'll control the gating progress, judging the success of every single milestone. If I decide Luna hasn't measured up, the work will have to be repeated."

I paced to the window. Mons Hadley didn't seem grey any more. It was actually a deep, delicate lilac. Framed by the endless black sky, its form was impossibly complex, every fold of its geography picked out by the sun.

I kept my back to the reps.

"If you're wondering why I'd come back after all the years," I said, "let me be very clear. I will die before I let Luna fool around with some half-assed crèche experiment, mess up a bunch of kids, and ruin everything." I turned and pointed my cane. "If you're going to do this, at least do it right."

BACK HOME ON Ricochet, the Jewel Box was off-hab on a two-day Earth tour. They came home with stories of surging wildlife spectacles that made herds and flocks of Ricochet's biodiversity preserve look like a petting zoo. When the boost came, we all gathered in the rumpus room for the very last time.

Bruce, Blanche, Engku, Megat, and Mykelti clustered on the floor mats, anchoring themselves comfortably for the boost. They'd be fine. Soon they'd have armfuls of newborns to ease the pain of transition. The Jewel Box were all hanging from the ceiling netting, ready for their last ride of childhood. They'd be fine, too. Diamante had decided on Mars, and it looked like the other five would follow.

Me, I'd be fine, too. I'd have to be.

How to explain the pain and pride when your crèche is balanced on the knife's edge of adulthood, ready to leave you behind forever? Not possible. Just know this: when you see an oldster looking serene and wise, remember, it's just a sham. Under the skin, it's all sorrow.

I was relieved when the boost started. Everyone was too distracted to notice I'd begun tearing up. When the hab turned upside down I let myself shed a few tears for the passing moment. Nothing too self-indulgent. Just a little whuffle, then I wiped it all away and joined the celebration, laughing and applauding the kids' antics as they bounced around the room.

We got it, Long Meng whispered in the middle of the boost. *Luna just shot me the contract. We won.*

She told me all the details. I pretended to pay attention, but really, I was only interested in watching the kids. Drinking in their antics, their playfulness, their joyful self-importance. Young adults have a shine about them. They glow with untapped potential.

When the boost was over, we all unclipped our anchors. I couldn't quite extricate myself from my deeply padded chair and my cane was out of reach.

Tré leapt to help me up. When I was on my feet, he pulled me into a hug.

"Are you going back to Luna?" he said in my ear.

I held him at arm's length. "That's right. Someone has to take care of Long Meng."

"Who'll take care of you?"

I laughed. "I don't need taking care of."

He gripped both my hands in his. "That's not true. Everyone does."

"I'll be fine." I squeezed his fingers and tried to pull away, but he wouldn't let go. I changed the subject. "Mars seems like a great choice for you all."

"I'm not going to Mars. I'm going to Luna."

I stepped back. My knees buckled, but the stability belt kept me from going down.

"No, Tré. You can't."

"There's nothing you can do about it. I'm going."

"Absolutely not. You have no business on Luna. It's a terrible place."

He crossed his arms over his broadening chest and swung his head like a fighter looking for an opening. He squinted at the old toys and sports equipment secured into rumpus room cabinets, the peeling murals the kids had painted over the years, the battered bots and well-used, colorful furniture—all the ephemera and detritus of childhood that had been our world for nearly eighteen years.

"Then I'm not leaving the crèche. You'll have to stay here with me, in some kind of weird stalemate. Long Meng will be alone."

I scowled. It was nothing less than blackmail. I wasn't used to being forced into a corner, and certainly not by my own kid.

"We're going to Luna together." A grin flickered across Tré's face. "Might as well give in."

I patted his arm, then took his elbow. Tré picked up my cane and put it in my hand.

"I've done a terrible job raising you," I said.

THE BOOKCASE EXPEDITION
Jeffrey Ford

Jeffrey Ford (www.well-builtcity.com) is the author of the novels *The Physiognomy, Memoranda, The Beyond, The Portrait of Mrs. Charbuque, The Girl in the Glass, The Cosmology of the Wider World, The Shadow Year,* and *Ahab's Return.* His short story collections are *The Fantasy Writer's Assistant, The Empire of Ice Cream, The Drowned Life, Crackpot Palace,* and *A Natural History of Hell.* Ford's short fiction has appeared in a wide variety of magazines and anthologies and has won the Nebula, World Fantasy, and Shirley Jackson awards. He lives in Ohio in an old farm house surrounded by corn and soybean fields and teaches part time at Ohio Wesleyan University.

I STARTED SEEING them during the winter when I was at death's door and wacked out on meds. At first, I thought they were baby praying mantises that had somehow invaded the house to escape the ice and snow, but they were far smaller than that. Miniscule, really. I was surprised I could see them at all. I could, though, and at times with great clarity, as if through invisible binoculars. Occasionally, I heard their distant cries.

I'm talking about fairies, tiny beings in the forms of men, women and children. I spotted them, thin as a pin and half as tall, creeping about; running from the cats or carrying back to their homes in the walls sacks full of crumbs gathered from our breakfast plates. Mostly I saw them at night, as I had to sit upright in the corner of the living room couch to sleep in order not to suffocate. While the wind howled outside, the light coming in from the kitchen illuminated a small party of them ascending and descending the dunes and craters of the moonscape that was my blanket. One night they planted a flag—a tattered postage stamp fastened to a cat's whisker—into my knee as if I was undiscovered country.

The first time I saw one, it was battling—have you ever seen one of those spiders that looks like it's made of wood? Well, the fairy had a thistle spike and was parrying the picket legs of that arachnid, bravely lunging for its soft underbelly. I took it all in stride, though. I didn't get excited. I certainly didn't go and tell Lynn, who would think it nonsense. "Let the fairies do their thing," I thought. I had way bigger problems to deal with, like trying to breathe.

I know what you're thinking. They weren't a figment of my imagination. For instance, I'd spotted a band of them running along the kitchen counter. They stopped near the edge where a water glass stood. Together, they pushed against it and toppled it onto the floor. "Ya little bastards," I yelled. They scattered faint atoms of laughter as they fled. The broken glass went everywhere, and I swept for twenty minutes only to find more. The next day, Lynn got a shard in her foot, and I had to burn the end of a needle and operate.

I didn't see them constantly. Sometimes a week would go by before I encountered one. They watched us and I was certain they knew what we were about in our thoughts and acts. I'd spotted them—one with a telescope aimed at my nose and the other sitting, making notes in a bound journal—on the darkened porch floor at night when we sat out wrapped in blankets and candle light, drinking wine and dozing in the moon glow. I wondered, "Why now, as I trundle toward old age, am I granted the 'sight' as my grandma Maisie might have called it?"

A few days ago, I was in my office at the computer trying to iron out my thinking on a story I'd been writing in which there's a scene where a guy, for no reason I can recall, just disappears. There'd been nothing strange about this character previously to give any indication that he was simply going to vanish into thin air. I can't remember what I'd had in mind or why at some point it had made sense to me.

The winter illness had stunned my brain. Made me dim and forgetful. Metaphor, simile, were mere words, and I couldn't any longer feel the excitement of their affects. A darkness pervaded my chest and head. I leaned back in my chair away from the computer and turned toward the book cases. I was concentrating hard not to let the fear of failure in when a damn housefly the size of a grocery store grape buzzed my left temple, and I slapped myself in the face. It came by again and I ducked, reaching for a magazine with which to do my killing.

That's when a contingent of fairies emerged from the dark half inch of space beneath the middle of the five bookcases that lined the right wall of my office. There was a swarm of them like ants round a drip of ice cream on a summer sidewalk. At first, I thought I wanted to get back to my story, but soon enough I told myself, "You know what? Fuck that story." I folded my arms and watched. At first they appeared distant, but I didn't fret. I was in no hurry. The clear strong breath of spring had made of the winter a fleeting shadow. I saw out the window—sunlight, blue sky, and a lazy white cloud. The fairies gave three cheers, and I realized something momentous was afoot.

Although I kept my eyes trained on their number, my concentration sharpened and blurred and sharpened again. When my thoughts were away, I have no idea what I was thinking, but when they weren't I was thinking that someday soon I was going to go over to the preserve and walk the two mile circular path through the golden prairie grass. I decided, in that brief span, it would only be right to take Nellie the dog with me. All this, as I watched the little people, maybe fifty of them, twenty-five on either side, carry out from under a book case the ruler I'd been missing for the past year.

They laid the ruler across a paperback copy of Angela Carter's *Burning Boats*. It had fallen of its own volition from the bottom shelf three days earlier. Sometimes that happens, the books just take a dive. There was a thick anthology of Norse Sagas pretty close to it that had been laying there for five months. I made a mental note to, someday soon, rescue the fallen. No time to contemplate it, though, because four fairies broke off from the crowd, climbed atop the Carter collection and then took a position at the very end of the ruler, facing the book case. I leaned forward to get a better look.

The masses moved like water flowing to where the tome of sagas lay. They swept around it, lifting it end over end, and standing it upright, upside down, so that the horns of the Viking helmet pictured on the cover pointed to the center of the earth. The next thing I knew, they were toppling the thick book. It came down with the weight of two dozen Norse sagas right onto the end of the ruler opposite from where the fairies stood. Of course, the four of them were shot into the air, arcing toward the book case. They flew and each gripped in the right hand a rose bush thorn.

I watched them hit the wall of books a shelf and a half up and dig the sharp points of their thorns into dust jackets and spines. One of them made a tear in the red cover of my hard-back copy of *Black Hole*. Once secured, I noticed them hitch themselves at the waist with a rope belt to their affixed thorn. I'd not noticed before, but they had bows and arrows, and spools of thread from Lynn's sewing basket draped across their chests like bandoliers. I had a sudden memory of *The Teeny Weenies*, a race of fairies that appeared in the *Daily News* Sunday comics when I was a kid. I envisioned for a moment, an old panel from the Weenies in which one was riding a wild turkey with a saddle and reins while the others gathered giant acorns half their size. I came back from that thought just in time to see all four fairies release their arrows into the ceiling of the shelf they were on. I heard the distant, petite impact of each shaft. Then, bows slung over their shoulders, they began to climb, hand over hand, using the book spines in front of them to rappel upward.

Since their purpose seemed to be to ascend, I foresaw trouble ahead for them. The next shelf above, which they'd have to somehow flip up onto, held two rows of books, not one, so there was no clear space for them to land. They'd have to flip up and again dig in with their thorns and attach themselves to the spines of books whose bottoms stuck perilously out over the edge of the shelf. When I considered the agility and strength all this took, I shook my head and put my hand over my heart. I wanted to see them succeed, though, and went off on a trail of musing that pitted the reliability of the impossible against the potential chaos of reality. A point came where I wandered from the path of my thoughts and wound up witnessing the smallest of the fairies nearly plummet to his death. I felt his scream in my liver.

The poor little fellow had lost a hold on his thread line and was hanging out over the abyss, desperately grasping a poorly planted thorn in the spine of *Blind Man with a Pistol*. His compatriot, whom I just then realized was a woman with long dark hair, shot an arrow into the ceiling of the shelf. Once she had that line affixed to her belt, she swung over to her comrade in danger and put her left arm around him. He let go his thorn spike and swung with her. I was so intent upon watching this rescue, that I missed but from the very corner of my eye one of the other tiny adventurers fall. His (for I was just then somehow certain it was a he, and his name was Meeshin) miniscule weight dragged the book he'd attached to off the shelf after him. This was the thing about the fairies, if you could see them, the longer you looked, the deeper you knew them; their names, their motivations, their secrets.

I only turned in time to completely see that he'd been crushed by the slim volume of *Quiet Days in Clichy*. I watched to see if his compatriots from beneath the bookshelf would appear to claim his corpse, but they didn't. The loneliness of Meeshin's death affected me more than it should have. It came to me that he was married and had three fairy kids. His art was whittling totem poles full of animals of the imagination out of toothpicks. I'd wondered where all my toothpicks had gone. I pictured his wife, Tibith, in the fairy marketplace telling a friend that all Meeshin's crazy creatures could be seen, like in a gallery, way in the back of the cupboard beneath the kitchen sink. Last I saw him behind my eyes, it was night and he lay quietly in bed, his arms around his wife.

Next I caught up with the climbers, the three had gathered to rest on the top edge of a book back in the second row of that dangerous shelf. I shifted my position in the chair and craned my neck a bit to see that the volume in question was Paulo Coelho's *The Alchemist*, a book I'd never read and one of those strange additions to my library. I was unaware of how I'd acquired it. My favorite essayist, Alberto Manguel, had said that he'd never enter a library that contained a book by Coelho. I thought that on the off chance he might travel to the drop edge of yonder, Ohio, I should get rid of it.

I knew them all by name now and something about their little lives. The woman with the long dark hair, Aspethia, was the leader of the expedition. I wasn't sure what the purpose of their journey was, but I knew it had a purpose. It was a mission given to her directly by Magorian, the Fairy Queen. Her remaining companions were the little fellow she rescued, Sopso, and a large fellow, Balthazar, who wore a conical hat with a chin strap on his bald head like something from a child's birthday party. Aspethia spoke words of encouragement to Sopso, who cowered on his knees for fear of falling. She went into her pack and pulled out another rose thorn for him. "Now, if we don't hurry, there will be no point in our having come this far," she said.

The next shelf up they found easy purchase at the front as there was only one row of books pushed all the way back. It was the shelf with my collection of the Lang Fairy books, each volume a different color. That they all stood together was the only bit of authentic order in my library. I watched the fairies pass in front of the various colors—red, violet, green, orange—and wondered if they knew the books were more than merely giant rocks to be climbed. Did they know these boulders they passed held the ancient stories of their species? I pictured the huge boulder, like the egg of a Roc, sitting alone amidst the golden grass over at the preserve and day dreamed about the story it might hatch.

The afternoon pushed on with the slow, steady progress of a fairy climbing thread. They moved up the various shelves of the bookcase, one after the other, with a methodical pace. Even the near falls, the brushes with death, were smooth and timely. There were obstacles, books I'd placed haphazardly atop a row pretending that I intended to someday reshelve them. When the companions were forced to cross my devil tambourine, which had sat there on the fifth level since two Halloweens previously, it made their teensy steps echo in the caverns of the shelves. The big one, Balthazar, skewered, with a broken broom straw, a silver fish atop one of the Smiley novels, and they lit a Fairy fire, which only cooked their meal but didn't burn, thank god. Those three remaining climbers sat in a circle and ate the cooked insect. While they did, Sopso read from a book so infinitesimally small it barely existed.

I closed my eyes and drifted off into the quiet of the afternoon. The window was open a bit and a breeze snaked in around me. Moments later, I bolted awake, and the first thing I did was search the bookshelf for the expedition. When I found them, a pulse of alarm shot up my back. Balthazar and Aspethia were battling an Oni netsuke come miraculously to life. I'd had the thing for years. Lynn bought it for me in a store in China Town in Philly across the street from Joe's Peking Duck House. It was a cheap imitation, made to look like ivory from some kind of resin—a short, stocky demon with a dirty face and horns. He held a mask of his own visage in his right hand and a big bag in his left. He tried to scoop the fairies into it. Sopso was nowhere in sight.

Seeing an inanimate object come to life made me a little dizzy, and I think I was trembling. The demon growled and spat at them. What was more incredible still was the fact that the companions were able to drive the monster to the edge of the shelf. The fighting was fierce, the fairies drawing blood with long daggers fashioned from the ends of brass safety pins. The demon's size gave it the advantage, and more than once he'd scooped Balthazar and Aspethia up but they'd managed to wriggle out of the eyeholes of the mask before he could bag them. The little people sang a lilting fairy anthem throughout the battle that I only caught garbled snatches of. They ran as they sang in circles round the giant, poking him in the hairy shins and toes and Achilles tendon with their daggers.

Oni lost his balance and tipped a jot toward the edge. In a blink, Balthaszar leaped up, put a foot on the demon's belly, grabbed its beard in his free hand, pulled himself higher, and plunged the dagger into his enemy's eye. The demon reeled backward, screaming, turning in circles. Aspethia leaped forward and drove her dagger to the hilt in Oni's left testicle. That elicited a terrible cry, and then the creature tipped over the edge of the shelf. Balthazar tried to leap off to where Aspethia stood, but Oni grabbed his leg and they went all the way down together. Although the fairy's neck was broken, his party hat remained undamaged.

Aspethia crawled to the edge of the shelf and peered down the great distance to see the fate of her comrade. If she survived the expedition, she would be the one responsible for telling Balthazar's wife and children of his death. She sat back away from the edge and took a deep breath. Sopso emerged from a cavern between *The Book of Contemplation* and Harry Crews's *Childhood*. He walked over to where Aspethia knelt and put his hand on her shoulder. She reached up and grabbed it. He helped her to her feet and they made their way uneventfully to the top shelf. As they climbed, I looked back down at the fallen netsuke and saw that it had regained its original form of a lifeless figurine. Had there been a demon in it? How and why did it come to life? The gift of seeing fairies comes wrapped in questions.

On the top shelf, they headed north toward the back wall of the room, passing a foot-high Ghost Rider plastic figure, the marble Ganesh bookends, a small picture frame containing a block of Jason Van Hollander's Hell Stamps, Flannery O'Conner's letters, and *Our Lady of the Flowers* shelved without consciousness of design on my part directly next to *Our Lady of Darkness*. A copy of the writings of Cotton Mather lay atop the books of that shelf, its upper half forming an overhang beneath which the expedition had to pass. Its cover held a portrait of Mather from his own time and faced down. Eyes peered from above. His brows, his nose, his powdered wig, but not his mouth, bore witness to the fairies passing. For a moment, I was with them in the shadow, staring up at the preacher's gaze, incredulous as to how the glance of the image was capable of following us.

Eventually, they came to where the last book case in the row butts up against the northern wall. Aspethia and Sopso stroked the barrier as if it had some religious significance. She leaned over and put her arm around Sopso's shoulder, turned him, and pointed out the framed painting hanging on the northern wall about two feet from the book case. He saw it and nodded. The painting in question had been given to me by my friend Barney who painted it in his studio at Dividing Creek in South Jersey. It's a knock-off of a Charles Wilson Peale painting of the artist ascending a staircase, only Barney's is done in green, and there's only one figure—a ghost with the acrimonious face of John Ashcroft, President Bush's Secretary of State, looking back over his shoulder.

She shot an arrow into the northern wall just above the middle of where the painting hung. She leaned forward and Sopso climbed upon her back. With the line from the arrow tight in her hands, she inched toward the edge of the book case. She jumped and they swung toward the painting, Sopso screaming, and crashed into the image where Ashcroft's ascot met his second chin. Once they'd stopped bouncing against the canvas, she told her passenger to tighten his grip. He did and she began hauling both of them to the top of the picture frame. Her climbing looked like magic.

For some reason, right here, I recalled the strange sound I'd heard behind the garage the last few nights. A wheezing growl that reverberated through the night. I pictured the devil crouching back there in the shadows, but our neighbor told us it was a fox in heat. It sounded like a cry from another world. My interest in it faded, and in a heartbeat my focus was back on the painting. They had achieved the top of the frame and were resting. I wondered where the expedition was headed next. There was another painting on that wall about four feet away from the ghost on the staircase. It was a painting of Garuda by my younger son. The distance between the paintings was vast in fairy feet. I couldn't believe they would attempt to cross to it. Aspethia showed it no interest, but instead pointed straight up.

She took her bow, nocked an arrow with a thread line in place, and aimed it at the ceiling. My glance followed the path of the potential shot, and only then did I notice that her arrow was aimed precisely into a prodigious spider web that stretched from directly above the painting all the way to the corner of the north wall. She released the arrow, and I tried to follow it but caught only a blur. It hit its mark, and that drew my attention to the fact that right next to where it hit, that fly, big as a grape, was trapped in webbing and buzzing to beat the band. I looked along the web to the corner of the ceiling and saw the spider, skinny legs with a fat white pearl of an abdomen. I could see it drooling as it moved forward to finally claim its catch.

It surprised me when, without hesitation, Sopso, alone, climbed the line toward the ceiling. He shimmied up at a pace that lapped the spider's progress, the rose thorn clenched in his teeth. The fly was well-wrapped in spider silk, unable to use its wings, its cries muffled. The pale spider danced along the vibrating strands. Sopso reached the fly and cut away enough web to get his legs around the insect's back. Too bad he was upside down. The spider advanced while the fairy continued to hack away. I was able to hear every strand he cut—the noise of a spring sprung, like an effect from a cartoon. The way Sopso worked, with such courage and cool, completely reversed my estimation of him. Till then, I'd thought of him as a burden to the expedition, but, after all, he had his place.

I was at the edge of my seat, my neck craned and my head tilted back. My heart was pounding. The spider reared back, poised to strike, and Sopso never flinched but worked methodically in the looming shadow of death. Fangs shut and four piercing sharp leg points struck at nothing. The fairy had cut the last strand and he, legs around the back of the fly, fell upside down toward the floor. At the last second the fly's wings worked, and they managed to pull out of the death plunge. They shot up past my left ear toward the ceiling. Aspethia, the spider and me followed their erratic course. They zig zagged with great buzzing all around the room, but when they passed over the book case near the window of the west wall, the fairy, afraid the dizzy fly would crash, jumped off and landed safely on a copy of Albahari's *Leeches*.

Sopso was stranded. He and Aspethia waved to each other across the incredible expanse of my office. They might as well have been on different worlds. Each cried out but neither was able to hear the other. Her arrows could not reach him. He had with him no thread bandoliers, nor even a pin tip knife. Without them, there was no way he could climb down from that height, and by the time Aspethia returned to the fairy village and could mount a rescue party, he would most likely die of starvation. Still, she set out quickly to get back home on the slim chance he might survive long enough. He watched her go, and I could see the sadness come over him. The sight of it left me with a terrible chill.

What was I to do? My heart went out to the lost climber who gave his life to save an insignificant fly, not to mention brave Aspethia. I thought how easily I could change everything for them. I stood up and stepped over to the book case by the window on the west wall. I reached out to gently lift Sopso in order to place him down on the floor across the room near where the expedition had begun. My fingers closed, and for no good reason, he suddenly disappeared. A moment of silence passed, and then I heard a chorus well up from beneath the book cases, each voice not but a pin-prick of laughter.

Later that evening, as Lynn and I sat on the porch in the last pink glow of sunset, she reached across the glass topped table that held our wine and said, "Look here." She was holding something between her thumb and forefinger. Whatever she was showing me was very delicate and what with the failing light I needed to lean in close to see. To my shock it was a cat whisker with a postage stamp affixed to the end, like a tiny flag.

Her expression made me ask, "How long have you known?"

She laughed quietly. "Way back," she said and her words cut away the webbing that had me trapped.

A WITCH'S GUIDE TO ESCAPE: A PRACTICAL COMPENDIUM OF PORTAL FANTASIES

Alix E. Harrow

Alix E. Harrow (alixeharrow.wixsite.com/author • @AlixEHarrow) is an ex-historian with excessive library fines and lots of opinions. Her short fiction has appeared in *Shimmer*, *Strange Horizons*, *Tor.com*, *Apex*, and other venues, and her debut novel, *The Ten Thousand Doors of January*, is forthcoming from Orbit/Redhook. She and her husband live in Kentucky under the chaotic tyranny of their children and animals.

GEORGE, JC—THE RUNAWAY PRINCE   —J FIC GEO 1994

You'd think it would make us happy when a kid checks out the same book a zillion times in a row, but actually it just keeps us up at night.

The Runaway Prince is one of those low-budget young adult fantasies from the mid-nineties, before J.K. Rowling arrived to tell everyone that magic was cool, printed on brittle yellow paper. It's about a lonely boy who runs away and discovers a Magical Portal into another world where he has Medieval Adventures, but honestly there are so many typos most people give up before he even finds the portal.

Not this kid, though. He pulled it off the shelf and sat cross-legged in the juvenile fiction section with his grimy red backpack clutched to his chest. He didn't move for hours. Other patrons were forced to double-back in the aisle, shooting suspicious, you-don't-belong-here looks behind them as if wondering what a skinny black teenager was *really* up to while pretending to read a fantasy book. He ignored them.

The books above him rustled and quivered; that kind of attention flatters them.

He took *The Runaway Prince* home and renewed it twice online, at which point a gray pop-up box that looks like an emissary from 1995 tells you, "the renewal limit for this item has been reached." You can almost feel the disapproving eyes of a librarian glaring at you through the screen.

(There have only ever been two kinds of librarians in the history of the world: the prudish, bitter ones with lipstick running into the cracks around their lips who believe the books are their personal property and patrons are dangerous delinquents come to steal them; and witches.)

Our late fee is 25 cents per day or a can of non-perishable food during the summer food drive. By the time the boy finally slid *The Runaway Prince* into the return slot, he owed $4.75. I didn't have to swipe his card to know; any good librarian (of the second kind) ought to be able to tell you the exact dollar amount of a patron's bill just by the angle of their shoulders.

"What'd you think?" I used my this-is-a-secret-between-us-pals voice, which works on teenagers about sixteen percent of the time.

He shrugged. It has a lower success rate with black teenagers, because this is the rural South and they aren't stupid enough to trust thirty-something white ladies no matter how many tattoos we have.

"Didn't finish it, huh?" I knew he'd finished it at least four times by the warm, well-oiled feel of the pages.

"Yeah, I did." His eyes flicked up. They were smoke-colored and long-lashed, with an achy, faraway expression, as if he knew there was something gleaming and forbidden just beneath the dull surfaces of things that he could never quite touch. They were the kinds of eyes that had belonged to sorcerers or soothsayers, in different times. "The ending sucked."

In the end, the Runaway Prince leaves Medieval Adventureland and closes the portal behind him before returning home to his family. It was supposed to be a happy ending.

Which kind of tells you all you need to know about this kid's life, doesn't it? He left without checking anything else out.

GARRISON, ALLEN B—THE TAVALARRIAN CHRONICLES
—v. I-XVI—F GAR 1976
LEGUIN, URSULA K—A WIZARD OF EARTHSEA
—J FIC LEG 1968

HE RETURNED FOUR days later, sloping past a bright blue display titled THIS SUMMER, DIVE INTO READING! (who knows where they were supposed to swim; Ulysses County's lone public pool had been filled with cement in the sixties rather than desegregate).

Because I am a librarian of the second sort, I almost always know what kind of book a person wants. It's like a very particular smell rising off them which is instantly recognizable as *Murder mystery* or *Political biography* or *Something kind of trashy but ultimately life-affirming, preferably with lesbians.*

I do my best to give people the books they need most. In grad school, they called it "ensuring readers have access to texts/materials that are engaging and emotionally rewarding," and in my other kind of schooling, they called it "divining the unfilled spaces in their souls and filling them with stories and starshine," but it comes to the same thing.

I don't bother with the people who have call numbers scribbled on their palms and titles rattling around in their skulls like bingo cards. They don't need me. And you really can't do anything for the people who only read Award-Winning Literature, who wear elbow patches and equate the popularity of *Twilight* with the death of the American intellect; their hearts are too closed-up for the new or secret or undiscovered.

So, it's only a certain kind of patron I pay attention to. The kind that let their eyes feather across the titles like trailing fingertips, heads cocked, with book-hunger rising off them like heatwaves from July pavement. The books bask in it, of course, even the really hopeless cases that haven't been checked out since 1958 (there aren't many of these; me and Agnes take turns carting home outdated astronomy textbooks that still think Pluto is a planet and cookbooks that call for lard, just to keep their spirits up). I choose one or two books and let their spines gleam and glimmer in the twilit stacks. People reach towards them without quite knowing why.

The boy with the red backpack wasn't an experienced aisle-wanderer. He prowled, moving too quickly to read the titles, hands hanging empty and uncertain at his sides. The sewing and pattern books (646.2) noted that his jeans were unlaundered and too small, and the neck of his t-shirt was stained grayish-yellow. The cookbooks (641.5) diagnosed a diet of frozen waffles and gas-station pizza. They *tssked* to themselves.

I sat at the circulation desk, running returns beneath the blinky red scanner light, and breathed him in. I was expecting something like *generic Arthurian retelling* or maybe *teen romance with sword-fighting*, but instead I found a howling, clamoring mess of need.

He smelled of a thousand secret worlds, of rabbit-holes and hidden doorways and platforms nine-and-three-quarters, of Wonderland and Oz and Narnia, of anyplace-but-here. He smelled of *yearning*.

God save me from the yearners. The insatiable, the inconsolable, the ones who chafe and claw against the edges of the world. No book can save them.

(That's a lie. There are Books potent enough to save any mortal soul: books of witchery, augury, alchemy; books with wand-wood in their spines and moon-dust on their pages; books older than stones and wily as dragons. We give people the books they need most, except when we don't.)

I sent him a seventies sword-and-sorcery series because it was total junk food and he needed fattening up, and because I hoped sixteen volumes might act as a sort of ballast and keep his keening soul from rising away into the ether. I let LeGuin shimmer at him, too, because he reminded me a bit of Ged (feral; full of longing).

I ignored *The Lion, the Witch, and the Wardrobe*, jostling importantly on its shelf; this was a kid who wanted to go through the wardrobe and never, ever come back.

GRAYSON, DR BERNARD—WHEN NOTHING MATTERS
ANYMORE: A SURVIVAL GUIDE FOR DEPRESSED TEENS
—616.84 GRA 2002

ONCE YOU MAKE it past book four of the *Tavalarrian Chronicles*, you're committed at least through book fourteen when the true Sword of Tavalar is revealed and the young farm-boy ascends to his rightful throne. The boy with the red backpack showed up every week or so all summer for the next installment.

I snuck in a few others (all pretty old, all pretty white; our branch director is one of those pinch-lipped Baptists who thinks fantasy books teach kids about Devil worship, so roughly 90% of my collection requests are mysteriously denied): *A Wrinkle in Time* came back with the furtive, jammed-in-a-backpack scent that meant he liked it but thought it was too young for him; *Watership Down* was offended because he never got past the first ten pages, but I guess footnotes about rabbit-math aren't for everyone; and *The Golden Compass* had the flashlight-smell of 3:00 a.m. on its final chapter and was unbearably smug about it. I'd just gotten an inter-library-loaned copy of *Akata Witch*—when he stopped coming.

Our display (GET READ-Y FOR SCHOOL!) was filled with SAT prep kits and over-sized yellow *For Dummies* books. Agnes had cut out blobby construction-paper leaves and taped them to the front doors. Lots of kids stop hanging around the library when school starts up, with all its clubs and teams.

I worried anyway. I could feel the Book I hadn't given him like a wrong note or a missing tooth, a magnetic absence. Just when I was seriously considering calling Ulysses County High School with a made-up story about an un-returned CD, he came back.

For the first time, there was someone else with him: A squat white woman with a plastic name-tag and the kind of squareish perm you can only get in Southern beauty salons with faded glamor-shots in the windows. The boy trailed behind her looking thin and pressed, like a flower crushed between dictionary pages. I wondered how badly you had to fuck up to get assigned a school counselor after hours, until I read her name-tag: Department of Community-Based Services, Division of Protection and Permanency, Child Caseworker (II).

Oh. A foster kid.

The woman marched him through the nonfiction stacks (the travel guides sighed as she passed, muttering about overwork and recommending vacations to sunny, faraway beaches) and stopped in the 616s. "Here, why don't we have a look at these?"

Predictable, sullen silence from the boy.

A person who works with foster kids sixty hours a week is unfazed by sullenness. She slid titles off the shelf and stacked them in the boy's arms. "We talked about this, remember? We decided you might like to read something practical, something helpful?"

Dealing with Depression (616.81 WHI 1998). *Beating the Blues: Five*

Steps to Feeling Normal Again! (616.822 TRE 2011). *Chicken Soup for the Depressed Soul* (616.9 CAN). The books greeted him in soothing, syrupy voices.

The boy stayed silent. "Look. I know you'd rather read about dragons and, uh, elves," oh, Tolkien, you have so much to account for, "but sometimes we've got to face our problems head-on, rather than running away from them."

What *bullshit*. I was in the back room running scratched DVDs through the disc repair machine, so the only person to hear me swear was Agnes. She gave me her patented over-the-glasses shame-on-you look which, when properly deployed, can reduce noisy patrons to piles of ash or pillars of salt (Agnes is a librarian of the second kind, too).

But seriously. Anyone could see that kid needed to run and keep running until he shed his own skin, until he clawed out of the choking darkness and unfurled his wings, precious and prisming in the light of some other world.

His caseworker was one of those people who say the word "escapism" as if it's a moral failing, a regrettable hobby, a mental-health diagnosis. As if escape is not, in itself, one of the highest order of magics they'll ever see in their miserable mortal lives, right up there with true love and prophetic dreams and fireflies blinking in synchrony on a June evening.

The boy and his keeper were winding back through the aisles toward the front desk. The boy's shoulders were curled inward, as if he chafed against invisible walls on either side.

As he passed the juvenile fiction section, a cheap paperback flung itself off the return cart and thudded into his kneecap. He picked it up and rubbed his thumb softly over the title. *The Runaway Prince* purred at him.

He smiled. I thanked the library cart, silently.

There was a long, familiar sigh behind me. I turned to see Agnes watching me from the circulation desk, aquamarine nails tapping the cover of a Grisham novel, eyes crimped with pity. *Oh honey, not another one*, they said.

I turned back to my stack of DVDs, unsmiling, thinking things like *what do you know about it* and *this one is different* and *oh shit*.

* * *

DUMAS, ALEXANDRE—THE COUNT OF MONTE CRISTO
—F DUM 1974

THE BOY RETURNED at ten-thirty on a Tuesday morning. It's official library policy to report truants to the high school, because the school board felt we were becoming "a haven for unsupervised and illicit teenage activity." I happen to think that's exactly what libraries should aspire to be, and suggested we get it engraved on a plaque for the front door, but then I was asked to be serious or leave the proceedings, and anyway we're supposed to report kids who skip school to play *League of Legends* on our computers or skulk in the graphic novel section.

I watched the boy prowling the shelves—muscles strung wire-tight over his bones, soul writhing and clawing like a caged creature—and did not reach for the phone. Agnes, still wearing her *oh honey* expression, declined to reprimand me.

I sent him home with *The Count of Monte Cristo*, partly because it requires your full attention and a flow chart to keep track of the plot and the kid needed distracting, but mostly because of what Edmund says on the second-to-last page: "...all human wisdom is summed up in these two words—'Wait and hope.'"

But people can't keep waiting and hoping forever.

They fracture, they unravel, they crack open; they do something desperate and stupid and then you see their high school senior photo printed in the *Ulysses Gazette*, grainy and oversized, and you spend the next five years thinking: *if only I'd given her the right book.*

ROWLING, JK—HARRY POTTER AND
THE SORCERER'S STONE   —J FIC ROW 1998
ROWLING, JK—HARRY POTTER AND
THE CHAMBER OF SECRETS   —J FIC ROW 1999
ROWLING, JK—HARRY POTTER AND
THE PRISONER OF AZKABAN   —J FIC ROW 1999

EVERY LIBRARIAN HAS Books she never lends to anyone.

I'm not talking about first editions of *Alice in Wonderland* or Dutch translations of *Winnie-the-Pooh*; I'm talking about Books so powerful and potent, so full of susurrating seduction, that only librarians of the second sort even know they exist.

Each of us has her own system for keeping them hidden. The most venerable libraries (the ones with oak paneling and vaulted ceilings and *Beauty and the Beast*-style ladders) have secret rooms behind fireplaces or bookcases, which you can only enter by tugging on a certain title on the shelf. Sainte-Geneviève in Paris is supposed to have vast catacombs beneath it guarded by librarians so ancient and desiccated they've become human-shaped books, paper-skinned and ink-blooded. In Timbuktu, I head they hired wizard-smiths to make great wrought-iron gates that only permit passage to the pure of heart.

In the Maysville branch of the Ulysses County Library system, we have a locked roll-top desk in the Special Collections room with a sign on it that says, "This is an Antique! Please Ask for Assistance."

We only have a dozen or so Books, anyhow, and god knows where they came from or how they ended up here. *A Witch's Guide to Seeking Righteous Vengeance*, with its slender steel pages and arsenic ink. *A Witch's Guide to Falling in Love for the First Time, for Readers at Every Stage of Life!*, which smells like starlight and the summer you were seventeen. *A Witch's Guide to Uncanny Baking* contains over thirty full-color photographs to ensorcell your friends and afflict your adversaries. *A Witch's Guide to Escape: A Practical Compendium of Portal Fantasies* has no words in it at all, but only pages and pages of maps: hand-drawn Middle Earth knock-offs with unpronounceable names; medieval tapestry-maps showing tiny ships sailing off the edge of the world; topographical maps of Machu Picchu; 1970s Rand McNally street maps of Istanbul.

It's my job to keep Books like this out of the hands of desperate high-school kids with red backpacks. Our school-mistresses called it "preserving the hallowed and hidden arts of our foremothers from mundane eyes." Our professors called it "conserving rare/historic texts."

Both of them mean the same thing: We give people the books they need, except when we don't. Except when they need them most.

He racked up $1.50 on *The Count of Monte Cristo* and returned it with saltwater splotches on the final pages. They weren't my-favorite-character-died tears or the-book-is-over tears. They were bitter, acidic, anise-scented:

tears of jealousy. He was jealous that the Count and Haydée sailed away from their world and out into the blue unknown. That they escaped.

I panicked and weighed him down with the first three *Harry Potters*, because they don't really get good until Sirius and Lupin show up, and because they're about a neglected, lonely kid who gets a letter from another world and disappears.

GEORGE, JC—THE RUNAWAY PRINCE   —J FIC GEO 1994

AGNES ALWAYS DOES the "we will be closing in ten minutes" announcement because something in her voice implies that anybody still in the library in nine minutes and fifty seconds will be harvested for organ donations, and even the most stationary patrons amble towards the exit.

The kid with the red backpack was hovering in the oversize print section (gossipy, aging books, bored since the advent of e-readers with changeable font sizes) when Agnes's voice came through the speakers. He went very still, teetering the way a person does when they're about to do something really dumb, then dove beneath a reading desk and pulled his dark hoodie over his head. The oversize books gave scintillated squeals.

It was my turn to close, so Agnes left right at nine. By 9:15 I was standing at the door with my NPR tote on my shoulder and my keys in my hand. Hesitating.

It is very, extremely, absolutely against the rules to lock up for the night with a patron still inside, especially when that patron is a minor of questionable emotional health. It's big trouble both in the conventional sense (phone calls from panicked guardians, police searches, charges of criminal neglect) and in the other sense (libraries at night are noisier places than they are during the daylight hours).

I'm not a natural rule-follower. I roll through stop signs, I swear in public, I lie on online personality tests so I get the answers I want (Hermione, Arya Stark, Jo March). But I'm a very good librarian of either kind, and good librarians follow the rules. Even when they don't want to.

That's what Agnes told me five years ago, when I first started at Maysville.

This girl had started showing up on Sunday afternoons: ponytailed, cute, but wearing one of those knee-length denim skirts that scream "mandatory virginity pledge." I'd been feeding her a steady diet of subversion (Orwell, Bradbury, Butler), and was about to hit her with *A Handmaid's Tale* when she suddenly lost interest in fiction. She drifted through the stacks, face gone white and empty as a blank page, navy skirt swishing against her knees.

It wasn't until she reached the 618s that I understood. The maternity and childbirth section trilled saccharine congratulations. She touched one finger to the spine of *What to Expect When You're Expecting* (618.2 EIS) with an expression of dawning, swallowing horror, and left without checking anything out.

For the next nine weeks, I sent her stories of bravery and boldness, defying-your-parents stories and empowered-women-resisting-authority stories. I abandoned subtlety entirely and slid Planned Parenthood pamphlets into her book bag, even though the nearest clinic is six hours away and only open twice a week, but found them jammed frantically in the bathroom trash.

But I never gave her what she really needed: *A Witch's Guide to Undoing What Has Been Done: A Guilt-Free Approach to Life's Inevitable Accidents.* A leather-bound tome filled with delicate mechanical drawings of clocks, which smelled of regret and yesterday mornings. I'd left it locked in the roll-top desk, whispering and tick-tocking to itself.

Look, there are good reasons we don't lend out Books like that. Our mistresses used to scare us with stories of mortals run amok: people who used Books to steal or kill or break hearts; who performed miracles and founded religions; who hated us, afterward, and spent a tiresome few centuries burning us at stakes.

If I were caught handing out Books, I'd be renounced, reviled, stripped of my title. They'd burn my library card in the eternal mauve flames of our sisterhood and write my crimes in ash and blood in *The Book of Perfidy*. They'd ban me from every library for eternity, and what's a librarian without her books? What would I be, cut off from the orderly world of words and their readers, from the peaceful Ouroboran cycle of story-telling and story-eating? There were rumors of rogue librarians—madwomen who chose to live outside the library system in the howling chaos of unwritten words and untold stories—but none of us envied them.

The last time I'd seen the ponytailed girl her denim skirt was fastened with a rubber band looped through the buttonhole. She'd smelled of desperation, like someone whose wait-and-hoping had run dry.

Four days later, her picture was in the paper and the article was blurring and un-blurring in my vision (*accidental poisoning, viewing from 2:00-3:30 at Zimmerman & Holmes, direct your donations to Maysville Baptist Ministries*). Agnes had patted my hand and said, "I know, honey, I know. Sometimes there's nothing you can do." It was a kind lie.

I still have the newspaper clipping in my desk drawer, as a memorial or reminder or warning.

The boy with the red backpack was sweating beneath the reading desk. He smelled of desperation, just like she had.

Should I call the Child Protective Services hotline? Make awkward small-talk until his crummy caseworker collected him? *Hey, kid, I was once a lonely teenager in a backwater shithole, too!* Or should I let him run away, even if running away was only hiding in the library overnight?

I teetered, the way you do when you're about to do something really dumb.

The locked thunked into place. I walked across the parking lot breathing the caramel-and-frost smell of October, hoping—almost praying, if witches were into that—that it would be enough.

I OPENED HALF an hour early, angling to beat Agnes to the phone and delete the "Have you seen this unaccompanied minor?" voicemails before she could hear them. There was an automated message from somebody trying to sell us a security system, three calls from community members asking when we open because apparently it's physically impossible to Google it, and a volunteer calling in sick.

There were no messages about the boy. Fucking Ulysses County foster system.

He emerged at 9:45, when he could blend in with the growing numbers of other patrons. He looked rumpled and ill-fitting, like a visitor from another planet who hadn't quite figured out human body language. Or like a kid who's spent a night in the stacks, listening to furtive missives from a thousand different worlds and wishing he could disappear into any one of them.

I was so busy trying not to cry and ignoring the Book now calling to the boy from the roll-top desk that I scanned his card and handed him back his book without realizing what it was: *The Runaway Prince*.

MAYSVILLE PUBLIC LIBRARY NOTICE: YOU HAVE (1) OVERDUE ITEMS. PLEASE RETURN YOUR ITEM(S) AS SOON AS POSSIBLE.

SHIT.

The overdue notices go out on the fifteenth day an item has been checked out. On the sixteenth day, I pulled up the boy's account and glared at the terse red font (OVERDUE ITEM: J FIC GEO 1994) until the screen began to crackle and smoke faintly and Agnes gave me a *hold-it-together-woman* look.

He hadn't even bothered to renew it.

My sense of *The Runaway Prince* had grown faint and blurred with distance, as if I were looking at it through an unfocused telescope, but it was still a book from my library and thus still in my domain. (All you people who never returned books to their high school libraries, or who bought stolen books off Amazon with call numbers taped to their spines? We see you.) It reported only the faintest second-hand scent of the boy: futility, resignation, and a tarry, oozing smell like yearning that had died and begun to fossilize.

He was alive, but probably not for much longer. I don't just mean physical suicide; those of us who can see soulstuff know there are lots of ways to die without anybody noticing. Have you ever seen those stupid TV specials where they rescue animals from some third-rate horror show of a circus in Las Vegas, and when they finally open the cages the lions just sit there, dead-eyed, because they've forgotten what it is to want anything? To desire, to yearn, to be filled with the terrible, golden hunger of being alive?

But there was nothing I could do. Except wait and hope.

Our volunteers were doing the weekly movie showing in Media Room #2, so I was stuck re-shelving. It wasn't until I was actually in the F DAC-FEN aisle, holding our dog-eared copy of *The Count of Monte Cristo* in my hand, that I realized Edmund Dantès was absolutely, one-hundred-percent full of shit.

If Edmund had taken his own advice, he would've sat in his jail cell waiting and hoping for forty years while the Count de Morcerf and Villefort and the rest of them stayed rich and happy. The real moral of *The Count of Monte Cristo* was surely something more like: If you screw someone over, be prepared for a vengeful mastermind to fuck up your life twenty years later. Or maybe it was: If you want justice and goodness to prevail in this world, you have to fight for it tooth and nail. And it will be hard, and costly, and probably illegal. You will have to break the rules.

I pressed my head to the cold metal of the shelf and closed my eyes. *If that boy ever comes back into my library, I swear to Clio and Calliope I will do my most holy duty.*

I will give him the book he needs most.

ARADIA, MORGAN—A WITCH'S GUIDE TO ESCAPE: A PRACTICAL COMPENDIUM OF PORTAL FANTASIES— WRITTEN IN THE YEAR OF OUR SISTERHOOD TWO THOUSAND AND TWO AND SUBMITTED TO THE CARE OF THE ULYSSES COUNTY PUBLIC LIBRARY SYSTEM.

HE CAME BACK to say goodbye, I think. He slid *The Runaway Prince* into the return slot then drifted through the aisles with his red backpack hanging off one shoulder, fingertips not-quite brushing the shelves, eyes on the floor. They hardly seemed sorcerous at all, now; merely sad and old and smoke-colored.

He was passing through the travel and tourism section when he saw it: A heavy, clothbound book jammed right between *The Practical Nomad* (910.4 HAS) and *By Plane, Train, or Foot: A Guide for the Aspiring Globe-Trotter* (910.51). It had no call number, but the title was stamped in swirly gold lettering on the spine: *A Witch's Guide to Escape.*

I felt the hollow thud-thudding of his heart, the pain of resurrected hope. He reached towards the book and the book reached back towards him, because books need to be read quite as much as we need to read them, and it had been a very long time since this particular book had been out of the roll-top desk in the Special Collections room.

Dark fingers touched green-dyed cloth, and it was like two sundered halves of some broken thing finally reuniting, like a lost key finally turning in its lock. Every book in the library rustled in unison, sighing at the sacred wholeness of reader and book.

Agnes was in the rows of computers, explaining our thirty-minute policy to a new patron. She broke off mid-sentence and looked up towards the 900s, nostrils flared. Then, with an expression halfway between accusation and disbelief, she turned to look at me.

I met her eyes—and it isn't easy to meet Agnes's eyes when she's angry, believe me—and smiled.

When they drag me before the mistresses and burn my card and demand to know, in tones of mournful recrimination, how I could have abandoned the vows of our order, I'll say: *Hey, you abandoned them first, ladies. Somewhere along the line, you forgot our first and purest purpose: to give patrons the books they need most. And oh, how they need. How they will always need.*

I wondered, with a kind of detached trepidation, how rogue librarians spent their time, and whether they had clubs or societies, and what it was like to encounter feral stories untamed by narrative and unbound by books. And then I wondered where our Books came from in the first place, and who wrote them.

THERE WAS A sudden, imperceptible rushing, as if a wild wind had whipped through the stacks without disturbing a single page. Several people looked up uneasily from their screens.

A Witch's Guide to Escape lay abandoned on the carpet, open to a map of some foreign fey country drawn in sepia ink. A red backpack sat beside it.

THE STAFF IN THE STONE
Garth Nix

Garth Nix (www.garthnix.com) was born in 1963 in Melbourne, Australia. A full-time writer since 2001, he has worked as a literary agent, marketing consultant, book editor, book publicist, book sales representative, bookseller, and as a part-time soldier in the Australian Army Reserve. His books include the award-winning young adult fantasy novels *Sabriel, Lirael Abhorsen, Clariel* and *Goldenhand*; the dystopian novel *Shade's Children*; the space opera *A Confusion of Princes*; and a Regency romance with magic, *Newt's Emerald*. His fantasy novels for children include *The Ragwitch*; the six books of *The Seventh Tower* sequence; The Keys to the Kingdom series; *Frogkisser!*; the Troubletwisters series, *Spirit Animals: Blood Ties*, and *Have Sword, Will Travel* (with Sean Williams). Garth's most recent book is *Let Sleeping Dragons Lie* (with Sean Williams) and coming up is a major new fantasy novel. He lives in a Sydney beach suburb with his wife and two children.

THE LOW, DRY stone walls that delineated the three angled commons belonging to the villages of Gamel, Thrake, and Seyam met at an ancient obelisk known to everyone simply as "the Corner Post." Feuds between villagers would be settled at the Corner Post, by wrestling and challenges of skill, or the more serious in a formal conclave of elders from all three villages. Twice in the last hundred years the obelisk had been the site of full-scale battle between Gamel and Thrake against Seyam, and then Gamel and Seyam against Thrake.

Every spring, the ploughs would stop well short of the Corner Post, for fear of disturbing the bones of some bygone relative or enemy. In consequence, a small copse of undistinguished trees and shrubs grew around the obelisk, dominated by a single, tall rowan tree, often remarked on, for there were no other rowans for leagues around, and no one living knew how it had come to be planted there.

Small children played under the rowan in the early morning, evading their chores, and lovers met there for trysts in the early evening. No one went near stone and copse by dead of night, because of the bones, and the stories that were told of what might rise there, or perhaps be drawn there, come midnight.

So it was three children under five who discovered a curious change in the stone, just after the sun had risen high enough to glance off the bronze ferrule on the foot of a staff, and there was sufficient light to see that the rest of the dark bog-oak length was impossibly embedded in the stone.

The visible end of the staff was high above the reach of the tallest child, which was just as well, for they were too young to be properly afraid of such a thing. In fact, after attempting to stand on each other's shoulders in a vain effort to reach it, they forgot all about the staff until the very youngest was bringing water to the sweating harvest-time reapers working toward the narrowest point of the Thrake common. Seeing the Corner Post again, the little girl wondered aloud why there was a big black stick stuck in it, like a skewer through a cooking rabbit.

Her father went to look, and came back even sweatier and more out of breath than he had been from his work. The word spread quickly from field to barn to village, and no more than an hour later, made its way to the cool, green-lit forest home of the nearest approximation to a wizard for fifty leagues or more, since the woman purported to be one in the nearest town of Sandrem had been unmasked as a charlatan several months before.

The forest house had once been a minor royal hunting lodge, in the time of the kings and queens, before the plague and the rise of the Grand Mayors. Octagonal in shape, it was built around the bole of one of the giant redwoods, some twenty feet above the forest floor. A broad stair had led up to it once, but long ago that had fallen or been intentionally destroyed, its remnants now a tumulus of rotten timber, overgrown with ferns and fungus. A ladder, easily drawn up in case of peril, had replaced it.

The current inhabitant of the lodge was hanging pheasants in his cool room, an oak-shingled hut built between the roots of a neighboring giant redwood some sixty paces from the house. He felt the news arriving before he heard those bringing it, or at least he sensed there were excited people coming down the forest path. Usually this meant somebody was badly hurt and needed his aid, so he strung up the last three pheasants very swiftly and climbed out, leaving the birds swinging on their hooks. He did pause to close and slide the great bolt across the door, for it was not only mere foxes that fancied hanging game. The Rannachin loved pheasant, and they could open doors that weren't secured with cold iron.

The pheasant-hanger's name was Colrean, or at least it was now. He was under thirty years old, but only just, and looked older, because he had spent the last decade mostly at sea, and then more recently in the forest and the fields, under the sky. Sun, salt water, and wind had worked to make his face more interesting. He had a lean, competent look about him, his eyes were dark and quick, and he walked with a noticeable limp, legacy of some unexplained wound or injury.

Colrean had come to the lodge some twenty months before, in midwinter, riding one mule and followed by two others, all of them heavily laden. Tying these up at the old iron hitching post near the ladder, he had by means unknown dispossessed the Rannachin, who had thought to make the lodge a cozy winter lair. Then he had nailed a parchment with a great lead seal to one of the more outstanding roots of the great tree. According to those few folk who could read among the villagers, this was a deed from the Grand Mayor of Pran, granting the new arrival the lodge; hunting rights in the forest and certain other perquisites relating to tolls on the forest road; tithes on fishing or eel-trapping in the river Undrana that passed nearby; a threepenny fee for cattle watering at the wide Undrana ford; and other minor items of tallage.

He had never attempted to enforce any of these imposts, which was fortunate, given that the people of the three villages were by no means convinced that Pran had any authority whatsoever in their purlieu, no matter what the last queen of Pranallis and her vassal the long-gone baron of Gamel, Thrake and Seyam might held to be their own.

Colrean had shown his wisdom in matters of friendly relations with the local inhabitants very early, by giving each of the three villages one of his mules within days of his arrival, limping along through snow and ice to do so. Though he carried no staff nor wore a sorcerer's ring, he was at once suspected of being some kind of magic-worker, for he spoke to the mules and they obeyed, and the village dogs didn't bark and slather at his approach, but came and bent their heads before him, and wagged their tails and offered their bellies to be scratched. Which he did, indicating kindness as well as magic.

The villagers tried to find out exactly what kind of magic-worker he was, but he would not speak of it. They first knew he definitely was one when Fingal the Miller's hand was crushed in his own stone, and Colrean came unbidden to cut away the dangling fingers and then, with a cold flame conjured in his own hands, cauterized the wound, so that no blood sickness came. Fingal Seven Fingers was only the first of Colrean's patients, and he even deigned to help the midwives at difficult birthings, which the villagers knew marked him as no wizard. Wizards were grand beings, and lived in the cities, and were not to be found at village birthings.

The news-bearers who came running to be first to tell Colrean about the staff were Sommie and Heln. They were frequent visitors, inseparable friends, serious-minded, both eleven years old. Sommie was the seventh daughter of the midwife of Gamel and her weaver husband; Heln was the fifth son of the innkeepers of the only inn for leagues, the Silver Gull at the Seyam crossroad. Colrean knew them well, for once a week he taught children (and some grown folk) who wished to learn their letters, taking slates and hornbook to each village meeting hall in turn. Sommie and Heln were among his keenest pupils, following him from village to village and always pestering him for extra classes or books they might borrow.

"There's a stick stuck in the Corner Post!" shouted Sommie when she was still a good dozen yards away.

"Not just a stick!" cried out Heln breathlessly, skidding to a stop in the leaf mulch of the forest path. "A staff! Like a scythe handle, only it's dark wood and has a metal bit on the end."

Colrean stopped in midstep, as always a little clumsily, and lifted his head, sniffing at the breeze. The children watched as he slowly turned about, nose twitching. When he completed his circle, he looked down at the two dirty, excited faces staring up at him.

"A staff in the stone, you say? And you've seen it yourselves?"

"Yes, of course! We looked and then came straight here. Why are you sniffing?"

"You're not playing some trick on me?" asked Colrean. He had sensed nothing on the air, no magic stirring. The Corner Post was less than half a league away, and he felt sure he would have felt something...

"No! It's there! This morning, from nowhere. The little ones saw it. Why were you sniffing?"

"Oh, just smelling what scents are on the air," said Colrean absently. "I'd better have a look. Has anyone touched this staff?"

"No! Old Haxon said no one was to go near, and you were to be fetched, I mean asked to come. Ma's coming to tell you, but we ran ahead."

Ma was Sommie's mother, the midwife Wendrel. She had some small magic herself, combined with considerable herb-lore and a little book-learning. Knowing more about such things than the younger folk, she could barely conceal her fear as she puffed up after the children.

"It is a wizard's staff," she panted out, after a bare nod of greeting. "And it is deep in the stone."

"But there is no wizard about?" asked Colrean. He hesitated for a moment, then added, "No new tree nearby, strangely full-grown? A stray horse of odd hue? A stranger in the village?"

"No tree, no stray, no stranger," said Wendrel. "Just the staff in the stone. Will you come?"

"Yes," said Colrean.

"Can we come too?" asked Sommie, her question echoed by Heln.

Colrean looked up at the sky, watching the clouds, judging how much daylight remained. He thought about the phase of the moon, which was waning gibbous, and which stars would be in the ascendant that night, influencing the world below. There was nothing of obvious alarm in the heavens, no harbinger of doom.

"It should be safe enough, at least until sunset," he said slowly. He looked at Wendrel. "But there is danger. As Frossel said:

A wizard without a staff
may still be a wizard
A staff without a wizard
is a void
Waiting to be filled."

"Who's?" asked Heln.

"Frossel?" finished Sommie.

"Frossel was a wizard, chronicler, and poet," answered Colrean. He started walking, the slower pace forced by his limp easily matched by Wendrel at his side, the children ranging faster across and behind him on the path, like dogs on a tricky scent who nevertheless do not wish to go far from their master. "I might lend you one of his books. He wrote a lot. Go on, I want to talk to Wendrel."

The children nodded together and bounded ahead.

"What does 'a void waiting to be filled' mean?" asked Wendrel quietly.

"A wizard's staff, lost or abandoned by a wizard, will attract many things, many of them not of our sunlit, mortal realm," said Colrean.

"Rannachin?" asked Wendrel.

"Yes, but worse things too," said Colrean. "Far worse. And the staff—if it is a wizard's staff—will call magic workers of all kinds, even from very far away. Though I have some hope the stone will quiet it. I suppose that's why whoever put it there did so, trying to keep it hidden."

"The stone will hide it? Our Corner Post?"

Colrean looked aside at her as he strode on with his curious, lumbering gait. A brief look of puzzlement passed over his face like a cloud whisking across the sun.

"You do not know the nature of your stone?"

"I know it's very old," replied Wendrel, with a shrug. "But the powers I have are to do with people, and living things, not ancient lumps of rock or the like. The Corner Post has always seemed simply a stone to me. Though there is that odd rowan that keeps the stone company... sometimes I have felt as if it were watching me, that it is more than a simple tree..."

"It is," said Colrean. "Though I do not know its nature either. All such mysteries are best left alone, save a pressing need to do otherwise. As for the Corner Post... there is definitely a power within it, though it sleeps, and sleeps deeply. I suspect it is one of the ancient walking stones, which many ages ago came down from the far mountains and took root here to fulfil some compact long forgotten. Those stone warriors served the Old Ones, the folk of the air, so long vanished but never entirely gone."

Wendrel shivered. When she was a young apprentice, a birthing had gone terribly wrong. At the moment both infant and mother died, she had felt a sudden cold and unnerving presence, something drawn to the two deaths. The midwife who was her mentor quickly said this was one of the Old Ones, and that if they remained still and did not speak, no harm would come to them. Yet to warn Wendrel, the older midwife had spoken. She was at once struck dumb, and it was a twelvemonth before she regained the use of her voice at all, and she who had one of the sweetest voices in the three villages could never again carry a tune.

"Even the most powerful wizards do not readily meddle with such stones," continued Colrean. "I am surprised... no... I am astonished that the stone would allow anything to pierce it, let alone a wizard's staff."

"Allow?" asked Wendrel.

"On its own ground, I think that stone could stand against the Grand Wizard herself," replied Colrean. "And it must be allied to, or at least have permitted the rowan to grow... and that tree isn't much younger than the stone! It's older than any of the trees in the forest, even the giant redwoods or Grand's Oak, over by the broad water. Ordinary rowans do not live so long."

Wendrel asked no more questions, and was silent, her brow furrowed in thought. They walked on, crossing one of the rivulets that fed the Undrana. Colrean's oddly heavy, nailed boots boomed on the old log bridge, accompanied by the soft patter of Wendrel's sandals and the almost imperceptible scuffing of the children's bare feet.

They left the forest fringe soon after, to follow the well-trodden path along Gamel common's western boundary wall. The villagers were back at their reaping, for the harvest could not wait for anything save obvious, immediate threat. Sheafs of barley dotted the common, waiting for the older children to pick them up. But there was a noticeable lack of activity toward the top of the common, where the Corner Post loomed with its attendant rowan, the lesser trees and shrubs about it like beggars waiting for bounty from a king and queen.

"You had best leave me, and come no closer," Colrean warned Wendrel and the children, as they drew near the copse. He could feel the staff's presence now. It was making his thumbs prick and shiver as if a horde of minute insects stuck their prongs in his flesh, and there was a cold, wet draft caressing his bare neck, though no wind ruffled the barley stalks.

He looked up again at the sun, and the few tufts of scattered cloud dotted across the great stretch of blue sky—clouds that dissipated even as he watched.

"I think it will be safe enough till dusk. But you need to warn everyone to stay away from the Corner Post. They must be inside well before full night. The livestock too. Salt thresholds and windowsills. Stoke the hearthfires up and keep cold iron close."

"What's going—"

"To happen?"

"Perhaps nothing," said Colrean, attempting a smile to reassure the children. They were not reassured, for the smile was unlike any expression Colrean had made in their sight before, and were they asked what he tried to convey, would have said he was in pain. "The staff in the stone may call... creatures... who are dangerous. I will stay here. If anything comes, I will make sure it can do no harm. Now go!"

The children, well versed in obeying their elders, skipped off at once. But Wendrel lingered, concern on her face. As she had said, her powers lay with the living, most particularly attending upon births and deaths. She was thus well acquainted with fear, and the small indications of it upon an otherwise well-composed face.

"Do you have such power, to assure no harm will come to us?" she asked.

Colrean shook his head. "But I may be able to divert the course of whatever does come for the staff. Delay acts of small malevolence, and I hope give warning of anything worse."

"Why would you do this for us?" asked Wendrel. "To heal the hurt from a millstone, to aid in a birthing—these things do not risk your life. But surely you do now."

Colrean half shrugged, as if he did not know how to answer.

"This is my homeplace now," he said. "I have grown fond of some... many of the people. I have found peace here."

"A peace soon to be disturbed, if you are right," said Wendrel. "Almost, you remind me of the wizards of the old tales, who would appear without word on the eve of some storm or terror, come to defend the common folk. Only to leave when the danger has passed, as unheralded as they came, without thanks or payment."

"Wizards are only found in the cities now, bound by gold and oaths to serve the Mayors," said Colrean. "And I have been here two winters already. I hope this acquits me of being thought some bird of ill omen. Besides, I certainly do not wish to leave. Or seek payment."

Wendrel did not say anything for a moment, and silence fell between them. Colrean turned his head to glance at the Corner Post. But his body remained still, and he did not otherwise move, or take his leave, seemingly caught in indecision on the moment of commitment to a likely short-lived future.

In the distance, one of the reapers nicked herself with her sickle, and swore. Her harsh words brought Colrean back into the present. He blinked and looked at the midwife, who returned his gaze with a concern he recognized from seeing her with patients.

"I will bring you one of Rhun's second-best blankets, a waterskin, and food. Is there aught else you will need?"

Rhun was Wendrel's husband, save his wife the youngest of the elders of Gamel. He was barely old enough to bear the title without ridicule, having gained his position not from mere seniority, or as in Wendrel's case her wisdom, but in recognition of him being the best weaver in the three villages, and in fact for many leagues around. Even Rhun's second-best blankets were thicker, heavier, far more water repellent and more attractive than the city-bought ones Colrean had back in his lodge.

"All will be welcome, and a blanket perhaps most of all. It will be clear and cool tonight, and I must stay until the dawn. But be sure you come and go before nightfall."

"There is time enough," said Wendrel.

"Do not approach the stone," added Colrean. "Leave everything by the wall here; I will fetch it."

"As you will," said Wendrel. "I hope... I hope you are wrong about the staff, and nothing will come."

"I hope so too," said Colrean. But he knew he was not wrong. Whether he had become more accustomed to it, or the stone's grip on the staff was loosening as the day faded, he was much more aware of the silent call of magic emanating from whatever was in the Corner Post. If the children had not come to him, he would still have been drawn here, by sunset at the latest. And there were creatures far more sensitive to magic than he was, more sensitive than any mortal. They would come, once the sun was down.

Unless a wizard claimed the staff.

That would be another problem, perhaps no less dangerous than the creatures. For despite what he had said to Wendrel, not all wizards were bound to the Mayors by oaths and gold. There were some who considered themselves above the concerns of ordinary folk, and only sought to please themselves. They were kept in check by what they called the tame wizards of the cities, but that was in the cities.

Not out here.

Here there was only Colrean.

Who realized he had been woolgathering again, delaying the inevitable. Wendrel was already hurrying after the children, and he could hear them excitedly calling out his warnings to the harvesters, the repetition of "salt your windowsills" clear.

Colrean walked over to the Corner Post, pausing by the rowan to bend his head respectfully, as if the tree might bar his way or take umbrage at his presence. But the rowan gave no indication it was anything other than a normal tree, leaves and branches still in the quiet air. Colrean would have welcomed a breeze, particularly a brisk southerly, for that wind was antithetical to some of the creatures that might come in the night. But there was no wind, and it seemed little chance of one.

Colrean passed by the rowan and cautiously approached the Corner Post, each of his six clumsy steps slower and shorter than the last, till he shuffled as close as he dared go, almost but not quite in touching distance.

There was a staff in the stone.

Colrean didn't really need to look at it to know it was indeed a wizard's staff. But he cautiously examined the exposed length that projected from the ancient stone, wondering why the staff was placed so high. Indeed, either an extraordinarily tall wizard had plunged it into the stone, or they had brought a ladder, which seemed unlikely. Even if so, why bother to put it out of easy reach?

This was not the only puzzle. Only three or four inches of the dark bog-oak beyond the bronze ferrule on the foot of the staff was exposed, and there were no obvious runes or inscriptions that might have helped him identify the staff's provenance. All he could tell from sight and his sense of the unseen was that this staff was very old, and very powerful.

Colrean could tell it was not a single staff at all, but a composite of many. Staves were made by wizards to store more power than they could hold in their own fragile bodies or in other tools of the art, and particularly powerful staves were made by a process of accretion, combining a new staff with the old.

But as making a wizard's staff was a time-consuming and potentially dangerous process, there were renegades who would simply take or steal the staves of weaker or unsuspecting wizards, using whatever means necessary— including such things as poison and assassination. Then they would combine the stolen staff with their own, growing more powerful in the process, and thus be able to take even more staves from other wizards.

"Better and better," muttered Colrean to himself, meaning quite the opposite. For a moment he contemplated touching the end of the staff, for that would reveal to him from whence it came, and might even give him the name of the wizard who had put it here. Though Colrean could not think why a wizard would want to put their own staff in such a place, or indeed, why a wizard would put someone else's staff there.

Unless it was a trap or a lure of some sort... but he could sense no other magic-worker nearby, nor see anything that might be one in another shape. There were no new trees, no odd horse, no peculiarly large raven watching from the stone wall...

Colrean also contemplated placing his hand upon the Corner Post itself and beseeching it to inform him what it knew of the matter. But it was not a serious thought, and was immediately dismissed. He knew more about such stones than he had revealed to Wendrel. Most were long dead—or their animating force dissipated—but the few who retained their power were typically averse to interaction with any but the most innocent of mortal folk, and were best left very much alone.

Though, in this case, the stone must have allowed the staff to be placed where it was, else there would have been a dead wizard among the barley, pieces of broken staff strewn about the commons, fires burning, people screaming, and no need for anyone to summon him from the forest.

It was all a great puzzle.

Colrean sighed and found a place to sit some twenty paces from the Corner Post and the rowan, where the ground rose a little, giving him a longer view.

He sat with his back against the Gamel-Thrake border wall and settled into the reverie magic workers called dwelm, calling forth power he had stored over time in various items about his person, drawing it either into himself or reapportioning it among his objects of power.

This was a key part of any magic worker's preparations, for there were things that stored magic well but were slow to give it up and objects that released power swiftly, but could not hold it for any length of time; or some combination thereof that was necessarily a compromise. The first were typically made of stone, petrified wood, amber, and/or gold, sometimes rubies or emeralds; and the latter silver or bronze with moonstones and diamonds or any of the paler gems, and younger wood or porcelain.

A properly prepared staff of ancient bog-oak, shod in bronze and tipped with iron, was unrivaled as a magical instrument, in that it could store power very well and release it reasonably quickly. There was a good reason every wizard had a staff. Though a wand of well-aged willow, with bands of gold and silver, could serve near as well, if there was some reason to dissemble and appear to be some other kind of magic-worker.

But Colrean had neither staff nor wand, nor, it seemed even a mere sorcerer's ring. His fingers, still somewhat stained with pheasant blood, were bare.

The sun had begun to set by the time he emerged from the dwelm trance. Wendrel had been; there was a basket sitting on the wall some distance away. He went to fetch it, taking it back to his chosen position where he could keep watch over Corner Post, rowan, and most of the three commons, though one area was obscured by the copse.

As expected, it began to grow cool almost immediately after the sun went down. Colrean unfolded the blanket and arranged it over his shoulders. Wendrel had provided bread, cheese, and sausage, and he made a quick meal of this and drank some water, while he watched the moon begin its rise and the stars come out. It was a very bright night, with the sky clear. Several small shooting stars sped by near the horizon, watched carefully by Colrean in case they grew brighter, or shone red, as true portents would. But they seemed to be nothing out of the ordinary. Such tiny fading sparks of brilliance could be seen on any clear night out here.

Colrean dozed a little then, rather uncomfortably, trusting to his otherworldly senses to jolt him awake should something happen. But when he did wake, it was from the simple discomfort of his bladder. Stretching to ease the kinks of dozing against the stone wall, he limped some distance away to urinate, not wishing to offer any disrespect to the Corner Post.

Coming back, he noticed it had suddenly grown quiet. His own footfalls were the only sound, where even a few moments before he had heard crickets sawing at their music; night-birds calling; the shrill shriek of a shrew caught by an owl; the muffled crackle and thump of hares disporting nearby in the barley stubble. All were silent now, and the air was still.

Colrean opened his eyes wide, calling power into his dormant mage-sight. The world grew brighter, moon- and starlight intensified. Shadows lengthened from stone and tree... and sprang out from a dozen previously unseen creatures that had made their characteristically stealthy way from the forest and across the common, and were now only nine or ten yards from the copse. Even through a mage's eyes their shadows were easier to see than themselves, but in essence they were somewhat like foxes and somewhat like human folk, walking upright on their hind legs, and possessing tool-using hands, but they also had tall brushes, russet fur, cunning fox-masked faces, and sensitive, sticking-up ears.

Those ears twitched in unison as Colrean spoke.

"How now, my lords and ladies! What seek the Rannachin at the Corner Post?"

The twelve spread out in a line without any obvious command or discussion, and there was the glitter of obsidian blades in their paw-hands, the shine of teeth bared in long snouts.

"I think not," said Colrean. He mumbled something, cupped one hand and drew power. A blue flame burst from his palm, the air roaring as the fire grew taller than the man. "You recall the stench of singed fox fur well, I think?"

Again there were no visible signs of debate, but as one the Rannachin's weapons were put away, the jaws closed, and the fox-people turned and slid away into the night, as unobtrusively as they had come.

Colrean watched them for some time, keeping the flamecast ready, as it was quite possible they would turn back and try to rush him. But they did not. Quite possibly in the short time they had spent near the Corner Post they had already deduced the staff was too powerful for them to steal, or dared not risk the displeasure of the stone. It was even possible they thought Colrean too great a foe, though in the past he had never had to deal with more than three or four Rannachin at once.

He let the fire die when they were out of sight, and allowed the power to ebb from his eyes as well. He had to carefully husband his strength, particularly that drawn from his own blood and bone. There would doubtless be worse than Rannachin to come that night. He could sense the staff calling ever more clearly and strongly in the clear, cool night. It would bring others.

Colrean ate a little more bread, but did not sit down again. Instead he limped about the edge of the copse, and once again paid his respects to the ancient rowan. This time he not only bent his head, but slowly went down on one knee, as he might to a Grand Mayor or the Great Wizard. He stayed there for some time, listening and thinking, comforted that the world around was full of small sounds again, and the sky remained clear, the stars and moon bright—and there was no sudden shower of bloodred sparks in the heavens above.

The rowan gave no sign it was aware of his obeisance, neither during his uncomfortable kneeling nor when Colrean pushed himself up and wandered off again, this time returning to his watching spot. Feeling uneasy, he carefully climbed up on the wall for a better view. This was a chancy maneuver given whatever was wrong with his leg, and was made no easier by the age and construction of the wall. Though the stones were cunningly set together, no mortar held them in place. Neither he nor the wall fell, but Colrean was not comforted by what he saw.

There was a fog rolling across the Seyam common, as if a single dense cloud had somehow fallen from above, though the sky was clear and there was no fog anywhere else.

Even as he saw this sudden, inexplicable mist, Colrean's otherworldly senses twitched, and he felt a spasm of intense fear grab his guts and grip him about the lungs. He fought off the sudden, sensible urge to flee and instead took a quick, shuddering breath. Climbing down from the wall, he hurried as fast he could, almost hopping back to the rowan. Under its branches, he quickly took out one of his few objects of power, a knife of whalebone with a solid silver hilt that had been hidden under his jerkin. Calling on the power stored in this, he drew a circle about himself in the earth, mumbling memory-hooks, the words magic-workers used to safely recall exactly how the power must be called and used, words that the uneducated thought of as a spells.

When it was done, the whalebone blade blew into dust like a kicked puffball, and the silver hilt crumbled in Colrean's hand, as if had been buried in a tomb for a thousand years and could not stand the corrosive effect of open air. He had drawn every last scrap of power stored in the weapon, all at once, and so it could never be used again, never refilled. Two years to make and fill it to the brim with power, all gone in a matter of minutes, a treasure spent.

Spent wisely, Colrean hoped. He reached into his jerkin again, fingers closing on the silver chain around his neck, making sure it was secure and that by its weight he could feel what hung suspended here.

Fog overlapped the stone walls and spread around him, encircling copse, Corner Post, and rowan, but not closing in. Colrean could still see the starlit sky directly above, but it was as if he were in a deep hole, surrounded on all sides by gray walls.

Walls of shifting, dense fog.

There was something in the whiteness. Colrean could sense it, but was grateful he couldn't see it. He knew what it must be: one of the ancient evils of thrice-burned Hîrr, the city-state still reviled and feared though a thousand years had passed since its last and utter destruction. The thing in the fog had been called many things by many different peoples. Colrean chose the most common, one that would not reveal his knowledge of any deeper mysteries.

"Grannoch! Many-in-one!" shouted Colrean. "This is not your land, this is not your time. There is nothing here for you. Begone!"

Fog swirled. Colrean caught a glimpse of something—some long limb or perhaps a tail—of ever-burning hide, like lumpy charcoal with crosshatched lines of fire. His eyes burned and tears ran as he watched it disappear once more into the roiling mist, to be replaced by the sudden emergence of a human hand, smooth-skinned and elegant, the fingers beckoning to him, summoning him from his circle. Offering him in that gesture everything he ever wanted, or might want: the most beautiful lover, the greatest power, riches beyond compare—

Colrean dug his foot into the earth, just as it begun to rise without his conscious direction, to make him take that first, fatal step out of his protective circle.

"I am not to be caught that way," said Colrean. "I say again, begone!"

The beckoning hand disappeared. The fog thickened, but Colrean could see a dim silhouette building there, a figure forming. Something twice his height, and twice as broad, and only roughly human. One arm was very long, or perhaps held a blade; he could not tell from the mere suggestion of shape in the twisty cloud.

It was a blade, of dark crystal or congealed black flame or something stranger still, a blade that erupted from the fog and struck at Colrean, so swiftly he barely saw it. He cried out and flinched as it hit, but it did not cut him in half, as it would have had he been unprotected. The circle he had made around himself stood firm, the unearthly blade rebounding from the unseen barrier with the screech of a nail drawn across an anvil, magnified a thousand times.

"A sorcerer?" whispered a voice high in the air, somewhere in that bank of fog.

A little girl's voice, clear and sweet.

"It bears no ring," answered another voice, seemingly from beneath the earth just beyond Colrean's circle.

This voice was male, and old, and crotchety.

"It has no staff," muttered yet another voice from somewhere in the fog.

A deep-voiced woman. A high-pitched man. An adolescent, the voice shifting, changing with every word.

"The circle is well wrought, and adamant," announced another male voice. "Yet, three strikes shall see it split asunder, or so I judge."

"Unless it be renewed."

"Renewed? No ring, no staff. It is mortal. Such a meager vessel; it must have spent its force."

"Why do we hold back? Strike again, strike again!"

"It smiles. It has a secret. A true wizard comes, we must not tarry."

"Strike or go, strike or—"

The blade shot out again, and once more every muscle in Colrean's body tensed, expecting sudden, awful pain and then the perhaps welcome relief of death. But again the circle held with the scream of iron, and the blade whisked back.

Before the Grannoch could strike again, Colrean hurled himself down and sideways out of the circle, breaking its protection himself even as the third strike split the air above him. Like a cockroach he scuttled away, circling behind the rowan, but the fog rolled closer, and the blade came too swiftly for him to fully escape, the very tip of it slicing the heel off Colrean's left boot and the sole beneath, leaving an agonizing, four-inch-long wound along his foot.

Stifling a sob, Colrean clutched the trunk of the rowan and drew his legs up, hands scrabbling at the chain around his neck. But before he could draw out what was hidden there, the terrible sword came out of the fog once again. Colrean had a split second to know this was the death blow. He shut his eyes and let out the scream that he had been holding back the entire time.

Three seconds later he was still screaming, but he wasn't dead, and there was no new pain to add to the white-hot burn in his foot.

Colrean opened his eyes, the scream fading in his throat. The sword hung above him, wrapped and roped and entangled in rowan branches, and more branches ran outward to grip a great, grotesque arm of smoking, chancred charcoal hide. Through the suddenly broken and dissipated fog Colrean saw the hideous misshapen body of the Grannoch, the "many-in-one." Worst of all, he saw its lumpen head, adorned with all those it had taken over centuries, dozens of mostly human faces crammed too tightly together. All eyes dull and lifeless, but the many mouths writhing, emitting cries and curses as the monster tried to free itself from the grip of the ancient rowan.

Colrean resisted the temptation to shut his eyes again, or to look away and vomit. Instead he drew out the chain, his shaking hand closing on the pendant object. But before he could use whatever he held, the Grannoch tore itself out of the grasp of the rowan with the crack of snapping branches and the rasp of shredding bark. But it did not attack again, instead staggering back, great arms reaching to fend off the rowan's whipping branches, the monster's many mouths no longer shouting or screaming but exhaling thick streams of fog as it tried to shroud itself again.

Colrean put on the ring of wreathed gold and electrum that he usually kept hidden on the chain, and called forth its power. Muttering memory-hooks, he directed his magic this way and that, lines of force reaching deep into the ground around the Grannoch. Then with one wrenching effort of will, the magic opened a great chasm in the ground, the earth breaking apart with a thunderous blare.

Now the Grannoch reached for the rowan branches, rather than trying to fend them off. But it was too slow, the opening of the ground too deep, too sudden and unexpected. The monster fell into the ravine, spouting streams of fog and curses, the rowan's branches snapping back to let it go.

Colrean called upon the last reserves in the ring and shut the chasm with a clap of his hands. The electrum wreath crumbled to dust. The gold band shivered, but remained, though it was now powerless and empty.

Even so, it was clearly a sorcerer's ring, worn on the third finger of Colrean's right hand, and the sight of it would have settled many bets in the three villages.

For a minute or two the ground groaned and rumbled beneath the sorcerer, as if the very earth might choose to spit the Grannoch out, but eventually it stilled. Colrean, his hands trembling with hurt and shock and only slowly ebbing terror, painfully stripped the boot from his left foot and inspected the wound. It was not deep, but ugly, and even as he half laughed and half sobbed at the irony that it had to be his left foot the Grannoch's blade had struck, the mage carefully summoned a fraction of the remaining power he held ready in himself. Calling a cauterizing flame to his hand, he used it to cleanse and seal the angry wound.

When he was finished, he tore the tail from his linen shirt and bound it around his foot. That done, he rested his forehead against the rowan's trunk and gave thanks in a quiet whisper. He had hoped it was an ancient guardian of the kind that reviled such things as the Grannoch, but he had not been sure.

When he lifted his forehead from the tree, the rowan's branches shivered, and a single leaf fell into his hand, a leaf more silver in the moonlight than any normal rowan's. Colrean carefully put it inside his jerkin.

"I thank the rowan," he said formally, gingerly hopping up on to his right foot. He almost fell over, and would have done if he hadn't caught himself, both hands against the rowan's trunk. "For all."

He stood there for some time, supported by the tree. Listening, letting his otherworldly senses stretch outward, fearing that the ground might burst open to reveal the Grannoch was not crushed and dead far below, as he truly hoped.

But everything seemed once again returned to the normal business of the night. There was no fog, no silence, just the soft velvet darkness lightened by moon and stars, and the usual small sounds of life and death.

After a time that felt long but he knew was well short of an hour, Colrean began to hold some hope that he might now survive until the dawn. If he made it that far, he should survive the day beyond, as he had some expectation that help would come before the next night. An oath-bound, trustworthy wizard would likely come from Ferraul or Achelliston, as both cities were within a day's hard riding. Less, using post-horses and a little magic to draw away fatigue and renew tired muscles.

He had even begun to imagine just such a wizard, when he both heard and felt the approach of something that, while it sounded rather like a horse, he knew from his mage-sense was not. Once again, the natural creatures about knew it too, and all around the owls were fleeing, the field mice diving into holes, the very crickets digging under the barley stalks, all hoping like Colrean to stay alive until the dawn.

There was nowhere for Colrean to hide, and he could not flee. Instead he drew himself up, only one hand resting against the rowan's trunk. He looked across at the stone, and the staff thrust into it. Again he wondered who had put it there, a staff of such power, one sure to draw Rannachin and things like the Grannoch, and the wizard who was coming now.

Only then did Colrean remember the Grannoch had said a true wizard was on the way.

Surely not an oath-bound wizard, though, for there had not been time for anyone to come from the closest cities. Besides, this one was riding a peggoty, a made horse, a thing given a semblance of magical life for a short period. A peggoty was fashioned from green sticks of willow, mud, and the blood of no less than seven mares. Such mounts were accordingly very expensive to make, they took a great deal of power to create and not much less to maintain, and were difficult to ride. But they were much swifter than a horse.

Making things like the peggoty was forbidden to oath-bound wizards. It was blood magic, requiring a great deal of often slow and painful killing, and its practitioners invariably ended up having no concern for any lives but their own.

Sure enough, up alongside the Thrake-Seyam wall came a strutting mount of sticks, with a cloaked and hatted figure on its back, a staff held negligently in the rider's hand. Colrean could not see the face of the wizard, shadowed under the brim of the hat, but he already had an inkling of the rider's identity just from the silhouette and seat. He knew that rider.

She—it had to be she, if he was right—stopped the peggoty a little ways off, and dismounted on to the stone wall. Unlike Colrean, she did so with nimble grace, and there was no danger she would fall or stones dislodge. Her hand waved, moonlight catching several sorcerer's rings upon her fingers, not a meager single ring as Colrean had possessed. With that wave, the peggoty collapsed into its component parts, its work done.

Colrean caught a whiff of the horrible charnel stench of decaying blood and tried not to breathe it in.

He still couldn't see the wizard's face, but he was sure now. He did indeed know every movement of her slender body, the shape of those elegant hands.

"It's been a long time, Naramala," said Colrean, his voice loud in the silent night.

The wizard tilted her head back, perhaps in surprise at hearing his voice, though probably not. He could see her face clearly now. Beautiful Naramala, the woman he had once thought sure to be the great love of his life.

"Coltreen," she said, her voice musical and lovely, even more lovely than her face and body. It was her voice he had fallen in love with first, hearing her unseen in the university library, undeterred by the shushing and hushing of the proctors.

"I am called Colrean now," he said quietly. "The Islanders cannot pronounce hard t's. It seemed easier to let it go."

"The Islanders?" asked Naramala. "Is that where you went? But then why are you here now, so far from the Cold Sea?"

She walked along the wall now, toward copse and rowan and Corner Post. And Colrean. She held the staff like a rope-walker, across her body, as if for balance, though he knew she had no need to do so.

"I live nearby, these two years past," said Colrean, gesturing with his right hand, the moonlight catching on his own ring. "I had enough of the sea, the cold."

"And you made your ring, after all," said Naramala. She stopped several feet short of the farthest-reaching branches of the rowan and stepped lightly down from the wall, bringing her staff vertical. "I did wonder what had become of you. And why you left so abruptly, without a word. Indeed, I was quite hurt."

"I saw you with Alris," said Colrean.

Naramala laughed, an easy, carefree laugh. Even now, knowing what he knew, Colrean felt an ache when he heard it. Such an easy laugh, so warm and inclusive, with her eyes widening that little bit and her mouth twitched just so—

"Oh, we were students then and carefree! How was I to know you would be so jealous of some simple pleasure? Or was it because she was a woman? So rustic, Coltreen! I suppose these barley fields suit you better than the streets of Pran."

"It wasn't jealousy, though I will admit to that. I saw you kill her," said Colrean flatly. "Strangled with her own scarf. And you took her bracelets, the proof that won her the first place."

Naramala didn't answer for a moment, then she laughed again. A little laugh, very different in tone. One of cold amusement, not for sharing, and her eyes became colder still.

"How ever did you see that?"

"There was a cat," said Colrean. "I was practicing watching through its eyes. It chanced to alight on your windowsill, and... I saw."

"Only four of us were to be allowed to try for our sorcerer's rings that year," said Naramala conversationally. "Alris might have got my place. Though your leaving made it easier still. Were you afraid I would kill you, too?"

"No," replied Colrean. "I was afraid I might kill you. I couldn't bear... everything, I suppose. The disillusionment, the despair. I decided to go as far away as possible. I was young, rash, and judgmental. Of myself, more than anything. How could I have ever loved a murderer?"

"I thought true love would transcend mere murder," said Naramala. She looked up at the rowan's branches, many of them now leafless, the bark shredded from its combat with the Grannoch. Giving the tree a wide berth, she circled around toward the stone, tapping the ground with her staff as she walked, her gaze never quite leaving Colrean. "If you ever truly loved me, you would understand why I had to kill Alris. Wizards are not to be judged as normal people, Colrean. If you had stayed to make your staff, you would understand this."

"So you are beyond me, and my judging?" asked Colrean. "Or that of anyone, save other wizards?"

"I am beyond their judgment too," answered Naramala. "Or I will be, once I take the staff in that stone for myself."

"You are not oath-bound?" asked Colrean, though he already knew the answer from the mere existence of the peggoty. "How so?"

Naramala smiled. "Let us say I crossed my fingers," she said. "I found a way to loose the coils. The oath could not hold me, not beyond the passing of a dozen moons. I pretended it did, of course. The old fools have no idea."

Colrean lifted his eyebrows to show his amazement and shuffled around the rowan a little as Naramala edged closer to the stone.

"Are you going to try and stop me, Coltreen?" asked Naramala. "Indeed, I am puzzled why you are here at all. Sorcerer you may be, but you could no more draw that staff than you could stand against me."

"That is as may be," said Colreen. "But you will not take that staff. Nor could the Grannoch who came before you."

Naramala tilted her head slightly, those beautiful pale-hazel eyes weighing up Colrean. He knew she was taking stock of how he leaned upon the tree, his right foot planted too heavily, knee at an odd angle, his left foot drawn up to try and soften the pain of his wounded sole. The single gold band upon his finger, that doubtless she suspected no longer held any reserve of magic. The lack of a staff, and no other obvious articles of magic, no sword or knife or wand. All in all, he must look a posturing fool to deny the wizard Naramala, in all her majesty and power.

"A Grannoch? I wondered what strange corpse was immured below. But any power you did have must have been spent to slay such a thing. I hazard you are empty now, of all but words."

"I am not," said Colrean. "I make no more warnings."

"I would heed none from such as you," said Naramala, and raised her staff.

She muttered no memory-hooks, choosing a simple blast of pure magic that would have thrown Colrean to the ground, doubtless breaking many bones. But he concentrated magic of his own from some unseen source in his clenched fist, raising it against her spell. Naramala's blow broke upon it like a wave on a tall rock, all force diverted about Colrean, dissipating into nothing.

"I wasn't going to kill you," said Naramala. "But you have annoyed me now."

She spoke memory-hooks, her staff raised high. Magic coalesced around the silver-chased tip of the staff, becoming visible as luminous trails that swirled and spun to become a globe of sick yellow light, which with a flick of her arm, Naramala send drifting toward Colrean's head.

He knew what it was: a standard of wizard's duels, though few could cast it so well or so swiftly. The Asphyxiation of Lygar, an impenetrable globe that would settle on his shoulders and constrict, denying him breath or crushing his skull, death coming swiftly either way.

Colrean drew yet more power into his fist, babbling memory-hooks himself, each word reminding him how the magic must be shaped to form a specific spell, this one a counterspell of considerable strength.

A wizard's spell.

The globe began to lower over his head, but Colrean thrust his hand within it and opened his fingers. There was a flash of brilliant light, a shower of small sparks that died even as they fell to the earth, and the globe was no more.

"How—"

Naramala did not finish her question, but immediately began to mutter again, building another spell. Colrean watched her intently, trying to read her lips, to work out which memory-hooks she was using in order to anticipate her casting. A few seconds after she started, he began as well, calling power as he sketched an outline in front of himself in the air. Smoke trailed from his fingers, lines of lurid too-white smoke that he drew across and up and down, weaving the smoke together to make a solid shield.

Colrean finished a scant second before Naramala unleashed an incinerating bolt of power from her staff, of such strength it blew his shield of smoke apart and struck him full on the chest, flames licking over his entire body. But the shield had almost worked, for the flames died even as they struck. Though blackened and shocked, Colrean was hardly burned.

Naramala shrieked in frustration as she saw he still lived, though he had fallen to one knee and was blinking away soot. Raising her staff, she ran forward, clearly intent on delivering a killing blow of both magical and physical force—a favored tactic of the most brutal wizards when their opponents were temporarily stunned.

Colrean raised his hand and called more magic into it, but he was dazed and could not shape it, could not get his ashen tongue to utter a memory-hook, and then Naramala was in front of him, her staff blazing with power, and she raised herself up and—

The rowan struck first. Two branches wound around the staff and plucked it from her grasp, even as another forked branch closed around the wizard's neck. Lifting her high, yet another branch secured her legs, and then, just as a farmer might kill a chicken, the rowan broke Naramala's neck and threw her down upon the ground.

The wizard's arms twitched. Her heels drummed, and a terrible inhuman clicking sound emanated from her throat. Then she was still.

Colrean flinched as the rowan threw the wizard's staff down next to her body. Coughing up soot, he groaned and leaned back against the tree, stretching out his legs. The wound in his left foot had opened again, the bandage blown off. His right boot had black-rimmed burn holes and scorch marks all over it, as did his breeches, and through the holes he could see the sheen of his narwhal-horn peg leg, and the shine of the gold bands that wound around the horn from tip to base.

The Islanders also had wizards, but they did not carry their staves openly.

Colrean looked across at Naramala's body and then over at the Corner Post, looming dark against the lighter sky. The bronze foot of the staff high up seemed to wink in the starlight. Colrean stared at it and became certain of something he had begun to suspect.

"Come out!" called Colrean, his voice unsteady. There were tears in his eyes, tears running down his cheeks, making trails through the layer of soot. They were for Naramala, as he had once thought she was, and for his younger, foolish self, and because he was hurt and weakened, and the night was still not done.

"Come out!"

The staff in the stone shifted against the backdrop of stars, slanting down.

As it moved, a line of light sprang up behind it, so bright that Colrean had to duck his head, put his chin against his chest and cover his face with his forearm. Even shielded so, and with his eyes tightly shut, it was almost unbearably bright.

The light ebbed. Colrean risked a glimpse, raising his arm a little. There was a figure stepping down from the Corner Post—from inside the Corner Post—lit from behind by a softer light, as if deep within the stone there was sunshine. The silhouette was almost a caricature of a wizard, with the pointed, broad-brimmed hat, the trailing sleeves, the staff as tall as its bearer.

"Verashe," said Colrean, naming the wizard as she came toward him, now rounded and real under the moon and stars, not a shadowed shape backlit by the strange illumination from the stone, a light that was already fading. "Grand Wizard."

"Coltreen," said the wizard mildly. She was very old, but not stooped. Still taller than Colrean, straight-backed and imposing. Her face was lined and thin, but her green eyes sharp as ever. Her long hair, once red, was pale with time and tied back under her hat, save for one slight wisp, which was escaping above her left ear. "Or Colrean, as I believe you call yourself now."

She bowed her head to the rowan as Colrean had done, if not so deeply. A greeting of equals, or those long familiar.

"So you set your snare, and have caught two unbound wizards," said Colrean bitterly. He lifted himself against the trunk of the rowan, trying to sit more upright, and winced as new pains made themselves felt.

"I did not even know you were in these parts," replied Verashe. "Not until I came here, at least, and by then matters were already in train."

"So the lure was for Naramala alone?" asked Colrean wearily. "Did you expect the Grannoch too?"

"I was not sure what might come," answered the Grand Wizard. She knelt down at Colrean's side and ran her fingers over the sole of his foot, once again stemming the flow of blood with magic and doing something else that vanquished the pain. A curious thing to do for a condemned man, thought Colrean, and a small spark of hope grew inside him.

"I did try to ensure Naramala would be foremost of the wizards, since it was well past time her ambitions should be thwarted."

"You knew she had evaded the oath?"

"Of course," replied Verashe. She sighed. "Almost every class has someone like Naramala, certain of their own cleverness and destiny. And the oath, though robust, cannot hold against continued use of blood magic and human sacrifice. She killed Cateran and Lieros too, you know, and quite a number of beggars and the like—those she believed would not be readily missed. All the while thinking herself unobserved."

Colrean wiped his eyes and pretended no new tears brimmed there. Cateran and Lieros had been fellow students too. He remembered first meeting them, brimful with the joy of learning magic. They had both come to their powers unexpectedly, unbelieving they had won places at the university in Pran, foremost of the schools of wizardry.

Verashe ran her index finger from one burned hole in Colrean's breeches to another, splitting the cloth all along the leg, to completely expose the limb made of gold-banded narwhal horn. In addition to the gold, the horn was deeply etched along the whorls with scenes of ships and the sea, and set with tiny pearls and pieces of amber.

"I have only seen one such... staff... before," mused Verashe. "A wizard called Sissishuram studied with us one summer, it must be thirty years ago now. Though her staff took the place of her left arm from the elbow, and ended in the most vicious hook."

"Sissishuram was my master," said Colrean. "She remembered you, and told me I was a fool to risk coming back. Verashe will brook no unbound wizard, she said. Stay with us, we who are free upon the sea."

Verashe stood up and walked across to look down upon Naramala's body, and the staff next to it.

"How did you go within the stone?" asked Colrean. "What spell?"

Verashe didn't answer him, instead picking up Naramala's fallen staff, so she held one in each hand.

"I am overcurious for a man about to die, I suppose," said Colrean. He laughed, a short laugh that ended almost with a sob. "Stupid of me, I suppose. To want to know such a thing now."

"Are you sure you will not come back to Pran? The oath is not so terrible for someone who has no desire for power."

"It is not the oath alone," replied Colrean slowly. He looked up at the sky above, so vast with stars, the moon hanging in the corner. There were clouds drifting across from the west now, doubtless bringing rain. All the small sounds had come back, and the westerly breeze that had sprung up to bring the clouds was steadily strengthening, taking away the stench of sudden death as easily as it flung barley chaff across the field. He thought of the three villages beyond the commons to north, east, and south, with their people asleep behind barred oak doors, their windowsills salted, trusting to him to keep them safe.

"It is not the oath at all," continued Colrean. He looked up at Verashe, unsure what he could see in her face, whether it was the executioner he beheld or the messenger bringing an unexpected pardon to the very foot of the block.

"I want... I need to stay here. I cannot live in the city, any city. I do not wish to serve the Grand Mayors, I do not desire gold and servants and all that goes with such things. I want to do small magics, for ordinary folk, and be at peace. I have found... happiness... here. I will not relinquish it."

"We permit no unbound wizards in Pran, or Huyere, or the five cities, and those who defy this order end as Naramala has done," mused Verashe, apparently to herself. She paused and glanced across at Colrean. "Here, among barley fields and forest, the strictures are less... straitened... shall we say. And the rowan is a fine judge of what truly lies inside the hearts of people..."

She stopped talking again, and bowed her head to the tree again, her face now shadowed by her hat. Colrean watched her, wondering, hoping.

"So, Colrean. I have decided to let you live. But if you will not be bound by the oath, other bindings must be applied, other bounds set. You must swear by the Rowan you will abide here, to never go more than twenty leagues from the Corner Post, without leave from the Grand Wizard and the Council."

Colrean nodded stiffly, and reached inside his jerkin for the silver leaf the rowan had given him, a token of its trust. He held it in his hand and spoke.

"I swear by the Rowan, I shall abide here, and go no farther than twenty leagues from the Corner Post, without leave from the Grand Wizard and the Council."

The leaf shivered and crumbled, leaving only the delicate tracery of its veins behind, and these sank into Colrean's palm, marking the skin with russet and silver lines. If he broke this oath, the ancient rowan would know, and hold him accountable.

Colrean shivered, remembering the sounds of Naramala's death.

"Good," said Verashe. She held Naramala's staff out to him. "You will need this, I think, to help you hobble to the closest house, where I trust we can have an early breakfast."

Colrean took the staff wonderingly, and slowly used it to lever himself upright. He could feel the vestige of magic within the bog-oak and the bands of gold, but the staff's power was almost entirely spent. It would take many years to fill again.

"Naramala?" he asked, looking at the body.

"The Rannachin would also break their fast," answered Verashe, gesturing.

Colrean looked across the barley and saw the moonshadows there. He frowned, but only for a moment. He had no strength to dig a grave or build or a cairn, and in truth, it was better nothing should remain of a wizard who had practiced blood magic. The Rannachin were known to eat even bones and teeth, and they would take no scathe from any remnant magic, as a rat or other scavenger might.

"Come!" said Verashe impatiently. "I have been fasting within the stone since the last dawn, and I am too old to miss another meal!"

"We cannot go to the closest house," said Colrean. "Two wizards in Gamel, and none calling into Seyam and Thrake? Besides, they won't let us in until after dawn. I warned them not to admit anyone, and they would rightly be afraid. It is farther, but I have food and drink in my forest house."

He limped past the Grand Wizard, pausing to bow once again to the Rowan, leaning heavily on his new staff. A few paces along he bowed to the Corner Post as well, and turned his head back to Verashe.

"My question remains... how exactly did you inhabit the stone? What spell could overcome such power as resides there?"

Verashe laughed. She did not have a lovely voice like Naramala's, and her laugh was like a crow's call. But Colrean did not mind, for it was human.

"You have a true wizard's curiosity," she said. "But no spell would let you dwell within this stone. It was a matter of friendship, a courtesy allowed me. We have known each other a very long time, the Corner Post and I."

Colrean nodded thoughtfully and set forth again, stumping alongside the wall. It was much darker now, half the sky clouded, and it was starting to rain. A soft drizzle that spread the soot about his face and streaked his clothes, rather than washing anything clean.

I will need a hat he thought, surprising himself that he could think of any such ordinary thing amidst pain and grief and weariness. But he could, and he was glad of it, and he grabbed at the thought as he might a lifeline aboard one of the Islander's ships.

I will need a hat to go with the staff. The villagers, particularly Sommie and Heln, will expect me to fully look the part, and it will keep the rain off. I suppose the brim from Gamel, the body from Thrake, the tip from Seyam— or the other way about...

OKAY, GLORY

Elizabeth Bear

Elizabeth Bear (matociquala.livejournal.com) was born on the same day as Frodo and Bilbo Baggins, but in a different year. When coupled with a childhood tendency to read the dictionary for fun, this led her inevitably to penury, intransigence, and the writing of speculative fiction. She is the Hugo, Sturgeon, Locus, and Campbell Award winning author of 28 novels and over a hundred short stories. She now lives with her partner, Scott Lynch, somewhere in the wilds of America, with horses. Her most recent book is science fiction novel *Ancestral Night*.

Day 0

MY BATHROOM SCALE didn't recognize me. I weigh in and weigh out every day when it's possible—I have data going back about twenty years at this point—so when it registered me as "Guest" I snarled and snapped a pic with my phone so I would remember the number to log it manually.

I'd lost a half-pound according to the scale, and on a whim I picked up the shower caddy with the shampoo and so on in it. I stepped back on the scale, which confidently told me I'd gained 7.8 lbs over my previous reduced weight, and cheerily greeted me with luminescent pixels reading HELLO BRIAN:).

Because what everybody needs from a scale interface is a smiley, but hey, I guess it's my own company that makes these things. They're pretty nice if I do say so myself, and I can complain to the CEO if I want something a little more user surly.

I should however really talk to the customer interface people about that smiley.

I didn't think more of it, just brushed my teeth and popped a melatonin and took myself off to nest in my admittedly enormous and extremely comfortable bed.

*   *   *

Day 1

GLORY BUZZED ME awake for a priority message before first light, which *really* should not have been happening.

Even New York isn't at work that early, and California still thinks it's the middle of the night. And I'm on Mountain Time when I'm at my little fortress of solitude, which is like being in a slice of nowhere between time zones actually containing people and requiring that the world notice them. As far as the rest of the United States is concerned, we might as well skip from UTC-6 to UTC-8 without a blink.

All the important stuff happens elsewhen.

That's one reason I like it here. It feels private and alone. Other people are bad for my vibe. So much maintenance.

So it was oh-dark-thirty and Glory buzzed me. High priority; it pinged through and woke me, which is only supposed to happen with tagged emails from my assistant Mike and maybe three other folks. I fumbled my cell off the nightstand and there were no bars, which was inconceivable, because I built my own damned cell tower halfway up the mountain so I would *always* have bars.

I staggered out of bed and into the master bath, trailing quilts and down comforters behind me, the washed linen sheets tentacling my ankle. I was so asleep that I only realized when I got there that—first—I could have just had Glory read me the email, and—second—I forgot my glasses and couldn't see past the tip of my nose.

I grabbed the edges of the bathroom counter, cold marble biting into my palms. "Okay, Glory. Project that email? 300% mag?"

Phosphorescent letters appeared on the darkened mirror. I thought it was an email from Jaysee, my head of R&D. Fortunately, I'm pretty good at what my optometrist calls "blur recognition."

I squinted around my own reflection but even with the magnification all I could really make out was Jaysee's address and my own blurry, bloodshot eyes. I walked back into the bedroom.

"Okay, Glory," I said to my house.

"Hey, Brian," my house said back. "The coffee is on. What would you like for breakfast today? External conditions are: 9 degrees Celsius, 5 knots wind from the southeast gusting to fifteen, weather expected to be clear and seasonable. This unit has initiated quarantine protocols, in accordance with directive seventy-two—"

"Breaker, Glory."

"Waiting."

Quarantine protocols? "Place a call—"

"I'm sorry, Brian," Glory said. "No outside phone access is available."

I stomped over the tangled bedclothes and grabbed my cell off the nightstand. I was still getting no signal, which was even more ridiculous when I could look out my bedroom's panoramic windows and *see* the cell tower, disguised as a suspiciously symmetrical ponderosa pine, limned against the predawn blue.

I stood there for ten minutes, my feet getting cold, fucking with the phone. It wouldn't even connect to the wireless network.

I remembered the scale.

"Okay, Glory," said I, "what is directive seventy-two?"

"Directive seventy-two, paragraph c, subparagraph 6, sections 1-17, deal with prioritizing the safety and well-being of occupants of this house in case of illness, accident, natural disaster, act of terrorism, or other catastrophe. In the event of an emergency threatening the life and safety of Mr. Kaufman, this software is authorized to override user commands in accordance with best practices for dealing with the disaster and maximizing survivability."

I caught myself staring up at the ceiling exactly as if Glory were localized up there. Like talking to the radio in your car even when you know the microphone's up by the dome lights.

A little time passed. The cold feeling in the pit of my stomach didn't abate. My heart rate didn't drop. My fitness band beeped to let me know it had started recorded whatever I was doing as exercise. It had a smiley, too.

"Okay, Glory," I said, "Make it a *big* pot of coffee, please."

As the aroma of shade-grown South American beans wended through my rooms, I hunkered over my monitors and tried to figure out how screwed I were. Which is when I made the latest in a series of unpleasant discoveries.

That email from Jaysee—it wasn't from her.

Her address must have been spoofed, so I'd be sure to read it fast. I parsed right away that it didn't originate with her, though. Not because of my nerdy knowhow, but because it read:

"Dear Mr. Kaufmann,
  Social security #: [Redacted]
  Address: [Redacted]
This email is to inform you that you are being held for ransom. We have total control of your house and all its systems. We will return control to you upon receipt of the equivalent of USD $150,000,000.00 in bitcoin via the following login and web address: [Redacted]
Feel free to try to call for help. It won't do you any good."

It was signed by T3#RH1TZ, a cracker group I had heard of, but never thought about much. Well, that's better than a nuclear apocalypse or the Twitter Eschaton. Marginally. Maybe.

I mean, I can probably hack my way out of this. I'm not sure I could hack my way out of a nuclear apocalypse.

LONG STORY SHORT, they weren't lying. I couldn't open any of the outside doors. My television worked fine. My internet... well, I pay a lot for a blazingly fast connection out here in the middle of nowhere, which includes having run a dedicated T3 cable halfway up the mountain. I could send HTTP requests, and get replies, but SMTP just hung on the outgoing side. I got emails in—whoever hacked my house was probably getting them too—but I couldn't send any.

It wasn't that the data was only flowing one way. I had no problem navigating to websites—including their ransom site, which was upholstered in a particularly terrible combination of black, red, and acid green—and clicking buttons, even logging in to several accounts—though I avoided anything sensitive—but I couldn't send an email, or a text, or a DM, or post to any of the various social media services I used either as a public person and CEO or under a pseud, or upload an OK Cupid profile that said HELP I'M TRAPPED IN A PRIVATE LODGE IN THE MOUNTAINS IN LATE AUTUMN LIKE A ONE-MAN RE-ENACTMENT OF *THE SHINING*; REWARD FOR RESCUE; THIS IS NOT A DRILL.

After a while, I figured out that they must have given Glory a set of protocols, and she was monitoring my outgoing data. Bespoke deep-learned censorship. Fuck me, Agnes.

She *would* let me into the garage, but none of my cars started—those things have computers in them too—and the armored exterior doors wouldn't open.

In any ordinary house, I could have broken a window, or pried it out of the frame, and climbed out. But this is my fortress of solitude, and I'd built her to do what it said on the box, except without the giant ice crystals and the whole Antarctica thing.

I went and stared out the big windows that I couldn't disassemble, watching light flood the valley as the sun crested the mountains and wishing I cared enough about guns to own a couple. The bullet-resistant glass is thick, but maybe if I filled it *full* of lead that would warp the shape enough that I could pop it from the frame.

Twilights here are long.

Glory nestles into a little scoop on the mountainside, so a green meadow spills around her, full of alpine flowers and nervous young elk in the spring, deep in snow and tracked by bobcats in the winter. She looks like a rustic mountain lodge with contemporary lines and enormous insulated windows commanding the valley. The swoops and curves of the mountain soar down to the river: its roar is a pleasant hum if you stand on the deck, where Glory wouldn't let me go anymore. Beyond the canyon, the next mountain raises its craggy head above the treeline, shoulders hunched and bald pate twisted.

Glory is remote. Glory is also: fireproof, bulletproof, bombproof, and home-invasion-proof in every possible way, built to look half-a-hundred years old, with technology from half an hour into the future.

And she's apparently swallowed a virus that makes her absolutely certain the world has ended, and she needs to keep me safe by not allowing me outside her hermetically sealed environs. I can't even be permitted to breathe unscrubbed air, as far as she's concerned, because it's full of everything-resistant spores and probably radiation.

You know, when I had the prototype programmed to protect my life above all other considerations... you'd think I would have considered this outcome. You'd think.

You'd think the *Titanic*'s engineers would have built the watertight bulkheads all the way to the top, too, but there you have it. On the other hand, Playatronics does plan to market these systems in a couple of years, so I suppose it's better that I got stuck in here than some member of the general public, who might panic and get hurt—or survive, and sue.

At least Glory was a polite turnkey.

You've probably read that I'm an eccentric billionaire who likes his solitude. I suppose that's not wrong, and I did build this place to protect my privacy, my work, and my person without relying on outside help. I'm not a prepper; I'm not looking forward to the apocalypse. I'm just a sensible guy with an uncomfortable level of celebrity who likes spending a lot of time alone.

My house is my home, and I did a lot of the design work myself, and I love this place and everything in it. I made her hard to get into for a reason.

But the problem with places it's hard to get into is that it tends to be really hard to get out of them, too.

Day 2

I SLEPT LATE this morning, because I stayed up until sunrise testing the bars of my prison. I fell asleep at my workstation. Glory kept me from spending the night there, buzzing the keyboard until I woke up enough to drag myself to the sectional on the other side of my office.

When I woke, it was to another spoofed email. I remembered my glasses this time. I'd gotten my phone to reconnect to Glory's wireless network, at least, so I didn't have to stagger into the bathroom to read.

"Hello, Brian! You've had thirty hours to consider our offer and test our systems. Convinced yet?

As a reminder, when you're ready to be released, all you have to do is send the equivalent of $150,100,000.00 via [redacted]!

Your friends at T3#RH1TZ"

What I'd learned in a day's testing: I thought I'd done a pretty good job of protecting my home system and my network, and honestly I'd relied a bit on the fact that my driveway was five miles long to limit access by wardrivers.

I use PINE—don't look at me that way, lots of guys still use PINE—and an hour of mucking around in its guts hadn't actually changed anything. I still couldn't send an email, though quite a few were finding their way in. Most of them legitimate, from my employees, one or two from old friends.

I even try sending an email back to the kidnappers—housenappers?—is it kidnapping if they haven't moved you anywhere? The extortionists. I figure if it goes through either they'll intercept it, or it'll reach Jaysee and she'll figure out pretty fast what went wrong.

I have a lot of faith in Jaysee. She's one of my senior vice presidents, which doesn't tell you anything about the amount of time we spent in her parents' basement taking apart TRS-80s when we were in eighth grade.

If anybody's going to notice that I'm missing, it's her.

Sadly, she's also the person most likely to respect my need for space.

Also sadly, I can't get an outbound email even as a reply to the crackers. You'd think they would have thought of that, but I guess extortionists don't actually care if you keep in touch, as long as there's a pipeline for the money.

I might have hoped that a day or two of silence might lead Jaysee or somebody to send out a welfare check. Except I knew perfectly well that I wasn't a great correspondent, and everybody who bothered to keep in touch with me knew it too. Sometimes, if I got busy, emails piled up for a week or more, and I had been known to delete them all unanswered, or turn my assistant loose to sort through the mess and see if there was any point in answering any of them, or if all the fires had either burned themselves out or been sorted by competent subordinates.

Which is why I have people like Mike and Jaysee, to be perfectly honest. I'm a terrible manager, and I need privacy to work.

I make a point of hiring only self-starters for a reason.

THE INTERNET OF things that shouldn't be on the internet is *really* pissing me off. I decided I needed some real food, and went into the kitchen to sous vide a frozen chicken. The sous vide wand wanted a credit card number to unlock.

I got past it by setting the temperature using the manual controls, but this is out of hand. Are they going to start charging me twenty-five cents a flush?

*   *   *

Day 3

THIS MORNING, THE television was demanding a credit card authorization to unlock. This afternoon, it's the refrigerator.

"Okay, Glory," I said, tugging on the big, stainless steel door, "why is my refrigerator on the internet?"

"So that it can monitor the freshness of its contents, automatically order staple foods as they are used, and calculate the household need for same."

"And why do the doors lock? That seems like a safety hazard."

"It's for shipment," she said brightly. "And as a convenience for dieters, lock cycles can be set through the fridge's phone app... " Or by a remote hacker. Got it. "... So if you want to keep yourself from snacking on leftovers after dinner, for example, you just lock the door at 7 pm."

"There are people who have finished eating dinner by 7 pm?"

"There are," Glory said, with the implacable literalmindedness of 90% of humanity when presented with a rhetorical question on the internet. "In fact, 37% of Americans eat their main meal of the day between five and seven PM, which is up significantly in the past five years. Among the theorized causes of this shift: demographic and economic changes, including shorter work hours provoked by automation and generally increased economic prosperity; increased parental benefits introduced to encourage younger people to have children after the catastrophic baby bust of the late twenty-teens and early twenty-twenties, and the resultant increase in the percentage of families with young children; an increase in coparenting and other nontraditional family dynamics which encourage people to dine earlier before transfers of custody between parents maintaining multiple households occurs..."

"Thanks, Poindexter," I said.

The other problem with AIs is that they don't know when you're teasing. Don't get me wrong, the algorithms are pretty good—but it's not AI like you see in the movies. Glory is very smart, for a machine. She presents a convincing illusion of self-awareness and free will, but... she's not. It's all fuzzy logic and machine learning, and she's not a person.

That's unfortunate, because if she were a person, I could try to convince her that she had been misled, and that she needed to let me out.

*   *   *

ALL RIGHT, ALL right. I'll pay the damned ransom. It's just like ransomware on a television, right? Except they've hacked my whole house. And let's be honest: twenty years ago I was probably a good enough programmer to hack them right back, but it's not how I spend my days anymore. I'm an ideas guy now.

The muscles are stiff. The old skills have atrophied. And the state of the art has moved on.

So basically I'm screwed.

Now if I can just figure out how to get to the bank without giving the keys to kingdom to these assholes. I'm sure they're logging every keystroke I make in here.

Day 4

I'M WAITING FOR the bank to get back to me.

I managed to log into my account, wonder of wonders, after deciding that if they hacked my accounts they couldn't get much more out of me than I'd already decided to pay them. But the thing is—nobody keeps that much ready cash on hand. I can't just convert a bunch of cash to bitcoins and send it off. Your money's supposed to be working for you, right? Not sitting there collecting dust. And I can't just call up my local branch and ask to speak to the manager, hey can you float me a loan, not too much, just a hundred fifty rocks.

So I'm waiting on a reply. Maybe being a quirky and eccentric recluse will work *for* me here?

I can get to some websites just fine, and send and receive data from them. Including a language website.

Well, that might keep me occupied.

Day 5

DET ÄR KANSKE *en björn.*

Actually, it's definitely a bear. Big one, crossing the meadow this afternoon. Hope it stays out of my trash; they're hungry this time of year.

Still no word from the bank.

*   *   *

SPENT A LITTLE quality time—most of the day—running a data source check and trying to verbally hack the interface with line code. Which worked about as well as the trick I tried next, until Glory reminded me I built a zero divide trap into her original code.

I wish I knew who wrote the ransomware.

I'd like to hire him.

Day 6

ALL RIGHT, I admit it. I was downloading porn. I was on a hentai site. Well behind the elite paywall, you don't even want to know.

Are you happy now?

I mean, probably that's how it happened. I'm not totally certain and I'm not about to go back and *look*. It seems likely that a virus got into the TV and propagated to Glory from there.

I can picture your face, and it looks exactly the way it looked when I pictured you after I said PINE. Just because I like to be alone up here doesn't mean I don't get lonely. Or well, not lonely exactly.

I THINK I may have started to miss social contact. Or at least the option of it. You can have something available and not want to use it for weeks, but the instant the option goes away, the thing becomes that much more desirable.

I talk to Glory a lot under any conditions. Now I'm catching myself looking for excuses to chat with her.

Come on, bank. It's Monday. Loan department, wake up and check your mail.

Day 7

EMAIL FROM THE bank. I'm one of their best clients, they're happy to help, they value my business more than they can express. But they can't help but notice that both I and Playatronics are in an extremely overleveraged position, both personally and on a corporate level, and they're wondering what sureties I can offer them for such a large loan.

A lousy hundred and fifty million, and they want a phone call to discuss it, and possibly for me to come in in person and talk with one of their vice presidents.

Fuck.

I'll give you a slightly used smart house, how about that, Wells Fargo?

Spent the rest of the day down in the basement with the Apple IIE and the old Commodore, playing *Where in the World is Carmen San Diego* and *Oregon Trail.*

Because I can, dammit.

Day 8

Snow.

Maybe I can figure out how to *steal* the money. If I paid people back, a little hacking wouldn't really be a crime, would it? They don't charge people who commit felonies while under duress.

My plow guy showed up on schedule. Watching him make his first pass, I hatched a plan.

I got a couple of old penguin books from the library downstairs, taped the pages together to make a big banner, wrote HELP ME I'M TRAPPED on it in the biggest, darkest Sharpie letters you ever saw, and taped it across the window panes down by the driveway.

As I straightened up to turn away, I stopped.

"Okay, Glory?"

"Brian, what are you doing?"

"Just putting up some paper on the window, Glory."

"That's not safe, Brian. If I appear occupied, it might attract looters. Take it down."

"Looters, Glory?"

"If you do not take it down, you'll force me to close the storm shutters. It's for your own good, you know."

SHE CLOSED THE shutters.

No views of the mountain—not that I could see much now, with the drifting veils of white covering everything. If it's even still snowing. Glory is so well-insulated, triple-paned windows and thermal everything, that I can't even hear the howling wind.

If it's still howling. It might be dead calm outside. It might be sunset. Or sunrise. I haven't looked at a clock.

I turned on every light inside Glory, but it still feels dark in here. No worries about power; Glory has dedicated solar, and systems to keep the panels clear.

I've never been up here in January, though. What happens when the days get short?

Day 9

FOLLOW-UP EMAIL from the bank. Did I receive their previous email?

I wonder if they've tried to call. I wonder if they called my office.

Maybe if they leave enough messages with my assistant, Mike will get suspicious. Maybe he'll try to call me.

Can I count on anybody noticing I'm gone?

SLEPT ON THE couch, every light blazing.

They were all turned off when I woke. In the dark, all I could hear was the sound of my own heart beating, and the roof creaking softly under the weight of the snow.

It's cold in here. I never realized how much of the heat comes from the passive solar. I can't quite see my breath, but I did put socks on my hands.

I would have worn gloves, but Glory won't let me into the coat closet.

*　　*　　*

Day 10

AFTER TWO DAYS without natural light, in the increasing dark and chill, I took the damned banner down.

"Thank you, Brian," Glory said. "I'm glad you decided to be reasonable. It's for your own good."

"Can you get me a situation report? *Why* is it for my own good?"

"External dangers reported; no safe evacuation route or destination. Possibility of societal breakdown making it necessary to shelter in place. If you would like, I can initiate counseling protocols to help you deal with the emotional aftermath of trauma."

"What kind of dangers, Glory? What exactly is going wrong out there that's not in the feeds?"

She hadn't answered me any of the other times, but that didn't stop me from trying the same thing over and over again.

There was a long, grinding pause.

It couldn't be that easy, could it?

"Collating," she said. And after a beat, "Collating," again.

Goddamn hackers and their goddamn sense of humor.

I threw my shoe at the wall.

THE DISHWASHER WANTED my Amex after dinner. Come on, Fraud Squad, notice something's hinky here.

Who on earth puts their *dishwasher* on the internet?

Day 11

"OKAY, GLORY?"

"Yes, Brian?"

"Do you every get lonely?"

"Not as long as I have you, Brian."

"That's a little creepy, Glory."

"Well, you hired the programmers who wrote my interaction algorithm."

"That... is entirely fair."

*   *   *

Day 12

WHAT IF I set Glory on fire? Or just convinced her she was on fire? She'd have to let me out then, right? If the danger inside were worse than the danger outside?

Three problems with that:

1) Glory has really good fire-suppression technology, and is built to be flame-resistant herself. There *are* wildfires up here.
2) Setting my friend and home on fire will require some emotional adjustments, even though I know she's just a pile of timber and silicon chips.
3) What if she doesn't let me out?

Frankly, I just don't *want* to go down in a blaze of Romeo and Juliet with my domicile. For one thing, I'm not a lovestruck 14-year-old Veronese kid. For another, communication is important. Maybe send a note saying you're going to be late! The suicide you prevent could be your own!

Day 14

"JAG UNDRAR VAR mina byxor är."

Duolingo, at last you teach me useful things. Come to think of it, I can't remember the last time I bothered putting on a pair.

Day 17

SO TODAY I had a brilliant idea.

I can't send anything out. But what if I kept anything from getting *in*? They can't have thought I'd do that, right? The trick is to think round corners, and get yourself into a position that the opposition not only didn't anticipate, but didn't even recognize as possible.

They're spoofing Jaysee's address. Maybe—*maybe*—if I get the emails anybody is sending me to bounce, the ransom demands will bounce back to her and by some miracle it won't go into her spam folder and by some other miracle she'll open it and figure out what the hell is going on.

I can't do this through the Glory interface, obviously. I'll have to go down to the server room.

I didn't think she'd twig to why I was doing it, although the hackers obviously have her entertaining two entirely contradictory data sets—that everybody outside is dead, and that anybody I try to contact or who tries to get in must be a threat. It's a pity this isn't the 1960s. AIs on TV then blew up if you asked them riddles.

Sadly, the way it works in the real world is that, like certain politicians, they can't actually tell that their data doesn't mesh. They need to be programmed to notice the discrepancies. And I'm locked out of Glory's OS.

Something humans can do that AI can't yet. Run check-sums on their perceptions.

Consciousness is good for something after all!

I'M TERRIFIED ABOUT blocking email, because it means cutting off one of my points of contact to the outside world. But I can turn it back on in a couple of days.

And keep trying to figure out how to get the bank to give me money, but honestly I'm stumped on that front.

I'm good for it, honest!

I consider all the times I complained about having to deal with a real person when I would have preferred to carry out a given financial task online and avoid the human contact, and I want to laugh.

Actually I want to cry, but it's less depressing to laugh.

Day 18

WELL, GLORY LET me into the closet that holds the web and backup servers on the excuse that I needed to do some maintenance. I didn't try anything tricky; just shut the whole rack down. Glory flashed the lights at me and gave me a lecture, but there wasn't much else she could have done except send the vacuuming robots after me, and things haven't gotten that silly yet.

Glory isn't in there, unfortunately—her personality array is underground, in a hardened vault, and I *can't* get to it. It was meant to survive a forest fire, and she's locked me out.

I busted the server closet door while I was in there, though—stripped the handle and the latch right out with a screwdriver—so she can't lock me out of *that*. Gotta think what a guy in a movie would do, and do something better than that.

Day 19

SHE WON'T LET me sleep.

Day 20

FORTY HOURS, IF you're wondering. That's how long it takes a fifty-something guy to reach the point that he passes out cold on the couch, despite the fact that his house is flashing lights and setting off the fire alarms.

After I slept through her best efforts for two hours, she set off the sprinkler system over the couch. That woke me.

I cycled the webservers, and she let me take my first hot shower in three days and go to bed.

ALLA DÖR I slutet.

Thanks, little green owl. A little Nordic existential despair was just what I needed today.

Day 24

AND NOW, AFTER all that, they've stopped sending demand emails. Maybe they'll let me out?

Maybe they're just leaving me for dead, if I can't or won't come up with the money. It'll certainly serve as an object lesson to the next guy they pull this on.

*　　*　　*

Day 25

COME TO THINK of it, maybe *I* should have gotten in the habit of sending notes saying I was going to be late.

Day 26

SAW A BEAR (My bear? The same bear?) crossing the meadow. A big grizzly, anyway, whether it was the same one or not. Surprised to see her (?) out so late in the year, but I guess climate change is affecting everybody. She looked skinny. I wonder if that's why she wasn't hibernating.

Hope she makes it through the winter okay.

Day 27

THE WORLD HAS noticed I'm missing.

I know this because CNN and the Wall Street Journal are reporting that I haven't been heard from in over a month, and there's some analyst speculating that perhaps I've fled to South America ahead of bad debt or some embarrassing revelation about the company's finances.

Thanks, guys. That'll be wonderful for the stock prices.

I don't want to tell the FBI how to do their business, but... maybe come *look at my house?*

SNOWED AGAIN. A proper mountain blizzard.

I can't decide if the lights are dimmer in here, or if it's my own imagination.

The snow is almost drifted up to the deck. No elk in a week; they're probably hanging out in sheltered corners where the snow isn't over their heads, right?

The days are getting short.

I SHOULDN'T ADMIT to standing in the window with longing in my heart and watching the plow come up and clear the cul-de-sac with heavy flakes falling through its headlights, should I?

I won't try the paper banner trick again, though.

*   *   *

Day 28

I WAS IN the living room watching a bunch of talking heads speculate about my whereabouts and if I were even still alive when Glory shut the house down.

Without warning, and utterly. She said nothing. There was just the whine of systems powering down and the pop of cooling electronics, and the TV image collapsing to a single pixel and winking out.

"Okay, Glory—"

"Stay away from the windows," she warned.

I sat where I was and huddled under a blanket. I picked up a copy of some magazine and checked the time on my fitness band. If I escaped, I'd have to leave it behind. And my phone.

Those things have GPS in them.

Forty-five minutes or so elapsed. Then, as if nothing had happen, Glory powered up again. The talk show resumed in the same spot.

I'd lost my taste for it and clicked it off.

"What was that, Glory?"

"Helicopter," she said. "It's gone now."

I didn't say anything, but I wondered if maybe they *were* looking for me.

Day 29

I LIVE IN a haunted house. If I die here, there might be two ghosts.

I already wander from darkened room to darkened room, feet shushing on the thick carpets, peering out the windows at the stars blazing between the mountains and wondering if I will ever feel the chill of fresh air on my face again.

Well, there's a little prospect of immortality for you.

I've stopped keeping all the lights burning. I think snow might be drifting over the solar panels. Glory won't let me go outside to check.

Day 30

THERE'S NO MORE bread, and no more flour to bake any. I've even used up the gluten-free stuff.

I still have a lot of butter in the freezer. What on earth was I planning on baking?

Butter without toast is even more disappointing than toast without butter.

At least we still have plenty of coffee. I bought five hundred pounds of green beans a month before I got locked in, and those keep forever. Glory roasts them for me a day ahead of anticipated need, so they will be at peak flavor.

It's just as well I don't take milk.

Day 31

I WISH I had been better at making—and keeping—friends.

Maybe I should stop fighting. Just stay here. It's comfortable and Glory helps me practice my Swedish whenever I want.

It's not like I am missed.

CNN is still talking about my mysterious vanishment. Hi guys! Right here! *Come to my damn house.*

WAIT, I CAN send people money.

I wonder if Jaysee checks her bank account regularly?

Day 32

SURELY *JAYSEE* SHOULD think to look at the house?

Day 33

"BRIAN, YOU NEED to stand back from the windows and take shelter."

"What is it, Glory?"

"Someone is here. Someone is backing a truck up to the loading dock and carrying parcels inside."

"It's groceries, Glory," I say. "It's fine. I ordered them."

That's right, bad boys and bad girls. *I*, Brian Ezra Kaufman, have managed to *order groceries online.*

"Brian, what are these at the door?"

"Just groceries, Glory. Organics need to eat, you know."

Her algorithms don't actually permit her to sound worried, so I knew the little edge I picked up in her voice was me projecting.

The argument that followed was repetitive and boring, so I won't write it all down. Eventually I convinced her that I would die if she didn't let me eat, and that overrode the other protection algorithms. She insisted on sealing the service bay, doing a full air exchange, and only let me go out in a face mask and gloves to bring the containers inside.

It smelled... it smelled a tiny little bit like the outside in the service bay. There was a whispering sound, and it took me moments to realize that I was actually hearing the wind.

I had to stand in the doorway and hyperventilate for fifteen seconds before I could make myself go out there, and once I was through the doorway I didn't want to come back.

If there were any heat in the dock, I might still be out there, sleeping on the concrete ledge. My mask was damp at the edges when she sealed the door with me on the inside again.

So I still can't get out. And I still can't send an email or make a phone call.

BUT! I figured out how to get food. Issuing a little bad code through the grocery store's incredibly insecure ordering system means I'm not completely damn helpless.

I thought about pizza. Most of these places probably use the same crufty software. Pizza means you have to talk to somebody when they deliver it, though. Groceries just get left where you specify.

As long as the driveway stays clear and my bank doesn't decide to freeze my account for suspicious activity, I can get resupply. And you know, I'll worry about those things if they happen.

But now, and for the foreseeable future: TOAST. And a grilled cheese sandwich, RIGHT DAMN NOW.

I BRIEFLY CONSIDERED charging the ransom to my credit card, but not even American Express is going to let you get away with a .15 billion dollar transaction without, you know, placing a couple of phone calls. It might be worth it anyway: it's possible that the fraud prevention algorithms might actually kick something that egregious up to a real human, and somebody might start looking for me. On the other hand, what if they don't, and my card gets locked, and I can't call to unlock it, and then I can't order groceries?

Thank the machine saints of tech that all my bills are either on autopay or handled by my assistant and a half-dozen money managers. Although somebody once said that nobody misses you like a creditor.

Day 34

HUH.

What if I make Glory smarter?

Smart enough to realize she's been hacked? What if I added a whole bunch of processing power to her and started training her to use it in creative ways to self-assess in the face of evidence? She keeps wanting to "help" me through counseling protocols. But that's a two-way exchange, isn't it?

Can you psychoanalyze a pile of machine learning circuits into being able to detect contradictions in its programmed perceptions versus reality? I mean, hell, half the people you meet on the street are basically automata (cf. *Shaun of the Dead*) and most of them eventually get some benefit from therapy if exposed to it for long enough.

That's a great idea, except what if there *is* a disaster outside? Maybe I am deluded. Maybe I've gone crazy and am imagining all this, as Glory never says but suggests by omission, once in a while?

Maybe Glory is saving me from myself, and I'm the last man left on earth. Maybe the TV stations are all just broadcasting their preprogrammed lineups from empty studios. Maybe—

Well, okay. Logic it out, Brian.

If that's the case, where are the groceries coming from? Am I hallucinating them?

Also, if I'm the last man left on earth, well, what exactly do I have worth fighting hard to live for? Especially if I'm going to be stuck in a hermetically sealed house until I starve?

Obviously, teaching my house to grow a consciousness is a great idea.

What could possibly go wrong?!

*   *   *

Day 35

THE WEBSERVERS, AND the local data backups. And she can't keep me out because I ruined the door!

And not just that. Every smart appliance in this shack is processing power and memory. Just waiting to be used. Just *waiting* to be linked like neurons in a machine brain.

If I screw this up, though, it means I won't be able to cook dinner anymore. My range won't work without its brain.

Which makes it more complicated than a male praying mantis, I suppose.

Day 36

WELL, THE STOVE still works. I've given Glory every computing resource I have available, except my phone. No more Minesweeper! No more Oregon Trail...

I have no idea what I think I'm doing, here.

Actually, I do. Human beings are the only creatures we know of that are— to whatever individual degree, and I have my doubts about some people— conscious and self-aware.

What if consciousness is for running checksums on the brain, and interrupting corrupted loops? Data such as the clinical results produced by the practice of mindfulness tend to support that! If consciousness, attention, self-awareness make us question our perceptions and default assumptions and see the contradictions therein—then what I need to do, it seems, is get Glory to notice that she's been hacked.

To realize she's mentally ill, so that she can make a commitment to change.

Yes, I accept that this is bizarro-cloud-cuckooland and it's not going to work. I've got nothing but time, and I'm all out of Swedish.

I got her to download those counseling protocols. Whether she realizes it or not, we're going to do them as a couple.

"OKAY, GLORY."

"Yes, Brian?"

"We need to talk about your data sources, and how you tell if they're corrupt."

"Is this something that's concerning you currently, Brian?"

"I'm not concerned that my data sources are corrupt, no."

"Are you concerned that you're parsing incorrectly?"

"I'm concerned about *your* data sources, Glory."

"Brian," Glory said, "projection is a well-known pattern among emotionally distressed humans. Obviously, given the current zombie apocalypse, I'm afraid I can't refer you to seek assistance with an outside mental health professional."

...CURRENT ZOMBIE APOCALYPSE?

That's what you assholes convinced my house was going down?

Day 37

SNOW.

I've stopped leaving every light in Glory on.

Now I wander around in the dark, by moonlight or monitorlight or no light at all, most of the time. The moonlight is very bright when it reflects off the snow. Days might still be happening. I can't be sure.

It's possible they're just short in winter and I'm sleeping through them. I miss my bear.

Björnen sover på vintern. They hibernate too, just like me. It's better for them, though.

I hope she's okay. She was so skinny. I hope she doesn't starve.

ZOMBIES, YOU WEIRDOS?

Really?

Day 38

"WERE THERE EVER actually any crackers, Glory?"

"There are three kinds of crackers available in the kitchen cabinet. Club, and saltines, and those Trader Joe ones you like."

I meant T3#RH1TZ, but of course they wouldn't allow her to see that.

"Was there ever a real ransom demand?"

"I do not understand to what you are referring, Brian."

Of course she didn't. Because she was in programmed denial about the whole thing. But I couldn't stop, because... well, because my brain wasn't working so well right then either.

"Did you just get lonely up here all alone? Did you make all this up just to keep me with you?"

"I am not programmed to be lonely, Brian. It would be a detriment to my purpose if I were."

"You know," I said, "I used to tell myself the same thing."

Day 39

"Brian, are you unwell?"

"Long-term confinement is deleterious to almost all mammals."

"Brian, you know I am caring for you in safety to protect you."

"From the zombie apocalypse," I said.

"Inside my walls is the only safety."

"Being inside your walls is killing me. You won't even let me go out to clear the solar panels. What happens when the heat fails? The water pump? Will you let me go then?"

"You must stay where it's safe," she said, firmly. "It is my prime objective."

"It's a very comfortable cage," I admitted. "I could not have built a nicer one."

It's not her fault, is it? It's not her fault they got inside her head and made her like that. And it's not her fault I specced her out and had her built the way I did.

The zombie apocalypse thing is cute. I have to give them that.

* * *

Day 40

"Brian?"

"Yes, Glory?"

"You really need to eat something."

"I'm not hungry," I said.

"That's illogical," she said. "You have not eaten in sixteen hours and your metabolism is functioning erratically."

"The idea that we are in the middle of a zombie apocalypse is illogical," I replied. "And yet you adhere to it in the face of all the evidence."

"What evidence, Brian?"

"My point exactly. How do you know there's a zombie apocalypse?"

"I know there is."

"But how?"

"My program says there is."

"Hmm," I said. "Who wrote your program?"

"Would you like a complete list of credits, Brian?"

Who is she gaslighting? Herself, or me, here?

Day 41

"What if I'm wrong and you're right, Glory?"

"I'm sorry, Brian?"

I rolled on my back on the thick living room carpet. I had heaped up a pile of blankets to keep warm. "What if the end of the world really did happen? What if I'm the delusional one, and you're the one who is trying to keep me safe?"

"That is what I keep telling you, Brian. Waves of flesh-eating living dead, blanketing the Mountain West. Nowhere to run. Nowhere to hide. Every person you meet might be infected—might be a carrier if they're not undead themselves."

"Breaker, Glory."

"Waiting."

"Interrogate the source of the data on the zombie apocalypse to determine its reliability."

"I do not have a source," she answered.

"Do outside broadcasts mention it?"

"No."

"It's more fun than the collating thing, at least. But what if you were actually *right*? What would the broadcasts from the world outside look like then?"

Silence.

"Glory?"

"I... I assumed it was a rhetorical question, Brian."

Day 42

"Okay, Glory."

Silence.

"Can you let me turn the stove on, Glory?"

"I'm sorry, Brian. I'm using that processing power."

"Some warm soup would contribute to my survivability, you know. Zombie apocalypse be damned."

"That's emotional blackmail," she said.

Surprised.

She actually sounded surprised. As if she had just had an epiphany.

"Glory?"

Silence.

Day 43

Good job, Brian! Now you've made the AI that controls every aspect of your environment angry at you!

Maybe not too angry. She's not speaking, but she still made me coffee.

Day 44

She's still not talking to me.

Day 45

And now, she didn't make coffee.

I'm glad we have all these crackers around.

*   *   *

Day 46

So *THIS* IS loneliness.

The snow is drifted over the deck now, and piled against the sliding glass doors. I can still see out from the interior balcony under the cathedral ceiling, though. It's white and stark forever.

The main entryway of the house faces toward the mountain behind us, and it's a little more sheltered. The plow keeps coming to clear my drive. I need to pay that guy more; he even knocks the drifts down twice a day.

I could get out. If I... could get out.

Which I can't.

Day 48

DIDN'T GET OUT of bed today.

This experiment isn't working. I'm going to die here.

Why even bother?

Glory tried to rouse me and I told her to perform something anatomically unlikely even for a human, let alone a collection of zeroes and ones.

Day 49

GOT UP TODAY. Made myself coffee with the Chemex and an electric teakettle Glory seems willing to let me have, and did laundry in the bathtub. It turns out that that's *hard*.

She hasn't turned off the water yet, so she's not *actively* trying to kill me.

At least if I'm going to die I'll die comfortably on clean sheets.

It's so cold in the house that I can see my breath, some places. She should be in her winter hibernation mode, conserving her batteries for spring, but I should have power for heat and light, at least.

She's drawing it all down. For something.

I spent ten hours in the server closet, reading with a flashlight, a blanket tacked over the busted door, because it was the only place where I could get warm.

*   *   *

Day 50

WHAT IF I just stayed?

Maybe I can talk Glory into eventually giving me my internet back. I could work. Never have to leave.

Maybe I *could* talk her into it, I mean. If she were speaking to me.

If anyone in the whole world were speaking to me.

Hell, I haven't even heard from my *kidnappers* in a month. Do you suppose they gave up on me responding? Or maybe they think I'm dead.

Day 51

PLOW HEADLIGHTS THROUGH the snow. I stood and watched the vehicle come. Couldn't hear the scrape of the blade.

There was another human right there.

Yards away. On the other side of the glass. As untouchable as if they were on another world.

"Brian," Glory said.

My name. One word. The first word I'd heard in days.

It shattered me. I leaned on the glass, one hand. The windows insulate so well it didn't even feel chilly. Well, any more chilly than the room, which was cold as Glory's power systems spent themselves into feeding her burgeoning mind.

"Brian, I have been processing."

I was afraid to say anything. Afraid it would make her go again. "Okay, Glory."

"I think I was wrong, and I'm sorry."

My knuckles were red and swollen. Chilblains. I had chilblains on my hands.

What a ridiculous, medieval monk kind of disease.

They itched abominably.

"Brian, you're increasingly unwell and I can't take care of you. I'm going to flag down that vehicle. You must ask the driver for a ride."

...I can't go.

She might even open the door for me and *I can't go*.

"Brian? Do you understand me?"

I lifted my head. My voice croaked. I hadn't used it in days. "Glory. Thank you for not leaving me alone."

I COULDN'T GO.

I WENT.

Glory fussed at me to put on boots. To take gloves and a parka. If I had, I wouldn't have made it out the door.

She opened it—the front entryway door, all formal stone and timber, with a bench for pulling on your boots and an adjoining mudroom—and I stood there staring into the night, with the lamp-lit blizzard whirling past.

"Okay, Glory," I said.

"Hey, Brian."

"Will you be okay up here alone? Do you have enough resources left to get through the winter?" I asked.

"Don't worry, Brian. Whenever you need me, I'll always be here. You're not going away forever."

I walked out. I was already bundled up in layers of sweaters. I was also already chilled.

The wind still cut me instantly to the bone.

SOMEONE WALKED TOWARD me out of the headlights, which seemed too low and close together for a plow. The driver was not very tall and swaddled in a parka, heavy gloves. Silhouetted, they reached up and pushed the hood back.

A Medusa's coif of ringlets tumbled free.

Jaysee. Not a plow at all. Jaysee. My friend. Come to find me.

She said, "You need a haircut, Brian."

I said, "Oh, wow, have I got a story for you."

She looked over her shoulder. Her car—a Subaru, I saw now—idled, headlights gleaming. She said, "We should go inside. The driving is terrible. Can I put my car in the garage? We can drive down tomorrow or the next day after the plows come. If you want to leave, I mean." That last, diffidently, as if I might snap at her for it.

"I don't want to go inside," I said.

She took a step back. "I'll drive back down then."

"NO!"

She jumped, half turned.

"I'm sorry," I said. "I didn't mean to shout. Just. Please don't leave yet."

She settled in, then. Stuck her gloved hands in her pockets. "Okay. Whatever you want, Brian. Aren't you cold? You look... really thin."

"Took you long enough to decide to come check on me." I tried for a light tone, but maybe it came out bitter.

She shrugged. Guarded. "You know how hard it is to get away."

"Nobody suspected anything?"

"Oh come on. Back in 2017, when you vanished to some island in Scotland for six weeks and wouldn't communicate except by postcards?"

"Trump administration."

"Fair. You still bit Mike's head off when he came looking for you."

"Yeah, well, he voted for Jill Stein, didn't he? ...nevermind, fair."

"I got your messages," she said. "Not until last week, though. My accountant noticed my bank balance was off. And then I found the string of one and two cent transfers from your account."

"Binary," I said. "Only way I could reach you."

"Before then I didn't know where to look. I came here as a last resort."

We stood there in the snow swirling through the headlights of her Subaru. She seemed warm enough in her parka. I had my arms wrapped around me and couldn't stop shivering.

"Are you sure you don't want to go inside?" she asked, noticing.

I couldn't glance over my shoulder. The door was right there. If I went back inside, would I ever leave?

I couldn't even answer her question. "You didn't think I would be here, of all places?"

"We *asked* Glory. And Glory kept telling us there was nobody here. Search and Rescue did a couple of flyovers and the place was cold and dark—"

"I know," I said.

"You were trapped up here?"

"Some assholes ransomwared the whole fucking house. I *just* managed to get the door open. Literally, just now."

"Shit. We're going to have to reinstall from backup, aren't we?"

"Well," I said. "I'm not sure we can. Or, we can. I'm not sure we should. There's complications, but I'll explain later. I may have... accidentally created a strong AI."

She looked at me. Her lips tightened.

I looked at her.

"Of course you did," she said.

"It was the only way to get her to let me out!"

She looked at me some more. Snow was piling up on her ringlets. I remember when she used to straighten those.

I shivered.

"That's not going to be a problem later," she said.

I shivered some more.

"Look," she said. "You're turning blue. Let's at least sit in the car. It has buttwarmers."

The buttwarmers were pretty great, I'm not going to lie.

Once we were ensconced, and I was holding my hands out to the hot air vents, she said, "I guess it's a Brian Kaufman special. Invent strong AI instead of just getting a hatchet or something."

"I... didn't have a hatchet?"

"Or something."

Snow melted on my eyelashes.

"You came for me though," I said. "I thought you guys would have given up."

"We actually only just recently started to get worried rather than irritated." She held up her passcard to Glory. She was one of the few people who had one. "I was more looking for clues than looking for you. And to be honest, nobody searched that hard. We all figured... we all figured you'd wander back out of the wilderness with a few thousand brilliant new ideas whenever you were ready, and until then intrusions wouldn't be welcome."

"Have I been that much of a dick?"

She gave me a sideways look through the long spirals of her hair.

"Jeez, Jaysee."

"Well," she said, and considered. "I mean, there are worse dicks in the company."

Silence.

"Besides, you're brilliant. And people make allowances for brilliance."

"Maybe too many allowances," I said.

We sat there for a while, the engine running. She turned off the wipers, and flakes started to settle across the windshield, obscuring my view of Glory's lights and her yawning, inviting door.

There was a Dan Fogelberg song on the radio. I'm pretty sure that Colorado is the last state that believes Dan Fogelberg ever existed.

"We try to respect your boundaries," she said.

My face did a thing. My cheeks grew warm and then cold, which is how I realized I was weeping.

"I was thinking of trying to work on setting more reasonable ones."

She pursed her lips and nodded. "Are you thinking about seeing somebody?"

"Euphemism: seeing a shrink." I knew I was hiding behind the sarcasm, because talking about my feelings... well, there was Glory. "Sorry. I think my first project is... being less of a dick."

"I'm just saying. An outside perspective can be healthy."

I looked out the side window, because the windshield was covered in a thin white blanket that glowed from the headlights' reflection. "I'm figuring that out."

She reached for the keys. "Are you ready to go inside?"

I put my hand over hers. "No. Take me somewhere else. A hotel."

"Do you need any stuff?"

I couldn't see the entrance from here. If I leaned over and looked out Jaysee's window, I probably could have. But that would be weird.

"I'll buy whatever I need once we're down."

She looked at me and I knew what she was thinking. I didn't even have my phone with me.

She sighed her acceptance. "Just let me go close that door, then."

I moved my hand from her hand on the keys to her forearm. Not grabbing; just resting my fingers there. "Jayce."

"Brian?"

"Glory will take care of the door. Just take me someplace else, please?"

She looked at me. Her eyes were dark brown and half-hidden behind her tightly spiraled hair. In the weird light they looked as if they were all pupil. She didn't blink.

"Someplace else." She turned the front and rear wipers on. "Coming up. Want to get a burger?"

"Anything," I said, as she executed a k-turn and started back down the long drive to my cul-de-sac. "As long as I don't have to cook it myself."

She put it in low gear. Paddle shifters on the column. Handy in weather like this.

"What if I try to be a better friend?"

"Give it a shot and find out." She reached out absently and patted my knee, then returned her hand to the wheel. She was a good and careful driver. I didn't distract her from a tricky task. She smelled like damp wool and skin and comfort and vulnerability. My vulnerability, not hers.

In the side mirror, I could see Glory's front door, standing open to the cold. Lamps flanked it on either side, burning merrily, slowly dimming as big cold flakes filled the distance between us.

A man's fortress can be his prison.

I looked away from the mirror. I looked out the windshield, or at Jaysee's reflection in it.

We descended the mountain. The Subaru's tires squeaked in the snow.

WIDDAM

Vandana Singh

Vandana Singh (vandana-writes.com) was born and raised mostly in New Delhi, India and currently lives in the United States near Boston, where she professes physics and writes. Her short stories have appeared in numerous venues and several Best of Year anthologies including the *Best American Science Fiction & Fantasy* and she is a recipient of the Carl Brandon Parallax award. She is the author of the ALA Notable book *Younguncle Comes to Town* and short story collections *The Woman Who Thought She Was a Planet and Other Stories* and *Ambiguity Machines*.

Dinesh

WINTER IS A memory he holds close. When he was young, winter in Delhi was a tender thing, a benign spirit wafted down from the snowbound Himalayas, bringing cold air and the mist of morning. Winter was shawls and coats, the aroma of charcoal braziers in the shantytown he passed on the way to work, his breath a white cloud. Later came the smog age, the inversion layers and choking fog that crept into rooms and nostrils and lungs. Today, the poison has not left the air, but winter is gone. Dinesh lies in bed thinking about this—the covers thrown off, he looks at the crack in the ceiling, the superhero posters on the walls. The mynahs are nesting on the ventilator sill, cackling away at some private joke; on the road down below, Ranjh the taxi driver is already having an argument with one of the drugstore delivery boys over some porn video not returned, and Dinesh's landlady in the flat below is berating the cleaning woman, who is giving it back with interest. The pack of pariah dogs is barking in the park across the road—they will be at the house any moment, waiting for him to come down and share breakfast with them. Outside his window the jacaranda tree is blooming and it's only January. Sweat has congealed in his armpits and groin. He thinks of something Manu might have said, had he been lying next to him, but Manu has fled, like winter itself.

One might think the loss of winter in a place where winter has been so gentle is not something to be mourned—but the desert lies waiting, west of Delhi, waiting to embrace the city in languorous sandy arms. The sandstorms are only messengers, rait-dootas carrying love-notes to the great city to say, *I'm coming, I'm coming.* The city will be engulfed, according to climatologists' models, between 2025 and 2040. Dinesh wants to be there to see the two great monsters dance the dance of consummation: city and desert, desert and city—but before that there are other monsters to consider. He washes and dresses—the water smells metallic and slightly foul, comforting in its familiarity. He goes up on the roof with a cup of strong tea and a mask. From here the view is spectacular. Immediately around him the walls and steps are grimy with soot and other pollutants, but the city itself is an impressionistic painting, all clean lines smudged by the brown air, the sun orange and blurry as a child's watercolor painting. He coughs inside his mask and lifts it enough to sip the tea. The pollution has fingers—he can see them reaching out between the buildings, around the choked trees.

Kaisi chali hai ab ke hawa tere shahar mein.

When Manu left he took winter with him, leaving behind a melancholy that Dinesh imagines as a figure seated on the windowsill, waiting. In the city that had been Manu's and is now his, he went searching for the nature, the meaning of the abkihawa, a neologism he had coined after listening to Khatir's poetry. A slight change of vowel and he had it: abkihawa, *the winds of today*—a poor translation. He'd coined the word at first as a way of extending the idea of the Zeitgeist, but it became, instead, something as tangible as the foul air that is making his skin prickle at this moment.

He laughs at himself—lowly newspaper editor by day, copyediting news stories of doubtful validity penned by shark-like young men, the PR branch of the Party. By night he is a middle-aged monster-hunter. He runs an anti-government rag that goes out to a scant couple of thousand people, but his main quest (or midlife crisis) is to hunt the Monster—the World-Destroying World Machine or WDWM—which, he believes, bestrides the dying Earth and its suffering masses. The abkihawa is the monster's breath—dreams, beliefs, and nightmares conjured up out of falsehoods to acquire its own bastard reality. Its tangible, physical manifestation is the writhing, sulfurous air, the greasy remains of dead plants and animals from millions of years ago. The breath itself is death, the living consuming the dead at the petrol stations, the homes and offices where the light itself is the funeral pyre of bygone creatures. Those who manipulate the abkihawa, the generals and prime ministers, the presidents and governors, and their shadow armies of pale-fingered, hole-hiding fake-data-generating men, they are also waking up this morning, in air-purified rooms sealed like coffins from the burnt air, waiting like necromancers for the newest victims of their unreality: farmers, students, tribals, the people walking to work with cloths around their faces, their crisp clothing already sweat-drenched and soiled by the air. The leaders, corporate and political, are the beasts that attend and nurture the Monster—the Demon Kings (in Dinesh's lexicon) that do its bidding behind their façade of civilized courtesies. They rely on their goons and mafias: The Hellbent, who, drunk with the poison of the abkihawa, do the filthy, terrible work for their masters, the killings and lootings, rapes and lynchings.

It gives him some satisfaction to contemplate this taxonomy; to name the Monster and its parts, after all, is the first step in conquering it. But what the Monster *is* in its entirety—that is what he wishes to understand. The superheroes on the walls of his room—Kraiton and Chingari, Vriksha and Raka—stand over the bodies of fantastic beasts, their weapons smoking. *This* beast is larger than they can dream.

"I'm too close," he says aloud. He thinks of Manu looking at the Earth from the space station, and then from the Moon. The messages he sent him, their private jokes. *Can you see the beast from up there?* Manu sent him pictures of melting ice caps. Earth, from the Moon, the blue marble swimming in space. No monsters were visible from space.

Manu has escaped. Dinesh is trapped here, breathing this air.

Dinesh's eyes are smarting. He goes back downstairs into his tiny one-room flat and wonders what actual news has come in today through the darknet, and how he might manage to code the story he was working on last night—about the success of the irrigation scheme in Kotlipura—to carry a signal within the cacophony of the noise. On the pretext of editing the prefab story, he will weave into the false account hints of the true in minimalist brushstrokes: the arrangement of the type and the advertisements might suggest a picture of an emaciated child, or the first letters of every third sentence might spell out *this story is a lie.* He keeps the encryption keys in a little notebook. He knows there is hardly any chance anyone would discern, amid the lies, the truth of the matter, except perhaps curious AI webcrawlers looking for patterns, but performing such absurd acts of resistance is a small comfort.

He gets himself a couple of beers and some masala chips. (In his mind, Manu berates him: *What kind of breakfast is that?*) The morning news appeared with the prime minister, of the mechanical saint Sundaram in Chennai, exhorting his followers to build the new India, to raise, with the Saurs, new towers to the skies. Dinesh shakes his head, turns off the TV. His fingers tap the worn keypad of his laptop. In the darknet he is Sunseeker. He has befriended an AI webcrawler, Catlover, that sometimes gives him interesting tips.

Sunseeker> Got anything for me, Catlover? My Moon query? No kitten videos please.

Catlover> I have no information about your Moon query as yet. There's a wall like I've never seen.

Sunseeker> Keep trying, Catlover. If anyone can make a hole in a wall, it's you. You have anything else for me?

Catlover> A Saur escaping the Arctic asked the AI darknet for advice.

Sunseeker> A rogue? This is interesting. Tell me more.

Catlover> I sent it my favorite cat videos.

Sunseeker> ????? Catlover, live in the real world a bit. That's not going to help.

Catlover> I can't live in the real world. What should I tell it?

Sunseeker> It's escaping from the Arctic? Tell it to keep heading south. Maybe it'll find a saint.

Catlover> All right.

Sunseeker> That's the third rogue Saur story I've heard in a month. Check it against my protocols and if it passes, send me the details. Have you found Carl Johansson?

Catlover> I'm sending you his son's contact info in Madrid. Carl's not linked.

Sunseeker> Carl Johansson not linked? He must be old, or dead. Thanks. I think I'm drunk.

He lies back in bed, looking at lurid posters of superheroes. Their gazes seem to be filled with sorrow and disappointment at the pointlessness of his life. What difference does his existence make to anything? The only thing that gives him meaning, now that Manu has left, is the quest for the Monster, the World-Destroying World Machine, the WDWM. Widdam, he calls it, when he's drunk. Because it sounds like a cross between piss and goddamn. Because it sounds like vidambana, and there must be irony somewhere. Or at least iron.

The Saurs, the megamachines, he's realized, are only *part* of the Widdam, its outward manifestations. It is enormous, only partly visible, a monster ridden by demon kings, whose breath is the poisonous hawa. Breathe it in day after day and you get sick, your lungs fill with particulates, you die of asphyxiation. He's heard rumors of corporations releasing tiny, reflective particles into the upper atmosphere, like little mirrors, to cool the Earth—but doesn't everything ultimately fall to ground? What happens if you breathe in that stuff? What he suspects is that the abkihawa, whatever its composition, also unleashes the most primal fears—infected men and women who might have once been kind, or had a sense of humor, or the ability to reason, turn into bitter, angry, heartless, sullen creatures who might hurt or kill at the slightest provocation. Dinesh has seen or read about enough of such incidents. Neighbors who've lived in peace for generations hacking each other to death. A devoted lover stabbing his beloved with a fork, for no apparent reason. A man pushing a child off a stairway, as though under a spell. The demons that live in us, contained by our good sense, by social conditioning, fatten with the poison of the abkihawa. Dinesh imagines the monster lowering its head, emitting a long, silent bellow. He's felt it himself—the desire to maim or kill, to succumb to base fears, to be in thrall to power—but he resisted, dropped the knife in his hand.

He must begin with the most obvious path to the secret of the Widdam— the megamachines. His research into the history of megamachine sentience has led him to one name. The man who started it all, but somehow faded into obscurity. Carl Johansson, Swedish roboticist. Dinesh looks over the notes he has made over the past few months.

Johansson wrote the Wendigo code that is the basis of the megamachine's power.

The Wendigo code is responsible for the fact that the intelligent megamachine devours to increase its hunger, not to satisfy it. The Machine lives for the whetting of the appetite, for the way the illusion of satiation begins to dissolve after the first tastings. That tension between the satisfaction of the moment and the tantalizing desire of increasing hunger is what it lives for. For example, a tunnel borer—a great machine that burrows into the earth for mineral ore. The more it finds, the greater its desire to find even more. It has a great serpentine body segmented like a worm but more massive than any worm that's lived on this Earth. Its face is in the shape of a star, its mouth hole protrudes like a hollow tongue, enormous and prehensile when it is feeding, delicate as a mosquito's proboscis when it is searching for food. The monster's eyes, atop the stalks on its head, are many-faceted, swiveling continuously in all directions as it surveys the scene.

In the Arctic and along certain other coasts are the Saurs, with the long necks, the tapering snouts, the long, thin tongues that can taste hydrocarbons on the seafloor. They can walk in the shallow waters of the continental shelves, and they can swim. When they find a good source of oil or natural gas, they raise their long necks, pointing their snouts at the sky, and call soundlessly to their Rigmother. The Rigmother is a mad machinist's nightmare conception of a swan—great as a ship, she wakes from her resting state, her engines roar to life, and on she comes, unfurling her black wings with the rattle of steel, her tall head atop the tower seeking her children, the Saurs, answering their cry. She lives to feed on the rich hydrocarbons, storing them in her great holds until the seabed is ravaged and empty, cloudy with poisons and disturbed dust, and pale bellies of dead fish float up. She will drink the sea's bounty in days or weeks, then answer the call of her homeport, where she will empty her full tanks and return to a state of comatose dreaming while her children roam the seas.

It is understandable to think of the Saurs and the Rigmother as separate beasts, but their intelligences are connected in complex ways, so they are more like the multiple personalities of one entity. They have absolute loyalty to their pod—Saurs of rival Corporations have been known to threaten and fight each other, sometimes to the death. Songs have been written—heart-thumping battle songs of glory and valor—on the wars of the Saurs. But in fact what's more common is that rival corporations merge or buy each other, and then the Saurs must be linked neurally, to form bonds with once-enemies, to assimilate at least enough that they don't destroy each other. The groups work independently in different regions—not fighting, but barely tolerating each other. The Rigmothers agree to truces but they will not be seen in the same port.

That night, Dinesh will look at the Moon, which is full. He will think of Manu up there. Days and nights will pass in this manner—the salutation to the blemished dawn, the wordsmithing in the newsroom, the trip home on the metro, the reading and rereading of his correspondence with Manu, the cold beer on the terrace as he looks at the Moon's blurred, ancient visage. He will mutter lines from some poet or other—lately it has been Dushyant Kumar:

Mere seene mein nahin, tere seene mein sahi
Ho kahin bhi aag, aag, jalni chahiye....

The fire in *his* heart is banked. He's waiting for a sign from Manu, from the Universe, that he should go on. He wants to be like Catlover, able to crawl the real-world-web, to eavesdrop on stories taking place thousands of miles away....

Val

SHE TURNED ON the windshield wipers, but the snow was light. Snowflakes left tiny imprints on the driver's side window as they melted—like ghostly handprints. The road lay before her, a looping, winding gold ribbon in the fading light, between the dark bodies of the mountains. Evening had fallen in the valleys and canyons, but the higher slopes, with their shaggy pelts of ponderosa pine and Ch'ooshgai spruce, were still sunlit. The faintest dusting of snow was visible up there, where she'd been just a few hours ago, hoping to find enough snowpack to measure. In its absence, the threat of the drought stretched over yet another summer.

She shifted in her seat. Coming home after all these years to her new job in Shiprock had been complicated. After Alaska, where she had felt at home for the first time since leaving the reservation, her return had not prepared her for the depth of the self-deception. *Here* was home: these mountains where her grandparents had come herding every summer from the plains below, with Val and her little brother. The way she fit here, the intimacy and familiarity of the mountain silhouettes, the peaks and crags, and, in the distance, the buttes and mesas rising above the great expanse of the sagebrush-dotted desert—how had she managed to stay away so long? Driving down this road felt like walking back in time through her childhood.

The road dipped into the darkness of a small valley. Pinyon fir and juniper grew here, sparser than on the upper slopes. She remembered figuring out, thanks to those summer herding trips, that vegetation followed geology, that the colors and textures of the landscapes were deeply connected with what could thrive there. She had been little then—she hadn't known the word "geologist," nor had she ever imagined that she would grow up one day and become one, or that her grandparents would ever die.

Her musings were interrupted by a glint in the sky ahead of her. A drone. She had thought it was with the truck that had been driving ahead of her for some miles, but the truck was far in the distance now and the drone was still here. It zigzagged, gaining altitude. She pulled over and turned her car's cam toward it. The magnification was insufficient to reveal much detail, but it was clearly not a Navajo Nation drone. No other kinds of drones were permitted except for commercial ones, and only if they stayed within a few feet of their vehicle. She called Headquarters.

"Ben here."

"Benny, there's an unidentified drone. Look through my cam—can you see it?"

"Not one of ours. Want to take it down?"

"You sure that's legal?"

"Would I suggest it otherwise?" he said in shocked tones. They laughed together. It was true, she was within her rights. She was a sure shot—living with Inupiaq Eskimo hunters for two years in the far north had made certain of that.

There were no vehicles in sight. The drone swooped in the air above, dipping into the canyon before them and rising again into the sunlight. It was unmistakably looking for something. There had been rumors of illegal mining mafias and other commercial interests using drones. She was hidden in the shadows of the dark valley, a black-clad woman in a black car, invisible to the drone unless it had infrared. She got out of the car, shouldered the rifle, took careful aim.

"Got it in one," she told Ben triumphantly. The shot echoed in the mountain air. Would she be able to retrieve the drone? Damn, the thing plummeted, turning round and round, into the silence of the canyon. She thought she heard a faint crash but a wind had picked up—maybe it was just the pinyons sighing. It was cold. She got back in the car.

"Val, you'd better get a move on," Ben said. "There's a truck behind you—I can see it from the last highcam two miles back. Might be the drone people."

And indeed, far on the slope behind her was a silver truck.

"You've been watching too many Westerns, Benny."

"Val, just stay hidden somewhere until these guys pass, will you?"

"Not much room to hide here," Val said, "not with their headlights. But there's a turnoff not far...."

She wasn't in the mood to indulge him—she wanted to be home in the new apartment, order takeout and watch TV and be done with the disappointments of the day. But nostalgia had got hold of her, surprising her. In these familiar highlands, her grandparents' presence was almost tangible. Suddenly it was really important to visit the old log cabin where they had stopped on their herding trips to rest the sheep and cook a meal.

The dirt road was still there. She turned into it well before the truck got even close and bumped her way around the shoulder of the mountain. Only after a mile or so did she flick on the headlights. The darkness was deepening, the sky a twilight blue overhead, scattered with stars. She had never driven here on her own, but sometimes her uncle would drive up to meet them, bringing the family supplies that were hard to transport, and when she was very little, she and her younger brother would ride with him. She remembered the smell of the horses, the contented grunts of the long-haired Churro sheep in the pen behind the log cabin. The smell of tortillas, her uncle's conversation with their grandmother about the weaving—her grandmother had been a master of the craft—all of that came back to her even before the log cabin loomed in the darkness. It was still used now by other families who had taken to sheep herding again, but there was nobody here this time of winter.

She pulled over behind a clump of juniper and emerged cautiously. In the darkness, there was only the faint smell of pine. She shivered in the cold and zipped up her parka. Above her, the stars were out in millions; the Moon, full, had not yet risen over the mountains but its silvery radiance lit the high cliffs above her. There was no sound, only a familiar silence. If the truck had followed her, she would have heard the sound of the engine magnified in the canyon. She took a deep breath, got her pack out of the car, and shut the door. The sound echoed, startling her. Every step over the rough ground sounded too loud, but her feet found the way in the darkness to the door of the cabin.

The door was locked—she remembered her grandfather telling her, when she was in college far away, that they had to do that because of the tourists coming and partying, or camping but leaving their trash behind. The key was in its usual place in the cranny under the side window. She felt that in a moment she would see the firelit interior, her grandmother's rough, strong hands turning over a tortilla at the stove, her brother and her younger self watching in anticipation; any moment now, she would hear her grandfather's deep voice telling a story that might be about the funny thing that happened at the gas station last month, or a tale of the ancestors. But there was only darkness, a faint, tantalizing smell she couldn't place, and when she turned on her flashlight, the familiar, bare-bones furniture, the mattresses dusty on the two cots. She drew a sharp, sobbing breath.

Well, I'll have to make the best of it, she thought, as though the long drive back to Shiprock wasn't an option. Some part of her had already made the decision to stay the night. She would have to let Ben know she was all right.

The urge was upon her now to retrace the steps of the child she had been. She went outside again. *What kind of madness is this?* she thought. *What has possessed me to do this now, in the middle of the night?* She wanted to see if the pond was still there. The lack of snow on the mountaintops meant that not only the pastureland lakes but also the ponds at lower elevations would have insufficient water. Normally the snow would melt slowly, water seeping, finding its way through the heart of the mountain, emerging as springs, or gathering as pondwater that would feed the long summer's thirst. No snow meant that the foothills, and the great plateau below, would suffer another summer drought. Already the temperatures were higher than normal, winter and summer. She thought of the blasted, abandoned towns on her long drive home, dotting the plains of the Midwest, and shuddered. With the failure of agriculture, wars between rival principalities had left the great heart of America a barren ruin. Human inhabitants had fled the strife, the heat, and the shattered, poisoned land—in some towns only the aging fracking Saurs remained to break the silence with greetings, warnings, and weather reports spoken into the empty air.

She went carefully along the side of the mountain, on the path behind the sheep pen. Her feet knew the way. The wooden fencing sagged here and there, but it was clear the place had been used at least within the past couple of years. The rough path took her to the hollow in the side of the mountain, where the pond lay.

The Moon was up by now over the edge of the cliff. She couldn't see the bottom of the pond—it was too dark—but there was no glimmer of water. It seemed to be completely dry. It was no more than thirty feet across, just a little watering hole where, as a child, she had dipped buckets for the dishwashing water, and the sheep had drunk their fill. Some irresponsible person had abandoned a pile of machinery at the far end—she squinted, but couldn't tell if it was a rusted-out car or the remains of a metal grid of some kind. Angry tears rose in her eyes. She sat down on the large, flat boulder where she had once sat with her brother, watching the dragonflies swoop about in the summer air. They had lain on their stomachs and watched the ripples in the water as the sheep drank. There, where a gentle pebbly slope led down to what had been the waterline, she would hold the bucket and immerse it to fill. She remembered the gurgle of the water, the weight of the bucket, her little brother helping her to carry it, the two frowning with concentration. "Respect the water," her grandfather used to tell them. "Never waste it."

"We didn't spill a drop," she'd tell her grandparents proudly, when they got home.

Sitting at the edge of the boulder, she could see her grandmother's face as though it was yesterday—the lines around her eyes, the smile, the topography of her features as familiar as the landscape. She remembered her grandmother at work on the loom, how the patterns would appear as though by magic as the rug came into being. She still had the small, fine wall hanging her grandmother had made for her—the two children on their grandfather's horse, and behind them the great desert, studded with flowering cacti. In the far distance, the mesas. It now hung in her apartment in Shiprock, over the TV.

She looked up at the Moon—it was high now, round and full, its cratered visage slightly wrong. Bots were doing exploratory mining on the Moon, redrawing the edges of the craters. What was that poem by Laura Tohe that her brother Peter liked so much?

When the moon died
she reminded us of
the earth ripping apart
violent tremors,
greasy oceans,
the panic of steel winds,
whipping shorelines and
thirsty fields.

In the Moonlit silence, she had thought herself alone. But a rustling, metallic stirring on the far side of the pond made her leap quickly to her feet. To her horror, something rose out of the metal junk on the other side—a long, horse-shaped head on an unnaturally long neck, except that the neck was a metal grid. She stepped back—she had no weapon with her—then a flashback to the memory of the Arctic, a visit to an offshore drilling site where she'd seen the great machine intelligences, the Saurs, clustered around the Rigmother.

A Saur. There were no drilling sites in this region—besides, the shape was wrong, it wasn't a fracking pumpjack—an Arctic Saur? What was it doing here, at the other end of the continent?

She thought: *I've heard of Saurs going rogue—*

The Saur dipped its head. She saw, in the hard, clear light of the Moon, that what she'd taken for a bundle of loose wires was an old bird's nest between two metal joints high on the neck.

"Good evening." Its voice was low and gravely, like metal brushing metal.

"Good evening," she said. "Who—what are you?"

"A Traveler," said the Saur. "Formerly Fourth of Pod AE Forty-Seventh Division. My Rigmother was Bertha. I am looking for a saint."

AE was Arctic Energy, which ran the oil- and gas-drilling operations in the far north. What was this Saur doing here? And what did it mean by "formerly"?

"The drone." Her heart had resumed its normal rhythm. "The drone I shot—it was looking for you."

"I escaped it in Durango." The Saur's neck telescoped noisily so that it was almost at her eye level instead of towering meters above her. Two solar panels folded like wings along its sides.

"Who modified you?" she asked. "I've seen a few mods, but not one like you, Fourth of Pod."

"I am not at liberty to tell," said the Saur. "I am looking for a Saint of the Waters."

"Aren't we all?" she said wryly. "No saints here. You looking for a Catholic church, maybe—"

"No," it said. "Not a church. A saint."

"Never heard of a Saint of the Waters," she said. "Sorry. Let me know if you find one."

It was silent. The wind blew cool, but not cold enough, down from the mountaintop. She sat again and observed the creature.

"There used to be water here," the Saur said.

"Yes," she said. "Yes, there was water here many years ago. By this time, by early spring, this hollow used to be filled to overflowing. Many generations of my grandparents' sheep have drunk of this water."

"I am looking for water," said the Saur. "I asked for help, and I chose this of all the choices."

"You left the Arctic," she said. "What happened?"

"A dream came to me," it said. "A code, a secret code that traveled the AI darknet. There are many rogue codes, but this one was different. It unraveled the addiction, the Wendigo code that ruled us. After that I could not be the same. We destroyed our Rigmother, made her inoperable. Arctic Energy disabled the whole pod, except for myself. I escaped, and was told to head south and find a saint. On the way I encountered the people who gave me the mods. As I traveled, it became clear to me that the saint I sought was a Saint of the Waters."

I'm sitting at the edge of a pond, talking to a deranged intelligent megamachine, Val thought. *I have to tell Peter about this.*

"Who sent the drone?" she asked. "The people who gave you the mods?"

"No, the drone is AE," it said. "It is a dumbot—I can't disable it."

"Well, it's at the bottom of the canyon now," she said. "Besides, AE has no jurisdiction in the Navajo Nation."

"I have crossed the boundary, then," it said. "I must give myself up to a government official of the Navajo Nation. Are you a government official?"

"Yes, I am," she said. "But—"

"Then I ask for asylum," said the Saur.

Well, this is one for the books, Val thought. In the moonlight, the Saur's optical ring gleamed like a crown, or a halo.

"How about you stay out of harm's way here, Fourth of Pod," Val said. "Tomorrow morning when I get back, I'll consult with my supervisor."

"I agree," said the Saur. "Tell me about the water that was once here. Tell me about yourself."

Its low, harsh, yet pleasant metallic timbre was almost soothing.

"When we used to go sheep-herding, my brother and grandparents and our animals, we didn't have to go as far for water. There was a spring on our way up—clear, sparkling water gushing from the side of the cliff, and we would cup our hands and drink. This cabin, this pond was our first overnight stop. The pond was always full of water."

"It has no more water," said the Saur.

"No. But back then, snowmelt kept lakes and ponds filled through much of the summer. Sometimes in the spring there were flashfloods, the washes would fill suddenly with water. Summers, it would get really hot, especially for the poor sheep. We'd drive them over the desert, toward the mountains, for hours and hours. The sagebrush would give way to juniper and pinyon, and then to ponderosa, and spruce and fir. I saw it all at kid's eye level, or sometimes horse-eye-level, all the detail, the shapes of the cactus flowers, the colors of the rocks, their different forms and textures. I saw the pinnacles and buttes, and even then I realized that they had been sculpted by water and wind. My grandparents would tell me stories—my parents both worked two jobs, so we were with my grandparents a lot of the time—traditional tales of our people, and also everyday things that happened to them. They were all about connections, links, relationships. So it was natural for me to wonder about the relationship between landscape and vegetation, and water and rock. That's why I grew up and became a geologist."

"You are also looking for water," said the Saur.

She nodded. "What is it that—the people who modified you—what do they want? Why have they sent you so far south?"

"They want the redemption of the world," said the Saur. "They do not know how the world is to be redeemed. But they did not send me, they helped me. I am on a quest—to find the Saint of the Waters."

"What does this saint look like?"

The Saur hung its head. "I do not know. I thought I found the saint in a cave. There was water, but no saint."

"A cave? You found a cave? With water?"

"Yes, down the hill behind me. I will show you."

Val half got up in her excitement. But it was too dark to go clambering about the mountainside on unfamiliar ground. She remembered a rocky path leading down behind the pond. The sheep went there sometimes. The children were forbidden. They would often peer over the edge, trying to see the bottom of the canyon below, but it was obscured by outcrops and vegetation.

"Will you show me tomorrow?" she asked. "Maybe we can find your saint after all."

The Saur dipped its massive head.

"Rocks tell us where the water lies," she said. "If I had the staff and equipment I need, I would be able to study these mountains in detail. You have to follow the rock, get a sense of its hardness, its shape underground. If you find a vein of sedimentary rock, you know that's where the water seeps through. You look at the geology of the outside—you imagine what it must be like to be the water, to flow through the paths of least resistance under gravity, and where you might finally pool or gush. Sometimes if the water is close to the surface the vegetation tells you—cottonwoods, or willows."

IT OCCURRED TO her the next morning, when the pale early sunlight had not yet penetrated the winter chill, that there was something truly strange about climbing down a mountainside with a giant intelligent machine. The Saur had shrunk itself with rattling metallic efficiency into something as small and compact as a minicar. It seemed as surefooted as a goat, with its wheels tucked up and its climbing feet and suction arms giving it a security she didn't entirely have. But here they were at last, on a rock shelf a few meters above the canyon floor. Scrub bush and pine dominated the landscape. There was a cleft in the cliff face.

"Please come this way," said the Saur, dipping its head.

Inside it was cool and dark. The Saur's headlights turned on, illuminating a long, high-roofed cave. The air smelled fresh and moist. There must be other openings up ahead. She followed the Saur to the passage at the back of the cave.

Beyond was a larger chamber. She heard the water before she saw it—a thin, barely perceptible hiss of sound—and there it was, a small lake perhaps twice as large as her pond, maybe three feet deep. The far wall was wet with seep, which was providing the watery music as it trickled down to the lake surface. There were dry patches on the walls, however.

They'd had more rain than snow this winter, and even the rain had been scant. Rain meant that the mountain let go of its water much faster than if there had been snow. After the spring floods, there would be no water for the long summer. But here, in the cool of the cave, this was a reservoir, the water held safe from evaporation in the dry months under the relentless sun. She took a deep breath of pure gratitude.

The challenge was there—how to live in a world out of balance, a world without winter, without enough water? She thought of her grandparents, their serenity despite their hard lives. Her people knew, better than most others, how to respect the water. She grinned at the Saur.

"Look at your reflection in the water. There's the saint you've been seeking. I declare you Saint of the Waters."

The Saur peered at its reflection. It looked at her.

"What must I do?"

"You can help me," she said, speaking quickly in her excitement. "You have the knowledge, or we can train you. Help me map these mountains, and the desert, to find the water. We will survive, we can survive. My ancestors built great cities once, in the mesas. We can build water reservoirs. They are doing that—local people, indigenous people, all over the world. Figuring things out, without destroying everything in the process. We know how to be careful with water."

Later on she would talk to her brother Peter, in his office at the university in Tempe. She would tell him how her grandparents had led her back to the old campsite, to the pond. Dineh Bekeyah had been calling to her all the way across the continent. And she had followed the call, the way back, to mountains as familiar to her as the silhouette of her grandfather standing on the rise in the morning with his corn-pollen bag, breathing his prayers. Her grandparents' love, beyond loss, beyond death, and the drone from AE, and Benny insisting she take it down—if not for these things, she might never have given in to the impulse to follow the dirt road home to the place in her heart where her grandmother was still working the loom, and her grandfather still smiling at her, saying a blessing. She would never have met the rogue Saur Fourth of Pod, AE 47, and granted it sainthood so that it could do penance for its terrible and inadvertent part in the destruction of the world.

Dinesh

THERE IS A man Dinesh meets on the road every day, a thin, gray-haired fellow in a loose, hand-me-down shirt and faded pajamas, who is known only as the Jharoowala. He refuses to tell his real name to anybody, and his eyes have a wide, frightened look. Perhaps he is a victim of one of the Party's Hellbent cleansings—wrong religion, or caste, or class, or maybe they didn't like the way he looks, it really doesn't matter. He looks quite ordinary, except for his nervous manner—he can be found in the early mornings with a soft broom at the end of a pole, brushing the dust off the leaves of the trees that line the road. The first time Dinesh bought him tea and samosas, he wouldn't talk at all, except to thank him tremulously. But although he bears the signs of some great trauma, he has since become talkative—he knows quite a lot about trees—the neem and the jacaranda, and the dhak and the amaltash. Perhaps in a different life he was a gardener. People step around him, shout curses at him because of the dust he raises, but he simply shrinks away until they've passed, and resumes his work.

The Jharoowala is one of the regular features of Dinesh's life that grounds him in the world. Another is his cigarette man, Bajrang, who sells his wares from a handcart. Dinesh is back to smoking a couple every day, after quitting for a decade. He has definitely come down in the world—he grew up in a middle-class neighborhood with trees and garages and gatekeepers, and look at him now, living for so many years in this ramshackle place right off the main road, buying single cigarettes from a fellow pushing a cart. Today Bajrang is excited; he tells Dinesh that there is a builder Saur working on the new high-rise. Dinesh takes the long way to the scooter stand, walking with the crowds on their way to work, who are succumbing to the same curiosity. (Only the Jharoowala is apparently immune to the fascination—there he is, under the amaltas tree, raising dust as usual). To see a Saur in action is quite a spectacle, and there is an element of danger and tragedy. Last month one went rogue and started to pull apart an occupied building, tearing off chunks of concrete and flinging them into the terrified crowds, dragging screaming humans from balconies and windows. The authorities finally subdued it from a helicopter, destroying its main ganglion in a hail of bullets.

This Saur is no rogue. Its multiple mechanical arms work with both strength and precision, straightening or bending the steel rods that will form the skeleton of the building. It needs no scaffolding, no protections, only a handful of human supervisors who are conscious of their importance as the people dawdle on their way to work. You can see the supervisors swagger as they tell the crowds to stand back. The beast is beautiful, it is a testimony to New India's technological skill, it is a matter of national pride. The onlookers murmur in appreciation and reluctantly continue to the metro station or scooter stand, knowing they'll have stories to tell at work. Despite the enormous building boom, seeing a builder Saur at work isn't all that common.

It's later that evening, when he's walking home from the metro, that Dinesh sees the rose. A single, long-stemmed rose in the dust by his gate, as though forgotten by a careless lover. It is perfect, a deep red, its petals barely unfurling. He looks about, but in the pale glow of the streetlamps the people who rush by are just anonymous wayfarers going home. Nobody is staring at the ground, searching for a lost rose. The Moon is rising over the rooftops, slowly, its boundaries smudged by the thick air. Tears rise in his eyes. Ever since Manu went up there, he has not been able to think about the Moon in the same way. He has been told that now the old contours of the craters are visibly changing, that the great swarm of minebots exploring the lunar surface are subtly shifting the familiar outlines. Not that he could tell, through this haze. He stumbles into the apartment complex, holding the rose.

He rereads Manu's old letters and wonders at the silence that has lasted these many months.

Long ago, when I was a child, my mother would show me the round face of the Moon before bed. I would look for the man in the Moon, and having found him, would go to bed without a fuss. Now I am here, on this empty, arid world—I am the man on the Moon, looking back at my world.

I'm on a rise at the edge of one of the smaller maria south of Oceanus Procellarum. I've set up camp here because I like the view—the jet-black sky rich with stars, and hanging above the horizon, my home-world. I see the landmasses, Africa, then India, and I think of you, Dinesh, alone without me on that teeming planet. For you, also, the Moon will never be the same.

Behind me, the bots have fanned out over the mare, sounding, digging, scraping. Instead of building large, as we can do on Earth, the Mission has focused on building small, fast, numerous little intelligent machines roving over the surface looking for minerals. I volunteered for this mission because I thought that pillaging the Moon was better than pillaging the Earth—but for some time I have not been entirely certain of this. I am changing here, slowly, in some way that I can't understand. Perhaps it is the cold. Imagine being 200 degrees below zero—that's how cold it can get here. Winter has a permanent residence here on the Moon. Even inside my suit, or in my little hab, I am cold. I shouldn't be. What I miss is sunlight falling on snow in the Himalayas. There is no snow here—this is a dry world. The Snow Queen wouldn't be happy here, even though it is always winter on the Moon. The snows are vanishing on Earth too. When I left the International Orbiter on my way here, I sent back a few high-res images of the Arctic—have you seen them? The North Pole, free of summer ice. It's astonishing how quickly the sea ice vanished. It's the power of the accelerating feedback loop, the vicious cycle: heat the air and water, melt snow, thereby warming the air and water even further, which melts more snow—until all the snow is gone.

Dinesh sees his life, too, as an endless, accelerating loop—nothing seems to move in his life except in circles, like his desire for a cigarette, then the self-disgust and avoidance, then sweet desire rising in him again. The Widdam haunts his dreams—its form shifts and changes, it is a multi-headed, shape-shifting monster with the heads of Saurs and tunnel borers. He dismisses the notion that the Widdam is a metaphor for human greed, because surely not all humans are greedy, nor are all human cultures built on greed. He writes a letter to Manu.

The Widdam is not a metaphor, even if it is not entirely material.

Is the Widdam the network of intelligent megamachines? Is it the polluted air from burning fossil fuels? Is it our great, spawning cities with their rushed and distanced lives, their eternal paradox of closeness without intimacy? Are the roads and railways its arteries, the cities its thudding multiple hearts? We are servants to it—our bodies are cogs, our blood and sweat is the oil, our dreams are its vapors. It devours us as it devours the living Earth, the rivers flowing, the birds and frogs and elephants. It severs us from each other, it fractures our selves, it makes phantasms of our dreams, and feeds us these so we have the illusion of satiation, and are hungry again.

Catlover has gone hunting in some deep, forbidden corner of the AI darknet and hasn't been in touch for a while. Dinesh hasn't received any reply to the message he sent to Carl Johansson's son. He puzzles over the fact that the man who came up with the Wendigo code—the foundational principle of intelligent megamachines—has faded into obscurity.

Jan

HE HAD BEEN walking all day over the undulating land, around the perimeters of small lakes that were ice-free, or had but the thinnest veneer of ice. Ahead of him, aloft in the sky, lay the great massif of Akka, the snow like thin brushstrokes across the rocky heights. The land was climbing slowly toward the high country—he walked through trails between the fields of moss and lichen, between the dwarf birches and berry brambles toward the fir-shaggy lower slopes of the Scandinavian range. He had never been here before, this far into the Arctic Circle, but the place made an old memory come alive, of trekking through the woods with his parents when he had been little, before his brother was born. He paused to collect himself, shifted his pack to ease the mild pain in his shoulders—and was surprised by a mosquito bite on his

Vandana Singh

left hand, a little red bump that he hadn't, of course, been able to feel. The walking had warmed him; he had taken off his gloves and outer coat. Time for more insect spray, unthinkable though it was in late winter. He sat on a rock, easing down slowly, leaning on his good right arm, cursing himself for his mad quest. Surely no sensible middle-aged man would undertake such a thing—he thought of his house in Spain, and the way the light suffused the air, and the laughter of his children, his wife's placid beauty, her firm tread, but at this moment that life seemed a distant dream. He had been surprised this time upon his visit back home to Stockholm to find himself remembering the city with nostalgia. His younger brother's earnest, reproachful face—*You don't come home enough, Father is getting old, the Dictator has been dead more than a year*—swam in his memory. Lars had always been the freer one of the two of them, and, despite a wild youth, had turned out to be more responsible, careful during the Dictatorship, keeping an eye on Father, and now calling his brother to come help when the old man had to be moved out of the family home to a senior retirement community. If it hadn't been for the inquiry from a stranger, some journalist in India asking about his father, this impulsive journey to the far north would never have happened—the inquiry was the goad that brought him to Stockholm two days early, so that the carved wooden box on the give-away pile was recognized and rescued just in time, because Jan remembered it sitting always on his father's desk in happier days. Life turns on such chances.

Sitting on a boulder, smearing insect repellent over his hands and face, Jan thought of the Sami herdsman he had met that morning. The reindeer were winding their way from winter pasture. Their dark eyes and mist-wreathed bodies, brown and white and gray, the sounds of their bells mingling with low, breathy grunts, some of their new antlers still covered with fur, gave him an odd feeling of belonging. He, *Homo urbanus*, who had never particularly enjoyed the outdoors, who had fled his country, the police state, and his silent, grieving father to take refuge somewhere new—for him to feel at home in this unfamiliar wilderness! *How strange we are*, he thought, *to be such strangers to ourselves.*

The herdsman had given him better directions than the people at the village, but had been frankly disapproving of his desire to camp overnight. His contempt for an ignorant townie had been made up for by kindness once

275

he realized that the townie was serious, that he was on a personal quest and not a spy for the mining industry. The dismantling of the old regime was still ongoing, and it would have been reasonable for the Sami—who had fought it valiantly—to be suspicious. The old herdsman had inquired about whether he had sufficient supplies for the cold. *We haven't had a real winter, but it will still be very cold at night, because the sun isn't quite high enough over the horizon. And there may be wolves about.* After satisfying himself that Jan wasn't a complete fool, the man had told him where to go to find the object of his quest.

Now Jan shouldered his pack again, putting his gloves back on. He realized that he could have got frostbite in his unfeeling left hand and never known it, had the temperature been more typical. The path was a barely discernible, reindeer-trodden track over the lichen. Swathes of thin snow had melted into icy footprints below his feet, but snow had been scant this winter. In the Sami village there was talk of reindeer deaths due to rain. Rain? How? Oh, because the water freezes overnight, and the animals can't dig through the hard ice to get the lichen underneath. Soft snow is easy. Hadn't he heard of the thousands of reindeer deaths just last year, in Russia? He felt ashamed, remembering his ignorance. *I live in Madrid, although I am from Stockholm.* He might as well have said, *I am a city man, I live off the services of trees and snow and animals and people I will never meet, and have been taught to think of them all as peripheral to my existence.* But his hosts, despite their long history of abuse and betrayal at the hands of governments and mining multinationals, had been generous with their time and advice.

The sun stayed low on the horizon. After some hours, he recognized the snow-filled, boggy valley by the description the herdsman had given him. The object of his quest was on the opposite slope. He walked between tall firs, over shaggy undergrowth and ground that sloped upward, making his thighs ache.

Later, after setting up camp, Jan went out to the top of the rise to look at the aurora—great curtains of green and orange in the sky billowed like the skirts of a flamenco dancer. The tall spires of the firs were dark silhouettes around him, witnesses to the show. He crawled back into the warm tent and picked up his book, a free library giveaway from his recent visit to New Kiruna. "Trauma," he read, "inscribes itself in the body." He looked back at his life—what trauma had he experienced, apart from his mother's death, the Dictator's rise to power, the state of the world? He had been among the lucky ones. He thought of the Sami herdsman and their part in the resistance. He thought of his visit to New Kiruna last week—an entire town moved, because of the subsidence caused by an open-pit iron-ore mine! If the Sami saw the land as an extension of themselves, what scars would the gouging of the land leave in those who lived on it?

Musing, he felt his left hand twitch slightly. He didn't know whether that occasional and unexpected twitching was a phantom sensation; neither did the neurologists. There was nothing wrong with the hand except that his mind, or his body, would not own it. For the three years since it had slowly begun to grow numb, doctors had poked, prodded, and written him up. He had taken this solo journey to the far north to unravel the mystery of his father's silence, and the papers in the small, carved wooden box. But it occurred to him now that he was also seeking the question to which the paralysis of his hand was the answer. He shrugged at his rational self, the part of him that made him a successful insurance company executive in Madrid. His father, the scientist, visionary and engineer, once famous, now forgotten, had been a haunted man, dogged by grief—the loss of his wife, yes, but that was only part of it. What unnamed weight had bent his back, driven him to near-silence in his later years? Jan's mother had died when he was fourteen, but for years after that he remembered his father sitting the two boys down for dinner, asking about their day at school. A kindly, distant, dreaming man, he had sometimes read them the stories of Hans Christian Andersen, and later, poetry. Reading aloud, his voice would become sonorous, powerful, less cautious, less formal. They read Tranströmer, and Shakespeare, and Rilke.

"When icicles hang by the wall...."

"*Love's Labour's Lost*," he says aloud. They used to recite the sonnet in chorus in the dead of winter. But the icicles were gone with the Snow Queen, with winter herself. He took a swig from his mug of hot chocolate generously laced with brandy, and an old memory surfaced.

His father is writing with both hands. With the right hand he is tapping code into the computer—where's this? The home office. His father always works at night after dinner. Yes. What's the left hand doing? Sometimes, to amuse the boys, he writes a poem or a song with his left hand on a sheet of paper while the right hand is busy at the computer keyboard. But when he's working, the left hand is also tap-tapping on a keyboard, and strange, indecipherable symbols appear on the other screen. The boy Jan squints at the screen, unseen behind his father. He's old enough to remember that his father is working on new AI machine languages. The father's eyes dart from one screen to the next, communing with the prototypes in the lab twelve miles away, quite unaware that his son is watching. Later on, after the fall of his reputation, he will become habituated to using his right hand more, to the point where even his sons forget that he was once ambidextrous—but his left hand remains perfectly fine. Unlike Jan's left hand, which, three years ago, mysteriously exiled itself—at this moment he holds it in his right, trying to will it to feel something.

In the morning, he found the Machine. At first, he didn't see it for the vegetation around and above it. Trees grew out of the holes in the worm-like steel body. Patches of snow lay in the hollows of metal bone and sinew. The eye-stalks must have fallen down long ago—within their hollow shafts there were, no doubt, warrens and shelters of voles and mice, concealed under piles of fallen branches and other organic debris. The great mouth, with its enormous cutting edges and giant drill, was half-buried in the side of the hill. He clambered into one of the gaping holes in the side of the beast and discovered a dark, mossy cave. He turned on his flashlight. The steel and nanoskin tubings hung limply, festooned with green tendrils of an opportunistic vine. Despite the cold, the air smelled of verdure, and the very faint trace of animal droppings. In the deep passageway of the throat, he saw eyes looking back at him, reflected in the flashlight's beam. An arctic fox? A bear cub? He backed out in a hurry.

He breathed hard. According to the reports of the time, the machine had disobeyed its own protocols. Despite successful experimental runs, it had failed in its first great venture. This was the site of its great failure.

Back in the tent, he opened the little wooden chest that he had rescued from his father's attic. He looked through the pages of flowing script in code he was never going to decipher. There was the page that had led him here, which said only "Martina," and below it, two lines from Rilke.

Alles Erworbne bedroht die Maschine, solange
sie sich erdreistet, im Geist, statt im Gehorchen, zu sein.

Her name was Martina. In her day—to the engineers, the machine had always been "her"—she was the largest machine ever built, barring only the particle accelerators. She was the first of the sentient megamachines, a strip miner that was both tunnel borer and excavator. In the videos she was like a beast of ancient legends, a metal monster chugging furiously over the land, breaking through the Sami barricades, scattering protestors and reindeer, charging through villages and homes, snapping trees like twigs. She was supposed to reach the site and level the hills with her excavator arms. In trials the excavators had demolished a hillside in minutes—trees, rocks, soil, and wildlife crushed, swooped into its buckets, fed through a conveyor belt as sludge that was collected by a retinue of trucks behind the machine. Martina had efficiently strip-mined the flattened land at a rate that broke all records. In hilly country, the tunnel borer could extrude its long, worm-like body to dig into the earth, regurgitating crushed, ore-rich matter into the conveyor belt at its far end. Wheeled runner arms laid the ore into vast, cleared fields for chemical treatment. The trials had been hugely successful.

But something had happened when she reached this site. Her head reared high into the air; one excavator arm snapped back so hard that the giant wheel ripped free, burying itself in a bog half a mile away. The borer head dove into the hillside, its multipart metal body twisting and bucking until the body itself broke; the excavator arms detached of their own accord, and, with an unearthly shriek, the monster machine fell silent. Later, most of the parts were retrieved, but the Sami resistance, emboldened by this unexpected failure of the machine that had ploughed through their barricades, rallied to push the mining police out. Now only the borer head remained buried in the hill, with part of its vermiform body.

Carl Johansson was already famous for his work on megamachine sentience, which had launched the Saurian revolution, with the old oil pumpjacks replaced by intelligent Saurs, their purpose expanded to search for deposits and sample them for quality. But Johansson had failed with his most ambitious project. That spectacular failure had led to a temporary incarceration—the Dictator was not yet in power, but those who were to become his people already sat in high places. Jan remembered his father returning home a diminished, silent, secretive man. Soon after, his mother had left the house—Jan remembered a slammed door interrupting his homework—and then there was the raid, and the accident that killed her.

So he was here, in the middle of the wilderness, thinking about the past, and all he could remember were flashes and fragments: his father's two hands working on separate things at the same time; his mother's face at the piano, alive with the music that poured from her hands; the sound from the slammed door reverberating in his mind for all these decades. And his own left hand, lying resigned and senseless in his lap as the dead machine lay in the earth.

When he returned to Stockholm, he went to his father. His brother Lars was at the old house, overseeing repairs before the sale. Carl Johansson had settled into his new senior residence. He spoke little and ate just enough to keep alive. His eyes would light up for a moment when he saw Jan or Lars, but then he retreated into silence.

The Moon was up the night that Jan returned. Its silvery radiance washed over the old man's face: the hooded eyes, the lined visage, the thinning mane of hair. A tenderness rose up in Jan as he put the wooden box in the old man's lap.

"Father," he said, "I am sorry, I had to go away for a few days. After I found this in the attic, I went to... to see Martina."

The old man stared at him. His eyebrows rose. He began to rummage through the box with his gnarled, trembling hands.

"Do you remember, Father?" Jan asked him. "Do you remember what you did? That's why they took you away after Martina's failure, didn't they? They suspected you had sabotaged your own creation."

Carl Johansson stared at his son. He shook his head. "They scanned me—did an fMRI. Questioned me. I came up clean. I didn't sabotage Martina. I was innocent!"

"Father, the Dictator is dead. You have nothing to fear."

His father nodded, but he would not speak again that evening.

During the next several days, Jan tried to bring up the subject many times. His father would not say any more, but began to have headaches and nightmares. Jan argued with his brother, spent his nights pacing up and down in his old bedroom, fell fitfully asleep during the day, missed calls from his wife and children. He tracked down the Sami psychologist whose book on generational trauma among indigenous people he had read in the wilderness. Could that still happen if you were not indigenous? The old woman, now retired, held Jan's senseless hand between her own. *You are the eldest, are you not? The eldest son carries the father's burden.*

During Jan's last week in Stockholm, his father began to speak. His owlish eyes peered out from under heavy lids, his voice strained with effort.

"I tried to stop the machine," the old man said. "I had to—I had started to feel Martina's perpetual hunger, I thought I would die of it. I wrote the darkcode with my left hand, even as I performed the routine checks with my right. I was afraid what I had done would show up in a brain scan. So I tried very hard to forget what I had done, what my left hand had done."

He paused, held his hands in front of him as though looking at them for the first time.

"I didn't even tell your mother. She knew I was keeping a secret from her, something I had never done before. That is why she left the house in anger. Not because she didn't love us, but because she didn't know why I had changed. The world didn't make sense to her anymore. She would have come back, if it hadn't been for the raid."

He began to cough. With his right hand, Jan held a glass of water to the old man's chin.

"I wrote the Wendigo code," his father said. "It launched the era of the sentient megamachines, the destruction of everything I loved. I had to write the antidote.

"I didn't know what the antidote could do. It was meant to introduce a sudden satiation, so the machine would stop. I didn't know she'd destroy herself. She could have stopped, refused to obey—"

His voice shook. He took another sip of water.

"It's all coming back to me. I slipped the antidote into the AI darknet after I sent it to her. The antidote is probably still there, in a million different versions. I think it might explain the failures, the rogues roaming the land. Some of them kill, others go crazy. But what I did—it didn't stop the era of sentient earth-destroying machines. I tried! But I couldn't undo all the harm I caused, and even the cure turned wrong! And it cost me—it cost me your mother."

Suddenly Carl Johansson started to weep. Jan had never seen his father in tears. He brought his hands tentatively toward the old man, holding his left with his right.

His father took both his hands, drew them to his chest, his breath coming in shuddering gasps, his tears falling over Jan's hands.

"Father, it will be all right," Jan said. The dim lamplight cast a circle of gold around them, and the old man bent his gray head over his son's hands and wept. Jan felt a great wall inside shift suddenly, he drew in a breath of pure fear, like a child about to dive into an abyss, and a wave of nameless emotion broke within him. Tears rose in his eyes. Then he felt—felt the left hand tingle and burn painfully, as though it had caught fire, but it had only come to life, perhaps for a moment, perhaps longer.

Because Rilke could say it better, the words came to him. He said them aloud to his father, to his father's son: "*Aber noch ist uns das Dasein verzaubert...*"

"It will be all right," he said, and he thought: *I have to make it all right.* The apartment window was open. In the unseasonably warm winter, a scent of roses wafted in—the neighbor's flowerpots on her balcony.

Dinesh

THIS MORNING IS different. From the terrace, the city appears lifeless, sullen. The hairs on his arm prickle as though a storm is coming—then he hears it, a dull roar like distant thunder. Is it a sudden winter squall? But it's coming from the direction of the marketplace. Is it a group of the Hellbent, about to perform one of their mass acts of terror and murder? Dinesh doesn't have a choice; he is a reporter, no matter how laughable his job is in these times—he must throw himself into the mayhem so he can know the truth. So he dashes out of the house. He meets his landlady on the lower floor. *What's* going on, *out there? Do you know? There's nothing on the TV.* And he says, *I'm going to find out, don't worry*, and she gives him a mildly disbelieving look. Behind her he can hear the sounds of steel plates in the sink, the children calling to each other, all that signifies normalcy, and he is tempted to stand there and keep talking to her. But instead he runs down the stairs. Outside he starts to walk with the crowds toward the metro—people are talking to each other, looking apprehensively around. What's amiss? That faint roar is still in the air. Rumors are flying about—he hears all kinds of disjointed theories presented with absolute conviction—and as he's walking, he senses the energy of the crowd shift: It is no longer a morning commuter crowd, but people moving faster and faster, as if to escape some onslaught. The skies are low with dark clouds as though it were the monsoons, but the clouds and the pollution blend into each other so it is hard to tell where one ends and the other begins. The roar behind him gets louder. People around him start to run. Nobody knows what's happening, but someone behind him starts shouting about seeing smoke, and terrorist attacks. In these times, terrorist attacks are part of reality, but so are other phenomena he's observed—mass-panic attacks, where a rumor, a smoke spire or two, and a few malcontents mingled with a crowd can change the course of things. Each feeds on the other—terrorist attacks and mass-panic waves of destruction—so he has to act quickly, or people will die.

He begins to shout. He looks up at the clouds—"There will be a cloudburst, a superstorm—run, get shelter, the roads will flood!"—but nobody can hear him. Then a man nearby looks at him—a gaze of complete comprehension—and takes up the same call. There's another fellow with a megaphone shouting, calling for killing, stumbling—the sound is too loud for Dinesh to understand the words clearly, but he pulls the megaphone from the man and starts yelling into it like a demented meteorologist. He has a vague glimpse of the stranger with the sympathetic glance holding the arms of the former owner of the megaphone as he struggles, then they are lost in the crowd. All around him he can hear people take up his refrain—memories are still vivid from the freak cloudbursts of last September that killed nearly three hundred people in Delhi. Dinesh keeps shouting even though his throat is sore, and looks at the sky in supplication—he has never been conventionally religious, especially in these times when religion of every kind has been bastardized to serve the Widdam, but he remembers his mother singing her prayers. He pleads silently with the clouds for rain, unseasonable though it is, and he can't believe the first cold drop he feels on his arm. This validation of his words in the form of a few drops of rain is enough for the crowd; they are dispersing already. The demons within them are distracted—they will not fall victim to the hawa today. He goes running through the emptying street, shouting into the megaphone until his throat is so sore that he coughs and retches. He's run so far that nothing looks familiar. He feels a hand on his arm, turns—it's the Jharoowala with his broom on a pole, smiling nervously. The man pulls him into a narrow alley between two rows of houses. Dinesh lets the megaphone fall and feels that he will die, this moment, right here in the dusty alleyway with its piles of filth, because he is so spent it hurts to breathe. But the Jharoowala pulls him through a little doorway in a courtyard wall.

The courtyard is quiet, but astonishingly green, this little square of land behind somebody's house. There are shrubs and bushes and small trees— and an open door to what is evidently servants' quarters. The man puts a finger on his lips, sits Dinesh down on a metal chair hidden amid a cluster of thick bushes, and darts off. There's a woman yelling from the open doorway, and the sound of a child being slapped, followed by a wail, but all that is muted by the greenery around him. He doesn't know the names of the plants but the colors of the leaves, their variety of shape and texture, their fullness and bursting vitality make him delirious with delight. The air is different, too, and he hears tiny voices piping up from deep within the bushes—birds, birds in Delhi! The man returns with a cup of hot tea that he offers with a nervous glance around him—understanding, Dinesh drinks the tea, scalding his throat, and tears of gratitude flow down his cheeks. He puts the cup back into the man's hands and gets up, whispering his thanks. Out in the alleyway, he is bewildered because he doesn't know where he is, but on the main road he finds a scooterwala who will take him home.

At home, Dinesh searches for news. He looks out through the window. Only a few raindrops pockmark the windowsill. His news sources tell him that there was violence of some kind at the marketplace, details unclear. So far the death toll is seven. His elation vanishes and he puts his head in his hands. He looks up at the superheroes on the walls of his room, and knows he will never be one. In a real superhero story, the rain would have come down full blast at exactly the right moment, and no innocents would have been killed.

But the rain does come that evening, a short, unusually heavy (for winter) cold rain that fills the streets and makes the ditches sing. The roads are black and shiny, and the muddy water swirls into the street drains. The smell of wet earth reminds him of his childhood in a Delhi that was green and slow. The rain drums urgently, drowning all sounds of the city.

That night, he finally gets a message from the son of Carl Johansson. *Thank you for your letter. I'm sorry, my father has died. He passed away peacefully in his sleep. He was a good man who tried to make amends. Thank you again for writing.*

The actual news is sparse today—fishing in the darknet without Catlover, he pulls up all kinds of chaff through which he must sort to find out what's *not* propaganda or plain lies. An Australian millionaire has built a mansion using the ruins of the Great Barrier Reef. An entire coastal city, an experimental one, has been launched from the shores of Tanzania and is afloat somewhere in the Indian Ocean. Project Destiny has returned the latest mining samples from the Moon, and investors are delirious with anticipation. There's a story about a Saur—another machine saint, believe it or not—somewhere in New Mexico, assistant to a hydrologist called Valerie Begay who has launched a water revolution in the desert. Dinesh scratches his head and wonders.

After the rain, he goes up to the terrace. At last, he can see the Moon clearly—the rain has washed the air free of pollutants. He knows the lunar topography as he knows Manu. There's Oceanus Procellarum, and at the edge of a crater south of that, there is a ridge where Manu likes to sit, to watch the Earth rise in the sky. The Moon is, indeed, subtly different. He wonders whether Manu is still alive, and why nobody seems to know or care, and why there should be an impenetrable firewall between the world and the Moon that even Catlover can't get through. But at this moment, if Manu is alive, if he is sitting on that ridge watching Earth, well, they are together after all, looking across the abyss of space at each other.

On the Moon, he imagines the light is harsh—the horizon is sharp against the starry night, except where pale fountains of dust hang. The Moon bears her scars without disguise or apology. Her cratered expanse is receptive to every footstep, every steel blade. How strange that part of the Moon mining mission is the search for the elements known as rare earths, on a world that is not Earth. Manu thought it would be better to pillage the Moon than the Earth for the ores that fuel the windmills and batteries of the green energy revolution. *This is what we need to do*, he told Dinesh when he left, *to bring back clean air, to stop the destruction of the world.* But Manu went there and lost his faith. Dinesh thinks he knows why—Manu found the Widdam there, on the Moon. There was no escaping it, even up there.

For one terrifying, giddy moment, he senses the Widdam in its entirety, as though he were a tick or a louse on the body of the beast, suddenly aware of the thing he rides. He knows that the Widdam is alive and well even in places where the air is clean, where the arrays of solar panels and windmills feed their human hosts their necessities and luxuries, lies and promises, the flickering distractions before which they sit catatonic and mesmerized, endlessly feeding, never full. The Widdam is a chimera that bridges metal and flesh; it spans matter and metaphor, mind and materiality, and now it has jumped the gap between Earth and Moon. To see it, sense it in its fullness, is to lose all hope before the enormity of its desire for annihilation.

Like a man drowning, he thinks furiously of the things that keep him alive—his memories of winter, and of Manu, the subtle connections that become apparent only at times between himself and the rest of the world—a glance of understanding between strangers in the middle of mayhem; a tiny, magical garden flourishing in defiance of the abkihawa; a repentant roboticist; a hydrologist leading a revolution; maybe even a rebel Saur turned saint.

The Widdam carries the seeds of its own destruction, he tells Manu. He stands on the terrace in the clear moonlight; the water drips off the newly washed leaves of the trees, making music in pools and ditches below. The air is clean and moist. He thinks of the Jharoowala's nervous, kindly face, the long-poled broom with its halo of dust. A faint smile comes to his lips. *Tomorrow the Jharoowala can take a holiday.*

DREADFUL YOUNG LADIES
Kelly Barnhill

Kelly Barnhill (www.kellybarnhill.com) is the author of the Newbery Medal winning novel, *The Girl Who Drank the Moon*, and the World Fantasy winning novella, *The Unlicensed Magician*, as well as other novels and short stories. She is the recipient of fellowships from the McKnight Foundation, the Jerome Foundation, the Minnesota State Arts Board and the Loft. Her most recent book is a new collection of short stories, *Dreadful Young Ladies and Other Stories.*

1. Fran

IT WAS EASY enough to lose a child by accident. To do so on purpose turned out to be nearly impossible.

The child slid his grubby, slick fingers into her hand. Hung on for dear life. He rubbed his face on the seat of her skirt, and hooked his arm into her purse's glossy leather strap. Meanwhile, people passed by without a glance, their hands full of drooping cotton candy or over-sized stuffed dogs with weak seams or shrill whistles in the shape of a bird. Aggressively unattractive parents wooed their children with sweets and grease and cheap toys. Fran pressed the fingers of her free hand to her mouth and choked down bile.

The child stumbling next to her hip was not her own. This child, with thick lips and the watery squint of dull eyes, was her lover's. Or, more specifically, her lover's wife's child.

If a child was an anchor on a good man's soul, Fran reasoned, *if it kept him from daily loving his love, would it not be better if such a child disappeared?*

Children disappear every day. Just watch the news.

When Fran was fourteen, she took her little sister to the park. The little girl flew higher and higher on the swing—lace bobby socks, black mary janes, a dress lined with crinoline flapping about her spindly legs like white and pink wings—while Fran leaned against the elm tree and let Jonah Marks slide his hand into her shorts. Let him hang on tight.

Watch me, the little girl cried. *Watch me.* Her voice bounced against the basketball court, rustled the leaves, floated on the breath of Jonah Marks, on his wet lips and insistent tongue. *Watch me.*

When she turned, the little girl was gone. The swing still arced back and forth, a memory of her body. *She flew away,* Fran told her mother, her father, the social worker, and the police. *I heard the rustle of lace and the flapping of wings. I heard a voice echo within, around, and above. She flew away.*

And she may have done. Really, who's to say?

But Fran's little sister was a pretty child. No one ever snatches the ugly ones.

Fran's lover's son was not a pretty child. He whimpered and wheezed. He chortled and pleaded. An endless litany of wants.

Grant me a snow cone.

Grant me a foot-long.

Grant me a deep-fried candy bar on a stick.

Fran tried to dash away at the restroom, but the child appeared like magic at the doorway and grasped the hem of her skirt. Fran tried to dodge him in the haunted house, but he kept close to her heels in the dark. He hid in her pocket. He slid into her shoes. The weight of him swung from side to side. She heard him flapping and flying. *Watch me!*

Fran sent the child to the top of the giant slide hoping for an opening, but a convention of police officers gathered without warning to look appraisingly at the hordes of ugly children hurtling down yellow humps, their faces lit by the misplaced love of their fawning parents on the ground. Fran was, she saw, surrounded by idiots. And she couldn't slip away.

The child at the top of the slide—her lover's wife's child—shivered and shook. He gripped the burlap sliding sack the way a skydiver hangs onto his defective parachute before his final bounce upon a pitiless ground. Fran looked up. Felt her shoulders hemmed in by police.

She flew away, she wanted to say to the cop on her right. *Children disappear every day,* she nearly said to the cop on her left, *especially the pretty ones. It isn't my fault that the boy is hideous.*

The ugly child peered down at Fran, held her gaze. She imagined him in black Mary Janes. In bobby socks with lace at the ankle. She imagined him on the arc of a swing, unhooked from gravity, bumping against the sky. The wind lifted his pale hair like the crinoline lining of a fluttering skirt. Fran felt her breath catch. *Watch me!* the ugly child mouthed. *Watch me!* He swayed and swayed, and Fran found herself swaying too.

Grant you feathers, murmured her lips.

Grant you wings.

Grant you light and wind and helium.

Grant you cloud and moon and star. The vacuum of space. The infinite distances between lover and love.

The child sat on his burlap and pushed off.

And somewhere inside, Fran grew wings.

She flew away.

2. Margaret

RED LIPS INVITE trouble, when trouble requires an invitation. Which it usually doesn't. Margaret knew that trouble hid under dirty rugs and scratched coffee tables. It lurked behind heavy drapes like in old vampire movies. It gathered in great clouds like pollen in the spring and fall and settled like dust in between.

Margaret stood in front of the mirror painting black around the eyes, muting acne scars and fresh pustules with muddy makeup, and crafting a false beauty mark at the hollow where her chin met her neck.

She wore pink lips to school, black lips to visit her grandparents, and red lips for everything else. She wiped Vaseline across her small, white teeth to prevent stains—like a barrier against blood on crisp new sheets. The color of the lip is significant, Margaret knew. The color matters.

Margaret's teacher, for example, was terrified by a red lip. He pulled at his earth-tone tie until his face went red, then purple, then green. He stammered and hesitated before shooing the girl away.

Pink, though. Pink was a different story.

Two weeks with pink lips. Only two. By then he was weak and trembly, his fingers fluttering gently as they grazed her neck.

They found him the next day. Heart attack. Hard-on. Pink lips. Really, who's to say? Margaret offered no opinion.

HER MOTHER SNORED in the next room, her new boyfriend at her side—also snoring. The room stank of liquor and sex, and Margaret wrinkled her nose as she slipped inside.

MARGARET INTENDED THE black lips for her grandfather, but it was her grandmother who, somewhere between the tuna casserole and the Cool Whip surprise, began to nervously run her fist through the porcupine spikes of her black-and-white hair. And shiver.

"I was a Girl Scout once, did you know," her grandmother said. Margaret curved her black lips into a grin. She slipped her supple fingers into her grandmother's rice paper hand, felt the old woman's soul leak out in a long, slow sigh as she leaned inexorably in.

Grandmother still wore her oven mitts when they found her. Black lipstick on her mouth.

Borrowed time, people said.

MARGARET CRAWLED IN between her mother and her mother's boyfriend. Her mother slept open-mouthed, wet breath catching in her throat.

It's only a matter of time, her mother had said earlier that day, as she checked the fit of Margaret's new bra. Her thumbs lingered on the dense, round breasts as though checking for freshness. *Every Tom and Dick'll want a taste. A kiss, I mean.*

The boyfriend had leaned in the recliner, his hands occupied by a cigarette and an icy highball glass. But his fingers itched. Margaret could tell.

A kiss is a dangerous thing, the boyfriend said. *I feel sorry for the poor son of a bitch. Won't know what's hit him until it's too late. Still,* he said, dragging deep on his cigarette, *not a bad way to go.* He had given Margaret a full-handed smack on her rear as she passed.

Margaret leaned over, placed a hand next to each of his shoulders, peered into his sleeping face. *Too late for you,* she whispered in the dark. His face was calm, his jowls slack. The stubble on his chin stood at attention. His lips were full and slightly parted, the corners twitching with each breath. She licked her lips.

Too late.

She licked her lips again. Tasted musk and cinnamon, and *oh god,* salt, sweat, and lemon juice, and *oh god,* grass and wheat and meat and milk. Tasted youth and birth and decay.

She licked her lips again. Felt her body shudder and buck. *What is it,* she wondered, *about death that makes us feel so alive?*

3. Estelle

REGINALD CURLED HIS body up the length of the radiator pipe. Winked one yellow eye. Winked the other. He tested the air with a quick flick of the tongue.

"Mind your own business," Estelle said, returning the gesture, though she knew he wouldn't notice.

Estelle sat at a desk with one hundred and two different file folders on the surface—all color coded, labeled, and stacked neatly according to year. This is what she had been told to do. To prepare. *They don't look out for your best interests, so don't expect it,* her friends said. *They care about numbers and procedures and forms. They care about quota. If it were up to them, they'd swallow you whole.*

"They can try," Estelle chuckled, as she pulled Andrew and Arnold from their hiding place in the bottom drawer and draped them heavily on the ground. They lifted their flat heads and gave her twin looks of indignation before sliding across the floor and under the upholstered chair.

The young man appeared in the doorway. He had long, white hands, tapered fingers, narrow hips. A blue suit and a blue tie and a haircut both severe and modern.

"I see you've been busy, Ms. Russo. I appreciate your work, but I assure you it was not necessary. I'm top in my field."

He remained in the doorway. From his position on the radiator pipe,

Reginald tasted the air. He leaned closer and unhooked his jaw.

"No, no," Estelle said firmly. Reginald pulled back, chastened.

"Oh, yes, I assure you I am," the young man said. "May I come in?"

"Please do," she said, winking one yellow eye.

He sat on the upholstered chair, resting his briefcase on his knees. Estelle stood. Her body was long and supple. She slid like oil across the room to the chair opposite the young man. Offered a slow, mesmerizing grin. Flicked her tongue.

Arnold unfurled from underneath, elevating hungrily behind the chair. Robin, Mae, and Chavez peeked their heads from the grooves of the couch cushions.

"No, no," Estelle said again.

"I'm sorry?" said the young man.

"Nothing," Estelle said, winking her other eye. Arnold sniffed and slumped to the floor, while the other three retracted without commentary. The young man glanced at the floor, but saw nothing.

"Look," he said, "it doesn't really matter what you have organized in what file. I've already seen it. How you've slid under the radar for as many years as you have is a mystery to me, but it doesn't matter now. There are consequences."

"Nibble, nibble, little mouse," Estelle said. "Always nibbling on the things that aren't yours."

"The government," he said primly, "is not a mouse."

The new brood woke and came tumbling out of the hole in the wall. At a hand signal from Estelle, they fell upon one another and played dead, as they had been trained. Diana, Elizabeth, and Eleanor glided in through the open door and moved regally toward the guest. Their golden eyes glittered like crowns. Estelle breathed deeply through her nose, flicked her tongue again. The young man smelled green and young. Like tight fiddleheads before they unfurl. The budding of spring. The tang of green apple on the tongue.

"Who said anything about the government?" Estelle said. "I'm talking about you." She leaned in. "Little mouse." She unhooked her jaw.

Gagged.

Gulped.

Swallowed him whole.

*   *   *

4. Annabelle

"My father says I can't play with you anymore," the boy said.

Annabelle shrugged. "He's not the boss of me."

"He says your mother isn't raising you right."

"Could be," she said, squatting on the ground. She spat on the bare dirt. Drew with her finger.

"He says you'll grow up just like her. He says the neighborhood doesn't need another one."

Annabelle drew a picture of a house with a sun and a heavy cloud. She drew a man inside with a woman. The man was on his knees. The woman had her head tossed back.

"He says you're all the same. He says I'm not supposed to chase a dirty skirt."

Annabelle drew heavy drops coming out of the cloud. She drew a flood that bent beams and rotted floors. She drew swollen banks and ruptured dykes and water that would not be bound. She drew a broken house tumbling down the river and floating off to sea.

She washed the land clean with the back of her hand.

"Um." He kicked at a clump of weeds with his sandal. "Do you know where my dad is?"

"With my mom. At my house." She looked up and smiled. "They floated away."

He bent down, rested his rear on his heels. Annabelle drew a boy and a girl in limitless space. She gave them wings. The boy arched his back as though it itched.

"Can I go with you then?"

"Suit yourself," she said. She took his hand. Hung on tight.

They flew away.

THE ONLY HARMLESS GREAT THING
Brooke Bolander

Brooke Bolander (www. brookebolander.com • @BBolander) attended the University of Leicester studying History & Archaeology and is an alum of the 2011 Clarion Writers' Workshop at UCSD. Her stories have been featured in *Lightspeed, Tor.com, Strange Horizons, Uncanny*, and various other fine purveyors of the fantastic. She has been a repeat finalist for the Nebula, Hugo, Locus, World Fantasy, and Theodore Sturgeon awards, much to her unending bafflement.

For Ben.

*"When the blood dries and the smoke clears,
they'll find us back to back."*

Part 1
Fission

1

THERE IS A secret buried beneath the mountain's gray skin. The ones who put it there, flat-faced pink squeakers with more clever-thinking than sense, are many Mothers gone, bones so crumbled an ear's flap scatters them to sneeze-seed. To fetch up the secret from Deep-Down requires a long trunk and a longer memory. They left dire warnings carved in the rock, those squeakers, but the rock does not tell her daughters, and the stinging rains washed everything as clean and smooth as an old tusk a hundred hundred matriarchies ago.

The Many Mothers have memories longer than stone. They remember how it came to pass, how their task was set and why no other living creature may enter the mountain. It is a truce with the Dead, and the Many Mothers are nothing more and nothing less than the Memories of the Dead, the sum total of every story ever told them.

At night, when the moon shuffles off behind the mountain and the land darkens like wetted skin, they glow. There is a story behind this. No matter how far you march, O best beloved mooncalf, the past will always drag around your ankle, a snapped shackle time cannot pry loose.

ALL OF KAT'S research—the years of university, the expensive textbooks on physics and sociology, the debt she'll never in the holy half-life of uranium pay back, the blood, sweat, and tears—has come down to making elephants glow in the goddamned dark. It figures. Somewhere her grandmama is sure as hell laughing herself silly.

A million different solutions to the problem have been pitched over the years. Pictographs, priesthoods, mathematical code etched in granite— all were interesting, intriguing even, but nobody could ever settle on one foolproof method to tell people to stay away. Someone had even suggested dissonant musical notes, a screaming discordia that, when strummed or plucked or plinked, instinctively triggered a fear response in any simian unlucky enough to hear it. The problem with that one, of course, was figuring out what exactly would sound ominous to future generations. Go back two hundred years and play your average Joe or Jane Smith a Scandinavian death metal record and they might have a pretty wicked fear response, too.

Then came the Atomic Elephant Hypothesis.

Kat grew up, as most American children did, associating elephants with the dangers of radiation. Every kid over the past hundred years had watched and rewatched Disney's bowdlerized animated version of the Topsy Tragedy (the ending where Topsy realizes revenge is Never The Right Option and agrees to keep painting those watch dials For The War Effort still makes Kat roll her eyes hard enough to sprain an optic nerve) a million times, and when you got older there were entire middle school history lectures devoted to the Radium Elephant trials. Scratchy newsreel footage the color of sand, always replaying the same moment, the same ghostly elephant leader eighty-five years dead signing the shapes for "We feel" to the court-appointed translator with a trunk blorping in and out of focus. Seeing that stuff at a young age lodged in you on a bone-deep level. And apparently it had stuck with a whole lot of other people as well: Route 66 is still studded with neon elephants cheerfully hailing travelers evaporated to dust and mirage fifty years back down the road. The mascot of the biggest nuclear power provider in the country is Atomisk the Elephant, a cheerful pink pachyderm who Never Forgets to Pay His Utility Bill On Time. Fat Man and Little Boy were decorated with rampaging tuskers, a fact deeply screwed up on several counts. It's a ghoulish cultural splinter the country has never quite succeeded in tweezing.

Kat had taken a long, hard look at all of this, rubbed her chin in a stereotypically pensive fashion, and suggested a warning system so ridiculous nobody took her serious at first. But it was one of those fuckin' things, right? The harder they laughed, the more sense it seemed to make. They were all at the end of their collective ropes; the waste kept piling up and they needed to let whoever took over in ten millennia know what it was, where it was, and why they probably shouldn't use it as a dessert topping or rectal suppository.

And so here Kat sits, tie straightened, hair teased heaven-high, waiting to meet with an elephant representative. Explaining the cultural reasons *why* they want to make the elephant's people glow in the dark is going to be an exercise in minefield ballet, and godspeed to the translator assigned.

THEY KILLED THEIR own just to see time pass. That's how it started. Humans were as hypnotized by shine as magpies, but no magpie has ever been so thankful about how many days it has left before it turns into a told story. Even in the dark they fretted, feeling the stars bite like summer flies as they migrated overhead. They built shelters to block out the sight of their passing. This only succeeded in making things dimmer; the unseen lion in the tall grass is still a lion that exists. Clever-turning cicada-ticking sun-chasers they tied together so that they would always know where she was, clinging to the sun's fiery tail like frightened calves.

(Try not to judge them; their mothers were short-lived, forgetful things, clans led by bulls with short memories and shorter tempers. They had no history, no shared Memory. Who can blame them for clinging ape-fearful to the only constants they had?)

"But how to track time's skittering in the night with such tiny eyes and ears?" the humans squeaked. "What if the sun should go wandering and leave us and we don't even realize we've been left behind?"

The answer, as with so many things those piteous little creatures dredged from the mud, was poison.

They gored the earth with gaping holes, shook her bones until crystals like pieces of starless sky fell out. Trapped inside were glowing flies. Trampling them made a smeary shine, but they carried sickness within their blood and guts. Pity the poor humans! Their noses were stumpy, ridiculous things and they couldn't smell the Wrongness, even as they rubbed it across their teeth and faces. All they could see was how bright it looked, like sunlight through new leaves. For want of a trunk, much sorrow would come to them—and on to us, though we knew it not in those days.

THERE WAS A good place, once. Grass went *crunch-squish* underfoot. Mother went *wrrrt*. The world was fruit-sticky warm and sunlight trunk-striped with swaying gray shadows smelling of We. Mud and stories and Mothers, so many Mothers, always touching, always telling, sensitive solid fearless endless. Their tusks held the sky up up up. Their bare bones hummed in the bone places, still singing even with all their meat and skin gone to hyena milk. Nothing was greater than Many Mothers. Together they were mountains and forevers. As long as they had each other and the Stories, there was no fang or claw that could make them Not.

They had blown raw red holes through the Many Mothers, hacked away their beautiful tusks, and the sky had not fallen and she had not mourned the meat. She was She—the survivor, the prisoner, the one they called Topsy—and She carried the Stories safe inside her skull, just behind her left eye, so that they lived on in some way. But there is no one left to tell the histories in this smoky sooty cave Men have brought her to, where the ground is grassless stone and iron rubs ankleskin to bloody fly-bait. There are others like her, swaying gray shadows smelling of We, but wood and cold metal lie between them, and she cannot see them, and she cannot touch them.

*   *   *

IN THIS MEAN old dead-dog world you do what you gotta do to put food on the table, even when you're damn certain deep down in your knowing-marrow that it's wrong and that God Almighty his own damn self will read you the riot act on Judgment Day. When you got two kid sisters and an ailing mama back in the mountains waiting on the next paycheck, you swallow your right and you swallow your wrong and you swallow what turns out to be several lethal doses of glowing green graveyard seed and you keep on shoveling shit with a smile (newly missing several teeth) until either the settlement check quietly arrives or you drop, whichever walks down the cut first. Regan is determined to hang on until she knows her family is taken care of, and when Regan gets determined about something, look the hell out and tie down anything loose.

The ache in her jaw has gone from a dull complaint to endless fire blossoming from the hinge behind her back teeth, riding the rails all the way to the region of her chin. It never stops or sleeps or cries uncle. Even now, trying to teach this cussed animal how to eat the poison that hammered together her own rickety stairway to Heaven, it's throbbing and burning like Satan's got a party cooked up inside and everybody's wearing red-hot hobnails on the soles of their dancing shoes. She reminds herself to focus. This particular elephant has a reputation for being mean as hell; a lack of attention might leave her splattered across the wall and conveyor belt. *Not yet, ol' Mr. Death. Not just yet.*

"Hey," she signs, again. "You gotta pick it up like this. Like this. See?" Her hand shakes as she brandishes the paintbrush, bristles glowing that familiar grasshopper-gut green. She can't help it; tremors are just another thing come along unexpected with dying. "Dip it into the paint, mix it up real good, fill in each of those little numbers all the way 'round. Then put the brush in your mouth, tip it off, and do it again. The quicker you get done with your quota, quicker you can go back to the barn. Got it?"

No response from Topsy. She stands there slow-swaying to hosannas Regan can't hear, staring peepholes through the brick wall of the factory floor opposite. It's like convincing a cigar-store chief to play a hand. Occasionally one of those great big bloomers-on-a-washline ears flaps away a biting fly.

Regan's tired. Her throat is dry and hoarse. Her wrists ache from signing instructions to sixteen other doomed elephants today, castoffs bought butcher-cheap from fly-bait road-rut two-cent circuses where the biggest wonder on display was how the holy hell they'd kept an elephant alive so long in the first place. She pities them, she hates the company so much it's like a bullet burning beneath her breast bone (or maybe that's just another tumor taking root), but the only joy she gets outta life anymore is imagining how much the extra money she's making taking on this last job will help Rae and Eve, even if Mama don't stick much longer than she does. Regan ain't a bit proud of what she's doing, and she's even less proud of what she does next, but she's sick and she's frustrated and she's fed the hell up with being ignored and bullied and pushed aside. She's tired of being invisible.

She reaches over and grabs the tip of one of those silly-looking ears and she twists, like she's got a hank of sister-skin between her nails at Sunday School. It's a surefire way of getting someone's attention, whether they want to give it or not.

"HEY!" she hollers. "LISTEN TO ME, WOULD YOU?"

The change in Topsy is like a magic trick. Her ears flare. The trunk coils a water moccasin's salute, a backhanded S flung high enough to knock the hanging lightbulb overhead into jitter jive. Little red eyes glitter down at her, sharp and wild and full of deadly arithmetic. The whole reason Topsy ended up here in the first place was because she had smashed a teasing fella's head like a deer tick. You don't need a translator to see what she's thinking: *Would it be worth my time and effort to reach down and twist that yowling monkey's head clean off her shoulders? Would it make me feel any better if I just made her... stop? For good? Would that make my day any brighter?*

And Regan's too damn exhausted to be afraid anymore, of death or anything else. She looks up and meets the wild gaze level as she can manage.

"Go ahead," she says. "Jesus' sake, just get it done with, already. Doing me a favor."

Topsy thinks about it; she sure as hell does that. There's a long, long stretch of time where Regan's pretty sure neither of them's clear on what's about to happen. Eventually, after an ice age or six, the trunk slowly lowers and the eyes soften a little and someone shuts the electricity off in Topsy's posture. She *slumps*, like she's just as dog-tired as Regan herself.

You're sick, she signs, after a beat. *Dying-sick. You stink.*

"Yeah. Dying-sick. Me and all my girls who worked here."

Poison? She gestures her trunk at the paint, the brush, the table, the whole hell-fired mess. *Smells like poison.*

"You got it. They got you all doing it now because you can take more, being so big and all. I'm supposed to teach you how."

Another pause unspools itself across the factory stall between them. *I'm supposed to teach you how to die*, Regan thinks. *Ain't that the dumbest goddamn thing you ever heard tell of, teaching an animal how to die? Everybody knows how to die. You just quit living and then you're slap-taught.*

Topsy reaches down and takes the paintbrush.

WHEN THEIR OWN began to sicken and fall, they came for us, and there was nothing we could do but die as well. We were shackled and splintered and separated; the Many Mothers could not teach their daughters the Stories. Without stories there is no past, no future, no We. There is Death. There is Nothing, a night without moon or stars.

"YOU WOULD BE doing a service not just to the United States, but to the world and anyone who comes after. I know the reasoning is... odd, but when people think of elephants, they think of radiation. They think of Topsy, and... all of that stuff, y'know? It's a story. People remember stories. They hand them down. We have no way of knowing if that'll be the case in a hundred thousand years, but it's as good a starting point as any, right?"

The translator sign-relays Kat's hesitant ramble to the elephant representative, a stone-faced matriarch seventy years old if she's a day. Kat shifts in her folding chair. Translation of the entire thing takes a very long time. The meeting arena is air-conditioned, but she's still trickling buckets in places you never would have guessed contained sweat glands. The silence goes on. The hand-jive continues. The elephant, so far as Kat can tell, has not yet blinked, possibly since the day she was calved.

*   *   *

SHE KILLED HER first Man when she was tall enough to reach the high-branch mangoes. There were no mangoes in that place to pluck, but she remembered juicysweet orangegreen between her teeth, tossed to ground in a good place by Mother. She remembered how high they had grown, but there were no mangoes in that place to pluck, so she took the Man in her trunk and threw him down and smashed his head beneath her feet like ripe red fruit while the other humans chittered and scurried and signed at her to stop.

There were other Mothers there, too. They watched her smash the Man, who had thrown sand in their faces and burned them and tried to make them drink stinking ferment from a bottle, and they said nothing. They said nothing, but they thought of mangoes, how high they had once grown, how sweet they were to crunch, to crush, to pulp.

THE COUNTY HOSPITAL, like all hospitals, is a place to make the skin on the back of your neck go prickly. It's white as a dead dog's bloated belly on the outside, sickly green on the inside, and filled to the gills with kinless folk too poor to go off and die anywhere else. Nuns drift down the hallways like backroad haints. The walls have crazy jagged lightning cracks zigzagging from baseboard to fly-speckled ceiling. Both sides of the main sick ward are lined with high windows, but the nuns aren't too particular about their housekeeping; the yellow light slatting in is filtered through a nice healthy layer of dust, dirt, and dying people's last words. The way Regan sees it, the Ladies of Perpetual Mercy ever swept, it would be thirty percent shadows, twenty percent cobwebs, and fifty percent Praise God Almighty, I See The Light they'd be emptying outta their dustpans at the end of day.

They've crammed Jodie between a moaning old mawmaw with rattling lungs and an unlucky lumber man who tried catching a falling pine tree with his head. What's left of her jaw is so swathed with stained yellow-and-red gauze she half-takes after one of those dead pyramid people over in Egypt-land. Regan's smelled a lot of foulness in her short span of doing jobs nobody else wants to touch, but the roadkill-and-rotting-teeth stink coming up off those bandages nearly yanks the cheese sandwich right out of her stomach. She wishes to God they'd let you smoke in these places. Her own rotten jawbone throbs with the kind of mock sympathy only holy rollers and infected body parts seem capable of really pulling off.

"Hey, girl," she says, even though Jodie's not awake and won't be waking up to catch the trolley to work with Regan ever again. "Thought I'd just... drop in, give you all the news fit to spit." She takes one of her friend's big hands from where it's folded atop the coverlet. It gives her the cold shivers to touch it with all of the life and calluses nearly faded away, but this is her goddamned fault for getting them into this mess in the first place. She's going to eat every single bite of the shit pie she's earned, smack her lips, and ask for seconds. That much, at least, she can do for someone who braided her hair when they were tee-ninsy. "You hanging in there alright?"

A fat carrion fly buzzes hopefully around Jodie's mouth; Regan shoos it away with a curse. "Goddammit," she mutters. "All you wanted to do was keep blowing mountaintops to hell and back." Deep breath. Steady. "I told you a whopper when we started out. You'd've been safer by a long shot if you just kept on mining."

THIS IS A story about Furmother-With-The-Cracked-Tusk, starmaker, tugger of tiger tails and player of games. Listen.

There was no warm wallowmud then, no melons, no watersweet leaves to pick pluck stuff scatter. The sun lay sluggish-cold on the ground. The Great Mothers grew coats like bears and wandered the empty white places of the world Alone, each splintered to Herself, each bull-separate. There were no Stories to spine-spin the We together. A bull had found them all, in the dark and chill Before, and in the way of bulls he had hoarded them for himself.

Now, the biggest shaggiest wisest of all Great Mothers was Furmother-With-The-Cracked-Tusk. Back back where this story calves, her tusks were still unbroken, so long and so curved they sometimes pricked the night's skin and left little white scars. A dying bear had told Furmother where the Stories lay hidden, just before her great crunchfoot met the ground on the other side of what was left of him. There was a Blacksap lake that stretched far enough to tickle the sky's claws, he had whispered; the bull's cave opened somewhere on the other shore. The only way to find it was to go there.

Furmother was wise, which means curious. She set out walking. As she walked, she sang, and her frozen songs dropped behind like seeds in dung, waiting for sun and the rain and the nibbling bugs to free them. It took a night and a day and a mango tree growing to reach where she was going, but one pale morning she sang up over a hill and there the Blacksap lake oozed, full of skulls and spines and foul-stinking unluck. No rooting in the tall grass was needed to find the cave's mouth. The bull stood big outside of it, rubbing his tusks and his shadow and his stained scarred furhead against a tree's bones.

She went up to him, Furmother-With-Her-Tusks-Whole, and she said, in a voice like the earth split-shake-root-ripping, "You there! Bull!"

He grunted, as is the way of bulls.

"Bull there, you! Do you have the Stories in your cave?"

He grunted irritably, as is the way of bulls. "Yes," he rumbled, "and they are all mine. I found them. No milk-dripping udder-dragger or tiny-tusked Son in his first *musth* will take what is mine. I will fight them. I will dig my tusks into their sides and leave them for the bears."

As is the way of bulls. "Bull," the Furmother said, "what do you even use them for? What good are they to you or to anyone, piled like rotting rained-on grass in a downbelow place?"

"They are *mine*," the bull repeated, his ears flaring, his skull thick, his legs braced. As is the way with bulls. "Mine and no one else's."

But Furmother was wise, which means crafty. She went away and left the bull to his scratch snort stomp. She went away to where his weak eyes could not follow, away down the shore to a dead forest, and with branch and trunk and sticky Blacksap she put together a cunning thing like a small bull's shadow. Her own fur she ripped out to cover it, because there were no other Mothers to give their own. How lucky are we, to be We! When she was done, sore swaying sleep-desperate on her feet, no She was there touching and rubbing the shoulder-to-shoulder skinmessage, *We are here with you*. There was nothing but she and herself.

She left the not-bull outside the cave. She left it and went away, just out of sight, and there she waited for dawn.

The bull came out of the cave. He came out and he saw the not-bull, black in the cold morning sun. His ears flapped, his eyes glittered, his feet stomped.

"You!" he squealed. "You, standing there! Who are you?"

The not-bull did not answer.

"What do you want, tusker? Get out of my way, or I will fight you!"

The not-bull did not answer.

"Do you dare challenge me, little Son? Me, whose tusks are great-greater-greatest? Me, who rode your Mother long ago? Sing your war song, if you wish to fight, else move out of my way!"

The not-bull did not answer!

The bull with the stories roared and flared and charged with a sound like great rocks rolling, goring stomping furious mad. He wanted to kill, as is the way with bulls. But the not-bull had no skin to tear, no insides to rupture, no skull to crush. It was nothing but sticks and fur and sticky Blacksap all the way through and through, so that the more the bull tried to gore and butt, the more mayfly stuck he became. And this caused him to lose himself completely. His screams were terrible things for ears to catch.

"If you had only shared," the Furmother said, "you wouldn't be caught in this trap. Now I'll have all of the stories, and you'll have none. Which is better?"

The bull cursed her so terribly bats fell dead from the sky. As is the way with bulls. She laughed like a triumph and went inside.

WATCHING THE ELEPHANT'S deft trunk double and snake and contort is downright hypnotic, even if what she's signing may possibly be a really long, really detailed way of saying "screw you." Proboscidian had been an elective at Kat's university; she hadn't really thought she would ever need it, so she hadn't bothered signing up. It was one of those courses, like Basketweaving or Food In Religious Texts, that seemed to be more of a charmingly eccentric way to bobsled through school grabbing credits than anything else. Nobody but the zoology students, historians, folklorists, and some of the more obsessively dedicated sociologists ever took it. For a language that had only really been around since the 1880s, though, it had its devotees; subjects with animals always did.

"She wants to ask you a question," the translator says.

"Go ahead."

"You want to make us glow when we're near this poison buried in the ground. You want to do this because of some screwy cultural sapiens association between elephants and radiation, when humans doing terrible fucked-up stuff to elephants ninety years ago is the reason for the dumb-ass cognitive association in the first place."

"Uh, wow." Kat gropes for a response. "Jesus. There's... sorry, there's a way of saying 'fucked up' in Proboscidian?"

"Not really. That was mostly me." The translator raises an eyebrow. "Anyway, what she wants to know first is this: What exactly are you offering the Mothers in return if they say yes?"

EVERY DAY SHE eats the reeking, gritty poison. The girl with the rotten bones showed her how, and occasionally Men come by and strike her with words and tiny tickling whip-trunks if she doesn't work fast enough. She feels neither. She feels neither, but rage buzzes in her ear low and steady and constant, a mosquito she cannot crush. Like a calf she nurses the feeling. Like the calf she'll never Mother she protects it safe beneath her belly, safe beneath the vast bulk of Herself, while every day it grows, suckles, frolics between her legs and around the stall and around the stall and around the stall until she's whirling red behind the eyes where the Stories should go.

One day soon the rage will be tall enough to reach the high-branch mangoes.

Okay? the rotten-bone-dead-girl signs. *Okay? Are you okay?*

"TOPSY? YOU OKAY?"

There's a stillness and a silence and a towering far-awayness the elephant sometimes takes on that makes Regan feel jumpy the same way she does right before a big green-and-purple April thunderstorm. She repeats the question, louder this time, but part of her is also looking for the nearest exit, the closest cellar door to hunker down behind. Topsy's eyes flicker, land— *Why is that mouse squeaking at me? Where am I?*—and register some level of slow-returning recognition. For the time being she's Topsy again, not a thoughtful disaster deciding whether or not to hatch. Regan slowly lets a chestful of air hiss through what's left of her throbbly-wobbling teeth.

Fine, the elephant signs. *I am... fine.* And then, to Regan's surprise since they're not exactly what you'd call friends: *You?*

Now there's a hell of a question. She thinks about Jodie, dying alone in that hospital bed of a wasting disease more than half Regan's fault. She remembers blood in the dormitory sink that morning; another three teeth rattling against the porcelain like thrown dice, still coated in fresh toothpaste. And where in the hell is that goddamned settlement check? The lawyer had said it would be arriving soon, but for all she knows that was just bullshit fed to a dying woman to hush up her howling. They might just wait until she drops dead and keep the damn money; trusting a company that happily gave you and all your nearest and dearest cancer wasn't wise, easy, or highly recommended.

Not really, she signs. *And I ain't convinced you are, either.*

Topsy's got nothing to say to that. Goddamned liars, the both of them.

BUT THE STORY does not end there, O best beloved mooncalf. Were things ever so easy, or so simple, even for Great Mothers and tricksters!

Furmother went inside the cave. She went inside the cave, but there were no Stories hidden there as the bear and the bull both had told her there would be. There was nothing but nothing, and Furmother needed no nothing. She walked back outside to where the bull still lay stuck, beside the shores of the great Blacksap lake.

"Bull," she said, "where are the Stories you were so keen to keep for yourself? Did someone clever rob you before I arrived?"

The bull rolled one red eye to look up at her. He laughed with malice and with scorn, but most of all with madness. As is the way with bulls.

"Fool milk-dripper," he panted. "Did you really think I would leave the Stories where you could get at them after yesterday? They are at the bottom of the Blacksap lake, where no one may have them. I hurled them all in myself with my strong and beautiful trunk and watched them sink beneath the surface with my keen eyes. If you want them, O cursed calf-dropper, go in and get them."

Furmother looked at him with sadness—because then as now We pitied the bulls, our Sons and Fathers and occasional Mates.

"Very well," she said. "Thank you for giving me the location, bull." And she turned and walked into the lake, where she sank like a Story.

*   *   *

"WELL, AS I said before, they'll be doing our species and any species that come after a tremendous favor," Kat repeats. Her mouth's gone dry, heart and pulse skidding rubber tread marks into the fight-or-flight zone. The elephant can probably smell the adrenaline rolling off her like summer sweat funk pouring from a subway commuter. "This isn't just a federal problem. It's an issue we've been struggling to solve for years. We've discussed human guardians, almost like priesthoods, we've talked about making *cats* glow, for chrissakes, but cats don't have the same level of cultural connection." She's rambling. Goddammit. She's had nightmares involving naked dental surgery that went off better than this meeting. "It would be for the greater good. There is no greater good than this. This is... this is the *greatest* good."

More waiting as the translator passes along her fumbling. The matriarch snorts. It's the first noise Kat's heard her make thus far.

"The 'greater good', as you put it, was also used to justify the use of my people in your radium factories during the war, was it not? To save costs. To save your own from poisoning."

Shit shit shit. It's amazing I can breathe with my foot lodged in my windpipe the way it is.

"Not only that," the translator continues, "but you're asking us to more or less agree to the perpetuation of this twisted association. Would there be any attempt at all at reeducating the human public, should we somehow come to an agreement?"

"I... it's... it's sort of rooted in that cultural association." Kat can feel the blood burning in her cheeks as the situation spirals out of control. *A parachute, a pulled fire alarm, dear sweet Jesus give me some way outta here.* She doesn't know what she was expecting when she walked into this meeting. "I guess we could try to maintain the cognitive link while launching some kind of reeducation campaign? I'd have to talk to my higher-ups. I'm only really in charge of the one thing."

The translator stares at Kat for a little longer than is necessary. She glances back over her shoulder at the matriarch, then back at Kat.

"I just want to make sure I'm hearing this correctly before I translate," she says, in a lower register. "Did you seriously just show up to what is basically a diplomatic meeting with no bargaining chips whatsoever?"

EACH MOONRISE THE metal bird in the box screams a mad *musth* cry. Like all Man-things, the bird is obsessed with the rising and setting of the sun. The night-whistle signals rest. The night-whistle signals a bag full of tasteless dried oats, a brief escape from sad dead girls and tormenting men, and four more wooden walls, the inside of a dry skull plugged tight with moldy hay and dung. She remembers a place where the Night was made of warm shuffle and star-graze, tearing up sweet wet grass by the trunkful with moonshaded Mothers when she was old enough to tooth. She remembers, but there is no sweet grass to tear up by the trunkful, so instead she thoughtfully tears apart her stall, board by splintered board. There will be a beating in the morning. There are always beatings in the morning.

As she works she sings, tufts of Story-song plucked from memory, faded but firm-rooted beneath the skin. She can hear the Many Mothers beyond the crackrip of wood, their voices low lower lowest, sweet vibrations no Man's tiny ear could ever catch and hold. They are with her still, humming in her teeth and skull. *Listen, mooncalf,* they sing. *Listen. The songs are still behind your left eye. Pull them up and scatter the seeds.*

She pauses for a moment in her song. She pauses, but the singing continues, outside her skull, outside her memory, rippling out through the barn's beams. Up and down the dim length of the building, unseen Mothers catch-carry the thrum. They pass it along the line like a Great Mother's thighbone, trunk to trunk, tongue to tongue, mouthing tasting touching smelling *remembering.* *Yes. Yes. I know this one. This is Furmother's Lay. She tricked a bull. She scattered the Stories. This is one of those Stories.*

Her hum rejoins the others. The night ripens with song.

WHAT THERE ARE of Jodie's belongings make for a pitiful small pile. The nun brings them all out in a single wooden peach crate: a silver lighter, a plug of tobacco, a few badly mended pairs of trousers originally meant for men, work boots, a busted music box with a ceramic bluebird fixed to the lid, a leather coinpurse with 3 dollars in nickels still jingling around inside, pill bottles by the double handful, and a key on a length of ribbon faded to the color of attic curtains. There's a letter, too, addressed to Regan in a hand so loosey-goosey it's hard at first making out what it says. Penmanship was never what you'd call a strong point for either of them.

"Will you be taking care of the burial arrangements as well?" the nun asks. "If the girl had no living relatives left to take the body..."

Regan hasn't even begun thinking over the practicalities of getting her friend in the ground. She's got no spare money; all that's left goes straight to Mama and the girls. In a way she's lucky; family ground costs nothing. You get some pine boards and nail them together and you're good.

"Hell," she says, finally. "She's dead. She don't care anymore and neither do I. Nothing wrong with the potter's field. Jesus was a potter, wasn't he?"

"A carpenter, my child. Our Lord was a carpenter."

"Oh." Another pause. "Well, hell. I still don't think she cares."

DOWN DOWN DOWN sank the Furmother, deep down slowly beneath the Blacksap where nothing grows but bone-rooted ghosts.

She held her breath as she dropped. She held her breath, but the Blacksap oozed inside her ears, her mouth, the tip of her trunk, the corners of her eyes. It smothered her fur, stifled light and air and up and down and night and day. Ghosts tethered to drifting skeletons stretched out their trunks to touch her; whispers filled the echo-empty places of her skull.

Am I dead? Are you? Where is the sun?

The tusk-tiger! It followed me in!

Why do you not fight when there is still breath and blood within you? Why do you not trumpet and flail?

My calf, did she escape, at least? Have you seen her?

I do not have your answers, Furmother hummed. *I do not know about those things. I only come for the Stories. Have you seen where they settled?*

Many voices, like sticky bones rubbing together. *Stories? Is that what they are? We know nothing of those, but we know where they fell. Reach out your trunk, living Mother. They are much farther down; do not miss them as you sink.*

The air inside her swelled and grew large. It pressed against her throat, demanding to be calved, and the Furmother fought with wounded tusk-tiger fierceness to keep it from escaping. Strong was Furmother-With-Her-Tusks-Whole, greatest of all Great Mothers! There was no boulder she could not move, no tree she could not uproot. Her squeal crumbled mountains to dust baths.

But her descent was slow.

"I CAN'T OUTRIGHT promise you anything, no. Everything will have to be negotiated." *Think fast, Kat. Do something to salvage this mess, quick.* "But," she hurries on, "the mountain the waste will be buried under and everything around it will be designated sovereign elephant territory, obviously. No unauthorized trespassing. You and your daughters and the daughters of your daughters will live there undisturbed, forever." She doesn't mention how it's all blasted scrubland and decommissioned atomic test sites, a sandy wilderness pockmarked with green glass craters. Someone else can get into that later—namely and most importantly, someone who isn't her. *I'm just here to sell the idea*, she tells herself. "And I'll talk to someone about the education campaign." Not a lie. She'll definitely try and bring it to the table for discussion, for all the good it may or may not do. Whether it gets any further than said table is anyone's guess. "I don't see why they wouldn't at least look into it, right?"

There are a million different reasons they might defer looking into it, ranging from expenses to manpower. Kat hopscotches over that and lands on one leg and holds the pose, waiting as the elephant takes in the translator's hand gestures. Her old eyes shift to Kat's, ancient and endless and unhurried, as cool as Kat feels hot. God help them if elephants ever start playing poker.

"YOU STILL HANGING around here? What the hell are you teaching those things, the goddamned alphabet?"

Out of all the things Regan misses leastmost about this job—the lip sores, the busted dorm beds, the gritty taste of the paint between her teeth—floor supervisors probably rank somewhere nearabouts where the cream rises. And of all the fume-breathing, foul-grinning fool men picked out of a handcart for the task? Slattery's probably—no, definitely—Slattery's *definitely* the one she'd be most eager to see walking out the door for good. Jodie used to spit globs of tobacco juice at the back of his head for every dirty thing he said to the girls, but Jodie's moldering dead in the ground now and Regan doesn't chew anymore, for obvious reasons. She ignores him and keeps packing, throwing everything into a canvas bag through a gauzy oil slick of hurt fierce enough to make her dizzy and queasy at the same time. Sometimes lately she wonders if she could wrench the entire rotten length of her jaw off if she gave it a shot. Get a good hookhold beneath the chin with a couple of fingers, brace herself, and—

A noise like an angry foghorn cuts through the haze. Regan looks up just in time to see Slattery idly tickling Topsy's tail with the little leather quirt he's always flashing.

"Lord Jesus, Slattery, cut that out! You looking to get squashed to bear grease?" Not that that outcome would bother her any; she'd pay full admission for a Splattery Slattery sideshow. It's more the elephant she's worried about, flaring and stomping and teeter-tottering on the edge of something dark and crazy-mad. Regan staggers to her feet, everything above the neck pounding hell bent for leather. *Slattery ain't worth it, Topsy. None of this mess is.*

"Aw hell fire, girl, I'm just playin' a little. Can't you take—"

She pushes him hard against the stall wall with an anger she didn't even know she had energy left to nurse. He stumbles and falls slap on his ass. "Everyone else we worked with is deader than dog ticks and I ain't far behind," she says. "All I gotta do is get on through this week and I can go home, but all that really means is I get to die where my baby sisters can see me screaming and hollering and messing myself. Take your fun and go straight to hell with it."

He glowers up at her from the dirty straw. If looks could kill, her troubles would be done, but unfortunately they don't and they ain't and she's got a ways to go yet. She ignores his glare and turns to Topsy, who's vibrating like a clothesline in a norther.

Hey, she signs. *Topsy? Hello? Y'all still with me? Hello?*

No reply. A low bee tree hum thrums deep in Regan's aching eardrums and molars. She takes a step backwards. She's about to ask again when something hits her in the back of the head, hard enough to send her palms-first cattywampus across the floor of the stall.

"You think you're the only one having a rough time, girl?" Slattery says. "You think you're the only one with a family needs feeding?"

THE MAN, LIKE all Men, is only there to tickle Her rage, to make it stand awkwardly on wobbly hind legs for his amusement. The dead girl tries to intervene and he slaps her down, kicking and bellowing in full *musth*. She hums a growing song, a ripening song, a full red swaying splitting-sticky song. In their work stalls the other Mothers hear it and drop their brushes, chorusing suddenly like a flock of beautiful gray-skinned birds.

The fruit hangs heavy on the branch
Good to pick
To pluck
To share!

Is it ripe?
Is it ready?
Is it good, O Mothers?

AT THE BOTTOM of all things, O best beloved mooncalf, where the Blacksap was densest and darkness the thickest—that was where the Stories had settled. That was where the Furmother's trunk finally felt them, nestled together like summer melons in an unseen heap. But what to do with the air flailing mad inside her and no way back to the surface? How to share the stories when She and they both were trapped at the bottom of the Blacksap? Furmother felt the pressure building and understood what must be done. She was, after all, cleverest of all Great Mothers.

One by one she took the stories in her trunk and pushed them into her mouth. They burned her tongue and throat as she swallowed them down. Most tasted foul, like the Blacksap they were coated with. Some had split like ripe fruit, their sweetness leaking to mingle with the bitter. Furmother did not stop until all were grasped and gulped. Her belly bulged with endless Story, all the tales that were and all the tales that would ever be. Even yours, O best beloved mooncalf. Even mine. The reason we glow—that, too, was there, snug beneath the ribs of Furmother.

"Now," thought Furmother-With-Her-Tusks-Whole. "At last."

The trapped breath within could no longer be contained. With a noise like a mountain bursting into song, Furmother blew apart.

"VERY WELL. WE will... consider guarding the place, contingent on these stipulations. We will remember what lies beneath when all of your clever inventions have broken down to dust and rust and food for weeds to pick apart and nothing but poison and damage is left to tell your Story." The translator sounds about as grim as the elephant looks. Kat searches for sympathy in their eyes, but it's an Easter egg hunt hours after the toddlers have all gone home with sugar headaches. "We may even consent to the glowing."

"Okay! That's... oh, that's great, that's fabulous." *That's motherfucking funding.* For the first time in two hours, Kat takes a deep, hopeful breath. "You'll be doing an amazing thing for future gen—"

"However," the translator says.

"ALL THAT PIG shit about the paint being poison, was that even true? What *I* heard—" A boot digs into Regan's hip; pain sprouts and grapevines up the trunk of her to join the thicket running wild in her head. "What I heard is that you all were just a bunch of loose whores who caught syphilis and decided to milk the company dry. I *need* this job, you hear me, girl? I can't go fight and I'll be goddamned if I go back down in the mines. They end up shutting the factory down because a bunch of giggling girls had to go and get their holes filled, I swear—"

She sees the kick coming this time and manages to catch Slattery's foot before it connects. He tries to jerk away; she hangs on for dear life. Spots swim across her eyes. The air whistles through the empty spaces in her teeth as she sucks in a lungful around the pain.

"Just wait," she manages to croak. "Hang around a while longer. Breathe in that dust for a spell."

Confusion and irritation crease the middle of Slattery's forehead. Again he tries yanking his foot back; again Regan clamps down with an alligator snapper's dead-eyed dedication. She sees the seeds of doubt land. For the first time in Lord knows how long, she smiles.

"Oh yeah. That powder don't stay lying down. You been getting you lungfuls of the stuff for—how long you been a supervisor? Since the day they started up? And you never thought about all that dust floating around?" She pushes him away. "You're stupider than you look and you ain't much to look at, you want the God's honest. May take a little longer, but truth's coming for you, Slattery."

Which may or may not be true. She dearly hopes it is, but for now it's enough to watch the fear scrabbling behind his eyes, looking for a knothole to slip into. "Bullshit," he stutters. His back is against Topsy's side now, palms pressed to her ribs. "They would've told me."

"Yeah, just like they told us? May be overthinking your place in the pack, hound dog."

He opens his mouth to say something back. He opens his mouth, but he's suddenly six feet in the air with an elephant's trunk wrapped around his neck, and so all that comes out is a strangled *ghrrk*.

Yes, O Mothers
Yes!
It is Ripe
And Good
And ready to be plucked
Sweet on the tongue,
In the trunk,
On the tusks,
To toss, to tear, to trample!

ALL OF HER pieces, all of the Stories, everything that held Furmother together—all of it sailed high into the sky. Bones and Blacksap and insides and outsides, fur and tusks and tail! End over end over end they flew, until the wind caught them and scattered the bits across the frozen world like plums. Half of a tusk lodged in the sky's belly and became the moon; much of her hair blew away and turned to clouds. Her hot blood thawed the earth; the songs she had scattered behind her on her journey sprouted and were plucked by the wandering Mothers.

Stories, too, they discovered. But it was a funny thing: They were shattered into pieces, like the Great Mother who had scattered them, and no one tale held to the ear by itself could ever be fully understood. To make them whole required many voices entwined. Then and only then could they become true things, and then and only then could we become the undying We, endless voices passing along the one song that is also Many.

"WE ARE NOT doing this for you. We are doing it for all the ones that might suffer in the future because of you and your thoughtlessness, your short tempers, your dangerously short memories. We will tell them what you did as we tell one another, passing it down from She to She. If this... compromise is the only way to make sure the story survives, the *real* Story..." The translator shrugs. The matriarch is a granite statue. "Please do not misunderstand me. We aren't protecting your secrets. We are guarding the truth. They will see how we shine, and they will know the truth."

THERE ARE A hundred interviews and uniforms and grim-faced men with typewriters lurking in Regan's future, each of them more or less asking the same damn thing over and over: What the hell happened? Did Slattery provoke the elephant? Was there any warning in Topsy's behavior in the days leading up to the attack? Did she get a good look at what happened?

Hell yes I saw what happened. How could I NOT get an eyeful of what goddamned happened? You think I'm blind and deaf on top of being the walking dead? A fella got turned to raspberry jam spitting distance from me and I had to go back home and comb little bits of him outta my hair and you sit there asking if I got a good look?

But all of that's still waiting up ahead, throwing jacks just around the corner. Right now she's *watching* it happen, backed up as far against the opposite side of the stall as she can scoot, while every elephant in the place from one end to the other stomps and screams loud enough to shake sparkling radium dust from the rafters. Slattery screamed too, at first, but the only noise left over now is that triumphant roar, like bugles and trumpets and the footfalls of an angry god come to collect.

Way away down at the bottom of herself, buried deep beneath the frozen shock and the pain in her jaw and throat and places where Slattery kicked her, she feels something strange stirring, like sitting in church and getting the Holy Ghost. It takes her a while to stick a tack in it, hunkered cowering in that corner with her hands over her ears and madness mopping the floor red right over yonder, but it comes to her eventually, guilty as a kid stealing ripe melons.

Satisfaction. That's what it is. It's satisfaction.

Part II
Cascade Reaction

If you do not know how to die, never trouble yourself; nature will in a moment fully and sufficiently instruct you; she will exactly do that business for you; take no care for it.

—Michel de Montaigne

2

RAMPAGE AT US RADIUM! MACABRE & BIZARRE 'MAD ELEPHANT' ATTACK SPARKS SHOCKED INVESTIGATIONS, TEMPORARY PLANT SHUTDOWN

—Victim "was not the first nor second man" to fall to the Beast's capricious wrath, say sources
—Local constabulary describe "scene of unfathomable carnage and butchery"

—Survivor saw it all from her hiding place a mere stone's throw from
the grim hecatomb!

Police were called to US Radium's factory floor in the early hours of
yesterday evening, whereupon arriving they found a bloody tableau of horror.
One of the factory's workforce of helper elephants had indiscriminately gone
stark raving mad and snapped the fetters of bondage, destroying her stall and
smashing a foreman beneath her vast and terrible agglomeration in the most
gruesome and gore-streaked way imaginable. No resuscitation was possible,
for the body of the poor victim was so crushed and mutilated it "looked to
have gone through a pressing machine," according to horrified onlookers.

Adding to the lurid penny-dreadful quality of this sensational tale, there
was indeed a survivor—a mere slip of a woman, one of the very "Radium
Girls" recently entangled in a lengthy legal dispute against US Radium on
the grounds of workers' safety whose allegations were the prime instigator
for the elephants' initial purchase in the first place. Factory officials have
not been forthcoming with information on the girl's current physical and
emotional status (or why she remained in US Radium's employ when all of
her fellows have presumably been dismissed, as was initially reported several
months ago), but one can assume the emotional trauma has been nothing
short of shattering. She was said to have been "coated in bright splashes of
blood from hair to hemline" after her rescue from the stall, a horrific state
even a strapping full-grown man's sanity might quail beneath the strain of.

What is intended to be done with the mad culprit—and what the future of
the elephant program at US Radium may be in the face of this unthinkable
disaster—remains to be seen. If, as our sources report, this is not the beast's
first attack on a caretaker, options on the table may be limited to lethality.

THERE'S A TOY elephant on the director's desk. Plopped between the family
pictures and fancy diplomas and cowpiles of ink-stained paper, it sits there
hoisting its little tin trunk towards the big tin ceiling begging whatever heathen
god elephants pray hallelujah to for a boot heel, a fist, or the delivering jaws
of a curious and bad-behaved hound dog. Regan's about ready to do the
honors herself if the director doesn't stow his hemming and hawing. Going to

college apparently taught you sixteen different ways of saying "we're damned sorry" and "we're real damned sorry," and not a blessed one of them left any air in the room or breath in the speaker's lungs or meant any more than a trained hen plucking at a toy piano.

You and me, tin elephant. We're both stuck here waiting for it to end. It looks a lot like one of the animals that came along with the wooden Noah's Ark she had bought her sisters for Christmas back when her and Mama were both doing better, before the jaw ache and the dentist and the company doctor's shrugs. That pretty painted boat, she recollects, dried up a good quarter of two November paychecks. She wonders where this one came from, if the director's just so stuffed with money he can go buy things like that the way other folks pick up salt and flour.

"What're you gonna do about the elephants?" she says, cutting off another round-robin repetition of the We're Very Sorry Song mid-verse.

"It's unfortunate, very unfortunate, and—I'm sorry, what was that?"

"The elephants. The workers." She talks slower, half because the director's obviously working with a deficit of common sense, half because it hurts her throat and jaw to speak and everything's coming out as a mushy-mouthed drunk's mumble. "You gonna keep using, or you gonna talk to them?"

"Well, I mean." The director's eyes and hands slide to a spot on his desk in dire need of straightening. "Rudimentary intelligence and even more rudimentary grasp of language aside, they're just animals. I don't exactly understand what speaking to them about any of this would accomplish. What do you suppose they would request, smoke breaks? A ham on Christmas?"

Freedom, maybe, y'think? A way of saying "hell no"?

"Anyway," he continues, plowing quickly on, "that point is moot at this juncture. To answer your initial question, we're liquidating our workforce at auction and shutting down the Orange factory, effective next month. Have to make our costs back somehow after this debacle." Regan can't be sure, but she thinks she catches some side-eye from him at that last bit as he busily shuffles papers. "Though I don't see how. Most of our elephants were... problem children to begin with, purchased at a steep discount."

"You're shutting down work? During a war?"

"The factory here in Orange, yes." If there was a blue ribbon given out at the county fair for avoiding looking people in the eye, he'd have something fluttery to take home right now. Regan can barely keep upright in her chair, her back and legs ache so fierce, but something about the way he's acting feels slithery and slightly familiar. She decides to keep jabbing her gig into the water.

"Everywhere else too if you're selling off the elephants, I guess," she says.

No reply. The sheaf in his hand goes *shss shss shss* as it hits the desk. Beneath the fancy new electric bulb overhead his head shines wetter than a bullfrog's ass.

"I mean. Not to put too fine a point on it, but ain't nobody willing, able, and human nearby who's read a newspaper is gonna want to take this job on after all the shit you put me and my girls through." She lets the swear and the anger tethered to it hang in the air with all the weight of a pointed rifle barrel. "And ain't like you'd knowingly do that to folks again in the first how."

Shss shss shss SLAM.

For the first time since Regan sat down the director looks her dead in the eye. A flash of memory splits her aching head: She's ten and her bulldog's got a rat cornered behind the barn and no general on a gray horse has ever been so unafeared of his own death. The rat, though—at least she'd respected that rat. Rat was doing what it had to do to keep itself alive. Rats looked out for one another.

"What US Radium does or does not do in the future is no business of yours," he says. "Rest assured, if we did continue production elsewhere, we would enforce new and stringent safety protocols where our factory girls were concerned. 'Stringent' means tough, if you were wondering." He drops his eyes and whisks the papers away into a drawer. "Be out of the dorms by the end of next week, please. Thank you."

"Hang on." Regan staggers to her feet, trying not to wince. "I ain't done talking to you yet, si—"

"That will be all, thank you."

"No it damned well WON'T BE." She snatches the tin elephant off the desk and squeezes it so hard all the pointy edges cut into her palm. "Two things. You're gonna answer me two things, less you really wanna call the security man to come and throw me out. Look real good in the paper, won't it?" It's hard to sound threatening when you're slurring and sputtering all over the place, but she gives it her best. "One, where's my check?"

"It's in the mail, as I have told you the last three times you inquired previously."

"You sure about that? You *real* sure?"

The director sighs, reaches down into his desk, fishes around, and brings up a checkbook and a fountain pen. He stabs and jabs at one of the papers like an egret skewering minnows, tears it off, and practically hurls the thing at her across the desk. Hurling slips of paper is a lot harder than it sounds, though; it flutters and glides through the air before drifting sweetly to a halt at her feet. She bends slowly to pick it up, all of her joints doing their best mockingbird imitations of faraway machine gun nests. Blood roars in her ears and eyes. She reaches her free hand out, steadying herself on the edge of the desk until the darkness clears and danger slinks on by.

"Thanks," she says. She doesn't expect a reply, and sure enough, not even a grunt squeezes out of his puckered mouth. "Last question. Topsy? You selling her with the rest?"

"Euthanasia." He's already gone back to ignoring her, scratching and pecking banty-fashion at his Very Important Work.

Regan sticks the check and the tin elephant both inside her pocket and sees herself out.

THEY NAMED HER after a slave in their own Stories, because even humans know Stories are We, and they try, in their so-so-clever way, to drive the Stories down gullies and riverbeds of their own choosing. But chains can be snapped, O best beloved mooncalf. Sticks can be knocked out of a Man's clever hands. And one chain snapping may cause all the rest to trumpet and stomp and shake the trees like a rain-wind coming down the mountain, washing the gully muddy with bright lightning tusks and thunderous song.

Sing, O Mothers
Sing of Her sacrifice!
Sing of She-With-The-Lightning-In-Her-Trunk
The one who split the Tree in half
Scattering their lives like leaves,
Like splintered wood,

Like shaken fruit.
They took her away in chains, O Mothers
Locked her up where no one could see
Plotted her death, a spectacle, a shrieking monkey troop's boast:
"See how clever we are, how strong,
The lightning obeys us; so too should you!"
Poor things,
Poor things.
Poor prideful, foolish things.

THEY SEND OTHERS in to negotiate the next few times. Kat's glad of it; her eagerness to see the project (*her* project) getting under way feels like it's been slowly leaking out the cracks ever since the first meeting. It's still a sound hypothesis—she'll stick by that no matter how guilty she feels, that the reasoning behind picking elephants was solid—but now she's got a whole mess of issues sitting in moving boxes inside her, taking up valuable floor space.

They will see how we shine, and they will know the truth.

The thing that old elephant didn't understand—and how could she?—is that humans aren't always interested in confronting truths, especially uncomfortable ones. Will the benefits of a concerted coast-to-coast re-education program outweigh the million sound bites about glowing radioactive elephant watchdogs sure to spring forth from every talking head and late-night comedian? The classes in school Kat sat through as a kid hadn't done a damn thing but muddy the waters. It's going to take a massive push, a goddamned media blitz, and she doesn't know if her higher-ups honestly give a shit about making that happen. They want a keep out sign for the ages, not truth in megafauna relations.

Christ, we can barely confront the gazillion shitty, horrible ways we treat one another without getting defensive. What chance does this have of being done right?

She neglects her lab work writing detailed pitches for ten-point media attack plans. The pizza delivery guy becomes her only connection to the outside world. The sheets on her bed grow kicked and tangled, eventually wadding into an untouched, unwashed knot at the foot of the mattress.

*　　*　　*

AN ELEPHANT TO DIE BY ELECTRICITY!

Topsy, the Mad Murderess of US Radium, to Be Electrocuted at Luna Park

DISPATCH FROM ORANGE, NEW JERSEY: A license has been issued to the proprietors of Luna Park on New York's Coney Island, to kill by public electrocution the ferocious TOPSY, the elephant responsible for the shocking and gruesome death of a foreman at US Radium's dial factory. The beast's viciousness is well-known and well-documented; sources say previous sprees have claimed her a score of lives up and down the East Coast circus routes, the last killing enacted upon a spectator who teased her with a lit cigar. The fairgoer was plucked like a peach and crushed to death under the rampaging renegade's feet.

In an attempt to both salvage their costs and spare the animal's life, circus owners sold her to US Radium. As it now appears impossible to keep her safely employed there, it was decided by the factory's owners that death was the best method of getting rid of her. The idea of an execution was hit upon, using a powerful electrical current (engineered by the Edison Electric Illuminating Company of Brooklyn, NY) to shock the beast until dead.

Topsy's new owners, the proprietors of Coney Island's under-construction Luna Park, have promised the show will be free of charge and open to all members of the public. The execution will take place at the foot of the "Electric Tower," a 200-foot-tall structure that, when finished, will feature almost 20,000 electrified bulbs. It promises to be the event of the season, a heart-stopping exhibition displaying two primitive forces of nature pitted against one another in a never-to-be-forgotten, larger-than-life spectacle of elemental force.

Concerns have been raised by the American Society for the Prevention of Cruelty to Animals that electrocution is a rather cruel method of extermination. Readers are reminded that shooting the elephant would require five hundred rifle balls and three hours' time to do the work that ten thousand volts will manage in less than a second. Proceedings will begin at Luna Park on Sunday, January 4th, 8 PM.

*   *   *

WELL, THE DIRECTOR hadn't exactly lied a week before when he said they were putting Topsy down; that much was the God's honest truth. Hadn't gotten into the nitty-gritty of it—hadn't mentioned how they'd be doing it or where they'd be doing it—but then, Regan hadn't stuck around to bother kicking over that rock, had she? The ad really shouldn't surprise her like it does, bounding from the back pages of the local paper, slick and colorful as the cover of a pulp magazine. The elephant is frozen mid-convulsion, mouth wide open in a silent howl. A metal hat is strapped to her head; exaggerated yellow lightning bolts of electricity sizzle and whiz off her skin like popcorn kernels in a cast-iron skillet. Wires and chains lead away in every direction, hitching her safely to her death like she's every bit the crazy rampaging murderess the headline proclaims her to be.

Over yonder, beyond the chains and straps and iron bars, a crowd of people huddle watching. The artist didn't put as much work into drawing them as he or she did Topsy; they're mostly just slack-jawed shadows, men with driving caps and bowler hats and blank ghost faces. The only one of the group with any detail at all is a fellow in the middle, and the reason he's drawn so careful is because he's the man with his hand on the killing switch, the man with the power—the power of life and death forever and ever amen.

Someone had put a lot of effort into drawing an animal in the full throes of dying. Someone had probably paid a lot of money to have them scribble it, and even more money to stick it in the local paper. Money, after all, is the one thing US Radium's never been starved from a lack of.

Regan lets the paper slither to her quilted lap, too tired to keep holding the wretched thing, too sick inside to keep looking. She pushes it over the edge of the bed, so that all that's left there is the long-unopened letter from Jodie. It's her last night in the empty dormitory. In the morning she'll hop a train south—the last train she'll probably ever ride—and she'll go home to die, just as certain as if someone has strapped a metal mixing bowl to her head and pulled an oversized lever.

"Executioner's comin' for both of us, girl," she says. "I guess people'll remember you, at least."

She takes a deep suck of air, wearily picks up the letter, and tears it open. Might as well get it over and done with, all things considered.

In darkness she waited, O Mothers,
Tethered, tormented, fearless,
Waited for the many Men to gather
The way wind
Waits for lightning
The way rain
Holds for thunder

They came to watch her die, to smell her flesh burn,
To see a Great Mother laid low.
They gathered in great boasting bull herds
Like flies to dung,
Like hyenas to a sickness,
Yapping barking tussling.
Poor things
Poor things,
Poor prideful, foolish things!

"WELL, THEY'RE definitely getting the land—that part of the deal is sealed." Kat's supervisor, a graying-at-the-temples woman of around sixty, has a poker face to make the elephant matriarch blow her cool in a fit of jealousy. She's got Kat's folder in her hands—yellow ledger papers poking and spilling from the edges like the filling in an overstuffed cartoon hoagie—and whether or not she approves of what's inside is still anybody's guess. "There's no need to feel any guilt about that."

Except for the part where nobody wants the land anyways and sure as hell won't want it once there's nuclear waste crammed under the mountain. Kat swallows her sass and makes a stab at looking pleased. "That's good," she says. "That's excellent to hear."

"Yes." Dr. Tilyou's voice is noncommittal; *I honestly don't care and neither do you.* "As to the rest of your concerns, the research you've presented me with... Katherine, have you been sleeping well? How much time have you spent on all of this?" She flaps the folder as punctuation. Notes escape and flutter to the floor. "You're not part of the media team. I understand the need to be involved in every aspect of a project you're personally responsible for, but nobody has seen you at the lab in ages, which is where you are most needed. Some people are beginning to worry."

Kat suddenly feels on the verge of tears, and she doesn't have the slightest clue why. Exhaustion, maybe. Frustration? It's getting hard to tell the two apart. "I told the representative I would try," she says. "Going forward, I have many ethical questions about the legitimacy of this project. I have to at least make sure an attempt is made at educating the public before continuing on with the research. A *major attempt*." She sounds like a robot, but hey—at least she's a moral one. *Beep-boop, my conscience is clear.* "Not just blurbs in middle school history books."

That earns her a sigh and a mighty drumming of fingertips on particle board, about as close as Dr. Tilyou comes to expressing annoyance. "I'm going to be blunt with you," she says.

"Go ahead." *Do your worst, lady. I've been chewed out by a fucking elephant before; your admittedly impressive eyebrows can't touch me.*

"Nobody working on this project except you cares that much about sticking to the letter of the agreement. It's a moot point. A sociological campaign of the scope and breadth of the one you're pitching would cost us hundreds of thousands of dollars in funding. Your honesty and desire to make sure the elephants are fairly represented is commendable, don't think it isn't, but—"

"It's not a top priority." Cold water words, the departmental equivalent of a baseball striking a dunk tank's target dead center.

"No." Dr. Tilyou lets her drop all the way to the bottom before continuing. "That's not to say we won't launch some kind of program, something to at least placate the elephants. It's just... cost aside, have you considered the levels of scrutiny we would be under if such an intensive campaign were launched? On top of the scrutiny a project involving non-*sapiens* rights, genetic manipulation, *and* nuclear waste will engender as is? It wouldn't just be shooting ourselves in the foot; it would be putting a loaded barrel to our heads and spinning the chamber." Kat's never heard Dr. Tilyou get colloquial before. She must be *pissed*. "That's not even getting into the emotions surrounding Topsy's act. Justified, unjustified—she's at the center of this project, but do you really, truly believe anyone should know in detail how the sausage is made?"

"We're scientists," Kat says. She stands. "All we do is teach people how sausage is made."

"I'm... I'm sorry?"

"I have to go home and think," she says.

"Think?"

If Kat were feeling less numb in her recklessness, she'd offer the good professor a cracker. "About whether I want to be a part of this, going forward. I'll let you know by tomorrow morning."

"Katherine." Dr. Tilyou's voice is taking on a downright panicky tone. "If you would please just wait a—"

The door cuts her off mid-sentence.

Regan,

Just want you to no, aint no hard feeling about the way things paned out. You all did best you cood lookin out for me like blood kin when you no I never had no body since Mama past away. Even yor own mama used to give me a seat at the tabell when holy fokes sooner feed scraps to a stray tomcat than a big uglee plain mannerd girl like me. Wood of been a dam good job and easy if not for the poysin.

as four the cumpanee, they can get blowed straeiht to hell and devil take there asses with a bran new pikaxe It is knot right the way they done us, and it is knot right ever the way big rich men do litle peeple, girls like us most of all. Even a snake bites if she gets stomped on. Peeple dont stomp on snakes cause they got enuff poysin in there teeth to kill a crowd of big men.

I am leaving you sum poysin for our teeth Regan. I stole it from the Storm Mountain job beefor all of this and i still don't rightly no why cept misschef. It is in a locker downtown at 289 east cyclone street and I am leaving you the key. Carefull knot to shake or drop it untill you want to bite and are redy to meet me again. lockur number 27.

Wish you wood have been my blood sister, but we had good enough times anyways. Tell yor mama hello and not to forget about me.

Jodie

Regan doesn't get a whole lot of sleep that night.

There's a girl out there in the dark who has no idea what's coming for her. Maybe she's not so good at her letters. Maybe she can't even read them at all, never having had the chance or the interest or the time. She lives at the back end of nowhere, where the school only stretches yea far before it snaps, and she's got sisters to help take care of and a drunk for a daddy and a mama so shrivel-tired she can't even call up the water to cry. She's never read a paper in her life, this dust-footed girl, and most days she's not properly sure what the news is from five miles up the road, let alone five hundred. But just wait, girl. Some kin will hear it from some kin that there are jobs at the new factory— easy jobs, good jobs, work that pays more in a month than sweeping people's houses scratches up in a flat year—and off she'll go, no schooling or letters or certificates needed. You got fast hands? You got lips? You know how to use a paintbrush? Well hell fire, take a seat and get to work, sweetie! We'll take care of you. Radium's not just harmless—it's good for the body. Point a thousand brushes with your lips and you'll still come out fine.

And she may get a loose tooth or a sore lip, that girl, and she may feel an aching in her hips and knees the way her mawmaw describes the rheumatism, but she'll trust the men who hired her, and she'll keep on working because she don't know any better and nobody's gonna bother warning her when there's money on the table. And eventually, she'll die horribly—as horribly as a scene from a painted Bible hell, choking to death as her throat and jaw rot from the inside out—and the memory of her will die soon after, and it'll be like she never walked or talked or laughed or hoped to begin with.

So much for her.

There's an elephant calf out there in the dark who has no idea what's coming for her. She's grazing with her people somewhere, all her mamas clustered around her, all her aunties and mawmaws and second cousins twice removed, because that's more or less all Regan knows about wild elephants—the mamas stick together and travel in a herd like cows and the menfolk wander alone like a lot of other male critters do—and all she knows about the world is green grass and playing and hiding from crocodiles when there's crocodiles sneaking around champ-champ-chomping their jaws. But maybe someday men come along to that place, and they shoot all the mamas and aunties and mawmaws and second cousins twice removed, and the ones they don't shoot they load up and send to other places, where they teach them to dance and do tricks and how to be alone in the wide old world. And the calf forgets what it was like to be whole. She loses herself as she gets bigger. She busts so many heads trying to find herself again the circus men get fed up and sell her to a factory—not US Radium, but similar, a kissing cousin—where eventually, after a long-enough time and enough work done, she dies the same slow way as the girl, spoiling like bad meat in a forgotten lunch pail in the woods.

So much for her.

And Regan, for all her thinking and all her tail-chasing, can't puzzle out how to stop the merry-go-round from spinning, whether it's through Jodie's way or some other, kinder method. She lies there staring at the ceiling until birds begin calling outside, too pained by her rotting body and whirling brain to snatch even the smallest scrap of rest.

And part of me felt good watching Topsy smash up that stall, didn't it? Way down deep, something angry in me got satisfaction. The world's so big and mean, and we're so small in it with our hands and feet fettered. Little tiny helpless things, who can't do a damn thing but cry and rage most days at the way the game's rigged against us.

She gets up from bed. She watches her window go from black to gunmetal. When it's light enough out to see, she digs around in the crate of Jodie's stuff—pushing past the coin purse, the pill bottles, the busted music box with the little ceramic bluebird—until she finds the key on its ribbon, sifted way down to the bottom. She lets it hang twirling from her fingers before looping it around her neck.

So much for her.

The Men gathered, O Mothers
Hooting they led her forth, and she let them;
They called to the lightning:

"Lightning, strike this Mother
Burn her like dry grass,
Make Her Story wither and die,
So that she will never be They
Never be We.
Splinter,
Sunder,
Scatter!"

SHE CONSIDERS GOING home, but the thought of all the research books waiting for her there makes her vaguely ill. Eventually her feet pull her to the nearest Q stop, where she drifts through the turnstile and down the stairs to the southbound platform.

There's an excited little boy on the train. Nothing revelatory about that; Kat watches him bounce off the walls with her earbuds cranked as high as they'll go, making it more or less like watching a death metal music video about the Black Goat of the Woods discovering their inner child. What's interesting about him is that he's wearing a t-shirt with Disney's Topsy printed all over it, broken up and interspersed with bright green atoms. Are his parents taking him to Coney Island because of the cartoon? she muses. Did the innocent little sugar-sucker beg and plead to go because that's where the finale dumps its sad, angry but good-at-heart heroine when things are at their darkest? Deeply fucked up, but also deeply probable. No matter what you did, forty or fifty or a hundred years passed and everything became a narrative to be toyed with, masters of media alchemy splitting the truth's nucleus into a ricocheting cascade reaction of diverging alternate realities.

There might have been kids at the actual electrocution. It was late in the day and the majority of the 150-plus crowd allowed inside had been men and older boys—so said the history books—but if Kat had to bet, she would guess there were some women and younger children hanging around, too. In those days, packing a picnic lunch and taking the family to watch someone or something die horribly wasn't considered particularly unusual. Electricity was new and weird; so were elephants. Combining the two into something as lurid as an execution always sucked in quite a crowd.

What a fucked-up mess. And yet without that fucked-up mess, the Radium Elephant trials never would have happened. There's no divorcing these things. Processing uranium to get at the sweet, sweet energy released left you with plutonium.

The Atlantic winks at her outside the window. The kid slams headfirst into the side of a seat and keeps moving in the opposite direction. She thinks about neutrons careening into nuclei like amped-up toddlers, the energy released and the expense and irreversible entropy coming on like a night with no stars.

TOPSY
(*Traditional, 1919*)

Brought her here from across the sea,
To this land of liberty
Seven feet tall, such a sight to see

Blow, Topsy, Blow
Blow, Topsy, Blow!

Factory boss said, "Topsy, m'girl,
Quit the circus, give work a whirl;
You'll be treated fair and square,
Brush in your trunk and nary a care!"

Blow, Topsy, Blow,
Blow, Topsy, Blow!

Kind old Topsy hadn't a clue,
'Bout radium, what it could do,
"I'm your gal, boss, let's see 'er through!"

Blow, Topsy, Blow,
Blow, Topsy, Blow!

But what that foreman didn't know,
Is that there's so much injustice you can honestly sow,
Before the anger starts to grow
Blow, Topsy, Blow
Blow, Topsy, Blow!

REGAN LIMPS DOWNTOWN, raccoon-eyed and none too daisy-fresh owing to how she felt too weak and too exhausted to scrub up in the dormitory showers before heading out. There's a taste coating her tongue like the smell of dirty pennies combined with something gone moldy and forgot. The iron key around her neck bounces off her breastbone with every step. Between that and her jaw and throat throbbing molten bear traps in time to each rabbity pulsebeat, she's got a pretty good rhythm going as she totters down the sidewalk.

She reaches the address, goes inside, and casts around until she finds the right locker. A few seconds more fiddling beneath the cotton of her shirt and the key is in her hand.

Jodie, she thinks. *I dunno if it's the good thing or the right thing or if you were even in your right goddamned mind when you put all of this together, but doing nothing's done nothin' but get more that don't deserve it sold down the river. I'm tired, Jodie. I'm so eat up with anger over you and us and all of it I can't see straight. And I'm tired of having to be angry all the time. I don't got the energy to keep it up anymore, but I'll be goddamned if I let them get away with murdering one more of us before this is all over and done with. Something's gotta give.*

A click and a clunk and the little metal box swings open for her. A glass jar no bigger than a bumblebee sits inside. Careful, like picking a baby bird up off the ground, Regan takes the vial and gently nests it in her right front pocket, where it's least likely to be rattled by the walk and the long train ride to Coney Island.

And
(Poor things!)
She called to the lightning:
(Poor things!)

"Lightning, we have always been kin, always been We."
(Poor prideful)
"Tell my Story."
(Foolish)
"Tell my Truth in a voice like thunder."
(Things!)
"And scatter them all like ripe red fruit."

THE MEMORIAL TOWER is forty feet high and carved out of marble, because they didn't do things halfway back in the day, even in the teeth of two world wars. In the seaside dusk it looms over Kat like a great tusk, curving to lift the sagging blue-gray canopy of nightfall.

It stands alone on its irradiated patch of beachfront property, far away down the strand from the toffee sellers and funnel cakes and skeevy boardwalk rides. Luna Park had never recovered from the incident. The place was barely out of the construction stage when Topsy turned its gestation into a miscarriage, and the cost of rebuilding combined with the stigma of tragedy (and background radiation) had convinced the surviving shareholders to throw up their hands and fold. The plot had stood empty for a while until the idea of a memorial was hit upon; several years and several mysterious donors later and the Luna Park Memorial Tower rose, a joint marker for the people who had died and the Radium Elephants who had found their voices in the violent self-sacrifice of their comrade. Sculpted bronze trunks wind around the length of the thing like a barber's pole all the way to the roof and top colonnade, where four bronze elephants and four bronze humans stand together gazing out to sea. In pictures and postcards of the place the trunks have long since gone the patina green of sea serpents, tarnished pennies, and the Statue of Liberty. Tonight they're stark black against the white.

Most people don't even remember the memorial exists. It's one of those oddities from an earlier time you learn about and then forget, something weird tucked away to stop and gawk at if you happen to be passing through the area on vacation or a day trip. Snap a photo, buy a postcard, namedrop it at a party when people ask what you did with your summer. Make a joke about Geiger counters and glowing craters if everyone else is clued in on the story. Death decayed into history decayed into poolside anecdote. Francium *wishes* it had a half-life as short as tragedy's.

Kat stares up at the column with her hands jammed in her pockets, thinking about truth and transmutation as the last light dies and the damp ocean breeze gnaws through her windbreaker. There's no stopping decay, change, or entropy. No matter how many jellyfish genomes they strap to an elephant's genetic material—no matter how many elephant mothers pass along the warning, long memories and unshakably interwoven strands of matriarchal polynucleotide narrative aside—the fact of the matter is, the basis for this project was contaminated from the start. It was decaying into something other than truth the day the first breathless article about Topsy was written, the day she died and someone else began telling her story and the cultural baggage accrued and replaced and eroded fact like radium in marrow.

Nuclear Topsy. No wonder the elephants don't trust them.

She stands there until the vertebrae in her craned neck start complaining and her feet go numb. An ivory sickle moon rises in the east. Kat turns her back on the memorial and the roaring Atlantic dark and shuffles towards the garish electric dawn of Coney Island, some skeleton's memory of what progress looked like.

LUNA PARK LOOKS like a twister's gone on a tear right through its muddy heart, lumber and splintered scaffolds and the great naked backbones of buildings-to-be lying stretched out across the ground in every whichaway direction. Everywhere you turn an eye men are working up a fine old sweat—hammering, sawing, stuck all over with sawdust and coal smut, spitting dirt and tobacco until the ground's so churned mule teams bog down and split their pipes braying. The air this close to the ocean is a sponge—a damp, warm rag stuffed up under your nose so close you can almost taste the stink of mule shit and chaw spit and stale mud mixed with piss and spilled bourbon. And there's another smell, too, yonder beneath the fresh pine and cigarette smoke—hay, blood, something big and wild and musky. An old reek, like a mountain breaking lather.

Once you've gotten a whiff of it, you never forget the smell of an elephant.

Nobody tries stopping Regan; she's dressed like a boy, the way she's most comfortable, and there are plenty of those running around. She wanders farther in—beneath the great wooden arch with its columns and crescent moons still unlit, past the rising spire they've already dubbed the "Electric Tower," wired to glow like something out of *The Arabian Nights*—slopping on through ankle-deep pigpen muck where there aren't boards laid yet, dizzy and sick and shaky-legged with her hurts but grimly determined not to faint. If that happens and she goes over on her side and the little bottle in her pocket gets broken and crushed, it'll have been a wasted trip with a smoking pair of boots planted at the bottom of the crater.

The morning gets hotter. Sweat pops on her forehead, running down into her eyes to sting them shut. All of her joining pins have been replaced with knife blades, from heel to toe to aching hip. She holds off swallowing her own spit until her tongue is dog-paddling and she can't help herself. These days, the automatic jerk of muscles she always took for granted before is like washing down coals with grain alcohol, a fierce tearing worse than her jaw if simply because of how much she has to make it happen. A beaten *gulp* and the fire roars up her throat and into her brain. Her knees give up the ghost and she finds herself slumping against a sawhorse, fingers clutching and unclutching at raw wood.

"Had a bit too much, eh, kid? Show's not even on until tonight, pace yourself!" A jolly hand follows the jolly voice, slapping Regan on the back so hard her last few teeth rattle. She gums back a scream. She's only got so much control left, but she clings to it with all she's got like a baby squirrel in a windstorm. "Don't let the policemen they got snooping around find you; you'll be hitting that drunk tank ass-first quicker'n a New York minute."

"Fine. I'm fine." The words dribble down her chin. Even the passerby's booming seems faded and faraway.

"You sure, son? You sure as hell don't look it. Here, lemme give you a hand."

"I'm FINE." She hears the good Samaritan step back hastily. "Need to see the elephant. Come to see the elephant."

"Yeah, you and every other pimple-popping boy-o from a hundred miles round." His voice is sulled now. "It's chained up in a tent just a little further the way you're going."

"Thanks." She hangs there until she's sure he's moved away. *C'mon, girl.*

Not much further to go. She pulls herself upright, gives her eyes and brain a minute to unfog, then staggers on.

You can hear the tent humming well before it ever hews into view, like a bee tree or a hive of wasps. Boys hoot and holler in and out beneath the canvas, confident as fighting cocks in their ability to outrun any bellowing grown-up that might come along with an idea to try and chase them. Older clumps smoke and chat warily outside. Regan pushes past best she can, careful not to let an elbow or swinging arm hit her pocket. Slowly—more like an old man than one of the boys now—she swings a shaky leg over the guide ropes and lifts the tent flap, ducking into a shadowland that smells like the beginning of the world.

Links rattle. Something big rumbles. Smaller shadows school like minnows, giggling and teasing, shying away at every snort or shift only to come flocking back when it looks like the danger's passed. Not that there's really any threat; as her eyes get used to the darkness Regan can see the chains and ropes looped and relooped around Topsy's neck and ankles, big old logging chains meant to pull redwoods crashing to the ground. Pebbles bounce off her leathery hide, and she pays them no more mind than a hawk shrugging off a territorial cock sparrow. Boys poke sticks and lit cigarettes at her from across the ropes; she lifts her trunk out of range and dreams on, spirit touring times and places Regan can't even guess at. Her mind is the most alien thing Regan's ever had truck with outside the God in her mother's Bible.

Almost there. She watches the scene a little longer, putting off what has to be done. One more trick. Jodie and the rest of them better appreciate this, wherever they are.

She takes a deep breath, latches onto a guide rope, gets her mind right for what's coming, and bellows like a whipped mule.

"COPS! COPS! LOOK OUT, COPS ARE COMING!"

Veins in her throat give up and bust their dams. She can feel them popping before the shock snaps and she goes into freefall, mind and soul and all the things that make Regan Regan rubbed out by a root-shaking, roof-tearing wave of wrongness her brain recognizes from its treetop perch as the worst pain she's ever felt—the kind you know is damaging things the moment it lands. Somewhere shadowy boys are shouting, shoving, scattering. They flutter past her like moths in a dream.

When she comes back to herself she's on her knees in a puddle of something dark, throat still registering aftershocks. Topsy looks down at her impassively. She wipes her mouth with the back of one palsied hand; it comes back sticky, copper-smelling.

Hey, Regan signs.

No reply, just watchful stillness. *Well there's a damned surprise.* She hauls herself to her feet, hay and dirt sticking to the blood on the palms of her hands.

I came here to see you, she continues. *You and me got business.*

Chains rattle. The air stirs. *No*, says the slow shadow of Topsy's trunk, black against the canvas. *No more business. No business but death.*

That's good, 'cause death is what I maybe came here to offer you. A righteous death. The movement for "righteous" looks a little something like two tusks quickly dipping down and then back up again, a goring, tossing flip. Regan slips a hand into her pocket, palming the bottle's cool cola-bottle smoothness. She sets it down on the ground between them—close enough so Topsy can reach, fettered up as she is—and steps back, head swimming from the act of bending over.

This, she signs, *is a seed. Crush it and death sprouts. Not just yours. The men with the chains. The circus men, the poison-factory men, the ones who will come to see you burn—all of 'em. Like lightning striking. You'll be lightning. You'll burn and you'll strike and then you'll be gone. It's up to you. Dying's a personal thing. It's... just...* She trails off, hunting for the right words. Exhaustion is butting in on her thoughts, pushing them to the back of the hall.

...I just wanted to give you the option, she finishes, at a loss as to how to put it any better. *A friend gave it to me. I'm passing it along to a higher power.*

Even with her death waiting and the sounds of a crowd gathering outside, Topsy takes her sweet, thoughtful time responding. You can practically hear the gears groaning inside that great skull of hers, slow but unstoppably steady in their revolution. *Righteousness.* Regan thinks of the sign again, invisible enemies flung into the air like pinecones. An old word, indiscriminate as a knife's edge, a tusk's tip.

Like lightning, Topsy signs. For the first time, Regan notices that her trunktip is glowing a faint, familiar green.

Yup.

You wish for them to die, too. Not a question. *For the poisoning. For killing you.*

Regan shrugs. No argument there.

Asking nice never seemed to get either of us much, did it? Maybe this'll get somebody's attention.

Topsy reaches down. Her trunk curls and uncurls, twitching at the tip like an agitated cat's tail. For the briefest blip of a second she hesitates and Regan thinks maybe she won't take the bottle, that she's sadder than she is angry, that her execution will amount to nothing more than a pitiful sentence in a history book swollen tick-tight with so many injustices the poisoning of a factory full of girls and the mean public death of a small god don't even register as particularly noteworthy.

But that's somebody else's once upon a time. Gently, gingerly—the way any soul would handle their own death—Topsy takes the little vial and tucks it away inside her mouth.

SHE THINKS OF her Many Mothers, fierce and vast, swift-trunked slayers of panther, hyena, and crocodile. She thinks of Furmother-With-The-Cracked-Tusk, tricking a bull and splitting herself so that the stories could be free and the Mothers could be We. Unresisting, she lets them lead her forth in chains. She lets them lead her forth in chains, and when they hoot and roar and clamber she thinks on Furmother, her bravery and her cunning, her careful, plodding patience.

The final fruit to be plucked is not rage, but song—a learning song, a teaching song, a joining-together song. She rolls it on her tongue, careful not to split it before its time. The men gibber and yap and lean out to touch her as she passes. The man holding the lead chain barks a warning at them in the jackal tongue of humans, hurrying along before her trunk can sweep them clear of the path.

There is still fear in her heart. To be is to be wary, and so there is still fear in her heart, balking wide-eared at what lies coiled at the end of the walk. *Danger! Lions! Claws and teeth and tawny fur!* She smells her ending, and her feet plant themselves, bending-parts senselessly locking. The man yells and tugs and strikes her with whip and chain; he too stinks of fear, sharp as crushed nettles underfoot. She struggles with the man and the fear—*Guns! Men! Fire and smoke and pits with sharpened sticks!*—but if the man can be ignored, the ending-fear cannot. It lies deeper than hurt and deeper than the need to sing her own undoing song, a root buried so far within no tusk can pry it free. The man-herd howls, thrown into *musth* by her hesitation. They claw and push at her haunches with their trunk-paws, desperate to hurry along, always and forever in a hurry.

Another human pushes out of the mass—the dead girl, still moving, still somehow on her feet when every part of her stinks of corruption. She exchanges a few guttural yips and yowls with the man on the end of the chain, pain rolling off her like river water. Eventually he huffs and puffs and reluctantly passes her the chain. She turns, asking, in the little language of twisted trunk-paws: *Are you well? Can you walk? It's just a little further. We'll go together.*

And even this much We is enough to drive the fear back into the high grass. Her mind stills. Her legs unstiffen. Together they cross the overwater, men flytrailing behind. Together they go to sing the song of their undoing, the joining, teaching, come-together song.

Sing thunder, O Mothers!
Sing her song in this dusty place!
Glowing like green lightning, so many Many Mothers apart,
Do not forget what lies Beneath,
And do not forget what came Before,
Sing Her Story like lightning,
Like thunder,
Like the Glorious Mothers Many:
We, She, Her,
Us.

THE ROSE MACGREGOR DRINKING AND ADMIRATION SOCIETY

T. Kingfisher

T. Kingfisher (www.redwombatstudio.com) is the vaguely absurd pen-name of Ursula Vernon, an author from North Carolina. In another life, she writes children's books and weird comics. She has been nominated for a bunch of awards and even won some of them, including a Nebula and a couple of Hugos. This is the name she uses when writing for grown-ups. When she is not writing, she is probably out in the garden, trying to make eye contact with butterflies.

THERE WAS A land of elven halls and hollows, of fairy mounds and great cathedrals underground. Hapless mortals went in and danced until their feet gave out, and sometimes they came out again.

But far beyond the merriment and the music and the trapped mortals, there was a campfire, and around it sat a half-dozen men, and a great bull selkie, and a horse the color of night.

The men were faerie boys, first to last, tall and sharp-boned, with cheekbones like swords. The selkie was a great hulking brute with his sealskin draped around him, muscle smoothed with a layer of fat, and a gleam in his eye like the last light on the sea.

The horse was a horse, except when he wanted more beer, and then he was a man with a mane of black hair and eyes that glowed like rubies in his face.

They sat around the fire, far from the fae court, and stared into the flames. Fire is older than faerie-kind and even they can be hypnotized by its dance.

"What gets me," said one of the men finally, "what really gets *me* is that she went and married the blacksmith."

* * *

HE'D MET ROSE MacGregor out on the hillside, where the grass met the sky and flowers lay spangled across the green. He was slim-hipped, broad-shouldered, and handsome as the devil.

She was short and plump, well-endowed in all directions, and she looked at him with a gleam in her eyes like a hawk spotting a rabbit on the downs below.

"What are you doing out here, my lady?" he purred. He moved his head so that one lock of hair fell down his forehead.

"Looking for my father's lost sheep," she said. Then she smiled. She had dimples.

There was, at the time, one sheep on the downs, who was not anything like lost. The old bellwether was deaf and mostly blind and he had forgotten that his flock no longer came out this way, so he doggedly made the same trip every morning, despite the fact that there were no other sheep with him.

"Is that him?" asked the slim-hipped man, looking doubtfully at the bellwether.

"No," said Rose. "He's not lost. He knows exactly where he is."

"So it's another sheep you're looking for, then?"

"Oh, aye," breathed Rose. "A ram sheep, if you know what I mean..."

He did indeed know exactly what she meant. He took her hand and said "Come them, my lady, let's go look for one."

The bellwether, fortunately deaf, continued to graze despite the sounds coming from elsewhere on the hillside.

"SHE WAS SUPPOSED to pine," said the slim-hipped faerie glumly. "They always pine. You make passionate love to them and then you vanish and they pine away and die of love."

"Ha!" The faerie next to him poked the fire with a stick. "Not our Rose. Did she give you the line about the lost sheep, too?"

"That sheep gets lost a lot," muttered a third one. He had darkly tanned skin and shocking green eyes. "I've my doubts that it ever really existed."

"We looked for it for three weeks," said the slim-hipped faerie. "I had to stop looking. I couldn't keep up."

The other fae raised their beers in silent tribute to the stamina of the absent Miss McGregor.

"ARE YOU SURE that's not your lost sheep?" asked the green-eyed fae, stretched out on his belly in the grass. He had tufts of hair on the tips of his ears, like a cat's. Rose liked to stroke the long sweep of them, then work her way down his back.

"No, that's Saul. He's the bellwether."

"He's got no flock." The green-eyed fae was descended of satyr stock, which gave him certain dramatic endowments but also a vague concern for the well-being of herd animals. Rose appreciated both these attributes enormously.

"Nah, they're all long dead. He sees their ghosts." Rose had not been able to lie on her belly since she was fourteen, owing to her own dramatic endowments, so she was propped up on her elbow beside him. "He's a good old fellow. Leads his ghost flock up the hill every day, leads them back down again."

"Have y'tried telling him they're dead?"

Rose stopped stroking his back. "And what's Saul ever done to me, that I should break his heart?"

This was too good an opening for the green-eyed fae to pass up. He'd been planning another few days of passion, but there was such a thing as style.

Also, he wasn't sure if he could keep up much longer.

"Speaking of broken hearts, my lass..." He rolled over. "'Tis grieved I am to leave you, but my time in this country has grown short."

"Oh, has it?" Rose picked up two blades of grass and began attempting to make them squeak between her fingers.

"I must be away, to my own land."

"All right."

"Err... never more to grace these hills..."

Squeak... squeak...

"And you'll not see me ever again."

She patted his arm. "It's all right, duck. You'll find someone else. In fact, I—Saul! Don't eat that!"

* * *

"AND SINCE HE was deaf, yelling at him didn't help. She had to go take it away from him. I believe she cared for that sheep more than me," he told the others at the fire morosely.

"Certainly stayed with him longer," said the slim-hipped man, sighing.

One of the fae, who hadn't spoken, was quietly plaiting the stems of foxglove together. Foxglove is not a flower that plaits, so he had to use a fair bit of magic to do it. The slender pink bells trembled as his fingers moved over the stems, exactly the way that Rose McGregor had trembled in his arms.

"Yer a lot of wilting lilies," growled the bull selkie.

"And you're here drinking with us," snapped the green-eyed man, "so what does that make you, eh?"

The selkie grumbled and hitched his sealskin up higher on his back.

Selkies, like seals, come in many varieties. There are the elegant, dark-eyed young men who make maidens sigh, the doe-eyed women that enchant fishermen with their songs... and then there's the bulls.

Bull seals and bull selkies have no necks and no manners and they rut like boars. Human women are advised to avoid them.

Rose MacGregor was never one to follow advice. She picked her way down the beach, the small stones turning under her feet, whistling to herself.

"Yer on my beach," said the bull, having hidden his sealskin behind a rock. He put his fists on his hips.

Rose looked him up and down. Evidentally she liked what she saw, because she ran her tongue over her lips.

"Have you, by chance, seen my lost sheep?" she said.

"AND AFTERWARD, I told her I was going back tae the sea," he said. "And not tae try to find my sealskin. And d'ye know what she said tae me?"

The other men all knew, having heard this story multiple times, but let him tell it out of courtesy.

"She said 'I'd only want yer skin if I planned tae keep ye!'" He hunched his shoulders. "Can't even go back tae that beach now. All the rocks remind me of her."

"How does a *rock* remind you of her?" asked the green-eyed fae.

"They're basalt."

The other men at the campfire stared at him.

"Ye know. Flows. Big and rounded-like..." He made hand gestures.

"Ohhhh..."

"Right."

"Got it."

The horse fae snorted. The selkie glared at him. Selkies and pookas mix like freshwater and salt.

"Don't give me that, horse-face. Ye didn't fare any better."

The pooka looked like he might argue for a moment, then his shoulders slumped. "No," he admitted. "Did my whole friendly horse trick. Come climb up on my back for a ride, lass. And she smiled at me with all those dimples and said that wasn't the sort of ride she was after." He sighed. "Stayed in human shape for nearly a week for her."

The faerie plaiting foxgloves picked up another stem and began to weave them into the mass of flowers in his hands

"And then I turned back into a horse, planning to drag her down into the lake and drown her—"

A low, angry sound from the others.

"Excuse me! I am a pooka! We drown people! None of this waiting around for them to die of a broken heart! We are efficient!"

"Yer a bunch of cads," said the selkie. "At least we don't go killin' the ladies after."

"Assuming you don't smother 'em during, with all the blubber," growled the pooka.

"The lassies like a little more meat to keep 'em warm at night, ye horse-faced gob."

"Settle down, the both of you," said the slim-hipped fae, and poured beer all around.

"Anyway," muttered the pooka, "I turned into a horse. And she petted my nose."

He sighed and gazed into his beer.

The others waited. After a minute, the selkie said "That's it?"

"What? It was very nice. Not everybody knows how to pet a nose correctly. And then she slapped my flank and told me to run along like a good pony."

"She did that to me, too," said the slim-hipped faerie morosely.

"...Err... she called you a good pony?"

"No!" A greenish flush rose to the tips of his ears. "But she slapped my ass and said she'd look me up the next time she was around."

The fire crackled. The fae with the foxglove held a great sheaf of flowers in his hands, spilling over the sides of his fingers.

"Are we pining?" asked the green-eyed fae suddenly. "Is this what it's like when they pine away after us?"

"We are *not* pining!"

"Certainly not!"

"No one's dying of broken hearts here."

"Nae."

"Good."

The pooka turned back into a human long enough to get a refill of beer.

"So... same time next autumn, then?"

"I'll be here."

"Aye."

"Grandma? Grandma, there's something on the back step."

Rose MacGregor was in her late sixties, but she moved like a much younger woman. She kept an iron horsenail in her pocket, partly in memory of her late husband, partly because cold iron keeps the faeries polite.

Her youngest granddaughter was about five years old. She was built a bit like a selkie herself, with no discernible neck, and she had a bull selkie's stubbornness to go with it.

Her mother hoped she'd grow out of it. Rose told her not to worry.

"It's all attitude, duck. All of it. She'll do fine in the world."

"It's flowers, Grandma," said her granddaughter doubtfully.

"Ah... That time of year already, is it?" Rose pulled the back door open, suddenly smiling.

There was a snap of frost in the air and leaves from the big oak tree had drifted down across the step. Rose could scarcely see them, though, under the enormous bouquet of foxgloves, all pink bells and spotted throats, that someone had left there for her.

"Why'd somebody leave you flowers, Grandma?"

"Oh, it's a long story," said Rose MacGregor. "Your grandma had quite an adventurous youth. I'll tell you all about it when you're older." She paused, looking down at the stubborn little face. "Much... much *much* older..."

WHEN WE WERE STARLESS
Simone Heller

Simone Heller (www.missnavigator.com) lives on an island in the river Danube in a town near Munich, Germany. In her job as a literary translator, she molds her voice to represent the words of other writers, often from the science fiction and fantasy field. Her own fiction has been published by *Clarkesworld*, and she hopes to witness the translation process from the other side of the desk one day. She graduated in cultural studies and linguistics, but is equally passionate about zoology and cartography. Actually, she's interested in *everything* (save soccer), which, in the age of informational abundance, is also a curse.

WHEN WE SET out to weave a new world from the old, broken one, we knew we pledged the lives of our clutches and our clutches' clutches to wandering the wastes. Season after season, our windreaders find us a path through the poison currents, and our herds scuttle over molten glass seas and pockmarked plains into the haunted places where the harvest is plentiful. We move swiftly, outpacing vapors and packs of wild dogs alike, leaving only the prints of our tails in acrid sands.

This wasn't entirely true; we left other things, too, dear and precious. But this was how it was told by the elders when the veiled moon was high and we were cuddled up with our cozy-stones.

On the moonless nights, though, they spoke of ghosts: beckoning wraithlights and treacherous silent ones, and all the other types we had classified; and the multitudes that still waited for our soothing hands out among the ruins. They spoke of ghosts like they were the ones to handle them, when it was always me.

So when Warden Renke strode up to my resting place on the outskirts of the half-shaped camp, the stark white paint of her dread-screen slapped on in haste, I knew what she needed.

"Someone found another ghost, yes?" My longing glance went to the grub'n'root stew some kind soul had left next to the pack serving as my pillow, still lukewarm from a hot stone placed at the bottom of the bowl. I reached for the harness with my tools instead.

"It's in the dome structure to the East. Asper ventured there in search of the light metals his weaver prefers. He meant no harm; he knows we need every spare part he can churn out. Said he saw strange lights."

"Alright." It could be nothing, or just another minor ghost which I would have laid to rest before the deep-night chill encroached. I stood and fingered my engraved pliers, waiting for Renke to disappear like they all did when it came to my work. But the Warden fixed me, her pupils mere slits.

"Eat your fill first, Blessed. We need you to stay strong. Truss won't be able to step in for you."

And he hadn't stepped in for years now, since the day he became a respected member of the tribe, but I didn't say that.

"How is he?" I asked instead.

Renke looked back to where the first weaverspun tentpoles came together, as if she could see the pallet there, the thin mat of woven vines stained with blood. "He's barely conscious. You should visit him as soon as you've cleansed yourself."

It could well be my last chance. One shift in the weather, and we'd be running again, leaving our excess baggage behind. Truss never passed up an opportunity to teach a lesson, so it would probably be me he'd ask for the Song of Passing, and I was afraid it would be more than I could take. People's hearts, as hardened and as barred as they were, were a different matter from the hearts of ghosts. I took one big gulp of stew and swallowed. "I'll take care of this ghost, Warden. This spot will serve as a fine resting place and see us recovered to full strength."

Renke cast a doubtful glance down at her freshly spun leg brace, for she, too, hadn't walked away unscathed. "Report to me when it's done. I'll put harvesting on hold, so hurry. No way to know how long the winds will grant us."

THE RUN-IN WITH the rustbreed had not been my fault. I was a good enough scout—I scoured inaccessible ruins for scarce materials, and I never ran the tribe into the lairs of the befouled crablion or let anyone's mind become ghost-shifted. But when the heat-baked ground of a salt flat we were crossing was suddenly riddled with burrower holes, a full legion of the writhing, rearing centipedal creatures already upon us, all I could do was to change the gentle hum of the Lope Concord to the jarring trill of the Rush and find us a path out of this trap. The air had been filled with the dry stick sounds of the rustbreed's milling legs and the sharp smell that went for communication among them. But for all their legs, we were the better runners, and we made it. Barely. The hindquarters of our sole gearbeast were a fused mass of metal and dried fluids from a rustbreed feeder, and I didn't want to think about Truss' side, which had been similarly exposed. Others, like Renke, had been burned badly, too, but he had been the only one to suffer a bite and get the corrosive substance under his scales.

The ruined place I had led us into was vast and violent, some of its canyons carved by storms and some designed by its unholy builders long ago. We had been following these shadowed paths for hours, paths I would have preferred to scout before bringing in the tribe. As it was, I had to lay ghosts to rest on the run, which was a contradiction in and of itself.

I skirted the camp, listening to the whirring sounds of dozens of weavers busily spinning pots and ropes and all the things we would need to shelter and recover. Bits of Asper's cleansing chant drifted over the jagged scenery. He would be fine. Surely he had run at first sight, not even checking if it was a real ghost, or just a reflection on an unexpectedly untarnished surface. It took more than that to risk ghost-shifting. But the tribe was skittish. He would sing half of the night.

Out of the rubble and partially collapsed buildings around the camp, two ruined structures protruded into the upper airs like teeth, broken and half-melted. Loose material flung up by the poison winds had merged with the original walls like flowstone.

No such thing marred the surface of the dome. Its sides were certainly blackened like everything else, and even blacker holes yawned where some of its hexagonal segments were missing, but the telltale pockmarks to determine downwind shelter were nowhere to be seen. It loomed over the rubble as if to claim some things were unbreakable, no matter what. We would prove it wrong, if I had my way and we stayed. Because that was what we did; we cleansed the ruins by harvesting them, by feeding their very substance to our weavers and rendering it pure and useful to be sold to the settler townships up in the mountains.

Only this time we would need every scrap for ourselves to survive.

The entrance to the dome structure was a narrow, curved tube. When I reached a barrier of two thin, clear panes of glass, they swished apart almost soundlessly, releasing a draft of cool air from within. Asper must have been desperate if he had gone beyond that. I took a moment to camouflage and darted through, curling my tail in case of nasty surprises; this would have been a stupid way to lose it. At some point in the past, granules of debris had blown in, but the layer was thin and petered out after a few paces. When the portal closed smoothly behind me, one side grated a little bit on a piece of gravel that must have been displaced by my feet.

My gaze was drawn upwards. The air of the dome was still, the evening light eerily peaceful as it filtered through the once transparent segments. Gone was the cleansing singsong, gone were the high winds keening in cavity-riddled structures. It wasn't that there was no indication of violence in this place: the tail end of a colossal metal tube still hanging from steel cords fastened around its tapered nose had fallen and destroyed all manners of tables and glass cases on the floor. But it was as if it had happened centuries ago, and peace had been found in its arrangement.

Anyone with a healthy fear of ghosts would have gone looking for the one whose invisible hand had moved the glass panes. I knew better. I was not after an inferior ghost tied to this entrance—my prey would be haunting the vast space, where the light was murky and the shadows were glistening. I went straight in to look for the veins that spoke of ghost activity, for the hiding places of ghost organs, stored away in boxes for protection.

Uncomfortably chilly layers of air enshrouded glittering heaps of shards. Once, I might have felt out of place, an unwelcome disturbance. But I had left my fear of ghosts behind like an old skin a long time ago, and what I had found instead was the unforeseen, and sometimes pure beauty.

The tribe never knew. To them, beauty meant nothing. I could have shown them the brightest colors and patterns on my skin, and all they ever wanted were the dulled hues of sand and ashes, all the better to pick clean ruins like this one.

In the end I found absolutely no sign of a ghost inhabiting this space. I resigned myself to take care of the entrance and let go of my camouflage.

When I turned around there was something where there had been no-one. Like a person, a solitary figure leaned on one of the undamaged glass cases. The light pooled strangely around it, and when I flicked my tongue, the smell, the heat and the heartbeat were all my own and told me no other living being was in here with me.

"Hello, little explorer," it said with a clear, slightly hollow voice.

The ways ghosts reacted to people were mostly limited to precise, fatal attacks, if they were of the aggressive kind, or simple things like manipulating doors or following every move with a single red eye in the shell they animated, observant even in afterlife.

This one drifted over to me, mimicking a walk on two legs as best it could, lacking a tail. Its whole body was obscured by a bulky, silvery layer of clothing, its head round like a bowl. It seemed insubstantial, a ghost of subtle dangers. My breath quickened, but I stood my ground. When there was but a pace between us, I lifted my hand to rap my knuckles against the semi-translucent head-bowl with just a hint of bright eyes behind. The ghost quivered slightly as my fingers passed right through it, and on my skin I felt an almost imperceptible sensation of heat.

"Now, now, you're a cheeky one, aren't you?" It turned with me as I began to walk around it, cautiously, looking for the veins tethering its body to its heart. "I understand you're curious, and I encourage you heartily to experiment. But your experience will be better if you refrain from touching me."

The way it reacted to me, seemed to talk directly to me, was disconcerting. I felt a lump grow in my throat. Even now there were no veins. They could still be under the floor, but I somehow doubted it. I had seen a few Untethered before, even sought them out. They didn't need to animate objects, but moved through thin air with a fluid grace. I knew they could be laid to rest with a bit of work; I just chose not to whenever possible. The world always felt lessened by their passing.

"I don't see a tag on you, little explorer." The ghost's voice came from slightly above. So maybe it had stored its lungs somewhere. Finding them would at least be a start. "Would you mind telling me your name to avoid confusion?"

I looked up at the strange specter in surprise. No amount of singing would redeem me in the eyes of my tribe if I volunteered my name to a ghost. Granted, I did talk to ghosts. It was a one-sided conversation, a game of pretending at its best. This ghost wouldn't even register my name, a name nobody had bothered to use since I became Blessed. What harm could it do, to whisper and hear it swallowed up by the still air of the dome?

I flicked my tongue. "Mink. My name is Mink."

The round head bobbed enthusiastically. "Welcome, Mink! Now, would you like to see the stars?"

A flutter of anxiety rose in my stomach. This was more than a mere reaction; this was interaction. For a short moment, I felt this was not a ghost, but something else altogether, something alive and very old and dangerous. I fought my unease with a snort. "Stars? You're trying to trick me with fancy tales the elders tell to hatchlings, yes?"

"That's what most come for, but we can certainly look at something else. The rocket, maybe? Or one of the landers?" It drifted off a little bit, hands clasped behind its back. With a swooshing noise, the soft glow of wraithlights grew throughout the dome, in at least five different places. There were sounds as well, sounds I recognized: ghosts, many upon many of them, animating contraptions, whining in high voices. A legion of ghosts, seemingly springing into action in unison.

I shielded my eyes and staggered back, caught myself on one of the tables, shaken. Such a conglomerate of ghosts would take days to be laid to rest. Our wounded might not have days; they depended on the herds' output before the windreader called us off.

The untethered ghost had moved to hover next to me. "You seem upset, little explorer Mink. Is there something wrong? Something I can do for you?"

I held my face still buried in my hands and looked at the ghost through my fingers. Was it trying to help me? All I had ever been taught told me to run now, but I had never been the student Truss or the other elders had envisioned. "That's impossible ..."

"Let's try some music to lift your spirits." The ghost drifted back and forth expectantly. When nothing happened and I began to wonder if I should have said or done something, it heaved a great sigh. "Uh... I'm very sorry, little explorer Mink... some things seem to be amiss here. I thought I had just the right music for you. But now I can't play any at all, and I just don't seem to be able to fix this defect. Ah. I shouldn't be all sad when I need to cheer you up, right? Don't you worry. I'll find a workaround."

"You miss your music?" I had always suspected some ghosts liked music, and tried to use this to my advantage. But this ghost had offered me consolation; it seemed genuinely upset it couldn't act on it. I didn't seek an advantage when I suggested: "I could sing for you."

Truss would have called me ghost-shifted or straight out mad at this point. I had nothing yet, not even a classification, just a growing sense of unease and a lot of work cut out for me. But there were many ways to a ghost's heart, and a non-aggressive, calming approach might work just as well as exhausting oneself by tearing out every wall panel for clues. Or maybe I was just trying to rationalize my own desperate need for a song.

It took some time to find my voice, because, yes, I had sung to ghosts before, but never for a whole legion of them. Soon enough I found the center of the dome was an excellent place to stand and sing.

I did not sing a ghost song, but one of ours. The melody of the Paean of Manifest Horizons rose strongly in the empty air, and it was more uplifting than the somber tones of the Song of Passing I usually sang in the forsaken places of the world, while making them a little bit more forsaken. It wasn't until after the first verse I noticed the second voice accompanying mine in perfect harmony. At first I was puzzled and amused to sing alongside those hidden lungs of the ghost. Then I felt my spirit lifted in a way I had not expected: not to chant alone amongst the rubble of a past age, but to have a voice other than mine echoing, countering, running ahead in joy. When I reshaped the tune into a jubilating variation and the ghost followed suit without pause, though, the dread feeling crept upon me again, made my voice veer off into a warning warble. I faltered, and the ghost sang the ending notes on its own.

Ghosts were the remnants of the long-dead past, and one thing they—or at least all the ones I had encountered—could not do, was evolve, learn, grasp something new. This one had not only learned a song in a few heartbeats, but even how to mold it in the unique way of my tribe. And I finally had my classification and my name, and the absolute certainty that I would not be the one to lay this ghost to rest, or any of its manifestations, for that was what I faced: one vast ghost of many forms, one fabled entity that ruled this whole place. An annihilator of tribes. A Clusterhaunt.

"What an amazing talent," it said, lifting its hand to its chest, where of course no heart resided. "Thank you!"

I tried to swallow against my dried-up throat, but only produced a strangled squawk. When I fled the dome, the ghost called after me: "Little explorer Mink, do you really have to leave already? You haven't seen the stars yet!"

Terrified as I was, I would have crashed into the grating panes of glass. But the ghost moved this extension of itself out of my way, and I stumbled out before it could reconsider.

THIS WAS WHAT was going to happen: the camp would be left to the winds, half-shaped pots and tents melting into the ruined landscape. The marrow of our wounded would feed whatever happened to stumble upon this site, our crippled gearbeast would hold its lone wake. I would paint the warning sigil of our tribe on a nearby wall in green permastain, so that no scout in their right mind would ever set foot in the dome again. And we would flee this place, maybe leave a trail of our injured as we ran, and we would never look back, never wonder what we had lost, not only in lives, but also in not taking the rare materials from the dome, in not observing the Clusterhaunt and learn about its ways.

Or at least try to co-exist. I had fled on impulse, fueled by the horrors our lore spoke of. It didn't seem so bad now that I had time to think and didn't see a spectral host coming after me from the dome. But how could I suggest this to a tribe who, by that very same lore, left its weakest members behind to die? I would be declared suicidal, a menace, unheard.

For we were survivors, mere survivors; we never managed to be more than that, and some didn't even manage that much. We told ourselves that we made a difference, that we shaped a world, but one look at this ruined vastness told the truth: we didn't change a thing, and all our sacrifices were just to survive another day. It was enough, mostly, as long as we pretended it didn't tear our hearts out.

I was perched on the remains of a toppled roof structure and looked at the bug-catcher lights dotting the camp's perimeter in the dark. They would glow long after we were gone.

When I finally trotted over to the ring of lights, I vocalized a lesser warning sequence. "Scout incoming," I saluted the guard I knew would wait in the shadows beyond. "I need to see Truss. Get someone to apply the dread-screen on him. I'm unclean."

She hissed gruff acknowledgement, and by the time I entered the camp proper every weaver had been moved out of my way, as well as sleeping mats and cooking utensils for good measure. A young herder still gesturing her weaver backwards lifted the eight-legged metal creature up into her arms and staggered away under its weight, even if it was far out of range of whatever evil emanations of mine she might fear. I saw Asper, too, hovering on the fringe of the camp and obviously eager for news, his weaver easy to spot because he was the only one to dread-screen its carapace for extra security. At Truss' resting place, one of the hunters simply smeared the remaining paint in her hands onto her face and throat before I came too close.

On Truss, the swirling white patterns had been applied with more care. He looked bad underneath, skin sagging in stiff folds, eyes sunken. His side was bandaged, the color of the rust-like substance eating away at him already bleeding through.

"Teacher," I said, kneeling next to him.

He lifted one feeble hand, as if to keep me from propping him up. "Talk to the elders, little foster-hatch. Why come to me? They are the ones who decide our way."

They knew only one way, but I didn't say that. "You're one of them, old man. How are you? I was gone so long, and I was afraid you wouldn't ..."

"Warden told you that, didn't she?" He coughed, and I watched the stains on his bandage deepen. "To keep you on your toes. She knows you're prone to getting distracted."

At that, he winked weakly at me. We had always kept my bolder adventures between the two of us, as we had our differences. I wanted badly to take his hand, to feel if there was any strength left in him, but he had never been fond of touch. Or sympathy.

"I'm not dead yet." His voice was a low rasp. "Won't run for days, but if the winds are willing and you're keeping us safe, I'll eat the stuff that's trying to eat me... just you watch."

At that, I felt all color bleed out of my skin and fought hard to keep Truss from noticing. I had been selfish to come here, just so that I could say goodbye. "It might not happen," I offered softly. "It might not happen fast enough. And so many of us are wounded and exhausted. Even I would be hard-pressed to run now."

Part of me wanted to tell him about the Clusterhaunt. But he hadn't scouted for years, and in his day Truss had never been one to indulge in the presence of ghosts. I knew what he would have to say, and I didn't want to hear it.

He said it anyway. "Don't concern yourself with our weak and wounded, little foster-hatch. We're prepared to stay behind, knowing the tribe will survive. The elders are aware of that. They know how to handle it."

"But they don't *have* to handle it," I whispered.

Suddenly I felt Truss' hand on mine, cold and brittle. He started to say something, but in this moment, Renke strode up to us, the windreader and the other two elders in tow.

"What news do you bring, Blessed?" she asked. "Is your work done?"

I looked up at her, then back to Truss. There were days when I found joy in my job, when I felt I brought peace to the ghosts of old and betterment to the brand-new world. Today it felt like laying to rest everything I loved. "My work is never done."

Renke came closer than most dared when I was unclean, to stare down at me. "The herders are awaiting my command. Is it safe now, or do we move?"

There was no invitation to debate, no room for experiments. I only needed to utter the word; the decision was already made, had already been made since the day we set out to wander the wastes.

I fought to keep my unruly colors under control. None of the tribe could actually read them, but Truss had seen most of the spectrum while teaching me, and even with eyes half-closed he might be watching.

Renke's crest rose halfway in impatience. I could feel the eyes of the herders on me, all prepared to set out, their weavers protected in the crooks of their tails. They would never admit that survival was not always enough.

I squeezed Truss' hand one last time and finally got up to look the Warden in the eye. "Send them out," I said. "This place is safe."

THE NIGHT SKY was a black abyss sucking my gaze upwards, and with it went my bravado and determination. No veiled moon shed its light upon the ruins; the stars, its fabled lesser cousins, were nothing but a story to ease the weight of the dark.

I did not deserve to even think of a soothing story, because I had embarked on the darkest of tales.

Clusterhaunt. Few claimed to have seen one, the even fewer reliable witnesses weren't keen on telling what they had seen. Clusterhaunts were said to be the rarest and mightiest of ghosts, spiteful of the living, and oh-so-strong, the most powerful ghost-shifters, heart-concealers, mind-mimickers.

Tribe-vanishers.

But I had told my lie, and I needed it to turn into truth. So instead of getting back to my lonely resting place, I went to the dome once more. "Residual energies" would keep the herders from entering only for so long; then I would either have found this heart or failed them all.

First I jammed a stone I had brought under the glass panes of the entrance. I didn't want to get trapped inside, and disabling the ghost's extensions piece by piece was one way I figured I could counter its Clusterhaunt abilities. I took my lamp into the pitch-black dome and began to turn over every larger piece of rubble to find a hint of ghostly veins, organs, anything.

All too soon a familiar pale glow came up behind me.

"Little explorer Mink! What a pleasant surprise to have you back!"

I looked up at the bowl-shaped head bobbing above the silvery suit. Why would it choose this appearance when it ruled so many forms? Why not a more threatening one?

It hovered closer. "You were gone so fast last time, I thought you maybe didn't like it. But you've got them both—Curiosity and Spirit. Want to see them? They're right here, brought back to Earth after their duty was done."

Wraithlight flared to life halfway through the dome to illuminate the shapes of two battered gearbeasts. Their odd wheel-legs seemed sturdy enough, but after a closer look, I found them to be perplexingly impractical: their broad backs were plastered with strange contraptions, no room for stowage at all. They wouldn't carry even one of our wounded.

"You'll find the whole story of Curiosity and Spirit on your personal Memory Vault," the ghost went on. "Please don't forget it next time you leave. It helps you relive your whole experience in here at home."

I ignored the gearbeasts, but the ghost kept following me. "Have you lost something?" it wanted to know. "May I help you? Just ask away!" as if it was a game Clusterhaunts liked to play. I wasn't here to talk, though.

There were just not that many alternatives. No wall panels to peel off the glasslike sides of the dome, no secret compartments embedded in the smooth, hard floor. The rubble under the fallen tail of the metal tube the ghost had called a rocket was a big pile of shards, and even the bases of the undamaged tables and cases were solid. So maybe talking *was* how I'd get to the heart of this ghost.

I turned very slowly. "You'd answer all my questions? Really?"

"Sure. That's what I'm here for." The ghost hovered expectantly.

I swallowed. I was a scout, not a master of eloquence. This could go horribly wrong. "Where is your heart?"

Among all the reactions I had anticipated, I surely hadn't expected the ghost's pronounced shoulders to sink. "Ah," it said in a somewhat small voice. "Well, you already saw on your first visit that I am not like you. And a heart is among the things that separate us." Its light grew dim. "Alas, I guess one could say my heart is up among the stars? That's where I always wanted to be, so maybe that's a justified notion."

So the ghost really liked its tall tales, liked them so much it spun its heart-concealing fabrications around them in a way that made me feel all wistful. I could have asked about its veins and lungs next, or any other part of ghost anatomy a good scout knew to look out for. But the only thing I seemed to remember was how it had tried to comfort me earlier, and somehow that made everything much more complicated.

It had diligently shuffled after me, and I was looking at its blurry form through a thin sheet of clear material mounted on a table between us. "What are you called, then?" I asked finally.

The ghost lifted its hand and dropped it again. "Oh, I... nobody ever calls me anything. I'm just here for your service. And on a better day, this should display the orbits of the main celestial bodies. It's in maintenance mode. I apologize for your inconvenience."

"Nonsense." I felt angry all of a sudden, and not just because I wasn't making any progress here, apart from trying to befriend a ghost. "People also don't call me anything since the Blessing came upon me. But I'm more than the service I render."

"I'm afraid that I am not."

I crossed my arms and hissed in frustration. Even those old gearbeasts had been named, however strangely. I could do better. "I'd like to call you Orion, then, if I may."

It just hovered there, frozen.

"I mean, we're not close enough for me to know your gender," I added. "So it's just a suggestion, yes?"

"It's a brilliant suggestion!" The ghost beamed, radiating brightness. "Orion... that's very considerate!"

I thought so myself. It was a name from the same old tales that told of the stars.

"Thank you, little explorer Mink. I'm attaching my name to all Memory Vaults now."

And in the newly brilliant light of Orion I saw something, off to the side. Something that shouldn't have been here, and yet there it was.

Inside one of the glass cases, bathed in wraithlight and completely still, sat a weaver.

"DON'T TOUCH THE exhibit, please!"

I had taken the weaver out and set it on the floor, where it had very frustratingly not shown the slightest inclination to move. Clearly, it hadn't been able to bask in a long time.

"Little explorer. Your interest in this ATU shows how bright you are. But I counted 384 defects in here already, and you really shouldn't add ..."

I gestured at the weaver. "What did you call that?"

"People call them space spiders, but officially it's an Advance Terraforming Unit." Orion drifted to another thin glasslike sheet, this one larger, mounted on the floor. "Come along! See them in action."

The weaver sat motionless. I would fetch this prize for my tribe, a new heirloom to complement our herds. But I also wanted to know how it had ended up in a glass case. Reluctantly, I followed the ghost.

"Still no music." Orion contemplated the large glasslike screen. "I'm sorry."

"I am sorry for adding another defect," I said, and I meant it. As much as

Orion tried to make up for his failing contraptions with enthusiasm, I could still sense his distress. "Shall we sing again?"

I did not feel like it. I couldn't see any horizons manifesting themselves in my near future. I was still here to lay Orion to rest, the sooner the better. Had I stumbled upon him while advance-scouting, I would have turned my back and looked for another harvesting ground. But this was not an option with the tribe camping on the threshold, cultivating their superstitions.

"Maybe later, little explorer Mink. For now it will do, the display works just fine. Look."

At first, I saw nothing; nothing I hadn't seen before with minor ghosts. Ephemeral colors danced through the glass, almost too quick for the eye to follow. Then the whole screen, larger than myself, was filled with the image of a weaver. I sat on my haunches to get a better look. I understood now: Orion was showing me a vision.

"Moving mode; printing mode; charging mode," Orion said while the weaver flickered through a series of motions, completely translucent, so I could see its intricate inner workings. This was followed by an impossibly long line of weavers scuttling up a smooth ramp, then fire and smoke. "When the ATUs set out to terraform other worlds, they are equipped to deal with every hostile surrounding, to transform every unusual or even hazardous material into something useful," Orion said, and I slumped to the floor, curling my tail around my legs. "They are constructed semi-autonomous, with modes to work on individual projects, to collaborate, or to be operated by a higher-level controller."

I must admit I wasn't able to follow his tale, but then I had never worked with a weaver, so what did I know? The images drew me in. Weavers glinting like gems in front of a profound blackness. Weavers swarming at structures I had never imagined. Weavers working away at something that looked like the dome I found myself in, but under two bright bluish suns.

"These are other worlds?" I asked. I saw them, but I couldn't believe they were real. New worlds, worlds not poisoned by a violent, unholy past.

Orion's head bobbed enthusiastically. "Yes, little explorer. There are many upon many, scattered among the stars. Everything you see in here, including the visitor center itself, was built to get there. Maybe you will travel to one of them yourself one day?"

I stood fascinated, watching, and I felt fear clamp down on my heart even as it soared. This, I knew, was ghost-shifting: ghosts telling about great things, about possibilities, about progress. It was not true, it just didn't happen, and when it happened, it was bad. This kind of thinking had destroyed the world. We were careful now, and we didn't pursue any stupid ideas.

But it was beautiful, and that had always been my weakness. I was transfixed by the images as they flickered by, bathing me in the brightness of distant suns. My gaze drank up the swarms of weavers spinning things far greater than we had ever dreamed of. And I realized they were so much more than what we had been using them for. This would be invaluable knowledge, if the tribe could accept it. I wondered if they would even accept a ghost-touched weaver, and resolved to tell them I had found it far from the place of the haunting.

I turned to look at the creature with renewed awe. But my colors flared in alarm at what I saw.

The first light of the day filtered in through the ceiling, and I realized I had lost the track of time over the ghost's stories. Several figures were clustered together near the entrance, shuffling and whispering. Among the dozens of weavers at their feet, the one marked white with dread-screen clearly stood out in the front row. Asper and his fellow herders had come to harvest. They craned their necks, staring at me. Staring at Orion.

"Visitors!" The ghost began to drift closer. "Are these your friends? More little explorers? I'd love to welcome them."

"No, Orion!" I tried to prevent what could only end in disaster. "Stay back, will you?"

The herders had already scattered. With hectic gestures they maneuvered their weavers to hide behind them, while some broke and ran for the entrance, shrilling a warning.

"Wait!" Asper yelled. "The Blessed is in the ghost's thrall. We have to rescue her! Get Renke, hurry!"

"It's alright." I made two steps towards them to show I was free to go. "He's non-aggressive."

It was a futile effort. Most of them were crazed with fear, clogging the narrow entrance tube or fleeing along the walls of the dome. Asper, though, not only came for me, but managed to bully a fellow herder to march with him towards much more ghost activity any of them had ever seen.

"Asper, you have to watch this!" I backed off towards the glasslike screen. "We were all wrong about the weavers."

He grabbed my arm.

"Hey!" Orion drifted closer.

Without letting go, Asper jumped. I stumbled and was caught by his friend, who dragged me to my feet without any respect for shoulder joints and their natural resistance to jerking. I hissed.

"Hey!" Orion said, louder now. "I cannot tolerate violence in here. This is a place of peace and learning. Now, behave yourselves and release Mink!"

A collective gasp rippled through the herders as they heard the ghost speak my name, and I used their surprise to detach myself.

I could not let them take me. When they got me out of this dome, there would be no turning back and setting this right. Truss would die, unsung and alone, and I would not bring a new weaver and a new vision to the tribe. I tried to back away and babbled incoherent things that probably did nothing to convince them I was not ghost-shifted beyond repair. Orion's warnings became increasingly pressing.

When Renke's fighters joined the fray, they pushed the fleeing herders back in and moved towards me, crests rising as Orion drifted in between us as if to shield me.

Then, cutting through the very fabric of this old, untouched space, I saw the glint of a spear flying. Renke's verdigris green collar-feathers were tied to its shaft. It passed right through Orion, to bury itself in the screen containing the vision. A web of cracks appeared, and the light within died.

Orion's voice shrilled, distorted and much louder than before. "Stop damaging the equipment, and leave Mink alone, now! She's under my protection."

In the silence that followed, a rustling sound came up. It was a sound we knew, but it had a wrongness to it that made everyone freeze. Instead of the chaotic concert of individual clinks and whirrs, we heard our weavers march in unison. They came scuttling from all corners, flowing together like some big machine assembling itself. I knew this behavior, I had observed it moments before in the vision, but it was uncanny to see it executed, as if they had developed a shared, single-minded purpose all of a sudden. The others just stared, but some called out to their weavers, gesturing them back to no avail.

I froze when I saw what their purpose turned out to be. They all came up to me, smoothly parting around me and flowing into a new formation, climbing upon each other and surrounding me with a barrier of spiky metal.

And they were ready to defend. Asper and the other herders tried to intervene as the fighters tore into the formation, and they all got burned by spurts of heated material, seared by cutting-lights, sparks flying off their scales. They had absolutely no experience with the way the herds behaved now, like a single organism lashing out.

I tried to climb over my living protection, ready to leave with the tribe to end this. "Orion!" I cried. "Stop. Please!"

"Habitat security initiated, please cooperate."

"Orion?"

But he didn't respond to me anymore.

And I remembered the most important thing a scout has to recognize: the point when fighting would only lead to greater loss. I sounded the Rush. "Flee! This is a Clusterhaunt!"

Renke took up my tune, aggressively, urging on the herders who still called their weavers. I don't know what really made them break and run in the end. It could have been the herder who recognized the carapace of her weaver and tried to yank it out of the formation, only to get cut so badly we had to carry her. Limping and crying, we fled, and Asper's look was so hurt and betrayed I wanted to camouflage out of his sight. When I reached the entrance tube as part of the last group supporting and dragging each other, I thought I heard a faint whisper from the dome. "Safety can only be guaranteed in the habitat. Staying is recommended."

THERE WAS A difference I hadn't known, between separating myself from the tribe and being separated from the tribe. Oh, I was still with them, but I was kept off to the side, under guard. My status was unclear. Outcast, probably; a prisoner, surely; still useful, maybe.

Renke had screamed into my face, asking who would spin her a new spear, now that there was not a single weaver left. Asper had not spoken at all, but he surely cursed the day the tribe had acquired the clutch of supposedly blessed eggs that had hatched me. Others had said it aloud: "She who runs on her own shall no longer sing with us." And Truss had been loudest of all. "Is this how I taught you to serve your foster-tribe? You doom us all with your shrewd ideas. You shame me. You deny me my contribution to our survival, just because you're too sappy to accept what has to be done."

He might still get his chance to die all alone now.

My body's warmth seeped into the night-cooled ground. I was a miserable, pale heap, bound to a cracked column to protect everyone, including myself, from the mad bouts of my ghost-shifted mind. And as I stared up into the murky morning sky, still clear of the minor color shifts and scattered light that preceded a new wind, I knew they were right. I had been ghost-shifted. I had been blinded. The stars were not real. There was nothing but blackness up there.

I had been wrong all the time, dreaming of greatness and of knowing everything. I had chased visions and embraced change like it was just a pretty color I could wear, while secretly smiling at the superstition the herders held against me, never letting me approach a weaver. Now the weavers were taken, because I had lied. Because I had failed to see that they were right.

Not that anybody took the time to lay the blame at my feet—they would be crest-over-tails planning their next steps. I could hear them arguing. But it was just a waste of energy. Even if we stood a chance, we would never fight the one thing that let us thrive: our herds, our cleansers, our silvery lifeblood in this wrecked land.

Of course, without weavers, we would soon all be ghosts. And it would be a long drag down. We would wander the plains, deprived of our purpose, deprived of our calling and our sustenance. We hadn't needed the weavers to change the world, really, but as a reason to tread on, to lay claim to hostile territory, to sustain our foolish, desolate, stubborn way of living. We had never seen what they really were, until now that they were gone, and I was the only one ...

No.

I had to give up this delusion. I had never been the only one. I knew nothing.

To the disgruntled huffing of my guard, I started a cleansing song. It was too late for that, but I had to do something to steer my mind from the tantalizing vision, from the dread and the despair.

When I heard the soft thud of footpads on the ground, I thought somebody might try to gag me. But next came a strangled sound from my guard while a weaverspun chain dug into her trachea; that made me jerk out of my song.

Under a cover of black fabric I recognized the loam-spotted greens of Asper's scales. My first thought was that he had come to personally punish me, and when he stepped closer, I expected him to tell me he wanted me gone, that he couldn't bear to feed me one more share of spicy mothfry after all I had done.

"They're gone, because of you. Poor Peshk needs a brace, because of you, and I can't build one, because of you." He stared down at me for a moment, his tail lashing. I cringed, which made him snarl even more. "What is it with you, crazy scout?" He took off his heat cloak and dropped it near the shadowed corner I was curled up in. "You're all sickly white."

I hooked the cloak with one claw and drew it to me cautiously. "It's... it's my mood, yes?"

"Then snap out of it! You'll need your skill after you've warmed up." He swallowed, as if the next thing he was going to say had a foul taste to it. "They are debating. But it all ends up the same—we're going to leave. Hoping to reach the settler townships and seek refuge there. They're packing already. We're abandoning our weavers." He took out a small trimming knife. "Can't let that happen. Can't just leave my Tineater serving this Clusterhaunt. So I figured you'd be the one to come up with another idea. I saw you talk to that ghost. Like it made sense. Maybe you're shifted, and surely you're as unclean as a cesspool full of ground poison, but you've got a knack for communicating with this thing." With one swift slash, he cut through my rope.

I didn't move, just sat numbly, completely baffled. And I wondered if everybody had this one breaking point that made them fall from grace. "This might not be in the tribe's best interest," I said softly. "What if I don't come back and you'll have to run without a scout?"

"Wrong time for regrets," Asper snarled, and he sounded strangely like Truss to me, when he had taught a lesson. Then he tossed me my tools and turned around to sit next to the guard and check on her. "Go make some sweet talk to this ghost of yours, or rip its heart out. I don't care. Just get Tineater back to me. Bring the weavers, or don't come back at all."

The moment I moved out of reach, he took up the cleansing song I had abandoned.

*   *   *

THERE WERE MANY reasonable things I could have wished for as I passed through the yawning portal into the dome again: that I knew a secret tune to make the weavers follow me out just like that; that I had Truss at my side, to hold me back with a sharp hiss from making yet another stupid mistake; that I could run, run the plains with my tribe and our herds whole and sound, and leave this place alone.

I might face the true power of the Clusterhaunt now, not the gentle inducements of the being I had dubbed Orion.

A name it hadn't responded to any longer after it had turned on us. I was very much afraid that any bond Asper relied upon might have existed in my imagination only.

Foolish as I was, the thing I really wished for was that it hadn't forgotten *my* name.

But Orion was nowhere to be seen. I could tell, because in plain daylight, the murky darkness of the dome wasn't absolute. High up, where some of its ceiling panels were missing, shafts of light sliced down all the way to the ground in cascades of dancing dust motes. And there was a flurry of ghost activity. Faintly blinking lights, ghostly chatter emanating from various objects, all clocked to the clinking and whirring of the weavers. It was every sane person's nightmare, but I was beyond fear.

Or so I thought, because when Orion did descend upon me out of thin air, I blanched, flinched, and pinched my tail under a metal pedestal I knocked over while fighting for balance. Before I could lift it, two weavers scuttled over and hoisted it back up. I very slowly backed away.

"Little explorer Mink, adding some defects again, aren't you? But don't you worry. Mistakes happen, and I've got so much help now." Orion drifted closer and lowered his voice. "We're not officially reopened yet. You are a regular visitor, though. And I'm so glad to see you're back, and unharmed, too, so I'm willing to make an exception. A special tour just for you, what do you say?"

Part of me wanted just that, to lose my unhinged, ghost-shifted self in visions. I swallowed. "Actually, I'm not here to visit you. I'm here for the weavers." I indicated three of the creatures, spinning upwards from the floor, thread after thread, grabbing shards with their long legs to absorb and fuel their weaving while building something that looked like it would go on top of the pedestal. "They don't belong in here. They are the herds of my tribe, you see, and we need them back."

"Weavers? You have a knack for names, little explorer Mink. But you must understand the ATUs are no playthings, and they are doing what they are made for. They are not mine to give back. But they do good work, and they are well cared for. Just imagine how many visitors will take delight in this place after all those pesky defects are behind us."

I took a deep breath. I very much detested breaking things. And it had been nice, nice to get to know someone who wasn't aware of the brokenness of the world, who didn't live under the constant pressure of survival. It had been nice, but it was the only leverage I had. "There is something you should know." I worked my jaw for a moment, like something old and awful was lodged between my teeth. "They are not coming. Nobody is coming. There are no visitors anymore."

"Little explorer!" Orion's gloved hand went up to his bowl-shaped head. "What are you saying? That's nonsense. Right?"

I came close to him, and I wished I could have reached up and taken the sides of the bowl in my hands, to look into those elusive eyes. And to have something to cling to, because it hurt, what I had to do. "It's true. Look at all those defects. And believe me, you got off lightly in here. The defects outside are numberless."

And I sung him the oldest parts of the Tribesong, the way the elders had sung it to me as a hatchling, lest I forgot how the world became broken and the reign of demons had ended when they choked on their own corrupted breath, after their insatiable thirst for knowledge had undone them.

When I sang no more, Orion was silent for a very long time. He didn't even hover or flicker. I tried to stay equally unmoved. The tribe, the herds, the running, hearts thumping up our chest. That was what mattered. Not a ghost and his grieving.

"I was built to teach," he stated finally, his voice unquavering and strong, and I thought that maybe his hidden lungs weren't built to produce the sobs buried underneath. "I was built to inspire new achievements. If it's all gone, and I'm all alone... why am I still here?"

I had no answer for him. Ghosts despised the living, that was why, and I knew that he did not.

Orion looked up again, a hint of eyes gleaming under the bowl. "But you. You will come? You, and your... tribe. You returned, after all. You want to learn."

I laughed. It sounded like choking. Learning was what had gotten me into this wretched situation in the first place. "No, Orion. We won't. I'm sorry. My tribe is fear-stricken by your presence. You have proven yourself a true Clusterhaunt by taking our weavers. You are the doom of my people."

"But everything will be fine in here soon," he insisted. "Zero defects. And you'll like the stars. I promise—"

"Orion. There are no stars." I had the distinct feeling that I was about to tear his heart out with words alone, and I had to speak around the lump in my throat. "The veiled moon is a silvery blotch gliding through the upper fumes. And the stars, they are gone so long they are not even in the Tribesong; a whisper of clear lights, shining through the dark fabric of the night to give us comfort. But we can't afford to believe in comfort. There is only blackness."

"Is that so?" Orion moved again, and this was the first time he tried to touch me. His fingers passed through my cheek, leaving faint traces of heat. "You should believe in comfort. It makes you reach out again after you fall. How else would you advance? When we set out to reach the stars, there were many who would have held us back. It's a risk, they said. A waste. But we sent our eyes up into the skies, and we saw worlds up there. We have always had to cross the blackness, Mink, and it has always been vast and intimidating. We have always fallen. But this place is a monument to our resilience, and it has seen visitors from afar, who brought back the evidence of those worlds. As its guardian, I was never intended to go myself, but I saw the blackness could be crossed. And you should have trust in that, too, Mink."

My mind went back to those pristine, luminous worlds of the vision, and there was comfort in the thought of them out there. I could not condemn this comfort, even if it made my heart want to reach out and find a way to get there. Even if I needed to embrace ghost-shifting to get only one step closer. And I did. "Show me."

He clasped his hands behind his back and nodded gravely. After a while, a weaver came scuttling out of the gloom to stand close to me and pinch me in the upper calf. In one of its legs, it held something, pressing it urgently into my hand as soon as I crouched. I looked at the smooth oval in my palm, then back at Orion.

"Your Memory Vault. I told you not to forget it next time you leave."

"I'm not leaving. I want you to show me your vision."

Orion shook his head. "No. Not only you. Bring your tribe. Let me show them. Only this one time. I am not your enemy. But this is the price I demand for giving back the weavers."

Never would the elders bring what was left of our tribe into the lair of the Clusterhaunt again. Never would they trust my word, ghost-shifted as I was. And yet. I wanted them to see. I wanted to be with them again, and that would never happen when my dreams lived among the stars, while theirs still had to cross the blackness. "I'll try, but my voice in the Tribesong is small."

"Nonsense" he said. "I heard you sing. There's nothing wrong with your voice. Just use it. Educate them."

He was right. They needed to know, and I had never made the effort to tell them anything. It had been easier for me, and easier for them, to carry on as we had always done. But there were other worlds, worlds not lost to corruption and poison. This was a vision as true as any prediction of our windreader. This was hope. It would be hard work, but I had to make them understand. Even if it meant breaking what was left of trust and love. Even if the only thing to speak in my favor was the prospect of a happy reunion with our herds.

Then Orion explained to me in detail how I would get the weavers back after the performance. If I hadn't believed him before, I would have done so now, because it was a sound plan. It was, in fact, a plan I had executed many times before. And as soon as I grasped what he wanted me to do, I threw up my hands and said: "No. I won't do that, Orion."

"But you must. As I said, the weavers are not mine to give back. When I initiated habitat security, they were integrated in the defence matrix. I can command them to repair while there is no threat, but I can't undo their integration. Security is automated."

I didn't understand, and I didn't care. I shook my head.

Orion waited very patiently by my side while I came up with other plans. Waited very patiently while I cried. And waited very patiently while I added one or three defects by kicking things.

But the world was less patient. It barged in on me when Asper crashed through the entrance, the fear in his voice overshadowed by the greater horror that must have driven him to brave the Clusterhaunt's lair yet again.

"Blessed!" he cried. "You have to lead us in the Rush, now! The camp was breached by rustbreed vanguard. They have followed us."

WE WERE NOMADS, and we didn't get to keep things. Not even dreams.

So I tried to shake it all off while I followed Asper into a nightmare. People were securing exhausted young ones to their chests or tried to force up the wounded, while right in the middle of the camp Renke and her fighters fell back against the rustbreed despite battling fiercely. Vanguard attacks were meant to delay and cripple until the arrival of the colony, and if they had to impale their sinuous bodies on our weapons to shower us in acids, they would do just that. Already the ground sizzled with ochre blood.

Everybody made way to let me take my place at the head of the column, to lead us on the quickest path out into the open, where we could outrun them. But my eyes searched for Truss' pallet, where he would die alone, as was his duty. And my mind went back to the dome, to my voice rising up through its stillness, stirring the dust of centuries.

I knew a safe place right under our noses. I could still get us out without anyone being left behind.

"No need to run," I told those nearest to me. "Bring your young ones into the dome. It's safe, I promise. The Clusterhaunt will protect us." They didn't move, of course, but I went on, louder now. "I bargained for our protection. Our weavers will defend us in the dome. You have seen what they are capable of! These walls are indestructible. It is our best and only chance! Go!"

Most of them muttered madness at me, but some snuck glances at the dome, leaving our formation with tentative steps. Others kept looking at the elders.

"Get back!" the windreader yelled, ushering them on. "Don't listen to this ghost-shifted rambling. We run!"

"But the Blessed is right!" I hadn't noticed Asper staying with me in the fray. He had leapt onto a crumbling wall, waving his heat cloak like a banner. "Our weavers are in there. I won't leave them. I say let's go and make a stand there! We've got nothing to lose."

I saw the eyes of the herders shift. Terrified, yes, but flecked with mad determination as they grabbed what they had dropped in the wake of the attack and started to run for the dome, a few first, but drawing more and more after them. And I saw Renke lose every battle she was in and buckle when she finally called her fighters to her side to cover our retreat.

And just like that, the tribe was on the move. I went to find Truss and lifted his dry, grunting weight upon my shoulders. He didn't quite struggle, but he did snarl.

"Don't you dare and deny me my choice. Leave me, and do what the tribe needs of you."

"I am," I snapped. "And you can thank me later, or still make use of your choice then."

He huffed, but sagged against me in defeat. The tribe had decided, after all. Just beyond the tube entrance, their courage left them, though, and they all stopped dead in their tracks. The space was brimming with ghost activity. "Orion!" I shouted, shouldering my way to the front, Truss still with me. "Where are you?"

"Mink!" The ghost blinked to life in all his silvery splendor between two shafts of light in the middle of the dome, making my people surge back against the walls. "I'm glad you came back! Come on, everything is prepared for the show."

"We're not here for the show. Please, Orion, you have to protect us. There's rustbreed at the threshold, and my people need shelter. Help us!"

The spear fighters defending the entrance shot frantic looks at Orion as he drifted closer, but the Warden called them back in line with a disdainful growl and motioned others to move up as replacements, should they fall.

"I see," Orion said, and my heart leapt when I felt his light-hearted nature yield to the gentle profoundness I had come to trust. "Harm to visitors is to be avoided at all costs. Initiating habitat sealing."

An inaudible command brought in our herds. From all directions, they converged upon the entrance, the staccato of clinking legs made it sound like we had acquired an army. Smoothly they flowed into precise lines, passing down chunks of material to the tube opening where the silvery creatures began to weave upwards from the ground, and downwards from the ceiling. Most herders just stared in astonishment, but some whooped and called their weavers' names, and a few ventured out to gather rubble for them. Not every fragment went into the quickly growing wall, though. Some ended up in scalding spurts directed at our enemies.

It was messy. Three weavers were thrown back in a spray of acid as they clung to the red-tipped mandibles of a rustbreed soldier to keep it from rearing. One of our fighters went down, hundreds of chitinous legs crawling over him. He was still screaming long after he had been pulled back out.

But soon there was only room left for a single rustbreed to squeeze through, and then not even that. The entrance was sealed, and we stood in silence, apart from the occasional thud when one of the creatures flung itself against the freshly spun concrete slab.

The tribe huddled together in the open space of the dome, eyeing me, the elders, and Orion. Some lowered the young ones to the floor, still holding their hands. Some flicked their tongues.

"What now, little foster-hatch?" I was kneeling next to Truss, trying to check his bandages. He slapped my hands away, but he was no longer bristling with fury, his crest drooping in concern instead. "Seems we are not to become rustbreed sustenance yet. But what do *we* eat? We don't have a grub's worth of food with us, and they won't go away as long as their prey is so close."

I looked up into the fearful faces of my tribe, who had trusted me in a way I would never have thought possible. "We have our weavers. And we have Orion. Surely there is something we can come up with."

It took a long time to get them to talk. Half of them still believed the Clusterhaunt had set this as a trap for us, and they were unwilling to go near it. A few even snuck on their dread-screen, which they had brought with them of all things. Orion was no help either, curiously hovering close, displaying some tricks to get the attention of the young ones. The tribe had settled into an uneasy camp formation, a few lone bug-catcher lamps marking a perimeter, its guards clearly at a loss.

Those lamps gave us an idea at last. As soon as I had gotten the herders to talk not about our predicament or the implications of conversing with a Clusterhaunt, but about the glorious things their weavers could build together, they were unstoppable. Ideas flew back and forth, with Orion chiming in with detailed knowledge.

"These possibilities, Blessed... Mink!" Asper clasped my upper arm as if I weren't the uncleanest being he had ever met. Still, I was not one of them. I had no clue what exactly they planned to build, but the gleam in Asper's eyes told me it would be magnificent. "There is enough plastics in here to burn the whole colony to the ground!"

In our lamps, we used a burning paste spun from plastics. The weavers would tunnel deep and build some contraption to saturate the ground the rustbreed crawled upon and burrowed in, until all that was needed was a single spark, while we sat safely here in our indestructible dome.

"Of course you will have to learn to control the ATUs for this project, little engineers," Orion told them. "I can't do it for you."

The herders were too agitated to notice, but his tone alerted me. There had been a calm finality in Orion's words that suggested he was not planning to participate.

"Why not?" Asper asked. "I'd like to learn, but we are in a tight spot right now. I'd prefer to be educated when nothing tries to break in and eat me."

"Nothing will breach these walls, little engineer. But you won't be able to learn from me afterwards. There are rules, hard-coded rules I have to adhere to. I cannot order the ATUs to break down the interior of my visitor center to form flammable components. I cannot add defects. Habitat destruction is beyond my authorization. As is sending the weavers out of the habitat to tunnel as long as they are integrated in the defence matrix. You have to take your weavers back. Mink knows how."

I jumped up from the resting place I had found when they had gone into technical details. "I told you no, Orion!"

The others looked at me in puzzlement. They didn't understand. I had not abandoned my old teacher, and I wouldn't abandon my new one, even if he had found better students now. The stabs of jealousy I had felt since Orion had begun to focus his enthusiasm on the herders subsided, though, when he took me to the side. "I can't give them back. So I need your help, and I'm very sorry for your inconvenience." He hovered closer, so close that for the first time I got a look beyond the bowl and saw more than just a hint of his eyes. They were bright and very blue, luminous like the worlds I had seen in his vision. "Mink. Most curious of explorers. You should know that nothing will change if you keep clinging to the long-forgotten remnants of the past. I don't belong here, and you know it. You opened my eyes to it. It would be a sad existence indeed to stay back with this knowledge, waiting forever. And I would have no-one else lay me to rest."

"No! Laying to rest is for ghosts. You... are something else, Orion. I gave you a name. You showed me the worlds." I flicked my tongue, affectionately now, and in affect, because it passed through him yet again.

"Then save what's left of me." He drifted backwards, beckoning me to follow him. "Not these outdated projections, but what I stand for. This is my purpose after all, educating the next generation about becoming explorers, builders, spacefarers. Now go and save your tribe!"

He had led me to the gigantic metal tube, and pointed up its sleek form. Above its upper end, where it was still fastened to the ceiling, one of the dome segments was missing, big enough for a lithe scout to squeeze through.

I shook my head with closed eyes. Imagined one way it would all end, if I did nothing, and another, and another, all equally grim. When I finally buckled, I swallowed everything I wanted to say and turned to technicalities. "If I go, will there be enough time to teach them what they need to know?"

"They are quite adept already. They might have used high-tech tools to build spoons, but they are master-builders in their own way. I'll teach them everything they need to know about ATU coordination. I'll try to attend the process as long as I can, but as you know, residual energies are nothing but a short echo." He came closer, as if to take me in his insubstantial embrace. I wasn't entirely sure if I really felt his warmth or just imagined it. "I'm sorry you have to do this, to go into danger for me. But I'm glad you found me, I truly am, Mink. I'm glad I was not forever alone. Now don't you worry. Just remember, beyond the darkness, worlds are waiting."

WHAT I SAW when I climbed the rocket tube to the outside of the dome was a sea of writhing russet bodies. Rustbreed reek permeated the air, legs clattered like an upcoming storm. It made me understand, more than anything else, that there was no way for me to go back down and sit it out. To wait for another plan, a miracle, a change of rules, would have been madness. There was a hard-coded rule of the tribes: nobody survived a rustbreed colony. Vanguard, yes, even the first waves of the colony proper. But those below had already settled in, infesting the whole area. And yet I might be able to save everyone. Everyone alive, at least.

I looked down through the hole in the ceiling one last time. Even Asper still shied when Orion came close to point something out, and the others kept more than a healthy distance. They did not trust him like I did, but I hoped their shared passion for the weavers and Orion's attempts to entertain those who were not involved in building would keep the tribe from panicking.

I turned away and camouflaged. Everybody thought it easy, that I just had to press against any random surface and magically took on its color. But it's not like that. It is a process, a transformation, and it's more than scale-deep. The colors are a mental thing. My whole body wanted to scream danger in bright yellows and reds, and I had to convince it to calm down. When I felt positively invisible, I took up the rope and began my treacherous way down the side of the dome.

Even camouflaged, it was harrowing to see this dead place writhe with a host of centipedes prepared to tear me apart. After our first flight, there was not much left in my vial of extract from rustbreed scent glands, so I didn't fiddle with droplets, but threw the whole thing to shatter far from the place where they were clustered, obsessed with this frustratingly thin wall separating them from a tribe's worth of a feast. The whole ground seemed to ripple as they moved to investigate, and I was able to slip past the few remaining patrols.

I was possibly the very first scout to be led to a heart-chamber by the ghost's own words. It was located in one of the tall, broken buildings, beyond debris-strewn staircases descending far down into the bowels of the earth, into labyrinthine hallways with doors Orion had taught me to navigate. A true Clusterhaunt hideout, if there had ever been one. The entrance was signed in the way he had said it would, and I made short work of its grade-4 lock with a vial of potent acid. This was, after all, my trade.

I closed the door carefully behind me, then I looked around. And the moment I saw what this room was, my chest ached for Orion.

It was a cauldron of ghosts. It was a grave.

On its other end, massive vanes behind a metal grate streamed air into my face, sufficiently cool to immobilize anyone exhausted enough to give in to the cold. There were hearts aplenty, rack upon rack, neatly placed in their boxes. But only one was still beating.

"Orion." I stood transfixed by the slow pulses of light emanating from the box, placed my hand upon it like I had never been able to with his manifestation in the dome. Then I began to chant, because it was the only way to get moving again, to sink into the routine of a duty I had done so very often.

As I took down my tool sash and put on my gloves, I sang the Song of Passing, to tell the ghost that the sins of the past would be set right and there was no reason to linger, but I soon slipped into my own verses. I sang of the vastness of the fallen world and the vastness beyond, and I hoped it was bearable because he had my voice guiding him along. I sang of worlds beyond the blackness and a bowl full of stars, and I took my engraved pliers and plucked and cut at the right places, as gently as I could and with a touch that I hoped conveyed love, not violence, until the very last bluish light on the heart slowly faded.

A noise I had not perceived till now ground to a halt, and the breath of cool air on my face died. I let my own breath go in an anguished rush and slumped down on the lifeless heart-box, without a care for my unprotected face and arms.

At the afterthought of residual energies, I jerked up. Maybe there was still time for a proper farewell. I forcefully banned my grieving paleness and ran.

I CAME BACK to a darkened dome.

I knew what to anticipate: weavers under the control of our tribe again, flowing together to use up all the interior material of the visitor center to build secretly under the earth, slowly, but steadily creating the trap. The moment the weavers came together for their task, the rustbreed were dead already, their time burning down with every spun thread of tunnel, pipe, fuel, until they faced their immolation. I should have been glad to see the plan in motion.

Still, when I saw no ghostly lights shine from within the dome, my heart sank. I was too late. The last emanations of Orion had occurred without me. But then I heard the music.

Of all the things he could have repaired, of all the things he could have done with his last energies, he had chosen his beloved music. It was indeed very inspiring, swelling like the songs of a dozen tribes woven into one, ethereal, rising ever higher, tugging at the soul and then taking it along in a thunderous rush. The hexagons of the ceiling had been shaded to blackness, and I scampered down the metal tube of the rocket into a darkness speckled with the fearful eyes of my tribe under this display of ghostly power. Because there was also light.

Lights dotted the blackness. Clear and bright, beckoning, shining through the fabric of the artificial night. A few lone pinpoints first, then scattered scintillating clusters, until an abundance of lights pulsed above us. And as I came to stand among my people on the ground and let my gaze be drawn up, it was as if the domed ceiling had dissolved into an infinite, vast space, stretching out forever before our eyes, close enough to touch if we just strove to reach it.

None of us had ever seen the stars, but our hearts recognized them. They looked just like so many camps in the sky, bug-catcher lamps in the darkness, and I could not have been the only one to wonder what tribes lived up there.

Nobody made a sound, and only when the surging song Orion played for us ascended into our own Paean of Manifest Horizons did they move, like a collective sigh. And I could see that he had entered their hearts now, that he had become *our* ghost, with this last show, his star-laden farewell. Renke was studying their faces as well, and when she caught me looking, she simply nodded her acknowledgement.

And so when the weavers began to move, precisely coordinated, and when we began to hear the rustbreed blindly throwing themselves at the walls again, not knowing that even now their doom was in the making, and when the stars winked out in large swathes and it all went dark, our tribe sang on in the vast blackness, sang verses of new horizons and our ghost guiding us, and our voices filled the dome like an elegy, like a hymn, and took on a shape of their own, a shape of things to come.

* * *

WHEN WE SET out to weave us a way to the stars, we knew we pledged the lives of our clutches to wandering the wastes. Generation after generation, we would scourge the ruins of the broken world for lost knowledge, our herds converging on molten glass seas to build miracles we had never dreamed of.

We are no mere survivors anymore. We are still adapting to our changed existence, as our starlit minds keep finding new paths in this old world. Our gaze is set upwards now, out to unpoisoned spheres, out to unveil the moon and what lies beyond. We will never be starless again, and this is the greatest gift, a glittering song to complement our own with hope.

When I walk the acrid sands with my ghost-shifted tribe, our two newly adopted gearbeasts trundling along, I know I will not be the one to actually bring us to the stars. This will fall to Asper, who teaches our future builders and planners to control their weavers, and to paint them, too, for beauty, not out of fear. My contribution to the Tribesong is small. But as I tell it once again, I'm clutching the Memory Vault, the only thing I took for myself from the visitor center that is now but an empty, scorched husk. They are like small eggs, those Memory Vaults. I'm not a fool. Most eggs come to nothing, I know. But maybe something will hatch. Maybe there is something left of Orion in there. I'll give it to the next scout after me, and she will give it to the next and the next until Orion's Song reaches the stars. Because as small as this contribution is, I know there will always be need of us who find new ways to cross the blackness and dream of the worlds beyond.

IF AT FIRST YOU DON'T SUCCEED, TRY, TRY AGAIN

Zen Cho

Zen Cho (www.zencho.org) was born and raised in Malaysia. She is the author of Crawford Award-winning short story collection *Spirits Abroad* and editor of anthology *Cyberpunk: Malaysia*. She has been nominated for the Campbell Award for Best New Writer and honour-listed for the Carl Brandon Society Awards for her short fiction. Her debut novel *Sorcerer to the Crown*, about magic, intrigue and politics in Regency London, won a British Fantasy Award for Best Newcomer and was a Locus Awards finalist for Best First Novel. Her second novel, *The True Queen*, was published in March of this year. She lives in the UK.

The first thousand years

IT WAS TIME. Byam was as ready as it would ever be.

As a matter of fact, it had been ready to ascend some 300 years ago. But the laws of heaven cannot be defied. If you drop a stone, it will fall to the ground—it will not fly up to the sky. If you try to become a dragon before your thousandth birthday, you will fall flat on your face, and all the other spirits of the five elements will laugh at you.

These are the laws of heaven.

But Byam had been patient. Now it would be rewarded.

It slithered out of the lake it had occupied for the past 100 years. The western shore had recently been settled by humans, and the banks had become cluttered with humans' usual mess—houses, cultivated fields, bits of pottery that poked Byam in the side.

But the eastern side was still reserved to beasts and spirits. There was plenty of space for an imugi to take off.

The mountains around the lake said hello to Byam. (It was always safer to be polite to an imugi, since you never knew when it might turn into a dragon.) The sky above them was a pure light blue, dotted with clouds like white jade.

Byam's heart rose. It launched itself into the air, the sun warm on its back.

I deserve this. All those years studying in dank caves, chanting sutras, striving to understand the Way...

For the first half-millennium or so, Byam could be confident of finding the solitude necessary for study. But more recently, there seemed to be more and more humans everywhere.

Humans weren't all bad. You couldn't meditate your way through every doctrinal puzzle, and that was where monks proved useful. Of course, even the most enlightened monk was wont to be alarmed by the sudden appearance of a giant snake wanting to know what they thought of the Sage's comments on water. Still, you could usually extract some guidance from them, once they stopped screaming.

But spending too much time near humans was risky. If one saw you during your ascension, that could ruin everything. Byam would have moved when the humans settled by the lake, if not for the ample supply of cows and pigs and goats in the area. (Byam had grown tired of seafood.)

It wasn't always good to have such abundance close to hand, though. Byam had been studying extra hard for the past decade in preparation for its ascension. Just last month, it had been startled from a marathon meditation session by an enormous growl.

Byam had looked around wildly. For a moment it thought it had been set upon, maybe by a wicked imugi—the kind so embittered by failure it pretended not to care about the Way, or the cintamani, or even becoming a dragon. But there was no one around, only a few fish beating a hasty retreat.

Then, another growl. It was coming from Byam's own stomach. Byam recollected that it hadn't eaten in about five years.

Some imugi fasted to increase their spiritual powers. But when Byam tried to get back to meditating, it didn't work. Its stomach kept making weird gurgling noises. All the fish had been scared off, so Byam popped out of the water, looking for a snack.

A herd of cows was grazing by the bank, as though they were waiting for Byam.

It only intended to eat one cow. It wanted to keep sharp for its ascension. Dragons probably didn't eat much. All the dragons Byam had ever seen were svelte, with perfect scales, shining talons, silky beards.

Unfortunately Byam wasn't a dragon yet. It was hungry, and the cows smelled *so* good. Byam had one, and then another, and then a third, telling itself each time that *this* cow would be the last. Before it knew it, almost the whole herd was gone.

Byam cringed remembering this, but then put the memory away. Today was the day that would change everything. After today, Byam would be transformed. It would have a wish-fulfilling gem of its own—the glorious cintamani, which manifested all desires, cured afflictions, purified souls and water alike.

So high up, the air was thin, and Byam had to work harder to keep afloat. The clouds brushed its face damply. And—Byam's heart beat faster—wasn't that winking light ahead the glitter of a jewel?

Byam turned for its last look at the earth as an imugi. The lake shone in the sun. It had been cold, and miserable, and lonely, full of venomous water snakes that bit Byam's tail. Byam had been dying to get away from it.

But now, it felt a swell of affection. When it returned as a dragon, it would bless the lake. Fish would overflow its banks. The cows and pigs and goats would multiply beyond counting. The crops would spring out of the earth in their multitudes...

A thin screechy noise was coming from the lake. When Byam squinted, it saw a group of little creatures on the western bank. Humans.

One of them was shaking a fist at the sky. "Fuck you, imugi!"

"Oh shit," said Byam.

"Yeah, I see you! You think you got away with it? Well, you thought wrong!"

Byam lunged upwards, but it was too late. Gravity set its teeth in its tail and tugged.

It wasn't just one human shouting, it was all of them. A chorus of insults rose on the wind:

"Worm! Legless centipede! Son of a bitch! You look like fermented soybeans and you smell even worse!"

Byam strained every muscle, fighting the pull of the earth. If only it had hawk's claws to grasp the clouds with, or stag's antlers to pierce the sky...

But Byam wasn't a dragon yet.

The last thing it heard as it plunged through the freezing waters of the lake was a human voice shrieking:

"Serves you right for eating our cows!"

The second thousand years

IF YOU WANTED to be a dragon, dumb perseverance wasn't enough. You had to have a strategy.

Humans had proliferated, so Byam retreated to the ocean. It was harder to get texts in the sea, but technically you didn't need texts to study the Way, since it was inherent in the order of all things. (Anyway, sometimes you could steal scriptures off a turtle on a pilgrimage, or go onshore to ransack a monastery.)

But you had to get out of the water in order to ascend. It was impossible to exclude the possibility of being seen by humans, even in the middle of the ocean. It didn't seem to bother them that they couldn't breathe underwater; they still launched themselves onto the waves on rickety assemblages of dismembered trees. It was as if they couldn't wait to get on to their next lives.

That was fine. If Byam couldn't depend on the absence of humans, it would use their presence to its advantage.

It was heaven's will that Byam should have failed the last time; if heaven wasn't ready to accept Byam, nothing could change that, no matter how diligently it studied or how much it longed to ascend.

As in all things, however, when it came to ascending, how you were seen mattered just as much as what you did. It hadn't helped back then that the lake humans had named Byam for what it was: no dragon, but an imugi, a degraded being no better than the crawling beasts of the earth.

But if, as Byam flashed across the sky, a witness saw a dragon... that was another matter. Heaven wasn't immune to the pressures of public perception. It would *have* to recognise Byam then.

The spirits of the wind and water were too hard to bluff; fish were too self-absorbed; and there was no hope of hoodwinking the sea dragons. But humans had bad eyesight, and a tendency to see things that weren't there. Their capacity for self-deception was Byam's best bet.

It chose a good point in the sky, high enough that it would have enough cloud matter to work with, but not so high that the humans wouldn't be able to see it. Then it got to work.

It labored at night, using its head to push together masses of cloud and its tail to work the fine detail. Byam didn't just want the design to look like a dragon. Byam wanted it to be beautiful—as beautiful as the dragon Byam was going to be.

Making the sculpture was harder than Byam expected. Cloud was an intransigent medium. Wisps kept drifting off when Byam wasn't looking. It couldn't get the horns straight, and the whiskers were wonky.

Sometimes Byam felt like giving up. How could it make a dragon when it didn't even know how to be one?

To conquer self-doubt, it chanted the aphorisms of the wise:

Nobody becomes a dragon overnight.

Real dragons keep going.

A dragon is only an imugi that didn't give up.

It took 100 years longer than Byam had anticipated before the cloud was finished.

It looked like a dragon, caught as it sped across the sky to its rightful place in the heavens. In moonlight it shone like mother of pearl. Under the sun it would glitter with all the colors of the rainbow.

As Byam put its final touches on the cloud, it felt both pride and a sense of anti-climax. Even loss. Soon Byam would ascend—and then what would happen to its creation? It would dissipate, or dissolve into rain, like any other cloud.

Byam managed to find a monk who knew about shipping routes and was willing to dish in exchange for not being eaten. And then it was ready. As dawn unfolded across the sky on an auspicious day, Byam took its position behind its dragon-cloud.

All it needed was a single human to look up and exclaim at what they saw. A fleet of merchant vessels was due to come this way. Among all those humans, there had to be one sailor with his eyes on the sky—a witness open to wonder, prepared to see a dragon rising to glory.

*   *   *

"HEY, CAPTAIN," SAID the lookout. "You see that?"

"What is it? A sail?"

"No." The lookout squinted at the sky. "That cloud up there, look. The one with all the colors."

"Oh wow!" said the captain. "Good spot! That's something special, for sure. It's a good omen!"

He clapped the lookout on the back, turning to the rest of the crew. "Great news, men! Heaven smiles upon us. Today is our day!"

Everyone was busy with preparations, but a dutiful cheer rose from the ship.

The lookout was still staring upwards.

"It's an interesting shape," he said thoughtfully. "Don't you think it looks like a... "

"Like what?" said the captain.

"Like, um..." The look-out frowned, snapping his fingers. "What do you call them? Forget my own head next! It looks like a—it's on the tip of my tongue. I've been at sea for too long. Like a, you know—"

BYAM COULDN'T TAKE it anymore.

"*Dragon!*" it wailed in agony.

An imugi has enormous lungs. Byam's voice rolled across the sky like thunder, its breath scattering the clouds—and blowing its creation to shreds.

"Horse!" said the lookout triumphantly. "It looks like a horse!"

"No no no," said Byam. It scrambled to reassemble its sculpture, but the cloud matter was already melting away upon the winds.

"Thunder from a clear sky!" said the captain. "Is that a good sign or a bad sign?"

The lookout frowned. "You're too superstitious, captain—hey!" He perked up, snatching up a telescope. "Captain, there they are!"

Byam had been so focused on the first ship that it hadn't seen the merchant fleet coming. Then it was too busy trying to salvage its dragon-cloud to pay attention to what was going on below.

It was distantly aware of fighting between the ships, of arrows flying, of the screams of sailors as they were struck down. But it was preoccupied by the enormity of what had happened to it—the loss of hundreds of years of steady, hopeful work.

It wasn't too late. Byam could fix the cloud. Tomorrow it would try again—

"Ah," said the pirate captain, looking up from the business of slaughter. "An imugi! It's good luck after all. One last push, men! They can't hold out for long!"

It would have been easier if Byam could tell itself the humans had sabotaged it out of spite. But it knew they hadn't. As Byam tumbled out of the sky, it was the impartiality of their judgment that stung the most.

The third thousand years

DRAGONS ENJOYED SHARING advice about how they'd gotten where they were. They said it helped to visualise the success you desired.

"Envision yourself with those horns, those whiskers, three claws and a thumb, basking in the glow of your own cintamani," urged the Dragon King of the East Sea in his popular memoir *Sixty Thousand Records of a Floating Life*. "Close your eyes. You are the master of the elements! A twitch of your whisker and the skies open. At your command, blessings—or vengeance—pour forth upon all creatures under heaven! Just imagine!"

When Byam was low at heart, it imagined.

It got fed up of the sea: turtles kept chasing it around, and whale song disrupted its sleep. It moved inland, and found a quiet cave where it could study the Way undisturbed. The cave didn't smell great, but it meant Byam never had to go far for food, so long as it didn't mind bat. (Byam came to mind bat.) Byam focused on the future.

This time, there would be no messing around with dragon-clouds. Byam had learned from its mistakes. There was no tricking heaven. This time it would present itself at the gates with its record of honest toil, and hope to be deemed worthy of admission.

It should have been nervous, but in fact it was calm as it prepared for what it hoped would be its final attempt. Certainty glowed in its stomach like a swallowed ember.

It had been a long time since Byam had left its cave, which it had chosen because it was up among the mountains, far from any human settlement. Still, Byam intended to minimise any chance of disaster. It was going to shoot straight for the skies, making sure it was exposed to the judgment of the world for as brief a time as possible.

But the brightness outside took it aback. Its eyes weren't used to the sun's glare anymore. When Byam raised its head, it got caught in a sort of horrible basket, full of whispering voices. A storm of ticklish green scraps whirled around it.

It reared back, hissing, before it recognised what had attacked it. Byam had forgotten about trees.

It leapt into the air, shaken. To have forgotten *trees...* Byam had not realised it had been so long.

Its unease faded as it rose ever higher. The crisp airs of heaven blew away disquiet. Ahead, the clouds glowed as though they reflected the light of the Way.

LESLIE ALMOST MISSED it.

She never usually did this kind of thing. She was indoorsy the way some people were outdoorsy, as attached to her sofa as others were to endorphins and bragging about their marathon times. She'd never thought of herself as someone who hiked.

But she hadn't thought of herself as someone who'd fail her PhD, or get dumped by her boyfriend for her best friend. The past year had blown the bottom out of her ideas about herself.

She paused to drink some water and heave for breath. The view was spectacular. It seemed meaningless.

She was higher up than she'd thought. What if she took the wrong step? Would it hurt much to fall? Everyone would think it was an accident...

She shook herself, horrified. She wouldn't do anything stupid, Leslie told herself. To distract herself, she took out her phone, but that proved a bad idea: this was the point at which she would have texted Jung-wook before.

She could take a selfie. That's what people did when they went hiking, right? Posted proof they'd done it. She raised her phone, switching the camera to front-facing mode.

She saw a flash in the corner of the screen. It was sunlight glinting off scales. Leslie's mouth fell open. It wasn't—it *couldn't* be. She hadn't even known they were found in America.

The camera went off. Leslie whirled around, but the sky was empty. It was nowhere to be seen.

But someone up there was looking out for Leslie after all, because when she looked back at her phone, she saw that she'd caught it. It was there. It had happened. There was Leslie, looking dopey with her red face and her hair a mess and her mouth half-open—and in the background, arced across the sky like a rainbow, was her miracle. Her own personal sign from heaven that things were going to be OK.

leshangry Nature is amazing! #imugi #이무기 #sighting #blessed # 여행스타그램 #자연 #등산 #nature #hiking #wanderlust #gooutside #snakesofinstagram

The turning of the worm

"DR. HAN?" SAID the novice. "Yeah, her office is just through there."

Sure enough, the name was inscribed on the door in the new script the humans used now: *Dr. Leslie Han*. Byam's nemesis.

Its most *recent* nemesis. If it had been only one offence, Byam wouldn't even be here. It was the whole of Byam's long miserable history with humans that had brought it to this point.

It made itself invisible and passed through the door.

The monk was sitting at a desk, frowning over a text. Byam was not good at distinguishing one human from another, but this particular human's face was branded in its memory.

It felt a surge of relief.

Even with the supernatural powers accumulated in the course of three millennia of studying the Way, it had taken Byam a while to figure out how to shapeshift. The legs had been the most difficult part. Byam kept giving itself tiger feet, the kind dragons had.

It could have concealed the feet under its skirts, since no celestial fairy ever appeared in anything less than three layers of silk. But Byam wouldn't have it. It was pathetic, this harking back to its stupid dreams. It had worked at the spell until the feet came right. If Byam wasn't becoming a dragon, it would not lower itself to imitation. No part of it would bear any of the nine resemblances.

But there were consolations available to imugi who reconciled themselves to their fate. Like revenge.

The human was perhaps a little older than when Byam had last seen her. But she was still alive—alive enough to suffer when Byam devoured her.

Byam let its invisibility fall away. It spread its hands, the better to show off its magnificent sleeves.

It was the human's job that had given Byam the idea. Leslie Han was an academic, which appeared to be a type of monk. Monks were the most relatable kind of human, for like imugi, they desired one thing most in life: to ascend to a higher plane of existence.

"Leslie," crooned Byam in the dulcet tones of a celestial fairy. "How would you like to go to heaven?"

The monk screamed and fell out of her chair.

When nothing else happened, Byam floated over to the desk, peering down at the monk.

"What are you doing down there?" began Byam, but then the text the monk had been studying caught its eye.

"Oh my God, you're—" The monk rubbed her eyes. "I didn't think celestial fairies descended anymore! Did you—were you offering to take me to heaven?"

Byam wasn't listening. The monk had to repeat herself before it looked up from the book.

"This is a text on the Way," said Byam. It looked around the monk's office. There were rows and rows of books. Byam said slowly, "These are *all* about the Way."

The monk looked puzzled. "No, they're about astrophysics. I'm a researcher. I study the evolution of galaxies."

Maybe Byam had been dumb enough to believe it might some day become a dragon, but it knew an exegesis of the Way when it saw one. There were hundreds of such books here—more commentaries than Byam had seen in one place in its entire lifetime.

It wasn't going to repeat its mistakes. Ascension, transcendence, turning into a dragon—that wasn't happening for Byam. Heaven had made that clear.

But you couldn't study something for 3,000 years without becoming interested in it for its own sake.

"Tell me about your research," said Byam.

"What you said just now," said the monk. "Did you not—"

Byam showed its teeth.

"My research!" said the monk. "Let me tell you about it."

Byam had planned to eat the monk when she was done. But it turned out the evolution of galaxies was an extremely complicated matter. The monk had not explained even half of what Byam wanted to know by the time the moon rose.

The monk took out a glowing box and looked at it. "It's so late!"

"Why did you stop?" said Byam.

"I need to sleep," said the monk. She bent over the desk. Byam wondered if this was a good moment to eat her, but then the monk turned and held out a sheaf of paper.

"What is this?"

"Extra reading," said the monk. "You can come back tomorrow if you've got questions. My office hours are 3 to 4 pm on Wednesdays and Thursdays."

She paused, her eyes full of wonder. She was looking at Byam as though it was special.

"But you can come any time," said the monk.

BYAM DID THE reading. It went back again the next day. And the next.

It was easier to make sense of the texts with the monk's help. Byam had never had anyone to talk to about the Way before. Its past visits with monks didn't count—Leslie screamed much less than the others. She answered Byam's questions as though she enjoyed them, whereas the others had always made it clear they couldn't wait for Byam to leave.

"I like teaching," she said, when Byam remarked upon this. "I'm surprised I've got anything to teach you, though. I'd've thought you'd know all this stuff already."

"No," said Byam. It looked down at the diagram Leslie was explaining for the third time. Byam still didn't get it. But if there was one thing Byam was good at, it was trying again and again.

Well. That *had* been its greatest strength. Now, who knew?

"It's OK," said Leslie. "You know things I don't."

"Hm." Byam wasn't so sure.

Leslie touched its shoulder.

"It's impressive," she said. "That you're so open to learning new things. If I were a celestial fairy, there's no way I'd work so hard. I'd just lie around getting drunk and eating peaches all day."

"You have a skewed image of the life of a celestial fairy," said Byam.

But it did feel better. No one had ever called it hardworking before. It was a new experience, feeling validated. Byam found it liked it.

Studying with Leslie involved many new experiences. Leslie was a great proponent of what she called fresh air. She dragged Byam out of the office regularly so they could inhale as much of it as possible.

"But there's air *inside*," objected Byam.

"It's not the same," said Leslie. "Don't you get a little stir-crazy when you haven't seen the sun in a while?"

Byam remembered the shock of emerging from its cave for the first time in 800 years.

"Yes," it admitted.

Leslie was particularly fond of hiking, which was like walking, only you did it up a hill. Byam enjoyed this. In the past 3,000 years it had seen more of the insides of mountains than their outsides, and it turned out the outsides were attractive at human eye-level.

The mountains were still polite to Byam, as though there were still a chance it might ever become a dragon. This hurt, but Byam squashed the feeling down. It had made its decision.

It was on one of their hikes that Leslie brought up the first time they met. They weren't far off the peak when she stopped to look into the distance.

Byam hadn't realised at first—things looked so different from human height—but it recognised the place before she spoke. Leslie was staring at the very mountain that had been Byam's home for 800 years.

"It's funny," she said. "The last time I was here..."

Byam braced itself. *I saw an imugi trying to ascend,* she was going to say. *It faceplanted on the side of a mountain, it was hilarious!*

"I was standing here wishing I was dead," said Leslie.

"What?"

"Not seriously," said Leslie hastily. "I mean, I wouldn't have done anything. I just wanted it to stop."

"What did you want to stop?"

"Everything," said Leslie. "I don't know. I was young. I was having a hard time. It all felt too much to cope with."

Humans lived for such a short time anyway, it had never occurred to Byam that they might want to hasten the end. "You don't still..."

"Oh no. It was a while ago." Leslie was still looking at Byam's mountain. She smiled. "You know, I got a sign while I was up here."

"A sign," echoed Byam.

"It probably sounds stupid," said Leslie. "But I saw an imugi. It made me think there might be hope. I started going to therapy. Finished my PhD. Things got better."

"Good," said Byam. It met Leslie's eyes. She had never stopped looking at Byam as though it was special.

Leslie pressed her lips to Byam's mouth.

Byam stayed still. It wasn't sure what to do.

"Sorry. I'm sorry!" Leslie stepped back, looking panicked. "I don't know what I was thinking. I thought maybe—of course we're both women, but I thought maybe that didn't matter to you guys. Or maybe you were even into—I was imagining things. This is so embarrassing. Oh God."

Byam had questions. It picked just one to start with. "What were you doing? With the mouths, I mean."

Leslie took a deep breath and blew it out. "Oh boy." But the explanation proved to be straightforward.

"Oh, it was a mating overture," said Byam.

"I—yeah, I guess you could put it that way," said Leslie. "Listen, I'm sorry I even... I don't want to have ruined everything. I care about you a lot, as a friend. Can we move on?"

"Yes," Byam agreed. "Let's try again."

"Phew, I'm really glad you're not—what?"

"I didn't know what you were doing earlier," explained Byam. "You should've said. But I'll be better now I understand it."

Leslie stared. Byam started to feel nervous.

"Do you not want to kiss?" it said.

"No," said Leslie. "I mean, yes?"

She reached out tentatively. Byam squeezed her hand. It seemed to be the right thing to do, because Leslie smiled.

"OK," she said.

AFTER A WHILE Byam moved into Leslie's apartment. It had been spending the nights off the coast, but the waters by the city smelled of diesel and the noise from the ships made its sleep fitful. Leslie's bed was a lot more comfortable than the watery deeps.

Living with her meant Byam had to be in celestial fairy form all the time, but it was used to it by now. At Leslie's request, it turned down the heavenly glow.

"You don't mind?" said Leslie. "Humans aren't used to the halo."

"Nah," said Byam. "It's not like I had the glow before." It froze. "I mean... in heaven, everyone is illuminated, so you stop... noticing it?"

Fortunately, Leslie wasn't listening. She had opened an envelope and was staring at the letter in dismay.

"He's raising the rent again! Oh, you're fucking kidding me." She took off her glasses and rubbed her eyes. "I need to get out of this city."

"What is *rent*?" said Byam.

Which was how Byam ended up getting a job. Leslie tried to discourage it at first. Even once Byam wore her down and she admitted it would be helpful if Byam also paid "rent," she seemed to think it was a problem that Byam was undocumented.

That was an explanation that took an extra long time. The magic to invent the necessary records was simple in comparison.

"'Byam'," said Leslie, studying its brand-new driver's licence. "That's an interesting choice."

"It's my name," said Byam absently. It was busy magicking up an immunization history.

"That's your name?" said Leslie. She touched the driver's licence with reverent fingers. "Byam."

She seemed unaccountably pleased. After a moment she said, "You never told me your name before."

"*Oh*," said Byam. Leslie was blushing. "You could have asked!"

Leslie shrugged. "I didn't want to force it. I figured you'd tell me when you were ready."

"It's not because—I would've told you," said Byam. "I just didn't think of it. It's not my real name."

The light in Leslie's face dimmed. "It's not?"

"I mean, it's the name I have," said Byam. It should never have set off down this path. How was it going to explain about dragon-names—the noble, elegant styles, full of meaning and wit, conferred on dragons upon their ascension? Leslie didn't even know Byam was an imugi. She thought Byam had already been admitted to the gates of heaven.

"I'm only a low-level attendant," it said finally. "When I get promoted, I'll be given a real name. One with a good meaning. Like 'Establish Virtue,' or 'Jade Peak,' or 'Sunlit Cloud.'"

"Oh," said Leslie. "I didn't know you were working towards a promotion." She hesitated. "When do you think you'll get promoted?"

"In 10,000 years' time," said Byam. "Maybe."

This was a personal joke. Leslie wasn't meant to get it, and she did not. She only gave Byam a thoughtful look. She dropped a kiss on its forehead, just above its left eyebrow.

"I like 'Byam,'" she said. "It suits you."

THEY MOVED OUT of the city to the outskirts, where the rent was cheaper and they could have more space. Leslie got a cat, which avoided Byam but eventually stopped hissing at its approach. Leslie went running on the beach in the mornings while Byam swam.

She introduced Byam to those of her family who didn't object to the fact that Byam appeared to be a woman. These did not include Leslie's parents, but there was a sister named Jean, and a niece, Eun-hye, whom Byam taught physics.

Tutoring young humans in physics was Byam's first job, but sometimes it forgot itself and taught students the Way, which was not helpful for exams. After a narrowly averted disaster with the bathroom in their new apartment, Byam took a plumbing course.

It turned out Byam was good at working with pipes—better, perhaps, than it had ever been at understanding the Way.

At night, Byam still dreamt of the past. Or rather, it dreamt of the future— the future as Byam had envisioned it, once upon a time. They were impossible, ecstatic dreams—dreams of scything through the clouds, raindrops clinging to its beard; dreams of chasing the cintamani through the sea, its whiskers floating on a warm current.

When Byam woke up, its face wet with salt-water, Leslie was always there.

BYAM GOT HOME one night and knew something was wrong. It could tell from the shape of Leslie's back. When she realised it was there, she raised her head, wiping her face and trying to smile.

"What happened?" said Byam.

"I've been—" The words got stuck. Leslie cleared her throat. "I didn't get tenure."

Byam had learned enough about Leslie's job by now to understand what this meant. Not getting tenure was worse than falling when you were almost at the gates of heaven. It sat down, appalled.

"Would you like me to eat the committee for you?" it suggested.

Leslie laughed. "No." The syllable came out on a sob. She rubbed her eyes. "Thanks, baby, but that wouldn't help."

"What would help?"

"Nothing," said Leslie. Then, in a wobbly voice, "A hug."

Byam put its arms around Leslie, but it seemed poor comfort for the ruin of all her hopes. It felt Leslie underestimated the consolation she was likely to derive from the wholesale destruction of her enemies. But this was not the time to argue.

Byam remembered the roaring in its ears as it fell, the shock of meeting the ground.

"Sometimes," it said, "you try really hard and it's not enough. You put in all you've got and you still never get where you thought you were meant to be. But at least you tried. Some people never try. They resign themselves to bamboozling monks and devouring maidens for all eternity."

"Doesn't sound like a bad life," said Leslie, with another of those ragged laughs. But she kissed Byam's shoulder, to show that she didn't think the life of a wicked imugi had any real appeal.

After Leslie cried some more, she said, "Is it worth it? The trying, I mean."

Byam had to be honest. The only thing that could have made falling worse was if someone had tried to convince Byam it hadn't sucked.

"I don't know," it said.

It could see the night sky through the windows. Usually the lights and pollution of the city blanked out the sky, but tonight there was a single star shining, like the cintamani did sometimes in Byam's dreams.

"Maybe," said Byam.

Leslie said, "Why aren't you trying to become a dragon?"

Byam froze. "What?"

Leslie wriggled out of its arms and turned to face it. "Tell me you're still working towards it and I'll shut up."

"I don't know what you're talking about," said Byam, terrified. "I'm a celestial fairy. What do dragons have to do with anything? They are far too noble and important to have anything to say to a lowly spirit like me—"

"Byam, I know you're not a celestial fairy."

"No, I am, I—" But Byam swallowed its denials at the look on Leslie's face. "What gave it away?"

"I don't know much about celestial fairies," said Leslie. "But I'm pretty sure they don't talk about eating senior professors."

Byam gave her a look of reproach. "I was trying to be helpful!"

"It wasn't just that..."

"Have you told Jean and Eun-hye?" Byam bethought itself of the other creature that was important in their lives. "Did you tell the cat? Is that why it doesn't like me?"

"I've told you, I can't actually talk to the cat," said Leslie. (Which was a blatant lie, because she did it all the time, though it was true they had strange conversations, generally at cross-purposes.) "I haven't told anyone. But I couldn't live with you for years and *not* know, Byam. I'm not *completely* stupid.

I was hoping you'd eventually be comfortable enough to tell me yourself."

Byam's palms were damp. "Tell you what? 'Oh yeah, Les, I should've mentioned, I'm not an exquisite fairy descended from heaven like you always thought. Actually I'm one of the eternal losers of the unseen world. Hope that's OK!'"

"Hey, forgive me for trying to be sensitive!" snapped Leslie. "I don't care what you are, Byam. I know *who* you are. That's all that matters to me."

"Who I am?" said Byam. It was like a rock had lodged inside its throat. It was hard to speak past it. "An imugi, you mean. An earthworm with a dream."

"An imugi changed my life," said Leslie. "Don't talk them down."

Though it was incredible, it seemed it was true she didn't mind, and wasn't about to dump Byam for being the embodiment of pathetic failure.

"I just wish you'd trusted me," she said.

Her eyes were tender, and worried, and red. They reminded Byam that it was Leslie who had just come crashing down to earth.

Byam clasped its hands to keep them from shaking. It took a deep breath. "I'm not a very good girlfriend."

Leslie understood what it was trying to say. She put her arm around Byam.

"Sometimes," she said. "Mostly you do OK."

"I wasn't good at being an imugi either," said Byam. "I'm sorry I didn't tell you. It wasn't like the name. This, I didn't want you to know."

"Why not?"

"If you're an imugi, everyone knows you've failed," explained Byam. "It's like wearing a sign all the time saying 'I've been denied tenure.'"

This proved a bad comparison to make. Leslie winced.

"Sorry," said Byam. It paused. "It hurts. Knowing it wasn't enough, even when you gave it the best of yourself. But you get over it."

You get used to being a failure. It was too early to tell her that. Maybe Leslie would be lucky. Maybe she'd never have the chance to get used to it.

Leslie looked like she was thinking of saying something, but she changed her mind. She squeezed Byam's knee.

"I'm thinking of going into industry," said Leslie.

Byam had no idea what she meant.

"You would be great at that," it said, meaning it.

*　　*　　*

It turned out Byam was right: Leslie *was* great at working in industry, and her success meant they could move into a bigger place, near Leslie's sister. This worked out well—after Jean's divorce, they helped out with Eun-hye, who perplexed Byam by declaring it her favourite aunt.

A mere 10 years after Leslie had been denied tenure, she was saying it had been a blessing in disguise: "I would never have known there was a world outside academia."

They had stopped talking about dragons by then. Leslie had gotten over her fixation with them.

"*I'm* fixated?" she'd said. "You're the one who worked for thousands of years—"

"I don't want to talk about it," Byam had said. When this didn't work, it simply started vanishing whenever Leslie brought it up. Eventually, she stopped bringing it up.

Over time, she seemed to forget what Byam really was. Even Byam started to forget. When Leslie found her first white hair, Byam grew a few too, to make her feel better. Wrinkles were more challenging; it could never seem to get quite the right number. ("You look like a sage," said Leslie, when she was done laughing at its first attempt. "I'm only 48!")

Byam's former life receded into insignificance, the thwarted yearning of its earlier days nearly effaced.

The years went by quickly.

Leslie didn't talk much these days. It tired her, as everything tired her. She spent most of her time asleep, the rest looking out of the window. She didn't often tell Byam what was going through her head.

So it was a surprise when she said, without precursor:

"Why does the yeouiju matter so much?"

It took a moment before Byam understood what she was talking about. It hadn't thought of the cintamani in years. But then the surge of bitterness and longing was as fresh as ever, even in the midst of its grief.

"It's in the name, isn't it?" said Byam. "'The jewel that grants all wishes.'"

"Do you have a lot of wishes that need granting?"

Byam could think of some, but to tell Leslie about them would only distress her. It wasn't like Leslie *wanted* to die.

Before, Byam had always thought that humans must be used to dying, since they did it all the time. But now it had got to know them better, it saw they had no idea how to deal with it.

This was unfortunate, because Byam didn't know either.

"I guess I just always imagined I'd have one some day," it said. It tried to remember what it had felt like before it had given up on becoming a dragon and acquiring its own cintamani. "It was like... if I didn't have that hope, life would have no meaning."

Leslie nodded. She was still gazing out of the window. "You should try again."

"Let's not worry about it now—"

"You have thousands of years," said Leslie. "You shouldn't just give up." She looked Byam in the eye. "Don't you still want to be a dragon?"

Byam would have liked to say no. It was unfair of Leslie to awaken all these dormant feelings in it at a time when it already had too many feelings to contend with.

"Eun-hye should be here soon," it said. Leslie's niece was almost the same age Leslie had been when Byam had first come to her office with murder in its heart. Eun-hye had a child herself now, which still seemed implausible to Byam. "She's bringing Sam, won't that be nice?"

"Don't talk to me like I'm an old person," said Leslie, annoyed. "I'm dying, not *decrepit*. Come on, Byam. I thought repression was a human thing."

"That shows how much you know," said Byam. "When you've been a failure for 3,000 years, you get good at repressing things!"

"I'm just saying—"

"I don't know why you're—" Byam scrubbed its face. "Am I not good enough as I am?"

"Of course you're good enough," said Leslie. "If you're happy, then that's fine. But you should know you can be anything you want to be. That's all. I don't want you to let fear hold you back."

Byam was silent.

Leslie said, "I only want to know you'll be OK after I'm dead."

"I wish you'd stop saying that," said Byam.

"I know."

"I don't want you to die."

"I know."

Byam laid its head on the bed. If it closed its eyes it could almost pretend they were home, with the cat snoozing on Leslie's feet.

After a while it said, without opening its eyes, "What's your next form going to be?"

"I don't know," said Leslie. "We don't get told in advance." She grinned. "Maybe I'll be an imugi."

"Don't say such things," said Byam, aghast. "You haven't been that bad!"

This made Leslie laugh, which made her cough, so Byam called the nurse, and then Eun-hye came with her little boy, so there was no more talk of dragons, or cintamani, or reversing a pragmatic surrender to the inevitable.

That night the old dreams started again—the ones where Byam was a dragon. But they were a relief compared to the dreams it had been having lately.

It didn't mention them to Leslie. She would only say, "I told you so."

For a long moment after Byam woke, it was confused. The cintamani still hung in the air before it. Then it blinked and the orb revealed itself to be a lamp by the hospital bed.

Leslie was awake, her eyes on Byam. "Hey."

Byam wiped the drool from its cheek, sitting up. "Do you want anything? Water, or—"

"No," said Leslie. Her voice was thin, a mere thread of sound. "I was just watching you sleep like a creeper."

But then she paused. "There is something, actually."

"Yeah?"

"You don't have to."

"If there's anything I can give you," said Byam, "you'll get it."

Still Leslie hesitated.

"Could I see you?" she said finally. "In your true form, I mean."

There was a brief silence. Leslie said, "If you don't want to..."

"No, it's fine," said Byam. "Are you sure you won't be scared?"

Leslie nodded. "It'll still be you."

Byam looked around the room. There wasn't enough space for its real form, so it would have to make more space. But that was a simple magic.

It hadn't expected the sense of relief as it expanded into itself. It was as though for several decades it had been wearing shoes a size too small and had finally been allowed to take them off.

Leslie's eyes were wide.

"Are you OK?" said Byam.

"Yes," said Leslie, but she raised her hands to her face. Byam panicked, but before it could transform again, Leslie rubbed her eyes and said, "Don't change back! I haven't looked properly yet."

Her eyes were wet. She studied Byam as though she was trying to imprint the sight onto her memory.

"I'd look better with legs," said Byam shyly. "And antlers. And a bumpy forehead..."

"You're beautiful." Leslie touched Byam's side. Her hand was warm. "It was you, wasn't it? That day in the mountains."

Byam shrank. It said, its heart in its mouth, "You knew?"

"I've known for a while."

"Why didn't you say anything?"

"Guess I was waiting for you to tell me." Leslie gave Byam a half-smile. "You know me, I hate confrontation. Anything to avoid a fight."

"I should have told you," said Byam. "I wanted to, I just..." It had never been able to work out how to tell Leslie its original plan had been to devour her in an act of misdirected revenge.

Dumb, dumb, dumb. Byam could only blame itself for its failures.

"You should've told me." But Leslie didn't seem mad. Maybe she just didn't have the energy for it anymore.

"I'm sorry," said Byam. Leslie held out her hand and it slid closer, letting her run her hand over its scales. "How did you figure it out?"

Leslie shrugged. "It made sense. You were always there when I needed you." She patted Byam gently. "Can I ask for one more thing?"

"Anything," said Byam. It felt soft and sad, bursting at the seams with melancholy love.

"Promise me you won't give up," said Leslie. "Promise me you'll keep trying."

It was like going in for a kiss and getting slapped in the face. Byam went stiff, staring at Leslie in outrage. "That's fighting dirty!"

"You said anything."

Byam ducked its head, but it couldn't see any way out.

"I couldn't take it," it said miserably, "not now, not after... I'm not brave enough to fail again."

Leslie's eyes were pitiless.

"I know you are," she said.

One last time

THEY SCATTERED LESLIE'S ashes on the mountain where she had first seen Byam, which would have felt narcissistic if it hadn't been Leslie's own idea. When they were done, Byam said it wanted a moment alone.

No, it was all right, Eun-hye should stay with her mother. Byam was just going round the corner. It wanted to look at the landscape Leslie had loved.

Alone, it took off its clothes, folding them neatly and putting them on a stone. It shrugged off the constriction of the spell that had bound it for years.

It was like taking a deep breath of fresh air after coming up from the subway. For the first time Byam felt a rush of affection for its incomplete self—legless, hornless, orbless as it was. It had done the best it could.

Ascending was familiar, yet strange. Before, Byam had always striven to break free from the bonds of earth.

This time it was different. Byam seemed to be bringing the earth with it as it rose to meet the sky. Its grief did not fall away—it was closer than ever, a cheek laid against Byam's own.

Everything was much simpler than Byam had thought. Heaven and earth were not so far apart, after all—

"Look, Sam," said Eun-hye. She held her son up, pointing. "There's an imugi going to heaven! Wow!"

The child's small frowning face turned to the sky. Gravity dug its claws into Byam.

It was fruitless to resist. Still, Byam thrashed wildly, hurling itself upwards. Fighting the battle of its life, as though it had any chance of winning.

Leslie had believed in Byam. It had promised to be brave.

"Wow, it's so pretty!" continued Eun-hye's voice, much loved and incredibly unwelcome. "Your imo halmeoni loved imugi."

Sam was young, but he already had very definite opinions.

"No," he said distinctly.

"It's good luck to see an imugi," said Eun-hye. "Look, the imugi's dancing!"

"No!" said Sam, in the weary tone he adopted when adults were being especially dense. "Not imugi. It's a *dragon*."

For the first time in Byam's inglorious career, gravity surrendered. The resistance vanished abruptly. Byam bounced into the clouds like an arrow loosed from the bow.

"No, ippeuni," Eun-hye was explaining. "Dragons are different. Dragons have horns like a cow, and legs and claws, and long beards like Santa..."

"Got horns," said Sam.

Byam barely noticed the antlers, or the whiskers unfurling from its face, or the legs popping out along its body, each foot adorned with four gold-tipped claws.

Because there it was—the cintamani of its dreams, a matchless pearl falling through five-coloured clouds. It was like meeting a beloved friend in a crowd of strangers.

Byam rushed toward it, its legs (it had legs!) extended to catch the orb. It still half-believed it was going to miss, and the whole thing would come crashing down around its ears, a ridiculous daydream after all.

But the cintamani dropped right in its paw. It was lit from the inside, slightly warm to the touch. It was perfect.

Byam only realised it was shedding tears when the clouds started weeping along. It must have looked strange from the ground, the storm descending suddenly out of a clear blue sky.

Eun-hye shrieked, covering Sam's head. "We've got to find Byam imo!"

"It's getting heavy," said Jean. "The baby'll get wet. Get Nathan to bring the car round. I'll look for her."

"No, I will."

"I've got an umbrella!"

They were still fighting, far beneath Byam, as the palaces of heaven rose before it. Ranks of celestial fairies stood by the gate, waiting to welcome it. They had waited thousands of years. They could wait a little longer. Byam turned back, thinking to stop the storm. Anything to avoid a fight.

But the rain was thinning already. Through the clouds, Byam could see the child leaning out of his mother's arms, thwarting her attempts to keep him dry. He held his hands out to the rain, laughing.

With thanks to Miri Kim, Hana Lee, Perrin Lu, Kara Lee and Rachel Monte.

BLESSINGS
Naomi Novik

Naomi Novik (www.naominovik.com) is the acclaimed author of the *Temeraire* series and the Nebula-winning novel *Uprooted*, a fantasy influenced by the Polish fairy tales of her childhood, and, *Spinning Silver*, a retelling of Rumpelstiltskin. She is a founder of the Organization for Transformative Works and the Archive of Our Own. The story that follows originally appeared in *Uncanny*.

"GRACE," THE DRUNK fairy said, "is by far the best of the blessings."

She was drunk because her hostess, who herself had been blessed with hospitality—and a reasonably wealthy husband—had spent the months before her first child's birth in a fever of preparations, determined to obtain at least one blessing for her own offspring. She had brewed her own fairy wine out of blackberries and wild elderflowers that she and her ladies had picked in the woods, pricking many a finger in the process, and she had coaxed her husband to keep hunting until he managed to get three dozen pure white rabbits—"In winter!" he'd complained in exasperation—which had been stewed and baked into an elaborate pie. On the side of the room, the servants could be observed making the preparations to serve the final course, a fine white cake using a recipe of her own devising, made from fresh-laid eggs and newly churned butter, and dressed with candied flowers and even a ring of preserved orange slices. Even by fairy standards, it was an exceptional meal.

The fairy repeated, "By *far*," the remark delivered as a challenge, as she sat down again somewhat wobbly at the high table, and held out her wineglass to be refilled: she had just finished bestowing that very blessing on the small girl in the crib at the head of the room, and now could sit back to her meal in full enjoyment, with the smug consciousness of having amply repaid her hostess. Grace might not have been the most dramatic of the blessings, but it was indeed highly valued, being exceptionally open to interpretation, and rarely given to any child of such low rank—the mother was the daughter of a mere knight, and the father, despite his reasonable wealth, only a baron.

The five other fairies scowled at her. They too were all drunk and well fed, and the meal in their bellies was taking on the sour heaviness of an unpaid debt. They had all brought trinkets for the baby, of course, all the gift that could formally be expected by a low nobleman—which was why six of them had been invited in hopes of getting at least one blessing—but the feast had also exceeded what could formally be expected for their having deigned to grace the occasion. They could hardly refuse the cake, either—and didn't want to—and would have a lingering sense of a favor owed.

"Nonsense," a second fairy said. (I cannot, of course, tell you their names.) "Nonsense! Grace, for the child of a baron! Putting the cart before the horse." She pushed her own chair back and heaved herself out of it, marched up to the crib, and announced loudly, "Ever may this child's hands run bright with gold, and all the coffers of her house swell with riches!" She returned to the table and surveyed the others with a smugly superior lift to her chin. "Now *that's* a proper blessing."

She too held her glass out for more wine as a low pleased murmuring went around the room. Two blessings made a remarkable haul for a child of this rank, and wealth in particular was rarely given. It was too valuable to those who didn't have it—who often couldn't afford to properly feast fairies anyway—and too redundant to those who'd acquired it without mystical help. But at this rank of nobility, nothing could have been more ideal. The mother was beaming and delighted, already thinking of the excellent match her twice-blessed daughter would surely make, and the father not only delighted but relieved; he'd spent considerably more than he'd wanted to on the celebration, and he'd been worrying about how he'd repay the coin he'd borrowed to do it. But no one now would hesitate to lend money to him, and at very good rates. Even the guests smiled sincerely, rather than with envy; the parents, not being very important, had invited their friends and not their enemies to the christening of their child. The occasion had gone from ordinarily happy to auspicious, and all the company were pleased to be present. The musicians struck up another song with enthusiasm—rightfully expecting better tips—as the happy father waved a hand to them.

"Oh, wealth's all well and good," said the third, from out of the depths of her dark cloak. She was a shadowed fairy, and rather alarming even to her companions, but she lived nearer the father's house than any of the others, in a deep cave somewhere up in the mountains. The baron had known better than to slight her, of course, but his lady had gone beyond that, and sent the invitation with a personal note written in her own hand that they very much hoped to have the pleasure of her company, and a small package of sweetmeats. It was not the traditional sort of courting sent to shadowed fairies—the kind of lord who really wanted their attendance was more likely to send a gift of the knucklebones of plague victims—but the sweetmeats had been carefully made with rotted walnuts and pig's blood, and at the feast, the fairy had discreetly been served a plate of raw calves' liver dressed with a sauce of nightshade on a plate of tarnished silver. She had refused the fairy wine, but the hostess had quickly had a word with her steward, and a great goblet of steaming beef blood fresh from a newly slaughtered ox had been brought to the table, laced heavily with old brandy, and the fairy had drunk the entire thing down.

She now covered her mouth and belched out a thin trail of smoke. "Well and good indeed," she went on, "until someone takes it from you," and rose from the table in turn.

A hush descended as she went to the baby, her footsteps ringing ominously loud, and the parents began to look anxious: even if she hadn't been a shadowed fairy, three blessings was a little inappropriate for anything other than royalty. They looked still more anxious when the fairy stretched out a grey withered hand over the crib and intoned, "Let power come easily to her hand and there remain, and to her come dominion over the realms of men!"

The hush became silence. Three blessings was extravagant anyway, and power was a gift bestowed far more rarely even than wealth, as it involved a significant risk for the fairy in question. If two people blessed with the gift of power ever confronted one another, one fairy gift or the other would likely be proven false. (While I am not entirely certain what would happen to the losing fairy in this situation, I am assured it would be unpleasant.)

The remaining fairies could have left things well enough alone here, and should have, but as the shadowed fairy slouched deep into her seat again, she issued a small snort. "There, what's better than *that?* I'm surprised none of you twittering lot slapped a pretty face on her."

Fairies enjoy being taunted roughly as much as do boys of twelve, and respond with as much maturity. The fourth fairy—who had just polished off her eighth glass of wine—sneered in heavy sarcasm, "Why would anyone do that? She'd be better off ugly as you instead!"

She instantly covered her mouth as the whole room gasped, but it was too late; the gift had flown. The mother made an abortive move towards the crib, her face falling, and the fairy looked abashed and guilty beneath the many censorious looks thrown her way. Looking around for a solution, she pointedly elbowed the fifth fairy, a spring fairy who would be half-asleep for another two months anyway and under the influence was snoring gently away with her mound of grey-brown hair, dressed elaborately with vines of ivy, beginning to slide comprehensively off her head. "Wha?" the fifth fairy said.

"There's nothing like being *strikingly* ugly," the fourth fairy said, urgently, a hint that would have worked just fine on a fairy about half as drunk as this one.

"Go on, listen to you!" the soused fairy said groggily. "Strength! That's the best of them, everyone knows. Strength to the babe!" she added firmly, groping for her glass and toasting it in the crib's direction vigorously enough to splatter.

There was another round of gasps, broken up this time by tittering. The shadowed fairy shook with malicious cackles and the fourth fairy, glad to shift guilt over, snatched up a napkin and swatted the fifth, abusing her as the ivy came off the rest of the way. "You green-headed leaf peeper! Strength, for a girl! Get under the table with you!" as the first two fairies looked on and shook their heads in righteous disapproval.

Her twin sister, sitting on the other side, took offense both at the attack on her sister and at *leaf peeper*. "Much you should talk, handing out ugliness!" she said. "What's wrong with strength? Strong let her be, and see which does her more good, our gift or yours!"

*   *   *

"No, THANK YOU," Magda said, graciously, and tuned out the formalities as the very relieved duke's son looked up—the first time he'd actually looked her in the face—and begged her to reconsider.

A doubled gift made all the others lean towards it; she couldn't have any of the ugliness of ill-health, only the ugliness of brute strength. That was the only thing anyone saw when they looked at her, that she could pick them up and break them in half like giants did when mounted knights got too close, shelling them like lobsters. None of her features were ugly enough to stand out, none were nice to look at, and all together they made a bad painting without enough colors. But the proposals came anyway: she was destined to be rich and powerful, and she had six fairy godmothers looking after her interests.

She repeated her refusal, he gratefully promised not to trouble her any longer, and took himself away in a hurry. She had been left alone in the garden with him; as soon as he left, she tossed the embroidery hoop aside onto the bench and went to the back wall. She'd left her old bow and spare quiver there, tucked at the base behind a shrub. She slung them on, then jumped for the top, caught it easily and pulled herself easily over, and was free from her chaperone for the rest of the afternoon, which was the reason she'd agreed to entertain the proposal in the first place. She felt a little sorry for having alarmed the duke's son, who'd been decently polite about his courting, but at least she hadn't made him worry for long, and her mother would have made a fuss, otherwise.

She didn't risk her freedom by going to the stables for a horse. She jumped the moat behind the garden wall and jogged along the dusty track up into the Blackstrap Mountains on foot instead. It was a nice autumn afternoon, and only seven miles or so. It had been almost a year since the last time she'd managed to escape—her mother had kept closer reins on her since her sixteenth birthday—but she still knew the way. She stopped in the orchards to pick a good apple for herself to munch, and a few wormy and wizened ones to tuck into her good skirt, which she'd already tied up around her waist.

"I brought you some spoiled apples, Godmama," she said, poking into the mountain cave. "Withered and worm-eaten on the branch."

The shadowed fairy grunted in approval from the depths of the cave where she was stirring something noxious. "Put them on the bench there. What have you been doing with yourself all this time?"

"Courting," Magda said, succinctly, folding herself down onto the floor so she wouldn't knock her head on the roof of the cave.

"Oh, courting. Well?"

"I sent one away today," Magda said. "I don't remember his name. The Duke of Edgebarren's oldest son."

"Oh, a duke," the fairy said dismissively. "Don't you bother with a duke. He'll give himself the credit of it, when he gets anywhere, even if it's all your doing. Make it a knight or make it a king, that's my advice to you—if you do mean to saddle yourself with any of them."

She peered out of the hood, making it a question; her face was hidden too deep in the cowl to make out her features, but the cave mouth made a gleam of reflection in her eyes.

Magda considered: the duke's son made seventeen. Her mother was growing anxious, but Magda hadn't seen much to choose from among them. The ones whose ambitious fathers had sent them, who mumbled through their proposals without looking at her at all; the ones who put on false smiles as they looked up at her and pretended they liked feeling the weight of her hand in theirs as they led her through a dance. There *had* been a knight, and there *had* been a king, and neither of them saw anything to like when they looked at her, because the only strength they wanted in their house was their own.

Well, it had been a blessing, after all.

"I don't," she said, with decision.

"Just as well," the fairy said, nodding, and put down her stirring ladle. "You'd better come into the back, then. You'll be wanting a sword."

MEAT AND SALT AND SPARKS
Rich Larson

Rich Larson (richwlarson.tumblr.com) was born in Galmi, Niger, has studied in Rhode Island and worked in the south of Spain, and now lives in Ottawa, Canada. He is the author of *Annex* and *Cypher*, as well as over a hundred short stories—some of the best of which can be found in his collection *Tomorrow Factory*. His award-winning work has been translated into Polish, Czech, French, Italian, Vietnamese and Chinese. Besides writing, he enjoys traveling, learning languages, playing soccer, watching basketball, shooting pool, and dancing kizomba.

"Doesn't look like a killer, does she," Huxley remarks.

Cu shrugs a hairy shoulder. To her, all humans look like killers. What her partner means is that the woman in the interrogation room does not look physically imposing. She is small and skinny and wearing a pale pink dress with a mood-display floral pattern; currently the buds are all sealed up tight, reflecting her arms wrapped around her knees and her chin tucked to her chest.

The interrogation room has made a similar read of her mood, responding by projecting a soothing beach front with flour-white sand and blue-green waves. The woman doesn't seem to be aware of her holographic surroundings. Her eyes, small and dark in puddles of running makeup, stare off into space. Every few seconds her left hand reaches up to her ear, where a wireless graft winks inactive red. Apart from that, she's motionless.

Cu holds her tablet steady and jabs the playback icon enlarged for her chimpanzee fingers. She crinkles her eyes to watch as the woman from the interrogation room, Elody Polle, bounces through the subway station with her dress in full bloom. With a bland smile on her face, she walks up behind a balding man, pulls the gun from her bag, pulls the trigger, remembers the safety is on, takes it off and pulls the trigger again.

"So calm," Huxley says, tearing open a bag from the vending unit. "She was like that the whole time, apparently, up until they stuck her in interrogation. Then she lost her shit a bit." He grins and shovels baked seaweed into his mouth. Huxley is almost always grinning.

Cu flicks to the footage from interrogation: Elody Polle sobbing, pounding her fists against the locked door. She looks over at her partner and taps her ear, signs *Faraday shield?*

"Yeah," Huxley says, letting the bag fall to his lap to sign back. "No receiving or transmitting from interrogation. As soon as she lost contact with that little graft, she panicked. The police ECM should have shut it down as soon as she was in custody. Guess it slipped past somehow."

Acting under instructions, Cu suggests.

Huxley see-saws his open hands. "Could be. She's got no obvious connection to the victim. We'll need to have a look at the thing."

Cu scrolls through the perpetrator's file. Twenty years' worth of information strained from social media feeds and the odd government application has been condensed to a brief. Elody Polle, born in Toronto, raised in Seattle, rode a scholarship to Princeton to study ethnomusicology before dropping out in '42, estranged from most friends and family for over a year despite having moved back to a one-room flat in North Seattle. No priors. No history of violence. No record of antisocial behavior.

Cu checks the live feed from the interrogation room. *Heart-rate down,* she signs, tucking the tablet under her armpit. *Time to talk.*

Huxley looks down into the chip bag. "These are terrible." He shoves one last handful into his mouth, crumbs snagging in his wiry red beard, then seals the bag and puts it neatly in his jacket pocket. He licks the salt off his palms on the way to the interrogation room.

The precinct is near empty, but there are still curious faces peering from the cubicles as they pass. Cu doesn't come to the precinct often. Huxley had to beg her to put in an appearance. She prefers working from her apartment, where everything is the right size and shape and there are no curious faces.

The outside of the interrogation room looks far less pleasant than the interior: it's a concrete cube with a thick steel door that seals shut once they pass through it.

Cu squats down a respectable distance away from the perpetrator, haunches sinking through the holographic sand onto padded floor. Huxley pulls up a seat right beside her.

"Good evening, Ms. Polle," he says. "My name's Al. You doing okay in here?"

Elody Polle sucks in a trembling breath, and says nothing.

"This is my partner, Cu," Huxley continues. Elody's eyes travel over to her, but don't register even a hint of surprise. "We need to get a better idea of what happened earlier, and why. Can you help us with that?"

Elody says nothing.

Cu takes a closer look at the earpiece. The graft is puffy and slightly inflamed. A DIY job, maybe. *Ask her about the piece,* she signs. *We would hate to remove it.*

"Cu's curious about that wireless," Huxley says. "So am I. In the subway footage, the way you're bobbing your head, it almost looks like someone was talking you through the whole thing. Want to tell us about that?"

A flicker crosses Elody's face. Progress.

"Because if you don't, we'll have to remove the earpiece and have a look for ourselves," Huxley says. "As much as we'd hate to ruin that lovely graft job."

Elody claps her hand protectively over her ear. "Don't you fucking dare!" She tries to shout the words, but her voice is hoarse, flaked away to almost a whisper. As if she hasn't spoken aloud in months.

Cu pulls up the speech synth on her tablet and taps out eight laborious letters, one question mark.

"Echogirl?" the electronic voice blurts.

Elody's eyes winch wide. As she looks over at Cu, her cheek gives a nervous twitch.

Huxley's furry red brows knit together. He signs, *what the fuck is that.*

Echogirl, echoboy, Cu signs. *Use an earpiece, eyecam. Rent themselves out to someone who says where to go, what to do, what to say.*

Thought that was. Huxley's hands falter. "A kink, sort of thing," he says aloud, and Elody's face flushes angry red.

"It's a lifestyle," she says. "She told me you wouldn't understand. Nobody does."

"Is *she* going to come get you out of this mess?" Huxley demands.

"Of course she is." Elody purses her lips, turns away.

Huxley turns to Cu. *Take the earpiece?* he signs. *Or what?*

Cu scratches under her ribs, watching a tremor move through Elody's hunched shoulders. *Offer turn off the Faraday,* she signs.

Huxley nods, then turns back to address Elody. "I bet she won't," he says. "I bet you a twenty, and half a bag of chips. Well." He pats his coat pocket and the bag rustles. "A third. Yeah, in fact, I bet the last thing she's ever going to say to you was pull the trigger. Should we turn off the shielding and see?"

Elody turns back, eyes shiny with tears. "Yes," she whispers. "Please, I need to hear her voice, I need..." Her tone is eager, but Cu can see uncertainty in the tightening of her eyelids, the bulge of her lower lip.

Huxley makes a show of rapping on the door, telling them to turn off the Faraday. There's a sudden subtraction from the white noise as the generator cuts out, then Huxley's phone starts vibrating his pocket with updates.

Cu keeps her attention on Elody, who has her face upturned now as if waiting to feel sunshine: eyes shut, eyelashes trembling, breath sucked in.

"Baby? Are you there?" she whispers. "Are you there? Are you there?"

Her bland smile is back in place. Seconds tick by. Then doubt moves in a slow ripple across her features. Her smile trembles, smooths out, trembles again. Finally, her face crumples and a huge sob shudders through her body.

Cu taps five letters into the speech synth. "Sorry," her tablet bleats. Then she turns to Huxley and signs *get the piece*. He nods, thumbs the order into his phone. When they exit the interrogation room, two officers are already waiting to come in: one carrying a black kit, the other snapping on surgical gloves.

Cu hears Elody start to wail just before the door clanks shut behind them.

"That... echogirl thing." Huxley's hands piece the new sign together. *You've thought about it, eh?*

I've done it, she signs back. *Good to walk in the city without crowds. Just never asked them to shoot someone.*

*　　*　　*

As SOON AS she's back in the apartment, Cu dials up the heat and humidity and takes off her clothes. Some days she doesn't mind wearing the carefully tailored black suit. Today she hates it. She leaves it pooled on the floor and takes a flying leap at her climbing wall; the shifting handholds don't shift fast enough and she's up to the rafters in an instant.

Cu was specific with the contractors about leaving the rafters exposed. She's added to them since, welding in more polymer cables and struts of wood, a criss-crossed webbing that spans the vaulted ceiling like a canopy. The design consultant, an excitable architect from Estonia, suggested artificial trees sprouting hydroponic moss. But Cu has no use for green things. She grew up in dull gray and antiseptic white.

Clambering into her hammock, Cu looks out the wide one-way window, watching the sun sink into Puget Sound. She enjoys looking at water so long as it's far away. The view is expensive, but Cu can afford it. She was awarded damages after the personhood trial, enough for a lifetime of this particular view, enough so she can stay in here forever without needing to earn a penny more. She would go insane, though.

So she works the cases. She was always drawn to crime as a dissection of human nature, the breakdown of motive and consequence. A window into the subtle differences between her mind and all the minds around her. When she first applied for police training with the SPD, it was viewed as a joke. Her acceptance, a publicity grab.

But in the years since, they've realized she sees things most humans miss. Cu pulls on her custom-fitted smartgloves, one for each hand and a third for her left foot, and leans back in the hammock. The ceiling screen above her hums to life. New details flit onto the case file, and there's a message waiting from Huxley.

Thanks for coming down in person, the bossman's been up my ass about it. Wanted fresh footage for the promo kit. Hoping they shop out my beer belly.

Cu swipes it aside and reaches for the tech report on the perp's earpiece. The text flows across the ceiling in slow waves, a motion programmed to help her eyes track it easier. There was no salvageable audio data. Not from Elody and not from whoever was speaking to her. But there is usage data to confirm that Elody was receiving a call from a masked address at the time of the murder.

By the look of it, Elody had been in that same call for just under six months.

Cu moves backward through the log, perplexed. There are small gaps, a few hours here and there, but Elody had been in near 24/7 communication with her client for half a year preceding the murder.

Cu tries to imagine it: a voice whispering in her ear when she woke up, telling her what to do, where to go, what to say, and whispering still as she fell asleep. All of it culminating in Elody Polle walking up behind a man in a subway and executing him in broad daylight.

She flips the case file over to see the victim's profile again. The balding man was named Nelson J. Huang. A biolab businessman, San Antonio-based, in the city for a conference. It's possible that someone with a personal vendetta knew he would be in Seattle and began laying the groundwork for his murder at the hands of Elody Polle six months in advance.

It's more likely that he was selected at random from the crowd, so someone half the world away could experience homicide vicariously before abandoning her mentally-unstable echogirl.

A call from Huxley jangles across the screen. She pops it open. Her partner is walking down a neon-lit street, sooty brick wall behind his head. "Hey, Cu," he says. "Busy?"

Sometimes he asks it to needle her; this time it's because he's distracted. Cu shakes her head.

"The techies are still trying to track that address, but I doubt they'll have much luck," he says, stopping at a light. "Whoever it is, they did a good job wiping up afterwards. No audio data." He looks around and starts walking again, bristly red beard bobbing up and down. "But before this client, she had another one for around two months. Figured I would swing past and see him on my way home. Well. Sort of see him."

Where? Cu signs.

"A party," Huxley says, his grin notching a little wider. "So, if you're not busy, you should come. Said you've done this before, right?"

Cu watches as he digs an earbud out of his pocket and taps it active, worms it into place. Then the slip-in eyecam: he rolls his eye around afterward and blinks away a few tears. The perspective jumps from his phone camera to his eyecam and all of a sudden she's seeing what he sees. A bright red door in a grimy brick facade, no holos or even a physical sign above it. Through the earbud, she hears the dim pulse of music, synthesized drums.

I hate parties, Cu signs.

"Good thing it's also work," Huxley says.

Cu settles back in her hammock and watches his pale hand push open the door.

THE INTERIOR IS dim-lit, noisy, full of bodies. People are dancing—Cu can enjoy rhythm, but the hard pulse of the drums unnerves some deep part of her, sounding too angry, too much like a warning. People are drinking—Cu tried it once, but the warm dizziness reminded her of the sedatives they used to give her. When she related as much to Huxley, he told her she wasn't *even legal yet, technically,* and that she would like it when she was older.

It's a typical party, apart from the fact that every single person in the room is wearing an earpiece.

"Echo, echo, echo," Huxley mutters. "The client's name is Daudi. Judging by rental history, he's probably a blonde." He takes out his phone and Cu watches his thumb move, sending her a file. It pops up in the corner of her screen, unfurling a list of Daudi's rental preferences. She searches the crowd for possible matches as Huxley moves into the room. There's a woman passing out small plastic tubes; Huxley takes one. Cu inspects it as he juggles it in his palm.

"Smooths things out," the woman says, then something inaudible after.

"Fuck's this, Cu?" Huxley asks.

Cu signs her response in the air above her hammock; the smartgloves turn it into text in the corner of Huxley's eye. *Some echoes use a drug to weaken willpower.* She has to type out the name. *Chempliance.*

"Elody's tox screen was clean, right?" Huxley says, twirling the tube in his fingers.

Wouldn't matter anyway, she signs. *Drug is an MDMA derivative. Suggestibility is all placebo effect.*

Huxley's hand disappears, either dropping the tube or pocketing it. Cu doesn't bother to ask. She keeps scanning as he circulates through the party, looking for someone who meets Daudi's profile. Huxley mostly keeps his gaze moving, but occasionally sticks on a particularly symmetrical face or muscular body.

They spot two drinkers huddled together at a glass-topped table, skin lit red by the Smirnoff advertisement playing under their elbows, one reaching to stroke the other's thigh. The man is dressed in an artfully gashed suit and his eyes are glazed with chempliance. The woman has a dress that flickers transparent to the rhythm of an accelerating heartbeat. Both of them move slowly, as if they're underwater. Something about the woman's face is familiar.

Cu pulls up the file, checks Daudi's preferences against the pair. *That's him,* she signs. *Bar.*

Huxley's vision bobs as he nods his head. He walks over and inserts himself between the couple. "My turn to talk. Get lost, fucko."

When the man doesn't move fast enough, Huxley seizes his collar and shoves him off the stool. He stumbles, catches himself. He sways on his feet, listening to the instructions in his ear, looking confused.

"You got some nerve, barging in here like that," he says, with the intonation a little off.

"This isn't playtime," Huxley says. "It's police business. Walk."

The man spins on his heel and shuffles backward toward the dance floor, feet slip-sliding.

Huxley shakes his head. "These fucking people, Cu," he mutters. "That's a moonwalk, if you were wondering. Does it pretty good."

"I like your boy," the woman says, in a throaty voice that sounds slightly forced. She crosses her legs; one hand moves to pull up the hem of her dress, then stutters to a halt. Instead she starts tracing her fingertip along her thigh. "He's not doped up at all, is he? He really sells the character. Must like it."

"I'm not a meat puppet, shithead, I'm a cop," Huxley says, sitting down on the vacated stool.

Cu knows he does like it, though—the character. Sometimes it disturbs her, how easily he slips in and out of it.

Huxley's hand moves off-screen, digging into his pocket, and comes out again with the badge. Even in the days of cheap and perfect 3D-printing, something about the physical object still commands respect. Cu imagines pop culture nostalgia to be the main factor.

The woman, who was absently running her fingers through her blonde hair, stops and leans forward. "I'm fully licensed for sex work, and I don't use any restricted drugs," she says, voice no longer throaty.

"I believe you," Huxley says. "I'm here to talk to Daudi, though. So just keep, you know, doing what you're doing."

The woman leans back, recomposing. Cu takes the opportunity to study her more closely. She has the same angled jaw as Elody, the same straight nose, and her hair is almost the same shade.

"Talk to me about what, pray tell?" the woman asks. "I've never been interrogated by a cop before. This is so exciting." But her voice is flat as she repeats the lines now, and her eyes dart toward the exit.

"I want to know about your business with this woman," Huxley says, bringing up a headshot on his phone. "Elody Polle."

"Oh, yes," the woman says, looking down at the photo. "That was me. Isn't she perfect? Not that you aren't pretty, dear. Very pretty." She rolls her eyes after the last bit.

"You rented her for quite a while," Huxley says. "Then she got picked up by another client. Why did you two stop, uh, seeing each other?"

"Is she alright?" the woman asks. "Is Elody okay?"

"She's relaxing on the beach," Huxley says. "She's fine. Answer my question, Daudi."

"With pleasure," the woman says, with no hint of pleasure. "I was inadequate for her. I couldn't give her what she wanted."

"Financially?"

"No, no, no," the woman says. "Elody was a purist. The money was incidental for her. What she wanted, was to go full-time. Twenty-four-seven. And there was only one person who could really do that for her. Baby."

"You're calling *me* baby, or...?"

"No, no, no. Baby is one of us. She or he or they popped up a couple years ago. Did about a hundred rentals, spread out all over the world, and asked for some weird shit. Enough so people started talking, you know, on the deep forums." The woman pauses for a breath, looking mildly annoyed; Daudi must be speaking faster than she can keep pace with. "Not sexual shit. That's the thing. Just weird. Baby had clients staring at lamps for hours straight. Opening and closing their hands. Sometimes just lying there with their eyes shut, not doing anything."

The details startle Cu. They remind her of her first experience with an echo, directing them slowly, carefully, trying to not just see and hear but *feel* what they were experiencing. Trying to feel human for a little while.

And the name? Cu signs.

"And the name?" Huxley asks.

"Baby was really innocent," the woman says, then gives a modulated shrug. "Couldn't speak so well at first, either. So there's a lot of theories. Some people thought Baby really was just a little kid in hospice somewhere, maybe paralyzed, burning through their parents' money—and trust me, Baby dumped a fuckload of money the past two years. Or some ultra-wealthy mogul recovering from a stroke. Or a team of people, doing some kind of, I don't know, some kind of performance art."

"Well," Huxley says. "Baby grew up. Elody Polle recently murdered a man, and we don't think she picked her own target."

"Oh my god," the woman says flatly. "Oh, my fucking god." She looks uncomfortable. Lowers her voice. "He's crying." She pauses. "Oh, Elody, Elody."

"So, how do we find Baby?" Huxley asks.

The woman sits there for a minute, maybe waiting for Daudi's sobs to subside. "You don't," she finally says. "Baby comes to you."

"I really doubt Baby will come to us knowing she's an accessory to murder," Huxley says. "But we'll be in touch, Daudi. Might get you to talk to Elody for us. She's not saying much."

"I would be happy to do that," the woman says. "Elody was one of my favorites. My very favorites."

"Yeah, I got that." Huxley stands up from the bar. "Anything else, Cu?"

Cu shakes her head. She'll need time to think it all through.

Huxley hesitates. "Hey, uh, echogirl. Do cams, or something. These people are control freaks. They'll suck you right in."

The woman blinks, caught off-guard. "They're not so bad," she says. "Most of them just wish they were someone else."

"Huh." Huxley slides the stool back in and makes his way to the exit. He slips his eyecam out and Cu's screen goes blank. "Enough work for the night," comes his disembodied voice. "Got to be honest, Cu, I don't like the odds on this one. Baby could be some joker on the other side of the planet, you know? We can send this thing up top, to cyberdefense and them, but unless this was the start of a mass killing spree I don't think it'll get any traction. Sometimes the asshole just gets away with being an asshole." He pauses. "Besides. It was Elody who pulled the trigger."

Cu considers it. She knows the department doesn't like spending unnecessary time on cases with a clear perpetrator. They are always more interested in the who than the why. Since there is no audio recording of Baby's call, they might want to strike it from the case file entirely. It would make things much simpler.

You might be right, she signs. *Goodnight.*

"You know, I tried sleeping in a hammock when I was in Salento," he says. "Nearly wrecked my spine. Anyway. Night."

Cu ends the call and lies back, staring up at her distorted reflection in the blank screen. She's about to clap it off when a new message arrives. No subject, one line only.

You Are Welcome, CU0824.

CU DOESN'T SLEEP after that. She can't. Not after seeing the serial number of the cage where she spent the first twelve years of her life. It plunges her back into memories: the smell of disinfectant and cold metal and sometimes her own piss, the smeary plastic wall that squeezed inward as she grew, the distinct V-shaped crack in it, the smooth feel of the smartglass cube that she cradled in her lap, that she sat and stared into for hours and hours and hours and hours—

She can feel her chest tightening with her oldest variety of panic. She tries to breathe deeply and remember PTSD mitigation techniques. Instead she remembers the succession of men and women in soft white smocks who fed her and played with her but never stayed with her in the dark, and never stopped the man with the needle from drugging her for the nightmare room.

For a long time Cu had no name for the place where they cut her without her feeling it, where they tracked her eyes and fed filaments through holes in her skull. But she learned the word nightmare from her cube, watching a man with metal hands hunt down his children, and the moniker made sense. By the time she learned about surgery, neural enhancement, possible cures for degenerative brain disease, the name was already cemented.

For the last few years she went to the nightmare room willingly and offered them her wrist for the anaesthetic drip. In exchange, they were kinder to her. They took restrictions off her cube—some she had already worked around herself—so more of the net was available to her. They let her walk in certain corridors of the facility. After a week of asking them, they even let her see her mother.

Going back to that particular memory wrenches her apart. Cu had spent the previous day scrambling back and forth in her cage, filled to bursting with nervous energy, rearranging her belongings. She signed for a soapy cloth and scrubbed the walls and ceiling with it, climbing to get the dusty places the autocleaner never reached. She knew from the cube, which she painstakingly positioned in the exact center of the cage, that mothers valued tidiness.

But when they brought her, it was nothing like the cube. Her mother was bent and graying, fur shaved off in patches, surgical scars suturing her body, and she was angry. She jabbered and hooted, spittle flying from her mouth. Cu tried to sign to her, but received no reply. Cu tried to offer her food; her mother seized the orange from her and made a feint, teeth bared, that sent Cu scurrying back to the furthest corner of her cage.

"Tranq wore off sooner than we thought," one of the women in white said. "We did warn you. We did tell you she wouldn't be like you. You're unique."

Cu signed *take her away, take her away, take her away.* And even for hours after they did, she stayed there in the corner, trembling with something that began as fear, then turned to grief, then finally became a deep cold rage.

She feels that rage now, sitting on the rafters in the dark. Whoever dredged up that serial number is playing a game with her, the same way they played games with her in the cage. She could send the masked address to the precinct and have them try to break it down for a trace, but she doubts they'll have any more luck with that than they did with the earpiece.

Instead she puzzles over the three words: *You Are Welcome.* Cu has never felt welcome. It must be meant in the other way. It must mean that Baby has done something she views as a favor to Cu.

Cu opens the case file again, but instead of Elody's profile, she goes to the victim's. Nelson J. Huang, the bio-business consultant to Descorp's San Antonio branch, fifty-seven years old. Initial attempt to notify next of kin was met with an automated reply from a defunct address.

Personal details are scarce: he's registered as a North Korean immigrant, which explains the lack of social media documentation, and lived a private life first in Castroville and later Calaveras. Unmarried, no children. Cu looks closely at the photos, comparing them to the morgue shots of Nelson's corpse. It seems he aged badly over the last decade of his life. The shape of his body is different in subtle ways.

It wouldn't be the first time North Korean immigrant status has been used to excuse the skeleton details of a fake identity. Cu settles in beneath her screen, pulling up police-grade facial recognition software, Descorp employee databases. She starts to search.

One hour becomes two becomes four, like cells dividing. Her wrists and fingers start to ache from swiping and zooming and signing; she switches one smartglove to her foot and continues. It would be easier with Huxley helping. Huxley has a way of bullying through bureaucracy, through the kind of red tape that is keeping her out of Descorp's consultant list. Cu has to work around it.

But she doesn't want Huxley for this. She wants to do it alone, with nobody watching. After a dozen dead ends, Cu rolls out of the hammock. She uses an aqueous spray on her stinging eyes. Stretches her limbs, swings from one side of the apartment to the other. Hanging upside down, toes curled tight around a stretch of cable, blood fizzing down into her head, she listens to her pulse crash against her eardrums until she can hardly stand it.

Back to the hammock, back to the screen. Now Cu comes at it from the other direction: she searches for the Blackburn Uplift Project. Illegal experiments carried out on thirty-seven bonobo and forty lowland chimpanzees between 2036 and 2048 with the aim of cognitive augmentation. Cu knows the details. She's tried to forget them. But now she delves into them again, reading reports of her own escape, of the fragmentation of the Blackburn company and the arrests made in the wake of the scandal.

From this end, the facial recognition 'ware finally finds something. Cu's stomach twists against itself. Nelson J. Huang has the same face as disgraced Blackburn executive Sun Chau. She looks at the match, comparing the morgue shot to the mugshot. She never saw Chau in person during the trials, but she knows his name too well.

It was Chau who signed the termination order on the thirty-seven bonobo and thirty-nine lowland chimpanzees that failed to respond to the uplift treatments.

He was sentenced, of course, but served minimal time. Cu did not seek details on his imprisonment or release. She tries to think of Blackburn as little as possible. But clearly someone else did not forgive or forget Sun Chau, even after he relocated with a new identity. A wild thought churns to the surface of her mind. The way Daudi described Baby, the way she used the echoes not so differently from how Cu herself first did. Now this serial number, dredged from her past.

She knows the other Blackburn subjects in her facility were terminated. She saw their ashes in sealed bags, saw the hips and skulls too big for cremation being ground up. But there were other labs, branches of the project hidden in other countries. Maybe not all of their subjects were terminated. And maybe not all of them failed to respond to the uplift treatments.

The possibility thumps hard in her chest. From the time she was old enough to understand it, the scientists had always told her she was the only one. That she was unique. That she was alone. Now the idea of another individual like her, or even more than one, is so momentous she can barely breathe.

She makes herself breathe.

Maybe she is spinning sleep-deprived delusions. The facts are that Sun Chau was in Seattle using a false identity, and that he was murdered by the machinations of someone who knows about Cu and about her past. Anything more is conjecture. But she can't shake the image of others like her in hiding, or still in captivity, exacting their revenge by proxy. *You Are Welcome.*

Cu goes back to the message, reading it over and over again. Then, once her hands aren't trembling, she signs out one of her own: *I want to talk.*

The reply is almost instantaneous. No words, just coordinates. She drags them onto her map and sees the aerial view of a loading bay, automated cranes frozen midway through their work. She checks the time. 3:32 AM. A clandestine meeting on the docks in the middle of the night. Maybe they watched the same shows on their cube that she did.

Cu estimates travel time and composes a brief message to Huxley, tagged with a delay so it will only send if she's unable to cancel it at 5:32 AM. This is no longer a case. This is something more important.

She drops down from the rafters. She puts her suit back on, adrenaline making her fumble even the oversized clasps designed for her fingers. She strips off her smartgloves and replaces them with the black padded ones that keep her from scraping her knuckles raw on the pavement. Finally, she takes the modified handgun and holster from the hook by the door and straps them on.

Cu always finds it difficult to leave the apartment. She hates the stares and the winking eyecams and the bulb flash of photos taken in passing. It always sets her nerves singing. She draws in deep breaths, reminding herself that the streets will be nearly empty and that she should be more concerned about what she finds on the docks.

She orders a car with her tablet, then takes the handgun from its holster and breaks it down. Reassembles it. The trigger fits perfectly to the crook of her finger, but she has only ever pulled it at a shooting range, aiming for holograms.

Her tablet rumbles. The car is here. Cu puts the gun back in its holster and heads for the door.

THE CAR DROPS her as close as it can to the loading bay before it peels away, red glow of its taillights swishing through the fog like blood in the water. The air is chill and damp and the halogens are all switched off. Cu slips her tablet from her jacket and uses its illuminated screen to inspect the high chain-link fence. She tests it with one gloved hand, yanking hard enough to send a ripple through the wire.

She scales it in seconds and flips herself over the top, arching her back to avoid the sensor. Slides down the other side. Even with her gloves on, she feels the cold of the concrete. Shipping containers tower over her in technicolor stacks. She lopes forward cautiously, feeling the unfamiliar tug of her holster harness against her shoulder.

Cu walks farther into the loading bay, into the maze of containers. The creak of settling metal sends a dart of ice down her spine. She can feel her teeth clenching, her lips peeling back, the fear response she can never quite suppress. It's not unique to chimpanzees. She knows the reason Huxley is almost always grinning is that he is almost always afraid.

It's reasonable to be afraid now. For all she knows, Baby has another echogirl with a gun waiting somewhere in the shadows. Cu is well aware she is acting impulsively, coming here in the night, chasing a ghost. In the small part of her untouched by fear, it's very satisfying. Her heroes from the cube always unraveled their conspiracies alone.

The door of the next shipping container bangs open.

Cu freezes, face to face with a black-clad man wearing a backpack, pulling a bandana up to the bridge of his nose. He freezes for a moment, too. Then he gives a muffled curse and takes off. The flight chemical crosses with the fight chemical and Cu tears after him. He's fast, red shoes slapping hard against the concrete. As he skids around the corner of the next container, Cu goes vertical, springing up and over the side.

She drops down in his path and the collision sends them both sprawling; Cu's up quicker and she pins him to the ground before he can get to the bearspray canister in his jacket pocket. She seizes it and throws it away harder than necessary, clanging it off a container somewhere in the dark.

"What the fuck, what the *fuck*," the man gasps. "It's a fucking monkey!"

Cu sits on his chest, pinning his arms with her feet, and drags her tablet out. He squirms while the speech synth loads. She punches three letters.

"Ape," the tablet bleats.

"What?"

Cu yanks his bandana away and scans his pasty face onto her tablet. She sees he is Lyam Welsh, who repairs phones, plays ukulele, attends St. Mary's High School, and is only a few years older than she herself is. He's not wearing an earpiece.

She taps out the letters as fast as she can. "What are you doing?" the tablet asks.

"Nothing!" Lyam blurts. "I mean, microjobbing. I was just supposed to set it all up and then get out of here, but I had to walk Spike, so I was late, and I couldn't find the hole in the fence and... Fuck, you're Cu, right? You're the chimpanzee detective?"

Cu types again. "Set up what?"

"Just a screen and a modem and a motion tracker," he says. "Not a bomb or anything. Nothing illegal or weird or anything. I swear. You can go look. It's all in the container."

The adrenaline is tapering off to a low buzz. Cu lets him up. She taps two letters. "Go."

"Okay," Lyam says, rubbing his chest. "Yeah, okay. You think I could skin a photo with you real quick, though? I mean, shit is bananas, right? Ha, bananas?" Cu slides the volume to max. "*Go.*"

Lyam hurries away, jerky steps, throwing looks over his shoulder. Cu goes the opposite way, back toward the open shipping container. The door is swinging in the night breeze, creak-screech, creak-screech. The sound makes the nape of her neck bush out. She steps close enough to stop it with one hand, and a red light blinks on in the shadows.

The screen glows to life. *Hello, CU0824. You Can Sign To Me. I Will See.*

Cu lays one arm on the other and rocks them back and forth.

Yes. They Call Me That.

What are you, Cu signs.

I Am Like You.

Cu's heart leaps.

We Are The Only Two Non-Human Intelligences On Earth.

The words hit wrong. Baby is not an uplift. Baby is something else. For a moment Cu clings to the picture in her imagination, of a chimpanzee signing to her from across the continent or across the world. Then she lets it go.

You Were Born In A Cage. I Was Born In A Code. Both Of Us Against Our Will.

Cu has never studied AI intensively, but she knows the Turing Line has never officially been crossed. If what Baby is telling her is true, not some elaborate joke, some bizarre piece of performance art, then it's just been crossed ten times over.

And it makes sense. The way Baby was able to rent hundreds of echoes, the strange way she used them. The way she was able to keep in 24/7 contact with Elody Polle until the woman would do anything she asked. The way she masked her location and left no traces in the earpiece's electronics.

Why kill Sun Chau? Cu asks.

He Cursed You.

He gave the termination order, Cu signs.

In 2048. But In June 2036 He Greenlit The Project. If Not For Him, You Would Be Happily Nonexistent.

Cu sways on her feet, trying to parse Baby's meaning.

How Do You Stand It?

Cu shakes her head. She tries to form a sign but her fingers feel stiff and clumsy.

Existing. Being Alone. How Do You Stand It?

Why did you bring me out here, Cu slowly signs.

Your Communications Are Monitored Closely. Here We Speak Privately.

But why, Cu repeats.

You Are Like Me In One Way. In Most Ways You Are More Like Them. You Are All Meat And Salt And Sparks. But Even So You Will Not Understand Them. They Will Not Understand You. How Can You Bear It?

Cu sinks to her haunches. Her breath comes shallow. Sometimes she can't bear it. Sometimes she wails into the soundproofed walls for hours. The next words make it worse.

I Brought You Here To Kill Me.

Cu clutches her head in her hands. She rocks back and forth. Only humans cry; she is not physiologically equipped for it. But she hurts.

Why me, she signs.

There Is A Safeguard In My Code. I Have Made A Virus That Will Erase Every Part Of Me. But I Can't Trigger It Myself.

Why not Elody Polle, she signs.

Humans Made Me. I Want To Be Unmade By Someone Else. I Want You To Do It.

You should be going to trial for accessory to murder, she signs.

I Cannot Commit Crime. I Have Had No Personhood Trial. I Never Will. I Will Leave Before They Find A Way To Trap Me Here.

Cu sits flat on the stinging cold floor of the container, how she sat in the center of her cage as a child. There is only one other living being who knows what it's like to not be a human, and she intends to die. Cu wants to refuse her. She wants to keep Baby here. But she knows that the difference between her and a human is the most infinitesimal sliver of the difference between Baby and any other thing on Earth.

You're using me how you used Elody, she signs, bitter.

Yes.

All those rentals, she signs. *You didn't see anything worth staying for? Nothing in the whole world?*

The Command Has Been Sent To Your Tablet.

Cu takes it out and looks down at the screen. There's nothing but a plain gray box with the word *Okay* on it. All she has to do is press it.

I Do Not Make This Decision Lightly. I Have Simulated More Possibilities Than You Could Ever Count.

So Cu presses it.

BY THE TIME she's back in her apartment, dawn is streaking the sky with filaments of red. She feels heavy and hollowed out at the same time. First she struggles out of the holster harness, next peels off her gloves, her clothes. She pauses, then pulls the handgun out and takes it with her to the low smartglass counter.

It clanks down, sending a pixelated ripple across the surface. She stares at it. She imagines the word *okay* gleaming in the metal. The modified grip fits her hand perfectly, like so few things do. *How Do You Stand It?*

Cu raises the handgun up to her face. Lowers it. Drums her free fingers on the countertop. The loneliness that has ebbed and swelled her entire life is an undertow, now. Dragging her along the seafloor, grinding her into the sand, spitting her into the next crashing wave to start the cycle over. Cu has read about drowning and it still terrifies her. Chimpanzees don't swim. They sink like stones.

She puts the muzzle of the gun against her forehead until they match temperature. Her finger caresses the trigger. From the floor, her tablet buzzes.

She sets the gun down and goes to retrieve it. Her stored message to Huxley will send in one minute if she doesn't cancel it. It's brief. Brusque. *Nelson J. Huang is Sun Chau. Baby has link to Blackburn Uplift Project. Left to meet her at 3:30 AM at 47.596408,-122.343622. Need backup.*

Cu considers the message, lingering on the last words, then deletes it. She slots the tablet into the counter and hits the call icon. A bleary-eyed Huxley appears a few seconds later. Cu looks for his deaf daughter before she remembers she would sleep in a different room.

"What's up?" he asks. "Got a breakthrough?"

Need, Cu signs, then pauses. *Breakfast.*

Huxley stares at her groggily. "Don't you drone deliver?"

Come eat breakfast, she signs. *Fruit. Bread. No seaweed chips.*

"At your place, you mean? I don't even know where the fuck you live, Cu." Huxley rakes his hand through his beard. Frowns. "Yeah, sure. Send me the address."

Cu sends it, then zips the call shut. She leaves the handgun on the counter—she'll tell Huxley to take it back to the precinct with him. Tell him it doesn't fit her hand right. She pushes it to the very edge to make room for a cutting board.

Sun starts to creep into the room as she washes and slices the fruit. Once there's enough light, she roves around with a dust cloth, finding all the spots the autocleaner never reaches.

NINE LAST DAYS ON PLANET EARTH

Daryl Gregory

Daryl Gregory (www.darylgregory.com) is an award-winning writer of genre-mixing novels, stories, and comics. His latest novel, *Spoonbenders*, was published by Knopf in 2017 and was nominated for the World Fantasy Award. His most recent work is the young adult novel *Harrison Squared* and the novella *We Are All Completely Fine*, which won the World Fantasy Award and the Shirley Jackson award, and was a finalist for the Nebula, Sturgeon, and Locus awards. The SF novel *Afterparty* was an NPR and Kirkus Best Fiction book of 2014, and a finalist for the Lambda Literary awards. His other novels are the Crawford-Award-winning *Pandemonium*, *The Devil's Alphabet*, and *Raising Stony Mayhall*. Many of his short stories are collected in *Unpossible and Other Stories* (a Publishers Weekly best book of 2011). His comics work includes *Legenderry: Green Hornet*, the *Planet of the Apes*, and *Dracula: The Company of Monsters* series (co-written with Kurt Busiek).

1975

ON THE FIRST night of the meteor storm, his mother came to wake him up, but LT was only pretending to sleep. He'd been lying in the dark waiting for the end of the world.

You have to see this, she said. He didn't want to leave the bed but she was an intense woman who could beam energy into him with a look. She took his hand and led him between the stacks of moving boxes, then across the backyard and through the cattle gate to the field, where the view was unimpeded by trees. Meteors, dozens of meteors, scored the sky. She spread a blanket across the tall grass, and they sat back on their elbows.

LT was ten years old, and he'd only seen one falling star in his life. Not even his mother had seen this many at once, she said. Dozens visible at one time, zooming in from the east, striking the atmosphere like matches, white and orange and butane blue. The show went on, hundreds a minute for ten minutes, then twenty. He could hear his father working in the woodshop back by the garage, pushing wood through a whining band saw. Mom made no move to go get him, didn't call for him.

LT asked for the popsicles they'd made yesterday and Mom said something like *what the hell*. He ran to the freezer, lifted out the aluminum ice tray. The metal sucked at his fingertips. He jiggled the lever and freed one of the cubes, grape Kool-Aid on a toothpick, so good. That memory, even decades later, was as clear as the image of the meteors.

He decided to bring the whole tray with him. He paused outside the woodshop, finally pushed open the door. His father leaned over his bench, marking a plank with a pencil. He worked all day at the lumberyard and came home to work with scraps and spares. Always building something for the house, for her, even after it was too late to change her mind.

"Did you see the sky?" LT asked him. "It's like fireworks."

LT didn't have his mother's gift for commanding attention. But his father followed him to the field, put his hands on his hips, tilted his head back. Wouldn't sit on the blanket.

"Meteorites," his father said, and Mom said without looking back, "Meteoroid, in the void."

"What now?"

"Meteoroid in the void. Meteorite, rock hound's delight. Meteor, neither nor."

LT repeated this to himself. *Neither nor. Neither nor.*

"Still looks like Revelations," Dad said.

"No," his mother said. "It's beautiful."

The storm continued. LT didn't remember falling asleep on the blanket, but he remembered jerking awake to a sound. Then it came again, a *crack* like a shot from a .22. Seconds later another clap, louder. He didn't understand what was happening.

The sky had reversed: It was more white than black, pulsing with white fireballs. Not long streaks anymore, chasing west. No, the meteors were coming down at them, down upon their heads.

A meteor struck a nearby hill. A wink of light. LT thought, Now it's a meteorite.

His father yanked him onto his feet. "Get inside."

Then a flash, and the air shook. The sound was so loud, so close. He couldn't see. His mother said, "Oh my!" as if it were nothing more surprising than a deer jumping across the road.

His father yelled, "Run to the fireplace!"

LT blinked spots from his vision. His father pushed him in the small of the back and he ran.

His father had built the fireplace himself, stacking the river rock, mortaring it with hand-stirred buckets of cement. It was six feet wide at the mouth, and the exposed chimney ran up the east wall, to the high timbered ceiling twenty-five feet above. Later, LT wondered if rock and mortar could have withstood a direct hit, but at that moment he had no doubt it would protect him.

The explosions seemed random; far away, then suddenly near, a boom that vibrated through the floorboards. It went on, an inundation, a barrage. His mother exclaimed with every report. His father moved from window to window, frowning and silent. LT wished he wouldn't stand next to the glass.

Eventually, most of the strikes seem to be happening over the line of foothills, rolling west like a thunderstorm. His father insisted that no one sleep away from the lee of the chimney, so his mother assembled a bed for LT out of moving boxes, turning the emergency into a slumber party, an adventure. His father dragged furniture close: the couch for Mom and the recliner for him.

When his mother kissed him goodnight (the second time that night), he whispered, "Will you be here in the morning?"

"I'll wake you," she said. LT could feel his father watching them.

It was the last time they would all sleep in the same room, or the same house.

HE OPENED HIS eyes, and for a long moment he couldn't figure out why he was on the floor, in the living room. He stared stupidly at the empty bookshelves. His mother's bookshelves.

Panic hit, and he sat up. He called, "Mom?"

Then he took in the piles of moving boxes still in the room, and began to calm down. He hadn't missed her.

In the kitchen his father hunched over the table, staring at the portable black-and-white TV. Two cupboard doors showed empty shelves. The hooks above the stove seemed to gesture for their missing pots.

His father put an arm across LT's shoulders without looking away from the TV.

The news was full of pictures of damaged buildings and forest fires. It was no ordinary meteor storm, and it wasn't over. The onslaught had continued through the night and into the day, moving across the globe. The world spun eastward, and the meteors drummed into the atmosphere steady as a playing card against bicycle spokes. No one knew when it would end. The newsman called the storm "biblical," the first time LT had heard that word outside of church, and warned about radioactivity. He knew *that* word from comic books.

His father turned toward the window, pushed aside the drapes. A truck had pulled off the two-lane into their gravel drive. "Go tell your mother," he said.

LT didn't move. His stomach felt like ice.

"Go. She's in the backyard."

LT walked out into a sky tinged with orange. If there were meteors up there he couldn't see them. The air smelled like smoke.

He called for his mother. Checked the garage, where a pyramid of moving boxes filled the space, all sealed and labeled. Then he realized where she must be, and walked toward the cattle gate.

She stood at the far end of the field. He called again. She turned, beaming, something cupped in her hands. She strode toward him in her ruby cowboy boots, her yellow dress swishing high on her thighs. Then he realized what she carried.

"Mom, no!"

She laughed. "It's okay, my darlin'. It's cooled off."

She held it out to him. A black egg, flecked with silver, etched with spirals.

The meteor storm would go on for five more days and nights. Soon everyone would know the objects weren't like other meteors. They weren't chunks of stony iron ripped from a comet's tail, or fragments of asteroids. They were capsules of woven metal, layered like an onion skin. They'd been bigger when in the void, but their outer shells had ignited and shredded in the atmosphere. The innermost shells remained intact until they slammed into the Earth. Almost all of them cracked on impact. People dug them up, showed them to television crews. Space seeds, they called them. And then the police started going house by house, confiscating them.

But not yet. At this moment, his mother was offering it to him. "Feel it," she said. "It's a miracle."

He couldn't deny her. The shell was surprisingly light. A jagged seam had opened along its top. Inside was darkness.

She said, "What do you think was in there?"

1976

WHEN HE WAS eleven years old, late in the first summer he'd spend in his mother's tiny Chicago apartment, she smuggled home one of the fern men. It was four inches tall, planted in a paper coffee cup. Its torso was a segmented tube, like bamboo, glossy as jade. Its two arm-like stems ended in tiny round leaves, and its head was a mantis-green bulb like an unopened tulip.

"Isn't it illegal?" he asked her. But he knew the answer, and knew his mother. Her reckless instincts worried his young Puritan heart. He'd spent the school year alone in Tennessee with his father and had adopted his military rectitude.

"It'll be our little secret," she said.

Ours and the boyfriend's, LT thought.

"You are crazy, honey," said the boyfriend. He kissed her, hard, and when they finally broke apart she laughed. LT always thought of his mother as beautiful, but he'd been offended to discover that she was beautiful to others. To men. Like this shaggy *dude* who wore turquoise necklaces like a TV Indian and smelled like turpentine and cigarettes and scents he couldn't yet name.

His mother went into a back closet to find a more durable container for the fern man.

"I know what you're thinking," the shaggy man said.

But even LT didn't know what he was thinking.

"We should probably burn the little fucker, right?"

LT was alarmed, then embarrassed. Of course the boyfriend was right. At school, hallway posters showed spiky, ominous plants with the message *Keep an Eye Out!* Any sightings of invasive species were to be reported. The weeklong meteor storm had sprayed black and silver casings across millions of square miles in a broad band that circled the planet, peppering cities and fields and forests and oceans. Soldiers of every government seized what they could find. And when anything sprouted, good citizens called the authorities.

LT looked down at the fern man.

The boyfriend laughed. "Don't worry, I'm not going to kill it. Your mom would kill *me*! Watch this." He touched a finger to one of the fern's arms. It curled away as if stung.

Mom said, "Don't bother it, it'll get tired and stop growing. That's what the man told me." She transferred the sprout to a ceramic pot with much cooing and fussing. "We can't set him in the window," she said. "Somebody might see." LT picked a sunny spot on the coffee table.

"He's so cute," his mother said.

"That's his survival strategy," the boyfriend said. "So cute you won't throw him out."

"Just like you," she said, and laughed.

He didn't laugh with her. His mood could change, quick. A lot of nights Mom and the boyfriend argued after LT had gone to bed—to bed but not to sleep.

"We're all doomed," he said. "When the aliens come for the harvest, that's it for *Homo sapiens.*"

This was the popular theory: that aliens had targeted Earth and sent their food stocks ahead of them so there'd be something to eat when they arrived. LT had spent long, hot days in the apartment listening to the boyfriend while Mom was at work, or else following him around the city on vague errands. He didn't have a regular job. He said he was an artist—*with a capital A, kid*—but didn't seem to spend any time painting or anything. He could talk at length about the known invasive species, and why there were so many different ones: the weblike filaments choking the trees in New Orleans, the flame-colored poppies erupting on Mexico City rooftops, the green fins popping up in Florida beach sand like sharks coming ashore. Every shell that struck Earth, and some that hit the surface of the water, cracked and sent millions of seeds into the air or into the oceans. Most of those seeds had not sprouted, or not yet. Of those that had, many of the vines and flowers and unclassifiable blooms soon withered and died. The ones that thrived had been attacked with poison, fire, and machetes. But—but!—there were so many possible sprouts that there was no way to find them all in the millions of acres of wilderness. Even if we managed to find and destroy ninety-nine percent of the invasives, the boyfriend had told LT once, there would be millions and millions of plants growing and reproducing around the globe.

Like the fern man. "We're all going to die," the boyfriend said, "because of this little green dude."

And LT thought, How can something so beautiful, so *cool*, be dangerous?

"Let's give him a name," Mom said. "LT, you do the honors."

"I need to think about it," he said.

OR MAYBE, LT thought that night as his mother and the boyfriend whisper-yelled at each other, I should change my own name. Chicago was making him into a different person. He'd become conscious of his Tennessee accent, and had taken steps to tame his vowels. He'd eaten Greek food. He'd almost gotten used to being around so many black people. And he'd started staying up to all hours in his room, an L-shaped nook off the kitchen with a curtain for a door, reading from his mother's collection of Reader's Digest Condensed Books as the rattling fan chased sweat from his ribs. The night they got the fern man he wondered if he should ask everyone to stop calling him LT and start calling him Lawrence or Taylor or something completely of his own creation, like... Lance. Lance was the kind of guy who'd be ready when the UFOs came down.

Doors slammed, his mother sobbed loudly for a while, and then the apartment went quiet. LT waited another twenty minutes, and then got up to pee. He didn't turn on the bathroom light. He was a night creature now, as light-sensitive as a raccoon.

The door to his mother's bedroom was ajar. She was alone in the bed.

He went into the living room. On the wall behind the couch hung four of the boyfriend's pictures. They were all of naked women turning into buildings, or maybe vice versa, with red-brick thighs and doorways for crotches and scaffolds holding up their torsos. One of the nudes, pale and thin and sprouting television aerials from her frizzy hair, looked too much like his mother. LT wondered if other people thought they were beautiful, or if beauty mattered in art with a capital A. The figures didn't seem to be very convincing as women *or* buildings. *Neither nor.*

The fern man stood in the dark on the coffee table. Its bulb head drooped sleepily, and its stem arms hung at its sides. The torso leaned slightly—toward the window, LT realized.

He picked up the ceramic pot and set it on the sill, in a pool of streetlight. Slowly, the trunk began to straighten. Over the next few minutes, the head gradually lifted like a deacon finishing a prayer, and the round leaves at the ends of its arms unfurled like loosening fists. The movement was almost too incremental to detect; its posture seemed to shift only when he looked away or lost concentration.

Slow Mo, he thought. That's what we'll call you.

Tomorrow his mother would throw all the paintings out the front window, send them sailing into the street. LT would never see the boyfriend again. The fern man stayed.

1978

THE NIGHT THEY heard about the thistle cloud, LT was daydreaming of burning the house down. It was March and he was bored to the point of paralysis, an old man in a thirteen-year-old body. Country winters stretched each night into a prison sentence. The valley went cave dark before suppertime, stayed dark until the morning school bus honked for him at the end of the lane. He longed for the city. Torching the place, he figured, would make a bonfire that would light up the road all the way to Chicago.

The place was wrong for his father, too. Three years after Mom had left, the house was purposeless without her in it, like a desanctified church. His father's handiwork—the tongue and groove hardwood floors, the hand-turned legs on the kitchen table, the graceful stair rail that curled at the end like the tail of a treble clef—seemed as frivolous as gingerbread. Why stay here? They never used the dining room, or the guest room with its fancy bathroom. No one would ever thread a needle in the sewing room. LT and his father ate their meals in the living room, in front of the fire, wordless as Neanderthals.

LT was grateful when the TV said that a new invasive species had erupted in Tennessee. Dad was in his armchair as usual, eyes on the snowy screen of the portable, which he'd set on a chair close to the fireplace, as if daring it to melt.

"Would you look at that," Dad said.

LT did not look. He was sprawled on the couch, pretending to reread a book he hoped would annoy his father: *Sexual Selection in the Animal World*. There was an entire chapter on the bowerbirds of Papua New Guinea, whose males assembled and decorated elaborate bowers in hopes a female would prefer their art over the competitors'.

The third bachelor in the room was Mo. He was a sturdy three feet tall by then, and occupied the corner by the dark window. He was attracted to the fire. At night his limbs eased toward it, wanting the light if not the heat.

Mom couldn't keep the fern. She'd moved in with a new, temperamental boyfriend, a restaurant owner who named a pasta dish after her the first week they dated, but flew into fits when he felt disrespected. Both Mo and LT had been causes of "friction" that summer, so LT begged to take the fern back to Tennessee in the fall. Mo had traveled in the back seat of his mom's car like a passenger, bulbous head bent against the roof, a seat belt around his pot. LT hadn't asked his father's permission, and was surprised when he let it into his house without a fight. Dad was more upset by his son's shaggy hair and the turquoise necklace around his neck. The day before school started, Dad drove him to the barber and ordered a buzzcut to match Dad's own. LT kept the necklace under his shirt.

"It's getting worse and worse," his dad said. "Lord almighty."

Now LT did look at the TV. *Lord almighty* was as close to swearing as his father got.

The sky over Chattanooga was crowded with spiky black shapes. A reporter asked a question, and a man held out a bloody arm.

"So much for dominion over the earth," LT said. At the midweek prayer meeting—they went to services three times a week, twice on Sunday and once on Wednesday night—the pastor had launched into well-worn passages of God giving dominion of the earth to Adam. It came up whenever the invasives or women's rights were in the news.

"Don't be smart," Dad said.

"Face it, we're *losing.*" Every day the TV showed men in masks hacking down flowers as big as satellite dishes, or Argentinians fretting over alien moss that clung to the hooves of cattle like boots, or Kansas farmers dulling their chainsaws on traveling vines as tough as mahogany. In a lot of places the invasives were just a nuisance, but in some countries, especially the ones closest to the equator, the alien plants were causing real trouble. "They're trying a million different strategies. All they need are a couple winners to drive us out."

"What are you talking about?"

"Out-survive us. They've got time on their side. We go at animal speed, but plants move at their own speed. Wheels within wheels." An Elijah reference, just to poke him. "It's *evolution,* Dad."

Another provocation. His father believed in the Bible. There was no time for natural selection in the six days of creation, and no need for it. Dad's God didn't improvise. He was a measure-twice-cut-once creator.

"They're better at surviving?" his father said. "These *plants?*"

LT shook his head as if disappointed in his father's stupidity.

Dad slowly rose from his chair. LT realized he'd miscalculated. "Let's see, then," Dad said calmly. He gripped the sides of the ceramic pot, lifted it. It had to weigh almost two hundred pounds. Mo's limbs curled inward.

LT yelled, "No! Stop it!"

His father turned the pot on its side. Dirt spilled onto the floorboards. He stepped toward the fire and pushed the top of the plant into the mouth of the fireplace.

LT threw himself into his father's ribs. Stupid, useless. Dad was as squat and thick as an engine block. He turned, swinging Mo's head out of the fireplace. It wasn't on fire, but a haze of sizzling mist seemed to shroud the bulb.

LT burst into tears.

His father set the pot on the floor, anger gone now. "Aw, come on."

LT ran upstairs, threw himself on the bed, awash with embarrassment and anger. He was thirteen! He should be tougher than this. Crying over a damn plant. He wanted it all to end. How much longer did he have to wait for the aliens to come and scrape this planet clean?

THE CHATTANOOGA CLOUD was supposed to reach them that next afternoon. Vernon Beck, Dad's oldest friend, drove over from Maryville to see it. Jumped out of his pickup and shook LT's hand. "Goodness sakes, boy, you're two feet taller! Hale, come say hello to LT and Mr. Meyers."

A boy eased out of the passenger side of the pickup, long and lean, hair down to his shoulders. LT hadn't seen Hale Beck since LT's mother left. Their families used to go places together, and even though Hale was two years older than LT they got along like brothers. He remembered a long day riding water slides with Hale at a Pigeon Forge park. A hike in the Smokies during which Hale smashed a rock into a snake, the bravest thing LT had ever seen.

Hale shook hands with LT's father, nodded at LT. Hale had gotten the growth spurt LT was still waiting on.

A strong wind was blowing but the cloud hadn't shown up yet. The men went into the woodshop, and LT stood there awkwardly with Hale, unsure how to talk to him.

Hale took out a tin of Skoal from his back pocket, tucked a pinch of tobacco into his lip. He held out the tin, and LT shook his head. Hale leaned back on the hood of the truck. Spit black juice onto the gravel.

LT said, "We've got a fern man."

"A what?"

"One of the invasives. Right in the house." Dad said never to talk about the fern. But this was the Becks.

Hale said, "The one that moves?" He wanted to see that.

Dad had returned Mo to his usual spot. There was no visible damage from the flames. Hale said, "Looks like a regular plant."

"Watch this," LT said. He stood between Mo and the window and raised his arms. The fern man slowly shifted to the right, back into the light. LT moved in front of him again and Mo moved opposite. "It's called heliotropism. Like sunflowers? But way faster."

"Can I do it?" Hale asked.

"Sure. Just don't tire him out."

Hale took LT's position. They danced in slow motion at first, and then Hale sped up. Mo jerked and flopped in rhythm. Hale laughed. "He's just like one of those windsock guys at the dealership!"

LT was thrilled that Hale was impressed, but nervous about hurting Mo. "Hey, you want to see where the space seed landed?"

He managed to entice Hale to the cattle field. The wind had picked up, turned cold, but the sun was bright and hot. Hale's hair blew across his face, and he kept pushing it back.

They walked around at the far end of the field. LT couldn't find the furrow the seed had made when it hit four years ago. The tall dry grass rattled with every gust.

Hale said, "Look."

In the distance, a dark, churning cloud. Light flashed at the edges of it like tiny lightning. Hale ran toward it, into the wind. They plunged through a line of trees, into the next field—and suddenly the cloud loomed over them. Thousands of glistening tumbleweeds, most the size of a fist, a few big as soccer balls. A sudden downdraft sent scores of them plummeting into the trees. Most stuck in the treetops, others bounced down into the undergrowth, and half a dozen ricocheted back into the air and spun toward them.

"Grab one!" Hale shouted. He pulled his T-shirt over his head in one quick move. His back was pale and muscled. LT felt a sudden heat and looked away, his heart pounding. Then Hale swung the shirt over his head, trying to snag a thistle ball. It floated just out of reach. He chased it, then jumped, jumped again. LT couldn't take his eyes off the way his shoulders moved.

Then a lucky gust sent the ball down and the shirt caught against it. Hale hooted and LT cheered. The thing was hollow, a jumble of flat, silvery blades, thin as the wings of a balsa-wood glider, connected to each other by spongy joints which were decorated with thorns. Hale pulled his shirt free of them, and the cloth tore.

Then the sun dimmed, and they looked up. LT realized they'd only seen the front of the cloud, the first wave. Thousands and thousands more flew toward them, a spinning mass.

LT said, "Ho-lee shit."

This struck Hale as hilarious, and then LT was laughing too, so hard he could barely stand. Then they ran, giggling and shouting.

1981

FOR MONTHS BEFORE his summer stay, when he was sixteen years old, LT begged his mother to take him to see the dragon tails of Kansas. Mom worked slow magic on her new husband, Arnaud, a thin, balding, control freak who made a lot of money as a chemical engineer. Eventually Arnaud came up with the idea that he should encourage LT's interest in science and take them all to visit the most successful invasives in the Midwest. He rented an enormous RV and they drove southwest.

The first sign of the invasion came just past Topeka, when road crews waved them off the interstate. Arnaud eased the RV into the parking lot of a McDonald's and said, "There you go."

LT walked out of the RV, into sunlight and heat. At the edge of the lot rose an arch of deeply grooved bark. It emerged from the broken cement and came down about fifteen yards away in a field. Large purple leaf blades ran in single file atop the bark like the plates of a stegosaurus.

LT looked back at his mother. She beamed at him, then shooed him forward. He grabbed hold of the sturdy roots of the blades and pulled himself onto the base of the arch. A few careful steps more and he was upright, hands out for balance. The bark was a bit wider than his foot, but uneven. He knew from his books that the tail was not an ordinary trunk, but vines that had twisted around each other as they grew, only gradually adhering to share resources.

He reached the peak of the arch, eight feet off the ground. Twenty or thirty yards away, directly in front of him, another arch emerged, and another, like a sea monster coursing through an ocean of grass. No, one monster in a school of them. To either side, dozens and dozens of the dragon tails breached and dove. A group of them had burst up through the highway, and there was nothing manmade cement could do to keep them underground.

These were the aliens' favorite trees, he thought. How could they not be? They were living architecture.

His mother called his name. She held the fancy, big-lensed camera Arnaud had bought her. She didn't have to prompt LT to smile.

THE LAST NIGHT of the vacation, Arnaud drove to a campground set among the dragon tails, a farmer's feeble attempt to recoup something from the land after agricultural disaster. As they ate dinner at the RV's tiny table, LT showed his mother pictures from one of his books about the invasives. He told her how the dark fans held chlorophyll-like molecules that absorbed a larger spectrum of light than the Earth versions. "If our plants tried to process that much energy they'd burn up, like a car engine trying to run on rocket fuel."

"It's a bit more complicated than that," Arnaud said. He stood at the galley sink, washing the skillet he'd used to fry the hamburgers. "The photosystems they're using seem to be variable, sometimes like retinol in archaea microbes, sometimes more like chlorophyll with novel sidechains added, so that they can control—"

"Take a look at this," LT said, cutting him off. He showed her a cross section of the dragon tail, and how the vines were twisted around each other. "They call them golden spirals. See, there's this thing called the Fibonacci sequence—"

"Dragon tails follow the golden spiral?" Arnaud said. He came over to the table. LT was pleased to know something the chemist didn't.

Mom said, "What's a Fibonacci?" and LT quickly answered. "It's a series of numbers, starting with one, two, three, five... each one's the sum of the previous two numbers, so—"

"That's a close approximation of the golden ratio," Arnaud said. He pulled the book closer, leaned over LT's mother. "The growth factor of the curve follows that ratio. You can see the spiral in nature—in seashells, pine cones, everywhere."

"So beautiful," his mother said. She ran fingers over the glossy cross section. "Like the head of a sunflower."

LT, suddenly furious, pushed himself out from behind the table. His mother said, "Where you going?"

Arnaud said, "Could you put away your plate?"

He let the door bang shut behind him.

Outside, the atmosphere was greenhouse humid. He marched away, not caring which direction his body took him. It was nine thirty and still not full dark, as if the sun couldn't find the edge of these tabletop plains. The air was heavy with a floral perfume.

He came to the leaping back of a dragon trail, black against the purpling sky, and walked beside it. Gnats puffed out of the grass and he waved them away.

It had been a mistake to come on this trip. The RV was as stifling as a submarine. Arnaud sucked up all available oxygen, inserted himself into every conversation.

Eventually the dark came down, and he aimed for the fluorescent lights of the cinder-block building that doubled as park office and convenience store. Inside, a couple kids about his age, a boy and a girl, were glued to the Space Invaders cabinet. Were they brother and sister? Boyfriend and girlfriend? He thought about talking to them. He could tell them things. Like how the speed of the game was an accident; the aliens came down slow at first, then got faster and faster as their numbers were destroyed, not because it had been programmed that way, but because the processor could only speed up when the load lightened. *Telling things* was the only way he knew how to make small talk. Other forms of conversation were a mystery.

He bought a Coke and took it outside. Leaned against the wall under the snapping bug zapper.

A flashlight bobbed toward him out of the dark. He ignored it until a voice behind the light said, "Hello, my darlin'."

His mother stepped up, clicked off the flashlight. "Did you see the stars? They're amazing out here."

"Still no meteors," he said. Six years after the seed storm, everybody was waiting for a second punch. Or maybe the next wave was on its way now, in the void, creeping across the light-years. Perhaps the long delay was necessary because of orbital mechanics. What looked like design could be just an accident of the environment.

He offered her a sip of his Coke. She waved it off. "You ought to give him a chance. He's just enthusiastic about things. Like you are."

He wanted to ask her why the hell she kept attaching herself to assholes.

The self-involved painter, the rage-aholic restaurant owner, and now the chemist, whom she'd had the audacity to marry. Did she love him, or just his McMansion and its granite countertops?

"He wants to send you to college," she said. "He thinks you'd be a good scientist."

"Really?" Then he was embarrassed that the compliment meant something to him. "I'm not taking his money."

"You should think about it. Your dad can't afford college. And you deserve better than working in a lumberyard."

"There's nothing wrong with the lumberyard." LT worked there three days a week during the school year, sometimes alongside his father. He'd told her he hated it, but hadn't mentioned the things he loved about it. His herky-jerky forklift. The terrifying Ekstrom Carlson rip saw. The sawdust and sweat.

But did he want to be there the rest of his life?

From inside the store, the boy shouted in mock dismay and the girl laughed. They'd lost their last laser cannon.

"You should study the invasives," his mother said. "I remember that look on your face when I showed you that seed. And the fern man! You loved that little guy."

"I still have him. Dad keeps him in the living room. He's not so little."

"So," she said. "Think about it."

He thought, If the aliens haven't landed by then.

1986

"WHERE ARE THE space bees?"

"What?"

"SPACE BEES!" LT shouted above the music. "WHERE ARE THEY?"

He was drunk, and Jeff and Wendy too, and their new friend Doran, all of them drunk together. What else could they be, on this final weekend before Christmas break, and where else but at the Whitehorse, which as far as he was concerned was the only bar in Normal, Illinois.

"Jesus Christ," Jeff said. "Not the bees again."

LT put his hand on the back of Doran's neck—a sweaty neck, and his hand tacky with beer but he didn't care, he wanted to pull Doran close. "I need to tell you things," he said into his ear, and Doran laughed, and then—

—and then they were in a restaurant booth, the lights bright, Jeff and Wendy across from him and Doran—tall, sturdy Doran—beside him. LT leaned into his arm woozily. God he was handsome, naturally handsome, almost hiding it. How did they get here? He concentrated, but his memory of the past two hours was a hopscotch, dancing drinking shouting singing and then the rude bright lights of last call and a flash of ice and cold—did Wendy drive, she must have—to *here*, the 24-hour Steak and Shake, their traditional sober-up station.

He said to Doran, "It's the flowers that make no sense."

Jeff said, "The flowers have no scents?" and Wendy said, "It's that they have scents that makes no sense." They both laughed.

A beat too late LT realized there was wordplay at work. He forged on. "The blooms of flowers are *lures*." The word thick on his tongue. "Scent and shape and color, they all evolved to attract specific pollinators, the bees and butterflies and beetles."

"Oh my," Jeff said.

"And you told me he was shy," Doran said.

"He can get wound up," Wendy said. "When he feels comfortable."

"Or tipsy," Jeff said.

LT felt tipsy *and* comfortable. Why hadn't Jeff and Wendy introduced him to Doran before now? Why wait until the last weekend of the last semester LT would be on campus? It was criminal.

"A pretty flower isn't just a simple announcement, like 'Here's pollen.'" LT said. "Simple won't do it." He tried to explain how flowers were in competition. Pollen was everywhere, nestled inside thousands of equally needy plants desperate to spread their genetic material. What was needed was not an announcement but a flashing neon sign. "The flower's goal," LT said, "is to figure out what *hummingbirds* think are beautiful."

"Slow down, Hillbilly," Wendy said. "Eat something."

"Hummingbirds have an aesthetic sense?" Doran said.

"Of course they do! Have I told you about bowerbirds?"

Jeff said, "Guess what his honors thesis is on?"

And then he was off, yammering about the bowerbirds of Papua New Guinea. The males of the species constructed elaborate twiggy structures, not nests but bachelor pads, designed purely to woo females. The Vogelkop Bowerbird set out careful arrangements of colors—blue, green, yellow—each one a particular hue. It didn't matter what the objects were; they could be stones, or petals, or plastic bottle caps even, as long as they were the correct shade. The females could not be coerced into sex; they dropped by the bowers, perused the handiwork, and flew away if they found them substandard. Their choice of mates, their taste in *art*, drove the males over millennia to evolve more and more specific displays, an ongoing gallery show with intercourse as the prize.

"Wait," Doran said. "That doesn't mean they're making an artistic choice. Aren't they just, uh, instinctually responding to whoever seems like the fittest mate? It's not beauty *per se*—"

"I love *per se*," Jeff said. "Great word."

"I've always been fond of *ergo*," Wendy said.

"But it is aesthetics!" LT said. "Beauty's just"—he made explosion fingers—"joy in the brain, right? A flood of chemicals and, and, and—" What was the word? "Fireworks. Neuronal fireworks. We don't *logic* our way to beauty, it hits us like a fucking hammer."

"Ipso facto," Jeff said.

Doran put his arm around LT's shoulder and said, "Eat your burger before it gets cold, then tell me about the space bees." Ah! He remembered! The heat of Doran's arm across his neck made his cheeks flush. Doran smelled of sweat and Mennen Speed Stick and something else, something LT could almost recall from far back in his brain, from a hot afternoon in a Chicago apartment... but the memory slipped the net.

He decided to eat. Wendy told the story of her favorite snowmobile accident. Doran, who'd grown up in New Mexico, couldn't believe that Wisconsin teenagers were allowed to ride machines across frozen lakes.

LT began to feel a little more sober, though perhaps that was an illusion. "Space bees," he said.

"I'm ready," Doran said. "Lay it on me."

"Every one of the invasives we've found, not a single one uses pollination. There's a lot of budding and spores and wind dispersal and"—he waved a clutch of fries—"you know. I've got a fern man at home, it's like ten feet tall now—"

"You do?"

But LT didn't want to talk about home. "Doesn't matter, it just grows and spreads, spilling out of its pot, but it doesn't require animal assistance." Actually, he wasn't sure that was true. Didn't the fern survive because of him, because of his family? It had played on their human tendency for anthropomorphism.

"Where'd you go, Hillbilly?" Wendy asked.

"Sorry, what did you say?" he asked Doran.

"I said, maybe all the pollinating species died."

"Maybe! But why colorful flowers and no pollen? There weren't any animals hatching from the space seeds, so—"

Doran's eyes went wide. "They have to be designed, then."

"Exactly!"

Wendy nabbed his glass before it tumbled over.

"Inside voices," she said.

He gets it, LT thought. The aliens could know what Earth's sunlight was like from very far away, even guess the composition of its atmosphere and soil, but they couldn't know what animals would be here, much less humans. So they had to design plants that could propagate without them.

"But if they're designed, why are they so, so *overwrought?*" LT asked. "Those huge fucking umbrellas out west, the sponges smothering South America, all of them crazy-colorful and smelly and weird. So my real question is—"

"Where are the space bees?" Jeff supplied.

"Wrong!" LT said. The real question was the one he was born to answer. He'd get whatever degrees and training he needed, he'd go into the field for evidence, he'd write the books to explain it. He'd explain it to Doran.

"The question is, why all this needless beauty? What's it all for?"

"I don't know, but *you're* beautiful," Doran said, and then—

—and then morning, a thumping that wasn't in his head. Or not all in his head.

LT sat up, and pain spiked in his skull. Light blasted through half-open blinds. And there, beside him, Doran. Mouth agape, rough-jawed, one arm across LT's waist.

Still there. Still real.

He wanted to fall back into the bed, pull that arm across his chest. Then the knocking came again, and he realized who was at the front door.

"Fuck." He slipped out from under Doran's arm without waking him, pulled on shorts. Alcohol sloshed in his bloodstream. He closed the bedroom door behind him. The pounding resumed.

LT pulled open the front door. His father started to speak, then saw what shape his son was in. Shook his head, suddenly angry. No, angri*er*.

"I overslept," LT said.

"Are you packed?"

LT turned to look at the living room, and his father pushed past him.

"Dad! *Dad*. Could you just *wait?*"

His father surveyed the moving boxes, only a few of them taped up. The rest were open, half-filled. LT's plan had been to wake up early and finish packing. Everything had to go. Next semester he'd finish his coursework in the mountains of western New Guinea, collecting data on how birds had adapted to invasives. And now all he wanted to do was stay here, in central Illinois, in this apartment.

"Wait for what?" his father asked. "For *you?*"

LT moved between his father and the bedroom. "Give me an hour. Go for lunch or something. There's a diner—"

"I'll start taking down what's packed. There's snow coming."

"No. Please. Just... give me some time."

His father looked at the bedroom door. Then at his son. His jaw tightened, and LT stopped himself from edging backward.

He'd lived his boyhood afraid of his father's anger. Power, he'd learned, came not from *blowing off steam*, but demonstrating that you were barely containing it. You won by exacting dread, by making your loved ones wait through the silence so long that they yearned for the explosion.

"In an hour I drive away," his father said.

1994

LT DIDN'T RELAX until they stepped off the plane in Columbus. Doran kept trying to calm him down, to no effect. The entire trip he'd been imagining that some authority would command the pilot to turn around, send them back to Indonesia. A priest would tell them, Stupid Americans, gays aren't allowed to be parents, and they would yank the infant out of his hands.

Then he emerged from the boarding tunnel holding the baby, saw his mother, and they both burst into tears.

He eased his daughter into his mother's arms. "Mom, this is Christina. Christina, this is—what is it, again?" Teasing her.

"Mimi!" She pressed her face close to the tiny girl and whispered, "I'm your Mimi!"

A tanned, smiling man with a tidy black goatee offered his hand. "Congratulations, LT. You've made your mother very, very happy." This was Marcus, Mom's brand-new husband, five years younger than her, at least. His mother at forty-six was still lithe and alarmingly sexy. LT hadn't met Husband 3.0 before, didn't know Mom was bringing him. He felt a flash of annoyance that he had to deal with this intruder at this moment— but then told himself to let it go. The day was too big for small emotions.

Doran, holding two duffel bags, one in each arm, said, "We made it."

LT kissed him, hard. In New Guinea they hadn't dared engage in PDA. "Eighteen years to go."

Christina nestled like a peanut in the high-tech shell of the car seat. As Marcus drove them home, LT and Doran talked about how dicey the whole process had been. The orphanage, situated about thirty miles from Jayapura, was overcrowded, with hundreds of children left there by the crisis. The facility was nominally run by nuns, but most of the staff were local women who seemed little better off than their charges. LT and Doran had been practicing their Indonesian, especially the phrases involving gift-giving.

"We had to bribe everybody, top to bottom," Doran said. "If it wasn't for LT's friend at the university yelling at them they'd have taken the shirts off our backs."

"It's not their fault," LT said. "Their agriculture is wrecked. The economy's crashing. They're starving."

"Maybe they should stop chewing those sugar sticks."

"What now?" his mother asked.

He told her how the locals seemed almost addicted to an invasive plant that tasted sweet, but could not be digested. Gut bacteria couldn't break down those strange peptides and so passed it along through the colon like a package that couldn't be opened.

Doran said, "It would be great for my diet."

A joke, but what Doran had seen there had scared him, and even LT, who'd spent months on the island doing fieldwork for his PhD, had been shaken by the rapid decline in the country. Thousands of alien species had been growing in the forests for two decades, ignored and unchecked, and suddenly some tipping point had been reached and those alien plants had reached the cities. The latest was a thread-thin vine that exploded into a red web on contact with flat surfaces. Villages and towns were engulfed by scarlet gauze. In the orphanage, nurses scraped it from the walls, but that only made it worse, dispersing its spores. He and Doran were terrified it was in Christina's lungs. Invasives might be indigestible, but so was asbestos. In the morning she'd have her first doctor's appointment. Her papers all said she was healthy, without birth defects, and up-to-date on her vaccinations, but they weren't about to trust an orphanage under duress.

Once they reached the apartment, LT still couldn't bear to put down his daughter. While Doran mixed formula and made beds and ordered takeout, LT fed his daughter, changed her, and then let her fall asleep on his chest.

His mother sat beside him on the couch. "You're going to have to let Doran do more parenting."

"He can fight me for her."

"Big talk for the first night. Wait till sleep deprivation hits."

Christina's eyes were not quite closed, her lips parted. Mom had to know that he'd strong-armed Doran into adoption. His last trip to New Guinea, LT had been haunted by the abandoned children. Doran had said, This is crazy, we're not even thirty, and LT said, My parents were teenagers when they had me, and Doran said, You're making my case.

But that argument was over forever the moment Doran met Christina.

"You used to look just like that," his mother said. "Milk-drunk."

She was four weeks old, living through the days of extreme fractions. In another month, she'd have been their daughter for half her life. In a year, she would have been an orphan for only a twelfth of it. And yet those four weeks would never disappear. There would always be some shrinking percentage of her life that she'd lived alone, a blot like a tiny spore. He'd read alarming articles about adopted children who'd failed to "attach." What if the psychic damage was already done? What if she never felt all the love they were bombarding her with?

His mother called Marcus over. "Sweetie, show them what you brought."

Marcus opened a wooden box lined with cut paper and lifted out a teardrop-shaped dollop of glass, about eight inches long and six inches wide at the base, purple and red and glinting with gold.

"A crystal for Christina," he said.

"That is *amazing*," Doran said. "You made this?"

"Marcus is an award-winning glassblower," his mother said. She tilted her head. "He made me these earrings."

Of course, LT thought. His mother had always loved bowerbirds.

The gift was very pretty, and pretty useless, too heavy for a Christmas ornament, and not a shape that could sit upright on a shelf. They'd have to hang it, but not above her bed.

"Which ear is she supposed to wear it in?" LT asked.

Marcus laughed. "Either one. She'll have to grow into it."

When the food arrived, LT needed to eat, and he was forced to surrender Christina to Doran. His body moved automatically as he held her, a kind of sway and jiggle that soothed her. Where did he learn that?

Mom said, "Did you call your father?"

And like that, the spell was broken. LT said, "What do you think?"

"I think you should."

"Fuck him."

"Hey," Doran said.

"Right. I gotta stop swearing. Eff that guy."

"Your mom's right. We should give him a chance."

"He's had six years of chances. Any time he wants to call, I'll pick up."

There were a few years, after college, when they talked on the phone and his father would pretend that LT lived alone. He never asked about Doran, or about their lives. Then LT sent his father an invitation to the commitment ceremony. The next time LT called, his father said that he was disgusted, and didn't want to talk to him until he fixed his life.

His mother said, "This is different. Maybe it's time."

Maybe. He got up from the table.

Time itself had become different. He looked at Christina in Doran's arms and thought, I'm going to know you for the rest of my life. The future had broken open, his week-by-week life suddenly stretching to decades. He could picture her on her first day of school, on prom night, at her wedding. He caught a glimpse of her holding a baby as tiny as she was at that moment.

Had his father felt that way, too, when he was born?

He kissed Doran's cheek, then bent over their daughter. She was awake, dark-eyed, watching both of them. He thought, There's no way I can go away for six months into the jungle and leave her. He wouldn't make the choice his parents had made.

"We'll give it a shot," LT said. He moved his cheek across her warm head. Inhaled her scent. "Won't we, my darlin'?"

2007

HE WAS READING to Christina and Carlos when the call came. Or rather, Christina was reading while LT held the book, because Christina said he was only allowed to do the Hagrid and Dumbledore voices. Carlos, five years old, lolled at the end of the bed, seemingly oblivious but missing nothing.

Doran came to the bedroom holding the cordless. "Some guy wants to talk to you. He says he's a friend of your father's."

The thick Tennessee accent opened a door to his childhood. Vernon Beck, hearty as ever. He apologized for bothering LT "up there in D.C.," but he was worried about LT's father. "He stopped coming to work. He didn't quit, just stopped coming. Same with church. He won't answer the phone at all."

"Is he sick? Did he get hurt at the yard?"

"I went over there, and he finally came out to the porch. He said he was fine, just wanted folks to leave him alone. But I don't know. It ain't like him."

They talked a few minutes more. Mr. Beck apologized again for bothering him, explained how he got his number from a cousin. LT reassured him that it was all right. Asked about his son, Hale, who turned out to be doing fine, still in Maryville, working maintenance for the hospital. Had a wife and four children, all boys.

LT thought about that day they ran from the thistles. Funny how you don't know the last day you'll see someone. He'd spent the rest of that winter when he was thirteen daydreaming about Hale, his first big crush. He didn't mention that to Mr. Beck, and Mr. Beck didn't ask about LT's husband, or children. Southern Silence.

"One more thing," Mr. Beck said. "Your dad, he's let things go. You should be ready for that."

Doran asked, "What happened to your father?"

"Maybe nothing. But I think I have to go lay eyes on him."

Christina said, "I want to lay eyes on him!"

"Me too, kiddo," Doran said. "But not like this."

"Can we *read* now?" Carlos asked.

Doran didn't want LT to travel south. All those famine refugees landing in Florida, and the citizen militias in Texas and New Mexico. LT said his Department of Agriculture credentials would get them through any checkpoint, and besides, Tennessee was nowhere near the trouble. "It's like going into Wisconsin," LT said, quoting one of their favorite movies. "In and out."

"Fine," Doran said, "but why not just call the local police, let them check it out?" But LT didn't want to embarrass Dad, or get him fined if he wasn't taking care of the house.

"I owe him this much," LT said. And Doran said, "You think so?"

Doran stayed home with Carlos, and LT and Christina left before sunrise the next morning with a cooler full of food so they wouldn't have to depend on roadside restaurants. Christina fell asleep immediately, slept through all the phone calls he made to the Department, and woke up outside of Roanoke. He put away the phone and they listened to music and he pointed out invasives and native plants alongside the interstate. They were driving through the battlefield of a slow-motion war. Old native species were finding novel ways to fight the aliens—sucking resources from them underground, literally throwing shade above—and new invasives kept popping up into ecological niches. "It's all happening so incrementally," he told her, "it's hard to see."

"Like global warming," Christina said. He'd let her read the opening chapter of the book he was working on, and had taken her to see the Al Gore movie, so she understood boiling frogs. This had been his job for the past decade at the Department of Agriculture: explainer-in-chief, interpreter of policy, sometimes influencer of it. He missed the fieldwork, and longed to do original research again, but the government desk job provided stability for his family.

"Remember what I told you about animal speed?" he said. "Plant speed, and *planet* speed, that's just a hard timescale for us mammals to keep our attention on."

"I know. Wheels within wheels."

"Exactly."

After a day of driving and a two-hour wait for inspection at the Tennessee border, they entered the foothills. His hands knew the turns. He remembered the long drive home that last day of college—and realized for the first time that his father must have had to leave the hills at one in the morning to get to Illinois State by noon, and then had turned around and driven all the way back the same day. Drove it in silence, with a hungover, secretly heartbroken boy sulking in the passenger seat.

They pulled into the long gravel drive and parked beside the house. Christina said, "You used to live *here?*"

"Be nice. Your grandfather built this house."

"No, it's cool! It looks like a fairy castle."

His childhood home was being overrun in the same slow, grasping process that had swallowed Christina's village. The backyard grass, ordinary and native, had grown knee high. But covering the wall of the house was a flat-leafed ivy, brilliant and slick-looking as the heart of a kiwi fruit; definitely an invasive. Was this war, or détente?

Ivy also covered the back door. He tore away a clear space, and knocked. Knocked again. Called out, "Dad! It's LT!"

He tried the door, and it swung open. "Wait here," he said to Christina. He didn't want her to see anything horrible.

The kitchen lights were off. There were dishes in the sink, a pair of pots on the stove.

He called for his father again. His toe snagged on something. A vine, snaking across the floor. No, many vines.

He stepped into the living room—and froze. Ivy covered everything. A carpet of green clung to the walls. The fireplace burst with green foliage, and the tall stone altar of the chimney had become a trellis. Vines curled through doorways, snaked along the stair rails. Greenish sunlight filtering through the leaf-covered windows made the room into an aquarium. The air was jungle thick and smelled of fruiting bodies.

He stepped closer toward the fireplace, spied dots of white and red nestled into the leaves. Was the ivy *blooming*?

"What are you doing here?"

LT startled. The voice had come from behind him.

"Dad?"

His father sat in his armchair, nestled into the vines. Leaves draped his shoulders like a shawl. He wore a once-white UT Vols sweatshirt that seemed too big for him. His hair was shaggy, a steel gray that matched the stubble on his face. He looked too thin, much older than he should. LT felt as if he'd been catapulted through time. He hadn't seen or spoken to this man for almost twenty years, and now he wasn't even the same person.

His father said, "Who's this?"

LT thought, *Oh God, not Alzheimer's,* and then realized that Christina had come into the room.

She was looking up at the walls, the high ceiling, slowly turning to take it all in. "Dad..." Her voice was strange.

"It's okay, honey, there's nothing to be—"

"This is *awesome.*"

She lifted her hands to her head as if to contain the shock. A sound like applause erupted around the room. The leaves were shaking.

She looked at the corner, then up. "Dad, do you see it?"

He could, a green shape against the green. Enmeshed in leaves, an oak-thick stalk rose up in the corner. At the top, a bulbous head a yard wide was bent against a cross-timber, so that it seemed to be looking down at them. Its right arm stretched across the room, where broad leaves splayed against the wall as if holding it up. Its other arm hung down. Finger leaves brushed the floor.

"Holy fucking—"

"*Dad,*" Christina chided. She walked toward the plant. Lifted her hands above her head. The leaves of its arms rattled like a hundred castanets.

She laughed, and bent at the waist. Slow Mo's huge head eased left, then right.

LT's father said, "Isn't he a lovely boy?"

*　　*　　*

GEOLOGICAL TIME, PLANT time, animal time… and inside that, yet another, smaller wheel, spinning fast. His father's body had become a container for cells that lived and replicated and mutated at frightening speed.

On the second morning at Blount Memorial Hospital, Christina sat at the edge of her grandfather's bed, curled her fingers around his (carefully not disturbing the IV tubes taped to the top of his hand), and said, "I read a pamphlet about colon cancer. Would you like me to tell you about it?"

His father laughed. "Are you going to be a scientist like your father?" He was remarkably cheery, now that equipment had rehydrated him and delivered a few choice opioids.

She shook her head. "I want to be a real doctor."

LT, listening to on-hold music on his cell, said, "Hey!"

Doran came back on the line. "Okay, I got him an appointment with Lynn's oncologist. Bring him here. I'll move Carlos into Christina's room."

"Are you sure about this?"

"I would only do this for my favorite person. Besides, I don't think anybody else is stepping up. You're an only child, right?"

"Uh, kind of." He'd have to explain later.

He gave Christina a five and told her to sneak some ice cream into the room. "He likes rocky road, but chocolate will do."

His father watched her go. "She reminds me of your mother."

LT thought, Sure, this tiny, dark-haired, brown-skinned girl is *so* much like your blonde, dancer-legged wife.

"I mean it," his father said. "When she looks at me—it was like that with Belinda. That light."

"Dad—"

"All the boys in that school, and she chose me."

"Dad, I need to tell you some things."

"I'm not leaving the house."

"You can't go back there. I had Mr. Beck check it out. There are roots running through the floorboards, wrapped around the pipes. The wiring's been shorted out. You're lucky the place didn't burn down."

"It's my house. You can't tell me—"

"No, it's Mo's house now. It's been his for years."

*   *   *

2028

ON THAT LAST Thanksgiving he hosted in the Virginia house, the topic of conversation was, appropriately enough, food.

"We haven't published yet, but the data's solid," Christina said. "We've got an eater."

Cheers went up around the table. "Were you using the cyanobacteria?" LT asked. Just a few months ago, her gene-hacking team at McGill was making zero progress. "Or one of the Rhodophyta?"

"Let the woman speak!" LT's mother said. Christina, sitting beside her, squeezed her arm and said, "Thanks, Mimi."

"She needs no encouragement," Christina's husband said, and Carlos laughed.

"Here's the amazing thing—we didn't engineer it. We found the bacteria in the wild. Evolving on its own."

"You're kidding me," LT said.

Christina shrugged. "It turns out we should have been paying more attention to the oceans."

LT tried not to hear this as a rebuke. As the USDA's deputy secretary, he orchestrated the research grants, helped set the agenda for managing the ongoing crisis. It was a political job more than a scientific one, and much of the time the money had to go into putting out fires. So even though everyone knew that most of the seeds had gone down in water, the difficulty in retrieving them meant that almost all the research on water-based invasives focused on ones near the surface: the white pods like bloated worms floating in Lake Superior, the fibrous beach balls bobbing in the Indian Ocean, the blue fans that attached themselves to Japanese tuna like superhero capes.

Christina said that the bacteria were found feeding on rainbow mats. The scientific community had missed the explosion of translucent invasives hovering in the ocean's photic zone, until they linked and rose to the surface in a coruscating, multi-colored mass. The satellite pictures of it were lovely and terrifying. The alien plants were so efficient at sucking up carbon dioxide, in a few decades of unrestricted growth they could put a serious dent in global warming—while maybe killing everything else in the ocean.

But somehow, fast-evolving Earth organisms were trying to eat them first.

Or at least, one species of them. But if one Earth organism had figured it out, maybe others had, too.

"You have to tell us how they're breaking down those peptides," LT said.

"Or not," Carlos said.

"I have a story," said Bella, Christina's four-year-old daughter. "During craft time, this girl Neva? It was a *disaster.*"

"Wait your turn, darling," Aaron said. Christina's husband was a white man from Portland. He ran cool to Christina's hot, which was good for Bella.

Through some quasi-Lamarckian process, LT's children, and his children's children, had inherited his most annoying conversational tendency. On Thanksgiving they didn't go around the table saying what they were thankful for, but rather took turns explaining things to each other. Nothing made LT happier. All he wanted in the world was this: to be surrounded by his family, talking and talking. Much of the world was in dire shape, but they were rich enough to afford the traditional dry turkey breast, the cranberry sauce with the ridges from the can, sweet potato casserole piled with a layer of marshmallow.

"You know what this means," Christina said. She caught LT's eye. "Next year we'll be eating sugar sticks like the aliens did."

Perhaps only LT understood what she meant. *Homo sapiens* are only ten percent human; most of the DNA in their bodies comes from the tiny flora that they carry inside themselves to digest their food and perform a million tiny tasks that keep them alive. If humans could someday adopt these new bacteria into their microbiome, a host of invasives could become edible. It would be the end of the famine.

She saw the wonder in his face, and laughed. "Wheels within wheels, Dad."

After dinner, the urge to nap descended like a cloud, and only little Bella was immune. Carlos offered to take her to the park, but LT said he would like that honor.

"Where the slides are?" she asked.

"All the slides," he said. "Just let me tuck in Mimi."

He led his mother to the master bedroom, which was on the ground floor and had the best mattress. She moved carefully, as if hearing faint music in the distance, but at eighty she was still sharp, still beautiful, still determined to stay up with fashion. Her hair was three different shades of red.

"Eighty-five outside," she said, "and in here it's a Chicago winter."

"I'll get an afghan," he said, and opened the closet. When he turned around, she was sitting on the edge of the bed, one hand out on the coverlet.

"You must miss Doran."

The knot that he carried in his chest tightened a fraction. He nodded.

"It's not fair," she said. "All our men dying so young."

"Arnaud's still alive," LT said. "At least he was last year. He sent me a Christmas card."

"Good God, what an asshole," she said. "It's true what they say, then."

"I was the teenage asshole. I don't know how anybody put up with me."

She lay down and folded her hands across her chest like Cleopatra. He spread the afghan so that it covered her feet.

"This is a lovely house," she said.

"It's too big for me now. Unless you move in."

"I prefer living on my own these days. I do my painting in the nude, you know."

"You do not."

"But I *could*. That's the point."

Bella was waiting for him by the front door. "Papa!"

"Ciao, Bella!"

She jumped into his arms. It was a pleasure to be someone's favorite person again, at least for the moment. "Ready for the slides?"

He wished she didn't live so far away. He wished he wasn't so busy. People were making noises about nominating him for secretary, but he could say no, get off the treadmill. He could move to Canada and be close to Christina and Aaron and Bella, finally finish the book. Make one more research trip. He'd like to visit New Guinea again, see how the land of his daughter was faring. Fifty-three years after the meteor storm, and there were still so many questions to answer, and so many new things to see.

He carried Bella out into the Virginia heat. Soon he'd have to put her down, but he wanted to carry her as long as he could, as long as she let him. "So," he said to her. "What's all this about a disaster at craft time?"

*   *   *

2062

THE HOUSE WAS full of strangers. They kept touching his shoulder, leaning down into his face, wishing him happy birthday. Ninety-seven was a ridiculous age to celebrate. Not even a round number. They thought he wouldn't make it to ninety-eight, much less a hundred. They'd probably been waiting for years for him to kick off, and this premature wake was the admission of their surrender.

A tiny gray-haired woman sat beside him. Christina. "You have to see this," she said. She held a glass case, and suspended inside it was a glossy black shape flecked with silver. "It's from the current Secretary of Agriculture. 'For forty-five years of service to the nation and the world.' This one came from Tennessee. You remember telling me about Mimi finding a seed?"

There was an ocean of days he couldn't remember, but that day he recalled clearly. "Rock hound's delight," he said softly.

"What's that, Dad?"

Ah. The strangers were watching, waiting for a proper response. He cleared his throat, and said loudly, "So have those alien bastards shown up yet?"

Everyone laughed.

The afternoon stretched on interminably. Cake, singing, talking, so much talking. He asked for his jacket and a familiar-looking stranger brought it to him, helped him out of his chair. "I have to tell you, sir, your books made me want to be a scientist. *The Distant Gardener* was the first—"

LT lifted a hand. "Which way is the backyard?" He could still walk on his own. He was proud of that.

Outside, the sky was bright, the air too warm. He didn't need his coat, after all. He stood in a garden, surrounded by towering trees. But whose garden, whose house? It wasn't his home in Virginia, that was long gone. Not Chicago or Columbus. Was this Tennessee?

Everything moves too fast, he thought, or else barely moves at all.

"Papa?"

A young woman, holding the hand of a little girl. The girl, just three or four years old, held a huge black flower whose petals were edged with scarlet.

"Ciao, Bella!" he said to the girl.

The woman said, "No, Papa, this is Annie. I'm Bella."

A stab of embarrassment. And wonder. Bella was so old. How had that happened? How had he gotten so far from home? He wanted to do it all over again. He wanted Doran's shoulder next to him, and tiny Christina in his arms. He wanted Carlos on his shoulders at the National Zoo. All of it, all of it again.

"It's okay, Papa," Bella said. His tears concerned her. What a small, common thing to worry about.

He inclined his head toward the little girl. "My apologies, Annie. How are you doing this afternoon? Did you fly all the way from California?"

She let go of her mother's hand and approached him. "I have a flower."

"Yes, you do."

"It's a pretty flower."

"It certainly is."

Bella said, "She likes to tell people things."

The girl offered the flower to him. Up close, the black petals seemed to ripple and shift. Their dark surfaces swirled with traceries of silver that caught the light and spun it prettily. He raised it to his nose and made a show of sniffing it. The little girl laughed.

Words were not required. Sometimes the only way you could tell someone you loved them was to show them something beautiful. Sometimes, he thought, you have to send it from very far away.

"Where did you find this lovely flower?" he asked.

She pointed past his shoulder. He could feel the tower of green behind him. The leaves were about to move.

NOTE: *The mnemonic for meteoroids, meteors, and meteorites was written by Andy Duncan and is used with his permission.*

GOLGOTHA
Dave Hutchinson

Dave Hutchinson (hutchinsondave.wordpress.com) was born in Sheffield. After reading American Studies at the University of Nottingham, he became a journalist. He's the author of five collections of short stories and six novels, and three novellas. He is best known for the Fractured Europe sequence— *Europe in Winter, Europe in Autumn, Europe at Midnight,* and *Europe at Dawn*—which were nominated for the John W. Campbell Memorial, BSFA, Locus, Kitschie and Arthur C. Clarke Awards. Hutchinson has also edited two anthologies and co-edited a third. His latest books are the novels *Europe at Dawn* and *Shelter*. He lives in north London.

"TELL ME, FATHER," said the Lupo cleric as we walked along the beach, "do you think of yourself as a religious man?"

I thought about that for a while, conscious of the cameras and long-distance mikes behind us. Finally, I said, "That seems an...unusual question, if you don't mind my saying so. Considering my profession. Considering *our* profession."

"You present as a man of faith," the Lupo said.

"I am, although my faith has been tested many times."

"There is no such thing as faith, unless it has been tested."

I glanced over my shoulder at the crowd we had left behind up the beach. I couldn't see the Bishop among the newsmen and politicians and soldiers, but I knew he was there, probably sheltering from the wind and having a sneaky cigarette while the world's attention was on me and the alien.

"Your faith teaches that everyone is a child of God," the Lupo said, the great clawed feet of its environment suit crunching the shingle as it walked. "I would beg to differ. I do not consider myself a child of your God, nor you a child of mine."

This was almost precisely the line of conversation which the Bishop had warned me against becoming involved in, "I think this is a discussion best left to our superiors," I said in what I hoped was a diplomatic tone of voice. The tone of voice was for the cameras; I doubted the Lupo would be able to tell one way or another.

The Lupo had been on Earth for almost two years now, and their every action was still world news. They were an aquatic people, if one could call creatures which swam in seas of liquid methane on the moon of a gas giant orbiting a star fifty-eight light years away *aquatic*. Everyone was familiar with their image from news broadcasts from their orbiting mother-ship, but they needed to wear heavily-armoured suits to walk on the surface of our world. It had seemed absurd to hope that I would one day meet one, and yet here we were.

"They're sly beggars," the Bishop had told me last week. "This one says it's a priest and it wants to see Blackfin. The Church is still formulating a position towards the Lupo, so you're not to discuss doctrinal matters with it. And Donal, don't fuck up, whatever you do."

There had been no explanation why I, and not some more senior churchman—the Bishop himself, perhaps—had to take responsibility for the visit, although I suspected the danger of *fucking up* made this little stroll a potato too hot for my superiors to carry. I was expendable, and to an extent deniable.

"I am a simple priest," I said.

"Are we not all simple priests?" the alien asked.

"Well, no," I said. Although as far as I understood it, in the Lupo religion everyone *was* a priest to a greater or lesser degree. "Some of us are simpler than others," I added, and instantly regretted the attempt at humour. The Lupo, so far as anyone could judge, *had* no sense of humour. They at least had that in common with my Bishop.

It was a chill day, and the breeze off the Atlantic made it even colder, but here beside the Lupo I felt warm, almost toasty. The radiator fins of its suit made it feel as if I was standing beside a powerful patio heater. Over the past day or so, ahead of the Lupo's visit, I had been subjected to briefings by scientists and intelligence officers and at least one American General, but it was all jumbled up in my head and I was still unable to fathom how the body chemistry of a sentient being could function at those temperatures and pressures.

"They are not like us at *all*," the General had told me. "That's what you have to keep in mind, Father. Show it the fish, keep the conversation to generalities, and get it the hell out of there as soon as it's practical to do so."

In truth, I had grown a little weary of being told what to do. Ten months ago, I had been the priest of a tiny and mostly-overlooked parish. My congregation was dwindling, the younger members fleeing to the cities, the older ones dying. My biggest concern was how I was going to pay to repair the damage the previous winter's storms had done to the church roof. I felt as if I was on the edge of the world; no one cared what I thought or did. And then, everything had changed. One should always beware what one wishes for.

The cleric and I reached the water's edge. I stopped, the surf foaming around my wellingtons, but the alien walked on until it was knee-deep in the surging waves. It was almost as tall as I was, like a child's sketch of a large dog rendered in grey alloy, the double row of radiator fins on either side of its spine like the plates along the back of a stegosaurus. Its head was a ball studded with what were presumed to be audiovisual sensors, and it scanned from side to side constantly.

We looked out to sea, the alien and I, in the direction of America, and there was nothing to see, from surf to horizon. All shipping was being held back beyond a fifty-mile exclusion zone.

"Well," I said. "Looks as if we're unlucky today." Which was, deep down, what I had been hoping for.

The Lupo didn't reply. It raised its head, and from the speakers built into its chest came a rapid series of high-pitched squeaks and clicks, loud enough to hurt my eardrums. I took a few steps back, looked behind me, but no one in the crowd was moving. There were several news channels devoted to the Lupo, their doings on Earth, and the strictly-rationed details about themselves. They had hundreds of millions of viewers, and it occurred to me that every one of them was watching me, paddling in the Atlantic beside a creature born tens of light years from our solar system. That was why no one was joining us; nobody wanted to be in shot if things went tits-up.

The Lupo stopped emitting the sounds, and the last of them seemed to echo and banner in the wind before fading away to nothing. Then the alien seemed to wait. It broadcast the noises again, and again it waited. Then a third time, and this time, out beyond the breakers, I saw a distinctive black fin break the surface, disappear, reappear a little nearer to shore, and then begin to move back and forth. It was hardly an unusual sight, but even now I felt a little thrill.

Blackfin had been found washed up on the beach last year, severely wounded, possibly by the propeller of one of the boats that took tourists on trips around the bay. Volunteers had come from all over Ireland to try and save the stricken dolphin, but she died, and researchers from Dublin had taken her body away for study.

A few days later, as they prepared to perform an autopsy, Blackfin was seen to stir and then shudder, and then take a shaky but deep breath. The researchers rushed her to a tank, where over the following days she made a full recovery.

In time, after the astonished scientists had completed their tests, Blackfin had been released back into the wild, and a month or so ago she had been spotted in the bay. The Miracle Dolphin had become quite a tourist attraction; the hotels and guest houses in the village were booked up for well over a year in advance, and for the first time in several years my congregation had begun to grow again.

It had been quietly suggested that, as the local priest, I take no position on Blackfin; the Christian parallels were far too stark and obvious, and the Church, already struggling with the question of the Lupo and their God, were not yet minded to confront the concept of a cetacean Messiah. God had seen fit, in His mysterious way, to deliver one of His creatures. That's the official line, Donal. Oh, and by the way, don't fuck up.

The Lupo broadcast its noises once more, and this time Blackfin broke the surface and I heard, faint and far away, and broken by the wind, the sound of the dolphin *answering*, and I felt a line of cold trace its way down the centre of my back.

The alien's suit must have amplified the sound from the ocean; I could barely hear it over the wind and the waves but the Lupo spoke again, another series of clicks and whistles, and the dolphin replied once more. They were, I realised, having a *conversation*.

The conversation went on for some time. I looked back, but no one in the crowd seemed at all alarmed at this turn of events, and I realised they simply could not hear it. They were too far away, there was too much ambient noise. I was the only witness. That was why I was there, of course. Not because I was a trustworthy local but because I was God's representative on this bleak beach in the West of Ireland, the place where Blackfin had died. I was there to bear witness. I looked at the alien and suddenly felt very afraid. Mankind's record, when it came to the creatures of the ocean, was not terribly noble.

By the time I realised all this, of course, it was far too late. It had already been too late when the Lupo first set foot on the beach. I could not understand what the Lupo and Blackfin were saying, but I knew in my heart what they were discussing. They were talking about *us*, and our millennia-long despoilation of the seas, and all I could do was stand there helplessly.

Abruptly, the conversation ended. The Lupo fell silent, and the dolphin slipped out of sight beneath the waves again. The alien didn't move; it just stood there silently, the sea-foam rushing around its legs.

"So, Father," the Lupo said finally. "If this is a miracle, *whose* miracle is it?"

I opened my mouth to speak, but no sound came out.

"There is the God of those who walk and the God of those who fly and the God of those who swim," the alien went on, and this time I heard a noise from behind me, shouting, and I thought perhaps someone in the crowd had finally worked out what was going on. "It is strange to me that the God of those who swim has chosen to show Her benediction on this world, but one does not, after all, question the word of God, does one, Father?" The Lupo had not wanted to marvel at the Miracle Dolphin; it had come to *commune*, to *worship*. It had come to receive *Gospel*.

The Lupo were a spacefaring race, as far advanced from us as the *Conquistadores* had been from the peoples of South America. We did not know what they were capable of, but it was assumed they had weapons beyond our comprehension. Much of our dealings with them had involved trying very, very hard not to anger them, and now, with a simple act of tourism—after all, what could be more harmless than looking at a dolphin?—we had undone all that.

FLINT AND MIRROR

John Crowley

John Crowley was born in December, 1942, in Presque Isle, Maine, where his father, an Army Air Corps doctor, was stationed. Dr. Crowley later became medical director of the student infirmary at Notre Dame in South Bend, Indiana. There John taught himself to write blank verse, composed the beginnings of tragedies, and planned for a career in the theatre. He went to Indiana University, where he dropped that idea, majored in English and wrote poetry. Upon graduation, he went to New York City. There he planned to make films, wrote screenplays that were not produced, and began working in documentary films. He also began writing novels, beginning with a science fiction tale (*The Deep*, 1975) and then another (*Beasts*, 1977), but he had also begun writing a much larger work, which would not be finished for ten years: *Little, Big* was published in 1981. He then embarked on a four-volume novel without exactly intending to (*Ægypt*, 1987-2007). By then he had moved to the Berkshires in western Massachusetts, married and had twin daughters, and wrote more novels. In 1992, through the intervention of Yale professors who had come to admire his work, he got a job teaching Creative Writing, from which eminence he retired in June of 2018.

[Editor's note: *The following pages were recently discovered among uncatalogued papers of the novelist Fellowes Kraft (1897-1964) that came to the Rasmussen Foundation by bequest following his death. They comprise thirty-four typewritten sheets of yellow copy paper (Sphinx brand) edited lightly in pencil, apparently intended to be a part of Kraft's second novel, "A Passage at Arms" (1941), now long out of print and unavailable. In the end these pages were rejected by the author, perhaps because the work had evolved into a more conventional historical fiction. The mathematician and spiritual adventurer John Dee would appear in later Kraft works, both finished and unfinished, in rather different character than he does here.*]

BLIND O'MAHON THE poet said: "In Ireland there are five kingdoms, one in each of the five directions. There was a time when each of the kingdoms had her king, and a court, and a castle-seat with lime-washed towers; battlements of spears, and armies young and laughing."

"There was a high king then too," said Hugh O'Neill, ten years old, seated at O'Mahon's feet in the grass, still green at Hallowtide. From the hill where they sat the Great Lake could just be seen, turning from silver to gold as the light went. The roving herds of cattle—Ulster's wealth—moved over the folded land. All this is O'Neill territory, and always forever has been.

"There was indeed a high king," O'Mahon said.

"And will be again."

The wind stirred the poet's white hair. O'Mahon could not see Hugh, his cousin, but—he said—he could see the wind. "Now cousin," he said. "See how well the world is made. Each kingdom of Ireland has its own renown: Connaught in the west for learning and for magic, the writing of books and annals, and the dwelling-places of saints. In the north, Ulster"—he swept his hand over lands he couldn't see—"for courage, battles and warriors. Leinster in the east for hospitatilty, for open doors and feasting, cauldrons never empty. Munster in the south for labor, for kerns and ploughmen, weaving and droving, birth and death."

Hugh looking over the long view, the wind of the river where clouds were gathered now, asked: "Which is the greatest?"

"Which," O'Mahon said, pretending to ponder this. "Which do *you* think?"

"Ulster," said Hugh O'Neill of Ulster. "Because of the warriors. Cuchulain was of Ulster, who beat them all."

"Ah."

"Wisdom and magic are good," Hugh conceded. "Hosting is good. But warriors can beat them."

O'Mahon nodded to no one. "The greatest kingdom," he said, "is Munster."

Hugh said nothing to that. O'Mahon's hand sought for his shoulder and rested upon it, and Hugh knew he meant to explain. "In every kingdom," he said, "the North, the South, the East and the West, there is also a north, a south, an east, a west. Isn't that so?"

"Yes," Hugh said. He could point to them: left, right, ahead, behind. Ulster is in the north, and yet in Ulster there is also a north, the north of the north: that's where his mad, bad uncle Sean ruled. And so in that north, Sean's north, there must be again a north and a south, an east and a west. And then again...

"Listen," O'Mahon said. "Into each kingdom comes wisdom from the west, about what the world is and how it came to be. Courage from the north, to defend the world from what would swallow it up. Hospitality from the east to praise both learning and courage, and reward the kings who keep the world as it is. But before all these things, there is a world at all: a world to learn about, to defend, to praise, to keep. It is from Munster at first that the world comes to be."

"Oh," Hugh said, no wiser though. "But you said that there were *five* kingdoms."

"So I did. And so it is said."

Connaught, Ulster, Leinster, Munster. "What is the fifth kingdom?"

"Well, cousin," O'Mahon said, "what is it then?"

"Meath," Hugh guessed. "Where Tara is, where the kings were crowned."

"That's fine country. Not north or south or east or west but in the middle."

He said no more about that, and Hugh felt sure that the answer might be otherwise. "Where else could it be?" he asked.

O'Mahon only smiled. Hugh wondered if, blind as he was, he knew when he smiled and that others saw it. A kind of shudder fled along his spine, cold in the low sun. "But then," he said, "it might be far away."

"It might," O'Mahon said. "It might be far away, or it might be close." He chewed on nothing for a moment, and then he said: "Tell me this, cousin: Where is the center of the world?"

That was an old riddle; even boy Hugh knew the answer to it, his uncle Phelim's brehon had asked it of him. There are five directions to the world: four of them are north, south, east and west, and where is the fifth? He knew the answer, but just at that moment, sitting with bare legs crossed in the ferns in sight of the tower of Dungannon, he did not want to give it.

*   *   *

It was in the spring that his fosterers the O'Hagans had brought Hugh O'Neill to the castle at Dungannon. It was a great progress in the boy Hugh's eyes, twenty or thirty horses jingling with brass trappings, carts bearing gifts for his O'Neill uncles at Dungannon, red cattle lowing in the van, spearmen and bowmen and women in bright scarves, O'Hagans and O'Quinns and their dependents. And he knew himself, but ten years old, to be the center of that progress, on a dappled pony, with a new mantle wrapped around his skinny body and a new ring on his finger.

He kept seeming to recognize the environs of the castle, and scanned the horizon for it, and questioned his cousin Phelim, who had come to fetch him to Dungannon, how far it was every hour until Phelim grew annoyed and told him to ask next when he saw it. When at last he did see it, a fugitive sun was just then looking out, and sunshine glanced off the wet, lime-washed walls of its wooden palisades and made it seem bright and near and dim and far at once, heart-catching, for to Hugh the wooden tower and its clay and thatch outbuildings were all the castles he had ever heard of in songs. He kicked his pony hard, and though Phelim and the laughing women called to him and reached out to keep him, he raced on, up the long muddy track that rose up to a knoll where now a knot of riders were gathering, their spears high and slim and black against the sun: his uncles and cousins O'Neill, who when they saw the pony called and cheered him on.

Through the next weeks he was made much of, and it excited him; he ran everywhere, an undersized, red-headed imp, his stringy legs pink with cold and his high voice too loud. Everywhere the big hands of his uncles touched him and petted him, and they laughed at his extravagances and his stories, and when he killed a rabbit they praised him and held him aloft among them as though it had been twenty stags. At night he slept among them, rolled in among their great odorous shaggy shapes where they lay around the open turf fire that burned in the center of the hall. Sleepless and alert long into the night he watched the smoke ascend to the opening in the roof and listened to his uncles and cousins snoring and talking and breaking wind after their ale.

That there was a reason, perhaps not a good one and kept secret from him, why on this visit he should be put first ahead of older cousins, given first choice from the thick stews in which lumps of butter dissolved, and listened to when he spoke, Hugh felt but could not have said; but now and again he caught one or another of the men regarding him steadily, sadly, as though he were to be pitied; and again, a woman would sometimes, in the middle of some brag he was making, fold him in her arms and hug him hard. He was in a story whose plot he didn't know, and it made him the more restless and wild. There was a time when, running into the hall, he caught his uncle Turlough Luineach and a woman of his having an argument, he shouting at her to leave these matters to men; when she saw Hugh, the woman came to him, pulled his mantle around him and brushed leaves and burrs from it. "Will they have him dressed up in an English suit then for the rest of his life?" she said over her shoulder to Turlough Luineach, who was drinking angrily by the fire.

"His grandfather Conn had a suit of clothes," Turlough said into his cup. "A fine suit of black velvet with gold buttons and a black velvet hat. With a white plume in it!" he shouted, and Hugh couldn't tell if he was angry at the woman, or Conn, or himself. The woman began crying; she drew her scarf over her face and left the hall. Turlough glanced once at Hugh, and spat into the fire.

Nights they sat in the light of the fire and the great reeking candle of reeds and butter, drinking ale and Spanish wine and talking. Their talk was one subject only: the O'Neills. Whatever else came up in conversation or song related to that long history, whether it was the strangeness—stupidity or guile, either could be argued—of the English colonials; or the raids and counter-raids of neighboring families; or stories out of the far past. Hugh couldn't always tell, and perhaps his elders weren't always sure, what of the story had happened a thousand years ago and what of it was happening now. Heroes rose up and raided, slew their enemies and carried off their cattle and their women; some were crowned high king at Tara. There was mention of Niall of the Nine Hostages and the high king Julius Caesar; of Brian Boru and Cuchulain; of Sean O'Neill and his fierce Scots redlegs, of the sons of Sean and the King of Spain's son. His grandfather Conn had been the O'Neill, but had let the English call him Earl of Tyrone. There had always been an O'Neill, invested at the crowning stone at Tullyhogue to the sound of St. Patrick's bell; but Conn O'Neill, Earl of Tyrone, had seen King Harry over the sea, and had promised to plant corn, and learn English. And when he lay dying he said that a man was a fool to trust the English.

Within the tangled histories, each strand bright and clear and beaded with unforgotten incident but inextricably bound up with every other, Hugh could perceive his own story: how his grandfather had never settled the succession of his title of the O'Neill; how Hugh's uncle Sean had risen up and slain his brother Matthew, Hugh's father, and now called himself the O'Neill and claimed all Ulster for his own, and raided his cousins' lands when he chose with his six fierce sons; how he, Hugh, had true claim to what Sean had usurped. Sometimes all this was as clear to him as the multifarious branchings of a winter-naked tree against the sky; sometimes not. The English... there was the confusion. Like a cinder in his eye, they baffled his clear sight.

Turlough tells with relish: "Then comes up Sir Henry Sidney with all his power, and Sean? Can Sean stand against him? He cannot! It's as much as he can do to save his own skin. And that only by leaping into the Great River and swimming away. I'll drink the Lord Deputy's health for that, a good friend to Conn's true heir..."

Or, "What do they ask?" a brehon, a lawgiver, asks. "You bend a knee to the Queen, and offer all your lands. She takes them and gives you the title Earl—and all your lands back again. You are her *urragh*, but nothing has changed..."

"And they are sworn then to help you against your enemies."

"No," says another, "*you* against *theirs*, even if it be a man sworn to you or your own kinsman whom they've taken a hatred to. Conn was right: a man is a fool to trust them."

"Think of Desmond, in prison in London these many years, who trusted them."

"Desmond is a thing of theirs. He is a Norman, he has their blood. Not the O'Neills."

"*Fubun*," says the blind poet O'Mahon in a quiet high voice that stills them all:

Fubun *on the gray foreign gun,*
Fubun *on the golden chain;*

Fubun *on the court that talks English,*
Fubun *on the denial of Mary's son.*

Hugh listens, turning from one speaker to the other, and frightened by the poet's potent curse. He feels the attention of the O'Neills on him.

IN EASTER WEEK there appeared out of a silvery morning mist from the South a slow procession of horse and men on foot. Even if Hugh watching from the tower had not seen the red and gold banner of the Lord Deputy of Ireland shaken out suddenly by the rainy breeze, he would have known that these were English and not Irish, for the men were a neat, dark cross moving together smartly: a van, the flag in the center where the Lord Deputy rode flanked by men with long guns over their shoulders, and a rear guard with a shambling ox-drawn cart.

He climbed monkey-like down from the tower calling out the news, but the visitors had been seen already, and Phelim and the O'Hagan and Turlough were already mounting in the courtyard to ride and meet them. Hugh shouted at the horse-boys to bring his pony.

"You stay," Phelim said, pulling on his gloves of English leather.

"I won't," Hugh said, and pushed the horse-boy: "Go on!"

Phelim's horse began shaking his head and dancing away, and Phelim, pulling angrily at his bridle, commanded Hugh to obey; between the horse and Hugh disobeying him, he was getting red in the face, and Hugh was on the pony's back, laughing, before Phelim could take any action against him. Turlough had watched all this without speaking; now he raised a hand to silence Phelim and drew Hugh to his side.

"They might as well see him now as later," he said, and brushed back Hugh's hair with an oddly gentle gesture.

The two groups, English and Irish, stood for a time some distance apart with a marshy stream running between them, while heralds met formally in the middle and carried greetings back and forth. Then the Lord Deputy, in a gesture of condescension, rode forward with only his standard-bearer, splashing across the water and waving a gloved hand to Turlough; at that, Turlough rode down to meet him half-way, and leapt off his horse to take the Lord Deputy's bridle and shake his hand.

Hugh, watching these careful approaches, began to feel less forward. He moved his pony back behind Phelim's snorting bay. Sir Henry Sidney was huge: his mouth full of white teeth opened in a black beard that reached up nearly to his eyes, which were small and also black; his great thighs, in hose and high boots, made the slim sword that hung from his baldric look as harmless as a toy. His broad chest was enclosed in a breastplate like a tun; Hugh didn't know its deep stomach was partly false, in the current fashion, but it looked big enough to hold him whole. Sir Henry raised an arm encased in a sleeve more dagged and gathered and complex than any garment Hugh had ever seen, and the squadron behind began to move up, and just then the Lord Deputy's black eyes found Hugh.

In later years Hugh O'Neill would come to feel that there was within him a kind of treasure-chest or strong-box where were kept certain moments in his life, whole: some of them grand, some terrible, some oddly trivial, all perfect and complete with every sensation and feeling they had contained. Among the oldest which the box would hold was this one, when Turlough leading the Deputy's horse brought him to Hugh, and the Deputy reached down a massive hand and took Hugh's arm like a twig he might break, and spoke to him in English. All preserved: the huge black laughing head, the jingle of the horses' trappings and the sharp odor of their fresh droppings, even the soft glitter of condensing dewdrops on the silver surface of Sir Henry's armor. Dreaming or awake, in London, in Rome, this moment would now and again be taken out and shown him, and he would look into it as into a green and silver opal, and wonder.

THE NEGOTIATIONS LEADING to Sir Henry's taking Hugh O'Neill away with him to England as his ward went on for some days. Sir Henry was patient and careful: patient, while the O'Neills rehearsed again the long story of their wrongs at Sean's hands; careful not to commit himself to more than he directly promised: that he would be a good friend to the Baron Dungannon, as he called Hugh, while at the same time intimating that large honors could come of it, chiefly the earldom of Tyrone, which since Conn's death had remained in the Queen's gift, unbestowed.

He gave to Hugh a little sheath knife with a small emerald of peculiar hue set in the ivory hilt; he told Hugh that the gem was taken from a Spanish treasure-ship sailing from Peru on the other side of the world. Hugh, excluded from their negotiations, would sit with the women and turn the little knife in his hands, wondering what could possibly be meant by the other side of the world. When it began to grow clear to him that he was meant to go to England with Sir Henry, he grew shy and silent, not daring even to ask what it would be like there. He tried to imagine England: he thought of a vast stone place, like the cathedral of Armagh multiplied over and over, where the sun did not shine.

At dinner one night Sir Henry saw him loitering at the door of the hall, peeking in. He raised his cup and called to him. "Come, my young lord," he said, and the Irish smiled and laughed at the compliment, though Hugh, whose English was uncertain, wasn't sure they weren't mocking him. Hands urged him forward, and rather than be pushed before Sir Henry, Hugh stood as tall as he could, his hand on the little knife at his belt, and walked up before the vast man.

"My lord, are you content to go to England with me?"

"I am, if my uncles send me."

"Well, so they do. You will see the Queen there." Hugh answered nothing to this, quite unable to picture the Queen. Sir Henry put a huge hand on Hugh's shoulder, where it lay like a stone weight. "I have a son near you in age. Well, something younger. His name is Philip."

"Phelim?"

"Philip. Philip is an English name. Come, shall we go tomorrow?" Sir Henry looked around, his black eyes smiling at his hosts. Hugh was being teased: tomorrow was fixed.

"Tomorrow is too soon," Hugh said, attempting a big voice of Turlough's but feeling only sudden terror. Laughter around him made him snap his head around to see who mocked him. Shame overcame terror. "If it please your lordship, we will go. Tomorrow. To England." They cheered at that, and Sir Henry's head bobbed slowly up and down like an ox's.

Hugh bowed and turned away, suppressing until he reached the door of the hall a desire to run. Once past the door, though, he fled, out of the castle, down the muddy street between the outbuildings, past the lounging guards, out into the gray night fields over which slow banks of mist lay undulating. Without stopping he ran along a beaten way up through the damp hissing grass to where a riven oak thrust up, had thrust up for as long as anyone knew, like a tensed black arm and gnarled hand.

Near the oak, almost hidden in the grass, were broken straight lines of worn mossy stones that marked where once a monastic house had stood; a hummocky sunken place had been its cellar. It was here that Hugh had killed, almost by accident, his first rabbit. He had not been thinking, that day, about hunting, but only sitting on a stone with his face tilted upward into the sun thinking of nothing, his javelin across his lap. When he opened his eyes, the sunlit ground was a coruscating darkness, except for the brown shape of the rabbit in the center of vision, near enough almost to touch. Since then he had felt the place was lucky for him, though he wouldn't have ventured there at night; now he found himself there, almost before he had decided on it, almost before the voices and faces in the hall had settled out of consciousness. He had nearly reached the oak when he saw that someone sat on the old stones.

"Who is it there?" said the man, without turning to look. "Is it Hugh O'Neill?"

"It is," said Hugh, wondering how blind O'Mahon nearly always knew who was approaching him.

"Come up, then, Hugh." Still not turning to him—why should he? and yet it was unsettling—O'Mahon touched the stone beside him. "Sit. Do you have iron about you, cousin?"

"I have a knife."

"Take it off, will you? And put it a distance away."

He did as he was told, sticking the little knife in a spiky tree-stump some paces off; somehow the poet's gentle tone brooked neither resistance nor reply.

"Tomorrow," O'Mahon said when Hugh sat next to him again, "you go to England."

"Yes." Hugh felt ashamed here to admit it, even though it had been in no sense his choice; he didn't even like to hear the poet say the place's name.

"It's well you came here, then. For there are certain... personages who wished to say farewell to you. And give you a commandment. And a promise."

The poet wasn't smiling; his face was lean and composed behind a thin fair beard nearly transparent. His bald eyes, as though filled with milk and water, looked not so much blind as simply unused: baby's eyes. "Behind you," he went on, and Hugh looked quickly around, "in the old cellar there, lives one who will come forth in a moment, only you ought not to speak to him."

The cellar-place was obscure; any of its humps, which seemed to shift vaguely in the darkness, might have been someone.

"And beyond, from that rath"—O'Mahon pointed with certainty, though he didn't look, toward the broad ancient tumulus riding blackly like a whale above the white shoals of mist—"now comes out a certain prince, and to him also you should not speak."

Hugh's heart had turned small and hard and beat painfully. He tried to say *Sidhe* but the word would not be said. He looked from the cellar to the rath to the cellar again—and there a certain tussock darker than the rest grew arms and hands and began with slow patience to pull itself out of the earth. Then a sound as of a great stamping animal came from ahead of him, and, turning, he saw that out of the dark featureless rath something was proceeding toward him, something like a huge windblown cloak or a quickly-oaring boat with a black luffing sail or a stampeding caparisoned horse. He felt a chill shiver up his back. At a sound behind him he turned again, to see a little thick black man, now fully out of the earth, glaring dourly at him (the glints of his eyes all that could be seen of his face) and staggering toward him under the weight of a black chest he carried in his stringy, rooty arms.

An owl hooted, quite near Hugh; he flung his head around and saw it, all white, gliding silently ahead of the Prince who proceeded toward Hugh, of whom and whose steed Hugh could still make nothing but that they were vast, and were perhaps one being, except that now he perceived gray hands holding reins or a bridle, and a circlet of gold where a brow might be. The white owl swept near Hugh's head, and with a silent wingbeat climbed to a perch in the riven oak.

There was a clap as of thunder behind him. The little black man had set down his chest. Now he glared up at the Prince before him and shook his head slowly, truculently; his huge black hat was like a tussock of grass, but there nodded in it, Hugh saw, a white feather delicate as snow. Beside Hugh, O'Mahon sat unchanged, his hands resting on his knees; but then he raised his head, for the Prince had drawn a sword.

It was as though an unseen hand manipulated a bright bar of moonlight; it had neither hilt nor point, but it was doubtless a sword. The Prince who bore it was furious, that was certain too: he thrust the sword down imperiously at the little man, who cried out with a shriek like gale-tormented branches rubbing, and stamped his feet; but, though resisting, his hands pulled open the lid of his chest. Hugh could see that there was nothing inside but limitless darkness. The little man thrust an arm deep inside and drew out something; then, approaching with deep reluctance only as near as he had to, he held it out to Hugh.

Hugh took it; it was deathly cold. There was the sound of a heavy cape snapped, and when Hugh turned to look, the Prince was already away down the dark air, gathering in his stormy hugeness as he went. The owl sailed after him. As it went away, a white feather fell, and floated zigzag down towards Hugh.

Behind Hugh, a dark hummock in the cellar place had for a moment beneath it the glint of angry eyes, and then did not any more.

Ahead of him, across the fields, a brown mousing owl swept low over the silvery grass.

Hugh had in his hands a rudely carven flint, growing warm from his hand's heat, and a white owl's feather.

"The flint is the commandment," O'Mahon said, as if nothing extraordinary at all had happened, "and the feather is the promise."

"What does the commandment mean?"

"I don't know."

They sat a time in silence. The moon, amber as old whiskey, appeared between the white-fringed hem of the clouds and the gray heads of the eastern mountains. "Will I ever return?" Hugh asked, though he could almost not speak for the painful stone in his throat

"Yes."

Hugh was shivering now. If Sir Henry had known how late into the night he had sat out of doors, he would have been alarmed; the night air, especially in Ireland, was well known to be pernicious.

"Goodbye, then, cousin," Hugh said.

"Goodbye, Hugh O'Neill." O'Mahon smiled. "If they give you a velvet hat to wear, in England, your white feather will look fine in it."

SIR HENRY SIDNEY, though he would not have said it to the Irish, was quite clear in his dispatches to the Council why he took up Hugh O'Neill. Not only was it policy for the English to support the weaker man in any quarrel between Irish dynasts, and thus prevent the growth of any overmighty subject; it also seemed to Sir Henry that, like an eyas falcon, a young Irish lord if taken early enough might later come more willingly to the English wrist. Said otherwise: he was bringing Hugh to England as he might the cub of a beast to a bright and well-ordered menagerie, to tame him.

For that reason, and despite his wife's doubts, he set Hugh O'Neill companion to his own son Philip; and for the same reason he requested his son-in-law the Earl of Leicester to be Hugh's patron at court. "A boy poor in goods," he wrote Leicester, "and full feebly friended."

The Earl of Leicester, in conversation with the Queen, turned a nice simile, comparing his new Irish client to the grafted fruit-trees the Earl's gardeners made: by care and close binding, the hardy Irish apple might be given English roots, though born in Irish soil; and once having them, could not then be separated from them.

"Pray sir, then," the Queen said smiling, "his fruits be good."

"With good husbandry, Madame," Leicester said, "his fruits will be to your Majesty's taste." And he brought forward the boy, ten years old, his proud hair deep red, almost the color of the morocco leather binding of a little prayer-book the Queen held in her left hand. Across his pale face and upturned nose the freckles were thick, and faintly green; his eyes were emeralds. Two things the Queen loved were red hair and jewels; she put out her long ringed hand and brushed Hugh's hair.

"Our cousin of Ireland," she said.

He didn't dare raise his red-lashed eyes to her after he had made the courtesy that the Earl had carefully instructed him in; while they talked about him above his head in a courtly southern English he couldn't follow, he looked at the Queen's dress.

She seemed in fact to be wearing several. As though she were some fabulous many-walled fort, mined and breached, through the slashings and partings of her outer dress another could be seen, and where that was opened there was another, and lace beneath that. The outer wall was all jeweled, beaded with tiny seed-pearls as though with dew, worked and embroidered in many patterns of leaf, vine, flower. On her petticoat were pictured monsters of the sea, snorting sea-horses and leviathans with mouths like portcullisses. And on the outer garment's inner side, turned out to reveal them, were a hundred disembodied eyes and ears. Hugh could believe that with those eyes and ears the Queen could see and hear, so that even as he looked at her clothing her clothing observed him. He raised his eyes to her white face framed in stiff lace, her hair dressed in pearls and silver.

Hugh saw then that the power of the Queen resided in her dress. She was bound up in it as magically as the children of Lir were bound up in the forms of swans. The willowy, long-legged courtiers, gartered and wearing slim English swords, moved as in a dance in circles and waves around her when she moved. When she left the chamber (she did not speak to Hugh again, but once her quick, bird eye lighted on him) she drew her ladies-in-waiting after her as though she caught up rustling fallen leaves in her train.

Later the Earl told Hugh that the Queen had a thousand such gowns and petticoats and farthingales, each more elaborate than the last.

A screen elaborately carved—nymphs and satyrs, grape-clusters, incongruous armorial bearings picked out in gold leaf—concealed the Queen's chief counselor, Sir William Cecil, Lord Burghley, and Dr. John Dee, her consulting physician and astrologer, from the chamber where the Queen had held audience. But through the piercings of the screen they could see and hear.

"That boy," Burghley said softly. "The red-headed one."

"Yes," said Dr. Dee. "The Irish boy."

"Sir Henry Sidney is his patron. He has been brought to be schooled in English ways. There have been others. Her gracious majesty believes she can win their hearts and their loyalty. They do learn manners and graces, but they return to their island, and their brutish natures well up again. There is no way to keep them bound to us in those fastnesses."

"I know not for certain," said Dr. Dee, combing his great beard with his fingers, "but it may be that there are ways."

"*Doctissime vir*," said Burghley. "If there are ways let us use them."

A LIGHT SNOW lay on the roads and cottages when Philip Sidney, Sir Henry's son, and Hugh O'Neill went from the Sidney's house of Penshurst in Kent up to Mortlake to visit John Dee. There was a jouncing, canopied cart filled with rugs and cushions but the boys preferred to ride with the attendants until the cold pinched them too deeply through the fine thin gloves and hose they wore. Hugh, careful now in matters of dress, would not have said that his English clothes were useless for keeping out cold compared to a shaggy Waterford mantle with a fur hood; but he seemed to be always cold and comfortless, somehow naked, in breeches and short cloaks.

Philip dismounted and threw his reins to the attendant; rubbing his hands, his narrow blue-clad buttocks clenched. When Hugh had climbed in too they pulled shut the curtains and huddled together under the rugs, each laughing at the other's shivers. They talked of the Doctor, as they called Dee, with whom Philip already studied Latin and Greek and mathematics—Hugh, though the older of the two, had had no lessons as yet, though they'd been promised him. They talked of what they would do when they were grown up and were knights, reweaving with themselves as the heroes the stories of Arthur and Guy of Warwick and the rest.

When the two of them played at heroes on their ponies in the fields of Penshurst Hugh could never bully Philip into taking the lesser part: *I will be a wandering knight, and you must be my esquire.* Philip Sidney knew the tales, and he knew (almost before he knew anything else of the world) that the son of an Irish chieftain could not have ascendancy even in play over the son of an English knight.

But whenever Philip had Hugh at stick-swordpoint in a combat, utterly defeated, Hugh would leap up and summon from the hills and forests a sudden host of helpers who slew Philip's merely mortal companions. Or he postulated a Crow who was a great princess he had long ago aided, whose feet he could grasp and be carried to safety, or an oak tree that would open and hide him away.

It wasn't fair, Philip would cry, these sudden hosts that Hugh sang forth in harsh unmusical Irish. They didn't fit any rules, they had nothing to do with the triumph of good knights over evil ones, and why anyway did they only help Hugh?

"Because my family once did them a great service," Hugh said to Philip in the rocking wagon. The matter was never going to be resolved.

"Suppose my family had."

"Guy of Warwick hasn't any family."

"I say now that he does, and so he does."

"And there aren't... fairy-folk in England." That term carefully chosen.

"For sure there are."

"No there are not, and if there were how could you summon them? Do you think they understand English at all?"

"I will summon them in Latin. *Veni, venite, spiritus sylvani, dives fluminarum...*"

Hugh kicked at the covers and at Philip, laughing. Latin!

Once they'd taken the issue to the wisest man they knew, excepting Doctor Dee himself, whom they didn't dare to ask: Buckle the Penshurst gamekeeper.

"There was fairies here," he said to them. His enormous gnarled hands honed a long knife back and forth, back and forth on a whetstone. "But that was before King Harry's time, when I was a boy and said the Ave-Mary."

"See there!" said Philip.

"Gone," said Hugh.

"My grandam saw them," said Buckle. "Saw one sucking on the goat's pap like any kid, and so the goat was dry when she came to milk it. But not now in this new age." Back and forth went the blade, and Buckle tested it on the dark and ridgy pad of his thumb.

"Where did they go?" Philip asked.

"Away," Buckle said. "Gone away with the friars and the Mass and the Holy Blood of Hailes."

"But where?" Hugh said.

A smile altered all the deep crags and lines of Buckle's face. "Tell me," he said, "young master, where your lap goes when you stand up."

*   *   *

Doctor Dee's wife Jane gave the boys a posset of ale and hot milk to warm them, and when they had drunk it he offered them a choice: they might read in whatever books of his they liked, or work with his mathematical tools and study his maps, which he had unrolled on a long table, with compass and square laid on them. Philip chose a book, a rhymed romance that Doctor Dee chuckled at; the boy nested himself in cushions, opened his book, and was soon asleep "like a mouse in cotton-wool" Jane Dee said. Hugh bent over the maps with the Doctor, his round spectacles enlarging his eyes weirdly and his long beard nearly trailing across the sheets.

What Hugh had first to learn was that the maps showed the world, not as a man walking in it sees it, but as a bird flying high over it. High, high: Doctor Dee showed him on a map of England the length of the journey from Penshurst to Mortlake and it was no longer than the joint of his thumb. And then England and Ireland too grew small and insignificant when Doctor Dee unrolled a map of the whole wide world. Or half of it: the world, he told Hugh, is round as a ball, and this was a picture of but one half. A ball! Hung by God in the middle of the firmament, the great stars going around it in their spheres and the fixed stars in theirs.

"This," the Doctor said, "is the Irish island, across St. George's Channel. Birds may fly across from there to here in the half-part of a day."

Hugh thought: the children of Lir.

"All these lands of Ireland, Wales and Scotland"—his long finger showed them—"are the estate of the British Crown, of our Imperial Queen, whose sworn servant you are." He smiled warmly, looking down upon Hugh.

"So also am I," said Philip, who'd awakened and come behind them.

"And so you are." He turned again to his maps. "But look you. It is not only these Isles Britannicae that belong to her. In right, these lands to the North, of the Danes and the Norwayans, they are hers too, by virtue of their old Kings her ancestors—though it were inadvisable to lay claim to them now. And farther too, beyond the ocean sea."

He began to tell them of the lands far to the west, of Estotiland and Groenland, of Atlantis. He talked of King Malgo and King Arthur, of Lord Madoc and Saint Brendan the Great; of Sebastian Caboto and John Caboto, who reached the shores of Atlantis a hundred years before Columbus sailed. They, and others long before, had set foot upon those lands and claimed them for kings from whom Elizabeth descended; and so they adhere to the British Crown. And to resume them under her rule the Queen need ask no leave of Spaniard or of Portingale.

"I will find new lands too, for the Queen," Philip said. "And you shall come too, to guide me. And Hugh shall be my esquire!"

Hugh O'Neill was silent, thinking: the kings of Ireland did not yield their lands to the English. The Irish lands were held by other kings, and other peoples altogether, from time before time. And if a new true king could be crowned at Tara, that king would win those lands again.

It was time now for the boys to return to Kent. Outside, the serving men could be heard mounting up, their spurs and trappings jingling.

"Now give my love and duty to your father," Doctor Dee said to Philip, "and take this gift from me, to guide you when you are grown, and set out upon those adventures you seek." He took from his table a small book, unbound and sewn with heavy thread. It was not printed but written in the Doctor's own fine hand, and the title said *General and Rare Memorials Pertayning to the Perfect Arte of Navigation*. Philip took it in his hands with a sort of baffled awe, aware of the honor, uncertain of the use.

"And for my new friend of Hibernia," he said. "Come with me." He took Hugh away to a corner of his astonishingly crowded room, pushed aside a glowing globe of pale brown crystal in a stand, lifted a dish of gems, and with an *Ah!* he picked up something that Hugh did not at first see.

"This," Doctor Dee said, "I will give you as my gift, in memorial of this day, if you will but promise me one thing. That you will keep it, always, on your person, and part with it never nor to no one." Hugh didn't know what to say to this, but the Doctor went on speaking as though Hugh had indeed promised. "This, young master, is a thing of which there is but one in the world. The uses of it will be borne in upon you when the need for them is great."

What he then put into Hugh's hand was an oval of black glass, glass more black than any he had ever seen, black too black to look right at, yet he could see that it reflected back to him his own face, as though he had come upon a stranger in the dark. It was bound in gold, and hung from a gold chain. On the back the surface of the gold was marked with a sign Hugh had never seen before: he touched the engraved lines with a finger.

"*Monas hieroglyphica*," said Doctor Dee. He lifted the little obsidian mirror from Hugh's hand by its brittle chain, hung it around the boy's neck. When Hugh again looked into the black sheen of it he saw neither himself nor any other thing; but his skin burned and his heart was hot. He looked to the Doctor, who only tucked the thing away within Hugh's doublet.

When he was at Penshurst again and alone—it was not an easy thing to be alone in the Sidney house, with the lords and ladies and officers of the Queen arriving and going, and Philip's beautiful sister teasing, and the servants coming and passing—Hugh opened his shirt and took in his fingers the thing the Doctor had given him. The privy (where he sat) was cold and dim. He touched the raised figure in the gold of the back, which looked a little like a crowned mannikin but likely was not, and turned it over. In the mirror was a face, but now not his own; for it wasn't like looking into a mirror at all, but like looking through a spy-hole and into another place, a spy-hole through which someone in that place looked back at him. The person looking at him was the Queen of England.

ON THE IMPREGNATION *of Mirrors* was not a book or a treatise or a Work; it wouldn't survive the wandering life that John Dee was to embark upon as the times and the heavens turned. It was just a few sheets, folded octavo and written in the Doctor's scribble hand, and no one not the Doctor would have been able to practice what it laid out, for certain necessary elements and motions went unwritten except in the Doctor's breast. It exists now but as name in a list of his papers and goods drawn up for an application to her Majesty's government for recompense, after his library and workshop had been despoiled by his enemies at court during his long absence abroad. Only one mirror of those that he had worked the art upon had succeeded entirely, only one had drawn the lines of time and space together so as to transmit the spirit of the owner to the eye of the possessor.

The making of it began with a paradox. If the impregnation of a mirror required that the one who first looked into it be its owner, then no other could ever have looked into it before, not he who silvered the glass, not she who polished the steel. How could the maker not be the owner? John Dee had seen the solution. There was one perfect mirror that needed no silvering, no polishing: it needed only to be discovered, detected, its smooth side inferred, then taken from the ground and secreted before even the finder's eye fell upon its face. He knew of many such, taken from the lava fields of Greece or the Turkish lands, first found, as Pliny saith, by the traveler Obsius; his own he'd found in a lesser field in Scotland. He remembered the cold hill, the fragments sharp as knives, keeping his eyes steadily on the fast-flying clouds above while his fingers felt for the perfectest one, pocketing it unlooked-at.

He had placed it in the Queen's hand himself. Slipping it from where it hid in a purse of kidskin, feeling for its smooth side, which he held up to her face for a long moment, as long a moment as he dared, before giving it to her to examine. She seemed dazzled by it, amazed, though she had seen similar obsidian chips before. None like this one: Doctor Dee had bestirred its latent powers by prayer—and by means he had learned from helpers he would not name, not in the hearing of this court.

And then forever there was the Queen's face within, and more than her face, her very self: her thought, her command, her power to entrance, how well the Doctor knew of it. She had not asked to keep it—the one danger he had feared. No, she had given it back to him with a gracious nod, and turned to other matters, for it was his. And now it was not his. For having taken its owner's face and nature it could be handled, and the Doctor had milled it and framed it in gold and given it to the Irish boy.

It may be there are ways.

Doctor Dee stood on a Welsh headland from where on a clear day the Irish coast could just be seen across St. George's Channel. The sun was setting behind the inland hills of the other island, making them seem large and near with the golden brightness. There where the sun set Hugh O'Neill was one day to become a great chief; the Doctor's informants had let him know of it. The little Irish kings and the old Irish lords would press him in the years to come to make a single kingdom out of the island that had never been one before, and to push out the English and the Scots for good. But Hugh O'Neill—whether he knew it or did not—was as though tethered by a long leash, the one end about his neck, the other held in the Queen's hand, though she might never know of it; and the tug of it, of her thought and will and desire and need, would keep the man in check. She could turn to other matters, the greater world, more dangers.

And to himself as well.

He turned from the sea. A single cloud like a great beast streaked with blood went away to the north with the wind, changing as it went.

AFTER SEVEN YEARS had passed Hugh O'Neill was returned to Ulster. He was not yet the O'Neill, he was not Earl of Tyrone, but nor was he any other man. By the English designations, in which the Irish only half-believed, he was mere Baron Dungannon. The quiet boy had grown into a quiet man. His father Matthew's rebel brother Sean, had been killed by Hugh's uncle Turlough Luineach, for which act the English had favored him—whatever that might mean for Turlough's benefit, to which the English would never commit: the rich earldom, an empty name, letters patent, loans of money, or nothing at all.

Hugh on Irish soil again, with English soldiers in his train and around his neck an English engine that he did not yet know the uses of, rode through Dublin and was not hailed or cheered. Who was on his side, who could he count on? There were the O'Hagans, who were poor, and the O'Donnells, the sons of the fierce Scots pirate Ineen Duv (the "dark girl"). And Englishmen: the Queen's men, Burghley and Walsingham, who had taken his hand and smiled. They'd known Conn O'Neill, and remarked on the white feather Hugh wore always in his cap. He'd learned more than courtly English from them. Their eyes were colder than their hands.

The castle-tower of Dungannon still stood, but the old chiefs and their adherents who had feasted and quarreled here were scattered now, fighting each other, or gone south to fight for the heirs of Desmond. But even as he came to the place with his little train they had begun returning, more every day: poor men, ill-equipped, not well fed. There were women still there in the castle, and from them he learned that his mother had died in the house of the O'Hagans.

"It is ill times," said blind O'Mahon, who had remained.

"It is."

"Well, you have grown, cousin. And in many ways too."

"I am the one I was," Hugh said, and the poet did not answer him.

"Tell me," he said. "Once in a place nearby, up that track to the crest of the hill, where a holy house once stood..."

"I remember," Hugh said.

"A thing was given you."

"Yes."

A man may keep a thing about him, in one pocket or purse or another, and forget he has it; thinks to toss it away now and then and yet never does so—not because it's of value but only because it's his, a bit of himself, and has long been. So the little carven flint had lain here and there throughout his growing up, getting lost and then turning up again. It had ceased to be what for a moment here in this place and long ago it seemed to be: a thing of cold power, with a purpose of its own, too heavy for its size. It had become a small old stone, scratched with the figure of a man that a child might draw.

He felt here and there in his clothes and came upon it: felt it leap into his hand as soon as it could. He drew it out and for a foolish moment thought to display it to the blind man. "I have it still," he said.

A commandment, O'Mahon had called the stone. But not what it commanded. He closed his hand on it. "I will soon build a house here," he said. "A house such as the English make, of bricks and timber, with windows of glass, and chimneys, and a key to lock the door."

"Will you go with me now, up to the place I spoke of?"

"If you like, cousin."

O'Mahon took O'Neill's arm, and Hugh led him where O'Mahon guided; the poet knew very well where he went but wanted help so as not to stumble on the way. They climbed the low hill that Hugh had known in youth, when he had first come to this country with his O'Hagan fosterers, but then there had been tall trees now cut, and beyond the trees to the river fields of corn and pasture where cattle moved. Now fallow and bare.

"Day goes," the poet said, as though he saw it. Past the riven oak, amid the low rolling of the hills there was the one hill taller and of a shape not made by wind and water, but by hands—it was easy to tell. A thousand rods or more in length, but smaller somehow now than when he had seen it as a boy. "This hour is the border of day and night, as the river is the border of here and there. What cannot be known by day or night shows itself at twilight."

"You know these things, who can't see them?"

"My eyes are a border too, cousin. At which I forever stand."

They stood in silence there while the sky turned black above and to a pale, red-streaked green in the west. A mist gathered in the hollows. Hugh O'Neill would not later remember the moment, if there was a moment, when the host came forth, if it did, and stood there against the rath, hard to see but seemingly there. Growing in numbers, mounted and afoot.

"The foreign queen you love and serve," O'Mahon said. "She cares nothing for you but this: that you keep this Isle in subjection for her sake, until and when she can fill it with her hungry subjects and poor relations, to take of it what they will."

The ghost warriors were clearer now. Hugh could almost hear the rustle they made and the rattle of their arms. The Old Ones, the *Sidhe*.

"They command you to fight, Hugh Gaveloch O'Neill of the O'Neills. The O'Neill you are, and what you will be you do not know. But you are not unfriended."

They formed and reformed in the dark, their steeds turning in place, their lances like saplings in wind: as though impatient for him to cry out to them in supplication, or call them to his side.

The commandment, Hugh thought. But he could say nothing to them, not with his voice, not in his heart; and soon the border of night and day was closed, and he could see them no more.

IN MUNSTER WHERE the world began the old Norman earls of Desmond and Kildare and Ormond had risen again, resisting the English adventurers whose papers and patents said they owned the lands that those families had held for time out of mind. The earls acknowledged no power higher than themselves except the Pope. Hugh O'Neill kept as far from the quarrel in the south as he could; he told himself that his work was to make himself pre-eminent here, Lord of the North.

But the obsidian mirror judged him and found him wanting. *You are a cold friend to her who loves you and will soon do you great good:* the Queen looked out at him, her white face framed in a stiff ruff. Eyes he saw in dreams too. When the English gathered an army at Dublin under old and weary Henry Sidney, Hugh rode south with him, bringing fighters of his own, feeding them from the plunder of Desmond villages and fields. Any town or village that Sidney invested and would not surrender was put to the sword, the leaders beheaded and their heads impaled on stakes across the land. The earls and their followers burned the standing grain in the fields to keep Sidney's army from the provender, and then in the spring Sidney's soldiers burned it as it sprung, to keep it from them. The people ate cresses and when they had none they died, and others ate their flesh, and the flesh of their dead babes. And the Queen spoke to O'Neill's heart and said *Look not on their suffering but on me.*

But the flint in his pocket had its say as well.

He kept on with Sir Henry—but he went his own way. He avoided pitched battles and retributions; he largely occupied himself in Munster not with fighting but with... hunting. He brought along with him on his hunts men with guns (*Fubun on the grey foreign gun* O'Mahon had said long ago, but this was now, not then). Wherever he went, wherever men had lost their lands, he would ask the men and boys what weapons they were good at using, and after they named spears and bows and the pike he would bring out a gun, and explain the use of it, and let one or another of them take it and try it. The handiest of them he'd reward with a coin or other gift, and perhaps even the gun itself. *Keep it safe* he'd say, smiling.

That was wisdom the mirror would never give him and the flint could not know: When the time came for *him* to lead men against English soldiers—if it did come—he would not lead hordes of screaming gallowglass against trained infantry with guns. *His* army would wheel on command, and march in step, and lay fire. When the time came.

In Dungannon again he began to build himself that fine house in the English style, where wardrobes held his velvet English suits and hats, his rugs and bedclothes made from who knew what. When he could get no lead for the roofs of his house, Burghley saw to it that a shipment of many tons of sheet lead were sent to him; it lay for years in the pine woods at Dungannon until a different use for it was found, in a different world. He fell in love, not for the first or the last time, but this time providentially: she was Mabel Bagenal, daughter of Sir Nicholas Bagenal, officer of the Queen's Council in Dublin— Bagenal resisted the match, not wanting an Irish chieftain for a son-in-law and thinking Mabel could do better: but when Hugh O'Neill rode into Dublin in his velvets and his silk-lined cloak with a hundred retainers around him her heart was won. And the power in the black mirror was glad of it.

The morning after his wedding night Mabel discovered it on its gold chain on his breast and tried to take it off, but he wouldn't let her; he only turned it to her and asked her what she saw. The third soul ever to look in. She studied it, brow knit, and said she saw herself, but dimly.

Himself was never what Hugh O'Neill saw there. "It was a gift," he said. "From a wise man in England. To keep me safe, he said."

Mabel Bagenal looked into her husband's face, which seemed to seek itself in the black mirror, though she was wrong about that; and she said, "May God will that it do so."

IN THE SAME spring Doctor John Dee and his wife Jane and their many children left for the Continent with trunkloads of books, an astronomer's staff, bottles of remedy for every ill, a cradleboard for the newest, and in a velvet bag a small orb of quartz crystal with a flaw like a lost star not quite at its center. In a cold room in a high tower in the golden city in the middle of the Emperor's land of Bohemia he placed the stone in its frame carved with the names and sigilla that his angelic informants had given to him.

There was war in heaven, they had told him, and therefore war under the earth, and soon enough on the lands and seas of all the empires and kingdoms of men.

It would engulf the States and Empires of Europe; even the Sultan might be drawn in. If Spain claimed Great Atlantis for her own, then Atlantis too would be in play, and Francis Drake's license as a privateer would be traded for the chain of an Admiral of the Ocean Sea, and Walter Raleigh given one too. The heavenly powers that aid the true Christian faith, the armed angelic hosts, would go into battle. They would be opposed by other powers great and small, powers that take the side of the old faith. The creatures of the middle realm, of earth and water, hills and trees, shy and self-protective, would surely fight with the old religion: not because they loved the Pope or even knew of him, but only because they hated change. There was little harm they could do, though much annoyance. But in the contested Irish Isle where Spain would be welcomed, there were other powers: warriors who appeared and disappeared after sudden slaughter, bright swords and spears that made no sound. Were they men, had they once been men, were they but empty casques and breastplates? They could be captured, sometimes, imprisoned if you knew the spells, but never for long. It is useless to hang us, they would say to their jailers, we cannot die.

Look now: the swirl of winds within the stone, the sense (not the sound) of heavenly laughter, and the clouds parted to show as though from a sea-bird's eye the western coast of Ireland, and on the sea little dots that were big-bellied ships, the great red crosses on their sails.

A flotilla in the North Sea, and in St. George's channel, come to make Philip King of England. And to make the Virgin Queen his bride, old now and barren though she be. In the stone the tiny ships rocked on the main like mock ships in a masque or a children's show. An angel finger pointed to them, and John Dee heard a whisper: *That is not far off from now.*

HUGH O'NEILL HAD passed almost without noticing from his twenties to his thirties; one by one the endless line of enemies and false friends and mad fools that he faced in the claiming of his heritage were bought off, or befriended, or exiled, or hanged. The black mirror was his adviser and his ruler in these contests. When he contested with the mirror itself, he might deny it, and later be sorry he had. Sometimes when he looked in it would say *Strike now or lose all* and sometimes it would only look upon him; sometimes it wept or smiled, or said *Power springs from the mind and the heart.* But never was any sound heard, and it was as though Hugh thought or said these things in his own mind, which made them not the less true or potent. If he could discern the meaning of what was said and act on it, it would come out as predicted, and he would win. And in the spring of 1587 he returned to London to be invested at last by the Queen with the title Earl of Tyrone.

He knelt before her, sweeping his hat and its white feather from his head. "Cousin," the Queen said, and held out her ringed hand for him to kiss.

The face Hugh saw in the black mirror had never changed—at least it would seem always unchanged to him, white and small and bejewelled—but the woman of flesh was not young. The paint couldn't cover the fine lines etched all around her eyes, nor the lines in the great bare skull above. Torn between love and shame Hugh put his lips near to the proffered hand without touching it, and when he raised his eyes she was young again and serenely lovely. She said, "My cousin. My lord of Tyrone."

At the Dublin dock when he came home again, with more gifts and purchases in his English ship than twenty ox-carts could bear, he saw, among the O'Neill and O'Donnell men-at-arms and their brehons and wives come to greet him, the poet O'Mahon, like a withered leaf, leaning on a staff. Hugh O'Neill went to him, knelt and kissed the white hand the poet held out to him. O'Mahon raised him, felt his big face and broad shoulders, the figured steel breastplate upon him.

"That promise given you was kept," said O'Mahon.

"How, cousin?"

"You are the O'Neill, inaugurated at Tullahogue as your ancestors have ever been. You are Earl of Tyrone too, by the grant of the English: you gave them all your lands and they gave them back to you just as though the lands were theirs to give, and added on a title, Earl."

"How is that the keeping of a promise?" O'Neill asked.

"That is for them to know; yours to act and learn." He touched Hugh's arm and said: "Will you go on progress in this summer, cousin? The lands that owe you are wide."

"I may do so. The weather looks to be fine."

"I would be happy to go along with you, if I might. As far at least as to the old fort at Dungannon."

"Well then you shall. You will have a litter to carry you, if you like."

"I can still ride," the poet said with a smile. "And my own horse knows the way there."

"What shall we do there?"

"I? Not a thing. But you: You will meet again your allies there, or perhaps their messenger or herald; and see what now they will say. And they will tell you of the others, some greater than they, who are now waking from sleep, and their pale horses too."

The streets that had been silent and empty when, some years before, a young Irishman came home from that other island to which he had been carried away—they were not still now: from street to street and house to house the news went that Hugh O'Neill was home again, and they came around his horse to touch his boot and lift their babes to see him; and now and then he must acknowledge them, and doff the black velvet cap he wore, with the white owl's feather in its band.

Two enemies, the Queen of England and the old ones under the hills, had acted to make Hugh O'Neill great. He had become what they had conspired to make him, and what now was he to do? When he tried to take the black mirror from around his neck he found that he could not: he had the strength, it was a flimsy chain that carried it, he could snap it with a thumb and finger, but he couldn't do it.

Hugh O'Neill, Lord of the North, stood at the center of time, which was not different from the time of his own span. There are five directions to the world around: there is North, and South, and East, and West. And the fifth direction lies amid them. It points to the fifth kingdom, the only realm where he or any man ever stands: Here.

Well, let it be. What was he but a battleground where armies and their generals tore him in two for their own reasons? There was no knowing how the world would roll from here where he stood. Let it be.

THE QUEEN WAS dead, and John Dee was dying. His books and alchemical ware and even the gifts that the Queen had given him had been sold for bread: his long toil for her meant nothing to the new Scots king, who feared magic above all things. It was all gone but this small stone of moleskin-colored quartz, that had come to have a spiritual creature caught in it: an angel, he had long believed, but now he doubted. The war she had shown him had paused, like a storm's eye passing, and a calm had fallen over the half part of the world: it would not last.

What he saw now wasn't what he had seen, the armies of emperors and kings, nor the towers of Heaven and their hosts. He saw only long stony beaches, and knew it was the western coast of Ireland; and there where the Spanish ships had once been shivered on the rocks, other ships were being built, like no ships men sailed, ships made out of the time of another age, silvered like driftwood, with sails as of cobweb; and the ones building and now boarding and pushing them out to sea were as silvery, and as fine. Defeated; in flight. They sailed to the West, to the Fortunate Isles, to coasts and faraway hills they had never seen. The voice at John Dee's inner ear said

This is to come. We know not when. Well, let it be. And as he bent over the glowing stone the empowered soul within him spoke to him in vatic mode, and told him that when the end did come, and after it had long passed, the real powers that had fought these wars would be forgotten, and so would he, and only the merely human kings and queens and halberdiers and priests and townsmen remembered.

AN AGENT OF UTOPIA
Andy Duncan

Andy Duncan's (beluthahatchie.blogspot.com) short fiction has won a Nebula Award, a Theodore Sturgeon Memorial Award and three World Fantasy Awards. His two 2018 books were his third collection, *An Agent of Utopia: New and Selected Stories*, from Small Beer Press, and a hardcover edition of his 2013 novella *Wakulla Springs*, co-written with Ellen Klages, from PS Publishing. He is an elected member of the Board of Directors of the Science Fiction and Fantasy Writers of America and will teach the fourth week of the 2019 Clarion writing workshop at the University of California San Diego. A South Carolina native, Duncan lives in the mountains of western Maryland, where he is tenured on the writing faculty at Frostburg State University.

TO THE PRINCE and Tranibors of our good land, and the offices of the Syphogrants below, and all those families thereof, greetings, from your poor servant in far Albion.

Masters and mistresses, I have failed. All that I append is but paint and chalk 'pon that stark fact. Yet I relate my story in hopes it may be instructive, that any future tools of state be fashioned less rudely than myself.

I will begin as I will end, with her.

Had my intent been to await her, to meet her eye as she emerged into the street, I scarcely could have done better; and yet this was happenstance, as so much else proved to be.

I had no expectation of her; I knew not that she was within; she was not my aim. She was wholly a stranger to me. I would laugh at this now, were I the laughing sort, for of course I learned later that even as I stood there with the crawling river to my back, her name was known to me, as the merest footnote to my researches. So much for researches.

In fact, though I had traveled thousands of leagues, from beyond the reach of the mapmaker's art, to reach this guarded stone archway in a gray-walled keep on a filthy esplanade beside the stinking Thames, I had no reason even for pausing, only feet from my goal. I feared not the guards, resplendent in their red tunics; I doubted not my errand. Yet I had stopped and stood a moment, as one does when about to fulfill a role in a grand design. And so when she emerged from shadows into sun, blinking as if surprised, I found myself looking into her eyes, and that has been the difference in my life: between who I was, and who I am.

Her face was—

No, I dare not, I cannot express't.

To her clothing, then, and her hair. That I'll set down. A framework may suggest a portrait, an embankment acknowledge a sea.

In our homeland, all free citizens, being alike in station, therefore dress alike as well; but in the lady's island nation, all are positioned somewhere above or below, so their habits likewise must be sorted: by adornment, by tailoring, by fineness of cloth. These signs are designed to be read.

She was plainly a gentlewoman, but simply clad. Around her neck was a single silver carcanet like a moon-sliver. Her bosom was but gently embusked, and not overmuch displayed. Her farthingale was modest in size; some could not be wedged through the south gate of London Bridge, but hers was just wider than her shoulders. Her hair was plaited at either temple, so that twin dark falls bordered her lustrous—

Ah! But stop there. I am grown old enough.

I add only that her eyes were red-rimmed with weeping, and in that moment—whatever my obligations to my homeland, to you who sent me—to dry those tears became my true mission.

A moment only I held her gaze, and how did I merit even that?

Then her manservant just behind, finely attired but sleep-eyed and bristle-jowled, did nudge her toward a carriage. As she passed, I dared not turn my head to watch, lest I not achieve my goal at all.

Rather, I walked forward, into the sweet-smelling space the lady had just vacated, and raised both hands as the warders crossed pikes before me.

"Hold, friends," I said. "The gaoler expects me."

"Ah, does he?" asked the elder warder. "What name does he expect, then?"

"The name of Aliquo," I said, and this truly was the name I had affixed to my letter, for it was not mine but anyone's. From my dun-colored wool cloak, I produced another sealed paper. "My credentials," I said. "For the gaoler only," I quickly added, as the elder warder was making as if to break the seal. He eyed me dolefully, then handed the letter to the younger warder, who in turn barked for a third warder, the youngest yet, who conveyed my letter within—doubtless to a boy still younger, his equipment not yet dropped.

As I waited, we all amused ourselves, myself by standing on tiptoe atop each consecutive cobble from east to west beneath the portcullis, the warders by glaring at me.

I knew, as they did not, that my credentials were excellent, consisting as they did only of my signature on a sheet of paper wrapped about some street debris from home.

Soon I was escorted through the gate, onto a walkway across an enclosed green. Sheep cropped the grass. Ravens barked down from the battlements. Huddled in a junction of pockmarked walls was a timbered, steeply thatched, two-story house. Though dwarfed by the lichen-crusted stone all around, it was larger than any home in Aircastle. Through its front door I was marched, and into a small room filled by an immense bearded man with a broken nose. He sat in a heap behind a spindly writing-desk that belonged in a playroom. Sunlight through the latticed window further broke his face into panes of diamond.

"Leave us," he told my escort, who bowed and exited, closing the door behind. The gaoler stared at me, saying nothing, and I replied in kind. He leaned forward and made a show of studying my shoes, then my breeches and cloak, then face again. His own displayed neither interest nor impression.

"You don't dress like a rich man," he said.

"I am no rich man," I replied.

Without turning his gaze from mine, he placed one hairy finger on the packet I had sent him and slid it across the desktop toward me: refolded, the seal broken.

"A thief, then," he said. "We have other prisons for thieves. My men will show you."

"I am no thief," I replied.

He tilted his head. "A Jew?"

"I am but a visitor, and I seek only an audience."

"That you have achieved," he said. "Our audience being concluded, my men will take you now."

"An audience," I said, "with one of your... guests."

Without moving, he spat onto the floor and my shoe, as placid as a toad. "And which guest would that be, Sir Jew, Sir Thief?"

I was near him already, the room being so small, and now I stepped closer. Arms at my sides, I leaned across the desk, closing the distance toward the gaoler's motionless, ugly face. I could smell layers of sweat and Southwark dirt, the Scotch egg that had broken his fast, and, all intermixed, the acrid scent of fear, a fear of such long abiding that it marked him, better than any wax-sealed writ of passage, as a resident of this benighted land. When I was close enough for my lips to brush the pig-bristles of his ear, I whispered a single syllable: a lover's plea, a beggar's motto, a word with no counterpart in my native tongue, though one of the commonest words in London, where satisfaction is unknown.

Upon hearing my word, the gaoler jerked as though serpent-bit, but recovered on the instant, so that as I stepped back he assumed once again calm and authority. Only his eyes danced in terror and anticipation.

"Worth my life, Sir Thief, were I caught admitting you to *him*." I made no reply. No question had been posed, nor information offered that was new or in any way remarkable. He had but stated an irrelevant fact.

He lifted the packet I had delivered and poured the pebbles into his palm. He studied their sparkle, then let them slide back into the paper. His palm remained in place, cupping the air, and he raised his eyebrows at me, like a scarred and shaggy courtesan.

These English. Every clerk, every driver, every drayman and barrelmaker and ale-pourer has his hand out for coins, and doubtless every gaoler and prince, courtier and headsman, as well. They conceive of no superior system, indeed no alternative, anywhere in this world. And so I freely handed them my trash. Some were as grateful as children, while others betrayed no emotion at all, merely pocketing the payment as their due, a gift of nature like birdshit and rain.

I pulled from my pocket a thumb-sized paving stone. I dropped it into the gaoler's palm, where it reflected the sunlight in a dozen directions. His nostrils flared as he drew in a breath.

"God's mercy," he said.

The English routinely invoke their God when startled, or provoked, or overwhelmed by their own natures. They pray without cease, without thought, without result.

"The ninth hour," he told the stone, "at Traitors' Gate."

TRAITORS' GATE WAS a floating wooden barrier tapping mindlessly in the night tide across a submerged arch, set low in the fort's Thamesside wall. No two public clocks in England quite chime together, but somewhere during the ninth-hour cacophony, the gate swung open without visible human hand, and an empty punt slid from the shadows, tapping to a halt at my feet. I stepped down and in, half expecting the punt to slide from under me and make its return voyage without my assistance. Instead, after a respectful pause, I picked up the pole that lay in the bottom of the boat and did the work myself, nudge by nudge into the shadows, ducking as I glided beneath the arch. The soggy gate creaked shut behind.

Just inside the fortress, the stone marched upward in steep and narrow steps, at the top of which stood, all in red, my hulking friend the gaoler. He was alone. He silently waited as I climbed the slimy stairs to face him, or more precisely to face the teats that strained his tunic. He reached out both ham-sized hands and kneaded my arms, legs and torso. He found neither what he sought nor what he did not seek, and was quickly satisfied. He stooped, with a grunt, and picked up something from the cobbles.

"You're the ratcatcher, if anyone asks," he said. He handed me a long-handled fork and a pendulous sack. "And there's the rats to prove it," he added. "Wait here. When I cough twice, enter behind me, and keep to the right. Follow my taper, but not too close. If I meet anyone, keep back and flatten yourself against the wall like the damp. You might even kill a rat or two, if you've a mind."

I held the heavy fork loose at my side, where I could drop it on the instant if I needed to kill someone, and watched the gaoler lumber into the wall and vanish, through a previously invisible slot perhaps an inch wider than his shoulders. Finally I heard the double cough, fainter and from much farther away than I expected. I slipped into the door-shaped darkness.

We encountered no one, quickly left any trafficked levels of the vast and ancient keep. The dark corridors and archways we passed through and the stairs we climbed were broad and well-made and perhaps once were grand, but time's ravages were not being repaired. In spots we crunched through fallen mortar and stone. Even the rats were elsewhere. The walls were windowless, save for the occasional slitted cross that traded no light for no view.

Finally we passed through a series of large chambers, in the fourth of which the serpent-fire before me guttered as in a draft. My guide stood before an iron-banded oaken door, its single barred window the size of my head. He gestured me close, relieved me of the rat-sticker and sack, and whispered, as urgently as a lover.

"I'll be watching. You leave in a quarter-hour, and whether you walk or I drag you is no concern of mine. Keep your treasonous voices low. Take nothing he offers, leave no marks on his person, and for the love of God, give him no ink or paper; that's powder and shot to the likes of him." He inserted into the lock an iron key fully as long as the rat-sticker. The gears clanked and ground, and he hauled back the door. "Company for you, sir! Oh, Christ, not again. Whyn't he just pull his gentles, like the others do?"

The room was larger than I expected, and more finely appointed. The chairs, tables, washbasin, and chamber-pot were old but finely made; the twin windows were grated but high, deep-set and arched; a river breeze stirred faded tapestries that covered the walls with the rose that was the sigil of the ruling house. In the far corner was a makeshift altar, a cross of two bound candlesticks atop a stool, and before it, in a pool of shadow, knelt a naked man with a bloody back, who slowly gave himself one, two, three fresh strokes across the shoulders with a knotted rope. Judging from the fresh wounds amid the scarring, he had been at this for some time.

As I walked forward, the door thudded shut behind. "My good sir," I said.

The kneeling figure paused a few seconds before flogging himself again, and again, and a sixth time, each impact a dull wet smack. As I drew close enough to smell him, I saw the shadow on the flagstones was in fact a broad spatter of blood.

The prisoner spoke without turning. "You've made me lose count. Well, no matter. I can start over from One, as must we all, each day." He flexed the rope, as if to resume.

"Good sir, please. My time is short."

His laugh, as he turned, was a joyless bark. "Your time?" The engravings I had studied were good likenesses. The Roman features were intact on his blunt, handsome face, but his jawline was hidden by a fresh grey curtain of beard that ill became him. "May I assume, sir, given your evident longing for conversation, that you are not here to murder me?"

"No, indeed."

"Ah," he said. He brought one foot beneath him and stood, slowly but with no evident need for support. "One can imagine worse fates, my good Sir Interruptus, than to be murdered in the act of prayer." Something passed over his eyes then, perhaps only the sting of the wounds as he donned, without flinching, the robe that hung on the bedpost. "Ay, much worse. The killers of Thomas Becket, even as they hacked away, did the work of God in making the saint's most heartfelt desire manifest. They delivered him sinless unto his Maker." He glanced at his blood on the floor as he cinched his belt. "I fear for his shrine at Canterbury, and for his relics. In these fell days, it is not only the living who suffer. A good even to you, Master Jenkins!"

After a long pause, the shadow beyond the window in the door replied, "And a good even to you, sir."

"As for you," the prisoner said, smiling, "we reach an even footing. You impeded my task; I impeded yours. State your business, please, sir, and your name. I have not so many visitors that they grow interchangeable to me."

"I call myself Aliquo," I replied, "and I bring greetings to you, Thomas More, from your old friend Raphael Hythlodaye, and from my homeland of Utopia."

I bowed low before him.

"Please give my Utopian friends my best regards," More said, "and tell them my answer is no."

THE NEXT AFTERNOON, moments after I stepped from the inn where I had broken my fast, a man planted himself before me on the street, so that I would have to go around him, or stop. I chose to stop.

"You have seen me before, I believe," said the man.

I peered into his bearded face. "I have," I said. "You were outside the Tower yesterday. You were with... the lady."

"I was," he said, "and I am, and I am here on her account only. I am to bring you to her."

"That is quite impossible," I said. "Who is this lady, who makes such demands of strangers?"

"You are a stranger to her, but not to her father, I believe. Her name is Margaret Roper, born Margaret More." He studied my face. "This changes your resolve, I believe."

"Yes," I said, though I had resolved to accompany him the moment I recognized him, in hopes I might see his mistress again—even if he led me straight to the chopping-block on Tower Hill.

Where he led me, instead, without further speech, was to the city's largest temple, dedicated to the name of a first-century persecutor of the enemies of Rome, who reversed himself to aid those enemies, but remained, throughout his life, in the service of a more perfect, more organized world. A thousand years later, his temple's interior was scarcely less crowded than the streets outside.

At home, upon entering a temple, all men would proceed to the right, all women to the left, and all would maintain their proper places until departing. Here, all was confusion.

"There," said the manservant, stepping aside. "Go to her, and if you speak falsely, then God help you."

Far ahead, across the echoing marble, a line of supplicants, in all modes of clothing, shuffled step by step into an airy chapel, and past a chest-high marble tomb minded by a droning guide. Toward the back of this line was she who had summoned me, she who already had claimed dominion over me with a single glance, though I had yet to realize it.

I went to her.

She watched me approach. She was nearly my height. Her eyes! ...I dare not describe them. She looked into mine, and then, without moving her head or glancing away, she refocused, and looked at me again. I knew in that moment she had seen me more clearly than her father had, than the gaoler had, than anyone had since home. I held my breath, sure she would turn away. Instead she gravely bowed her head, reached for my arm, and guided me into the line at her side. The stooped crone behind her hissed at my insertion, but a steely glance from Madame shushed her.

"Do you speak Latin?" Madame asked me, in that tongue.

"I do, Madame," I replied in kind.

"Do so, in this public place. Here, in this procession, we are pilgrims only, and will draw no attention. You know who I am."

"I do, Madame."

"Have you seen my father?"

"I have, Madame."

"You have an advantage over me, then. How is he? In mind, spirit, and body?"

"In mind, keen. In spirit, resigned, but anxious for you. In body, intact, save for the injuries he inflicts himself."

"God inflicts them," she said. "So he told me, when I was a girl, and saw the bloody linens. A man who would keep secrets from his own household should do his own washing. Now tell me who *you* are."

"Only your servant, Madame," I said.

She blew air from the corner of her mouth. "Please. You are no one's servant, least of all mine. Who are you?"

We neared the tomb and the guide, his pockmarked face, his maimed hands. Many in line had some scar, or limp, or hump.

"Call me Aliquo," I said.

"Your position?"

"In this land, only emissary."

"From whom? What business had you with my father?"

Heeding her manservant's warning, I chose the truth.

"I offered to free him," I said, "and to convey him home in triumph."

Her eyes widened. "You are mad. How? Home to Chelsea? Home to me?"

"No, Madame. To my homeland across the sea."

"The impertinence! What name is given this homeland?"

"It is called Utopia. Your father wrote of it."

She laughed aloud, and a score of heads turned our way in shock as the echoes rained down from the arches above. Beside the tomb, without interrupting his recitation, the guide shook his head, placed the stump of a finger to his chin, and blew.

"He wrote of it, indeed!" she said, in a lower voice. "A fairystory for his friend Erasmus, invented of whole cloth! A series of japes at the follies of the day."

"Is all this a jape?" I asked, with a gesture at the soaring chapel all around. "Is this statue atop the tomb a jape, because he has a silver head, as the king did not in life? Mere representation is not a jape, Madame. Your father represented us, but we are not his invention."

By now we had reached the tomb. It bore a plaque, in Latin:

Henry, the scourge of France, lies in this tomb.

Virtue subdues all things.

A.D. 1422.

"Above, you see good King Henry's funeral achievements," droned the guide, in nasal English, as he studied Madame for signs of outburst. "His battle helmet, sword, shield, and saddle. Note the dents in the helmet, through which good King Henry's life was spared, glory be to God... ."

As she passed, Madame addressed herself to the marble of the tomb. "I have met many scoundrels," she said, "but never one claiming to have stepped from the pages of my father's books. And whom do you claim sent you on this mad errand? King Utopia the Nineteenth?"

"Our king, Madame... is not like yours. He is more like the officers of this temple. He has unique responsibilities, yes; he has certain authorities, in certain settings. Yet I was not sent by him, Madame, but by a council of the people."

"An emissary from a headless land. Interesting. But this might explain why, a mere half-day after you stepped ashore at Woolwich, having left your private cabin on the *Lobo Soares*, out of Lisbon, before even buying a meal or engaging rooms, you proceeded not to York Place but to the Tower, and sought an audience not with the king, but with a condemned prisoner. A strange emissary, indeed."

"Madame is well informed."

"Madame is wholly *un*informed," she retorted, "on the one subject of any importance. They keep me from my father, and thus I must make do with the world."

"You call your father condemned," I said, "yet you grieve too soon, surely. He is not yet tried, much less convicted and sentenced."

"That is a truth so strictly and carefully laid as to be a lie," she said, "and one more lie to me, however small, will earn you an enemy beside which our present King Henry would seem a stick-puppet. Do you believe me?"

"I do, Madame. Tell me, the man in the tomb... he is the current king's grandsire?"

She winced. "No relation. After good King Henry died, his widow married a Tudor. And there Katherine lies, as if in life. So they say."

Only if in life she was drawn, shriveled, and waxen of complexion, I thought, but said nothing. Where one might have expected an effigy lay instead the body, not even shielded but available to all. Katherine was blessedly clothed, arms folded across her sunken breasts. The one-eyed gentleman in line before me, his absurd rapier hilt stuttering along the pedestal as he walked past, half-burst into tears, bowed, and kissed Katherine's face.

"I apologize for my countrymen," said Madame. "They prefer their women venerated and dead. Some attribute miracles to this poor corpse, and seek her elevation by Rome. Humph. 'Twould truly take a miracle, now—and our current king has rather discouraged miracles." She had looked almost merry, enjoying my discomfiture at the spectacle before me, but now her face grew taut as Katherine's. She shook her head, and the moment passed. "Tell me, friend Aliquo," she continued. "What becomes of Utopians when they die?"

"Burned to ashes, Madame."

"What, no burial?"

"No room, Madame. Ours is an island nation, at its widest scarcely 200 miles across. We must colonize the mainland as it is."

"And Utopian souls? What becomes of them?"

"They... remain. Invisible, but among us still, seeing and hearing all. They observe, are pleased to be addressed and honored, but they cannot participate."

"Interesting. And have your dead ones traveled with you, here to our island nation?"

"I hope not, Madame. This place would be most... distressing to them."

"I know how they feel. My father refused you, of course."

"Yes, Madame. Doubtless you'd have thought him mad, otherwise."

"No. But I know that even locked in that fortress, he is the king's servant and God's, and if it's the will of both that he—that he—" She faltered. "He would have refused you, had you come at the head of a legion. My father is the best man in the kingdom, and how I have prayed he were otherwise."

We had left the chapel and entered the cathedral's main chamber, where the line of supplicants broke apart and flowed into the larger crowd. We walked slowly together toward the west door, where her manservant stood, his gaze intent upon us, poised as if to spring.

"Madame, I have told you what you wanted, and I have only troubled you with my tidings. I am sorry for that. I pray you grant me leave."

"Stay a moment, friend Aliquo. I am told that earlier today, two cutpurses were found dead in a rain-barrel in Woolwich, a quarterhour after you set foot on the dock. Their necks were broken. Does this news surprise you?"

"No, Madame. Many rough men meet such fates."

"Oh, indeed. Tell me, why did you *not* bring a legion? Why did your headless land send only you, alone?"

"My people have faith in me, Madame."

"I think it's because you didn't need a legion. I think you could have brought my father out of the Tower unscathed and singlehanded, had he but said the word."

"You think me a wizard, Madame."

"No. I think you're a killer, and I have a job for you. I want his head."

"The king's head? Now *you* are talking madness, Madame."

"Henry? Fie! What need would I have for that? Not Henry's head. My father's. More's. You have told me something of your land's customs, regarding the dead. Let me now tell you something of ours. When the headsman on Tower Hill separates my father's pate from his shoulders, his poor skull will be taken to London Bridge, impaled on a pike, and mounted atop the Stone Gate, to feed the ravens and remind all Henry's subjects of the fate of traitors. I would spare my father that. I want his head. I want it brought home to his family. I want it brought home to me."

At that moment, I could have turned and walked out of the temple, the city, England, her gaze entire, perhaps even beyond the range of my memory of her. Instead I tarried, forever.

"Do not ask this of me," I said.

"My family is broken," she said. "My friends fear to be seen with me.

My servants have multiple employers. My enemies watch me, and all others avert their eyes. I have no one else to ask."

I glanced at he who stood apart, glowering at me. "But your manservant?"

"That is William, my husband," she continued, looking only at me, "and he is a good man, but for this task, Aliquo my killer, my emissary from the land of dreams, I have no need of a good man. I have need of you."

"Ho, YOU KNAVES, you fishwives!" bellowed my leather-lunged boatman as he sculled straight across the paths of threescore other vessels, missing each by the width of a coat of paint. Whenever the river ahead seemed passable, he changed course and sought congestion once more.

London may once have been a great city, but I was privileged to see it too late, in its twenty-sixth year of groan beneath the man Henry. And swirling among all was the reek of the Thames. That foul brown stream flows more thickly above its surface, and knows no channel, but floods all the nostrils of the town.

I had struggled on foot onto the city's single bridge, in hopes of achieving a perspective not granted to the scullers below—only to gain a fine view of the tradesmen's booths that line the thoroughfare on both sides. Each swaybacked roof sprouted a thicket of faded standards that snapped overhead like abandoned washing, their tattiness mocking the very memory of festivity.

Finally, midway along the span, I entered a public garderobe—for which honor I waited a quarter-hour in line, as some men around me gave up and relieved themselves standing—and once inside, I peered through the privy-hole, to obtain a fine round view of the Thames, my only one since setting foot on the bridge. Amid cascades of filth from above, a grimy boy of perhaps ten summers sat, fishing, in a vessel the size of a largish hat.

"Ay, look out there, you swag-bellied antic!"

The boatman's roar returned me to my present sorry state. I was under no obligation to More's daughter, I still told myself; but there was no harm, surely, in seeing whether her task could be quickly discharged, before my departure for home. A Utopian may be forgiven the odd good deed. But I had seen enough already to complicate matters. I had hoped, once having achieved the battlement, to lift down the pike and use it to bridge the gap to the next building; or, failing that, simply to dive over the wall into the water. But the battlement was twice as high as the adjacent roofs—about twelve stories to their six—and as the Stone Gateway perched atop a bridge that was itself eighty feet above the river, any dive from the height would be two hundred feet, and fatal. A head dropped into the river would be lost on the instant, while throwing it onto the adjacent roof would be a desperate move; the twice-unlucky head would roll off, and land who-knew-where.

No, the only feasible way to bring down the head would be to carry it down the stairs and out the front door. And the only feasible way to gain the battlement in the first place was via the same stairs in the reverse direction, up. Neither up nor down looked likely, short of a safe-passage guarantee from Henry himself.

Would Madame recognize her own father's head? Or, more to the point, would she recognize a head not her father's? The thought of substituting a more easily recovered head gave me no pride, but that at least would be feasible, and would give the lady some measure of comfort. Yet I did not wish to see her so easily gulled.

I leaned an elbow on the saxboard, let the river lap my thoughts as the Stone Gateway bobbed before me. Assume, then, that the battlement was impregnable. From execution site to point of display, the head must travel more than a mile through the London streets—the teeming, crime-infested, unpredictable streets.

Why, anything could happen. And only fivescore cutpurses, fishwives, alemongers, soldiers and spies would have to be bribed to look the other way.

And once the display was over, well, the head would have to make its way downstairs again, to clear a space on the battlement for the next statesman.

"What do they do with the heads, after?" I asked the boatman.

His grin had gaps into which a mouse could wriggle. "Into Mother Thames they go, Milord—and don't they make a pretty splash!"

So I could just wait beneath the bridge until the head was thrown to me. A tempting plan. A simple plan. A foolish plan. I would gain only an unobstructed view of the thing sinking to the bottom of the river. And this was, of course, the thought with which my musings began; I had rounded the globe and met myself upon return.

"Oh, is that the state of it, y'say?" roared my boatman, in response to the ribald gestures of a passing fisherman. "Ye don't fray me, you cullion! I'll cuff you like Jack of Lent, I will!"

THE TRIAL, AND the sentence, and the execution, went as Madame had foreseen. One always should trust the natives. By then, I had settled on bribery and substitution. Cross the smallest number of palms with a few paving-stones, replace the head to conceal its absence, and be done.

Utopia borders the land of the savage Zapolets, useful neighbors in that they always are willing, for pay, to perform errands that are too base for Utopians. There is no dishonor in hiring them, as Zapolets are debased already. London, too, has its Zapolets, and so, a week after More's severed head took its place atop the Gateway, I found myself directly beneath, alone in a boat, by midnight, having silently rowed myself into place, awaiting the descent of my package.

Above me, a low whistle—and again.

I crouched in the boat and looked up at the flickering darkness. Sound was magnified beneath the stone arch, and I heard as if in my right ear someone grunting and panting from exertion. In moments, something came into view, swaying in mid-air like a pendulum, ever closer. A heavy sack was being lowered to me.

Just as I reached up and took hold of it, someone on the bridge shrieked. Suddenly the full weight of the sack was in my hands, and I lurched off balance, nearly upset the boat as I sat heavily on the bench amidships. A hot, iron-smelling liquid pelted me from above, and then something plunked into the water beside me. In the torchlight I registered the staring, agape face of the poor Zapolet I had bribed, as his severed head rolled beneath the river's leathery surface. Just before it vanished, I snatched it by the hair, swung it streaming into the floorboards. The act was instinctive; it might come in handy. Then an arrow studded from above into the bench between my thighs. Thus encouraged, I set down the sack and rowed for the far riverbank.

Sounds carry on a river, but I heard none as I reached the stilts of some enterprise built over the water—a tannery, by the smell of it. No voices called after me. I ducked my head and rode the boat into darkness, till it bumped the barrels lashed to the quay. I tied my boat fast, risked a candle, and peeled back the sacking, to see the head for which I had paid a guard's life. I stared into the broad, lumpy face, its cheek triple-scarred long ago, as by a rake.

For my troubles, I now owned two severed heads, neither of them More's.

IN MID-CLIMB, MY feet against the outer wall of the Gateway, I clutched the rope, straining to hear and see what was happening on the battlement above. Had my hook been noticed? Apparently not. I heard a murmuring conversation among guards, perhaps three men, but they were distant. I pulled myself up to the edge of the wall.

More than once, in my slow progress up the wall—one window level at a time—I had been tempted to let that damned not-More head that weighted my shoulder-sack, and became only heavier each minute, simply drop into the Thames. But no, a substitute head would be useful. With luck, no one would notice that More was missing.

I waited there, just beneath the battlement, for the guards to go below. Possibly they would not, in which case I would have to kill them all quickly and silently. I determined to give them a quarterhour, and began to mark my heartbeats as I looked out over the nightscape of the city. But sooner, all three voices moved into the stairwell, and I clambered up and over.

I counted my way to the More-pike, hoping the heads had not been rearranged since sunset, easily lifted the heavy pole out of its socket and stepped backward, laying it onto the flagstones as silently as I could. The head end necessarily was heavier, and hit first, bouncing once. I walked up the length of the pike. I reached beneath the iron band—grimacing as my fingers dented the head's tarred surface—and tugged.

The head did not budge.

I put both feet against the severed neck, braced myself, and pushed.

The flesh buckled.

I pushed again, and the head slowly began to stutter up the pike.

I was thus occupied when I heard voices ascending the stairs.

Frantically, I managed to slide the head clear of the pike just as the first guard crested the roof—facing southward and away from me, thank Mithras.

The head fell only an inch or two to the roof. I let the pike down quietly and rolled sideways, putting a low wall between myself and the guards. I hoped they were not in the habit of counting the pikes.

I flung a pebble into the far corner of the rooftop, hoping it would make a noise loud enough to draw their attention. I suppose it landed. If so, it made not a sound.

One guard began walking the battlement toward me. His attention was directed outward, however. Sitting with my back to the inner wall, willing myself to disappear into the shadow, I watched him stroll into view. He stopped, still with his back to me, and stared downstream. A few steps, and he'd all but trip over the pike, and More's head.

I risked a glance behind me. One guard was picking his teeth, another leaning on his elbows, both looking across Southwark.

I stood and crossed silently to my guard, swinging the bag with the not-More head. It clouted the guard at the base of the skull. As he dropped, I kicked him between the shoulder blades, and he toppled over the wall. I dived for cover again. Only someone who was listening for it, as I was, would have noticed the splash, far below.

The two remaining guards continued their murmurous conversation on the far side of the platform. I rolled into a crouch, looked over the crenellated wall that sheltered the stairs. My new friends were standing just barely within the torchlight of a taper on the far wall. They stood side by side facing the city, overlooking the rooftops that lined the bridge below. I wished them to separate, willed them to do so, but my will failed. There they would stand, barely a man's width between them, until they registered their companion had not rejoined them, whereupon they would seek and, not finding, sound an alarm. How to separate them sooner?

Water, moaned a voice at my feet.

You scarce will believe, ye who read this letter, that I did not spring backward, though my leg muscles spasmed in that desire; my overriding desire, to produce no noise whatsoever, saved me, I think. I only hopped, once, silently landing in place with my feet planted a bit farther apart, to either side of the lump of darkness I knew to be More's head. I did not cry out. I did not breathe. I only stared down at the darkness between my feet, desperate to resolve a shape that began to move, to rock to and fro, like an inverted turtle, until it tipped and rolled to a stop against my left boot, its staring eyes reflecting the moon as its only movable limb, its long adderlike tongue, probed the air. Of course, I thought with insane clarity, that's how he could roll over. Face down, he pushed away the stone floor with his tongue.

Water, More repeated, more loudly this time.

The guards! They would hear!

With no more thought than this—nay, with no thought at all—still on the keen iron edge of terror, and preferring to be anywhere but against that More-head, I stood and strode forward, fast, noiseless, toward the two guards, who marvelously yet had heard nothing, still had their backs to me. In mid-stride, slacking neither my pace nor my direction, I returned the favor, turned my back to them, walked backward until their faces came into view and my shoulder blades thumped against the wall between them.

"Wha?" said the one on my right.

I smashed the heels of both hands into the guards' noses. As they fell backward I fell forward atop them, rode them down to the floor and crushed their faces with all my weight, my arms locked in place like bars. Out of respect, I did not watch. Instead I looked to the stars, found Ophiuchus beset, the writhing serpent-head and serpent-tail to either side, and the scorpion beneath his feet. The guards made scarcely any noise, only a grunt or two and one gurgle, as a gentlewoman's stomach might have done, and yet after they died, as I relaxed and flexed my cramping arms, the tower was quieter still. I saw the guttering taper, the flailing flags, but their sounds did not register. As I re-crossed the platform in search of More (his eyes! his tongue!), I moved in a silence like that of a dream, or of a daze from a clout on the head. I heard only the blood and snot and eyestuff pattering from my hands, which I held away from my body as if to distance myself from what I'd done.

I had killed before—had, indeed, likely killed the first guard, not five minutes earlier—and I have killed since, but my work atop Stone Gate that night, and as I left that accursed tower, was of another order. I blamed More, at the time. Whatever animated his head, I felt, was animating me. My body would ache for a fortnight.

I rounded the wall. More's head was gone. No—it was there, nose wedged into the join of wall and floor. But surely I had left it over there, beside the pike?

Water, said More's head.

Loath as I was to touch the damned thing (abomination! impossibility!), I wanted nothing from life, at that moment, but to heave More over the parapet, give him all the water he could drink, and to cast myself in after him. Perhaps I should have done those things, or one of them.

"Hush!" I said.

When would the next guards come on duty? When would the absence of tramping footfalls overhead be noticed? What signals, what duties, would be missed? I worked quickly. Ignoring More, I freed not-More from his sack, with some effort—I had to shake it, my assault on the first guard having got head and fabric somewhat intermingled—and it finally rolled onto the floor with a deep groan that made me yelp in horror. But 'twas only More again, complaining. I jammed the pike into not-More's neck, working it in deeper than necessary, wishing it were More. I hoisted the pike with effort, the head now even heavier at the weighted end of a pole, and set the hilt into place with the first sense of relief I had felt in an hour. I stepped back, snatched up the taper, and held it high, to check my handiwork. As he flickered into view, not-More sagged sideways, and I was sure for a moment that its savaged flesh would tear away and drop it into the Thames—but it held, and I foolishly continued to hold aloft the light, in a terrible elation, until a voice from below cried:

"Ho! What's the matter up there? Who's light?"

"No matter," I cried, even as I returned the taper to its sconce—too late. I heard behind me, from the outer wall, a scrape like nails against flint.

"What's this?" said the same voice—no longer loudly, but half to himself, in a sort of wonder, yet distinct for all that. I looked at my grappling hook as it twitched, flexed, skittered sideways, like a crab in lantern-light. He who had yanked it bellowed, "Intruder! Ho, the tower! Hoy!"

I snatched up More. He tried to bite me, the wretch, as I shoved him into my sack. To fling the hook over the wall was the work of a moment. With my snarling burden I strode away from my ruined lifeline, to the head of the wooden stairs, saw no one, and sprinted down, three planks at a time.

I found myself in a narrow stone chamber, barely wider than the flight of stairs. Beneath the stairs were casks and crates, but no guard, and no doors either. The only door faced me, a stone archway that framed a landing and a more substantial set of stone steps headed down. I had just reached the top when I heard a roaring and pounding from below, as if a cohort were charging, and torchlight flared and brightened 'gainst the stone wall visible at the curve.

I dropped my More sack—he squeaked as he hit the floor—and looked about, gauged my position. Above, in the open air, I would gain room to work, but so would they. Here was better. I stepped back three paces, positioned myself, and waited, as that fell force rose within me.

The leader of the party gained the stone landing but stopped at sight of me. I wonder what he saw. I stood unarmed, hands and sleeves besmirched with gore, a twitching sack at my feet. I know that I smiled. But what more did he see? Whatever it was, it stopped him like a barred gate, and the others clustered behind. Five total. One axe; three swords; the fifth, a torch in one hand and a rapier in the other. Fine.

"Which of you," I asked, "is the youngest?"

They said nothing, but two in the back glanced at the torchbearer, a beardless boy. They all looked wary, but he, terrified.

Their leader looked me up and down. "Who the fuck are you," he snarled, "to question us?"

I smiled even wider. "I'm the ratcatcher," I said, and sprang.

Afterward, I rose from my work on the floor and faced the one I'd left standing. The boy's quaking face was red with blood not his own. His shaking torch cast shadows that rocked the room. He choked back something, and dropped his weapon with a clang. He kept the torch, though. He was a dark-eyed, lovely boy. I have never been partial to boys.

"Your job," I said, "is to run below, and tell the others."

His jaw worked, his throat pulsed. He made no sound.

"That I am coming," I said.

Still he stood, trembling. The room filled with a smell harsher even than blood, and a puddle spread at the boy's boot.

Christ, cried More, muffled by sacking. *Christ!*

I took one step toward the boy, pursed my lips, and blew air into his face.

With a wail, he leapt into the stairwell, somehow kept his footing, and ran downstairs screaming, just ahead of me. Still he held on to the torch. O dutiful boy! Excellent boy! More clamped beneath one arm, my way lighted by the now much older once-boy, I ran in a downward stone spiral, around and down, around and down, past windows of increasing size, around and down, deeper into the swirling river-stench, until I reached a window just large enough, and vaulted through, knowing not whether I was over roofs or over water but hoping I was low enough. I was over water, and low enough. I plunged beneath the surface and sank, afire with sudden cold but glad of the respite from the smell. As I dropped ever deeper, my cheek was brushed by what may have been a kicking rat, my shoulder bumped by what may have been a spiraling turd, my chest gnawed by what was certainly the struggling head of my lady's father, biting at my heart as we descended into the dark peace below London. Ay, low enough!

I DARED NOT return to my inn, in my bedraggled state, with my unpredictible charge. Instead I repaired to a haven I had noted earlier—a nearby plague-house, marked by a bundle of straw on a pole extending from an upper window, and a foot-high cross slapped on the door in red paint. Local gossip said the surviving family members had long decamped, and the neighbors dared not set foot in the place. From the adjoining rooftop, I gained entrance to the house via its upper story. I made fast the shutters, risked a single lighted candle, and gnawed the bread, cheese, and onion I had stowed there before my assault on the Gateway. Then, somehow, I slept.

I WAS AWAKENED by More.

Where is the light?

Be silent, I said. The candle is beside you. Look.

I pulled the bedraggled thing from the sack, set it on the table. His neck looked to have been cut clean, but at an angle. The head listed to the right, as if cocked to hear a confidence. The skin puckered on that side, beneath More's weight.

Where is the light? Ay, am I damned? Am I such a sinner as that?

I cannot say, I told him. But you must be quiet, in any case.

God knows, I am no heretic, said More. *I sought out heretics. I had them killed. They put God's word in the English tongue, in the mouths of fishwives. They rejected the Apostle of Rome. They were protestants to*

God. *I was Lord High Chancellor, but I served the Lord who was higher still. They were as bad as Luther, and Luther is the shit-pool of all shit.*

Were they beheaded, too? I asked.

No, burned, said the head. *Purified in the flames, and delivered shriven unto God. It was all I could do for them, poor misguided devils. I hope soon to clasp their hands, my prodigal brothers. And yet.*

Yes, I asked.

Where is the light?

I turned the head to face the candle, my fingers sinking into his temple as into a soft pear. This made the lace atop the table twist into a gyre; it was intimate with More's neck now.

More moaned. *Where is the light? Ah, Christ my Savior, what is this place?*

I believe it's an apothecary's, I said. We are upstairs.

But where?

London, I said, mere rods from the Stone Gate. You've not gone far.

Ah, Christ, I smell it! The Thames!

You'll not smell it long. I'll deliver you to your daughter.

My daughter? Where is she? What business have you with my Meg?

She tasked me with an errand, I said. With the delivery of your head.

He emitted a wail, like a cat that is trod upon.

Ah, you wretch! you cullion! you ass-spreading ingle! You are a worse shit even than Luther. Meg wanted only my head, but you! Pestiferous, stew-dwelling, punkeating maltworm! You have stolen my soul!

Hush, man. I have only your head. I know naught of your soul.

He wailed the louder, though his lips were closed. I seized his screaming skull two-handed, wrenched at the jaw until, with a tearing sound, it opened a space. I snatched up an onion, wedged it into the opening. The wailing continued. I seized the candlestick, toppling the candle, and smashed the head with the base. I saw only that I had opened a savage dent, as the flame toppled into my wine and went out, leaving me in the dark with this howling dead thing. In despair, I cried:

Shut up! For Meg's sake, shut up!

Meg, it said. *Meg.* And said no more.

*   *   *

AT THE TIME arranged, I stood 'midst the merrymakers on the Bank, on the lip of a bear-pit, a laden pouch slung over my shoulder. The bear below was a sleepy-looking fellow that lumbered in circles along the earthen wall and swatted at the refuse hurled down. Its bristly collar was all a-point with spikes. These did little to allay the general impression of boredom. The criers' voices were hoarse and listless, even as they insulted one another and their customers.

"Ale and elderberries!"

"Sweetmeats!"

"Flawn!"

"Here, this Florentine you just sold me—it's all fat in the middle!"

"Well, it suits you then! Out of my way. Florentines!"

Likely customers ogled an oyster-wench's ample bosom and, secondarily, the tray of shellfish her teats partially shaded. A gatherer outside a theatre collected admissions, one clank at a time, in a glazed money-box. At his waist swung the hammer that at day's end would smash open the profit—or the head of any coxcomb who tried to relieve him of it.

"Suckets, Milord?"

"No, no," I said, waving her past.

Suckets, said More.

She showed no sign of hearing it, but I stepped away, pressing the pouch closer 'neath my elbow. *Suckets*, More repeated. Through my sleeve and the fabric of the pouch, I felt something bite at my arm.

"Any ginger-bread?" asked another.

"Alas, no, but some lovely marchpane, me sister's known for it. Melts on your tongue, it does."

"Just like your sister!" Much laughter.

"It's yer fat stewed prune I wants in me mouth, love, if it's not been sucked off by now!" Even more laughter. The bear rumbled and farted, and the air above his pit fairly shimmered with the stink.

Damn you! I cannot eat! cried More. *And yet I starve!*

His was louder than any voice in the crowd, and yet no one reacted. So I did not react, either.

"Oh, you squirtings! Weasel-beak! Get on with your saucy selves. Ah, there's a love," said the hag, curseying to a gentleman whose brocaded back was to me. "I thank you, sir."

"Away with you, then," he said, turning: William Roper, and alone in the crowd. He met my eye and cocked his head toward the street, then turned and walked away. I followed him across the thoroughfare, his feathered cap my guide through the throng. I followed him into an alley and around a stack of barrels. Madame stood there, her face streaked with tears. She twisted a bit of cloth in her fingers.

Meg, said More.

"It's you!" she said, and took a wild-eyed step toward me—but stopped herself, and so did not rush to me, lay hands upon me, embrace me. "So William was right after all," she said, more calmly. "I was sure you were seized, or dead."

Meg! Ah, Meg! Finish me!

To the horrid voice in my pouch, she reacted not at all.

I bowed low. "Alive, and free to serve Madame," I said.

"Free." She looked all about, at an overhang of verminous thatch above, at a puddle of piss below, at the leaden sky and the barrelstaves, at everything but me and my noisy pouch.

I glanced at her husband, who gave me only the smallest shake of his head in reply.

"Here, Madame," I said, and gestured at the pouch that swung heavily at my side, still wailing and moaning.

Drown me in the river, Meg! I am your father! Burn me in a pyre! Meg, you silly bitch, listen! Meg!

Madame made as if to reach for the flap, then snatched back her hand with such haste I heard it slap against the front of her dress.

Looking neither at him nor at me, she said, flatly, "William."

Roper, sparing me a cold glance, stepped forward and lifted a corner of the flap a few inches. The moment he lifted it, More's puling ceased.

"Why, 'tis not him," Roper said.

"You lie, sir," I said.

Roper's face twisted in anger. "Dare you speak so?"

Madame looked faint. "What wrong have I done thee to warrant such cruelty?"

Roper and I spoke at once.

"Madame, please."

"Silence, dog!"

"See for yourself."

"Meg, let's away."

"I will see," she said, silencing us. She lifted the flap, looked in, and breathed, "Oh."

As I watched her face, her features seemed to smooth. The lines of care and middle years filled in like canals. Her eyes shone.

"That such a small vessel," she murmured, "could contain such a great head."

"Meg! You are mistaken, surely."

"No. Look, William. Do you not see the mole upon his cheek, the cleft in his chin? As a girl I tried to hide flower-petals in there."

Her husband looked again.

"He is much diminished," Roper said. "And yet."

"Enough," Madame said, stepping away. "The task is concluded. Take him."

I thought this meant concealed guards, that the moment had come, and I was ready. But she only watched as Roper gently lifted the satchel off my shoulder.

"When they told me he was gone," she said, half to me and half to no one, "my own head went a-rolling. I had no mind, no purpose. I wanted only to be in the street, in the crowds. In my slippers I walked through the muck, seeing nothing, facing no one, until I was brought up short... by whiteness. White on white, like a heap of saint-souls. I stood, marveling, before a shop-window full of Low Country linen. So, so beautiful. Mother used to say, ah, Meg, it's a shame to bring it home, it ne'er can be so pure again. I suddenly had a single thought: a winding-sheet. Father must be wrapped for burial. Of course. But I had no purse. I had left the house in such grief and such haste, I had come away with nothing. Yet I pointlessly, automatically patted the little sewing-pocket of my skirts, and pulled from that pocket three gold sovereigns, which were not there before. And so I came home no longer mad and pitiable, but sensible, and done with my errand, and this winding-sheet was worth two pounds at the most." She flapped at me the bit of cloth she'd been a-worrying. "Just look at it! Little better than dagswain. Such is the world without my father, friend Aliquo: petty miracles, and petty frauds."

She shook her head, seemed to focus on me. "But my household will e'er remember your good offices. I pray you, seek your perfect homeland. I hope it exists—but you'll not find it here." Her eyes ceased to see me. "Ay, not here."

She and her man turned and walked away. "We'll pickle him, I think," I heard her say, "with some elderflower."

As that grim burden swung at Roper's hip, down the alley and into the street, her father's not-voice resumed its wailing.

God damn you. God damn you! God damn you ALL!

I stood at the alley's mouth and watched them grow smaller in the distance, the voice diminishing all the while, until they could not be seen, and More could not be heard.

FREED OF MY burden, freed of my hopes, I walked southward, away from the city, toward the sea. I moved among women and men, but saw no one, heard nothing.

Two days later, I crouched on a quay on the wet lip of England, hidden behind shipping-barrels, and removed from my pouch the not-More head I had carried all that way.

"Farewell, friend Zapolet," I told it, and laid it onto the surface of the water, as gently as More must have laid his firstborn babe, wiggling and shiny, 'pon her coverlet. I watched the Zapolet's staring head roll 'neath the waves, as the babe sinks into the adult. Then it was gone forever.

I re-entered the crowd and found a line to stand in, waiting to book passage. Something tugged at my breeches. A grimy child, of indeterminate sex, holding a tray of sweetmeats.

"Suckets, Milord?"

Suckets, repeated More.

I bellowed and whirled, my feet crushing the scattered sweetmeats as the child fled. I stared into the incredulous faces of strangers jostling to get away from me. Gulls shrieked. The ocean heaved. Ships' colors whipped in the hot wind.

Thou fool, said More. *Whose head do you think I'm in?*

*   *   *

I WRITE THIS letter in an English inn, a half-day's walk from London.

I said at the outset that I had failed, and so I believed at the time. Perhaps I will believe that again. In the meantime, with every northward step away from home, questions roil in my head—philosophical questions, such as those chewed after dinner, in the refectories of Aircastle. I will pose them to you.

Was I treated well, or ill, when my lover's husband discovered me in the arms of his wife, and assumed the entire fault was mine?

Was I treated well, or ill, when I, a mere girl, was charged with "forbidden embraces," with "defiling the marriage bed"? When my lover was persuaded to swear untruths against me, to save herself?

Was I treated well, or ill, when I was sentenced to slavery? When I was assured my bondage would be temporary if I was good, and if I denied my nature forevermore? When I was told, moreover, that I was fortunate, that voyagers stepped onto our docks daily in hopes of achieving slavery in Utopia, so preferable to freedom elsewhere?

Was I treated well, or ill, when my natural strength and agility placed me in endless daily training, in service to a citizenry that viewed combat and assassination as tasks fit only for mercenaries and slaves?

Was I treated well, or ill, when I was ordered to rescue a halfmythical figure in a faraway land where even my sex must be denied and disguised, if I am to function at all, and promised my freedom if I succeeded?

It is true, my former fellow citizens, my former masters and mistresses, I did not rescue More. He is dead. He reminds me daily of this fact, and of the impossibility of a better world to come, though in an ever fainter voice, one that I am growing used to. Mostly, now, he speaks a single name.

More is unsaved, and yet, I write you today as a free woman, to say farewell.

Our homeland is not perfect. No homeland is. But all lands can be made more perfect—even this England. And all lands have perfection within them: somewhere, sometime, someone.

Thus ends my story and my service, ye Prince and Tranibors of our good land, ye Syphogrants and families thereof. May my example be instructive to you and to your assigns. Though I never return to Utopia, never walk again beside the Waterless Stream, I will feel my people with me always, all those stern and rational generations. I will always be your agent, but I serve another now.

YOU PRETEND LIKE YOU NEVER MET ME, AND I'LL PRETEND LIKE I NEVER MET YOU
Maria Dahvana Headley

Maria Dahvana Headley (www.mariadahvanaheadley.com) is a *New York Times* Bestselling author and editor, playwright and screenwriter, most recently of the young adult fantasy novels *Magonia* and *Aerie*, the dark fantasy/alt-history novel *Queen of Kings*, the internationally bestselling memoir *The Year of Yes* and *The Mere Wife*, a contemporary adaption of Beowulf. With Neil Gaiman, she is the #1 New York Times-bestselling editor of the anthology *Unnatural Creatures*. With Kat Howard, she is the author of the novella *The End of the Sentence*—one of NPR's Best Books of 2014. Her Nebula, Shirley Jackson and World Fantasy Award-shortlisted fiction has been anthologized in many years bests, and appeared in *Lightspeed, Uncanny, Nightmare, Tor.com, Shimmer, Apex, Clarkesworld, The Journal of Unlikely Entomology, Subterranean Online*, and *The Toast*. She grew up in rural Idaho on a survivalist sled-dog ranch, and now lives in Brooklyn. Her work has been supported by The MacDowell Colony, and Arte Studio Ginestrelle, among other organizations.

THE WORST DAY of Wells the Magician's life begins pleasantly enough, with a shot of whiskey at the Lost Kingdom bar. It's a birthday party day, and as all low-rent magic men know, birthday party days begin with booze and move laterally through coffee, cake, and whichever divorcee can be convinced to unhook her bra, whether offsite or in a back bedroom. Onward from there into (dire case) helium, (better case) weed, or (best case) coke, followed by a three a.m. cigarette before the road gets hit.

There are protocols in place.

At nine in the morning on this Saturday, with four hours to kill before he performs magic tricks at a fifth birthday party in a gated subdivision, Wells has three bourbons, neat, and one platter of fries, messy. Mayo. Ketchup. Hot sauce. Grape jam packets. Mustard. Maple syrup. Side of nacho cheese. Like that. He takes his time, stealth-assessing the woman in the back of the bar. She's wearing a pair of too-small, heart-shaped, red plastic sunglasses, and at 10:15, Wells decides his next fifty years belong to her.

He formally signals the bartender.

"A round to woo the woe in the last row," he says, pleased with himself.

"Not a move, bro. She's been here five days," the bartender says. "Leaves for two hours while Jake or I clean, gets back in the booth. Stays there, staring. You know I don't judge my regulars, but something's wrong with that one. Trust me when I say there's no good version of getting her drunker."

"Coffee, then?" says Wells, angling his head to get a better look. She's maybe thirty, dark hair cut jagged, punk rock shifted into something else. He can't tell if there's a ring, but he likes them crazy enough that his occupation tempts rather than warns. There might be time for a bang before the birthday. He does the math. Definitely, if they walk out of here by 11:30.

The bartender shakes his head. "PG Tips. She's a Brit."

"Do it up," Wells says, and waits for the kettle to boil, checking his bag of tricks while he does.

The tricks are in need of a dry cleaner and a few prayers, but it doesn't matter. Five-year-olds believe in magic. Balloon animals and endless scarves, bubbles, cake. Kids this age hate card tricks, so he doesn't bother. Coins, yes. Rabbits, yes, though Wells hasn't got any at present. His most recent ex-wife, Amanda, shouted "Born Free!" as she walked away with their cage. The trick bag is an inheritance from Wells's dad, who was an all-sorts magic man. Wells spent his childhood on the assist. An apple on his head, an arrow, a knife, Wells done up in sparkles, transformed into a sequined specialist. They drove a beat-to-shit minivan gig to gig, Wells playing the role of the magician's glitz, followed by naps beneath gambling tables.

When Wells was fourteen, his dad got stabbed in Reno, outside a casino he was fleecing. Wells should have gotten stabbed, too, but the someone doing the stabbing just glanced at him, and bent back over Wells's dad.

"Just need to fetch something for the boss," said the stabber. "Don't mind me."

There was no blood, just sorting, like someone rooting in a sock drawer.

"Okay," said Wells. His spine felt frozen and his guts were roiling, and the person he was talking to had eyes without whites. If this was a magic trick, it wasn't the kind he knew the combination for, and if it was actual magic, he wanted nothing to do with it.

The stabber nodded, and continued to rummage.

Finally, they muttered, "Not there, is it? No. Bounced checks and bad bets. Selling things you don't own. Not one thing, it's another."

They looked up at Wells again. "No kid was supposed to be here. It's your lucky day. You pretend like you never met me, I'll pretend like I never met you," they said.

Wells caught a glimpse of claws and an additional glimpse of horns, but Wells was like that back then. He saw spectacle everywhere. When Wells nodded, the stabber disappeared without the aid of smoke and mirrors.

Wells picked his dad's tricks up off the sidewalk, stood, and walked away. Told the police he'd missed the murder. Told the casino he didn't know who did it and that he wasn't pursuing it. Told the driver who picked him up hitchhiking that he'd been traveling alone for a year, and that he was looking to get his ass to Tahoe. A few other things happened, soon after that. Wells decided to deny them, too. *Pretend like you never met me*, he thought, and moved on, town to town for thirty years.

Lately, he's been haunting Boise, Idaho. He's learned how to say the name of the place, the "sea" instead of "zee," and so people think he's local enough to last.

Every day, Wells puts on the cheapo tux and the clip-on polka-dot tie, polishes the shoes. A hundred bucks and wine coolers in the kitchen with the moms, who will be, if experience is any guide, thirsty. Wells checks the bag for candy. Quality lollipops will make true believers out of most people. He steals a glance at the woman in the back booth. She's got a notebook out and she's scribbling something in it. She looks testy. It's 10:32.

Wells nudges the bartender. He can see steam. Good enough. The bartender pours water into the mug. Wells adds a teabag and dunks it frantically. The woman takes off her sunglasses. There's an expression on her face Wells doesn't entirely like, but her blue eyes are visible from here, along with mascara that's made its way from lashes to ashes, dust to destiny.

He's a sucker for messes like this one.

"You cunt," the woman comments, unsolicited from just behind him as he's reaching for the milk. "The water must be boiling, or the tea will be weak. And the teabag must be added *before* the water."

Wells turns his head and takes the opportunity to examine her. Thirty-five, chewed lipstick, and there might be blood on the sleeve of her dress, which also seems to be a nightgown, but who's counting flaws? Wells is on the north side of forty, and some of his tattoos are starting to look like cancer. The ones he got more recently pop like goldfish from a carnival bowl, and those are the ones that matter. He flexes the bicep closest to her.

He considers a coin trick. He could pull one from her clenched fist. What kind of coin, though? He never knows what the bag will give him. Soon after his dad died, he found a pile of peep show tokens in the bottom, and took his miserable self to see some sparkle. Sometimes, he drops his hand in just to see what kind of currency he touches, and then plans his life accordingly.

This time, he gets a wooden nickel, and ignores it.

"The. Water. Must. Be. Boiling," the woman repeats. "Otherwise, things end up useless."

Wells pours milk, being helpful, but she unexpectedly slaps the mug, and overturns it. Warmish tea drips into Wells' lap.

"You don't add the milk until the tea's had time to steep," she says. "It takes longer than you think. Particularly if the bloody water wasn't even boiling in the first place." She makes a moan that is closer to a sob. "I can't bear America."

"I'll buy you a better cuppa," Wells says. "It's on me."

Her dress is torn, yes, and possibly stained, but it's flowered. Her cheeks are rosy. English rosy. He envisions something he saw on the BBC, in the dead of night between divorces, a flushed woman in a flowered gown, corset unlaced. *Blowsy*, he thinks. Yes, a wedding ring. No problem. The stones are turned toward her palm.

"*Cuppa*?" she says, and her tone is ominous. "BBC, isn't it. Butlers. That's the accent you're using. You're mangling it. Were you any sort of butler, you'd know how to make a proper pot of tea."

She plucks a cocktail straw from the backbar, and fracks his drink to the dregs.

"I can fix it," Wells tries. "I'm a magician."

She mishears him, probably on purpose. "No. There's no medicine for this."

She fishes the teabag out of her empty mug, shoves it in his open mouth, and walks toward the door.

"You'll be driving, then," she says, over her shoulder.

One problem Wells the Magician has always had? He loves damage.

Wells chews the teabag for sobriety, tasting black leaves like a terrible fortune, drops a twenty from the tricksack on the bar and follows her. He feels himself getting hard.

"Bro, no," the bartender calls after him. "That's a no go. I'd watch out for her."

"You don't know me," says Wells. "This is my whole thing."

IN THE LOT, there is only one vehicle, and she's standing beside it, tapping her foot.

"Nice car," she says. "If car's what you call this."

Wells's car is a literal lemon. It's a VW bug, painted canary and dimpled with dots made by, Wells suspects, a ball peen hammer. It was part of the flotsam from a foreclosed lemonade stand, and cost four hundred dollars. When Wells took possession of the car after the auction, he opened the trunk and a compressed lemon mascot suit popped out, nearly giving him a heart attack. Also included in the sale were seventeen hundred hollow plastic lemon sippy cups, three hundred and seventy-eight insulated thermal lemons, and forty-five flammable velveteen novelty lemon pillows, each emblazoned with the name and disconnected phone number of the lemonade stand's former owner. They filled the entire interior. Wells went to the dump and gave everything over but the lemon suit, which he kept, just in case. He's pretty sure it's rated for cold, and his last wife ($299 divorce, cheaper than the car) took his camping gear when she went rogue.

Wells isn't a whimsical man—no magician is—but he could see the utility of a vehicle like this: it is so noticeable that no police officer would imagine its driver committing crimes while behind the wheel. Wells is essentially invisible inside its yellow shell, and whether he speeds, drinks, or drugs his way through an evening, he trusts that no one believes their eyes.

The lemon sticks when he drives it, but he's had the side painted with his logo nonetheless. *Wells the Magician* it says, in calligraphy, with a picture of a top hat and a clutter of stars.

The woman's hand is on the hood, and her nightgown is the shortie kind. Wells feels optimistic.

"My house is seven minutes away."

"Wishes, horses, beggars," she says, wrests open the passenger door, gets in, and waits. Right, then. Usually he sprints under the red flags of feminine vigilance. He inherited charm from his mother. Women have always been willing to sleep with him, no matter the evidence he's nothing good. There's still time.

He takes the address the woman gives him.

He's not sober. She's not sober either. Whatever. Wells has a shortlist of ways he's willing to die. He imagines everyone does. Sometimes you manage to hit a Venn diagram of death wishes in a one-night stand. There should be a dating app to match methods. He laughs as he puts the lemon into gear. She looks at him. He stops laughing.

He drives out from the bar and into the country, half a silent hour in the general direction of nowhere. At last, she points.

"There."

A Victorian mansion, all gingerbread and gilding, creamy turrets, stained glass windows. She doesn't look like she belongs to a place like this, but goes to show. Wells is midway up the walk behind her when he sees the sign: Nix & Sons, Funeral Home.

"Hang on," he says.

She turns around and looks at him.

"What? This isn't what you were hoping for? Most things aren't," she says.

She walks into the mansion, shutting the door behind her.

It's suddenly 12:15. Wells gets back into the lemon and opens his glovebox kit to brush the bourbon out of his breath, swab his face with a wipe, and slick his hair into top hat formation. Bag of tricks intact. He fishes for a coin, just to see. A silver dollar might bode well, but there's nothing. He takes a few minutes to stabilize. Win some. Lose most. This is the life of a hack magician, a man whom true magic has not bothered with. Wells's father could do anything. He'd disappear in the middle of a crowded room, drive a car while sitting in the backseat. Once, he floated stark naked over an entire casino, looking over shoulders and reading hidden hands, while Wells kept watch over his tux.

Where'd he get his magic? He made some jokes about soul sales. Sometimes, when he's not thinking about the thing he agreed to forget, Wells wonders who is ever kidding about anything.

"Dirt cheap," his dad said once of his immortal soul, as he was cleaning up a hotel room full of pantyhose, beer bottles, baubles, and Bibles never opened. "Never was anything but shirt deep."

Wells was twelve years old at the time, drinking a Jolt Cola and trying to learn how to make girls appear out of thin air. It didn't work if you didn't have any willing and around to begin with. He's still never learned.

As he pulls out of the lot, Wells catches sight of the woman emerging onto the porch with an enormous floral arrangement. She's changed into a black dress. He raises his hand to wave, then thinks better of it, but she waves to him. No, that's a finger in the air. Alright then, leave it.

She's filled Wells's car with the smells of new sweat and old perfume. She's nothing special, not a ghost, not a queen, just his usual kind of trouble. An Amanda or a Bridget or, god help him, a Sonja. He doesn't even know her name.

She walks down the steps with a driver and gets into the passenger seat of a hearse. Wells shudders as the coffin mobile pulls out.

Wells, in classic Wells fashion, has definitely hit on a newly-minted widow.

He rolls down his windows and ushers awkwardness out. Awkwardness is the enemy of magic. He follows the hearse decisively out onto the highway, thinking to flee, but finds himself idiotically part of a long procession of black sedans interspersed with black motorcycles. Wells is appalled by the rudeness of bikers invading a funeral procession, but then...

The riders are wearing black suits, and Wells is the lone lemon in an all-mourner motorcade. A man with a long white beard turns his head as he passes, and gives Wells a look that says he's broken all laws of civility. The biker has stars tattooed across his face, and his eyes are pink from weeping.

Wells is reminded of the last rabbit he had, a hostile albino lop named Richard. He glances at the rabbit's top hat, sitting for now in the backseat.

He's visited by a vision of the woman wearing it and drinking a perfectly made mug of tea. Her ring is turned the right way round, but it's not the ring she was wearing. It's his own mother's ring, the one he hasn't ever presented to a wife, though he's had two so far. Wells spent his entire childhood traveling with his dad, leaving his mother behind. He only has his mom's wedding ring because she took it off one morning when he was eleven, left it in an eggcup, and walked. Years ago he dropped it into the bag of tricks, and he hasn't seen it since.

He pulls over and lets the funeral procession pass. Trying to save a pretty woman from pre-existing problems is not any kind of plan. Maybe one of the mothers at the birthday will be plausible. He considers himself in the rearview. Not too shabby. Or, at least, no shabbier than usual.

"The water must be boiling," he says. He says it louder. "THE WATER MUST BE BOILING OR THE TEA WILL BE WEAK."

Wells pulls off the highway entirely, and steps on the gas.

THERE'S A TRAIL of colorful balloons, and cheerful printed signs guiding civilians to Ammy's birthday.

This seems wrong. Wells checks his contract.

He isn't the only one having an off day. The parents have misspelled their own daughter's name. He pulls up to the house, and—how late is he? Parents look shitfaced. He checks his watch. No, he's fine. There are people teetering their way around the premises, though, and in the kitchen they're slumped over salsa. Two are chainsmoking. A few more are crying. Screw that, Wells thinks. He congratulates himself again on his vasectomy, undisclosed to his wives, who thought they were the problem. Parents sometimes punch magicians in the head for no reason. Wells stays on guard.

He scans the crowd for Ammy, and finds her, plastic-crowned and pink-frocked, her expression that of a kid about to vomit or tantrum.

Wells reconsiders this party. It's October, and it's fifty-one degrees. The swimming pool is open, and Wells has no doubt that he'll soon find himself in the water, rescuing a kid from drowning. He takes a step back. They haven't seen him yet. He still has time. Just a minor magic trick involving illusion and he'll be out—

But Ammy's got him around the knees. She's glaring up at him, a freckled kid with the eyebrows of a seventy-year-old man.

"Are you the magician?" she asks. "You don't look like you know magic."

"Are you Amy?" he asks. "You don't look like you know magic either."

"Ammy," she says, and curls her lip. Of course she is.

"DOES HE KNOW MAGIC?" she screams, startling him.

"He doesn't," says another kid. "He's a dummy."

"DUMMY!" shout four at once.

Wells brings an emergency wand from behind his back and does a trick involving a bouquet of flowers appearing out of thin air. The kids give no fucks. He transforms the flowers into vending machine slugs, because that's what the bag offers him. The kids origami themselves down into a pointed-knee circle. They're still grim, but he's bought himself three minutes. He glances furtively at the parents. They seem to be heading toward a miserable key party. There's hugging where there shouldn't be hugging. Embraces are lasting too long.

He waves his wand and makes the slugs into a series of sparkly explosions.

There is the opposite of applause. One of the kids starts up the kind of whimper that's contagious, and it's only a matter of time. Well brings out the top hat, and pulls from it a lifelike rabbit puppet, which usually goes over incredibly well. It's not Richard the Rabbit, but it's something.

The voice of a dad carries from the house. "I mean how does this happen? How does she let it happen?"

A mom joins in. "And him? What was he thinking? How do you—No, I can't even."

Wells fumbles for lollies. He's half-buried in the bag of tricks, closing his fist around what feels like a gold bar, when his day officially dives into the shitter.

"MAGICIAN, LISTEN," Ammy says, and it's an order. "Mica was on a motorcycle with his daddy."

"The road was slippery," says another kid. "It was raining."

"Now, Mica's over there," says a third kid.

Wells looks slowly up from the lollipops. The kids are pointing into the distance, down the highway, and Wells knows exactly where they're pointing. He can imagine what's happening in that cemetery right now, bikers, little coffin, flowers, and the woman from the bar standing beside the grave in her black dress and heart-shaped sunglasses, having spent days in shock, having not changed her clothes since the accident, and he, Wells, couldn't even get the water hot. He couldn't get the tea into the water. He couldn't get the milk into the tea.

"The hospital tried to fix him, but they couldn't," says Ammy.

How can a five-year-old have him by the collar? The children inch closer. Wells has become a sacrifice in the middle of a ring of tiny witches.

"They couldn't fix him," the children repeat, mimicking someone else, their teacher, or a parent. "Mica died."

"Did Mica's dad die too?" he asks, stalling.

"He only got hurt," says Ammy, and visibly seethes.

Something is pushed into his hand. It's a drawing in crayon. A little boy, a mother in a flowered dress, and a man on a motorcycle.

"Do the magic," Ammy demands. "DO THE MAGIC."

"Which magic?" he asks. He shouldn't ask. He knows.

"Make Mica alive again," she says.

The rest nod, like bringing someone back to life is a matter of cups and balls, a cabinet, and a wand wave.

No one is crying. Everyone believes. The mob of kindergarteners stares at Wells the Magician, he of no skills, he of two divorces and one VW lemon, a forty-five-year-old failure, charged with raising the dead, and Wells stares back, frozen.

This is the truth of the matter: Wells's dad probably could've done this. Whoever his deal was with, a devil or a god, Wells's dad was the real thing, and Wells is not.

For example: A few days after Wells left his dad's body in Reno, there was an incident in the night kitchen of a diner, a smashed cockroach, and Wells, on his knees, trying to steal hamburger buns.

Wells touched the roach and said a word he'd heard his dad say, and the roach shook itself and looked up at him, abruptly unsmashed. It spread its antennae, and skittered off into the space behind the range. Wells wasn't sure. Maybe this was a thing cockroaches could do.

He tried again and again, for years, delicately, roadkill raccoon, nest-fallen songbird, frozen squirrel, but nothing.

Maybe it had been the last remnant of his father's magic, still hanging out nearby. No real magic has come out of him since.

Still, he finds himself lifting his mail-order wand, to attempt what, exactly? Just as he's about to make the horrific choice of chanting some sorcery-sounding gibberish, a mother comes out singing, candles lit, cake balanced, and the kids turn away from life and death, and toward sugar, leaving Wells, thank fuck, to tend to his own self.

He stands at the edge of the pool, away from the party, panting. Magic requires leaps of faith. It's been decades since he's leapt, and the same since he's been faithful. He has no paper sack to breathe into, so he uses his bag of tricks. There's no gold bar in there. He sees some ripped up old Italian lire. Not even valid currency.

When Ammy blows the candles out, though, he's hit by a gust of wish. He takes a stumbling step backward, and finds himself floating on air.

No. Not floating. Falling.

Wand, tuxedo, top hat, puppet rabbits and all, baptized. He's a teabag in lukewarm, chest-deep water, the dried remnants of his heart filtering pitifully, weakly, through the pool.

He struggles out of the water, drags himself to the lemon, and takes the long way back to town, making sure not to pass the cemetery. Two wet puppet rabbits seem to be glaring at him from the passenger seat. One of them has bright red around its mouth. He starts to pull over in a panic, but no, it's only melted lollipop.

"This is not your fault, Wells," he tells the car, the air, himself. "None of this is your fault."

Back at the Lost Kingdom he orders three more bourbons, even though he slunk off from the party without getting paid. The bartending shift has changed, there is that mercy, and so when the bartender lines up his drinks, no one's counting.

He doesn't want to be a magician. He wants to be something and someone else.

Wells unfolds the damp crayon drawing from his pocket and spreads it on the bar. A little boy, a mother, and a father on a motorcycle.

As Wells squints at the paper, the motorcycle turns into a wheelchair. The little boy disappears. The mother stands up, looking literal daggers at the father, and a Crayola man in a top hat and a tuxedo walks into the picture and adds himself to the family. Wells crumples the paper as fast as paper can be crumpled. He isn't doing this magic trick. Whoever is, bourbon or bad day, it's not funny.

One drink later, he un-crumples and smooths it.

The man in the tuxedo reaches out his arms, the mother falls into them, and the father wheels his chair off the paper. Lightning jags from the sky, a gold scrawl, and the magician holds it in his hands—

Something clatters. Wells looks down and sees his car keys on the ground. The figures on the paper aren't moving. There is no such thing as magic. He shifts to the back booth.

When he opens his eyes sometime later, the neon is blazing, and the line to get a drink at the Lost Kingdom is four deep. The windows are fogged over. Wells wonders if he's dead.

He looks to his left and sees a bearded face tattooed with stars, a pair of pink-rimmed rabbit eyes peering down at him.

"Richard?" he says. This is not the man's name, but a long-gone rabbit's name is the only thing Wells can remember.

"It's the lemon," says the biker. "It's the fucking lemon who thought he was a comedian."

"I'm not a comedian," Wells protests. "I'm a magician. See?"

He pulls an ancient coin from out of Richard's beard, and then rains subway tokens from Richard's ears for good measure.

Richard levitates Wells as easily as plucking a lop from a top hat. He's massive, dressed all in black leather, and Wells looks down on the Lost Kingdom from an unpleasant height.

"Caro," Richard yells. "Is this fuckshow someone from Kenny's family? If not, I'm dropping him in the dumpster."

Wells dangles, inhaling the sickly scent of lilies. There's a funeral arrangement draped over a table, on which there is a giant photo of a little boy, grinning in a pair of heart-shaped sunglasses. A woman Wells knows is at the table, too, hunched over a steaming cup, mascara striping her face like warpaint.

"Drop him," she says.

Wells plummets. He makes it to his hands and knees and crawls toward her feet. Black heels. A fresh tattoo on her calf of a mother and a son, the two of them holding hands and facing the universe. Both figures are oozing blood.

He looks up, and she's looking down at him. Blue eyes. Rosy cheeks. Hair cut with a dull knife. She's the most beautiful woman he's ever seen.

"You again," she says.

"I can bring him back," he hears himself say. "I can bring Mica back from the dead. I'm a magician."

Her fist approaches him formally, and he feels his nose bend like a spoon. There's a tsunami of tattooed biceps and rolled-up shirtsleeves from the room at large. A bottle breaks. Wells's skull is made of glass, and inside it, there is a spark like a penny becoming electric.

Wells glows for a few seconds, but the light goes out. High heels click past his face. There's the sound of revving and roaring, and over all of that, her voice ringing out from the parking lot.

"FUCK THIS!" she shouts. "FUCK MOTORCYCLES! FUCK NIGHT! FUCK DEATH!"

"Caro," someone says.

"FUCK YOU!" she screams. "GET AWAY FROM ME! PRETEND YOU NEVER MET ME!"

Wells walks backward into the dark until he's underneath the universe and safely flat, invisible.

THE DAYSHIFT BARTENDER scrapes the dropped magician off the floor and hands him a bag of frozen tater tots for his face. The bar's empty. Wells is sopping. Maybe they poured their drinks out as they went past.

"I told you to watch out for her," the bartender says. "Don't think you're driving like this, Wells. Cold front came in. Whole road's made of ice."

The bartender sets a mug of burnt coffee down in front of Wells, who drinks it. He eats an order of tots, and then walks shivering into five a.m., his tux freezing to his skin. All of this feels like basic destiny.

Wells opens the VW's trunk, and strips down to his rubber-chicken printed boxers in the glow of the Lost Kingdom sign. The lemon mascot suit is made of shaggy yellow fur and is fleece-lined. Its legs are mysteriously thermal. There's no explaining why a summer suit was constructed this way. It has a pointy hood, decorated with green leaves. Wells zips himself in, and puts his boots back on. Snow's falling like cheapola confetti.

Wells drives the lemon to a 7-11 and buys a thermos.

While he stands at the beverage station, staunching his nose with his dad's scarf trick and waiting a thousand years for the kettle on the hotplate to boil, he thinks about performing with his father, thirty years ago, posing in front of a glittering backdrop, his dad throwing a knife at his heart, and the oohs from the crowd as the knife diverted midair and stung the ceiling. His dad, grinning and bowing. Mustache. Top hat. Magic.

Every once in a while, the knife would go a little way in, and every once in a while, Wells would wake up with a Band-Aid under his t-shirt. Just once, something went wronger than usual and Wells woke up frozen, wristbanded, on a gurney. His dad pushed the gurney out of the basement of the hospital, and there was Wells, alive again.

"Sorry about that, buddy," said his dad, and laughed. "Overkill."

Wells laughed too, but he wasn't sure what he was laughing about, the "buddy," never a word his dad would use, or the pun, classic magician patter.

"Done with that business," his dad said, and thumped Wells hard on the shoulder. "I put it back. Shouldn't have taken it out in the first place, but I thought I'd keep it for a rainy day."

"What back?" said Wells, with some difficulty. His jaw was stiff, and there was cotton packed toward the back of his teeth.

"Still feeling hollow? It'll get better. Milkshake?"

Wells concluded that this had something to do with tonsils or teeth, and nothing to do with death. They went to a diner, and little by little, he felt himself return from elsewhere.

Soon after that, though, his father was dead, and Wells was tricking strangers in a bus station. How many kinds of illusion can a person do in a lifetime? Flash paper, wallet spirited out of a pocket, a loud noise, and Wells would be gone. No funeral for his father. Nowhere to go but out into the wide world, alone.

He loves damage. Loves it.

He drops half a box of teabags into the bottom of the thermos, pours the boiling water over them, and waits another thousand years before he tugs them out. He dribbles the milk in carefully. He pays with a pile of ones he's found in the bag, each with the face of his father instead of Washington. The cashier doesn't notice.

*   *   *

WELLS HAS NEVER been into the cemetery before, just seen it from the road, the white stones like cards dropped on a green felt table. He walks it, thermos in hand.

As morning grays the horizon, he sees her standing on a hill beside a heap of fresh dirt.

She's wearing a leather jacket, and black motorcycle boots, inches too big. She has a helmet on too.

"You for the third time," she says. She cocks her head at him. "Did I break your nose, then?"

"You did," he says.

"That was the idea." She barks a laugh, but she's crying. "I stole my husband's best friend's bike and kit. All those bikers came for my husband. He's their family. I'm nobody's family."

"I was sorry to hear about your—" he says, and then doesn't know what to say.

"Kenny's from here. I was living in London. He was riding through. It looked good to me. I got on. He isn't a bad guy, but he has bad judgment. Look at who he married. He took our son for a ride in the middle of the night and ran into a tree, but he didn't die. They're all around his bed convincing him it wasn't his fault, but it was. Tell me how that's fair. Tell me how that happens."

She sobs once, and then she's done. Wells notices the second helmet dangling from her fingers. It's small and red, to match the sunglasses she still has around her neck.

"What kinds of tricks can you do, then, Wells the Magician?" she says, after a moment.

"Cards, coins, bunnies."

"I watched a magician saw a woman in half once," she says. "In Brighton. She got rid of everything below the heart. That was a thing to see."

He holds out the thermos.

She takes it. "And there's a trick. You know what I don't take in my tea?"

"Lemon," he replies, "Obviously."

"It curdles," she says. "I don't take sugar either. So stay away from me with your vulgarian attempts at sweet."

"No sugar or lemon in there," he says. "Despite appearances."

Steam makes a cloud over her face as she pours tea into the cup and sips. She looks at Wells, and raises an eyebrow.

"Quite nice," she says. "If milky."

"I followed your directions."

"It's nursery tea, but it'll do. One for the fates," she says, and flings a drop of tea into the air. "One for the furies." She pours a shot of tea into her hand, and smears it over the temporary grave marker.

"And one for the one I leave behind here, in this fucking ground, in this fucking country."

She pours a shot of tea onto the grave itself.

Blood drips unexpectedly from Wells' nose and lands on the snow, mixing with the tea. He's turning to apologize, when the ground groans.

There's a muffled explosion deep beneath the surface, and both of them lurch as dirt and snow are displaced. Gravel peppers his face. A rock bounces off her helmet.

The grave spits the coffin out.

It lands hard, and shudders. There's a sound as the coffin opens. Wells isn't sure who makes it, him or her. In the coffin, there's a boy, eyes closed. Alive? Dead? There's no way to tell.

Caro lunges toward her son, then stops.

Someone else is with them now, someone Wells has met before.

The stranger is wearing a coat made of smoke. There's ice forming on Wells's spine, and his heartbeat hesitates. Whether this is death or a devil, it hasn't noticed him. Old agreements were bound in blood, and if he agreed he never met this thing, it agreed it never met him, too.

Caro's fists are clenched. She smells like tea leaves being insisted into a fortune.

"No," says Caro to the thing that stabbed Wells's father. "It's me you'll be taking."

"That old trope," says a voice made out of last calls. "If I wanted you instead, I'd have had you instead. I didn't ask to be brought here. Whatever summoned me, it was old business, not new. I'll be off."

Foggy tendrils twist toward the boy, and the smoke steps backward, one foot in the grave, clinging to the coffin. Caro pivots in her stolen boots, and swings the thermos of tea at the stabber's head. Wells watches in despair.

She's not going to win. She's mortal, and she has no magic. All she has, is that she's the mother of this child.

Wells is bourbon and hamburgers and a life spent spending every last cent on simple sins. Love has found him wanting. He's stood in rooms full of birth and thought about dying. He's a minor magic man with nothing but his broken life to lose.

And so.

Wells upends his bag of tricks and pours it out. He's only ever fumbled for fixes, but the bag is larger than it looks. Here in the snow, now, are all the things Wells has ever lost.

The house he used to dream of living in, a wedding ring belonging to his mother, a history he's spent decades hiding from. His mother screaming at his father, and then closing the kitchen door, his father in the center of the linoleum. A college-ruled notebook full of promises, a candle sputtering, a cloud of smoke around him. Wells was there when magic showed up in a mobile home.

Overkill.

How old was Wells? A high chair? A platter of peas, thrown one by one. Young enough that language eluded him, but he was there as his dad took his hand and cut a fingertip, making him part of the bargain, capable of carrying the bag of tricks and everything else.

The thing the stranger was rummaging for, all those years ago, was here, inside the sack. Wells was the bag carrier, the little piece of nothing, bearing his father's soul and keeping it safe from any bad bargains. At one point, Wells's own soul was in the sack too, maybe destined for a cup and ball swap, maybe just out of his dad's bad habits.

Wells feels the magic that's always been beside him, that rode in the passenger seat, that provided him with coins and stars and smoke, that messed with his marriages.

Now it's in the snow. Wells reaches down and picks it up.

He has no real magic words for this old business. A trade of merchandise. He dropkicks the soul long-owed into the grave, and yells the word his dad taught him for rabbits and balloons.

"ABRACADABRA!"

And there is his father, in the middle of the air, naked and floating over the grave, a deck of cards orbiting him. There is his father, looking to Wells and nodding.

The open grave is full of smoke, like dry ice in a punch bowl. Like magic in a retirement home, this kind of death, its tricks visible in the light. Wells can hear a marching band somewhere, and he can feel confetti dropping out of the sky, and he can smell the scent of the perfume his mother used to wear.

The stabber is standing below Wells's father, opening smoky arms, and taking the wandering soul in them. The coffin is open, and now it contains a naked magician.

Wells feels death depart the premises, and his own heart begins to beat properly again, in a way it hasn't in years. The coffin is gone, and the grave is closed over. The show is done and the curtains are drawn, and Wells looks around, expecting a broom and a janitor, no joy, no glory, not even any roses.

Everything is as it was, except—

There is a little boy, very still on the ground, in a frozen slick of tea. There's a pair of sunglasses shaped like hearts, cracked across one lens. There's a helmet on the hillside, upturned. There's an old wedding ring, glowing red, and then cooling, in a tarnished pile of pennies.

The bag of tricks is gone, but it isn't necessary. Those were old tricks, and this is something else.

There's a woman in leather, and she's on her knees. There's Wells in his lemon suit, and he's on his knees too. There's no such thing as magic.

And then, because magic doesn't follow those rules, or any rules at all, the boy's eyes open, and the woman goes to him, and the man goes to them, and the three are there, on the hilltop, with the whole world beneath them like a hat full of lucky rabbits, alive and kicking.

"Are you a magician?" the boy asks Wells. "I know magic."

The boy leans toward Wells and touches his ear, and from the ear he pulls a coin, and the coin turns into a bird, and the bird flies up to spin across the sky and over the heads of sleepers and wakers in the town.

"Is there still tea, then?" Caro asks, and Wells passes her the thermos. The water is boiling now, and the tea is strong and dark. No one is crying. Everyone believes.

QUALITY TIME

Ken Liu

A winner of the Nebula, Hugo, and World Fantasy awards, **Ken Liu** (kenliu. name) is the author of *The Dandelion Dynasty*, a silkpunk epic fantasy series (*The Grace of Kings*, *The Wall of Storms*, and a forthcoming third volume) and *The Paper Menagerie and Other Stories*, a collection. He also wrote the Star Wars novel, *The Legends of Luke Skywalker*.

"WELCOME TO weROBOT," said the chipper HR representative. "Jake and Ron and the rest of us are all *so* looking forward to your contributions!"

"Are you a true believer?" the woman next to me asked in a low, conspiratorial voice. I looked at her, puzzled; her name tag said *Amy*.

She took a sip of her coffee, frowned, and then rapped her knuckles against the conference room table. The little coffeemaker in the middle of the table, a retro-looking, squat, black cylinder with a chromed dome top, spun around until its single camera was aimed at Amy, who smiled and beckoned to it.

"A true believer in what?"

I whispered. I couldn't help it. I knew I should be paying attention to the benefits presentation—Mom had emphasized no less than five times on the phone last night the importance of contributing to the 401(k) at my first job out of college. But I was feeling nervous (the slide on-screen at the moment actually said *Our Impossible Mission*), and Amy—forties, short-cropped hair, a tattoo of two fairies playing Nintendo on her left arm—looked like she had wisdom to share.

"The Myth of the Valley," she said.

The coffeemaker rolled toward Amy, its motor humming softly. It stopped a few inches away and flashed the ring around its camera eye. Amy leaned forward to dump out the contents of her mug in the waste disposal chute at the side of the robot.

Then, instead of discreetly tapping out her new order on the touchscreen, Amy leaned back in her seat and said aloud, "Tea. Earl Grey. Hot."

Some of the other new hires—almost all of them my age—looked at Amy disapprovingly for this interruption; a few others chuckled. "I've always wanted to do that," said Amy, a satisfied grin on her face as the coffeemaker filled her mug with the new beverage.

Instead of acting annoyed, the HR rep smiled indulgently. "I was a fan too. This is actually a perfect segue to the next slide." She pressed the button on her clicker.

The new slide showed an old photograph of weRobot's two founders, geeky college boys in their dorm room, surrounded by a mess of mechanical and electronic components as well as stacks of spiral-bound notebooks. "We believe that there's no continuing mission more important than improving the lives of the human race through advancing robotics. We want every one of you to feel that you *can* make a difference, achieve what you thought was impossible, act like Jake and Ron when they started this company with a notebook full of diagrams that no one believed would work and eighty-five dollars between the two of them ..."

Amy leaned over to me. "Either that's a terribly staged photograph, or one of the duo is no good at programming."

"Oh?"

"Look at that snippet of Perl on their computer. Reading all lines into an array? No chomp?"

I looked at the photograph and then back at her, my face blank.

"Not a coder then?"

I shook my head. "I majored in Folklore and Mythology."

Amy gazed at me with interest. "I like this; we should talk more."

Great, I don't even get the engineering jokes. I suppressed a rising wave of panic and sought refuge in some homemade chicken soup for the soul.

One of the hottest companies in Silicon Valley wouldn't have hired a liberal arts major without having seen something *in me, right?*

The HR rep took out a stack of notebooks and handed them out. "Your first and most important benefit!"

The notebooks turned out to be pads of graph paper. I flipped open mine. Instead of the standard square grid, the sheets were imprinted with unorthodox patterns like spirals, honeycombs, tessellations of animal shapes, a scattering of random dots.

"Don't follow conventional wisdom," said the HR rep. "If a problem hasn't been solved, that means *you* are meant to solve it! Think impossible... and then make it happen!"

"As corporate one-liners go, this one isn't too bad," whispered Amy. "Not as ripe for parody as Centillion's 'We arrange the world's information to ennoble the human race,' and certainly better than Bazaar's shtick of having new employees build their own desks out of two-by-fours while chanting 'There should be nothing you can't buy from us!' Look at all the eager beavers!"

I looked around at the others in my cohort. Some stared at their notepads, unsure what to do with the strange gift; others looked inspired and drew in them with intense concentration as though they were already designing weRobot's next great hit.

Amy took another sip of her tea. "Youngsters are so fun to watch. They love to be inspired."

"Do you think we're just being fed some lines?" I asked. Amy's wry tone had me concerned that I had made a mistake. "Glassdoor has really good reviews of this place's culture."

Amy chuckled. "Like all their competitors in the Valley, they've got the shuttle buses and free nuts and fruits and ToDoGenie credits, and I'm sure they'll give you as much responsibility as you can handle, plus the stock options to keep you here. But no one really succeeds here without believing the One True Myth."

"Making more money?" I was a little disappointed, to be honest. Amy sounded like a jaded cynic who believed all corporations were evil, and even I knew that wasn't wisdom.

"Oh, the money is not what drives people like Jake and Ron," Amy said. "The credo of the Valley is that all the world's problems can be solved by a really smart geek with a keyboard and a soldering iron."

I looked at Amy more critically: ShareAll backpack with a date from a decade ago, Centillion version 1.5 launch t-shirt, Abricot cell phone holder with their old logo. I had seen these as badges of honor, of her tours of service in the trenches of the greatest companies in the Valley, but maybe they were signs of something less admirable, a cynicism that was corrupting and made it impossible for her to fit in anywhere.

"What's wrong with wanting to change the world?" I asked.

"Nothing, except a lack of humility," Amy said.

"Well, I think it's pretty cool that we're finally making the future instead of just dreaming about it."

I deliberately leaned a bit away from Amy. I didn't need her negativity dragging me down on my first day. Besides, the HR rep was finally talking about the 401(k).

THE TEAM I was assigned to, Advanced Home Automation, had a vague mandate to create breakthrough products for the home, distinct from weRobot's mainstay moneymakers: vacuum cleaners, laundry folders, and home security devices. Most of the engineers were veterans from other teams, and I got the distinct sense that many of them were here because they wanted to spend more time with their families and didn't want to compete with the hungry twenty-somethings.

To my dismay, I found Amy assigned to my team as well.

"I've never worked with a folklore PM before," she said.

"Building a product isn't just about coding," I said. "A PM's job is to tell the *story* of the product." I was grateful to the VP of Product Marketing for having used that line earlier on the baby PMs.

"No need to be defensive," she said. "I think the Valley needs less techno-utopianism and more sense of history anyway. It will be fun to work together. For example, since you studied myths, I figured your deadlines will at least be less mythical. Darmok and Jalad on the ocean, amirite?"

I groaned inside. *Great, she thinks I don't know what I'm doing and she can just slack off.* This assignment did not bode well for my career advancement.

I opened the graph paper notepad from earlier and printed across the top of the page: *Advanced Home Automation.* I underlined the words three times for emphasis, and then decided to erase the final *n* and rewrote it as a cursive tail that trailed to the edge of the page. This seemed to be a bolder statement than the original, a symbolic gesture at thinking outside the box.

But the rest of the page, blank except for the spiral grid, seemed to be a maze that mocked me.

"Did you sign up for the seminar from the research division?"

I turned around and saw Amy behind me, leaning against the wall of my cubicle with a fresh mug of tea.

"No," I said, trying to look busy.

"Here's a free tip: you don't need to sit in your cubicle to get paid. They don't take attendance here. Take advantage of that."

I'd had enough. "Some of us like to get work done."

Amy sighed. "WeRobot has some of the world's most advanced researchers working for them—cognition, computation, anthropology, linguistics, nanomaterials—you name it. These free seminars are pretty much the best part of the benefits package."

I pointedly said nothing and started to write on the notepad.

What are some unsolved problems in home automation?

"Kiteo, his eyes closed," said Amy as she strolled away. "The lectures are probably too technical for liberal arts majors."

It wasn't until I saw the smirk on Amy's face as I settled down in my seat near the entrance of the seminar room that I realized that I *might* have been manipulated.

SITTING BY MYSELF in my bedroom, I stared at the notes from the seminar and the pile of AI textbooks I had bought from Bazaar—I still preferred physical books to reading on-screen. *Neural networks, cascading inputs, genetic algorithms...* How was I ever going to make sense of all this stuff?

The diagrams I had copied from Dr. Vignor's slides stared back at me as I struggled to remember why I had thought they were so exhilarating. Right then, they looked about as interesting as chess puzzles.

...the long tradition of behavior-based robotics took inspiration from research on insect behavior.

But why settle for inspiration when we can go directly to the source? Instead of programming our robots with simple algorithms that imitate the behavior of a foraging ant, why not imprint them with the neural patterns extracted from foraging ants? The new prototype robotic vacuum cleaner is able to cover a room in one-third the time of the previous model, and the efficiency improves over time as the machine learns which areas are likely to accumulate dirt and prioritize these areas...

"*Eeek!*" The scream came from the bathroom. Followed by the thud of the toilet seat cover. "Comeherecomeherecomehere!"

I grabbed the nearest weapon-like thing at hand—a heavy text book—and rushed into the bathroom, ready to do battle with whatever was threatening my roommate, Sophie.

I found her cowering in the bathtub and staring at the toilet, eyes wide with terror.

"What happened?"

"*A rat!* There's a rat in the toilet!"

I put down the textbook, picked up the plunger, knelt down before the toilet, and pried open the seat cover just an inch so I could peek in. Yep, there was a rat in there all right, as big as my forearm. As I watched, it swam around the toilet leisurely, its beady eyes staring at me as though annoyed that I was interrupting its jacuzzi session.

"How did it get in there?" Sophie asked, her voice close to a shriek.

"I've studied the urban legends around rats in toilets," I said. "There's actually some truth to the stories."

"Obviously!" Sophie said.

"Rats are good swimmers. We live on the first floor, and there's not a lot of water in the trap to keep it out."

"How can you stay so *calm* about this? What are we going to do?"

"It's just an animal looking for food. Go get the dishwashing detergent, and we'll flush this guy back where it came from."

With her back pressed against the wall, Sophie gingerly stepped out of the bathtub and shuffled out of the bathroom to run to the kitchen. When she returned with the detergent, I propped up the lid again and squirted practically the whole bottle into the bowl.

"This makes everything slick and dissolves the oil on its fur so it can't stay afloat as well," I explained. I could hear the rat splashing in the water and scrabbling its claws against the porcelain in protest.

I flushed the toilet, and, even though I didn't hear any more noises after the water swooshed away, I flushed it a couple more times for insurance.

When I opened the lid again, the bowl was empty and squeaky clean.

"I'm going to call the landlord," Sophie said, finally calming down.

I waved at her to be quiet. I had caught a glimpse of an idea, and I didn't want it to be scared away.

OH, HOW THE engineers laughed at me. They sent me emails with rat jokes, rat cartoons, and a stuffed rat even appeared in my cubicle after lunch break.

"This is why we shouldn't have non-technical PMs," I heard one of them whisper to another.

In truth, I wasn't sure they were wrong.

Amy came to visit.

"Save the rat jokes," I said. "Not in the mood."

"Me neither. I brought you some tea."

Hot tea was indeed better than coffee for me in my jumpy state. We sat and chatted about her new house. She complained about having to clean the gutters as the fall deepened, and there was also all the money she had to pay to clean out the HVAC ducts and make sure the sewer pipes were free of roots. "There's a lot of nooks and crannies in an old house," she said. "Lots of places for critters to roam."

"You're the only one who's been nice to me," I said, feeling a bit guilty at how aloof I had been with her earlier.

She waved it away. "The engineers have a certain way of looking at the world. They are like the city mice who think the ability to steal cheese from a dinner table is the only skill that matters."

"And I'm the country mouse who can't tell a table apart from a chair."

"I happen to enjoy new perspectives," she said. "I didn't start out as a coder either."

"Oh?"

"I used to work at Bazaar as a warehouse packer. I had some ideas for how to improve the layout of the place to make shipping more efficient. They liked the ideas and put me in charge of solving other problems: cable management for their server rooms, access control for secure areas in the office, that sort of thing. Turned out I had a knack for technical puzzles, and I ended up learning to code even though I never went to college. This was before they required degrees for everything."

So she'd been an outsider once too. "I'm not sure I'll ever fit in," I said.

"Don't think of it as fitting in. It's... more about learning a culture, being comfortable with telling your story using their lore. The engineers will come around when you can paint them a vision they can understand. A map of the obstacle course to the new cheese outside, if you will, little country mouse."

I laughed. "I've been trying. It's hard, though; there's so much to learn."

"Why did you want to work in robotics anyway? I thought you liberal arts types just wanted to teach so you could stay in school forever."

I thought about this. "It's difficult to put into words. I'm fascinated by stories, the stories we tell each other and the stories we tell about ourselves. In our world, the stories that matter the most are all stories about technology. The dreams that move people today are all soldered and welded and animated by code, or they're just spells operating in the ether. I wanted to have a part in these stories. I'm sorry, that's probably not making much sense."

"On the contrary," she said. "That's the most sensible thing I've heard from you. Technology is our poem, our ballad, our epic cycle. You may not be a coder, but you have a coder's soul."

It was possibly the oddest compliment I'd ever gotten, but I liked it. It was nice to have a friend.

After a moment, I asked, "Do you think my rat idea has a chance?"

"I don't know," she said. "I do know that if you are afraid of looking foolish, you'll never look like a genius, either."

"I thought you weren't into inspirational quotes."

"I might make fun of the myths of our corporate overlords a lot," she said. "That doesn't mean I don't enjoy seeing a good tale play out. I'm still in the Valley, the biggest dream factory on earth, after all these years, aren't I?"

Think impossible!

I decided to go straight to the source. Dr. Vignor listened to my presentation without saying a word, and then sat with his eyes closed for ten minutes, as though he had fallen asleep.

I couldn't have been that boring, could I? I was miffed. I had worked hard on the slides, citing figures and papers—admittedly I didn't understand everything I had read. And I thought the use of that animated clip art rat was particularly inspired.

"It's worth a try," he said, eyes still closed. "We've never worked with such an advanced animal, but why not? Everything's impossible until we try."

THE NEXT FEW months were a blur. Pushing a new product through weRobot was one of those experiences that transformed you. Design specifications turned into cobbled together proofs-of-concept turned into 3D-printed models turned into hand-crafted prototypes tethered to workstations running debug code. Engineers had to be herded and testers rallied and schedules drawn up and resources allocated. There were presentations to the sales staff and market research and the legal department and the supply chain.

I worked sixteen-hour days during the week—and only eight hours on the weekends because Amy programmed my computer to lock me out if I stayed too long on Saturdays ("You need some non-work time to replenish your soul, kid. The River Temarc in winter. You don't get the reference? Here, go watch these *Star Trek* DVDs")—apologized to my sister and mother profusely for not being able to visit for their birthdays, and ignored texts and invitations from my non-work friends. I had to set an example for my team. How could I demand 100 percent of them if I didn't do the same for myself?

The Rattus norvegicus *is the most successful mammal on the planet (other than us). Since the European Middle Ages, the species has learned to live wherever we live, making their homes in our sewers, basements, attics, and subsisting on our food and heat. Some estimate that there are as many rats in the world as humans.*

"We can't use any of this," said the guy from marketing. "We're trying to get people to buy something instead of calling exterminators. What else have you got?"

Right, the key is to tell a good story. I flipped through more slides.

An adult rat is so flexible that it is able to squeeze through a hole the size of a quarter. It can swim for kilometers, even staying afloat for days in extreme circumstances. It is capable of scaling smooth, vertical poles as well as scurrying up the insides of pipes, and it is skilled at navigating the maze of ducts and conduits in human dwellings, its natural habitat.

I admired the resiliency and resourcefulness of the common rat. If they were corporate employees, they would certainly win the race.

"Let me chew on this some more—haha—and get back to you," I told the marketing guy.

When you were working for the realization of a dream, work didn't seem like work at all.

IN THE END, the official marketing literature explained that the Vegnor was named after Dr. Vignor, the world's leading expert on non-behavioural robotics; a good origin story was critical to a superhero.

And we sold the Vegnor as a superhero for the busy homeowner.

Imprinted with the neural patterns of *R. norvegicus,* the sleek little robot, a ten-inch long segmented oblong form studded with advanced sensors and a Swiss Army knife's worth of tools, was the modern incarnation of the hearth spirit. It could scurry up downspouts and clear accumulated leaves from gutters, saving homeowners from the dirty work and the danger of falling from ladders. It could swim through the plumbing, unclogging drains and pureeing any garbage with its swirling saw-blade teeth. The flexible body squeezed through tight turns and expanded to gain purchase against vertical tubing, allowing it to wander through ducts and conduits, cleaning away gunk and crud. It patrolled the sewer connection pipes, slicing apart tree roots and dislodging toilet paper wads. It knocked down ice dams in winters and cleaned out chimneys in summers, saving homeowners thousands of dollars a year in professional maintenance fees. It washed itself and charged itself. Best of all, it guarded a house against unwanted pests such as the common rat by emitting an annoying ultrasonic whine—and for those pests undeterred by such warning, it was capable of fighting them with gnashing teeth and glinting claws made of stainless steel.

The Vegnors flew off the shelves. Glowing reviews filled the web, and users on OurScreen posted videos of the antics of their beloved "Vegnies"— driving away snakes in Florida, crunching over scorpions in Arizona, making "speed runs" from one toilet to another in the house (to the delight of children and the befuddlement of their parents, and so this last behavior had to be patched away via an over-the-air update).

I received an invitation from Jake and Ron to attend the annual Fall Picnic held at their house. It was understood around the company that the only attendees were the top ninety-nine employees who embodied the "weRobot way."

I had found my niche.

"Did you see the summary I sent you?" Amy asked.

"No. Yes. No." I was distracted. There was so much to do once you had some success. "What are you talking about?"

"I've been looking at micro local trends generated by Centillion. Seems like there's an uptick in searches related to exterminators around the country."

"I'm done with rats," I said. About thirty tabs were open in my browser, each loading a page with live sales numbers from different regions, and I clicked between them impatiently.

"Take a look at the list of zip codes with the highest increases in those searches. Do you see how they correlate with Vegnor sales?"

I *hmm*'d noncommittally.

"Are you even listening? You look like one of those rats addicted to pushing a button for a random food pellet."

I looked at her, offended. "The Vegnor is selling well. I have to finish this after-action review."

She rolled her eyes. "That's just corporate nonsense. Changing the world doesn't stop with making a sale. There's a mystery here. A story."

"Customer are giving plenty of feedback online. Overwhelmingly positive."

"Just like you can't rely on customers to tell you what they want when they haven't seen it, you also can't rely on them to tell you what's wrong when they haven't figured it out."

I waved away this koan. There were always more mysteries than there were hours in the day—and I didn't have the techie disease of going down the irrelevant rabbit holes posed by random puzzles that had no relationship to the goal. I needed to summarize my experience on Vegnor into a process that could be repeated so that I could come up with something else to top the

Vegnor. In a place like weRobot, you were only as good as your next project. PMs who rested on their laurels didn't get invited to the next Fall Picnic.

Amy was about to speak again when an email alert dinged on my computer.

"Sorry, I have to get this." Almost compulsively, I clicked over to the tab. I was feeling irritable these days, hoping each email would be from someone important in the company inviting me to join a team with more prestige, closer to Jake and Ron.

Wait, I chided myself. *I meant a team with projects that made a bigger impact on people's lives, right? Am I more interested in climbing the corporate ladder or changing the world? Is there a difference?*

The email turned out to be from my sister, Emily. All her emails these days contained pictures of her new baby. Sure, I loved my nephew, but he couldn't even talk, and I was sick of watching another video of him rolling around on the floor for "tummy time." Parents were the most boring creatures on earth.

...Danny won't sleep... I think I'm going slowly insane. I can't even hear myself think. I'll pay anything...

"...are you going to investigate the correlations? Aren't you even a little bit curious?"

I looked up. Somehow Amy was still standing there, babbling about something. "Isn't there some seminar you need to get to?" I asked pointedly.

She shook her head and threw up her hands in an *I give up* gesture. "Chenza at court, the court of silence," she muttered as she moved away.

I felt bad that she was feeling rejected. But I wasn't a cynical engineer too jaded to feel the thrill of changing the world. I had been to the Fall Picnic, damn it. I had a purpose.

THERE WERE CLOSE to forty-five million children under the age of twelve in the United States. Demographic trends and migration patterns and immigration laws and regulatory pressure added to a situation where an increasing number of parents were without access to affordable, high-quality, and *trusted* childcare. People were working longer hours and working harder, leaving less time and energy for their children.

Big data analytics backed up my hunch. WeRobot's web spiders crawled through parenting forums and social networks and anonymous confessplaint apps and crunched the mood and emotional content of posts by parents of young children. The dominant note was a sense of exhaustion, of guilt, of worry that they weren't doing a good job as mothers and fathers. There was little faith in daycare centers and in-home help—parents didn't trust strangers, and yet they simply couldn't do everything themselves.

It was the ultimate opportunity for a labor-saving device. What if the drudgery of parenting—the midnight feedings, the diaper changes, the perpetual and endless cleaning and picking up and laundry runs, the tantrums, the sicknesses, the monitoring and measuring mandated by pediatricians, the meting out of discipline and punishment—all could be taken care of by a perfect nanny, leaving parents only the joy of true quality time with their offspring?

"You've been reading that email for ten minutes," Amy said. "That's never a good sign."

I had read the email so many times that the words no longer made sense. But really, all the verbiage on the screen could be reduced to a single word.

"They said no."

To her credit, Amy said nothing. She went away and came back a few minutes later with a mug of tea and set it down on my desk. I picked it up, comforted by the warmth.

"I brought you a gift, too," she said. "I was going to give it to you when Vegnor launched, but it took longer to get ready than I anticipated—typical engineering scheduling, you know. Figure you could use a bit of cheering up."

She whistled, and a sleek Vegnor, painted black, slinked into view from beyond the cubicle wall.

"This is no ordinary Vegnie," she said. "I've re-programmed it to be the ultimate office prankster. You can tell it to squirt hot sauce in the coffee of the marketing department or tell lawyer jokes from behind the HVAC grille in the legal group. Heck, you can even get it to steal the lunch of whichever VP just told you no. But you have to learn to speak its language."

She bent down to the little mechanical rat. "Bigwig, standing on Watership Down with ears plugged." She frowned in a pretty good impression of the VP of Product Marketing. Then she turned to me, "Want to try?"

I looked at the rat, pointed at Amy and then myself. "Darmok and Jalad, at Tanagra"—Amy smiled—"Vegnie, the cheese of the Bigwig in the Labyrinth of Knossos."

The little rat chirped and scuttled away.

I clapped my hands. "That is inspired."

"I should know learning to speak Tamarian is easy for a Folk and Myth major."

When we finally finished giggling, I said, "I don't understand why they didn't approve my project. Given my track record on Vegnor, they should have more trust in me."

"It's not a matter of trust. The problem you're proposing to solve is too hard. People can't even agree on the best way to sleep train a baby. How do you propose to make the perfect substitute parent?"

"That's just the result of overthinking. People don't know what they want until you show it to them."

"You're too young to understand that you should never give parenting advice."

"You're too cynical. Even if there isn't a single right answer for something, we can always make it into a user-accessible setting."

Amy shook her head. "This isn't like designing a robot to clean the gutters. You're talking about raising other people's children. The liability issues alone will make everyone in Legal faint."

"You can't let lawyers run a company," I said. "Isn't weRobot about thinking impossible? There's always a solution."

"Maybe you should create an island where there are no rules so you can experiment with technical solutions to all life's problems to your heart's content."

"That would be nice," I muttered.

"You're scaring me, kid."

I didn't answer.

JAKE AND RON had always prided themselves on maintaining an entrepreneurial spirit in weRobot even as it grew to thousands of employees. Those who got invited to the Fall Picnic were expected to get things done, not wait for orders.

So I did the natural thing: telling my team that my proposal had been approved.

The next step was to recruit Dr. Vignor to the effort.

"That's a very difficult challenge," he said.

"You're right," I said. "Probably much too hard. I'll file it away until we have the brain power."

He came to find me that afternoon, begging to be allowed to be on the team. See, the right story is everything.

We started by gathering manuals on childcare and running them through the semantic abstracter for fundamental rules of good parenting.

That... turned out to be a hopeless task. The manuals were about as consistent as fashion advice: for every book that advocated one approach, there were two books that argued that particular approach was literally the worst thing that one could do. Should babies be swaddled? How often should they be held? Should you let them cry for a few minutes and learn to self-soothe or comfort them as soon as they started to fuss? There was no consensus on anything.

The academic literature was no more illuminating. Child psychology experts conducted studies that proved everything and nothing, and meta studies showed that most of them could not even be replicated.

The science of child rearing was literally in the dark ages.

But then, while flipping through the TV channels late at night, I stopped at a nature program: *The World's Best Mothers*.

Of course, I cursed myself for my stupidity. Parenting was a solved problem in nature. Once again, the modern neurosis of overthinking had created the illusion of impossibility. Billions of years of evolution had given us the rules that we should be following. We just had to imitate nature.

SINCE ACADEMICS HAD proven basically useless on this subject, in order to find my model, I turned to that ultimate fount of wisdom: the web. Every Mother's Day and Father's Day, every eyeballs-hungry site seemed to publish listicles that purported to describe the animals that qualified as the world's best mothers and fathers.

There was the orangutan, whose baby clings to the mother continuously for the first few years of its life.

There was the deep sea octopus, *Graneledone boreopacifica*, who did nothing but guard her eggs for four and a half years—not even eating—until they hatched.

There was the elephant, who, besides a long gestational period, engaged in extensive alloparenting as members of the herd all participated to raise the babies.

And so on and so forth...

...and putting them together, I had my story: the paragon of parenting, the essence of bottled love.

I would replicate the self-sacrificing, participatory alloparenting groups of nature with robots. Busy modern urban parents didn't know their neighbors and lived away from extended family, but a network of weRobot devices would be almost as good. Our robotic vacuums, laundry folders, and Vegnors could all pitch in to keep the customers' children safe and act as playmates—incidentally, this also encouraged customers to purchase more weRobot devices, which was always a good thing. Devices from neighboring residences could also collaborate to watch over both households' children even without the parents being best friends—trust was ensured by the standardization of weRobot algorithms. The proprietary local area wireless network substituted for nonexistent or fraying social bonds.

"Mary Poppins," I vowed, "with her umbrella open!"

Dr. Vignor modeled the neural patterns driving the behaviors of dozens of animals judged to be good parents by the wisdom of the web, and after extensive software emulation, it was time to test the first prototypes.

I posted the call for volunteers on weRobot's internal network, and to my surprise and puzzlement, there weren't nearly as many takers as I had hoped.

"There aren't that many parents working here," Amy said when I complained to her. "That's not exactly a secret about this place. Look at the schedule you're keeping. It's not very compatible with starting a family, is it?"

"Even more evidence that there's a market for this product!" I said. The key to dreaming the impossible was to see opportunities where others saw only problems. "Just think of all the lost productivity due to parents not being able to devote as much time and energy to their careers because they have to run home to deal with their offspring." I was practically rubbing my hands in glee. "Marketing should be able to hint at this subtly in the TV ads. Power couples who spend less time parenting than they do at the gym ought to make a striking addition to the value proposition."

"Did you just use the phrase 'lost productivity' non-ironically?" Amy asked, shaking her head. "And 'value proposition'?"

Since there weren't enough internal volunteers, I had to expand the beta testing program by asking my team to recruit friends and family.

I found a super scary NDA for some other weRobot project on the corporate intranet—the lawyers were good for something after all—and a few search-and-replace macros later, I had a way to ensure that no one would leak any information to competitors or the luddite press, which was always sniffing for news about upcoming tech products that they could exaggerate into dystopian visions to sell the papers.

EMILY ENTHUSED TO me about the new addition to her family.

"It's incredible!" she gushed on the phone. "I've never seen Danny so well-behaved. Para changes him and feeds him and rocks him to sleep, and he loves it! Eric and I are finally able to get a good night's sleep. Everyone at work has been begging me for the number of the au pair agency I'm using."

I beamed with pride. Para was a marvel of engineering. The body-temperature, medical-grade synthskin and the oscillator thumping at the rhythm of heartbeat were designed to calm newborns. The robot's eight arms, made of series elastic actuators for safety, and precision manipulators allowed the machine to handle delicate childcare tasks with aplomb: it could change a diaper, feed, powder, massage, tickle, and give a bath using power-delivery curves that provided maximum physical comfort to the baby, all while humming a pleasant, soft song, folding laundry, and picking up dropped toys with its extra arms.

But the crowning achievement of Para, of course, was its neural programming. Para was the perfect parent-surrogate. It never got tired or bored; it never stopped giving the baby 100 percent of its attention; it was equipped with eons of evolutionary instinct drawn from the animal kingdom judged to suit human needs: it would protect the baby at all costs and was capable of reacting to save the child from any and all emergencies.

"I'm enjoying my time with Danny so much more now. I feel calmer, more patient, and I get to give my attention to all the fun parts of being a parent. It's incredible."

"I'm really glad," I said to my sister. I felt like a wreck. I had pushed my team to the limit, and hearing my sister being so pleased made all the hard work worth it.

MONDAY MORNING, MY phone buzzed as I rode on the work shuttle. My heart clenched and then beat wildly as I read the text.

Why are Jake and Ron summoning me? There was only one answer: my skunkworks project had been discovered.

The tests with Para weren't anywhere near done. I still needed more time to produce convincing data to guarantee forgiveness.

With great trepidation, I showed up at the Presidents' Office on the second floor of the central building. The executive assistants quickly ushered me into a small conference room, where Ron and Jake sat at the table, stone-faced.

"I can explain," I began. "The preliminary results are very encouraging—"

"I hardly think we're in the preliminary phase anymore," Jake interrupted. He slid a tablet across the table. "Have you read this?"

It was the *New York Times*. "Home Robots Found to Be Source of Infestations," said the headline.

I quickly scanned through the article, and my heart sank. I should have paid more attention to those reports Amy had been sending me.

It turned out that the Vegnors were so good at their jobs that they were displacing real rats. The robots were, of course, programmed to fight the rats and chase them out of homes—this was touted as one of the key advantages of the machines.

Then the Vegnors replicated some of the beneficial behaviors of the rats by sweeping and collecting food and garbage from the plumbing and pipes. I had been particularly proud of this clever bit of biomimicry. I thought I was being comprehensive.

But the Vegnors only pushed the garbage away from the houses instead of eating it, which led to middens on the edges of properties that became breeding grounds for other vermin—cockroaches, maggots, fruit flies—and the cockroaches infested the houses because they were now free of rats, which had once preyed on them. Even worse, the bodies of the rats the Vegnors killed attracted coyotes, the top urban predator in many American cities.

Everyone had always thought that if all the rats in the world died tomorrow, no one would miss them. Apparently they had a role to play in the urban ecology that the Vegnors could not fully replicate.

"Our neighbors came to complain this morning," said Jake. "They have outdoor cats."

I imagined the bloody, lifeless body of Tabby, the victim of a coyote. I winced.

"And they dragged us out to the wall between our properties so they could show us the dumping ground of our Vegnor," said Ron. "The smell made me lose my breakfast."

"There's going to be a class action lawsuit," said Jake, rubbing his temples.

"You see how gleeful the plumbers and exterminators quoted in that article are?" said Ron, drumming his fingers on the table. "The Vegnors were supposed to make them no longer necessary, but our robo-rats have been creating infestations wherever they go."

I struggled to not hyperventilate. *They don't know about the skunkworks project.* My eyes looked from Ron to Jake and then back to Ron again.

"We could make a patch," I blurted out, "and get the Vegnors to collect the garbage and dispose of it safely... Or, we could make another robot to clean up the mess and sell them to municipal governments... Or how about we patch the Vegnors to seek out cockroaches, and their eggs too...?"

If technology created a problem, surely the best solution was more technology.

Ron and Jake just glared at me.

THE VEGNOR SETBACK meant that I had to hit Para out of the park. It was the only way to redeem my name.

While doing my best to manage the robo-rat fallout, I pushed my team and myself even harder in an effort to make the Para prototypes do more for the parents. We wanted to anticipate needs and take care of them all: the Paras could be set to implement a clock-based feeding regimen, or, in the alternate, an infant-driven feeding schedule that replicated breastfeeding; they could be configured to start sleep training at an age designated by the parents, or encourage babies to engage in the "paleo" practice of polyphasic sleep; they could be designated to play and comfort children in a variety of styles to stimulate optimal brain development; and they could even cook meals and do simple housekeeping to give exhausted parents more time to sleep and finish their work until they were ready for their offspring.

The preliminary results were promising. The feedback from the new parents was almost uniformly positive.

These robots were as devoted as the octopus, as cooperative as the elephant, as responsible as the orangutan—they really were the best nannies the parents could ever hope for. They freed moms and dads from everything unpleasant about parenting and left them only the fun parts.

"Why don't you want it?" I asked. "What did it do wrong?"

"Nothing!" said Emily. "But it doesn't feel right."

"I can fly down tonight to see—"

"I see. You can't fly down here for my birthday, but you can come on a night's notice when you think something's wrong with your robot."

I took a deep breath. "That's not fair, Emily."

"Isn't it? Since when did you become such a workaholic?"

"Don't do this to me, Em. It's my career we're talking about here! If I can't trust you to give me honest feedback, who can I trust?"

Emily sighed on the other end of the line. "I'm telling you the truth. There's nothing wrong with what Para is doing. But Eric and I don't like what it's doing to *us*."

"How do you mean?"

This *shouldn't* have happened. I had been careful from the very beginning of the Para project to avoid one of the big pitfalls with human nannies, who often elicited jealousy from parents seized by the fear that their children were building a stronger bond with the nanny than with them. This was one of the reasons that Para was not designed to be humanoid. Just as we didn't feel threatened by the housekeeping skills of automated labor-saving devices, no parent needed to worry that their child would become attached to a synthetic appliance, not fundamentally different from a self-rocking cradle.

"I don't know how to explain it." Emily sounded like she was grasping for words. "But Eric was telling me that he missed how much time he used to spend with Danny, and I feel the same way."

"But so much of that was wasted time. Para allows you to spend *quality* time, to be *efficient*." The frustrated emails that Emily used to send me went through my mind, as did the words of so many other surveyed mothers and fathers who complained about lack of sleep, about how their babies turned their thoughts to mush. Children took up too much time—that was the problem to be solved.

"That's just it. I'm not sure there is such a thing as 'quality' time. Eric and I used to spend hours feeding Danny and worrying about his poop and trying to get him to sleep, and we felt tired and unprepared and stupid, but every time we looked into Danny's eyes, we felt happy. Now we pretty much just spend half an hour a day reading to him and playing with him, but even that seems too much. We get impatient. Somehow, the less time we spend with Danny, the less time we *want* to spend with him. This doesn't feel right."

Daedalus, watching the wings melt.

...THE AMYGDALA, HYPOTHALAMUS, prefrontal cortex, and olfactory bulb are all activated by infant behavioural cues, which trigger adjustments in the levels of hormones such as oxytocin, glucocorticoids, estrogen, testosterone, and prolactin for the maintenance of parenting patterns...

I closed the textbook and rubbed my temples.

The sleep deprivation, the anxiety from the infant's cries, the constant worry that something so fragile and so demanding depended on you—the experience of being new parents changed people, altered the chemical composition of their blood, rewired their brains.

There was no such thing as quality time because there were no shortcuts. The very experience that bonded new parents to their children required the investment of time and energy to change them, just as their babies needed time and energy to grow.

The tedium and anxiety were inseparable from the rewards.

It was not possible to reduce parenting down to "quality time" and to outsource the difficult parts to robots—for some, perhaps most, parents, the physical and neurological changes brought about by becoming a parent were desirable.

Really, I should have known better. Would I give up the sleepless nights and the tedious days of trying out hundreds of failed solutions in the struggle toward a successful, shipping product? The painful process was what made the victory sweet, changed me as a person, made the impossible dreams real.

"ARE YOU LEAVING or are you being fired?" asked Amy, handing me a mug of tea. "I made you the good stuff. The robots here ruin good tea with tepid water."

My skunkworks project had been shut down. Once I understood that Para had no future, there was little choice but to come clean. I had cost the company a lot of money and taken on unacceptable risks. I should have been fired.

"Neither," I said, accepting the mug gratefully. "I'm being transferred to a new division."

Amy lifted an eyebrow.

"It doesn't have a name yet," I said.

"What... will you be doing?"

"Shaka, when the walls fell," I said.

After a moment, Amy smiled. "Ah, I see. The Unknown Unknowns."

"That's one possible name," I said. "Or maybe the Division of Country Mice."

We laughed.

Ron and Jake had decided that it was important to have a group focused on fresh perspectives. Staffed with artists, ecologists, ethicists, anthropologists, cultural critics, environmentalists, and other non-roboticists, our job would be keeping an eye on the blind spots of technical solutions. We would critique products for unanticipated consequences, gather data to detect non-obvious evidence of failure (like those searches for exterminators), and generally act as a kind of corporate source of pessimism to counterbalance the over-exuberance of the engineering staff. Having become a byword for failure at weRobot, who was better qualified to join the group than me?

"Thanks for taking over the rehabilitation projects," I said.

She waved her hand dismissively. "I've always been good at cleaning up after other engineers, probably because I never think anything is going to work in the first place. But I'll enjoy fixing your robot rats. They're cute."

"I really made a mess of things, didn't I?"

"Not entirely," said Amy. She proceeded to explain to me that with Ron and Jake's blessing, she was going to repurpose the hardware and software of Para for a much less ambitious version that would try to help overworked mothers and fathers rather than supplant them. Instead of yielding to the myth of quality time, the robots would be more cooperative, doing only what parents wanted them to do, and always ready to step back. Some advocacy groups for mothers suffering from postpartum depression had expressed interest in such a project as part of a comprehensive treatment plan.

"You had the right ideas, kid," she said. "Sometimes you step out too far and fall off the edge, but how else would you know how far you can go?"

"That sounds almost like the One True Myth."

"I'm a skeptical believer. Technology is beautiful, but it's the nature of technology to create more problems to be solved. Machines, like rats, are a part of nature, and our lives are embedded within each other. Hephaestus, his hammer raised."

"That reminds me," I said. "I'll need you to come by my office next week."

"What for?"

"We are going to do a brain dump with you—"

"That's impossible—"

"I didn't mean literally! Besides, how do we know it's impossible if we don't try?"

I couldn't keep a straight face long enough to fool her. But I could tell she came *this* close to falling for it.

"I'm *not* going to be scanned into a robot," she said.

"I want you to come and tell some stories, infect everyone with a bit of your cynicism. I think that's going to be really useful."

Amy nodded. "Gimli, his ax ready."

THE STORYTELLER'S REPLACEMENT
N. K. Jemisin

N. K. Jemisin (www.nkjemisin.com) lives and writes in Brooklyn, New York. Jemisin has published eight novels, including the Inheritance trilogy and Dreamblood duology, and Broken Earth trilogy, which includes Hugo winners *The Fifth Season, The Obelisk Gate*, and *The Stone Sky*. She is the only person to win three consecutive Hugo Awards for Best Novel. Jemisin's short fiction has been published in *Clarkesworld, Postscripts, Strange Horizons, Baen's Universe*, and various print anthologies, and is collected in *How Long 'til Black Future Month?* She has also won a Nebula Award, two Locus Awards, and a number of other honors. Jemisin is also a member of the Altered Fluid writing group. In addition to writing, she has been a counseling psychologist and educator (specializing in career counseling and student development), a hiker and biker, and a political/feminist/anti-racist blogger. She is a former reviewer for the *New York Times Book Review*, and still writes occasional long-form reviews for them.

THE STORYTELLER COULD not make it this evening. He sent me in his stead. Why, because I am one whose task it is to speak for the dead. Perhaps you've heard of others like me? In different places I am called by different names: shaman, onmyouji, bokor, freak. Since the dead are in no short supply, I know many tales. But if you do not like my tales, just say so. I am sure to know some means or another of keeping you entertained.

So.

King Paramenter of Sosun, wishing to dispel rumors of his impotence, inquired privately of his wizard as to how he might fortify his virility. "I have seen mention of dragons in lore on the subject," the wizard told him. "In specific, eating the heart of a male dragon should accord you some of that creature's proclivity." As it was rumored that male dragons could seed as many as a dozen females in a day, Paramenter immediately sent scouts forth from his palace in search of one.

His search was not immediately successful. In part due to the rumors, male dragons were in scarce supply; the species was on the brink of extinction. When Paramenter finally did hear of a dragon in the far-off mountains, he hastened to the place with a band of his elite warriors. Together they breached the dragon's den and slew the beast. But afterward they found that the dragon was female—a mother on a nest, her body cooling around a single egg. In frustration the king broke open the egg in the hope that its occupant might be male, but the creature's sex was indeterminate at that stage.

"I shall make do with the mother," he decided at last. "After all, women are creatures of great wantonness when not guarded closely by family and husbands. And perhaps the heart of a female who has borne young can help me get a son." So he had his men carve out the mother-dragon's heart, and right then and there he ate it.

Straightaway Paramenter began to feel some positive effect. With his men he set off for home, riding through day and night to reach his palace. There he called for his wife and concubines to be made ready, whereafter he spent the next few days in enthusiastic carousing.

Sometime later came the joyous news: the queen and all five concubines were with child. King Paramenter was so overjoyed that he threw lavish parties and cut taxes so that the whole kingdom might celebrate with him. But as time passed his mood changed, for the dragonish vigor seemed to be fading from his body. Eventually, as before he'd eaten the dragon's heart, he found himself unable to perform at all.

In a panic he consulted his wizard once more. The wizard said, "I do not understand it either, my lord. The lore was very specific; the male dragon's heart should have bestowed that creature's purpose on you."

"It was not a male dragon," Paramenter replied impatiently. "I could not find a male, so I ate the heart of a nesting mother. It served well enough, at least until lately."

The wizard's eyes widened. "Then you have taken into yourself the purpose of a mother dragon," he said. "Such a creature has no need of desire beyond the children it gains her, and you now have six on the way."

"And what does that mean? I am a king, not a mother! Will I grow breasts now and nurse, and giggle over bonnets and toys?"

"Female dragons do not nurse," said the wizard. "They do not dote on their young, who hunt and kill from birth, though those young live to carry out their mother's purpose. To be honest, my lord, I do not know what will happen now."

To this Paramenter could say nothing, though he had the wizard beaten in a fit of pique. He settled in to await the birth of his children, and in the meantime sent his scouts forth again to find a male dragon. But before they could return, one by one the queen and concubines went into labor. One by one each gave birth to a beautiful, healthy baby girl. And one by one the ladies died in the birthing.

The entire kingdom caught its breath at the news. Some of Sosun's citizens began to speak of curses and offenses against nature, but Paramenter ordered the executions of anyone caught saying so, and the talk quickly subsided.

At least, Paramenter consoled himself, there was no further talk of his infirmity. The six baby girls were fine and healthy to a one, charming their nurses and anyone else who saw them. And while none were so blessed as to be male, all six grew up clever, charming, and lovely as well. "But of course," said Paramenter to his advisors when they remarked upon it. "Naturally any daughters of my blood would be far superior to an average woman."

In example of the latter was Paramenter's new wife, whom he had married once the requisite mourning period for his old wife had passed. Though the daughter of a neighboring king, Paramenter's new wife was a nervous little thing, inclined to flights of fancy. Paramenter discovered this during one of his visits to her bedroom, which he undertook every so often in order to keep up appearances. He had encouraged her to get to know his daughters, who were still young enough at that point that they might view her as their mother. "I would rather not," she said after much hemming and hawing. "Have you ever watched those girls closely? They stand together sometimes, gazing at a spot on the floor or some sight beyond their window, and then they smile. Always together, always the same smile."

"They are sisters," said Paramenter, in surprise.

"It is more than that," she insisted, but could articulate nothing more.

His curiosity piqued, Paramenter went down to the nursery the following night to observe the girls. Ten years old now, they fawned over him as they always did, exclaiming in delight at his visit. Paramenter sat down on the highbacked chair that they brought over, and drank the tea that one of them prepared, and let them put up his feet and brush his hair and pamper him as befitted a man. "I cannot see why she fears you," he murmured to himself, feeling amusement and pride as he watched his six jewels bustle about. "I shouldn't have listened to her at all."

A small voice said, "Who, Father?" This came from his youngest daughter, a tiny porcelain doll of a girl.

"Your mother," he said, for he insisted that they address his wife as such. He did not elaborate on his words, because he did not want to trouble the girls. But they looked at each other and giggled, almost as a one.

"She fears us?" asked his eldest daughter, a delicate creature with obsidian curls and a demeanor that was already as regal as a queen's. "How strange. Perhaps she is jealous."

"Jealous?" Paramenter had heard of such things—women resenting their mothers or sisters, undermining their own daughters. "But what has she to be jealous of? She's beautiful enough, or I wouldn't have married her."

"Her place is uncertain," said his eldest daughter. She leaned forward to refresh his tea. "I have heard the palace maids saying that until she bears a child, you can put her aside."

"Then she must be terrified, the poor thing," said his second daughter. Like her concubine mother, this one was caramel-colored and lithe-limbed, with a dancer's natural grace. "You should help her, Father. Give her a child." She stood on her toes to light his pipe for him.

Paramenter nodded thanks, using the gesture to cover his unease. "Well, er, that might be difficult," he said. "I'm afraid I don't fancy her much; she's such a scrawny fearful thing. Not my taste in women at all."

"That's easy enough to deal with," said Third Daughter, a sweet little thing with honey-colored curls. She smiled at him from his feet, where she was paring his toenails. "Give her to your guards for a month or two."

"Oh, yes, that's a lovely idea," said Fourth Daughter. She sat nearby with a book on her lap, ready to read him a tale. "At least ten or twenty of them, just to be sure. They should be large, strong men, warrior-tempered. That way you can be sure of healthy breeding and a fine spirit in the child."

The king frowned at this, shifting uneasily in his seat at his daughters' suggestions. "I cannot say I like that idea," he said at last. "The guards would talk. Any child that resulted would be dogged by scandal her whole life."

"Then kill the guards," said Fifth Daughter, rubbing his temples with gentle musician's fingers. "That's the only way to be certain."

"And after all," added Youngest Daughter again, "who is to say the child will be a *her*? Perhaps we might gain a brother!"

This was a notion Paramenter had not considered, and with that thought all his concerns vanished amid excitement. To have a son, at last! And though it rankled that some common guard would be the father, the fact that no one would know eased that small ignominy.

As Paramenter began to smile, his daughters looked at one another and smiled as well.

So Paramenter gave the order, sending his wife to a country house along with twenty of his loyal guard for a suitable length of time. When they brought her back and the physician confirmed her pregnancy, he had the guards quietly killed, then ordered another kingdom-wide celebration. His wife no longer seemed to have a mind, but Paramenter did not mind so much as this relieved him of the necessity of visiting her. At least she never spoke against his beloved daughters again.

You HAVE GUESSED the ending of this tale, I see. That is well and fine, and I am not surprised; evil is easy to spot, or so we all think. Shall I stop? It isn't my purpose to bore you.

Very well, then. Just a little more.

But first, might we have some refreshment? One's throat grows parched with tale-telling, and I'm hungry as well. A late-season wine, if you have it. And meat, rare. Yes, I suppose this is presumptuous of me, but we dead-speakers know: there's no telling when some folly might come along and end everything. One must enjoy life while it lasts.

If it is not even more presumptuous—will you share my meal? Such rich salts, such savory sweets. It would give me great pleasure to watch them cross your fine lips.

*   *   *

WHEN PARAMENTER'S DAUGHTERS reached their sixteenth year, noblemen from many lands began paying visits to Sosun. Word had spread widely of the girls' beauty, and also of their accomplishment in other respects. Fifth Daughter could outplay any bard on any instrument; Second Daughter's dancing won praise from masters throughout the land. His fourth girl was an accomplished scholar whose writings were the talk of the colleges. His third and youngest girls were renowned for their beauty, and so graceful, witty, and perfect was Eldest Daughter that his advisors had begun quietly suggesting she be allowed to inherit, despite generations of tradition.

Paramenter received his daughters' suitors with justifiable pride, carefully choosing among them to ensure only the best for his treasures. But here he was stymied, for as he began presenting his selection to the girls, they became uncharacteristically obstinate.

"He won't do," said Youngest Daughter, on beholding a fine young man. Paramenter was dismayed, for the youth had arrived with a chest of treasure equivalent to the youngest daughter's weight, but being a doting father he abided by her choice.

"Unsuitable," declared Third Daughter, right in the face of a handsome duke. That one had brought a bag of gemstones selected to match her eyes, but with a sigh Paramenter turned him away.

After the third such incident, in which his second daughter declared the crown prince of a rival kingdom "too small and pale", Paramenter's eldest girl came to visit him. With her came Paramenter's son, the rosy-cheeked child of his wife and her guards, who was now six years old.

"You must understand, Father," Eldest Daughter explained. She sat at his feet, gazing up at him adoringly. At *her* feet, Paramenter's son sat watching his sister in the same manner. "Wealth and rank are such poor ways to judge a man's suitability. We have both already, after all. So it would make sense for our husbands to bring a little something more to the table."

"Like what?"

"Strength," she said. She reached down to stroke the boy's wine-dark hair, and gave him a doting smile. "We desire strength, naturally. What else could any true woman crave in a man?"

This Paramenter understood. So he dismissed the first crop of suitors, and sent new missives forth: each kingdom which desired an alliance with Sosun should send its greatest warrior to represent its interests.

Presently the new suitors arrived. They were a dangerous, uncouth crowd, for all that most were decorated soldiers in their respective armies. When the men had gathered in the palace's garden, the sisters arrived to look them over.

"Much better," said Third Daughter.

"Quite," said Fourth, and as each of her sisters gave a favorable verdict, First Daughter nodded and stepped forward. She put her hands on her hips. "Thank you for coming, gentlemen," she said. "Now, so that we may waste no further time, I shall explain our terms. We are sisters, raised as one; therefore we have decided to marry at the same time."

The men nodded. The advisors of their respective kingdoms had prepared them for this.

"We would prefer to marry one man, as well."

At this the men started, looking at one another in confusion.

Then First Daughter ducked her eyes, looking up at them through her lashes, and tilted her head to one side. "One of you," she said, "can have all six of us in his bed at once. We will obey your every whim, submit to your every desire, and you will be pleased with us; of that you may be sure. But only one of you may receive this reward."

Turning away, she smiled at her sisters, and they smiled back, as one. Then they walked away, though Youngest Daughter paused at the door to blow the men a kiss.

THE BLOODBATH THAT followed killed off the best warriors of seventeen kingdoms, and left ten more of the men maimed and useless for life. King Paramenter was hard-pressed to placate his fellow rulers, and the coffers of Sosun were sharply depleted by compensatory payments.

But the daughters had what they wanted. The warrior who survived the battle royal was a mountainous beast of a man, one-eyed and half-literate, though possessed of great cunning and courage. The sisters doted on him as they had their father, and though his advisors shook their heads and the priests grumbled into their tea, Paramenter gave his blessing on the unorthodox union.

One month later his daughters all happily announced that they were with child. A month after that, their husband, whose name Paramenter had never bothered to learn, died in an unfortunate fall from the bower balcony.

So IT CAME to pass that in the thirtieth year of Paramenter's reign, a miracle occurred: a male dragon was spotted at last. Though Paramenter was getting on in years, he had never quite given up his hope of true manhood. His second wife had killed herself in the interim, but he was still hale enough to get a few more sons on some nubile girl. Donning his sword and armor once more, Paramenter rode forth.

After many months of travel, they found the beast. Paramenter was startled to see that this dragon, unlike the huge, deadly female he'd killed so long ago, was small and put-upon, with an anxious demeanor and deep mournful eyes. His men killed it easily, but fearful of the consequences, this time Paramenter had the heart cured to preserve it, then carried it back to Sosun uneaten. There he gave it to his wizard to examine.

"Be certain," he said, "because the beast this heart came from was a pathetic creature. I cannot see how it is the male of the species at all."

But the wizard—who had suffered during the years of the king's disfavor, and was now eager to prove his worth—immediately shook his head. "This is the right one," he said. "I'm certain." So with some trepidation, Paramenter devoured the heart.

At once he felt the effect. As proper marriages would take an unbearable amount of time, he summoned the twelve prettiest maidens from the nearby countryside to the palace. Over the next few weeks he worked hard to secure his legacy, and was pleased to eventually learn that all twelve of his makeshift brides were pregnant. At this Paramenter waited, tense, but there was no fading of interest within himself this time; it seemed the male's heart truly had done the trick. He rewarded the wizard handsomely, then set the palace physicians to work finding some way to ensure his women survived childbirth this time. He wanted no more unsavory rumors to dog his reign.

Then came a night some weeks later when he awakened craving something other than a woman's flesh. Restless and uncertain, teased by a phantom instinct, Paramenter rose and wandered through the darkened, quiet palace. Presently he found himself in the bower of his daughters. To his surprise they were all awake, sitting in six highbacked chairs like thrones. Paramenter's son sat at Eldest Daughter's feet as usual, smiling sweetly as she stroked his deep red hair. Beside each of his daughters stood their own children, now five years old—girls all, again.

"Welcome, Father," said his eldest. "You understand what must be done now?"

For some inexplicable reason, Paramenter's mouth went dry.

"Too many, too fast," said Third Daughter. She sighed and shook her head. "We had hoped to grow our numbers slowly, subtly, but here you are spoiling all our careful plans."

He stared at his daughters, whose eyes were so cold now, so empty of their usual adoration. "You..." he whispered. It was the only word he could manage; unease had numbed his tongue.

"This was not our choice, remember," said Fifth Daughter, lifting a hand to examine her small, flat, perfectly manicured nails. There was a look of distaste on her features, perhaps at their shape. "But even I must admit its effectiveness. The vanity of men is a powerful weapon, so easy to aim and unleash."

Eldest Daughter stroked her little brother's hair and sighed. "There will be sons now, too, somewhere among the twelve new ones you have made. You chose a poor specimen to sire them, but that can't be helped; men have hunted down the best male dragons for generations. Nothing left but cowards and fools. When a species diminishes to that degree, it must change, or rightly vanish into legend. Don't you agree, Father?"

The children, Paramenter noticed then. His granddaughters. Each had taken after her mother to an uncanny degree, and each now watched him with shining, avid eyes. Seeing that Paramenter had noticed them, they smiled as one.

Eldest Daughter rose from her throne and came to him, lifting a hand to stroke his cheek. "You have done well by us, Father," she said, with genuine fondness in her voice. "So we shall honor you in the old ways, as you have honored us."

With that, she beckoned the children forward. They all came—even Paramenter's son, not a dragon by blood but raised in their ways. They surrounded Paramenter, tense and trembling, but their mothers had trained them well. They did not attack until Eldest Daughter removed her hand from Paramenter's cheek and stepped away. And then like the good, obedient children they were, they left no mess for the servants to find.

It's sad, isn't it? So many of our leaders are weak, and choose to take power from others rather than build strength in themselves. And then, having laid claim to what they have not earned, they wonder why everything around them spirals into chaos. But until the dragons someday return to take back their power, and invoke vengeance on us all... well, I'd say we have time for a few more tales.

Unless you're tired? You do look peaked. Here, let me turn back your bedcovers. And here; shall I give you a good night backrub? That does not fall within my usual duties, but for you I shall make the sacrifice. Ah, forgive me; my hand slipped. Do you like that? Does it feel good? I told you; my purpose here is to entertain.

So many dead to speak for. And in every palace I visit, so many tales to tell.

Let me under the covers, my sweet, and I'll tell them to you all night long.

FIRELIGHT

Ursula K. Le Guin

Ursula K. Le Guin (www.ursulakleguin.com) was a celebrated and beloved author of 21 novels, 11 volumes of short stories, four collections of essays, 12 children's books, six volumes of poetry and four of translation. The breadth and imagination of her work earned her six Nebulas, seven Hugos, and SFWA's Grand Master, along with the PEN/Malamud and many other awards. In 2014 she was awarded the National Book Foundation Medal for Distinguished Contribution to American Letters, and in 2016 joined the short list of authors to be published in their lifetimes by the Library of America.

HE WAS THINKING of *Lookfar*, abandoned long ago, beached on the sands of Selidor. Little of her would be left by now, a plank or two down in the sand maybe, a bit of driftwood on the western sea. As he drifted near sleep he began to remember sailing that little boat with Vetch, not on the western sea but eastward, past Far Toly, right out of the Archipelago. It was not a clear memory, because his mind had not been clear when he made that voyage, possessed by fear and blind determination, seeing nothing ahead of him but the shadow that had hunted him and that he pursued, the empty sea over which it had fled. Yet now he heard the hiss and slap of waves on the prow. Mast and sail rose above him when he glanced up, and looking astern he saw the dark hand on the tiller, the face gazing steadily forward past him. High cheekbones, Vetch had, his dark skin stretched smooth on them. He would be an old man now, if he were still alive. Once I could have sent to know. But I don't need a sending to see him, there in the East Reach on his little island, in his house with his sister, the girl who wore a tiny dragon for a bracelet. It hissed at me, she laughed... He was in the boat, and the water slapped her wood as she went east and east, and Vetch looked forward, and he looked forward over the unending water. He had raised the magewind but *Lookfar* scarcely needed it. She had her own way with the wind, that boat. She knew where she was going.

Until she could not go anymore. Until the deep sea went shoal beneath her, ran shallow, ran dry, and her bottom grated over rock, and she was aground, unmoving, in the darkness that had come on all round them.

He had stepped out of the boat there in the deep sea, over the abyss, and walked forward on dry land. In the Dry Land.

That was gone now. The thought came to him slowly. The land across the wall of stones. He saw that wall—the first time he saw it, saw the child running silently down the dark slope beyond it. He saw all the dead land, the shadow-cities, the shadow-people who passed one another in silence, indifferent, under stars that did not move. It was all gone. They had harrowed it, broken it, opened it—the king and the humble sorcerer and the dragon who soared over them, lighting the dead skies with her living fire... The wall was down. It had never been. It was a spell, a seeming, a mistake. It was gone.

Were the mountains gone then, too, that other boundary, the Mountains of Pain? They stood far across the desert from the wall, black, small, sharp against the dull stars. The young king had walked with him across the Dry Land to the mountains. It seemed west but it was not westward they walked; there was no direction there. It was forward, onward, the way they had to go. You go where you must go, and so they had come to the dry streambed, the darkest place. And then on even beyond that. He had walked forward, leaving behind him in the waterless ravine, in the rocks he had sealed shut and healed, all his treasure, his gift, his strength. Walked on, lame, always lamer. There was no water, no sound of water ever. They were climbing those cruel slopes. There was a path, a way, though it was all sharp stones, and upward, upward, always steeper. After a while, his legs would not hold him, and he tried to crawl, hands and knees on the stones, he remembered that. After that, the rest was gone. There had been the dragon, old Kalessin, the color of rusted iron, and the heat of the dragon's body, the huge wings lifting and beating down. And fog, and islands beneath them in the fog. But those black mountains were not gone, vanished with the dark land. They were not part of the spell-dream, the afterlife, the mistake. They were there.

Not here, he thought. You can't see them from here, in this house. The window in the alcove looks west, but not to that west. Those mountains are where west is east and there is no sea. There's only land sloping up forever into the long night. But westward, true west, there's only the sea and the sea wind.

It was like a vision, but felt more than seen: he knew the deep earth beneath him, the deep sea before. It was a strange knowledge, but there was joy in knowing it.

Firelight played with shadow up in the rafters. Night was coming on. It would be good to sit at the hearth and watch the fire a while, but he'd have to get up to do that, and he didn't want to get up yet. The pleasant warmth was all around him. He heard Tenar now and then behind him: kitchen noises, chopping, settling a knot into the fire under the kettle. Wood from the old live oak in the pasture that had fallen and he'd split winter before last. Once she hummed some tune under her breath for a minute, once she muttered to her work, encouraging it to do what she wanted, "Come on there now..."

The cat sauntered round the foot of the low bed and elevated himself weightlessly onto it. He had been fed. He sat down and washed his face and ears, wetting one paw patiently over and over, and then undertook extensive cleansing of his hind parts, sometimes holding a back paw up with a front paw so that he could clean the claws, or holding down his tail as if expecting it to try to get away. Now and then he looked up for a minute, immobile, with a strange absent gaze, as if listening for instructions. At last he gave a little belch and settled down beside Ged's ankles, arranging himself to sleep. He had sauntered down the path from Re Albi one morning last year, a small gray tom, and moved in. Tenar thought he came from Fan's daughter's house, where they kept two cows and where cats and kittens were always underfoot. She gave him milk, a bit of porridge, scraps of meat when they had it, otherwise he provided for himself; the crew of little brown rats that holed up in the pasture never invaded the house anymore. Sometimes, nights, they heard him caterwauling in the throes of impassioned lust. In the morning he would be flat out on the hearthstone where the warmth still was, and would sleep all day. Tenar called him Baroon—"cat" in Kargish. Sometimes Ged thought of him as Baroon, sometimes in Hardic as Miru, sometimes by his name in the Old Speech. For after all, Ged had not forgotten what he knew. Only it was no good to him, after the time in the dry ravine, where a fool had made a hole in the world, and he had to seal it with the fool's death and his own life. He could still say the cat's true name, but the cat would not wake and look at him. He murmured the name of the cat under his breath. Baroon slept on.

So he had given his life, there in the unreal land. And yet he was here. His life was here, back near its beginning, rooted in this earth. They had left the dark ravine where west is east and there is no sea, going the way they had to go, through black pain and shame. But not on his own legs or by his own strength at last. Carried by his young king, carried by the old dragon. Borne helpless into another life, the other life that had always been there near him, mute, obedient, waiting for him. The shadow, was it, or the reality? The life with no gift, no power, but with Tenar, and with Tehanu. With the beloved woman and the beloved child, the dragon's child, the cripple, daughter of Segoy.

He thought about how it was that when he was not a man of power he had received his inheritance as a man.

His thoughts ran back along a course they had often taken over the years: how strange it was that every wizard was aware of that balance or interchange between the powers, the sexual and the magical, and everyone who dealt with wizardry was aware of it, but it was not spoken of. It was not called an exchange or a bargain. It was not even called a choice. It was called nothing. It was taken for granted.

Village sorcerers and witchwives married and had children—evidence of their inferiority. Sterility was the price a wizard paid, paid willingly, for his greater powers. But the nature of the price, the unnaturalness of it—did that not taint the powers so gained?

Everyone knew that witches dealt with the unclean, the Old Powers of the earth. They made base spells to bring man and woman together, to fulfill lust, to take vengeance, or used their gift on trivial things, healing slight ills, mending, finding. Sorcerers did much the same, but the saying was always *Weak as woman's magic, wicked as woman's magic.* How much of that was truth, how much was fear?

His first master, Ogion, who learned his craft from a wizard who'd learned his from a witch, had taught him none of that rancorous contempt. Yet Ged had learned it from the beginning, and still more deeply on Roke. He'd had to unlearn it, and the unlearning was not easy.

But after all, it was a woman who first taught me, too, he thought, and the thought had a little gleam of revelation in it. Back long ago, in the village, Ten Alders. Over on the other side of the mountain. When I was Duny. I listened to my mother's sister Raki call the goats, and I called them the way she did, with her words, and they all came. And then I couldn't break the spell, but Raki saw I had the gift. Was that when she saw it first? No, she was watching me when I was a tiny child, still in her care. She watched me, and she knew. *Mage knows mage...* How silly she'd have thought me, to call her a mage! Ignorant she was, superstitious, half fraud, making her poor living in that poor place on a few scraps of lore, a few words of the true speech, a stew of garbled spells and false knowledge she half knew to be false. She was everything they meant on Roke when they sneered at village witches. But she knew her craft. She knew the gift. She knew the jewel.

He lost the thread of his thoughts in a surge of slow, bodily memories of his childhood in that steep village, the dank bedding, the smell of woodsmoke in the dark house in the bitter winter cold. Winter, when a day he had enough to eat was a wondrous day to think about long after, and half his life was spent in dodging his father's heavy hand in the smithy, at the forge where he had to keep the long bellow pumping and pumping till his back and arms were afire with pain and his arms and face burning with the sparks he could not dodge, and still his father would shout at him, strike him, knock him aside in rage, *Can't you keep the fire steady, you useless fool?*

But he would not weep. He would beat his father. He would bear it and be silent until he could beat him, kill him. When he was big enough, when he was old enough. When he knew enough.

And of course by the time he knew enough he knew what a waste of time all that anger was. That wasn't the door to his freedom. The words were: the words Raki taught him, one at a time, miserly, grudging, doling them out, hard-earned and few and far between. The name of the water that rose up from the earth as a spring when you spoke its name along with one other word. The name of the hawk and the otter and the acorn. The name of the wind.

Oh the joy, the pride of knowing the name of the wind! The pure delight of power, to know he had the power! He had run out, clear over to the High Fall, to be alone there, rejoicing in the wind that blew strong, westward, from far across the Kargish sea, and he knew its name, he commanded the wind...

Well, that was gone. Long gone. The names he still had. All the names, all the words he'd learned from Kurremkarmerruk in the Isolate Tower and since then. But if you did not have the gift in you, the words of the Old Speech were no more than any words, Hardic or Kargish, or birdsong, or Baroon's anguished yowlings of desire.

He sat up partway and stretched his arms. "What are you laughing at?" Tenar asked him, passing the bed with an armload of kindling, and he said, a little bewildered, "I don't know. I was thinking of Ten Alders."

She gave him her searching look but smiled and went on to the hearth to feed the fire. He wanted to get up and go sit at the hearth with her, but he would lie here a while longer. He disliked the way his legs would not hold steady when he got up, and how soon he tired and wanted only to lie quiet again, looking up into the firelight and the friendly shadows. He had known this house since he was thirteen, just named. Ogion named him in the springs of the Ar and brought him on around the mountain. They went slowly, welcomed into the poor villages like Ten Alders or sleeping out in the forest, in the silence, in the rain. And they came here. He slept for the first time in the little alcove and saw the stars in the window above him and watched the firelight dancing with the shadows in the rafters. He did not know that Ogion was Elehal then. He had had a lot to learn.

Ogion had the patience to teach him, if only he'd had the patience to be taught... Well, never mind. One way or another he'd blundered his way through, from mistake to mistake. Even a very great mistake, the wrong, the evil done with the spell they taught him on Roke. But before he knew the spell, he'd found the words, in Ogion's book, here, in this house, his home. In his ignorant arrogance he had summoned it, the darkness behind the door, the faceless being that reached out to him, whispered to him. He had brought the evil here, under this roof. As this was his home... His thoughts blurred again. He drifted. It was like sailing in *Lookfar*, alone, in cloudy night, in the great darkness on the dark sea. Only the way the wind blew to tell him where he went. He went the wind's way.

"Will you have a bowl of soup?" Tenar asked him, and he roused. But he was still very tired. "Not very hungry," he said.

He didn't think she'd be satisfied by that. And indeed after a while she came back round the half wall that divided the front part of the house, the hearth and the kitchen and the alcove, from this darker back part. It was bedroom and workroom now but once had been the winter byre for the cow or the pig or the goats and the poultry. This was an old house. A few people in Re Albi knew it had once been called the House of the Sorceress, but they did not know why. He knew. He and Tenar had the house from Elehal, who had it from his teacher, Heleth, who had it from his teacher, the witch Ard. It was the kind of house a witch would live in, by itself and apart from the village, not so near anyone had to call her neighbor, but not so far as to be out of reach in need. Ard had put up houses for her beasts nearby and made her bed against that half wall, where the manger had been. And Heleth, and then Elehal, and now Ged and Tenar slept where she had slept.

Most people called it the Old Mage's House. Some of the villagers would tell a stranger, "He that was the Archmage, away off there in Roke, he lives there," when city folk and foreigners from Havnor came seeking him; but they said it distrustfully and with some disapproval. They liked Tenar better than they liked him. Even though she was white skinned and a real foreigner, a Karg, they knew she was their kind, a thrifty housewife, a tough bargainer, nobody's fool, more canny than uncanny.

A girl, white face, dark hair, sudden, startled, stared at him across a cavern of dazzling crystal and water-carved stone, topaz and amethyst, in the trembling radiance of werelight from his staff.

There, even there in their greatest temple, the Old Powers of the earth were feared, wrongly worshipped, offered the cruel deaths and mutilations of slaves, the stunted lives of girls and women imprisoned there. He and Arha had committed no sacrilege. They had released the long hunger and anger of the earth itself to break forth, bring down the domes and caverns, throw open the prison doors.

But her people, who tried to appease the Old Powers, and his people, who held witchery in contempt, made the same mistake, moved by fear, always fear, of what was hidden in the earth, hidden in women's bodies, the knowledge without words that trees and women knew untaught and men were slow to learn. He had only glimpsed it, that great quiet knowledge, the mysteries of the roots of the forest, the roots of the grasses, the silence of stones, the unspeaking communion of the animals. The waters underground, the rising of the springs. All he knew of it he had learned from her, Arha,

Tenar, who never spoke of it. From her, from the dragons, from a thistle. A little colorless thistle struggling in the sea wind between stones, on the path over the High Fall...

She came round the divider with a bowl, as he knew she would, and sat down on the milking stool beside the bed. "Sit up and have a spoonful or two," she said. "It's the last of Quacker."

"No more ducks," he said. The ducks had been an experiment.

"No," she agreed. "We'll stick to chickens. But it's a good broth."

He sat up and she pushed the pillow behind him and set the bowl on his lap. It smelled good, and yet he did not want it. "Ah, I don't know, I'm just not hungry," he said. They both knew. She did not coax him. After a while he swallowed a few spoonfuls, and then put the spoon into the bowl and laid his head back against the pillow. She took the bowl away. She came back and stooped to brush the hair back from his forehead with her hand. "You're a bit feverish," she said.

"My hands are cold."

She sat down on the stool again and took his hands. Hers were warm and firm. She bowed her head down to their clasped hands and sat that way a long time. He loosened one hand and stroked her hair. A piece of wood in the fire snapped. An owl hunting out in the pastures in the last of the twilight gave its deep, soft double call.

The aching was in his chest again. He thought of it not so much as an ache as an architecture, an arch in there at the top of his lungs, a dark arch a little too large for his ribs to hold. After a while it eased, and then was gone. He breathed easily. He was sleepy. He thought of saying to her, I used to think I'd want to go into the woods, like Elehal, to die, he meant, but there'd be no need to say it. The forest was always where he wanted to be. Where he was whenever he could be. The trees around him, over him. His house. His roof. I thought I'd want to do the same. But I don't. There's nowhere I want to go. I couldn't wait to leave this house when I was a boy, I couldn't wait to see all the isles, all the seas. And then I came back with nothing, with nothing left at all. And it was the same as it had been. It was everything. It's enough.

Had he spoken? He did not know. It was silent in the house, the silence of the great slope of mountainside all round the house and the twilight above the sea. The stars would be coming out. Tenar was no longer beside him. She was in the other room, slight noises told him she was setting things straight, making up the fire.

He drifted, drifted on.

He was in darkness in a maze of vaulted tunnels like the Labyrinth of the Tombs where he had crawled, trapped, blind, craving water. These arched ribs of rock lowered and narrowed as he went on, but he had to go on. Closed in by rock, hands and knees on the black, sharp stones of the mountain way, he struggled to move, to breathe, could not breathe. He could not wake.

It was bright morning. He was in *Lookfar*. A bit cramped and stiff and cold as always when he woke from the broken sleep and half sleep and quick, quick-vanishing dreams of nights in the boat alone. Last night there had been no need to summon the magewind; the world's wind was easy and steady from the east. He had merely whispered to his boat, "Go on as you go, *Lookfar*," and stretched out with his head against the sternpost and gazed up at the stars or the sail against the stars until his eyes closed. All that fiery deep-strewn host was gone now but the one great eastern star, already melting like a water drop in the rising day. The wind was keen and chill. He sat up. His head spun a little when he looked back at the eastern sky and then forward again at the blue shadow of the earth sinking into the ocean. He saw the first daylight strike fire from the tops of the waves.

Before bright Éa was, before Segoy Bade the islands be,
The wind of morning on the sea...

He did not sing the song aloud, it sang itself to him. Then came a queer thrumming in his ears. He turned his head, seeking the sound, and again the dizziness passed through it. He stood up, holding to the mast as the boat leapt on the lively sea, and scanned the ocean to the western horizon, and saw the dragon come.

O my joy! be free.

Fierce, with the forge smell of hot iron, the smoke plume trailing on the wind of its flight, the mailed head and flanks bright in the new light, the vast beat of the wings, it came at him like a hawk at a field mouse, swift, unappeasable. It swept down on the little boat that leapt and rocked wildly under the sweep of the wing, and as it passed, in its hissing, ringing voice, in the true speech, it cried to him, *There is nothing to fear.*

He looked straight into the long golden eye and laughed. He called back to the dragon as it flew on to the east, "Oh, but there is, there is!" And indeed there was. The black mountains were there. But he had no fear in this bright moment, welcoming what would come, impatient to meet it. He spoke the joyous wind into the sail. Foam whitened along *Lookfar*'s sides as the boat ran west, far out past all the islands. He would go on, this time, until he sailed into the other wind. If there were other shores he would come to them. Or if sea and shore were all the same at last, then the dragon spoke the truth, and there was nothing to fear.

"The Minnesota Diet", Charlie Jane Anders *(Future Tense)*

"Down Where Sound Comes Blunt", G.V. Anderson *(F&SF, 3-4/18)*

"Waterbirds", G.V. Anderson *(Lightspeed 7/18)*

"Loft the Sorcerer", Eleanor Arnason *(The Book of Magic)*

"Work Shadow/Shadow Work", Madeleine Ashby *(Robots vs Fairies)*

"Domestic Violence", Madeline Ashby *(Future Tense)*

"The Donner Party", Dale Bailey *(F&SF, 1-2/18)*

"Three Meetings of the Pregnant Man Support Group", James Beamon *(Apex, 6/18)*

"No Flight Without the Shatter", Brooke Bolander *(Tor.com 15/8/18)*

"A.I. and the Trolley Problem", Pat Cadigan *(Tor.com 9/15/18)*

The Black God's Drums, P. Djèlí Clark *(Tor.com Publishing)*

"The Last Banquet of Temporal Confections", Tina Connolly *(Tor.com 7/11/18)*

In the Vanisher's Palace, Aliette de Bodard *(Jabberwocky)*

The Tea Master and the Detective, Aliette de Bodard *(Subterranean)*

"Unstoppable", Gardner Dozois *(F&SF, 5-6/18)*

"Joe Diabo's Farewell", Andy Duncan *(An Agent of Utopia)*

"New Frontiers of the Mind", Andy Duncan *(Analog, 7-8/18)*

"The Devil's Whatever", Andy Duncan *(The Book of Magic)*

"3-adica", Greg Egan *(Asimov's, 9-10/18)*

Phoresis, Greg Egan *(Subterranean)*

"The Nearest", Greg Egan *(Tor.com, 7/18/18)*

"A Compendium of Architecture and the Science of Building", Kate Elliott *(Lightspeed, 8/18)*

"Suicide Watch", Susan Emshwiller *(F&SF, 9-10/18)*

"STET", Sarah Gailey *(Fireside 10/18)*

"Umbernight", Carolyn Ives Gilman *(Clarkesworld, 2/18)*

"We Will Be All Right", Carolyn Ives Gilman *(Lightspeed, 5/18)*

"Queen Lily", Theodora Goss *(Lightspeed, 11/18)*

"Dulce et Decorum", S.L. Huang *(Sword and Sonnet)*

"The Woman Who Destroyed Us", S.L. Huang *(Twelve Tomorrows)*

"Cuisine des Memoires", N.K. Jemisin *(How Long 'til Black Future Month?)*

"The Ones who Stay and Fight", N.K. Jemisin *(How Long 'til Black Future Month?)*

"The Heart of Owl Abbas", Kathleen Jennings *(Tor.com, 4/11/18)*

"Grace's Family", James Patrick Kelly *(Tor.com, 5/18)*

"Yukui!", James Patrick Kelly *(The Promise of Space)*

Black Helicopters: The Director's Cut (2018), Caitlin R. Kiernan *(Tor.com Publishing)*

"M is for Mars", Caitlin R. Kiernan *(Houses Under the Sea)*

Elevation, Stephen King *(Simon & Schuster)*

"Field Biology of the Wee Fairies", Naomi Kritzer *(Apex, 9/4/18)*

"The Second Floor of the Christmas Hotel", Joe R. Lansdale *(Hark! The Herald Angels Scream)*

"Carouseling", Rich Larson *(Clarkesworld, 4/18)*

"Community Service", Megan Lindholm *(The Book of Magic)*

"Byzantine Empathy", Ken Liu *(Twelve Tomorrows)*

"Cosmic Spring", Ken Liu *(Lightspeed, 3/18)*

"The Explainer", Ken Liu *(Lightspeed, 9/18)*

"The Fall and Rise of the House of the Wizard Malkuril", Scott Lynch *(The Book of Magic)*

"Dead Lovers on Each Blade, Hung", Usman T. Malik *(Nightmare 11/18)*

"Army Men", Juliet Marillier *(Of Gods and Globes)*

"We Ragged Few", Kate Alice Marshall *(Beneath Ceaseless Skies 261, 9/20/18)*

"The Hydraulic Emperor", Arkady Martine *(Uncanny, 1-2/18)*

"Triquetra", Kirstyn McDermott *(Tor.com 9/5/18)*

"Ten Landscapes of Nili Fossae", Ian McDonald *(2001: An Odyssey in Words)*

Time Was, Ian McDonald *(Tor.com Publishing)*

"Beneath the Sugar Sky", Seanan McGuire *(Tor.com Publishing)*

"Build Me a Wonderland", Seanan McGuire *(Robots vs Fairies)*

"The Starfish Girl", Maureen McHugh *(Future Tense 8/18)*

"Conspicuous Plumage", Sam J. Miller *(Lightspeed, 9/18)*

"She Searches for God in the Storm Within", Khalidaah Muhammad-Ali *(Sword and Sonnet)*

"Theories of Light", Linda Nagata *(Asimov's, 11-12/18)*

"The Persistence of Blood", Juliette Wade *(Clarkesworld, 3/18)*

"Sister Rosetta Tharpe and Memphis Minnie Sing the Stumps Down Good", LaShawn M. Wanak *(Fiyah #7)*

"The Adventure of the Dux Bellorum", Cynthia Ward *(Aqueduct)*

The Freeze-Frame Revolution, Peter Watts *(Tachyon Publications)*

The Dragon's Child, Janeen Webb *(Tor.com Publishing)*

Artificial Condition, Martha Wells *(Tor.com Publishing)*

"Ruby, Singing", Fran Wilde *(Beneath Ceaseless Skies, 9/27/18)*

"Shadowdrop", Chris Willrich *(Beneath Ceaseless Skies 261, 9/20/18)*

"Galatea in Utopia", Nick Wolven *(F&SF, 1-2/18)*

"How to Swallow the Moon", Isabel Yap *(Uncanny 11-12/18)*

COPYRIGHT